GW01158538

Gloaming

The Tenebrous Trilogy, Volume 1

Addison Taylor Rich

Published by Addison Taylor Rich, 2022.

GLOAMING

First edition. June 18, 2022.

Copyright © 2022 Addison Taylor Rich.

ISBN: 979-8201174880

Written by Addison Taylor Rich.

Table of Contents

For JT, who heard it first.

Chapter 1

*G*reat. *Just great. First day of fall break, and a student's already been attacked.*

Ariel didn't have to examine the young woman's body to know she didn't have long. Her blood was already going cold on the asphalt, seeping out from between his fingers where his hands were pressed against her injuries.

Gina was on the other side of the city; there was no way the shambulance would make it here in time to help.

He heard a quiet whimper of pain accompany the sickening sizzle of flesh as his prosthetic fingers pressed against her skin. He hastened to readjust his grip on the blood-soaked cloth, trying to stall for time while he thought.

A flutter of wings, and then footsteps so quiet as to be almost inaudible reached his ears, and he turned to see the vampire at the end of the darkened alley, watching him warily from behind a large pair of sunglasses. He noted the faint movement of her head as she glanced at his silver-plated right hand, no longer hidden by its usual glove. After a moment that seemed to stretch on for too long, she looked down at the dead man beside him, before turning her attention to the injured woman whose bleeding wounds he was desperately trying to stem.

"I can help," Bella said.

Ariel snorted before he could stop himself. "You can't turn her," he said. "She's already been bitten."

He highly doubted Bella Graves was her true name, though he had to admit it made him chuckle when he first heard it. Typical vampire humour. Even when their current identity was meant to keep up with the times, he'd rarely met one that didn't try to slip a pun or two in.

"I wasn't planning to." Bella approached slowly, holding her hands up. "But we can't take her to a hospital—"

The mangled woman coughed weakly; blood splattered on Ariel's boots.

Bella slowly took off her sunglasses and tucked them over the neck of her shirt, crimson eyes meeting Ariel's. Her own gaze was pleading. Desperate. "Please. I mean no harm."

"Try anything, and—"

"Yeah, yeah, I know, you'll be well within your rights to kill me if I do," Bella said, crouching beside the woman, sniffing cautiously. "Oh. *Ew.* Smells like wet dog."

Ariel shook his head. "She won't make it if you stall much longer."

"I *know.* I know." Bella took a deep breath and held it before lowering her mouth to the gashes in the woman's neck.

Ariel watched warily, the fingers of his silver hand twitching, but Bella didn't drink to drain. Rather, she gagged as she ran her tongue over the wounds, her saliva accelerating healing and sealing the wounds shut; she spat out a mouthful of blood on the ground before continuing, moving from the deadliest wounds to the ones less urgently in need of attention. When she got to the woman's mangled leg, she paused to take a deep breath and looked up at him.

"I need you to help me set the bone," she said, and Ariel tried not to stare at the bloody stain around her mouth. "It... it won't be perfect, but she'll be able to use it, at least."

Ariel swore quietly, but tugged his glove on and nodded brusquely. "Show me what to do."

Bella directed him how to hold the leg, shifting the bone shattered by powerful jaws so it was set as well as she could manage.

"You have experience with this," Ariel noted, and Bella snorted.

"Do I ever," she said. "Got my first medical degree about a century back and was a nurse during World War II. Fat lot of appreciation I got for it then."

Ariel glanced at her dark brown skin and decided it would be best not to comment on that. "Well, then, I'm glad you happened to be passing by."

Bella lifted her mouth from the woman's mangled knee, stifling a gag. "Yeah, you and me both."

Ariel paused as he watched Bella gather the limp figure in her arms, brushing orange hair matted with blood out of the woman's face. "Where are you taking her?" he asked.

Bella gave him a look like he'd grown a second head. "Back to our dorm. She's my roommate, you foozler. Now, are you going to help me, or not?"

. . . .

When Lee woke up, she immediately wished she could go back to sleep again. Her entire body ached like she'd been run over by a small dump truck. And then, by a second, larger dump truck.

She groaned quietly, which attracted the attention of her roommate.

"Shh," Bella said, appearing by her side and taking her hand. "It's alright."

Lee's mouth felt dry, and she rasped, trying to swallow several times before a plastic cup was pressed into her hand, a straw hanging over the edge. Vaguely, she noted Bella wasn't wearing her usual sunglasses.

Maybe this was just a bad hangover, she thought as she sipped weakly at the water, squeezing her eyes shut against the brightness in the room. The corner of her mouth ached when she sucked on the straw, and she let it go with another groan.

3

"How're you feeling?" Bella asked, putting a cool hand to the back of Lee's forehead.

Lee's tongue was heavy in her mouth, and it took her a moment to answer. "Like shit."

Bella chuckled, though it sounded forced. "I'm not surprised. You were in pretty bad shape when we found you."

"We?" Lee strained as she tried to recall the events of the night before. Bella had gone out clubbing, and Lee had... she had gone out for a walk near Navy Pier...

The memories blurred together, concrete and forest, and Lee squeezed her eyes shut, shaking her head.

"You know that guy in our English class, Ariel Montgomery?" Bella asked, hauling herself up onto the bed and sitting by Lee's knees. "The cute blond twink with the prosthetic arm. We found you half-dead in an alley looking like you went through a meat grinder."

The memory came rushing back and Lee inhaled sharply, sitting up abruptly. "*Oh my god.* Oh my god, there was this, this man, he grabbed me a-and then he turned—Bella, this is going to sound insane, but you've gotta believe me, *please*—"

"He turned into a wolf, mauled you, and Ariel showed up just in time to kill him," Bella finished, swinging her legs. A corner of Lee's mind wildly noted she was wearing her bunny slippers. "And luckily for you, I decided to fly home. Caught the smell of blood, lots of it, and I was able to close the wounds before you bled out." She grinned, broadly, and Lee stared.

Fangs. Bella had fangs. About half an inch long and far sharper than any human tooth had any right to be.

Lee lifted shaking hands to see shiny pink scars on the heels of her hands where she'd fallen.

She checked herself over; Bella must have put her in pajamas while she was still unconscious. Everything hurt all over, but when she peeked down the neck of her shirt, the horrible, gaping wounds from the night before were scarred over.

But that would mean—

Lee lurched sideways off the bed and pain shot up her leg, and she collapsed to the floor with a yell.

"Lee!" Bella was by her side in an instant, helping her to roll over. "Jesus, girl, don't try to walk yet. Your knee was shattered. It'll take a while even with your accelerated healing to be better."

"The mirror," Lee said, pointing with a shaking hand, and Bella nodded, getting up to pull down the mirror they'd stuck to the wall. She passed it to Lee, who stared in dismay at her own reflection.

A wide, terrified green right eye stared back at her as her reflection touched its marred cheek with trembling fingers. The entire left half of her face looked like it had been torn off, jagged scars cutting across her eye, forcing it half-shut. The scars continued over the curve of her nose and cheek, only just missing the corner of her mouth.

"I know, it looks really bad," Bella said quietly, "but it will get better with time, and there's always... scar reduction surgeries and things—"

Lee put her head between her knees and threw up.

Bella scrambled for the trash bin and held it under Lee's face, catching the rest of the vomit. She rubbed Lee's back as she sobbed, hard enough to make her throw up again until her stomach was void of its contents.

"Little sips," Bella said brusquely as she handed Lee her cup of water, taking the bin away to begin cleaning the mess on the floor. "Not too quickly; we don't want to upset your stomach again."

Lee obediently did as she was told, watching as Bella threw the filthy paper towels into the trash. "You're a vampire," she said, and Bella glanced up.

"Well, that makes for a nice change of pace. Yes, I am."

"Is Ariel a vampire?" Lee asked.

Bella snorted. "No, he's a hunter. Pretty good one, too, it looked like from last night. Took down the werewolf that attacked you with his bare hands. Hand." She sat against the wardrobe, across the floor from Lee. "I'm not surprised, though. The Montgomeries are one of the best families in the business."

Lee nodded slowly, her mind spinning as she tried to take it all in. "Am I going to become a werewolf?"

"You already have," Bella said. She held out a hand to shake, and after a long moment, Lee took it. "Accalia Lowell, welcome to the world of Tenebrous."

Chapter 2

Bella always got a kick out of introducing newcomers to the world previously hidden under their noses. After she made sure Lee was settled more or less comfortably back on her bed, she sat beside her roommate and fluffed her hair puff as she thought.

"To start, Isabella Graves isn't my real name," she said. "It's just my current identity, so what I'm about to say doesn't leave our room, okay? My real name's Arabella Ward, and I was born in the Year of Our Lord 1835."

She couldn't help but laugh when Lee's mouth fell open. "I know! Still young by vampire standards, before you ask," she added. "But you can still just call me Bella. And to get the basic questions out of the way: no, sunlight doesn't burn us, it just takes away most of our powers; yes, holy stuff burns us; no, garlic doesn't repel us; yes, we can turn into bats; no, we don't need to be invited into places; the only way to kill us is with silver; and yes, my eyes are red."

Lee sniffled, and Bella leaned over to grab a box of tissues, handing them to her. Lee blew her nose, wincing as she did so.

"The scars," Lee said quietly. "They'll... you said they won't heal?"

Bella sighed. "They'll fade with time and get less achy, but there's a good chance you could have them forever," she said softly. "And I'll be surprised if you're able to walk without a limp after what that guy did to your leg. I set it as best I could, but the bone was pulverised and I didn't have access to tools. Werewolves have better healing than normal people, so who knows? Maybe you'll be alright." She attempted a smile. "And if not, once I've got my degree again, I'll fix your knee myself, free of charge."

Lee winced, looking down at her leg. Her fluffy rubber duck pajamas seemed too cheerful for the situation.

Bella patted her shoulder. "It's an awful way to find out, Lee. I'm sorry."

7

"I—I know it's selfish of me," Lee said, swallowing around the lump in her throat. "I mean, I'm glad I'm alive, I'm so glad... Thank you, Bella." She paused, and a hysterical giggle escaped her lips. "Hang on, you're a vampire and your name is—?"

"*Don't* start," Bella groaned. "And before you can bring it up, *no*, we don't *sparkle*."

Despite the awfulness of it all, Lee began to laugh, leaning back against the wall and holding her chest when it ached from the force of her guffaws. Bella chuckled, a bit less enthusiastically, her heart breaking as she watched Lee gasp with pain.

It wouldn't have been a stretch to call her beautiful, once—and some of that old beauty still shone through in the unmarred half of her freckle-kissed face. But surgery or not, this was going to mark her for the rest of her life, and any Tenebran worth their salt would know what those scars meant.

"Alright, then," Lee said, and took a shallow breath, gingerly patting her ribs. "So, go on. Enlighten me. Why aren't stories about vampires and werewolves on the news? *One* good reason for staying in hiding, if the only thing that can kill you is silver."

Bella kicked off her bunny slippers and tucked her feet up under her, pursing her lips. "Well, for one, we're really not as strong as books and movies make us out to be," she said. "I needed Ariel's help to get you back here without being seen. And for another, it's super easy to add silver to weapons," she added. "But just because silver's the best thing to finish the job doesn't mean we don't get hurt by other stuff. Most hunters use steel blades with silver inlay—steel to cut, and silver to burn the wounds. It prevents healing, you see. Though I fudged a bit; not that there aren't other things that can kill us, but silver's the easiest method."

"That... makes sense." Lee, Bella noticed, kept gingerly prodding at her face, and Bella sighed.

"I know it feels awful, but try to keep your hands off it. The scars will fade easier if you don't play with them."

Lee reluctantly let her hands drop. "How are we going to explain this to everyone?" she said, looking up at Bella. "The teachers, the other students? And the—the w-werewolf that attacked me..."

"Ariel arranged to get rid of the body, he didn't say how," Bella said, quietly noting Lee neglected to include her parents in that list. "But I was thinking we could say you got into some sort of accident—attacked by a dog, most likely. If you hide in the dorm for most of fall break, you should be able to get away with it." She smiled wryly. "My family and Ariel's both have some experience with this sort of thing."

Lee nodded slowly; Bella nudged her cup, and she took another sip of water. "Hang on," she said. "I met your family, when you moved in. Are they vampires, too? Are you guys even related?"

Bella's expression became rather fixed. "My little sister's not a vampire, but our parents are. They..." She paused for a moment, trying to decide how much she felt like sharing. "Well, let's just say they had me before they became vampires, and turned me when I was older."

"But your little sister," Lee said. "You said she was eight?"

This, at least, was easier. "Yeah," Bella said, smiling fondly as she leaned back against the wall. "Mum and Dad had to use a surrogate, but she's my bio sister. She can't wait to grow up and get vamped like the rest of us," she added with a laugh.

"Is that why she was wearing the sunglasses, too?" Lee asked.

"Pretty much." Bella pulled her hairband out and began to re-tie it as she spoke. "We're not sensitive to sunlight, but the red eyes are a dead giveaway as to what we are. Most people can't see through the Gloam—the barrier that separates magic and mundane. But of the ones who can, well, an even smaller handful of them are actually in the know. It just makes our lives a lot easier in the long run if we try to keep it all hush-hush, you just can't tell with most people."

Lee nodded and yawned, winced, and tried and failed to stifle another yawn. She grunted with pain and shifted on the bed, trying to make herself comfortable. "So that's why you never grinned at me before," she said tiredly.

"Got it in one. There were times I could've sworn you could see through it already, which was real fun." Bella considered her for a moment, tilting her head. "Tell you what," she said, sliding off the bed and turning to face Lee, "you get some sleep. Just because you're not in any immediate danger of dying doesn't mean you don't still need to heal, and rest is the best way to make that happen."

Lee nodded again and slumped back against the pillows; Bella helped her get comfortable and flipped the light off before settling on her own bed with a pair of headphones and a book, glancing up whenever she heard Lee whimper in her sleep.

Chapter 3

Ariel pulled his phone out as he left the dorm, double-checking the location he and Bella had agreed to meet. A text had come through from her while he slept, asking if he wanted coffee, and he sent a reply with his preferred order before he began walking. His long, gangly stride carried him quickly off campus and through the dusky streets of Chicago.

Nobody glanced twice at the tall, slender figure as he hurried along, blue coat flapping about his knees. There was a nip in the air; winter would soon be on its way, and with it came more monsters. Longer nights meant more work for hunters, and with it came more funerals.

Ariel glanced at the faces of pedestrians he passed, wondering which ones wouldn't live to see the sunrise. At least here in the city, though the Gloam spread thick through the streets, congealing in alleys and curling in shadowy entryways, the Gloambeasts knew to be careful where they tread, for hunters, vampires, werewolves, and magicians alike defended their territory fiercely.

But there would always be somebody who took a wrong turn, got separated from their group, or simply had no safe haven to return to, and then the darkness fed and fed well.

He found Bella on the pedestrian bridge, leaning against the railing and watching the cars pass by below. She turned at his approach, though he made barely any noise to alert her to his presence. He found himself looking at his own reflection in her mirrored sunglasses.

"You took your time," Bella said, holding out the coffee with a smile. Ariel accepted it with a nod of thanks and took a sip, sighing as he leaned back against the railing on his elbows.

"I'm not a morning person," Ariel said dryly, and Bella laughed. "You didn't text about your roommate. I assume she's doing well."

"She woke up long enough for me to bring her some soup from the dining hall," Bella said, shrugging. "She was sleeping again when I left. At least we were able to avoid the whole song and dance of 'But vampires are fictional!'" She waved her hands around, mock-hysterically, before letting them fall. "It'll make her transition easier, anyway. First person I've ever run into who accepted it that readily, though." She shrugged. "Not that I'm complaining."

"Mhm." Ariel glanced up at the darkening sky before turning to Bella, who sensed the sudden tension in the air and straightened up to her full height, which admittedly wasn't much. "Let's skip the pleasantries. This is a business meeting."

"Hey, I got you coffee, does that at least get me a thank you?" Bella asked.

"Thank you. Moving on to business."

Bella sighed and shook her head. "Yeah. I get it. I'm scared, too."

Ariel glanced at her out of the corner of his eye. "For now, try not to panic. The next council meeting is just in two weeks; I'm sure the Lunar Delegation will have their own incidents to discuss, and then we can share what happened."

"You think this wasn't a freak accident." It wasn't a question.

Ariel shook his head. "My brother's boyfriend runs the Chicago chapter of the support group," he said grimly. "I asked, after last night, if there had been similar attacks. Mind, this is all secondhand, but apparently members have been going missing."

Bella hissed; Ariel's hand twitched out of reflex, its motor whirring quietly. "Do you think it's a rogue hunter?"

Ariel was silent for a moment as he thought. "Honestly? I don't know," he said at long last. "But it can't be a coincidence. Werewolves going missing, going mad without the full moon?"

"Agreed." Bella sighed and tugged nervously on one of her pentagram earrings. "Lee can't be the only one who's been attacked.

Can you check in and see if there's anyone new at the next support meeting?" she paused. "Uh, when's that?"

"Always the day after the full moon," Ariel said, checking his watch. "...Which isn't for another twenty-one days. But those meetings are confidential. I won't be able to get names, just a general headcount if there are new members." He pursed his lips. "Though that's assuming any newly-turned werewolves have anyone to point them in the right direction, which they likely won't if they were attacked outside of the usual lunar cycle."

"Yeah." Bella sent her earring spinning with a soft tinkling noise. "Lee's lucky she's got us."

Ariel raised an eyebrow. "*Us? If you* want to adopt her, be my guest. *I'm* doing my job as a hunter, and that's it."

Bella scoffed and raised her eyebrows. "Too high and mighty to mingle, Montgomery?" she asked loftily, and grinned.

Ariel didn't smile back. "I work alone. My family has nothing to do with it."

"*I work alone*," Bella mimicked. "Sheesh. You lose your sense of humour along with your arm?" She clapped her hands over her mouth, but it was too late.

Ariel's cold blue eyes narrowed, an icy hand clenching around his heart. "I'll see you at the council meeting. Don't be late." He turned on his heel and stalked off, hurling the half-drunk coffee into a nearby bin as he passed.

· · · ·

"I'm an *idiot*," Bella groaned when Lee woke up sometime after midnight.

Lee rubbed her eyes and sat up, noting that most of the soreness seemed to have subsided. "What did you do, Bella?"

It took her a moment to register that Bella was pacing restlessly on the ceiling, her bunny slippers squeaking with each step. The

13

whole thing might have been rather comical were it not for the slightly crazed look in Bella's crimson eyes.

"What did I *do*? Only delivered what's possibly the lowest blow of my life, and I've had a *very* long life." Bella reached the door and walked down it to the floor, crossing their room to sit on her bed. She stared at Lee in dismay. "Ariel and I met up while you were asleep. And I made a crack about losing his arm."

Lee winced. "That's... not great."

"No shit, it's not great!"

"Did you try apologising?"

"No, he stormed off before I—wait. Oh, *hell*." Bella rubbed her eyes. "You don't know."

Lee stared blankly for a moment. "Remember I've only been a werewolf for, like, a day, and I slept through most of it."

"No, I mean, it was in the papers, it even made the human news." Bella pulled her phone out and quickly typed something on it, then tossed it to Lee, who fumbled before catching it in the crook of her elbow. She turned the screen around to read.

It was a news article from six years ago, about a car crash that had killed Jordan Montgomery and gravely injured his son, who was unnamed in the story. Lee looked up with wide eyes.

"Hang on, Ariel is from *the* Montgomery family? Silver Sword?" She pointed at her desk, where her laptop lay closed, a sword and star logo visible on the lid. "*Those* Montgomeries?"

"*Those* Montgomeries," Bella agreed heavily.

"No wonder he's pissed at you," Lee said, tossing the phone back.

Bella caught it and shook her head. "It gets worse," she said, her shoulders slumping. "The car crash was just a ruse, a coverup. His dad was killed on a hunt by a vampire and Ariel was left for dead. It's a super well-known story in Tenebrous, and I didn't *think*, I just went and shoved my foot in my stupid fanged mouth—"

14

"Okay, calm down," Lee said, holding up her hands, an unpleasant feeling curling in her stomach. "Why the hell would you joke about that in the first place?"

"It's just banter," Bella protested. "Lee, you've gotta understand, jokes like that are common in our world, it's just the reality we live in. Personal stuff is a big no-no, though, and I didn't just go for the throat, I kicked him in the balls while I was at it."

"Yeah, you're an idiot," Lee said, and Bella groaned, flopping back on her bed.

"Why don't you give me a nice paper cut and pour holy water on it?"

Lee watched her for a moment, wondering if all vampires were this dramatic. "Bells, not that I don't appreciate a good mope," she finally said, "but can you help me to the toilet? I've *really* gotta pee."

After checking that the coast was clear, Bella helped her limp down the hall to the communal bathrooms, where she stood guard while Lee took care of business.

When she limped from the stall to wash her hands, she caught sight of her reflection in the mirror, and her stomach lurched. She hastily averted her gaze, keeping her eyes fixed on her hands as she tried to steady her breathing.

You're alive. That's what matters.

You're alive, and Bella knows... she knows...

Lee splashed water on her face, trying to put the memory back where it belonged.

They snuck her back into the bedroom, and Lee collapsed into her chair with a soft groan, massaging her leg.

"You're walking better," Bella noted.

"It's definitely an improvement over falling off the bed," Lee said, attempting a smile. It felt forced, and the motion stretched her cheek, reminding her with another unpleasant jolt of the scars on her face. She felt her breathing speed up, and her heartbeat stuttered.

"Lee?" Bella said, frowning. "Your heart's going pretty fast."

I'm in my dorm with my chair. My chair has five wheels and spins around. My chair has firm cushions. The cushions are grey fabric.

"Panic attack," Lee bit out, before inhaling deeply, mentally counting to five.

I'm in my dorm with my pajamas. My pajamas are fluffy and soft. My pajamas have rubber ducks on them.

"Do you want some space or want me to leave?" Bella asked. Lee barely heard her.

I'm in my dorm with my roommate. My roommate's name is Bella. My roommate is a vampire.

She's a vampire and I'm now a werewolf and I can barely walk and my face looks horrible and monsters are real they're real this is really real they've always been real—

Lee bit down on her knuckle as she tried to muffle a wail. Bella was by her side in an instant, kneeling on the floor next to her.

"Lee, I'm here," Bella said, her voice soft. To Lee, it sounded like she was coming from far away, her voice muffled like she was underwater. "I'm right here, Lee, can you hear me? Can you nod if you can hear me?"

Lee nodded frantically, biting down harder. It stung, but wasn't enough to draw blood.

Not like him not like when he grabbed me by the face not like when they—

"Come on, take your finger out of your mouth, there you go," Bella said as Lee struggled to comply. "Can I touch you? I'm going to touch your hand, if that's okay."

Lee nodded again, and Bella took her hand, squeezing gently.

"You feel my hand? I'm squeezing your hand right now. I know it's hard, but try to breathe deeply for me," Bella said, and Lee nodded, whimpering quietly. "You're doing great, Lee. You're safe in the dorms, it's just you and me right now. You're safe."

Lee chased the words as they drifted in and out of focus, squeezing Bella's hand when it got to be too much.

Time always felt like it passed in an instant and forever when these attacks hit, and when Lee's breathing finally evened out, she glanced at the clock to orient herself. It wasn't even one in the morning yet.

"You with me again?" Bella asked, and Lee gave her a watery smile. "Glad to have you back."

Lee tapped herself on the chest, wincing slightly. "Thanks. For, um. For being here."

"Hey, what sort of doctor would I be if I left you to fend for yourself?" Bella asked, getting off the floor to sit in her own chair. She spun it around several times, and Lee took advantage of the opportunity to hastily dry her eyes. "Nothing to be ashamed of, you know? Your life's been thrown way out of whack. I think you're allowed a good cry or ten."

Lee chuckled weakly, and Bella beamed.

"There you go, laughing already."

"I stress laugh," Lee muttered, reaching for the tissues to blow her nose again.

Bella nodded, biting her lip. Her fangs pricked the skin, but just barely. "You know, there's support groups for this sort of thing," she said, and Lee let out a startled giggle. "Well, just the one, really, but there's a branch of it here in the city—"

"No," Lee said immediately, half-turning her chair away from Bella.

"Lee, I think it could help—"

"I said *no*," Lee snapped, and Bella sat back, visibly hurt. Lee hugged herself, glancing away. "...I'm sorry," she muttered. "For snapping at you, I mean. But I'm not going."

"...Okay," Bella said after a pause. "Nobody's going to make you. Just... think about it, alright? They meet after every full moon, since those nights can get... rough."

Lee turned back to her, dread settling in her stomach. "Don't tell me that we go nuts during the full moon."

Bella's mouth thinned to a line. "Yeah," she said. "You do."

"And I don't suppose there's some sort of potion I can take to fix that?" Lee said sarcastically, already sure she knew the answer.

"I wish," Bella said. "But no."

Lee felt her heart stutter again, and she flexed her hands open and closed, trying to stay calm. "What am I supposed to do, then?"

At this, Bella's usual smile made a ghost of a reappearance, though it still looked strained. "Luckily for you, I happen to know a guy."

"It's the guy you made a crack to about his dead father, isn't it."

"Yep."

"Fantastic."

Chapter 4

A riel normally slept through the mornings. He'd had another long night on patrol and collapsed into bed as dawn broke over the city, but there he laid awake, arm flung across his eyes to block out the sun that filtered in through the thin curtains. He listened to the noise of the city coming to life, set to the steady rhythm of his phone bleeping with updates as hunters checked in from their homes, letting their colleagues know they were still alive.

He knew Bella hadn't meant it, from the look of utter horror on her face the instant the words had left her mouth. Hell, he was no stranger to making the jokes, himself.

But right now, it was a little over two weeks until the anniversary of his father's death. He always felt more raw around this time of year. *"More prickly,"* Jessie liked to say. *"Prickly like a hedgehog."*

"Not a porcupine?" he'd asked grumpily.

His little sister had considered the question before shaking her head. "No, because even when porcupines are having a good day, you still shouldn't touch them. Hedgehogs, you can, you just gotta know how to pet them right."

And then she'd hugged him around the middle, and he couldn't stay annoyed at her. He never could. Not with Jessie.

His thoughts felt prickly now, trying to worm their way in, under his taut arm and eyelids squeezed tight, before Ariel gave up on sleep and swung his legs off the bed with a grunt.

Just another good thing about not having a roommate, he thought as he fumbled one-handed for the pack of smokes on his bedside table. *Nobody cares if you smoke inside.*

Well, not once you disabled the smoke detector, anyway.

He stuck a cigarette in his mouth, lit it, and tossed the lighter aside, exhaling with a heavy sigh when his phone chimed. Sometimes he wished he could just put his phone on silent when he wasn't on a hunt.

This time, it was another message from Bella, though not one of her many apologies she'd sent throughout the night. This one was a request for aid from him as a hunter, worded with the formal stiffness of a Victorian governess. Ariel set the phone on his lap and pulled the cigarette out of his mouth, letting it burn away while he considered the request.

The weak sunlight glinted off his silver arm, charging in the corner by his knives.

Maybe I'll mess with her first. Just a little.

Ariel smirked and bit down on the cigarette so he could send his reply.

• • • •

Lee, bless her, decided to catch up on an essay while they waited, which left Bella to pace the ceiling anxiously as she read Ariel's message over and over, the soft tapping of Lee's keyboard accompanying her footsteps.

k

Just one little letter, not even properly capitalised.

God, she'd really messed up.

Maybe she'd exaggerated a bit to Lee about this being the single most embarrassing moment of her life—after all, that incident with the fish oil had been mortifying—but it certainly ranked up there as one of those things that would keep her up during the day.

Not that she needed to sleep, but it was the principle of the thing.

If Ariel said something at the council meeting, she'd be a pariah. She would have to leave the school. She would turn into a bat and go live in the woods. She'd—

A firm rapping came from the door, and Bella nearly tripped in her haste to rush down the wall to answer it.

"I am so sorry," she said, wrenching the door open. "Ariel, I didn't even think, I just blurted it out, I should never have said such things and I can only offer my deepest apologies for my insensitive words, it's never going to happen again and I swear to you you'll never hear another thing from me after the current situation is resolved, but I'll do everything right going forward, you have my word as a vampire."

Bella fell silent when she realised she was starting to babble. She looked pleadingly up at Ariel's impassive face, resisting the urge to blink as he stared her down.

She became uncomfortably aware of the silence as it dragged on, measured only by the steady thrum of Ariel's heart and the nervous flutter of Lee's.

Just as the silence was becoming unbearable, she noticed a hint of a sparkle in Ariel's eye.

"No 'arm done," he said, and Lee tried and failed to stifle a snort.

Bella nearly sagged with relief before jabbing him in the chest. "You *ass!*"

Ariel snickered. "You deserved it."

"Yeah, yeah, you've made your point," Bella said, flapping a hand. "Did you bring the stuff?"

"As requested. So," Ariel said, brushing past Bella and sitting at her desk, setting the makeup case he was carrying down before turning the chair to face Lee, "Lee, right? You look pretty okay, all things considered." Lee unconsciously touched her face, but Ariel shook his head. "Got a glow to you," he continued, cracking the case open. "Healthy. You're taking to the transformation well."

"Is that a good thing?" Lee asked nervously, glancing at Bella.

Bella straightened up and cleared her throat. "Most definitely," she said. "Some people who get bitten find that changing shape at will comes more easily to them than others."

She grinned when Lee's good eye widened in amazement. "We can do that?" Lee asked.

"Yeah," Ariel said, pulling out several tubs of scar wax that looked close to Lee's skin tone and holding them up to compare. "If you don't mind shredding your clothes when you do."

"Oh," Lee said, visibly disappointed. "It's... that kind of lycanthropy."

"I've met a few werewolves who could keep their clothes when they transform," Bella offered; Ariel made his selection and packed the other containers away before pulling out more makeup supplies. "But they practiced with it, a lot. And with the, erm, generally traumatic nature of getting bitten, most prefer not to do that."

She saw Lee's unmarred eyebrow climb toward her hairline. "Does it help at all with the full moons?"

"No," Ariel said bluntly. "It's the curse of lycanthropy. That's the nature of the Tenebrans—nice powers, but the payoff's not worth it."

Bella huffed. "Just because some people aren't okay with the idea of drinking blood in exchange for living for literal centuries."

"Exactly." Ariel's fingers fluttered as he dithered over the colour pallets. "Also never being able to enjoy a hamburger again, constantly having to deal with hiding from government bureaucracy—"

"Wait, vampires can't eat human food?" Lee asked.

Bella rocked her hand back and forth. "We can, but our stomachs can't digest anything other than blood, so food literally rots inside unless we make ourselves puke it back up. Most vamps don't think it's worth the effort."

Lee wrinkled her nose.

"Can't eat food, but still with a working gag reflex," Ariel muttered as he set out the last of his supplies. He looked it over, nodded to himself, and grasped the scar wax container with his gloved hand, turning to Lee. "I'm gonna have to touch your face a lot," he warned.

Lee took a deep breath; Bella noticed her hands were trembling until she closed them on the arms of the chair. "Well, whatever it takes to get me out of the dorm, right?" she said, in a weak attempt at humour.

Bella and Ariel both decided not to comment that it fell massively flat.

"You've got the reference photos?" Ariel said brusquely, and Bella hurried to stand by his shoulder, waking up her laptop where she'd readied images of recently-sutured cuts, as close as possible to where Lee would ordinarily be in the healing process. Ariel studied them for a moment, nodded to himself, and reached towards Lee's face, moving slowly enough she could draw back if she so wished.

Bella heard her heartbeat speed up rapidly, and her knuckles went white where she gripped the chair, but Lee held still as Ariel began doctoring her face, pressing the scar wax over her actual scars before sealing it to her skin with liquid latex and carefully cutting it with a plastic sculpting tool. As he worked, Bella noted that his robotic hand seemed better at grasping and holding things than most prosthetics on the market. Of course the Montgomeries would have spared no expense for one of their own.

"Is this what you learn as a hunter?" Lee asked as Ariel started blending colour over the fake wounds. The quaver in her voice was so faint, Bella wasn't sure Ariel could hear it. "Fake scar makeup?"

Ariel snorted. "No," he said. "It's what I learn majoring in theatre and minoring in special effects makeup."

"Oh."

"We had to go around and say our name and our majors in English, remember?" Bella prompted.

Lee grimaced. "I might've been spacing for that one."

"Don't talk," Ariel said in exasperation. "Unless you want this to take even longer."

Lee swallowed and fell silent again, and Bella heard her heart rate increase once more. Lee's jaw was set, a thin sheen of sweat beading on her forehead before Ariel pinched a cloth between thumb and forefinger to dab it away, the soft whirring of the motor in his hand the only noise in the room save for the sounds of traffic outside.

He finally sat back to examine his work, and Bella winced. For all the world, it looked like Lee had fresh, gaping wounds in her face once again.

"Doctor," Ariel said, getting up from the chair with a slight bow, and Bella nodded, hurrying forward to take the vacated seat. "I'll finish the freckles after you're done with the sutures," Ariel added, sitting on Lee's bed. "Don't want you smudging them."

"Good call," Bella said, deftly threading a needle. It felt wrong to not wash her hands before doing this, even if the wound was fake. "Alright, Lee—if I'm going to make this look realistic, this is going to take a while."

"I'm going out for a smoke," Ariel said. "Don't touch my kit." He slouched out of the room, letting the door fall shut behind him.

Lee smiled uncertainly, and Bella had to fight the urge to grimace. She'd seen injuries far worse than this, infected wounds that oozed with pus and rot, the damage done by cannonballs and musket fire and tear gas and mortar shells.

But this was Lee. Her roommate, Lee, who she often caught bobbing her head along to a song stuck in her head, who always had a sharp retort at the ready, and laughed so readily at the stupidest puns, her bright smile enough to light up their dingy room...

It hurt to see her changed so much overnight.

"Want to put on some music?" Bella offered, and Lee let out a small sigh of relief, pulling up an alt rock playlist on her phone and hitting shuffle.

"And you thought he was gonna be furious," Lee said as Bella made herself comfortable. "I guess he found the situation pretty... humerus in the end?"

Bella groaned and rolled her eyes. "I guess there was no cause for al-arm after all."

Lee stuck her tongue out, and the pair shared a brief laugh.

"Alright, now, hold still for me," Bella said, readying the forceps.

"I'd hate for you to stab me in the face," Lee said. "You might ruin it."

Bella chuckled. "I'll be very careful," she promised, and leaned in.

Ariel had done phenomenal work; if it weren't for her keen smell or the fact she'd seen him putting the makeup on, Bella could very nearly believe the gashes were real. Even the scar wax felt uncannily realistic as she slid the needle in and out, drawing the lips of the fake wound together with her forceps.

"It's even slower going than normal," Bella said, "because I've got to make sure the sutures match the real scars."

Lee mumbled something, barely moving her mouth, and Bella drew back to let her speak. "You think people will notice that sort of thing?" Lee repeated.

"Chuckaboo, if there's one thing I've learned over the years," Bella said, going back to her work, "you can never be too careful. The witch hunts and vampire hunts and werewolf hunts were torches and pitchforks in the past, government scientists in the present. And there's no telling when you might end up photographed in the background of someone else's picture, and a nutter with no life posts about it on a conspiracy forum."

Lee swallowed. "Got it," she whispered.

"Hey, it's not *that* bad, really," Bella tried to backpedal. "I mean, yeah, it would *suck* to get cut up and dissected, but sometimes the government's stuffed so full of red tape they wouldn't be able to find their way out of a filing cabinet."

"What do you mean?"

"Remind me to tell you about the time my mum forgot which alias she was using between her birth certificate, driver's license, and marriage certificate," Bella said. "Long story short, the government refused to believe she was the same person, and she ended up killing off that identity and moving to San Fran for a while because that would have been less of a hassle."

"Wow." Lee held still while Bella sutured the curve of her nose. When she felt the thread get tied off and snipped, she asked, "So what's the deal with the Montgomery family?"

Bella sucked air through her teeth as she worked. "Well, the long and short of it is, two centuries back, they helped write up a peace treaty for Tenebrous. So vampires and werewolves don't kill humans, magicians don't outrageously warp the fabric of reality itself, and hunters don't go after the other three so long as the rules are followed."

"Which is why the werewolf who...?" Lee swallowed, gesturing at her face.

"Why Ariel was, by law of the Night Treaty, duty-bound to kill him," Bella said, nodding as she began work on Lee's eyebrow. "The Montgomeries are a huge family going back centuries, nearly all of them hunters. We were all devastated to hear what happened to his dad. Jordan was a good guy, and..." She sighed. "Well, it cast a bad light on the vampire community for a while after that. They never caught the guy, and a lot of folk suspect the Sanguine Lords know who it was and covered it up."

"Is that y'all's vampire council?" Lee asked.

"Mm. You could say that. The Tenebrous Council is a worldwide organisation, and the Sanguine Lords, Lunar Delegation, Arcane Conclave, and Gloam Hunters each have their own representatives for the local chapters. Ariel's mum is the rep for the hunters, of course," she said, frowning, "but, uh, from what I've heard, she's not been doing such a great job since his dad died—"

"She became a raging alcoholic who dumped her youngest kid on the older two to raise, if that's what you mean," Ariel said from the door, and Bella froze.

"...I was just asking Bella about how your world works," Lee said into the awkward silence.

"Figured as much." Ariel sat on Lee's bed again, propping his elbow up on his knee. "It's fine, it's pretty much an open secret at this point, anyway. Morgan's hoping to take the position when she resigns, if she ever does."

"Morgan?"

"My older brother," Ariel said. "He's a saint for all the shit Mom's put him through after..." He trailed off and sighed, shaking his head. "Anyway. You done yet?" he asked, looking at Bella.

"Just about!" she chirped, tying off the last suture. "Ta-da! Fake scars to wear until..."

"Until I have to show off my real ones," Lee said quietly.

Ariel shifted his shoulder so he was waving at Lee from the elbow, twiddling the fingers of his gloved prosthetic hand. "Once you've been touched by the Gloam, you're on a timer until you get hurt," he said. "You just got unlucky and had yours hit zero on the first day."

"Even I've got them," Bella added, and Lee turned to see her pull up her shirt to reveal a wicked-looking burn scar splashed across most of her right side, disappearing under her clothes.

"Was that...?" Lee asked, eyes wide, and Bella nodded, pulling her shirt back down.

"Holy water. Hurt like a mother for weeks."

Lee bit her lip. "How long ago?"

"Not long at all, funnily enough," Bella said. "You know about that whole..." She waved her hands, smiling with the ease of long

27

practice. "Satanic Panic thing, back in the Eighties? Yeah. Though that's the only scar I've got that I can show in polite company," she added with a wink, and was rewarded with Lee's face going a bright red that clashed with the orange of her hair.

"Save it for the nightclubs, bloodsucker," Ariel said, unamused. "Scoot, I need to finish her freckles so we can *go.*"

Bella rolled her eyes, but moved so Ariel could sit at her desk again.

Ariel did the freckles quickly, his tongue poking out of the corner of his mouth as he concentrated. Bella found herself somewhat transfixed by the sight of the normally-surly hunter focusing so intently on his project.

"Done," he said, and snapped the case closed.

"We *can't* stay long," Ariel stressed as they helped Lee limp across the football stadium's parking lot where freshmen were forced to leave their cars. "I've got patrol again tonight, and traffic is fucking horrendous during rush hour."

"I *know*, don't nag," Bella said. "Shotgun!" she added when they reached a sleek blue BMW. Ariel glowered at her and pointed towards what would normally be the driver's side, lifting his chin in the faintest hint of a challenge.

But Bella just cheerfully said, "Still shotgun!" and darted around to the other side.

Ariel slid into the driver's seat and turned the engine, and Lee hurried to get in the backseat, the slightest bit belatedly realising Ariel's car must have been imported from the UK or somewhere else where right-hand driver's sides were the norm.

At any rate, it was certainly the nicest car she'd ever been in. She almost felt bad about her worn-out Converse dragging dirt in with her, but then remembered his family owned Silver Sword. He could pay for the cleaning if he had to.

Despite what Ariel had said about Morgan, Lee still felt a knot forming in her stomach at the thought of going to meet the other Montgomeries. She'd managed to avoid being seen for now by pulling the hood of her purple sweatshirt low over her face, but sooner or later the band-aid was going to have to come off.

"It *should* just be Morgan and Jessie tonight," Ariel said, glancing back at her in the rear view mirror. "And maybe Morgan's boyfriend. Mom works late Wednesdays. Besides, she wouldn't have a problem with *you*."

"Wh—oh." Bella glanced down at her hands, then over at Ariel's pale blond head of hair. "Please tell me it's because of the fangs."

"It's because of the fangs," Ariel said, and Bella nodded.

"We'll make this quick, then."

• • • •

Maybe, Lee thought, as she watched the streets of steel and glass and concrete turn into green suburbs flashing past outside the window of Ariel's car, she could get used to this.

Maybe she could get used to Ariel's taciturn silence as he drove, to Bella loudly and merrily singing along to Queen, to wanting to be sick to her stomach whenever the memory of those nights forced their way back in uninvited. The makeup itched and was hot, and it was only by sitting on her own hands Lee was able to avoid scratching at it and ruining Ariel and Bella's hard work.

Her stomach growled and Lee wrapped her arms around herself instead, face flushing with embarrassment.

"We're almost there," Ariel said, pulling off the freeway and turning onto a lushly wooded main road, heading towards Lake Michigan.

"The houses out here are *huge*," Lee murmured.

"Yeah, and most of their inhabitants have more money than sense," Bella said. "Uh, sorry, Ariel."

"No, you're right and you should say it," Ariel muttered. The fingers of his prosthetic curled a little tighter around the steering wheel.

"...Hey, Ariel?" Lee asked. "Can I ask something personal?"

"Why do I get the feeling you will anyway."

"No, I wasn't!" Lee protested. "I won't, I'm sorry I brought it up."

Ariel drummed his flesh and blood fingers against the steering wheel, gnawing on the inside of his cheek while he debated how to answer. "If it's about the arm, there's not a question you can ask that I haven't heard already."

"Oh—I mean, I guess it sort of is. Kind of." Lee cleared her throat. "I was just wondering, about the glove?"

"The arm's plated with silver," Ariel said. "Got a minor little enchantment on it that lets it take a beating in a fight, but otherwise it's just a normal prosthetic."

"Oh. *Oh.* Is it to prevent argyria?" Lee asked, and Bella swung around to look at her with glee.

"You know about that?" Bella asked, smiling widely enough to show off her fangs.

"I know *of* it," Lee said awkwardly, rubbing the back of her neck. "Silver poisoning, right?"

Bella nodded. "Turns your skin blue. I'd wondered if that was the reason!"

"No, Bella, the oldest and largest clan of hunters who have been working with silver for centuries had no idea about argyria," Ariel said, deadpan. "I just wear the glove for shits and giggles."

"So with you," Lee said, grinning faintly, "if the gloves come off..."

"Quite literally, yes." Ariel kept his eyes on the road, but Lee could have sworn she caught the faintest trace of a smile.

Bella chuckled and stretched in her seat. "I like you, Montgomery."

"Truly, my joy knows no bounds." Ariel turned onto a driveway that wound through the trees, and Lee slouched a little lower in her seat, tugging her hood down over her face. Ariel paused only for a large gate that blocked the drive, which opened slowly as they approached.

"Is that a *chapel?*" Lee asked as they pulled up to the manor. The exterior of the house was a mix of red brick and grey stone, with a circular drive out front. She'd only caught a glimpse of a stone building in the trees just off the drive, but was certain she'd seen a steeple with a cross on top.

"Yeah," Ariel said, parking outside the front door and killing the engine. "Consecrated ground, means vampires and Gloambeasts can't enter. The crypt below is actually a bunker in case of a siege."

"Do you really think that could happen?" Lee asked as they got out.

Ariel twirled his key ring around a finger, looking pensive. "Dunno," he said at long last. "We've owned this land for centuries—"

Bella coughed loudly into her fist.

Ariel just looked resigned. "At least as long as since when the Night Treaty went into effect. One of my great-something grandmothers had it built because she didn't trust it was going to last."

"Does that mean religion is true, then?" Lee asked as Bella came around to offer her an arm to lean on.

"Hell if we know," Bella said, and Lee snorted. "Crucifixes, Stars of David, pasta water blessed by the Flying Spaghetti Monster, it all burns the same. Keep it away from me, please and thank you."

"But," Lee said, visible confusion on her face, "what if you're an atheist?"

Ariel shrugged. "Use silver?" he said. "Still just as effective."

"Silver can't be used to consecrate grounds, though," Lee pressed.

"Running water?" Bella suggested, and Lee swung around to look at her. "We can't cross running water."

Lee spluttered. "We drove across, like, fifty rivers and streams just to get here!"

"Well, *okay*, we can't wade through it," Bella said. "Which I guess would be super inconvenient if I had to cross a stream with a broken bridge in the middle of broad daylight for whatever godforsaken reason."

"Vampires don't make any sense," Lee decided.

"Yeah, well, wait until you grow a tail," Bella shot back.

Ariel rubbed his forehead. "Can we *please* just do what we came here to do and go ins—?"

The large, oak front door banged open to reveal a short, elven-faced man barely taller than Bella, his curly pompadour dyed a violent shade of blue. The black skinny jeans and flowing, pastel yellow shirt would have been enough of a statement on their own, but the ensemble was completed by a glittery green scarf that matched his eyes, and a small fang earring that dangled from his left ear.

Lee's eye widened slightly when she saw the jagged claw scars that cut across where his right ear should have been.

"Ariel, *DARLING!*" the man cried dramatically, and swooned against the door. "Whatever is taking you so long to come give your beloved big brother a hug?"

Ariel remained as impassive as ever. "Hullo, Mo."

Morgan Montgomery straightened up with a chuckle. "One of these days I'll get a reaction out of you."

"See, that's the problem," Ariel said, climbing up the short stone stairs to reach the front door. "You do this too often and I know you have an awful poker face."

"Bah, you know me too well," Morgan said, leaning up on tiptoe to ruffle Ariel's hair. With them this close together, it was clear Ariel easily stood a foot taller than his brother, but he leaned down obligingly to let Morgan muss his hair. "So, who're your friends?"

"These are my *classmates*," Ariel stressed. "Bella and Lee."

Lee fidgeted when Morgan turned his attention on her, studying her face. "Well," he said, and clapped Ariel's shoulder, "you did an excellent job with the makeup."

Ariel inclined his head. "Bella did the sutures. She's a doctor."

"M.D., D.O., *and* DNP," Bella said, giving a crisp salute. "Currently back in school looking to become an MD *again* since I'm a bit outdated with my credentials."

Lee's mouth fell open.

33

"Very impressive," Morgan said, nodding. "What about you, Lee?"

Lee shuffled her feet, only to hiss when pain shot up her leg and she stumbled backwards into Ariel's car, Bella only just managing to catch her before she hit the ground.

"Ooh, that looked like it was nasty," Morgan said, padding barefoot down the front steps to offer her a hand up. Lee accepted, noting his nails were well-manicured and painted a lurid shade of turquoise. "Come on, up you get—Ariel!" he barked. "Don't stand around like a lump, help your friend up these steps!"

Ariel looked like he would rather swallow crucifix nails, but he got his arm around Lee and helped her hobble up the stairs and into the manor.

The entryway was just as large and grand as the exterior suggested, with rich, warm wooden panelling on the walls and a curving grand staircase leading the way to the second floor. Lee, distracted by the pain as she was, wasn't paying much attention to the impromptu tour as Morgan led them in a beeline to the sitting room, where Ariel promptly deposited Lee onto a squashy armchair. Her vision briefly swam with stars, and she blinked them away to see a little girl who couldn't have been older than eight sitting in the armchair opposite with an enormous book on her lap, watching her curiously through a thick pair of round, purple-framed glasses. Between the pale blond hair and eerily piercing gaze, she could only be Ariel's younger sister.

"Did you win?" Jessie asked, tearing her eyes off Lee to look up at Morgan.

"Nah, this one goes to Ariel again, I'm afraid," Morgan said, planting his hands on his hips as he looked Lee over. He tapped a manicured finger against his cheek for a moment before snapping his fingers and rounding on Ariel and Bella. "You! What have you two been feeding this one? I'm sorry, darling, I forgot to ask your pronouns," Morgan said as an aside to Lee.

Lee blinked at him for a moment, temporarily confused, before finding her voice. "Um, I'll answer to any? But she/her is fine..."

"Right," Morgan said, and pointed at Ariel. "You of all people should know better!"

Ariel lifted one shoulder in a shrug. "Look, you're the werewolf expert, not me."

"I. Covered. This. In. Your. Lessons. Come. On. Ariel," Morgan said, slapping the back of his hand into the opposite palm. "Come on!" He snapped his fingers rapidly. "What-do-were-wolves-need-to-u-ti-lise-their-pow-ers?"

"Food," Jessie piped up. "Calories, lots of them."

Morgan gestured at Jessie, raising his eyebrows pointedly at Ariel.

Ariel rolled his eyes and looked away. "You know I never paid attention to that stuff."

"Bella? You've been around long enough to have learned a thing or two." Morgan turned to her, but she just shrugged.

"Hey, mate, I specialise in treating humans, not werewolves."

Morgan sighed and massaged his temples. "We're having pizza tonight," he announced, and Jessie cheered. "Lee, honey, you get your own, extra large, extra cheese, stuffed crust, as many toppings as you like. Wait, you don't have any dietary restrictions?"

Lee rapidly shook her head, her mouth already watering.

"Mo, we're not staying long," Ariel said.

Morgan held up a finger. "Don't be silly, of course you are. Ariel, the usual? Oh! Bella—and I've done it twice, what are your pronouns?"

"She/her," Bella said, smiling toothily. "I'll pass on the pizza, I'm not big on the regurgitation bit."

Jessie made an exaggerated retching noise, and Bella winked at her.

"*Mo*," Ariel said sharply. "We're not staying. I've got patrol tonight, and if Mom comes home and sees a vampire in the house, she's gonna *flip*."

For the first time, Bella looked visibly uncomfortable. "*Er*," she said, holding up a hand. "Me being here isn't going to end with the Night Treaty being broken, is it?"

"No, it won't, and don't you worry about our mother, dear Ariel," Morgan said, clapping him on the back. "I'll just handle her like I always do."

"Not always," Jessie murmured, going back to her book.

"What?" Morgan asked.

Jessie turned the page. "Nothing."

Morgan shrugged and folded his arms. "Fact of the matter is, Lee here needs food, and—what have you even been feeding her? Dining hall food?"

"I wasn't feeling well, to be fair," Lee said quietly.

"Mmm, yeah, vicious cycle," Morgan said, nodding. "You feel like crap 'cause you haven't eaten, and you haven't eaten 'cause you feel like crap."

"I think you can say 'shit' in front of them," Jessie piped up, and Morgan flapped his hands at her to be quiet. "What? *They're* adults."

"*Yes*, but *you're* not supposed to say it," Morgan said.

"Or what? The language inquisition will show up?" Bella asked.

"The Bad Language Beast!" Morgan said, and Jessie held up her hands curled like talons.

"Fuck!" Jessie roared, and Lee had to clamp her hands over her mouth to keep from laughing. "Shit! RAWR!"

"No Bad Language Beast is allowed in the Montgomery house while I draw breath!" Morgan declared, and leapt over the back of the sofa to chase after Jessie, who shrieked and, before Lee could really process what was happening, rolled out of the way of Morgan's grasping hands and between his legs. She jack-knifed to her feet behind him, pelting away at top speed while screaming profanities that echoed through the house.

Bella raised an eyebrow and glanced after the pair.

"She's allowed to swear until the Bad Language Beast gets defeated," Ariel said, shrugging. He rolled his shoulder and his arm shot forward to tap Jessie on the head when she went racing by in a blur of blonde hair. "Just like that."

"NOOOO! You have... slain... me..." Jessie made a series of increasingly dramatic convulsions and gags until she lay still on the floor, her tongue hanging out.

Morgan stood over Jessie and planted a light foot on her stomach, raising his fist in a dramatic pose. "And lo, I have slain the beast!"

"No you didn't, Ariel did!" Jessie protested from the floor.

"Ah, don't tell me the beast has already been slain?" a deep voice came from the doorway that led to the hall.

"Uncle Connor!" Jessie scrambled to her feet and ran over to the man, who knelt and held out his arms as Jessie leapt into them for a hug.

"Hey, Boo," Morgan said, moving to hug the newcomer, and Connor shifted his grip on Jessie so he could hug them both.

Where Morgan was a riot of colour and fashion, Connor looked... almost too normal by comparison. He was tall and mostly clean-shaven, with a five o'clock shadow threatening to grow in before the night came. Between khakis, a white dress shirt, and a grey tie with sensible blue pinstripes, he almost looked like he'd wandered in from an office job by complete accident.

"Hey, yourself," Connor said, stealing a quick kiss from Morgan before setting Jessie down. "Ariel! Long time no see. How's dorm life treating you?"

Ariel glanced sidelong at Lee. "It's delightful," he said, giving Connor a tight smile.

"Connor, this is Bella, she/her, and Lee, any, but female preferred," Morgan said, indicating which was which. "And this is my beautiful boyfriend, Connor, he/him."

Connor waved and pushed his wireframe glasses higher on his nose, looking a bit embarrassed. "Morgan asked me to come by after work," he said, going over to Lee and offering his hand to shake.

"What do you do for a living, Mr...?"

"O'Connor," Connor said, and Lee couldn't quite manage to stifle a snort. "I'm a cognitive and behavioural therapist."

The smile immediately slid off of Lee's face. "I see."

"Morgan mentioned there was a new werewolf in Ariel's year," Connor said, letting go. "What are you studying, Lee?"

"It's not as impressive as Bella," Lee said.

"Oh, nonsense, I've only got so many degrees because I love medicine," Bella said, waving her hand. "...That, and you can get *really* bored after enough decades, but that's just a bonus."

Lee glanced away. "English," she muttered.

Morgan, perhaps sensing her discomfort, jumped in. "Babe, I was thinking, since these three need to get back to the city before dark, we could do early pizza, and you can answer Lee's questions while we eat?"

"That sounds perfect," Connor said. "And Lee, if you'd like, I have some pamphlets in my car that we like to give to new werewolves. I run a support group, meets after every full moon."

"Great," Lee said, her tone clipped.

Connor hesitated a moment longer. "I'll go get that for you, then," he said, and headed to the door, brushing his hand against Morgan's as he left.

Chapter 6

Bella was a fan of observing things. She liked observing people even better; people were always so varied, so *unique*, that even after all these years, she still met people who surprised her.

Lee was not one of these people.

Bella watched the way Lee seemed to fold up on herself when Connor returned with the pamphlet, how she responded to his gentle coaxing with curt, one-word responses, before Connor seemed to realise she wasn't a fan, and sat on the floor where Jessie began telling him a story she'd concocted about her dolls.

The pizza arrived not long after, and Lee gratefully dived on the excuse not to talk, shovelling food into her mouth.

Bella took advantage of her distraction to slip the pamphlet into her pocket. She felt eyes on her and looked up to see Connor watching; he nodded, she nodded, and he went back to Jessie's story (which was now interrupted with long bouts of chewing).

Morgan relaxed on the sofa, a glass of wine in his hand and a fond smile on his face as he watched his boyfriend and sister play together.

"She's a cute kid," Bella said, sitting next to him, and Morgan glanced at her out of the corner of his eye in a manner very reminiscent of Ariel. "You know, I've got a little sister," she added conversationally. "Human, still. She's about Jessie's age, though my sort of adopted brother is younger."

"How old are they?" Morgan took a sip of wine.

"Eight and six."

"Hm. Jessie's eight as well." Morgan swirled his glass' contents, looking pensive. "You did a good thing, saving her," he said suddenly, and Bella tilted her head, confused by the abrupt turn of conversation. "The way you keep looking at her," Morgan said. "Sad,

39

a little lost. She'll take time to adjust, but things will... settle. Not go back to the way they were, no, but it will get better."

Bella huffed quietly. "Look at you being the voice of reason."

Morgan winked. "I'm more than just a pretty face, darling. I also give advice, and sometimes that advice is even good." He raised his voice a little. "Boo, how do you think our guest is faring?"

It took Connor a moment to pull himself away from Jessie's story, but he got up and approached Lee, holding out a hand. She eyed it warily, but he just offered an encouraging smile.

"Healing and transforming both take energy," he said. "I think after nearly three thousand calories of fried dough and cheese you might be feeling a little better. Want to see how you do standing up?"

Lee dithered for a moment, glancing at Morgan, who gave her a lazy thumbs-up. Lee grit her teeth and took the offered hand, instinctively wincing in anticipation of the pain.

Bella smiled as Lee looked up at Connor, still wary, but now with amazement in her eyes. "It... doesn't hurt."

"Healing takes energy," Connor stressed again. "Vampires have different magic than we do and get their energy from blood, but we still have to rely on food. Bit closer to humans, seeing as we're not undead."

"What happens if vampires don't get blood?" Lee asked, glancing over her shoulder at Bella.

Bella hesitated.

"Oh, go on, Graves," Ariel said, picking apart a piece of pizza crust with his long fingers. "Worst that can happen is you terrify her and she runs away screaming."

"You're being *mean*," Jessie said, making a face at Ariel and pushing her glasses imperiously up her nose. She turned to Lee, straightening her shoulders with the importance of an eight year old sharing confidential knowledge. "*Vampires need regular consumption of human blood, lest they become desiccated and feral,*" she recited, and

Bella shifted uncomfortably in her seat. "*Animal blood may satisfy a vampire's cravings in a pinch, but is not viable as a long-term solution to hunger.*"

"Not that you have to worry about that," Bella said quickly when Lee's eye widened slightly. "I make sure to keep up with regular feedings, a-and besides, you're a werewolf. Your blood tastes more animal than human, so..." She offered a nervous smile, careful not to show her teeth. "Um, I mean, not that you weren't safe with me before, but you're even safer now."

Lee smiled back, though she looked a touch worried. "I know, Bells. You did save my life." She looked to Ariel, her smile softening a little. "You and Ariel both."

Ariel grunted, not looking up from his task of dismantling the pizza crust, but Bella felt her stomach twist. "Just doing my job," Ariel said, shrugging. "I wasn't on patrol, but you were still on my route. Any other hunter would've done the same." He glowered down at the bits of crust like it had personally offended him.

"Yeah, but you were the one who was there," Lee said. "So... thank you. Both of you."

Bella opened her mouth to speak, but paused when she heard the soft sound of tyres on concrete. "Someone's driving up to the house."

Ariel sat up immediately, his eyes wide, and Jessie went pale, scrambling to pick up her dolls while Connor helped her sweep them into their bin. Ariel began stacking plates, a tic in his jaw.

"It's your mom," Lee said as Morgan got to his feet, heading for the front door. "Isn't it?"

"I thought she wasn't going to be back until late," Bella said, helping Ariel clean up.

"Mommy usually is," Jessie said, glancing worriedly up at Connor.

Connor slid the bin into a cabinet and snapped the door shut. "We'll handle her, Pumpkin. It's alright."

Jessie nodded and disappeared; Bella could hear her bare feet pattering against the wood floor of the stairs, but fell silent halfway up.

Probably listening in, Bella thought, pursing her lips. The front door rattled and opened, and Bella heard two pairs of feet, two pairs of sharp heels clacking on the marble floor in the entry.

"Mother," she heard Morgan say. "And Madame Blanchard. What a pleasant surprise."

Bella's blood ran cold at the name. She heard a woman laugh—which, she wasn't sure—and the jangle of keys being set in a glass bowl. "Get to the point, Morgan," the woman said sharply, though there was a slowness to her words, like she couldn't quite form them into thoughts before speaking. "Where's Ariel? Is he hiding from me? That boy knows I'm not stupid, I can see his car out front."

"No, Mother, we were cleaning up dinner," Morgan said.

Bella and Lee glanced at each other, Lee biting her lip.

"She's drunk," Lee whispered, and Bella nodded, sliding on her sunglasses.

Bella tensed as the footsteps approached, and then a blonde woman who looked almost too young to have college aged sons appeared in the doorway, leaning heavily against the frame. Her pale blue eyes, so similar to Ariel's, were bloodshot, but her smile widened when she saw them sitting in the living room.

"Ariel, baby, you came home!" she cried, kicking off her heels and striding across the sitting room to embrace her son. Ariel forced a smile and gave her a one-armed hug, glancing over her shoulder at Morgan, who slunk into the room, followed by a woman who Bella could only describe as *ethereal*, untouched by the ravages of time.

While Ariel's mother looked like an exhausted businesswoman, hair in a dishevelled bun with her pinstripe skirt suit slightly wrinkled, Madame Blanchard seemed to radiate the cold beauty of winter. Her bone-white hair was pulled up in a high ponytail that fell well past her hips, and her floaty, off-the-shoulder gown seemed to shimmer like crystals when she moved and the fabric caught the light. Rubies sparkled in her ears and at her throat in a delicate crystal netting; the only other colour Bella could see on her whole person was her bright red lipstick, like a rose emerging from freshly-fallen snow.

Bella could smell the stink of Gloam about her, and tensed. She had heard of the magician's reputation before—powerful, and unsettlingly *sane* in comparison to her peers.

This is bad.

"Where's Jessie?" Ariel's mother demanded, holding him at arm's length. "Where's my baby girl? I want to see her."

"She's already gone to bed, Mother," Morgan said carefully, coming around to stand beside Ariel. "Tomorrow's a school night for her, after all." He glanced at Bella and Lee. "Bella, Lee, my mother, Ashley. Mother, these are Ariel's friends. They were just leaving."

"Nonsense!" Ashley pouted, draping herself over Morgan's shoulders. Even without her heels, she was taller than her eldest son. "I never get to see him anymore! Ariel, stay, just for a little bit?"

"You're home earlier than expected," Ariel said stiffly.

Ashley waved a well-manicured hand; Bella caught the flash of a silver wedding band on her finger. "Stocks are doing well, so I called Neve! We went to that lovely cocktail lounge on the river."

"Don't worry," Madame Blanchard said, inclining her head with the sharpness of a bird. "I made sure to drive her home safely." Her accent was strange, one that Bella couldn't quite seem to place. "I take my leave."

She disappeared in a shimmer of snowflakes, and Lee's jaw dropped.

Bella relaxed slightly, but only slightly.

43

"Don't gawp, it's unbecoming," Ashley said, shaking a finger at Lee, and her mouth snapped shut. "You must be the new werewolf. Just look at you!" She reached for Lee's face, and Lee recoiled before Morgan grabbed his mother's wrist, forcing her hand down. "You look just like my Morgan. Though you still have both your ears, don't you? Yes, yes, I see the piercings." She laughed, sagging against Morgan.

"Mother, you're drunk," Morgan said firmly, mouthing an "*I'm sorry*" to Lee. "You'll feel better after you've had something to eat. You *have* eaten?"

"Just those little, those..." Ashely held up two fingers close together. "Martini cherries."

"Maraschino, Mother," Morgan said. "Look here, we have leftover pizza—"

"No, no, nonono," Ashley said, shaking her head. Several more strands of hair fell loose from her bun, curling around her face. "You know I'm on a diet, pizza will just go to—go to my—make me fat."

Bella could see that, though Ariel had inherited his high cheekbones from his mother, Ashley's were much more pronounced, giving her face a drawn, pinched appearance.

"There's teriyaki chicken in the fridge," Connor said, glancing sidelong at Ariel and lifting his chin in the direction of the hall. "Mrs Montgomery, please—"

"Where are my manners!" Ashley thrust her hand out to Lee, who just shook her head and shrank back; Ashley pivoted towards Bella, hand still outstretched. Bella hesitated for a moment, but not wanting to be rude, took it. "I'm Ashley. It's *so* good to meet Ariel's friends!"

Ariel grit his teeth, and Bella knew he was only holding back his usual protestations out of concern for escalating the situation.

Ashley was now squinting at her, like she wasn't quite sure what she was looking at. "You're wearing sunglasses."

"I have photophobia," Bella said, the well-practiced lie falling from her lips. "Sensitive eyes, Mrs Montgomery."

There was a long pause, and then Ashley clapped her left hand over Bella's. Burning pain shot up Bella's arm, and she jerked her hand free with a yell.

"*Vampire!*" Ashley shrieked, and Bella backpedalled as Ariel put himself between his mother and Bella as Ashley snatched a remote off the coffee table, hurling it with uncanny accuracy under Ariel's arm; Bella only barely ducked to the side, and the remote cracked against a framed photograph. The glass shattered and fell to the floor with a cascade of soft tinkles, the sound swallowed by Ashley's outraged shriek as Morgan restrained her. "Get out! Get the *fuck* out of my house! And stay away from my family!"

"Go," Ariel said over his shoulder, still standing between Bella and his mother, and Bella grabbed Lee's hand.

"*Murderer!*" Ashley shrieked as they ran for the front door, Lee's gait a lurching gallop as she compensated for her bad leg. "*Bloodsucking parasite! I hope when you get sent to Hell, you'll ROT!*"

Bella wrenched the front door open and ushered Lee through.

"*ARIEL JORDAN MONTGOMERY, YOU COME BACK RIGHT THIS INSTANT—!*"

Ariel was right behind them, slamming the door shut and sprinting to his car, unlocking it on the way. They piled in, and Ariel pulled out of the driveway, jaw clenched and knuckles white on the steering wheel.

It wasn't until they'd pulled onto the freeway that Ariel spoke. "You shouldn't have seen that."

Bella looked down at her hands, rubbing her thumb over the new scar. "I shouldn't have come."

Ariel shook his head. "If it hadn't been you, it would've been someone else," he said bitterly. "Maybe without the accusations of

45

being a murderer, but the shouting always starts once her good mood's worn off."

"I'm sorry," Lee said quietly.

"Yeah, well, fat lot of good *sorry* does," Ariel snapped, and Lee hunched her shoulders, turning away to look out the window.

The ride back to the city fell into tense silence, without even music to break it. Several times, Bella opened her mouth to speak, but every time, Ariel shot her a glare, before she finally took the hint and pulled out her phone, debating whether or not to text her parents.

No, Bella decided, going to answer several messages from her donors. The Night Treaty had not been violated; though Ashley Montgomery's reaction to her presence had been...

Bella's stomach twisted.

Well, it was hardly great, but she still had enough sense not to violate it. But this would be worth bringing up during the next council elections. Morgan seemed pleasant enough, and certainly more stable.

The point of the Night Treaty was to keep them all safe; if a leader of the Gloam Hunters, and a Montgomery at that, was actively hostile to other Tenebrans, it would destabilise the peace they'd worked so hard to attain.

They reached campus just as the sun was setting, and Ariel pulled into his parking spot and killed the engine. "Get out."

Lee and Bella hastened to comply; Ariel remained in his car, and when Bella glanced over her shoulder back at him, he was on his phone, brow furrowed in a scowl.

"Come on," Bella murmured, lightly touching Lee's elbow. "Let's go back."

"How's your hand?" Lee asked quietly as they made their way to their dorm.

Bella rubbed the scar and sighed. "It's fine," she said. "I'll live, anyway." She put on a smile, perfected through long years of practice. "Not the worst thing a hunter's done to me."

"I'm sorry," Lee said. "You didn't deserve that."

"Yeah, no dur," Bella said, kicking an empty beer can down the sidewalk. "But what could I do? I defend myself, and boom, she's got probable cause to believe that her life was in danger."

"But you'd have witnesses," Lee protested. "Me and Ariel and Morgan—"

"Lot of good that does me with a silver knife in my chest."

"We wouldn't have let her hurt you," Lee said quietly. "Ariel put himself between his mom and you. He cares, even if he pretends not to."

Bella sighed. "Lee, it's sweet that you're worried about me, but I'd just like to put tonight behind us, alright?" she said. "Even if you're walking better, you still need rest if you're going to heal well, and you'll have strained your knee running from the house." She paused. "How does it feel, by the way?"

"Stiff. A little swollen and warm."

"Hm. Ice and elevation, and ibuprofen to reduce the swelling and pain," Bella said, tapping her chin. "Four hundred milligrams every two hours."

Lee hesitated briefly, and Bella checked herself so she wouldn't leave her roommate behind. "Isn't that, like, way higher than you're supposed to take?"

"Werewolves have faster metabolisms than humans," Bella said, pulling out the pamphlet.

"*You kept—?*"

"If I'm going to treat you, I need to know," Bella said. "I don't know what bad experiences you had with therapists in the past, but Connor knows more about being a werewolf than I do. You're going to need to know this stuff, and like it or not, he's probably your best

47

source of answers." She glanced over at Lee, who scowled down at her shoes as they walked. "Besides, you're going to need *somewhere* to go during the full moon, and the support group maintains safe houses for werewolves who don't have the resources to build their own... containment rooms."

Lee nodded slowly, her mouth turning down in a frown. "When's the next full moon?"

"October 27th," Bella said automatically.

"So I've got a few weeks." Lee sighed and shoved her hands in her pockets. "Does it ever get any... easier? More normal?"

"I don't know if I can answer that." Bella held the door open to their building, and she and Lee slipped inside. "I was born into this life, I've known about Tenebrous since forever. And it was something I looked forward to, you know? I couldn't wait to grow up and get turned. So the circumstances are hardly the same." She bit her lip, fangs lightly pricking the skin. "I'm sorry."

"Nah, s'fine," Lee said, giving her a tight smile. "I was just wondering."

They reached their room and Lee collapsed on her bed, kicking off her shoes with a soft groan. Bella bustled about, retrieving painkillers for Lee before filling a baggie with ice from their minifridge, wrapping it in a towel and putting it on her knee.

"Right," Bella said, "*don't* fall asleep with that on your leg. Will you be alright on your own?"

"Where are you going?" Lee asked, propping herself up on her elbows.

Bella glanced out the window, closing her eyes briefly as the last rays of sun slipped below the horizon. The Gloam seeped forth, like a surge of power filling every fibre of her being.

She leaned over to unlatch the window, opening it just a crack.

"I'm going out to feed," Bella said, opening her eyes. "Don't worry, it's all very above board, willing donors and everything. Maybe next time I'll even let you tag along to see what it's like."

"What *is* it like?" Lee asked.

Bella inhaled slowly. Her senses were always keener at night, and the smell of warm bodies full of blood stood out among the stink of the city. "Intense," she said. "Like the greatest rush you've ever felt. I think after tonight, I deserve a little pick-me-up."

Lee nodded. "Be careful out there," she said, biting her lip. "You—you will be careful, right?"

She was only asking out of concern for a friend, that was all. Bella swallowed and grinned, flashing her fangs. "Don't worry," she said. "I know how to take care of myself."

The Gloam rose to surround her at her call, enveloping her in tendrils of shadow. When they dissipated, she gave her wings several powerful flaps, fluttering out the window and leaving Lee's startled laughter behind her.

Chapter 7

Lee lay on her bed, scrolling aimlessly on her phone while she waited for the painkillers to kick in. An email from the scholarship foundation, a news article about a shooting in South Chicago, and then, when the idea struck her, websites of plastic surgeons specialising in scar reduction. The more she read, the more her heart sank, especially in regards to the cost of such a procedure.

Bella had offered to do it herself for free, but the idea of accepting left a sour taste in Lee's mouth. Nothing was ever offered out of the goodness of someone's heart, especially not something as big as this; there would always be the unspoken assumption of a debt owed hanging over her head.

No, she would just have to deal with this on her own.

She set the melting ice bag aside and got off the bed, pulling the curtains shut before beginning to strip, tossing her clothes into the laundry bag under her bed. She was tempted to look down at her healed injuries, but her stomach churned at the thought, and she squeezed her eyes shut against the urge.

Naked and feeling very silly, Lee stood in the middle of the room and tried to imagine what being a wolf would feel like. If she was going to be stuck with this curse for the rest of her life, she might as well make the best of it.

The change was instant and as easy as slipping into a still pond. Where Lee expected pain from her bones rearranging, muscles shifting, and coppery fur erupting from her body, she felt as *right* in this body as her human form. She fell to all fours and shook herself out, staring down at her paws in awe before twisting to get a look at her bushy tail, which wagged.

There was a pervading smell of iron in the room that hadn't been there before; Lee snuffled around, and upon finding the source strongest on Bella's bed, decided it must have been *Bella* she was smelling. Iron like blood. That made sense.

She reared up on her hind legs, struggling to balance before bracing her front paws against the wardrobe on either side of the mirror.

The scarring carried over, but here, Lee could face her reflection with less disgust. Here, she looked like a noble beast, a survivor of many battles, with too-human eyes the same green as her own peering back at her.

She tilted her head and turned back, leaning in with a frown.

The makeup Ariel had done for her was still safely in place. And, she realised, though she'd forgotten to take her jewellery out, all of her earrings and facial piercings looked just fine as well.

"I wonder," Lee murmured, touching the mirror.

Surely, she should have ruined the makeup and shredded her ears, nose, and lip with the jewellery tearing through skin, but Bella had said some werewolves could keep their clothes with practice...

No time like the present.

Lee got dressed in a ratty T-shirt she wore to sleep in and a pair of holey sweatpants that she'd been meaning to get rid of for a while. She took a deep breath and let the change come over her.

Once again, she landed on her paws, no sign of shredded clothing anywhere. Lee's eye widened and she let out a yip of laughter, tail wagging fiercely as she shook herself, fur rippling across her body.

Lee was practically bursting with confidence as she changed back, trying to stand up as she did so. The transition from quadrupedal to bipedal was harder than the other way around, though, and she windmilled her arms for balance before catching herself on her chair.

Her stomach growled, and Lee made her decision.

Let them see her scars. Right then, she felt she could handle *anything,* even the monsters.

She got changed again, this time into black skinny jeans and a tank top, a green flannel thrown over her shoulders to guard against the chill. She paused before testing her transformation again.

What if it doesn't work this time?

No, she was being silly. She had no reason to doubt herself now.

Once again, she transformed without issue, and laughed to herself before returning to her human shape.

"Alright," she said out loud, tugging on her Converse and grabbing her keys, "let's do this."

Chapter 8

Ariel lightly touched his Bluetooth earpiece, listening to the sparse radio chatter as the Gloam Hunters did their work.

"3 November Charlie, just dispatched a pair of shadow crawlers. No casualties, but some property damage needing coverup. Over."

His boots carried him along the River Esplanade, rubber soles silent as he kept his ears pricked. Muting the radio wasn't an option in the event of an emergency, so most nights, all he had to occupy his thoughts were the sounds of the city.

"7 Whiskey Delta, requesting cleanup at Washington Square Park. Rogue vampire dispatched. Over."

"Copy that," Morgan's familiar voice came through. *"Aliyah, how close are you? Over."*

"On my way, just by Durso. Over."

In the past, it had normally been his mother who would record the calls, tracking where each incident happened, rerouting hunters for assists, and making the call on what story to feed the news if it came to that. Ariel had never gotten to hear her on the radio; it had always been Morgan for as long as he could remember.

Ariel heard the soft thudding steps of large paws racing towards him, and he turned, the fingers of his silver arm twitching as he reached for his hunting knife.

It was a werewolf, galloping directly at him, fur flashing orange as it passed through a pool of light cast by a lamp. Ariel's gaze zeroed in on its back left leg, which couldn't quite seem to keep up with the others, giving it an odd lurch to its gait...

"Lee?" he asked warily, and the wolf skidded to a stop before him, rearing back on its hind legs as its fur began to vanish.

"Whoa, hey!" Ariel automatically shielded her with his hands, but then he heard Lee laugh.

"It's alright, look!"

53

Ariel risked a peek, and then his eyes flew wide, staring at her incredulously. "You—impossible," he said. "No way you figured out clothes that fast."

Lee spread her arms wide. "Apparently, I did."

"*How?*" Ariel asked, then held up a finger when he heard his zone called.

"*6 November Charlie, requesting backup!*" Maria Lín's steady voice came through, almost drowned out by snarling. "*I repeat, requesting backup at the parking garage, over!*"

"*Copy! Ariel, how close are you? Over.*"

"Riverfront," Ariel said, and took off running, not checking to see if Lee kept up with him or not. "Almost to Fahey. Over."

"*It's a pack of prowlers,*" Maria said. "*Watch yourself. Over and out.*"

Her radio went dead, and Ariel kept running. He heard paws beside him and glanced down to see Lee running along with him, keeping pace easily.

He'd deal with that later.

They reached the stairs leading up to the bridge, and Ariel took them two at a time, whipping around the curve to find himself faced with a construction barrier blocking the last steps to the drawbridge.

Without breaking his stride, he leapt at the chainlink fence, scaling it with ease and sliding over the bar at the top to drop neatly on the other side.

He ducked reflexively when Lee went sailing over his head, landing on the pavement much less gracefully when her bad leg buckled under her weight. She righted herself and *boof*ed at Ariel, who nodded and carried on, across the river and into the subterranean streets dimly illuminated by flickering lights.

Several cars honked at them when Ariel made a dash across a crosswalk just as the light turned green. The entrance to the parking garage came into view, and Lee whined when the smell of something *wrong* hit their noses. It was a cloying stench of decay, of things that creep in the damp and the dark, the sort of stench that lingers in the nose long after it's gone.

The sound of snarling reached their ears, and Ariel ducked under the bar, drawing his knife as they raced deeper underground. The sounds of battle grew louder, and the stench stronger, and a young woman dressed in black danced backwards into view, leading a pack of shadowy monsters after her.

Lee drew up short, her good eye huge, but Ariel didn't falter as he approached.

The snarling *things* looked like they had crawled from the very shadows themselves, each one a twisted tangle of malformed limbs that stretched too long and thin, talons tipped in darkness that scraped on the ground. Their faces were gaunt and sunken, hollow sockets in place of eyes, mouths full of too many teeth open in a perpetual shriek as they clawed at the hunter. Their slinking movements were pantherlike, skin clinging so tightly they looked skeletal, with whiplike tails lashing behind them.

"Maria!" Ariel called, and Maria glanced up, nodded, and led the prowlers towards Ariel. One of the beasts leapt at her, and she ducked under its outstretched claws, jabbing her knife up into its chin. The prowler didn't even have time to shriek as its body disappeared into wispy tendrils of shadow.

Ariel joined the fray, stabbing viciously with his left hand while swinging his right arm like a club, using the momentum from his shoulder to drive his fist into a second prowler's jaw. Shadows rose like smoke from where he'd made contact, and the prowler hissed and fell back, giving the hunters space.

"Took you long enough!" Maria called, jumping over a tail that cracked at her ankles. She flipped the knife so she was holding it in a reverse grip and stabbed behind her, severing the prowler's spine. It, too, burst into smoke, and Ariel finished off the last one, plunging his knife through the top of its head.

The stench remained, but at last the parking garage was silent. It was all over so fast Lee had to take a moment to process what happened.

Ariel sheathed his knife and turned to Maria. "You call that a pack?"

Maria snorted. "I was picking them off one by one before you showed up. Who's the werewolf?" she added, nodding at Lee, who was still frozen in place, tail tucked between her legs and ears flat against her skull.

"Just a new acquaintance of mine," Ariel said, hoping Lee wasn't going to transform back—

Lee reverted back to human form, Maria's eyebrows going up as she took her in. Lee's face was ashen, but she gave Maria a shaky smile. "I'm—"

"She's accompanying me on patrol tonight," Ariel said, cutting her off. "Just to see what it's like, you know?"

Maria arched an eyebrow, tugging loose her bleached-ombre ponytail and shaking her hair out before re-tying it. "I thought you didn't make friends, Montgomery."

"I don't," Ariel said flatly, touching his earpiece. "6 November Charlie, garage is cleared, no casualties, over."

"*Copy that,*" Morgan said. "*Back to your route. Over.*"

"Copy. Over." Ariel let his hand drop. "Much as I'd love to stay and chat," he said, his voice dripping with sarcasm, "I gotta go."

"Uh-huh," Maria said, rolling her shoulders. "Well, don't be a stranger."

Ariel jerked his head back the way they'd come, motioning for Lee to follow.

"*That,*" he hissed, "was stupid."

"What did I do?" Lee asked, bewildered. She hurried along with him, her long stride almost able to make up for her limp.

Ariel still had to slow his pace to let her keep up, gritting his teeth. "Do you have *any* idea how unusual it is that you can transform with your clothes this early on? So unusual it's not something to just go showing off to anyone before we know a reason for it! That's the sort of thing that takes *years* of practice!"

"Really?" Lee asked. "I mean, I know Bella said it should, but it really wasn't hard. I just kind of thought about doing it, and did it."

"You just 'did it,'" Ariel repeated flatly. He tugged on his glove as they crossed the bridge, returning to the north side of the river.

"...Yes?" Lee hedged.

Ariel shook his head. "I've never heard of a werewolf being able to do anything like that before," he said.

"You also didn't know that bit where we need to eat a lot," Lee pointed out, crossing her arms.

"That's different," Ariel said. "That's not relevant to hunting."

Lee frowned. "Isn't it?"

"If the information doesn't help me kill it, it's not worth remembering." Ariel picked up his stride, and Lee struggled to keep up with him.

Lee made a small sound of disagreement in the back of her throat. "I don't know," she said. "I think this is all pretty fascinating stuff."

"Yeah, because to you, this is all new and exciting," Ariel said. They reached the stairs blocked by construction, and Ariel climbed over the barricade.

This time, when he reached the other side, he turned to watch Lee back up a few steps and shift, taking a running start at the barricade. He watched the strain in her bad leg as her muscles bunched like coiled springs, sending her jumping far higher than a human could hope to manage. She landed on the stairs, and stuck it this time, turning back with an out of breath but triumphant smile.

"I mean," Lee said, and the smile faded, "it *sucks*. It still aches to walk, and I look like Quasimodo, and I get to look forward to going crazy once a month and... risk doing to someone else what happened to me." It didn't escape Ariel's notice how she blanched beneath her freckles. "But I guess... maybe that's why I was able to get transforming down so fast?" she suggested. "Because if I can use this to... to help people, then maybe I could learn to live with it, you know? Make it... something to not be afraid of." She forced a grin. "And, hell, how many people would want to be able to turn into a wolf on command? It's just *cool*."

Despite himself, Ariel chuckled darkly. "You say that now, but you haven't yet experienced your first forced transformation," he said. "Wait until after that happens, and then tell me if joining Tenebrous is really worth it." They reached the bottom of the stairs, and Lee paused upon seeing the pooling Gloam lying in wait for them.

"Uh, Ariel?" she said nervously as he drew his knife, striding forward.

A hodag emerged from the Gloam, red eyes glowing with malice. Ariel twisted his shoulder and swung his silver arm around to hit it in the throat when it lunged for him, and it let out a choked wheeze. It fell to the ground, shadows rising from its burns, and Ariel stabbed it in the eye, sending it back to the Gloam from where it was formed.

"*Wow,*" Lee breathed, and he turned to see her watching him with something... almost like awe.

"These monsters don't terrify you?" he asked, continuing along the riverfront. He tapped his earpiece. "Six Romeo Echo, back in position, over."

"*Copy that. Over.*"

"I mean, they do, but... I don't know," Lee said, hooking her thumbs in her pockets as they walked. "Like, those things earlier, those skeletal panther things with the tails—"

"Prowlers," Ariel said.

"Yeah, those were terrifying, and whatever that thing is you just killed—was it a hodag?"

Ariel glanced over at her in surprise. "Yeah, actually," he said, eyebrow raising. "How'd you know?"

He saw the nervous bob of her throat as she swallowed. "Just—folklore, monsters. Read a lot about them as a kid," she muttered, and glanced away. "It's not that they're not absolutely terrifying, because they are, but... I think if you taught me about them, maybe..." Lee took a deep breath. "Maybe I could help you fight."

Ariel stopped short, and Lee almost ran into him. He turned around to glower at her, and she defiantly straightened herself up to her full height—which was almost as tall as him, he realised. "You want to help fight," he said flatly.

Lee nodded. "I do."

Ariel scoffed. "You can walk on that leg, but you can't run," he said, holding up his hand when she opened her mouth to protest. "Not well, and not for any length of time. You seemed to do fine as a wolf, but you can hardly use a blade like that."

"I've got teeth," Lee said stubbornly. "I've got claws."

"Do you know what these things are?" Ariel began walking again.

Lee thought for a moment, trying to think of earlier in the day. "You called them Gloambeasts."

Ariel nodded, turning to look when he heard something rustle in the bushes. A squirrel darted across a low wall, disappearing again. "You know how when kids are little, their parents tell them not to be afraid of the dark?" he said. "My parents weren't like that. They told me I was right to be afraid of the dark, because it is alive, and it is watching."

Lee swallowed.

"The Gloam is present in the night," Ariel said as they continued along the river. "The best we've been able to glean from the magicians who studied it—well." He let out a humourless laugh. "There's a reason the most powerful among them are also the most insane. They, like all Tenebrans, draw their power from the Gloam, but in doing so, they sacrifice a part of themselves for power."

"Like Madame Blanchard," Lee guessed, and Ariel glanced at her. "I kind of got the sense she wasn't... fully human."

Ariel sighed. "I'm not exactly thrilled by the relationship she has struck up with my mother," he admitted.

They climbed a wide set of stairs leading away from the river, between another bridge and a sleek glass building with an overhanging metal roof.

"But," Ariel said after a moment of silence, "she takes a lot of the responsibility of keeping my mother in line away from Morgan. It's given him a bit of relief."

Lee nodded, but didn't pry, and for that, Ariel was grateful. "So the Gloam makes you crazy."

"Not exactly." Ariel wasn't wholly sure of the particulars, but then again, nobody was. "It twists the minds of the ones who delve too deeply into its mysteries. Others, it simply curses with a twisted existence. Vampires, werewolves, your kind pass the curse on to one another."

"Bella seemed to think it was a blessing," Lee said, frowning. "Well, not that she worded it that way, but she mentioned how she couldn't wait to become a vampire when she was a child."

"They can try to justify it all they want, but it doesn't change the fact that they are undead creatures, feeding on the living to survive," Ariel said. "You know what we call creatures like that? Parasites."

He turned, hearing a rasp of claws over brick, and upon making eye contact with the ghoul, it shrieked, lunging from the alley at a blinding speed. Ariel sidestepped a moment before its talons could rake across his throat, and his knife shot out, ripping upwards and spilling shadowy entrails before the whole thing burst apart.

"Do you really think Bella's a parasite?" Lee asked, her voice small. "After all, she saved my life, she's a doctor, she helps people…"

Ariel grit his teeth. "She can be a good person and still be all those other things," he said. "Tell me, since she never would have let you out while you're still healing, where is she now?"

Lee hesitated.

"Feeding. Right?" Ariel shook his head. "Their saliva is addictive, you know. Not physically, psychologically. A vampire's bite triggers the pleasure centres of the brain, releases a flood of endorphins, so you keep coming back again and again, assuming you don't get drained dry to begin with."

"*Oh.*"

Ariel heard the squeak in her voice and glanced back. "Don't be getting any ideas," he said dryly. "Not only does your blood taste terrible to them, but a werewolf's saliva is toxic to vampires, too."

"I… see." Lee bobbed her head. "What about Gloambeasts?"

"No. The only thing that can send a Gloambeast back to the weave it came from is silver," Ariel said, unsheathing his hunting knife and showing Lee the silver inlay in the blade. "Which is why hunters are human. Silver burns all creatures of the Gloam—"

"Even mages?" Lee interrupted, and Ariel bit back a sharp retort.

"*No,*" he said patiently, "because mages are *not* creatures of the Gloam in the way vampires and werewolves are. They simply channel it to warp reality, though the smart ones prefer to stick to more subtle means of manipulation—like enhancing durability, for example." He raised his arm, twiddling the fingers. The motor in his hand whirred softly.

"That reality warping's why nobody looked twice at me as a wolf," Lee guessed, and Ariel nodded. "Bella mentioned it's why people never notice her fangs—well, not exactly, but I could extrapolate from what she said."

They turned onto Hubbard Street, the both of them silent for a moment.

"I could still hurt Gloambeasts, couldn't I?" Lee asked, glancing up at Ariel. "Like, I'm guessing there's not enough hunters for you to work in pairs? If Maria was anything to go by..."

"There's never enough of us," Ariel said heavily. "The winters are the worst. Longer nights, more monsters. The only time we have multiple hunters on a patrol is when one is training another."

"So you could really use the help," Lee said.

God help him, he was considering the idea.

"Tell you what," he said, "next patch we encounter, you take it on first. See if you can't make my job easier for me."

Lee's eyes shone. "And if I do, you'll take me on?"

"I'll *consider* it," Ariel said sharply. "The last thing I need is you slowing me down and making things worse. It's difficult enough as it is to keep up a patrol."

Lee snapped off a surprisingly crisp salute. "Sir, yes sir!"

Ariel rolled his eyes, fighting back a smile.

It was in an alley beside a donut shop that they found their next target. Ariel held up a hand, and Lee stilled, following his gaze to the writhing shadows.

"On it," she said, and her form shifted. Ariel kept his knife at the ready, and when Lee met the axehandle hound in a blur of teeth, he fully expected the creature to draw blood.

But Lee ducked under its bladed face, her fangs sinking into its throat in a spray of shadow, and she dragged it over to Ariel, who disposed of it at once.

Lee transformed back, spitting on the sidewalk. "Blegh! Tastes like rotten eggs!"

"Still want to accompany me on patrol?" Ariel said dryly, and Lee straightened up immediately.

"I do," she said. "I..." She glanced away and tried and failed to surreptitiously spit out the last of the taste in her mouth. "I think..." She took a deep breath and looked away. "I think this might help me with..." Lee trailed off, and looked up at him suddenly like she'd just remembered he was there. "Uh, I think it might help me with this, I mean." She gestured uncertainly at her face.

Ariel shrugged. "Maybe. Maybe not. People are gonna stare whether you like it or not. You can't control them, only you." He checked his watch. "Hope you're up to walking. It's another six and a half hours 'til we get relief, and the closer we get to midnight, the thicker the Gloambeasts come."

In response, Lee just smiled and cracked her knuckles.

Chapter 9

B ella landed in an alley across the street from the nightclub and transformed back, a sense of relief washing over her at the thought of the fresh blood that awaited her. She fluffed out her hair puff before unzipping a pocket of her leather jacket to pull out her compact eye shadow, taking a moment to touch up her makeup. After all, her donors were providing her a service; the least she could do was make the experience a good one.

Once she was satisfied, she snapped the case shut and crossed the street to the club, nodding at the hunter guarding the door as she passed.

Monica inclined her head in turn. "Alright there, Bella?"

"Just here for a quick nip," Bella said, smiling brightly, and Monica waved her in. She'd been coming here ever since the nightclub was founded; bouncers had come and gone, but they all knew the regulars on sight. Bella was familiar with the other clubs in the city, but Dark Desires was the only lesbian venue catered specifically for vampires and their clients that was backed by the Gloam Hunters' protection.

The inside was dim and lit with neon lights of magenta, turquoise, and lime, the pulsing beat of the music loud but not so loud as to deafen a vampire's sensitive ears. Cassandra, who had owned the place for a good four decades, had kept it running through police raids and public attacks alike, and defended her sanctuary fiercely. That night found her tending the bar, which was an illuminated glass affair that displayed colourful bottles of alcohol. Behind her was a large sign that said *NO DRINKS FOR THE DRINKS*, and underneath it a smaller sign, saying, *(After being drank)*.

"Back so soon?" Cassandra asked as Bella took a seat at the bar.

"Bad day," Bella said, pulling off her sunglasses and hanging them on the front of her shirt. "Charlotte should be here soon—can I get the usual for her?"

Cassandra made the screwdriver and passed it over to Bella, who nodded her thanks and turned to keep an eye on the entrance.

. . . .

Bella learned her lesson long ago not to try flying while drunk, so she opted to walk back to her dorm, a pleasant buzz running through her. Guilt pooled in her stomach, but she shoved it aside. Charlotte would understand she hadn't wanted to linger.

She made her way down Franklin Street, pausing to lean against one of the metal supports that held up the railroad tracks overhead. She could swear she smelled Lee had been here recently, and with a much stronger smell of wolf than before. And... was that Ariel?

Wait. Wait. Bella straightened up, peering blearily at the sign hanging from the underside of the tracks. Ontario Street—this was the north side of Ariel's patrol route. She'd sniffed it out ages ago.

Bella tried to work through the sluggish thoughts. If Lee was out here, that meant... that meant...

Oh, no.

Someone must have done to her what they were doing to the other werewolves. Which meant if she attacked someone, Ariel was well within his rights to kill her.

Lee is in trouble.

Bella took off running, trying to shake off the effects of the alcoholic blood.

Never should have left her alone. Stupid, stupid!

She heard a wolf snarl up ahead and her blood ran cold.

It was in a narrow alley she found them. Ariel's back was to her, but she could see his hunting knife in hand, and the smell of werewolf was stronger here... along with the smell of Gloam?

65

Bella frowned, then stumbled back when Ariel twisted aside, narrowly avoiding getting scalped by a shadow crawler's barbed tentacles. His arm shot forward and the Gloambeast burst apart, leaving no trace behind but a faintly lingering stench of Gloam.

"...Ariel?" Bella said tentatively, and he startled before realising who it was.

"Jesus *Christ*, Graves," he said, sheathing his knife. "Don't *do* that."

"Bella!" Lee came running, and Bella barely had time to register how much more easily Lee was moving before Lee had picked her up in an enthusiastic bear hug. "You weren't following us, were you?"

"You're..." Bella's legs flailed before Lee put her down, and Bella grabbed hold of Lee's shoulder for balance. "You're... thought you were in trouble..."

"Oh. Um." Lee rubbed the back of her neck, glancing behind her at Ariel. "I guess I should've texted, but I didn't want to disturb... whatever you were doing... are you drunk?"

"Little bit," Bella laughed, somewhat strained. "What are you doing out here?"

"Following me around like a lost puppy," Ariel said dryly. "Graves, I have a schedule to stick to. Either keep up or get lost."

"You go on ahead," Lee said, getting an arm around Bella, who sagged gratefully against her. "I'll get her back to our dorm."

Ariel didn't even hesitate; he simply turned and continued down his route, tapping his earpiece to update the hunters.

Lee supported Bella as they made their way back to campus, Bella clinging tightly to her roommate. "Your leg," she said woozily. "Doesn't it hurt?"

"Still aches, but it's getting there," Lee said. "Ariel and I got burritos about an hour ago, which helped. I thought you were feeding, not off getting drunk—I didn't even know vampires *could* get drunk."

Bella giggled. "Donor got drunk, I drank the donor, my drink got me drunk." She snorted, looking up at Lee. "Wanna drink you."

Lee glanced down at her. "I don't think I would taste very good," she said. "Werewolf, remember?"

"So?" Bella tried to put the words together into a coherent thought, but it was hard. She hadn't done this in a while. How long was a while, again? "Wanna show you it feels good."

Lee laughed awkwardly and shifted her grip around Bella's waist so she could unlock the door to their building. "Maybe some other time."

"Yay!"

Lee managed to get Bella up to their room, and Bella toed off her shoes before flopping onto her bed, rolling over to look up at Lee. "You know we get stronger when we feed?" she asked loudly.

"Shh, Bella, people are sleeping," Lee said, hanging up her flannel and pulling a bottle of vodka out from under her bed. "But no, I didn't."

"We do," Bella sighed, closing her eyes. "Was scared something happened to you. But maybe I'd be strong enough to protect you."

She heard Lee chuckle and the sound of a lid unscrewing. "I'm strong enough to protect myself now, but thank you. I'll tell you in the morning, Bella."

Chapter 10

When Lee gave Bella a rundown of the night before, she'd expected a scolding for straining her leg so early on. While Bella *did* scold her for that, she was much more intrigued by Lee's transformation abilities, but still seemed incredulous even after a demonstration.

"Have you ever heard of this before?" Lee asked anxiously, but Bella shook her head.

"No, never. But..." Bella gnawed her lip, thinking for a moment. "Tell you what. I'll put out some feelers—don't worry, I won't say it's about you specifically," she said when Lee opened her mouth to protest. "Just see if some of my old friends might have heard of something similar."

The wait to hear back was anxiety-inducing, but at least Lee now had patrol with Ariel to keep her mind occupied. Between that and finishing up homework she'd been neglecting, she didn't have any leftover time to *think* during fall break, which was exactly what she wanted. But as the week drew to a close, and none of Bella's contacts came up with definite answers, Lee felt her anxiety ramp up at the prospect of returning to a normal schedule—at knowing she would soon have to be among *people* again.

Bella might have been able to bring her meals from the dining hall until now, but there would be no escaping going to class.

Maybe I should ditch, she thought early Monday morning as she got dressed, raking a brush through her hair. *Maybe I should drop out of school. Not like an English degree would get me anywhere, anyway.*

But then what? Where would I go, what would I do?

Lee set her brush aside and poked gingerly at the makeup Ariel had re-done for her the night before.

I can't avoid people forever.

Heart heavy and stomach full of lead, Lee picked up her battered old backpack and slung it over her shoulder, slouching downstairs and out the door.

Every sense felt hyper-aware, and she was certain she could feel everyone's eyes on her as she limped across campus.

Stop being stupid. Not everyone's gawping at you. People have better things to do.

They're not all staring at you.

They're not.

Lee reached the humanities building and tapped in, her heart sinking when the woman behind the front desk gasped quietly. She hurriedly turned aside to head to her classroom, ducking her head when she passed students going in the opposite direction.

"Did you see her face?" she heard one whisper, and hot tears stung her eyes.

She wrenched open the door to her art history class, keeping her head down and using her hair like a curtain to shield herself. Though she normally liked it short, right then she wished it was longer than chin length.

"Lee!" she heard Professor Mallaby say, and she hunched her shoulders. "Did you have a good fall break?"

Without saying a word, Lee took her seat, and she heard the professor's breath catch when he caught sight of her face.

"...I'm not going to ask what happened," Professor Mallaby said after an intensely awkward silence that seemed to stretch on longer than it actually did. "It's none of my business. But my door's open if you want to talk."

Lee just pulled her textbook out and hid behind it, using it as a shield as other students began to trickle in. At least here in the front, nobody else was going to see her face.

• • • •

She made it until halfway through the day, when they were supposed to partner up in Spanish class to practice asking each other questions. Her partner openly stared, and when the professor called for a break, said, "Look, I've just gotta ask—what happened to your face?"

Lee burst into tears, crying harder when the class turned around to look at the commotion. She crammed her notebook into her bag and rushed out the door, going to the nearest bathroom and locking herself into a stall where she sagged against the door, her sobs echoing loudly off the tiled walls.

She wasn't sure how long it was before they died down to quiet hiccups, but the tears kept coming until she'd cried herself out.

The door opened and Lee bit down on her sleeve to muffle herself as she listened to footsteps approach her stall.

Someone knocked gently on the door. "Hey, are you okay in there?"

"I'm fine," Lee bit out.

"It's just, Katie said someone was crying in the bathroom—"

"I said I'm fine!" Lee snapped. "Leave me alone!"

A pause.

"Alright," the student said. "I hope you feel better soon."

Lee listened to the student leave before sniffling and reaching for more toilet paper to blow her nose. She was exhausted, and her stomach reminded her with an angry rumble that she hadn't eaten all day.

She checked her phone and winced. It would be dark soon, and she had several texts from students in her classes she'd gotten numbers of in case of missed homework, asking where she was. She ignored them and slunk out of the bathroom, the sound of her uneven footsteps seeming deafeningly loud in the deserted hallways.

Chapter 11

There was no patrol with Ariel tonight to even distract her from her thoughts. Lee lay in bed, staring at the ceiling while Judas Priest blasted from her phone's speakers.

Again, the thought that she would be better off dropping out crossed her mind, and she scowled. She hadn't busted her ass throughout high school to get a full ride scholarship only to drop out in her first semester.

But then again, she also hadn't expected to get half her face torn off by a werewolf, to get dragged into an alley, screaming as she clawed desperately at the asphalt when it seized her leg in its powerful jaws, hearing the awful crunch of bone—

Lee bit down on her knuckle, stifling a sob. She forced herself out of bed and pulled on her shoes.

She needed to run.

She headed outside and transformed out of sight before loping down the street, not really caring about where she was headed.

"Look, Mommy, a wolf!" a little boy cried as she passed.

"James, there aren't any wolves in the city, it's just a dog," she heard his mother say before she was of earshot.

Funny how she felt more like herself, on four legs and covered in fur, than she did in her own skin. Or maybe this was the only way to escape what had happened, by slipping into a different body. Maybe this way she could pretend all of that had happened to someone else.

Lee crossed the river, which reflected the lights of the skyscrapers on either side, twinkling like stars in the water. The moon's reflection loomed as well, growing fuller by the day.

What would it be like? She wondered. *To lose control, like the monster that attacked me? I don't want to hurt anybody. I won't.*

She raced through a patch of Gloam with a growl, teeth ripping into whatever creature tried to grab her from the darkness. She heard it reform behind her, but kept on running. This was Maria's territory, and the hunter was due to be by at any minute.

Lee's ears pricked up when she heard a yell of pain accompanied by snarling. She sprinted towards the yell, paws slamming against the sidewalk.

The smell of blood hit her nose as she reached an alley, and Lee rounded the corner to see an enormous grey wolf, snarling as it shook Maria by the arm. Her knives lay discarded on the ground behind her.

Lee's blood turned to ice, and for a moment, she froze in place, tail tucked between her legs. She couldn't think, couldn't breathe; her vision narrowed, and it wasn't *this* wolf but the *other*, and she was back in the alley again—

The werewolf flung Maria against a wall with a nasty *crack*, and the hunter slid down to the ground in a streak of blood.

It was enough to bring Lee back to the present. The adrenaline kicked in, and Lee launched herself at the werewolf with a howl.

They clawed at each other, snarling as they fought. The other werewolf was bigger, stronger, and soon gained the upper hand. Lee yowled as it bit down on the back of her neck, hot blood dripping down her fur, and the werewolf wrestled her to the ground.

Silver, a corner of Lee's mind whispered. *I need silver.*

She transformed back, snatched up one of Maria's fallen knives, and stabbed behind her. The blade sliced into the werewolf's leg and it let go with a yelp before baring its teeth at Lee. It tried to run, but collapsed, and before it could get up, Lee was on top of it, stabbing over and over as a wordless scream tore from her throat.

When her vision cleared, the werewolf was already dead, a naked, bloodied man sprawled on the ground and covered in stab wounds. Lee scrambled backwards, the knife slipping from her grasp, and she stared in horror before she heard a soft, groaning gurgle behind her.

Maria was still alive.

Lee crawled towards her, tapping anxiously on Maria's face and getting no response.

Stop the blood first. Then get help.

Lee ripped off her flannel shirt and, after a frantic search for the knife she'd dropped, began cutting it up into makeshift bandages, wrapping them around Maria's arm before using the rest to staunch the bleeding from the gashes in her side, blood beginning to soak through almost instantly. She was still bleeding heavily from the back of her head, and Lee groaned before pulling off her tank top as well, cradling Maria's head in her lap as she used her tank top to staunch the bleeding from the hunter's skull.

She pulled Maria's earpiece out with trembling, bloody fingers, and fumbled as she tried to put it in with one hand, using the other to hold the flannel against Maria's ribs.

"Um—um—Maria's down," she stuttered. "6, uh, 6—" She tried to remember how Ariel had explained the patrol system, but she could barely *think*.

"*Lee?*" Morgan's voice came through. "*Okay, darling, deep breaths. I'm seeing you're down by the Willis Tower; can you tell me where exactly you are? Over.*"

Lee looked up frantically, sucking in a shuddering breath. "I, I passed the, um, the—we're in an alley by a parking garage—"

"*Orange neon sign by the garage entrance? Over,*" Morgan's soothing voice said.

"Yeah," Lee stammered after a frantic glance to confirm it. "You gotta hurry, it's—it's bad—"

"*I'm just a few blocks away, over,*" a man said, but Lee shook her head even though they couldn't see.

"The werewolf's dead, Maria needs a doctor," Lee said, and her heart hammered as she waited for a response.

After what seemed an age, Morgan spoke again. "*Copy that, Lee. Hang tight. Help is coming. Over.*"

Lee remained huddled over Maria, goosebumps springing up on her exposed skin. Her sweat began to cool, the blood on the nape of her neck congealing and sticking down her hair.

Her legs were numb by the time a van pulled up to the alley's mouth, and a tall, burly woman got out, approaching carefully.

"Lee?" the woman called, and Lee nodded frantically, not trusting herself to speak. "My name is Gina. Morgan sent me."

Gina knelt beside Lee, beginning to check Maria over, working with the precision and speed of many years of practice, and Lee felt her breathing ease somewhat as Gina glanced up at her with a faint smile. She had a proud, handsome face, and long dark hair that fell in a tight plait down her back.

"How long has she been unconscious?" Gina asked as she finished wrapping bandages around Maria's wounds, holding Lee's makeshift dressings in place.

"I-I dunno," Lee stammered. "Five minutes?"

Gina sucked air through her teeth, pulling a penlight out and gently holding one of Maria's eyes open. "Normally not great, but once her healing factor kicks in, she'll be alright," she said, letting go. She tapped her earpiece. "Section 6, hunter is stabilised, confirmed bite." She nodded at Lee. "Hang on just a minute, and I'll be right back."

Lee nodded, hugging Maria a little more tightly.

Gina returned with a stretcher, and they eased Maria onto it, loading her into the van and onto a wide, padded bench built into the side. Lee realised the entire thing had been converted into a makeshift ambulance.

Gina opened a cabinet to pull out a blanket to cover Maria before strapping her in. "Here," Gina said, and Lee startled before looking up. Gina held out another blanket with a gentle smile. "You look cold."

Lee accepted the blanket, grateful Gina hadn't commented on her chest, painfully flat and lacking so much as the barest hint of breast. She wrapped the blanket tightly around herself and slowly sat on the bench opposite Maria, beginning to shiver harder despite the warmth. Gina climbed out the back and retrieved Maria's knives; just as she was returning, another van pulled up behind them, and a large man with a bushy beard climbed out. The two spoke for a moment, too low for Lee to hear, and then Gina shut the doors and climbed into the driver's seat.

"Where are we going?" Lee asked, her teeth chattering.

"My place," Gina said, and the van rumbled to life. "I'll be able to treat her better there."

Lee nodded, her good leg beginning to jitter. "Are you a doctor?"

Gina chuckled. "No, but I've got some experience as a paramedic. I actually work in IT, now." She glanced in the rearview mirror. "You did a proper number on that werewolf back there."

"It was attacking Maria," Lee said, her voice shaking. "Why? I thought—I thought w-we were only supposed to—to go crazy during the full moon..."

"Shit, kid, haven't you heard?" Gina asked. "Something's out there that's been making werewolves go feral."

Lee's mouth felt dry. "What do you mean?"

She saw Gina's shoulder rise in a slight shrug. "Whoever that poor bastard was, it's doubtful he just saw a hunter and decided to try his luck," she said. "Which means this was likely another one of the feral attacks."

"But *what's* been making werewolves go crazy?" Lee said, her voice shooting up an octave. "This is a whole *thing*? How come nobody told me?"

"Hey, hey, easy there," Gina said. "It's only been happening recently, like 'last couple of weeks' recently."

Lee looked down at her knees. Knee.

"You must be new," Gina said, and Lee looked back up, meeting her eyes in the mirror. "Did the Montgomery kid do your makeup?"

"How did you—?"

Gina chuckled. "He used to hang around my clinic so he could learn to copy wounds with his makeup kit. I still see him sometimes, making the rounds."

Lee nodded, hugging the blanket more tightly around her shoulders. "I was attacked last week," she said softly.

Gina let out a low whistle. "That's rough. I'm sorry."

"...Thanks." Lee gnawed on one of her snakebite piercings as she studied Maria's face. The hunter's olive skin was pale from blood loss. "You're sure she's going to be alright?"

"Mostly. She'll live, if that's what you mean," Gina said. "Might need physical therapy for her wrist, but we'll see how it's healing when she wakes up."

"So the werewolf that attacked me," Lee said, and swallowed. "I thought they just... sometimes... did that."

Gina made a small noise in the back of her throat. "Sometimes, but it's *incredibly* rare. Most werewolves are still decent people. I mean, look at you." She glanced over her shoulder, giving Lee a brief smile. "You saved Maria's life."

Guilt settled in Lee's stomach. If she hadn't frozen up, maybe Maria would be in better shape. Maybe she could have done something more, could have helped sooner...

Silence fell over the van before Gina turned on the radio, humming along as the van continued towards its destination.

Lee looked up when Gina spoke into the silence. "Copy, over," she said, and glanced over her shoulder again. "The werewolf's been ID'd."

76

Lee's heart leapt into her throat. "He... he has?"

"Mm-hm. One of the missing ones from the support group, apparently. Wasn't given any more information than that, sorry to say."

"Oh." Lee's toes curled in her shoes. "Ariel was the one who took care of my attack... do you know who did that?"

"I'd have to look at the logs, kid," Gina said, shaking her head. "Still, you've got guts, I'll give you that. You don't have anyone waiting for you back home, do you?"

"Just my... roommate," Lee said, grabbing her phone from her pocket. "*Shit.*"

There were several missed texts from Bella, and Lee hastily sent her a reply, vaguely saying she'd gone out.

She could tell Bella what had happened later.

Gina parked the van in the Lower West Side, outside a small, one-story brick house covered in peeling white paint. "Alright, easy does it," she said as she and Lee maneuvered Maria through the house and into the back room. It had been converted into a makeshift clinic set up with three different beds, one of which was occupied by a sleeping figure.

They got Maria settled, and Lee scrubbed the blood off her face and arms at the large, stainless steel basin before Gina shooed her out into the living room, which held a sagging, squashy sofa and a coffee table that had seen better days.

"Sit," Gina said, and Lee sat, glancing around.

Gina disappeared into another room and came back, holding a juice box and a sweatshirt with a picture of a giant lizard on it. "I'll let you know when you can come in," she said, and went back to the clinic room to attend her patients.

Lee pulled on the sweatshirt, breathing a small sigh of relief once it was over her head. She jabbed the straw into the juice box and sank back against the sofa cushions, closing her eyes as she sipped tiredly at her drink.

Chapter 12

Lee must have dozed off at some point, because she startled awake at hearing Gina's voice: "You can come see her."

Lee uncurled from the sofa and stretched, her joints cracking with a series of satisfying pops. She headed into the clinic, where she found Maria sitting up, her black and bleach-blonde ombre hair a dishevelled halo around her head.

Maria's eyebrows flew up when she saw Lee, but she quickly composed herself, giving Lee a tired smile. "Hey," she said hoarsely. "Gina told me what you did. Thank you."

So she didn't know that Lee had frozen up when Maria needed her help.

Lee tried to smile back. It felt forced. "I'm just glad you're still alive," she said, sitting next to Gina on the third bed. "How are you feeling?"

"Bit dizzy and I can't see straight," Maria admitted, "but considering how hard that mutt threw me into the wall, it could be a *lot* worse. Wrist hurts like a bitch, though," she added, lifting her arm for Lee to see it had been cleaned and re-bandaged properly.

"You should be able to take those off in the morning," Gina said. "As for how much mobility your hand will have, I can give you some exercises to do, but I'm no doctor."

"I know one," Lee piped up, and Gina looked at her interestedly. "Well, kind of. She's my roommate. And, um, a vampire." She winced, but neither Maria nor Gina seemed phased by this.

"Interesting," Gina said instead. "Do you think she'd be willing to give us a hand?"

"Pun intended?" Maria said dryly, and Lee giggled nervously.

"I *think* so," Lee said. "Her name's Bella, she's really nice. She helped me with..." She trailed off, gesturing at her face.

"Did a good job of it," Maria said, growing serious again. "You're the werewolf that was with Ariel last week, aren't you? I mean, unless I'm grossly mistaken, but I doubt it. I thought he was acting weird, so I looked you up."

Lee nodded, glancing down and biting her lip.

"*You're* Accalia Lowell?"

"Just Lee is fine," Lee said, rubbing the back of her neck. Her fingers came away sticky with blood.

"Hang on," Gina said, catching Lee's wrist. Lee flinched and pulled back out of reflex. "...Sorry. Can I see the back of your neck?"

Lee swallowed, but pulled her hair up for Gina to examine her.

"But you were turned just a week ago—how'd you figure out the clothes thing so fast?" Maria asked.

Lee flinched again when Gina began cleaning away the blood on her neck. "I don't know," she said. "I just... kind of did it."

"Wait, you can transform with your clothes already?" Gina asked incredulously, her hands pausing for a moment. "And you were bitten that recently?"

Ariel's going to be furious.

"I... yeah," Lee said, her face going a blotchy red.

Gina let out a low whistle. "You must have a gift, kid," she said, going back to her work. "Some werewolves are just like that, you know? Poor George, the fellow from earlier, was one of them. Never figured out clothes like that, though." She sighed. "Suppose he never will, now."

Lee swallowed, hands clenching on her thighs in an attempt to keep her hands from shaking. "Guess not," she whispered.

Maria just shook her head, rubbing her wrist. "I just hope I can pick it up that fast, too, since..." She trailed off, frowning into the distance. "Since I'm going to get taken off the roster."

"Why can't you keep hunting?" Lee asked. "I mean, I was able to use your knife to k-kill—"

80

She stuttered to a stop when she realised the implications. Though he'd been a savage beast at the time, the werewolf she'd killed had been a *person*. Just like whoever had attacked her.

That could have been me.

Lee felt like she'd been punched in the gut.

Maria didn't seem to notice, continuing like Lee wasn't having a crisis in front of her. "Conflict of interest," she said. "Gloam Hunters keep the other Tenebrans in line, so what happens if I'm out on patrol and run into a werewolf I know, who's gone rogue?"

"Makes sense," Lee whispered.

"Besides, I..." Maria rubbed her wrist again. "Well, dealing with the full moon, that's going to make me an unreliable asset, even if we know them in advance. My life as a hunter is over." She drew her knees to her chest, hugging them loosely with her good arm.

Gina dropped the bloodied alcoholic wipe into a covered bin and sat back down. "There's still freelancing," she said, and Maria wiped her eyes; Gina offered her a box of tissues, but Maria shook her head. "And I know you already know about the support group, but let me get you one of their pamphlets... Lee, do you have one?" she asked as she got up to rummage in a filing cabinet.

"I'm not going," Lee said stiffly, latching onto the distraction.

"Kid, I'm going to be blunt here," Gina said as she handed Maria one of the pamphlets, "if you didn't know about Tenebrous until last week, it's a hell of a lot of shock to take in all at once. And now on top of that, there's everything that happened *tonight*, too. I really recommend you at least give it a try."

Lee glared down at the offered pamphlet until Gina set it aside.

"It *would* be nice, not having to go alone," Maria said, and Lee glanced up at her. "Maybe consider it for me?"

Lee's face contorted. "You want to know what they do at those so-called 'support groups'?" she said, making sarcastic air quotes. "You introduce yourself, everyone says hi, you tell your story, whoever's running the thing for their own sick satisfaction says 'That's nice, dear, have a cookie, who's next?' and after they drug you up on their newest cocktail of happy pills, if you still aren't able to shape up enough for them, it's juvie for you."

Maria gave her a long look. "You sound like you're speaking from experience."

Lee bristled. "And what if I am?"

"Okay, girls, I think that's enough," Gina said, and Lee folded her arms, glowering. "Maria, I'd like to keep you overnight for observation, but if you're feeling well, I can take you back into the city?"

"My parents are going to freak if I'm not home for breakfast," Maria said, swinging her legs off the bed. "Please do."

Gina nodded and turned to Lee. "It's a long way to run back," she said meaningfully.

Lee was very tempted to tell her to piss off, but bit back a slew of choice words and nodded once. "Fine."

"I'll get the van running." Gina left, and Maria bent over to pull on her boots.

"You know," Maria said quietly, glancing up at Lee, "not all of them are like that."

Lee snorted. "Like you would know."

"I would, actually, yeah," Maria said, and pulled up the sleeve of her uninjured left arm, turning it over for Lee to see a series of white, parallel scars that ran up her forearm like the rungs of a ladder.

Lee's breath hitched, and Maria pulled her sleeve down.

"But go on," Maria said, and finished tying her shoes, "keep on acting like you're the only one who's ever had a hard life, here." She tugged her coat on with a wince and strode out the door.

Not for the first time that night, guilt gnawed at Lee's stomach, but she squashed it down and hurried to follow Maria.

They piled into the back of the van, and Gina started it up, taking them back to the city centre.

"I'm sorry," Lee said quietly, and Maria glanced up. Lee, however, looked away, sliding down a little lower in her seat. "I, um. Shouldn't have assumed."

Maria lightly kicked her shin, mindful not to hit her bad leg. "Hey, you couldn't have known," she said. "But does this at least mean you'll consider coming to the support group with me?"

Lee gnawed on one lip ring, then the other, before she sighed. "Okay," she muttered. "Promise I'll go. But just *one* meeting. That's *it.*"

She ignored the knowing smile Maria was giving her, opting to instead pull out her phone again.

She made a group chat, added Ariel and Bella, and sent the text that was the bane of everyone:

We need to talk.

Chapter 13

B ella had no idea what Lee wanted to talk about, and asking her for answers when her roommate got home was a bust; Lee simply mumbled something about being too tired to talk and promptly collapsed into bed, fully dressed.

Bella was certain she hadn't owned that sweatshirt before.

She tried waking Lee when the alarm rang, but Lee swatted her hand away and mumbled something incoherent into her pillow, so Bella decided to let her sleep.

She attended her classes, taking notes as dutifully as ever, even if she did already know the material; after all, the last time she'd been in university had been during the Seventies, and things had changed since then.

Around midday, she returned to her room to drop off her books and pick up the ones for her afternoon lessons, only to find Lee was gone, her smell mixed with the smell of alcohol faint, like she'd left at least a few hours prior. Whether she'd gone to class or somewhere else, Bella didn't know, but that wasn't her problem right now.

Off to her Japanese lesson, where she *did* have to pay attention—she'd already learned French, Spanish, Latin, and Dutch, so this was something new and exciting—and then chemistry, where once again Bella found herself *bored*.

It's been more than a few decades, she reminded herself sternly, her pen skating across the page in neat, loopy handwriting as she noted down equations she could solve in her sleep. *Just wait until you get past pre-med.*

Though, she considered, *maybe it wouldn't hurt to branch out, double major for a change.*

There was still plenty of time to decide, anyway.

When classes ended for the day, she packed her things neatly into her backpack and headed for Ariel's dorm, which was across campus from hers and Lee's. The smell of cigarette smoke hit her nose long before she found Ariel's room, where the smell was strongest; she double-checked she had the number right, took a deep breath, and knocked.

There was the sound of shuffling, and then Ariel answered. He was shirtless, and Bella found herself at eye level with his well-defined pectorals before she glanced down at his stomach, the muscles there just as prominent with a faint trail of pale hair disappearing below his waistband.

It was a good thing she was wearing sunglasses.

Ariel leaned his residual limb against the door frame, pulling the cigarette out of his mouth. "Well? You coming in, or what?"

Bella snorted and brushed past him to find Lee already in the room, a cigarette in hand as well.

"You know, that's *really* bad for your lungs," Bella said reproachfully.

"Healing, remember?" Lee said from where she sat against the wall, her bad leg stretched out in front of her and the other knee tucked against her chest.

"And I ain't exactly expecting to live past forty, anyway," Ariel said, shutting the door behind her and sprawling out on his bed, propping himself up on his elbow and taking another drag. "So go on, Lee, what did you want to talk to us about so bad? Cig?" he added to Bella, who shook her head as she sat next to Lee.

"A hunter was attacked by a werewolf last night," Lee said, and Bella twisted to look at her, wide-eyed.

Ariel, however, was unphased. "Yeah, wondered if that was what this was about," he said. "Mo told me," he said, when Bella turned to him in confusion. "Said there was another feral attack and Lee's the one who stopped it."

"That's—I mean, don't get me wrong, I'm glad you did, but are you hurt?" Bella asked urgently, and Lee glared at her.

"I'm *fine*, Bella," Lee said shortly. "I'm a little bit more worried about the hunter who got attacked, or, I don't know, the fact you both thought you could hide from me that something was causing werewolves to go crazy outside of the full moon?!"

Bella and Ariel glanced at each other.

"*Well?*" Lee demanded.

"We thought you knew," Bella said quietly. "Or at least, I thought you did. Werewolves don't just randomly attack people like that."

Lee let out a quiet whine of frustration before taking an angry pull on her cigarette, Bella watching anxiously as Lee exhaled. "I'm new to this, remember?" Lee said, gesturing at herself. "I don't know how this whole world works! I don't know what's normal, what's not normal—"

"I told you werewolves only lose themselves during the full moon," Bella protested. "You're smart, I didn't think it needed saying there was something weird going on with the one who attacked you—"

"How the hell was I supposed to know that?" Lee exploded. "How was I supposed to know there wasn't something that turned werewolves into mindless beasts otherwise, or, hell, just werewolves out there who like killing for the sake of killing—"

"The Night Treaty prevents them from—"

"To hell with your stupid Night Treaty!" Lee yelled, and Ariel slammed down his cigarette into the ashtray by his bed, sitting up.

"Shut the *FUCK* up, both of you!" he snarled. "Maria's lost hunting rights and very likely the use of her hand, and you two're just bickering about who forgot to tell who what!"

Lee shoved her cigarette between her lips and took a long drag, glaring at the wall.

"Look," Bella said after a moment, "what's done is done. Lee knows now, we're all up to the same page, we can figure out what to do going forward."

"Well, *clearly*," Ariel said, "what needs to be done is figure out what's causing the werewolves to go feral."

"Any ideas how to do that, wise guy?" Lee asked. "Unless you're planning on putting me out on the streets and waiting to see if I go feral or not..."

Bella shifted uncomfortably. "Lee, we're not going to use you as *bait*," she said firmly. "There's got to be another way."

"The Tenebrous Council meets this weekend," Ariel pointed out. "Between us, we've now personally witnessed two feral attacks, and I'm sure the Lunar Delegation will have their own concerns to bring up as well."

"Have the Gloam Hunters reported any other attacks?" Bella asked.

Ariel grimaced, and he nodded. "Just one that I know of, but I'm fairly certain if there were more, Mo would have told me," he said. "But it's another four nights until the council meeting."

"Four more nights for an attack to happen," Lee said quietly. She flicked the cigarette butt into Ariel's ashtray and hugged her good knee tightly to her chest.

"If whatever's causing this gets Lee, she's as good as dead," Bella said, looking up at Ariel.

"What do you want me to do about it?" Ariel said gruffly. "You know the rules, Graves. She attacks a human, I'm obligated to put her down."

Lee flinched, and Bella held out her arm; Lee slowly leaned against her, and Bella hugged her gently.

"Then I'm not leaving Lee's side," Bella declared. "At least until the meeting."

Ariel raised an eyebrow. "You'll be able to restrain a feral werewolf if it comes down to it?"

"Look, as long as I feed enough, I will," Bella said stubbornly, a plan already beginning to form in her mind. Donors she could contact, a route to take to hit up the clubs...

"You said vampires get stronger the more they feed," Lee said slowly. "How much stronger?"

Bella grinned, flashing her fangs. "Certainly strong enough to restrain a feral werewolf," she said. "'Course, that sort of feeding, we can't *all* drink like that, all the time. There just wouldn't be enough blood to go around. I'm going to need to get permission from the Sanguine Lords."

"Well," Ariel said, "if and when you do, let me know, and I can sign off on the emergency request and pass the information on to Mo. The Gloam Hunters will need to know there's going to be a temporary spike in vampire activity so they don't panic."

"What about me?" Lee asked, biting her lip. "I mean, is there anything I can do to, um, to help?"

Bella squeezed her a little more tightly. "Right now, I need *you* to start thinking about what you're going to wear for a night out on the town."

Chapter 14

Lee held still as Ariel put the finishing touches on her new makeup. Bella's emergency request for extended feeding permissions had been granted barely an hour after the sun had set. Now, Lee sat in her chair while Ariel cleaned up her scars, making it look like she'd had her sutures recently removed. In a way, she was glad all of the subterfuge surrounding her injuries was necessary; having to let him touch her face, though deeply uncomfortable at first, was something she had to get used to.

She still didn't have to like it, but at least it wasn't as bad as before.

"Luckily for you, facial wounds heal fast," Bella said, swinging her legs from where she was observing on her bed. "We can probably stop with the makeup charade next week. And look!" She passed Lee her hand mirror, and Lee held it up to look.

The scars were less eye-catching now, and even with the addition of Ariel's makeup, didn't look nearly as bad as they had the first day after the attack. They were paler, a little less taut, and Lee reached up to gingerly prod around the scars before Ariel swatted her hand away.

"I haven't put on the setting spray yet," he scolded. "Keep your hands off until I'm done."

"One minute, Drama Queen," Bella said, sliding off the bed and grabbing her own makeup case. "Before you spray anything on, it's my turn. Lee, close your eyes."

Lee obliged, closing her eyes and forcing herself to stay still while she felt Bella carefully apply eye shadow.

"Purple?" she heard Ariel ask sceptically.

"Trust me, blondie, I know what I'm doing," Bella said. "Besides, it'll match her flannel."

"Certainly not her hair," Ariel muttered.

Lee felt the brush lift briefly before Bella continued. "As a theatre student, you of all people should appreciate the beauty of a good sunset."

A long silence, and then—

"Alright," Ariel said grudgingly, "that does look pretty good."

Butterflies erupted in Lee's stomach, and she was tempted to look, but kept her eyes closed until Bella said she could open them, and handed Lee the mirror again.

"Wow," Lee breathed. Her eye shadow was dusky and dramatic, and did indeed evoke a sunset, with purple starting on her eyelids and blending into a dramatic, dark blue higher up. She covered half of her reflection to hide the scars and smiled, tentatively at first, and then a little wider. "It looks amazing, Bells."

"It helps I have a great canvas to work with," Bella said, winking, and Lee blushed underneath her freckles.

She closed her eyes again for Ariel to use his setting spray, and opened them once more to see him packing up his supplies. "Just be careful tonight, Bella. I'd hate to have to be the one to put either of you down."

"Aw, I knew you cared," Bella said, punching his shoulder.

Ariel just snorted. "Let's not get ahead of ourselves." He slouched out the door.

Bella flapped her hands excitedly. "Ready?" she asked, and Lee set the mirror down.

They'd both dressed for a night out, though Bella's clothes were both newer and cleaner; Lee, once again, was wearing her usual black jeans and an identical black tank top to the one she'd lost helping Maria, though this time she wore a purple flannel, having lost her favourite green. The main effort she'd made towards dressing up was switching out her industrial piercing, from a plain steel bar to a black bar adorned with a crescent moon.

Bella, however, had gone the whole nine yards. She'd donned a red halter minidress with a plunging neckline and dangerously short pleated skirt that flared around her hips as she moved. Nylon stockings clung to shapely legs, and a pair of black, strappy heels brought her height up almost to Lee's chin. A fitted leather jacket went over top of everything, emphasising her shoulders and waist, and dramatic red eye shadow and red lipstick completed the look.

When she'd first told Lee it was safe to look after getting dressed, Lee had to work very hard to keep her eyes on Bella's face. She looked every bit the modern vampire, sultry and seductive—and then she'd grinned and clapped her hands and gone to let Ariel in, which gave Lee a chance to compose herself.

Now, though, Lee felt her face heating up as Bella slung an arm around her waist, drawing her downstairs to the bus stop. Bella's skin was cool, Lee noticed, and a thought struck her.

"Hey, Bella," she said, glancing at her. "Do vampires have a body temperature?"

Bella laughed. "Whatever temperature room temperature is," she said. "Which can make winters annoying. Too cold and we can actually get frozen."

"So can humans," Lee pointed out.

"Yeah, but if we're thawed out, we're fine," Bella said, bumping her with her hip. "Ooh, this is our bus!"

They took seats near the back, and Bella dug her earbuds out, offering one to Lee.

"So what are these clubs, you know, *like?*" Lee asked as the bus headed south. "I'm not going to be out of place or anything?"

"Lee, between the flannel and the piercings, you'll be bang up the elephant," Bella said, patting her shoulder.

Lee nodded slowly. "And that's... a good thing?"

"You'll fit right in," Bella promised.

Still, Lee felt her nerve falter when they reached their destination; the door of Dark Desires was propped open, the music spilling out into the street. A sign by the door stated *No admittance to under 21s.*

"Uh, Bella, I'm not old enough—"

"It's fine, just come with me." Bella tugged on her sleeve, and Lee followed her to the door, where the bouncer raised an eyebrow at Lee.

"New donor tonight?" the bouncer asked.

"Not this time, Monica," Bella said. "My friend here's a little more in touch with the moon, you know." She winked.

Monica shrugged. "ID, please?"

Lee handed it over, glancing sidelong at Bella, but Monica just checked the birthday and passed it back, waving them inside.

"It's just to keep the cops off our asses," Bella explained. "You deal with the stuff we do all the time, Cassandra's of the opinion if you're eighteen, you're old enough to have a few drinks."

"Guess it would be hard to keep the Gloam a secret if the place is getting raided all the time," Lee muttered.

Bella shrugged. "Cassandra's been keeping the place going since before Stonewall," she said. "She's dealt with worse than cops trying to sniff out underage drinking. Now come on, help me find—"

"Bella!"

A human woman with a purple undercut pushed through the crowd, grinning widely. Her teeth looked oddly white against her black lipstick.

"Olivia," Bella said, letting go of Lee to embrace the woman. She sniffed the crook of Olivia's neck, and the woman's eyelids fluttered before Bella drew back. "You look great tonight!"

"You know me," Olivia said, her grin widening. "Couldn't wait to see my favourite vampire."

"You're too sweet," Bella said, trailing a hand over Olivia's bare shoulder, adorned with a large sugar skull tattoo. "Olivia, this is Lee," she added, gesturing at Lee, who waved awkwardly. Bella leaned in, looking up at Olivia through long eyelashes. "I thought maybe she could watch."

Oliva exhaled slowly and nodded. "Buy me a drink first?" she asked, but Bella shook her head.

"Not tonight, Liv. I need to keep a clear head." She grinned. "Next time?"

"*Definitely.*" Olivia held out her arm, and Bella latched on with a giggle as they began to make their way along the outside edge of the dance floor. Lee trailed along, glancing around the room, just taking in the atmosphere.

They made it to a series of large, private booths off to the side, some with their curtains already drawn. Another hunter stood watch in the centre of the curtained-off arches, a glittering silver chain wound prominently at her hip.

As Lee watched, one of the booths' hangings were pulled aside, and a pair of women stepped out, one supporting the other and both smiling at each other in a way that made Lee feel like she was intruding on something private. They stopped by the hunter, who stamped the back of the donor's hand, and the pair disappeared into the crowd.

"Hand?" the hunter asked, and Olivia extended her hand for the hunter to shine a UV light on the back of it. "And you?" the hunter said to Lee.

"She's not donating," Bella said quickly. "Just here to observe."

Apparently satisfied, the hunter waved them toward one of the empty booths, while a staff member approached the recently vacated one with cleaning supplies.

"Like I said, all very above board," Bella said, drawing the curtains shut behind her. The booth had a trio of black-draped lounge benches, a circular table in the middle. A red glass lamp hung from the ceiling, casting an eerie glow over the area.

Olivia made herself comfortable on one of the plush benches, Bella sitting next to her and brushing her hair away from her neck. Now that the long purple tresses were out of the way, Lee could see a pair of pinprick scars, still pink around the edges.

"Come on, have a seat," Bella said, sliding off her leather jacket, and Lee realised she was staring again. She sat, swallowing as she watched Bella trail her fingers over Olivia's neck and shoulders.

"It's usually at least common courtesy for vamps to give a bit of a show for their donors," Bella said to Lee as her fingers dipped beneath Olivia's neckline, trailing over her skin.

"A *bit of a show?*" Olivia said indignantly, and then shivered, biting her lip as Bella's fingers dipped lower.

"Oh, yes," Bella murmured. "Because that's part of the service, isn't it? You feed me, and I make you feel good..." Bella's lips brushed over Olivia's neck, just below her ear. "You've missed this, haven't you?" she murmured, and Olivia's breath hitched.

"Yes," Olivia breathed.

"You can't wait for me to sink my fangs into your neck and drink my fill of you," Bella purred.

"*Yes.*"

"If you're really so desperate," Bella said, and gently nibbled on Olivia's earlobe, "you know what to say."

"*Please,*" Olivia whimpered, and Bella chuckled, lowering her mouth to trail kisses along the curve of Olivia's throat. She reached the pinpricks, and bit down.

Olivia threw her head back with a groan, her eyes rolling back as Bella drank, sucking hard against her skin. Lee's fingernails dug into her palms, her own heart thudding erratically as Bella slid from the bench to straddle Olivia's lap, cradling the back of Olivia's head and keeping her neck exposed. Olivia got her arms around Bella, fingernails scraping over the bare skin of her back.

Before long, Bella sat up, and the bite marks on Olivia's neck were once again the taut pink of freshly-healed skin. Olivia's hands slid down to Bella's hips, and she leaned over to grin at Lee, her face pale from the blood loss.

"Like what you see?" Olivia teased, and Lee realised her mouth had fallen slightly open. She snapped it shut as Bella giggled and climbed off Olivia's lap.

"Sorry tonight had to be brief," Bella murmured, pressing a light kiss to the bite, and Olivia shivered, reaching up to cup Bella's face.

"I fully expect you to make it up to me next time," Olivia murmured, and slipped through the curtain.

Bella turned to Lee, her crimson eyes looking oddly brighter red than before, her pupils blown wide. "Well," she said, a touch breathlessly, "now that I've had my first drink—buy you something at the bar?"

. . . .

Lee ended up sitting at the bar nursing a sex on the beach, watching the dance floor. Bella had her hunt down to a science, approaching human patrons and inviting them to dance. She smiled widely, laughed openly, and, Lee noticed, was very handsy, whether it be a light brush of her fingers against her dance partner's hand, or pulling them closer together by their hips. Lee soon gave up counting after the fifth woman Bella escorted over to the booths.

She idly stirred her cocktail, glancing up when a very butch vampire sat beside her. "Buy you a drink?"

"No thanks, I'm good," Lee muttered. "You don't want to drink me, anyway."

The vampire leaned in, sniffed, and made a face. "Yeah, no. Sorry to waste your time." She got up and moved several stools down, approaching another patron.

Bella claimed the vacant seat, her dark skin noticeably rosier. "Look at you, chasing away your admirers."

Lee rolled her eyes and finished off her cocktail. "She just wanted a drink."

"And clearly thought you looked good enough to eat," Bella laughed. She reached over, holding out her hand, and Lee hesitated a moment before taking it. "So what do *you* think?"

"Of—of what?"

"Of giving it a try yourself, of course," Bella said, smiling easily.

Lee's breath caught. "Bells, I'm not going to taste good."

Bella waved her free hand. "Oh, pshaw, you never got the chance to try this before you got turned, right?"

"Well—I mean, no..."

Bella inclined her head, studying Lee. "Look, it's no pressure or anything, but the offer's there if you want."

"You're not..." Lee trailed off, glancing away, biting her lip. "You're not just offering because you feel sorry for me, are you?"

"What? No!" When she glanced back, Bella looked hurt she'd suggested the idea. "I'm offering because I think you'd enjoy it. And you've had a pretty rough go of it lately."

"And you think biting me would cheer me up," Lee said dryly, stalling for time while she tried to sort out her jumbled thoughts.

Bella shrugged. "I mean, it was just a thought." She turned her head, studying the dancers. "Hm. I think I'll just—"

Lee caught the sleeve of Bella's jacket as she made to slide off the stool. Bella turned back to her, eyebrows raised in a silent question.

"Let's..." Lee took a deep breath, trying to calm her racing heart. "Let's do this."

Bella positively beamed, and laced her fingers through Lee's, leading her to the curtained off booths. The hunter raised an eyebrow at their approach, but waved them to a vacant booth after checking the back of Lee's hand.

Lee sat, her leg jittering nervously as Bella drew the curtains shut.

"Hey, it's alright if you're nervous," Bella said, dropping her jacket on the table and sitting next to Lee. "I'll be gentle, I promise."

Lee bobbed her head, swallowing hard. "So all that, uh, all that stuff you did before, with Olivia...?"

"I don't have to go through it if you don't want me to," Bella said, and Lee shook her head, too embarrassed to admit she *did*. "Alright." Bella lifted a hand, moving slowly as she tucked Lee's hair behind her ear, fingers trailing over the right side of her neck. Lee shivered under her touch, and Bella drew back. "You okay?"

Lee took a deep breath and nodded. "Just... stay on that side?" she asked, her voice small. "Please?"

Bella smiled gently. "I will. Promise."

Goosebumps sprang up on Lee's skin as Bella lowered her mouth to the curve of her neck, and she felt the light scrape of fangs against her throat. When Bella didn't bite immediately, Lee realised she was trying to pick the right spot.

"Ready?" Bella murmured.

"Yes," Lee whispered.

And then Bella's fangs sank into her neck.

Lee gasped, her vision briefly going blank as the needle-sharp burst of pain was replaced with pleasure that coursed through her body when Bella withdrew her fangs, filling her with a heat that pooled low in her stomach and sent her heart racing. Bella sucked at her neck, tugging gently at her hair, and Lee bit down on her knuckle to stifle the moan that threatened to escape her lips.

It was over all too soon. She felt Bella's tongue slide over the bite like the caress of a lover's kiss before the vampire lifted her head, licking her lips and breathing heavily as they stared at each other.

"Wow," Lee said breathlessly, and Bella laughed, sounding equally out of breath. "That was... wow."

"Told you it was good," Bella said, grinning.

"It didn't taste too bad?" Lee asked, and Bella flapped her hands at her.

"Oh, shush, this was more for your benefit than mine," she said. "But don't worry, next donor will wash out the taste."

Lee nodded, lightly touching the bite, still feeling somewhat dazed. "Will we be here much longer?" she asked, and Bella considered.

"Half an hour," Bella decided. "You've got class early tomorrow, and I can't be hogging all the donors, after all. You get your hand stamped and go up to the bar, get yourself some juice and crisps—sorry, chips—they're free for donors, just show Cassandra your stamp. We'll head out once I'm done."

She hesitated, then leaned in, slowly enough that Lee could pull away if she so wished. Lee held still, her eye widening slightly as Bella pressed a gentle kiss to her unmarred cheek, then slipped out of the booth.

Lee stared after her as she lifted a hand to touch her cheek, which was still tingling from the touch of Bella's lips.

Chapter 15

"...Motion to approve the expansion of Gloam Hunter patrols in the Far Southeast Side and Far Southwest Side in response to the increase of missing persons cases..."

Ariel glanced at his watch, then over at Lee, whose leg had been bouncing gradually faster over the last hour and a half as the council proceedings dragged on. Bella, for her part, was on her phone, checking her social media and arranging to borrow donors in the event she needed to continue guarding Lee after the meeting.

Ariel sighed and slid a little lower in his chair, his arms crossed. There was a reason he normally skipped attending these meetings, as most of it involved the representatives of their respective factions discussing the minutiae of night-to-night life.

Why Morgan wanted to willingly subject himself to these meetings twice a month, he really had no idea.

Ashley Montgomery, at least, seemed mostly sober for tonight's meeting, though Ariel still avoided meeting her insistent gaze when she tried to catch his eye. To her left was Diana Guadalupe, a Latina woman whose hair was starting to show streaks of grey in part from age, but likely from the stress of acting as the elected leader of the Lunar Delegation, commanding enough respect to hold her seat for well over a decade and a half.

On Diana's other side sat Terry Nelson, a small, balding man whose appearance of a middle-aged, bespeckled accountant belied his status as representative for the Arcane Conclave. He was a new addition to the council, with his predecessor having been lost the year prior, in a failed experiment involving waterfowl.

At the far end of the table sat the last member of the Tenebrous Council of Chicago, Augustus Staker of the Sanguine Lords, looking painfully like every caricature of a classic vampire, with long black hair tied with a red ribbon at the nape of his neck and a high widow's peak. He'd been on the council since Chicago had grown large enough to demand their own representatives—in other words, nearly two hundred years, and had seen many a council member come and go.

The turnout for the evening was larger than Ariel remembered from the past, with a number of scarred faces that he guessed were werewolves, drawn by recent events. Among them was Maria, who'd waved at him across the room when they'd taken their seats, and Connor, looking grim. Morgan sat nearby, fingers laced together and elbows propped on his knees as he listened intently, and between them was Jessie, preoccupied with her book and completely ignoring the proceedings.

It was always a risky business, having Morgan off the radio even for a single night, but after recent events, it seemed prudent he attend the meeting. The Chicago Gloam Hunters would simply have to make do without him tonight.

The door opened behind him, and Ariel twisted around in his seat, scowling when he saw Madame Blanchard slip inside with a waft of cold air. She seemed to glide across the floor as she took a seat near the back, folding her hands in her lap. When Ariel turned back to the front, he saw his mother had perked up considerably, and his scowl deepened. He glanced over at Bella, who'd looked up at the intrusion, a slight frown furrowing her brow, and then at Lee, who shivered and tugged her scarf a little tighter.

"And now for Agenda Item Five," Augustus said, shuffling his papers. "Review of approvals for requests for extended hunting privileges."

Ariel sat up a little straighter, Lee's leg froze mid-jitter, and Bella slipped her phone back into her pocket.

"All items have been reviewed and signed off on, save one," Terry said, and Ashley and Diana nodded. "Augustus, you approved an emergency request from Arabella Ward, current alias Isabella Graves, with Ariel Montgomery as witness, on the night of Tuesday, October 13th, 2015, can you elaborate as to why?"

"Ah," Augustus said, steepling his fingers, "this is in regards to something I'm sure the Lunar Delegation also wishes to bring to the council's attention. Miss Ward and Mr Montgomery expressed concern for the safety of a newly-turned werewolf, Accalia Lowell. Diana, Ashley, I believe Ariel Montgomery filed the appropriate paperwork with you regarding this?"

"He did," Diana said, nodding. She gestured to the trio. "Would Ariel Montgomery please come forward?"

Ariel stood, shuffling past Lee before striding to the podium that stood before the council's table. They'd discussed this before they left, and agreed to let Ariel do the talking, since he had the most experience with this sort of thing.

That didn't necessarily mean he enjoyed it, though.

The microphone squealed with feedback when Ariel adjusted it, and the vampires in the room winced. "...Thank you, Council, for asking me to speak," Ariel said, glancing around. "On the night of October 5th, Lowell was bitten by a rogue werewolf who as of right now remains unidentified." He heard Lee's breath hitch behind him, but forced himself to keep his gaze shifting from one council member to another, never quite looking directly at his mother. "For those unaware, there was no full moon that night, yet the werewolf behaved as if feral, attacking Lowell unprovoked and ignoring calls to stand down. Lowell, Ward, and I discovered this was part of a growing pattern, which I have reason to believe Representative Guadalupe is already aware of. Ward submitted the emergency request with my approval, and I passed the information on to the Gloam Hunters as per protocol."

He felt his mother's accusatory gaze boring into his skull, but kept his eyes fixed on Diana, waiting for her to speak.

"Thank you, Mr Montgomery, you may sit," Diana said, and Ariel returned to his seat as she continued. "Augustus, you'll find the completed forms tomorrow."

"Thank you, Diana," Augustus said. "And accordingly, Arabella Ward's extended feeding privileges will be suspended now that the immediate concern has passed. This brings us to Agenda Item Six…" He held out a hand to Diana, who cleared her throat.

"The werewolves I represent have brought their concerns to me regarding the feral attacks that have begun in the last two weeks," Diana said, flipping through her notes. "All told, six have been reported by members of the Gloam Hunters; Accalia Lowell and Maria Lín are the only surviving victims of these attacks, with four human casualties. Four of the offending werewolves were disposed of in accordance with the Night Treaty's laws; the others remain as of yet unaccounted for." Her mouth twisted unhappily. "Three of the deceased werewolves have since been identified as long-standing and well respected members of the community: Iris Cooper, George Maclaren, and Shayona Watkins. The fourth was unknown to us in the Lunar Delegation, but has been identified as Brandon Steinbeck. I would like the council to observe a moment of silence for our fallen brothers and sisters."

The room went quiet save for the sounds of breathing; Ariel heard a quiet sniffle beside him and glanced over to see tears dripping down Lee's cheeks. Ariel glanced away, grit his teeth, and held his hand out without looking; after a moment, he felt Lee's hand creep into his, her long fingers cold against his.

"Now then," Diana continued after a minute, lifting her head, "it's important to stress that of the identified feral werewolves, they were all members of the local chapter of the werewolf support group, and attended regularly. However, I would like the record to show that Connor O'Connor, the present leader of the support group, alerted me that each of those members had gone missing, after the night of the full moons of July 31st, August 29th, and most recently, September 27th."

A ripple of murmurs ran around the room, and Ariel met Maria's eyes. Her jaw set, and she glanced away.

"Keeping this in mind, I want to ask that the Gloam Hunters temporarily use non-lethal means to subdue any werewolves who break the treaty and bring them in for detainment, from now until the full moon of October 27th," Diana said, raising her voice slightly. "In the meantime, I will be launching a full investigation into each incident, and request the aid of the Arcane Conclave to monitor lycanthropic activity in Chicago and its surrounding areas so we can start searching for answers."

"The Lunar Delegation will have the full support of the Arcane Conclave," Terry said.

"As well as the support of the Gloam Hunters," Ashley said, sitting up a little straighter. "Any hunters not in possession of silver bindings will be issued appropriate equipment before their next patrols."

"And, of course, if there is anything my people can do to aid your efforts, the Sanguine Lords' resources will be at your disposal," Augustus said. "This matter puts all of Tenebrous at risk, not just the werewolves." He rubbed his jaw as he thought. "I'll admit I'm concerned how this will affect the vampires as well. While Miss Lín sacrificed her humanity in the line of duty, my people, civilians, would be losing their lives."

"Nobody ever said there weren't enough vampires in the world," Ashley said darkly.

"*Shut up,*" Ariel growled under his breath.

Augustus' crimson eyes narrowed slightly. "Ashley, is there something you would like to say?"

"If I may," Madame Blanchard cut in, standing up. Heads turned to look at her as she glided to the podium, snowflakes trailing in her wake.

"Madame Blanchard, you were not called to the podium," Augustus said, but Ashley held up a hand.

"Show of hands, all in favour of letting Madame Blanchard speak?"

Ariel felt Lee's fingers tighten on his hand. "What's she doing?" Lee whispered as Diana and Terry raised their hands.

"Nothing good," Bella murmured.

Madame Blanchard flicked a finger, and the microphone adjusted itself. "We all know the Arcane Conclave is, how do I put this politely... less than powerful," she said. Though her back was to them, Ariel could just picture her frosty smile. "A project of this magnitude might just take more mages than you can afford."

"And I suppose you're offering your services," Diana said, arching an eyebrow.

Madame Blanchard laughed, a high, cold sound. "But of course, Diana! It's not like an opportunity such as this comes along every day."

"Terry?" Ashley said.

Terry hesitated, pushing his glasses up his nose. "These attacks are unprecedented," he said uncertainly. "We're working on devising spells that could be used to monitor the werewolves, but tracking down the source of the problem would risk more mages than I'd like."

"And, naturally, you don't mind when Madame Blanchard puts herself at risk," she said, putting a hand on her chest. "Not when it suits you, isn't that right, Terry?"

"Madame Blanchard, you are out of line," Augustus said sharply. "This is not appropriate for council meetings; take it up with your representative through the proper channels."

"My apologies," Madame Blanchard said, giving a sarcastic little bow.

She turned and swept out, and for a moment, her eyes landed on Lee, a small smile curling her ruby-red lips in a way that sent chills up Ariel's spine.

"Right," Diana said, calling attention back to the head table. "The next council meeting will be held October 31st. Unless there were any other orders of business, I move to adjourn this meeting."

The other representatives voiced their agreement, and the guests began talking amongst themselves, many of them standing to leave.

"Come on," Ariel muttered, standing up and helping Lee to her feet. The three of them joined the throng of people filing out of the underground chamber, but then Ariel pulled them into a waiting room and yanked the door closed behind them.

"Blanchard is up to something," Lee said immediately, and Ariel turned to her and Bella to see Bella nodding along.

"You read my mind," Ariel said, crossing his arms.

"What *is* her deal, anyway?" Lee asked.

Bella shuddered. "That's just it," she said. "Nobody really knows. Nobody really *trusts* her, because what kind of mage gets to be that powerful without also going barmy?"

"But *because* she seems sane, even if she's off-putting, she gets a pass," Ariel said darkly, pacing into the room with his hands clasped behind his back. "Because the fact of the matter is, the Arcane Conclave needs all the power it can get, and Blanchard's been their meal ticket for years."

"Do you think she's behind the attacks?" Bella asked as Lee limped over to the nearest armchair and sank gratefully into it.

"Can mages even *do* that?" Lee asked. "I mean, mind-control werewolves into..." She curled her fingers into claws. "You know, rawr?"

Ariel shook his head, turning on his heel. "The mind is the one area mages are incapable of influencing," he said, still pacing. "Nobody's really sure why."

"*I* think it's because only pure Gloam can warp somebody like that," Bella said, draping herself over a sofa and kicking her feet up onto the back of it. "I mean, mages can channel the stuff to do amazing things, but if they could control minds like that, they'd be able to..." She snapped her fingers. "Un-crazy themselves."

"Regardless of the reason, Blanchard's behaviour tonight was definitely suspicious," Ariel said, drumming his fingers against his other arm. The metal made a dull ringing noise beneath his coat sleeve. "But to accuse her without proof would reflect poorly on hunters, werewolves, and vampires alike—"

Bella held up a hand and sat bolt upright, her eyes narrowed.

"What—?" Lee began, but Bella hissed at her to be quiet.

And then the sound reached Ariel's ears, the soft footfalls of expensive leather dress shoes, which paused outside the door to the room. There came a knock, and Lee jumped, eye wide. Ariel glanced at his companions before going to the door and opening it.

Augustus Staker stood on the other side, looking much less threatening without the protection of the head table between him and the podium. Hair aside, in his red polo shirt and khaki slacks, he looked like an ordinary man.

Ariel stared silently down at him, but Augustus only smiled widely, his fangs gleaming in the low light. "I thought I might find you three in here," he said. "I wondered if I might speak to you in my office?"

Chapter 16

Augustus took them through the winding network of tunnels that ran beneath Chicago's pedway system, leading them to his office, where he ushered them inside.

"Alright, what's this about?" Ariel asked once the door was shut. Augustus took a seat behind his magnificent mahogany desk, motioning for them to sit in the chairs across from him. Ariel remained standing, though, and was gratified his companions opted to do the same, though he knew Lee's bad leg was likely sore.

Augustus propped his elbows up on the desk, leaning his chin on his hands while he studied them. A ruby signet ring glittered on his right hand. "To start with, I just wanted to warn you that these walls have ears," he said. "And a great number of its inhabitants have sensitive hearing. This room is warded so we may speak freely, but it would be wise to not discuss your suspicions where others might hear."

"Noted," Ariel said curtly. He was sure their room had been private, but then, if Augustus was calling them into his office to speak, maybe it hadn't been as private as he'd thought.

"Now then." Augustus pulled open a drawer in his desk, rummaging around until he found a file, which he placed on his desk. "I'm sure you've already guessed by now that this is about Madame Blanchard."

"You know something about her, Lord Staker?" Bella asked.

"Augustus, please. And... possibly, yes, I do," he said. He slid the folder across his desk, and Ariel reluctantly moved closer to open it. "I've been suspicious of her for years, of course, but within the last three months or so, her behaviour has become more... erratic," he said, watching as Ariel flipped through the folder. Notes on Blanchard's movement, photographs copied from the Conclave's files of Blanchard's experiments. Nothing particularly out of the ordinary, until Ariel noted that the most recent entry was dated to three months ago, save for a log of brief sightings around the city.

He glanced up, frown deepening. "What happened three months ago?" he said, and Augustus sighed, watching Ariel peruse the notes.

"That's just it. Her old laboratory was cleaned out, and aside from occasional appearances at council meetings, she seems to have vanished from the public eye." Ariel looked up again to see Augustus watching him with a guarded curiosity. "The only other times she's been spotted are in the company of your mother."

Ariel snapped the folder shut, knowing the vampires could hear the sudden increase in his heartbeat. "What are you implying?"

Augustus held up his hands. "Nothing, Ariel. May I call you Ariel?"

Ariel gave a jerky nod.

"Ariel." Augustus stood up, his fingers brushing over the cover of the folder, before he looked at each of them in turn. "Arabella. Accalia. I think whatever Blanchard is planning, the three of you are in a position to stop it."

"Why us?" Lee blurted out, and though Ariel wanted to turn around and snap at her to let him handle this, he had to admit the question had been on his mind.

"I was impressed by Arabella's initiative and response to the situation when I authorised the extra feeding privileges," Augustus said.

"Just Bella, please," Bella said, preening slightly.

"And Ariel is in a position to potentially learn more about Blanchard's plans without alerting her."

"You want me to spy on my own mother," Ariel said flatly.

Augustus' mouth set in a grim line. "I don't want to look at it that way," he said delicately. "But Ariel, please see sense. We all know it's a matter of time before your brother takes her place on the council. Blanchard may very well move on to a different target in such an event, and I would be left back at square one. But with the anniversary of your father's death approaching—"

Ariel's jaw set.

"—I'm concerned how this might be affecting your mother's mindset," Augustus said softly. "I'm very sorry to bring it up, but it has to be mentioned."

"You don't even know what she's planning," Lee said uncertainly. "If anything."

"Which brings me to you, Accalia," Augustus said. "You and Maria are the only survivors of these attacks. Ideally, I would like to see the both of you observed in the days leading up to the next full moon, and of course your subsequent transformation. There's simply no telling what the werewolves who attacked you might have passed on."

Lee's breath hitched, and she grabbed the back of the nearest chair for support. Bella moved forward, murmuring soothingly.

"And," Augustus added, glancing at Lee, "if I am correct in my thinking, Blanchard may very well want to get her hands on Accalia and Maria."

"You're assuming she's even the one behind this in the first place," Ariel said slowly. "What if we're chasing a red herring? What if this is just some freak variant on the curse?"

"Then we can rule her scheming out as a possible cause." Augustus sighed and rubbed his temples. "I'm just as worried by these attacks as you are. Which is why," he added, and looked up at Bella, "I'm granting you a permanent extension on your feeding rights."

Bella's mouth dropped open. "You're serious?"

"I am. And I'm sure Ashley will be thrilled," Augustus said dryly, and Ariel snorted. "I've already confirmed with Diana that Maria plans to use one of the support group's safe houses for the upcoming transformation, which just leaves the matter of Accalia."

"*Lee*," Ariel said, stressing the name, "is still deciding. She'll have her decision soon." He straightened up. "Thank you for informing us of this, Augustus."

Ariel turned to leave, pausing with his hand on the doorknob when Augustus spoke.

"What we discussed here doesn't leave this room. Is that understood?"

Ariel's mouth thinned. "Completely."

He wrenched the door open and stalked into the corridor, coat swishing around his knees. Bella and Lee hurried to keep pace, Bella with her short legs and Lee with her limp, as Ariel navigated them to one of the many hidden passages that exited into the pedway system, shielded from prying eyes with a Nevermind spell.

Lee had been astonished when Ariel and Bella showed her the door on the way in, but her astonishment was cut off by Ariel ushering them along to the council meeting. Lee opened her mouth to ask about it now, caught the look on Ariel's face, and fell silent until they reached the surface.

"So what do you think?" Lee asked as they blended into the crowd of pedestrians, but Ariel shook his head.

"Not here."

They ended up by Millennium Park, near the pedestrian bridge where Ariel and Bella had met what felt like so long ago. It was strange to think barely two weeks had passed since then.

Ariel was silent for a minute, enjoying the nip of cold wind on his face. It was soothing, in a way, and he felt his racing heart begin to calm now that they were out of the stale underground air of Augustus' office.

"I think my mother is worth keeping an eye on," he said grudgingly. "She's been getting more unstable since I moved out for college, and..." He sighed. "Well, you've seen what she's like."

"I'm sorry," Lee said, but Ariel shook his head.

"Sorry's not gonna help us figure out what's going on," he said. "I'm worried, for you, for Maria, for anyone else who'll get attacked. The werewolves that had to be put down were victims too. This *has* to stop."

"Agreed," Bella said, frowning. "Augustus made a good point at the meeting—vampires are in danger, too, and the longer this goes on, the worse it looks for the werewolves."

"Augustus thought I'd be able to help because of the—um, the circumstances surrounding my—my—" Lee broke off, gesturing awkwardly at her face. "I'm guessing you guys might have an idea how?"

"I do." Ariel folded his arms, slowing his steps until he stood at the edge of the pathway that passed the outdoor climbing wall. "We maintain a transformation space in our basement for Connor, but considering the circumstances, I think he would be willing to use one of the safe houses so we could monitor you."

Lee's eye widened. "You'd... do that for me?"

Ariel made a small noise of dissent in the back of his throat. "Not just for you," he said. "For everyone. Consider—if whatever is causing the werewolves to go feral goes worldwide. Nobody's noticed it here in Chicago yet, because people go missing all the time. It's a violent city. But if this keeps spreading, the Gloam Hunters won't be able to keep covering this up. All of Tenebrous will be at risk, and the Night Treaty would be dissolved."

"Open season on the mortals," Bella murmured, and Lee swung around to look at her. "Not all vampires are as friendly as I am," Bella said, catching her eye. "Mind, most of us just want to live and let live, but there's a... not insignificant number of vamps who aren't happy with the Sanguine Lords' rule. They think we should be allowed to feed as much as we like, war over territory, rule kingdoms full of human livestock." Her lip curled in disgust at the thought.

"It would be a nightmare," Ariel said.

"Yeah, that sounds... less than great," Lee said. She took a deep breath. "So I go back to your place, you... what, chain me up?"

"There's a soundproofed room with silver bars," Ariel said. "Plenty of space to pace while the moon is up, anyway."

"And then see if anything weird happens that night?" Lee finished.

Ariel nodded. "Lucky for us this didn't happen last full moon," he said thoughtfully.

"What do you mean?" Lee said, frowning.

Ariel shrugged. "Was a blood moon, wasn't it? Werewolves temporarily regain control during a total eclipse. If we're trying to observe any weirdness happening with you, best it's during a normal moon." He grinned. "Scientific method and all that."

Lee nodded, mentally filing the information away.

"What about your mother?" Bella asked. "She won't be...?" She glanced sidelong at Lee. "Well, the last time we saw her, she was screaming after us."

Ariel rubbed his jaw, considering. "Mostly screaming after you," he said to Bella, and she winced. "She knows we're still hanging out with you, but I think so long as you don't let yourself be seen, it'll be fine."

Bella gave a slow smile. "Bat?"

Ariel nodded. "Bat."

Bella pumped her fist. "Always wanted to sneak around inside a house full of vampire slayers!"

Lee stared. "You're—you're kidding, right?"

Bella snickered. "A bit," she said. "But you have to admit, this is pretty exciting stuff."

"Considering this is going to be my first full moon and I'm going to spend it as a supernatural science experiment," Lee said, "I'm a little *less* excited."

Ariel put a hand on her shoulder, grinning humourlessly. "Don't worry," he said, "you'll be in good hand."

When Lee giggled, Ariel's smile in return felt a little more genuine.

Chapter 17

Rosehill Cemetery was locked for the night, but Bella flew over the wall, her wings strong from the fresh blood that filled her with energy. Extended privileges or not, she still had to be careful not to overfish the population and leave other vampires without sustenance.

She really shouldn't have been surprised to smell Ariel's scent outside the Montgomery mausoleum, but paused when she landed outside, clinging by her feet to the roof. It seemed wrong to intrude, but maybe...

Bella let go and flew off to the nearest convenience store, which thankfully hadn't yet closed for the night. She returned and transformed back, Ariel's scent still fresh.

She knocked gently on the door and stuck her head inside.

Ariel sat on a stone bench in the centre of the room, his elbows resting on his knees. He didn't glance up when Bella quietly crossed the floor to perch beside him, a small bouquet of lilies in her arms. The only source of light in the room was the moon, which filtered through a stained glass window depicting the Montgomery family crest of a sword and star.

"I didn't realise you'd be here," she said softly, leaning forward to place the bouquet in front of Jordan Montgomery's tomb. "I guess I should have, though. I just wanted to pay my respects..." She trailed off, watching him carefully. "I can leave."

Ariel sighed and sat back. "It's fine," he said, and though his words were steady, Bella heard the strain in his voice. "It was... nice of you to come, really." He glanced at her. "You never have before."

"You come every year?" Bella asked.

"Yeah." Ariel sighed again. "Everyone did, that first year. Now it's just me. Mom's probably drunk again tonight, and Jessie was too

114

little to remember him when he died. Dunno if Mo would rather come or not, but he's always said he has to stay to look after her."

"I'm—" Bella let the word *sorry* die on her lips. Ariel had always been disdainful of it before. "...I'm here, for what it's worth," she said after a long pause. "You shouldn't have to be alone." She bit her lip, glancing away. "Especially not today."

Ariel was silent, and for a moment, Bella wondered if he was ignoring her. But then the smell of salt hit her nose, and she glanced over to see tears rolling down Ariel's cheeks.

"Oh, *shit*, I shouldn't have said—" Bella dug into her pockets and produced a travel pack of tissues. "Here—"

Ariel stared at them for a moment before accepting one, blowing his nose. "S'fine," he muttered thickly. "Haven't celebrated in years. Feels wrong."

Bella hesitated before putting a careful hand on his shoulder. She didn't speak, not wanting to make things worse, but Ariel took a deep breath.

"It was my first hunt, you know?" he said, and blew his nose again; Bella silently offered him another tissue, which he took. "Montgomery tradition, get our first field experience when we turn thirteen. It wasn't supposed to even be a full night, wasn't supposed to be dangerous. One kill, and then he'd take me home to open presents." Ariel's gloved hand clenched slowly around the tissues. "It wasn't a 'wrong place at the wrong time' thing, either. I lost my arm first, and then my dad, and then the bastard left. He left me *alive*. He killed Dad and left me alive and didn't even bother to drain me of blood. It wasn't a feral kill. It was *deliberate*." He laughed mirthlessly and finally looked up at Bella, his eyes filled with tears. "And now here you are leaving flowers at his grave."

"Your father was a good man," Bella said, squeezing Ariel's shoulder. "I know I didn't know him personally, but the city was safer when he was alive. Tenebrous lost a protector that day." She let her hands drop to her lap. "I guess, now that I'm working with you, it just felt right to pay my respects."

Another long silence passed between them, and several times, Bella opened her mouth to speak before deciding against it.

To her surprise, it was Ariel who finally broke the silence. "Thanks," he muttered. "For coming, I mean. It... means a lot."

"I didn't know you would be here," Bella said awkwardly.

Ariel huffed, letting out a quiet laugh. "I know. You said. But you still brought flowers and everything."

"I did have those before, on my way over," Bella said, rubbing the back of her neck. "But I got here and smelled you inside, and thought I should bring something for you, too..." She pulled a packet of cigarettes out of her pocket and lightly tossed them at Ariel, who caught it.

He turned it over in his hand, then looked up at Bella. "Thought you didn't approve," he said, a hint of amusement creeping back into his voice.

"I don't," Bella said, "but you like your tar-infused cancer sticks, and I wanted to get you something that might cheer you up a little."

She let out a tiny sigh of relief when Ariel's lips twitched in a faint approximation of a smile. "You're alright, Graves," he said.

"Ward," Bella said, and Ariel glanced up. "You can call me Ward, I mean. I think we're there." She nudged his shoulder, smiling back.

Ariel stuck a cigarette in his mouth. "Thanks, Ward." He shook his head. "Thanks... Bella."

"Hey, what are friends for?" Bella said, stifling a cough as Ariel lit the cigarette and blew out a cloud of smoke, turning his head away from her.

"We ain't friends." Ariel did his best to fan the smoke into dissipating, but when Bella's eyes watered, he stood up, inclining his head in the direction of the exit.

They slipped out of the mausoleum and made their way through the darkened graves, Ariel puffing on his cigarette while Bella stayed upwind of him.

"You don't have to walk with me," Ariel said. "I'm sure you're anxious to get back to Lee."

Bella waved a hand. "She got her hands on some vodka, passed out on her bed before I came here. She's fine, don't worry," she added. "I made sure of it."

"Well, that certainly explains why you're not worried about her going feral in the dorms," Ariel muttered. They reached the wall, and Ariel hauled himself up and over, keeping the cigarette clamped between his teeth.

Bella simply turned back into a bat and flew over, landing beside Ariel in her human form once more. "I am," she said, taking a moment to straighten her shirt. "But nothing's gotten any werewolves that weren't out on the streets before. I think she'll be okay for one evening."

"Yeah, that's a fair shout." Ariel pulled his cigarette out of his mouth, frowning. "Six days until the full moon. Do you think she's ready?"

"Is anyone ever?"

"Good point."

Bella inclined her head as they rounded a corner of the wall, heading for Ariel's car. "Any word from Maria? How's she doing?"

"About as well as can be expected. She's been having to hide what happened from her parents, but apparently they never paid much attention to her to begin with." Ariel flicked the cigarette butt into a garbage bin and pulled out his car keys. "Aliyah's been keeping watch outside her house, so at least we'll know if something happens before then."

"Another Gloam Hunter?" Bella guessed, and Ariel nodded. "That's... something, anyway." She watched as Ariel pulled open the driver's side door and sat, leaving it open. "Do you think anything's going to happen? Either then or on the full moon?"

Ariel shrugged and stuck his keys in the ignition. "I don't know, and I don't want to waste my time worrying," he said. "We'll deal with it as it comes. You want a ride back?"

Bella wasn't sure if he was offering out of a sense of obligation, but decided it would be best to play it safe. "Thanks, but no thanks—I'd like to stretch my wings some more before sunup."

A flicker of emotion crossed Ariel's face, but it was gone before Bella could figure out what it was. "Suit yourself," he said, and pulled the door shut.

Bella watched his tail lights before he turned a corner and was gone; it was only then that she transformed, following his car from the air to make sure he made it safely back to his dorm.

Chapter 18

Though classes were still a painful reminder of the normalcy she'd lost, Lee found they were easier to get through once the other students got used to her face.

The stares were replaced with shunning. It was like they thought her scars were contagious, though really, Lee felt it was more that looking at her made the other students uncomfortable. It stung, but this, at least, she could deal with. She'd hoped things would be better in college, but this was nothing, really.

Besides, she had Bella and Ariel, now.

Bella was always ready with a kind word and a smile, and often welcomed her home from classes with a high five and dinner from the dining hall. Lee wasn't sure if Bella knew her financial situation, but she certainly wasn't about to turn down free food and good company.

Ariel was a bit harder to parse, but beneath his gruff exterior, he was a kind soul who, she felt, just had a difficult time showing it. But he let her accompany him on patrols, and he understood what it was like to look *different* in a way that people were unused to.

Maybe it was a bit pathetic, but she was glad she at least had them to turn to.

Now, though, their presence wasn't nearly as much of a comfort as she'd hoped it would be as they sped along the interstate in the late afternoon, Lee anxiously watching the sun turn more vibrant shades of orange the further it slipped down towards the horizon. Her good leg jittered anxiously, and she gnawed on one of her lip rings, spinning it through the piercing hole.

"Nervous?" Bella asked from the back seat, and Lee jumped.

"Little bit," she said, unable to meet Bella's eyes.

"It's gonna be fine," Ariel said, though Lee could hear the doubt that crept into his voice. "We know Mom's at home so she can't surprise us, and Mo said she'd already started in on the wine before we left. The safe room's all prepped and ready for you, Bella's full up on blood, and I'll be right there and ready in case this all goes to hell."

"Well, you're just Mister Optimism today, aren't you?" Bella asked.

Ariel's hand tightened on the steering wheel. "I'd rather be safe than sorry tonight," he said. "Even with all the precautions we're taking, there's still a dozen different ways this can go wrong."

"Only a dozen?" Lee asked, trying to keep her voice light. "I like those odds."

"Lee, I'm serious," Ariel bit out. "We don't know what to expect tonight."

"Look, I'm scared too," Lee said, wrapping her arms around herself. "Even under *normal* circumstances I don't know what this is supposed to be like. Add everything else on top of that..." She swallowed and looked away. "So, sorry for trying to bring the mood up a little," she muttered.

The car was silent save for Ariel's music playing softly through the speakers. Bella glanced between the two of them, biting her lip.

Ariel finally sighed heavily, turning onto the main road leading to his house. "I think we're all just a little tense," he said. "I'll feel a lot better once Lee's secure in the safe room." As he spoke, he glanced at the sun, now barely a silver of orange above the horizon; they still had plenty of time to get there, but the faster night fell, the faster Lee could feel her heart go, pounding an unsteady rhythm in her chest.

"Hey," Bella said, reaching between the seats and holding out her hand. Lee took it, and Bella squeezed gently. "Deep breaths, remember? In through your nose, out through your mouth, count to five."

Lee nodded, swallowing hard before forcing herself to steady her breathing. It helped a little, her heart gradually returning to a more normal tempo.

They reached the driveway, and Bella transformed into a bat, Lee reaching behind her to scoop her now-tiny roommate into her hand, depositing her safely in a pocket.

"Come on," Ariel muttered when they parked. He and Lee got out of the car and climbed the front steps, and the front door opened to reveal Ashley, wine in hand and Morgan trying to pull her out of the way.

"Ariel, I missed you," Ashley crooned, and Ariel stiffened as she pulled him into a hug, wine nearly sloshing out of her glass.

"Mother, we're wasting time," Morgan said, tugging on her shoulder, and Ashley scoffed but let go. Morgan ushered them inside and shut the door. "Stop bothering Ariel for me, I need to get on the radio."

"You're going to have to talk to me sooner or later," Ashley said, catching Ariel by his upper arm, and Ariel went rigid. "I'm your *mother*."

"Tomorrow," Ariel promised through gritted teeth. He twisted out of Ashley's grip. "On the *phone*. I've got a job to do now, in case you've forgotten."

"I never see you anymore," Ashley yelled over her shoulder as Morgan steered her away.

"For good reason," Ariel said under his breath. He jerked his chin at Lee. "C'mon, it's this way."

Lee trailed after him, glancing around as they walked. Now that she wasn't half-blinded from pain, she could finally appreciate the decor, which reminded her more of old colonial houses rather than the generic Midwestern mansions that they passed on the drive up. Bella poked her head out of Lee's pocket to watch, then climbed up Lee's torso to her shoulder, tiny claws digging into the purple flannel.

They passed a large mirror showing tarnishing around the frame, and Lee realised she couldn't see Bella's reflection. She opened her mouth to ask.

"Mirror's made with silver, so that's why she's not showing up," Ariel murmured before she could speak, and Bella let out a tiny squeak of agreement.

"So how come I can still see myself?" Lee asked.

"Fuck if I know." Ariel held open the door to the basement, giving a sarcastic bow. "Werewolves first."

Lee snorted despite herself and headed downstairs, gripping the railing for support. She was getting better at going up stairs, but down was another matter entirely.

The basement was just as large and grand as the rest of the house, though felt distinctly more modern than the rest of it. Lee hesitated on the slate floor at the bottom, taking in the bar with its many bottles scattered on the countertop, to the sitting area with its enormous television and long sofas. "Where...?"

"This way." Ariel led her away from the sitting area to another door set in the far wall, in the deepest part under the house.

The inside of the door, along with the rest of the room, was lined with soundproof padding, and in the middle of the room was a cage of silver bars, just like Ariel had said. Even though she'd known what to expect, Lee's heart began racing again, and she took a few deep breaths to try to steady herself once more.

"Easy there," Ariel said, grabbing a stool from the bar and dragging it into the room. "No point panicking over nothing."

"Easy for *you* to say," Lee gasped, her fingernails digging into her palms.

Bella let go of Lee to flutter to the floor, transforming back. "Lee? Are you alright?"

"Hey," Ariel said, shutting the door behind them and reaching out for Lee. She let him carefully grasp her wrist in his gloved hand, using the other to prise open her clenched fingers. She forced her hand to relax, and Ariel smiled. "Whatever happens, I'm gonna be right here all night. You'll be frustrated trying to attack me, but after you figure out the bars hurt, you'll just spend the rest of the time pissy and growling."

Lee bit her lip hard enough for it to hurt. "Promise?"

Ariel hesitated. "Well, promise as much as I can. I ain't making any I can't keep."

"I guess that's as good as anything," Lee said, giggling somewhat hysterically. "So do I just—?" She grabbed the cell's latch and yelled, letting go and shaking her burned hand.

Ariel just stared at her for a long moment. "It's *silver*," he said, with the air of someone talking to a toddler. "What did you think was gonna happen?"

Lee blew on her blistered fingers and scowled. "I *knew* that, I just wasn't paying attention."

Bella leaned over to look at the blisters and winced. "Ooh, that looks painful."

Ariel arched an eyebrow, but flipped the latch up and pulled the cage's door open. Lee hesitated, glancing over at him; she trusted him, but that didn't take away the instinct of very much not wanting to willingly walk into a cage.

She squared her shoulders and stepped inside, and Ariel latched the door behind her. She turned around to see him settling on the stool.

"How much longer is it until moonrise?" Lee asked.

Ariel checked his smart watch. "Should be five minutes."

Bella whistled. "Cutting it a bit close there, aren't you?"

"If I had to choose between dealing with a crazed werewolf or my mother, I'd pick the werewolf," Ariel said shortly. "Lee, you might want to go ahead and change now... you won't exactly keep your clothes if you transform unwittingly."

Lee grimaced. "And I rather like this flannel."

Bella reached through the silver bars, and Lee grasped her hand, seeking comfort in Bella's cool touch. "You're going to be okay, Lee,"

Bella said quietly, lacing their fingers together. "Me and Ariel will look out for you."

"Promise?" Lee asked, hating how her voice cracked.

Bella gave her a small smile, squeezing her hand. "Promise." She gently disentangled their fingers and pulled her hand back out of the cage. "Catch you on the flip side."

Lee let out a shaky laugh and nodded, closing her eyes as she let the transformation come over her. She fell to all fours and shook herself out, her coppery fur rippling with the motion.

She caught Bella staring at her, and *boof*ed curiously.

"I'm never going to get over how cute you are as a wolf," Bella said, laughing as she rubbed the back of her neck. "You're so *fluffy*."

Lee yipped in agreement, and let out a huff of laughter as Ariel rolled his eyes.

"She's a fucking wolf, what did you expect?" he said. "She won't be so cute once moonrise comes."

Lee's tail drooped, and she hung her head, turning away to pad in a tight circle and lay down, her nose on her paws.

"Don't be mean," Bella scolded, sitting on the floor by Ariel's stool. "Lee? How're you feeling?"

Lee slowly lifted her head to give Bella a hard look.

"Uh, right," Bella said, a touch sheepishly. "I guess you can't really talk... um... one bark for no, two for yes?"

Lee barked twice, and Bella laughed, clapping her hands delightedly. Even Ariel cracked a grin at that.

"Guess that means you're feeling alright?" Bella asked, and Lee barked in confirmation. "Good. I just..." She sighed. "I just wish there was more I could do, you know?"

"You're here to wrestle her into submission if need be," Ariel said. "I think that's more than enough."

Lee's ears flattened and she let out a quiet whine.

"I'll be as gentle as I can," Bella reassured her. Lee shook her head. "That's not what you're worried about?"

Lee barked.

"You're... not worried about hurting *me*, are you?" Bella asked, and Lee whined anxiously, her ears flattening against her skull. "Hey..." Bella put a hand through the bars of the cage again, settling it between Lee's ears. Her fingers scratched gently, tugging at the fur, and Lee's tail thumped. "You won't, alright? At least nothing that I won't recover from. It's not like you're forcing me into doing this. I want to help you in any way I can."

Lee tried to smile. It looked more like she was baring her teeth, and winced when Bella snatched her hand back.

"Everything will be just dilly come morning," Bella said, settling cross-legged on the floor. "You'll see."

Ariel glanced at his watch again, before pulling out his phone to see the alerts coming in from the hunters. "Looks like everyone's ready to go," he said, setting his phone on his leg so he could keep an eye on it. "Everyone's anxious—first full moon since the attacks started. People are gonna get hurt tonight."

Bella pursed her lips. "Hopefully, though, we'll be able to get some answers, or at least some clues to this mystery."

"Maybe. But I'm not holding my breath." Another anxious glance at his watch. "Here we go."

Lee grit her teeth and braced herself, her fur standing on end in anticipation of whatever was going to come next.

The seconds ticked by, and Lee hesitantly cocked an ear, looking at the others. She let out a piteous whine.

"...Gimme a second," Ariel said after a long moment of staring at Lee expectantly. He got up and went to the door, slipping outside.

"You still with us, Lee?" Bella asked, and Lee barked twice.

Ariel returned to the room and shut the door behind him with a harrowed expression. "Moon's up."

"But Lee's still... well." Bella gestured at her, and Lee bobbed her great, furry head.

Ariel swore violently and turned away for a second, fingers raking through his hair. "I thought we'd be getting answers, not even more fucking questions!"

Lee whined again and tapped a claw on the floor in Morse Code for SOS. Ariel whirled to look at her anxiously, but Lee shook herself, scratching on the floor like she was writing.

"Lee? What is it?" Bella asked anxiously.

"Hang on," Ariel said, and darted out of the room once more.

Lee's ears flattened, her tail tucking between her legs, but then Ariel returned holding an Ouija board triumphantly aloft.

"Ohhh, that's clever!" Bella said as Ariel slipped the board through the bars, using his silver hand to do so just as a precaution. The planchette joined it, and Lee's tail wagged as she put a paw on the planchette to begin moving it around. It was painstakingly slow, but Ariel soon pulled a notepad out of his coat pocket and began scribbling down letters, guessing out loud what Lee was trying to spell with fairly decent accuracy.

So this is weird even 4 werewolves?

"You have no idea," Bella said, glancing at Ariel. "I mean, this is... unheard of."

"What she said," Ariel said. He pursed his lips. "Honestly? Until we've got more of an idea of what the hell is going on here, I don't want word of this getting out."

Lee nodded in agreement. *Blanchard?* She spelled out.

"Read my mind," Ariel said, nodding.

Lee nodded as well, and her front paw scrabbled as she moved the planchette again. *Maria?*

"Ooh, that's a good point," Bella said. "She's the only other survivor of the feral attacks; if she's also unaffected by the full moon, then we might just have ourselves a lead!"

"Ever the optimist, aren't you?" Ariel muttered. "Though you *also* bring up an interesting point..." His eyes narrowed as he studied Lee. "If she's actually, totally unaffected by the full moon...."

Bella sat up straighter, her eyes huge. "Ariel, you're a genius! " she said, and threw her arms around his neck, only to let go when he recoiled, apologising quickly to him. "Lee, try transforming back!" she said excitedly.

Lee looked uncertainly from Bella, who was watching her excitedly, practically bouncing in her seat, to Ariel, whose gaze had fixed on her in a way that reminded her uncomfortably of a predator studying its prey.

She shook herself. He was just being cautious, and she knew well enough that the night could easily go sour at the drop of a hat. Lee took a deep breath and focused on the change again.

And as easily as it ever was, her fur receded, her snout flattened, her ears migrated down to the sides of her head as her paws split into fingers. Lee stared down at her hand, wiggling her fingers in disbelief, and looked up to see her companions staring back at her with equally dumbfounded expressions.

"Tonight's now officially gone from freakishly weird to..." Ariel shook his head, a snarky reaction failing him. "Fuck me," he said instead, and sat back on his stool, looking rather like he'd been beaten over the head with a shovel.

"I have the coolest roommate *ever!*" Bella declared, and Lee burst into nervous giggles.

. . . .

Lee spent the rest of the night in the cage, just as a precaution. But Ariel slipped out of the room again to return with snacks, along with a pillow and blankets, and Lee made a makeshift nest on the floor of the cage. The three of them settled in to wait out the moon, at first waiting in an uncomfortable silence, then a more companionable atmosphere as they found ways to entertain themselves. By unspoken agreement, the night had gotten too weird to think about, and was better spent watching terrible vampire movies on Bella's phone, eating junk food and discussing the upcoming campus Halloween party.

"You know," Lee said, tossing a piece of popcorn into the air and crunching loudly when she caught it in her mouth, "if you'd told me these wild college parties I was warned about in high school would involve sitting up all night in a cage in a rich guy's basement, waiting to see if I snap and try to murder my friend—"

"I ain't your friend," Ariel said automatically.

Lee plucked another piece of popcorn from the bowl and lobbed it through the bars at Ariel's head. He let it bounce off his cheek to land in his lap. "You're sitting down here keeping me and Bells company to make sure I'm alright," she said, smirking.

"All part of the job, Lee," Ariel said, rolling his eyes.

"*And*, before all this, you introduced us to your family—"

"—you've met my mother, that's usually reserved for people I can't stand—"

"—*and* you let me accompany you on patrol—"

"—overworked and not enough hunters to cover if one got hurt—"

"*And!*" Lee said, lifting a triumphant finger, "You let me hold your hand while I was crying in the council meeting. Face it, Ariel, we're friends now."

Ariel rolled his eyes, but picked up the piece of popcorn that had fallen into his lap and stuck it in his mouth, crunching pointedly back at her.

"Ha! I remember that," Bella said, grinning. "The hand-holding, specifically. That was cute."

A pink flush crept into Ariel's cheeks. "Now hold on a damn second," he said. "We've only *maybe* progressed to 'friends'. Don't be jumping the gun, vamp."

Lee had no such dignified blush; her face went a blotchy red that clashed horribly with her hair as she nodded in agreement. "Please let's not make tonight any weirder than it already is?" she said.

Bella let out a theatrical sigh, but held up her hands in defeat. "How about some *good* vampire films now?" she said, changing the subject, and Ariel and Lee shared a brief glance before looking away, allowing Bella to distract them again.

When the moon finally set and Ariel unlocked the door to let Lee out, she'd barely taken a step in the direction of the exit before Bella tackled her in a hug, lifting Lee clean off her feet despite being over a head taller than the enthusiastic vampire. "You did it!"

"That's just the thing," Lee said, flailing for a moment before Bella let out a tiny 'oop' of apology and set her back down, "I'm not exactly sure *what* I did..."

"We'll figure it out later," Ariel said. "Right now, it's coffee, classes, and then..."

Lee's smile faded. "Support group?" she said, very unenthusiastically.

"Support group."

Chapter 19

L ee was no stranger to running on zero hours of sleep, but the transformations the night before seemed to make the deficit even worse, despite the quadruple-shot espresso Ariel picked up for her on their way to English class. It was all Lee could do to look like she was paying attention to the professor as he went over the finer points of rhetoric, her brain tuning the lecture out completely.

"I'll let you borrow my notes," Bella promised when they were dismissed.

Lee could only yawn in response as she crammed her loose handouts into her backpack.

"Look on the bright side," Ariel said when he joined them, "next one, assuming nothing changes, you can just stay in the dorm and... sleep."

"And I'll be there to take you out if need be," Bella added, winking.

"Only if you buy me a drink first," Lee said around another massive yawn, and slouched her way out of the classroom, making a concentrated effort to keep her gait even.

She was so tired she could have sworn she'd heard Ariel say behind her, "She lobbed that one right over the plate, at least take a swing!"

• • • •

Lee felt a little more revitalised after lunch (and another too-strong coffee), and almost felt like she was ready to face Maria and the rest of the support group when evening rolled around and rainclouds began to gather overhead.

Almost.

Bella was out feeding again, which left Lee alone with her thoughts as she sat on the edge of her bed, letting her good leg swing as she stared down at her injured knee, the scars hidden beneath black denim. She held a now very crumpled brochure for the support group in her hands, turning it over and over with her fingertips.

She could just not go. Ariel had said on the drive back that plenty of werewolves didn't attend, didn't feel comfortable or simply didn't want to acknowledge that facet of their lives. It wasn't like she would be dragged back to juvie if she didn't turn up to her mandated therapy sessions.

It would be a bit hard to send her to juvie now that she was eighteen, anyway.

Lee shook herself, taking several deep breaths to calm herself. It did little to help, but she stood and stuffed the brochure in her pocket before tugging her tank top straight and grabbing her purple flannel, slinging it over her shoulders as she headed out.

A promise was a promise, after all, and she'd promised Maria she would be there.

"I've got to start making my promises more carefully," Lee muttered to herself as she made her way down the stairs. She'd found that if she braced herself against the railing to swing herself forward, it was faster than she could manage taking the steps one at a time.

It was undignified as hell, but it got the job done.

Lee caught the bus north, head bobbing awkwardly along to her thrash metal playlist she put on in the hopes it might help psych her up. She caught herself drumming out a completely unrelated rhythm on her thighs, her good leg jittering as the bus headed further north, and she grit her teeth, sitting on her hands so she wouldn't draw any more stares.

Before, it had only been curious glances. Lee was well aware she tended to be disruptive just by nature of existing, but *before*, all it took was a quick look from strangers to determine the source of whatever noise she was making before they lost interest. Now, all it did was serve as an invitation for them to stare openly at her face.

Lee's hands clenched into fists under her thighs, and she closed her eyes so she could at least pretend nobody was looking at her.

She got off the bus to continue the next several blocks on foot. She ignored the twinge in her knee as she walked, her head still bobbing along to the music. Lee only realised she'd reached the community centre when she caught sight of a familiar black-and-blonde ombre ponytail, and she drew up short, blushing furiously as she pulled out her earbuds to hear Maria laughing.

"Good song, then, Lee?" Maria called from the steps as Lee, face burning, limped her way up to meet Maria at the top, winding her earbuds as she went.

Maria looked about as tired as Lee felt, but she grinned, holding out a hand for a fistbump that Lee hesitantly returned. The ex-hunter's arm was no longer bandaged, but she wore long sleeves, so Lee couldn't see the extent of the scarring.

Lee thought she'd been subtle in her glancing, but then Maria grinned wryly and pulled her sleeve up to show the angry red teeth marks. "Still needing to do PT exercises, trying to get my hand's mobility back," she said, flexing to demonstrate. Her hand couldn't quite close into a fist, and she let it relax. "Could've been worse. *Would* have been worse, if not for you."

"Right," Lee said, mortified that she'd been caught doing the exact thing she wished others wouldn't do to her. "Maria, I'm sorry, that was... rude of me."

Maria waved her off. "No harm, no foul," she said. She gave Lee a wry smile. "I've been fielding unwanted stares for years. I don't mind indulging the curiosity of someone I trust."

"...Right," Lee said again. "Maria, last night, was there anything weird about what happened?"

Maria frowned slightly, idly scratching her nose. "I don't think so," she said. "Textbook moon, wasn't it? Sucked, but..." She sighed. "I guess that's just life for us now, huh?"

"Right," Lee said, and winced, painfully aware that that was the third time she'd said that in response to Maria. "I mean... yeah. Sucks."

Maria bumped her hip gently and jerked her head to the community centre's doors. "Come on," she said. "Plenty of time to discuss it inside. I've already met a couple of the others who were in the safe house last night; they seem like alright people."

Lee nodded, her heart climbing into her throat as she followed Maria into the building; Maria nodded at the receptionist, who glanced up at them before going back to his work.

"So..." Lee pulled the battered pamphlet out of her pocket, futilely attempting to smooth out the creases. "What exactly kind of room number is '1/0th', anyway? That wasn't a typo of 'tenth', was it?"

Maria stopped when they reached a bend in the hallway; Lee almost kept going before she did a doubletake at the door that she could have sworn hadn't been there a moment before. She cursed internally. Of course it was going to be hidden by magic, just like the council rooms.

"Just a little joke by whatever mage cast the Nevermind spell," Maria said, shrugging as she pushed the door open. "Since, you know, can't divide by zero and all."

"I know it's hard to believe seeing as I'm an English major," Lee said, following Maria into a hallway brightly illuminated by witchlights, "but I do know a little more about math than just two plus two."

Maria grinned. "Yeah? Like what?"

"Four plus four."

Maria just snorted, shaking her head.

"What *is* a Nevermind spell, anyway?" Lee asked. "Ariel never did explain, and..." She winced. "I kinda forgot to ask about them until now. I know that's what's guarding the passages into the council's, uh, den? Warren? Labyrinth?"

"Offices?" Maria suggested. "And Nevermind spells are pretty nifty—the magician just... encourages the Gloam to do its thing of making people not notice anything out of the ordinary, only in this case, it's amplified. Gloamtouched can see through it once somebody shows them whatever's hidden, but normal folk have a harder time, even when it's been pointed out."

"Like a perception filter," Lee murmured with a grin.

"Yeah, only we don't get sonic screwdrivers to go with it," Maria, and she and Lee shared a brief laugh.

The corridor was short and lined with doors that Lee realised should have led into the middle of the street, and she grinned, wondering how that particular feat of magic had been managed. Pocket dimension? Twisting space so the community centre was bigger on the inside? Or did the hidden door act as a portal, transporting them to a completely different location seemingly seamlessly?

"Offices for the Lunar Delegation," Maria said, nodding at the doors as she passed. "You ever need to contact one of its members for anything, they've even got a directory and everything." She tapped the board as they passed, and Lee paused to snap a picture with her phone before hurrying on.

The last door opened up onto a room that was by all means completely innocent looking, a plain tile floor and ugly wallpaper that belonged to the Seventies. A circle of plastic chairs was set up in the centre, and a long plastic table full of cookies, pretzels, juice, and coffee stood against one wall beside the stack of extra chairs. It looked like almost every seat in the circle was already filled, and Lee braced herself as she and Maria walked in.

The faces that looked back at her could have been her own: almost all of them exhausted, some scared, some scarred.

Connor sat at the head of the circle, inasmuch as a circle could have a head, ankle crossed over his knee and balancing a clipboard on his lap. He gave a small wave when Maria and Lee walked in. "Go ahead and have a seat, we'll be getting started shortly," he said in that generically-friendly tone, and Lee felt her hackles rise again.

Maria, unconcerned, claimed one of the empty seats, and motioned for Lee to sit next to her. Lee hesitated, her gaze darting back to the door, before she sternly reminded herself of her promise and sat, mentally kicking her past self for agreeing to do this.

"We'll give it another five minutes before we get started," Connor said. "Anyone who hasn't gotten refreshments yet and wants them, go ahead and get 'em now." He glanced up at Lee, who stiffened at the eye contact before looking away.

"Relax," Maria whispered to Lee. "Nobody's going to bite you."

Lee shot her a tired glare and slouched lower in her seat, crossing her arms tightly as her good leg went straight back to jittering rapidly. Almost immediately, she uncrossed her arms again, untangling her earbuds and sticking them back in to continue listening to music, rather than let her nerves fray any further from having to hear the idle chatter in the room.

She resolutely ignored Maria tapping her on the shoulder, Maria getting up to help herself to cookies and coffee, Maria waving a double chocolate chip cookie enticingly under her nose before giving up and biting into it herself.

Lee thought she might explode by the time the room settled, and Connor shot her a meaningful look, tapping his ear. A tic jumped in her jaw as she yanked her earbuds out and rewound them, stuffing her phone roughly back in her pocket.

"Alright, it seems like that's everyone," Connor said, looking down at his clipboard briefly before looking back up at the circle of gathered werewolves. "Thank you everyone for coming; I know how stressful the day after the full moon can be, just like the rest of you, so it means a lot you took the time to come today and provide some support to your fellow lycans."

Lee slid lower in her chair. Much lower and she would be resting her back on the seat; as it was, her backside was already half-off the chair, and Maria nudged her, prompting Lee to reluctantly sit up straight. Her leg went back to bouncing.

Connor continued speaking, but Lee's mind had already wandered elsewhere, off to a memory of her last patrol with Ariel, before the daydream shifted to the nightclub she'd gone to with Bella, and Lee heard the chorus to that song playing on repeat in her head as she imagined what it might be like to go back and dance with Bella on a night she didn't have to worry about feeding.

She jumped when Maria nudged her again, and glared at her. "*What?*" she hissed.

Maria raised her eyebrows and gave the smallest jerk of her head at the waiting faces.

"Sometimes our minds tend to wander, especially when we're tired," Connor said sympathetically. "Would you like to share why you're here today?"

Lee scowled and jabbed a thumb in Maria's direction. "Because I promised her I'd show up."

A ripple of chuckles went around the room, but Connor shook his head, and the laughter quieted. "Sometimes just showing up to be supportive of a friend can be a step in your own healing process," he said. "It can feel awkward the first few times, coming to group therapy like this, but it doesn't have to. We're all here for the same reasons, after all." He gave Lee an understanding smile, which she returned with a deeper scowl. "Just share what you feel comfortable with, okay?"

Lee let out a heavy sigh. Why the hell not? It wasn't like she ever planned on coming back. "Uh... hi," she began, and smirked humourlessly. "I'm Lee, and I'm an alcoholic."

Nobody laughed.

Connor sat back, briefly taking off his glasses and polishing them before replacing them on his nose. "Lee, if you don't wish to share, then that's fine, but please don't make a joke out of this for everyone else."

Lee let out a bark of laughter. "You want to know what's a fucking joke?" she said, looking Connor in the eye as she awaited the reprimand for her language. When none came, her gaze slid away, and she shook her head. "This was supposed to be my out. Work hard, they tell you, study hard, get into college, get a degree, get a job, stay off the streets. I busted my *ass* to get into college trying to make a better life for myself, and for all of two months, life was finally going well, you know?"

She inhaled sharply, feeling the betraying sting of tears in her eyes, and she blinked several times, shaking her head. "And then, about a month ago, I thought, what's the worst that could happen? It's fall break, I can take one day for myself, and what do I do? I take a nice, normal walk, and the next thing I know I'm waking up missing half my face, leg so messed up I'm lucky I can even walk at all, and my roommate's telling me she's a vampire and I'm a werewolf and oh, by the way, monsters are real! And they *eat* people!"

"SHUT UP!" she yelled, head whipping around when she realised several of the werewolves were nodding along. "Just—shut up, stop acting like you know, because you *don't—!*" Her voice cracked and she squeezed her eyes shut.

"Lee, if you want to shout, by all means, shout," Connor said, "but not at the other people here."

Lee began to laugh, pressing a hand to her mouth. She realised she was crying.

She couldn't bring herself to care.

"You know, most people would think the worst part about this was the transformations, no. Or the scars, no," Lee said, propping her elbows on her knees. "Or even finding out about this whole secret little underworld of night y'all have got going here—no!" She angrily wiped her eyes on her sleeve. "It's realising that ever since you were four years old, you've been bounced from foster homes to psych wards to group homes to more foster homes to the streets to juvie to more *fucking* psych wards like a goddamn pinball, unwanted and unloved and doped up on meds you don't need because nobody believed the monsters you were seeing were real!"

There was silence in the room for a second, but to Lee, the second seemed to stretch on for eternity.

"Fuck this," Lee said, and there was that stress-laugh coming back as she stood abruptly, knocking her chair over from the force of the motion. She bit down on her knuckle to stop the laughter as she stalked to the door, the clatter of the chair echoing behind her.

Chapter 20

O utside the community centre, Lee fumbled with her earbuds before she managed to put them back in, and she cranked the volume up, uncaring about hearing damage. What did it matter, after all, if she could just heal it away?

At some point while she'd been inside, the clouds had burst and it was starting to drizzle. Lee tilted her head back to feel the bitterly cold water on her face. It was strangely soothing after her explosion of pent-up emotions, a breath of fresh air after the stifling atmosphere of the support group.

Stupid to keep her promise. Maria probably hated her now, and though the former hunter *shouldn't* tell Ariel what had happened, Ariel would probably guess. It didn't exactly take a genius.

Whatever. If he hated her, too, that was fine. That was just fine.

"I'm fine," Lee whispered, and took a deep breath, starting down the sidewalk as the drizzle became a downpour.

It had been too long since she'd done this, she realised, just put on a favourite playlist on a walk to lose herself in the music. Lee smiled faintly despite herself, her stride no longer lopsided but rhythmic in her footsteps, almost dancing to the music only she could hear as she made her way along the sidewalk.

The songs, she'd listened to hundreds of times on similar walks whenever she needed an escape, and her body settled into the familiar rhythm, arms joining in the dance.

She knew she was drawing stares, and she laughed to herself when she realised she didn't care. She might as well have been lost in her own little world free of monsters, where the music painted a story in her head that was just begging to be let out. Her tattered shoes came down on the mirror surface of puddles in sprays of water that refracted the lights of the city.

So this was what it came down to, in the end: stealing the moments of a childhood she never got to have.

Lee didn't even realise how far she'd wandered until she reached the river, and she leaned against the railing, blinking water out of her eyes. Her hair was plastered to her skull, and the unpleasant ache in her knee had returned. Lee began to laugh again, almost doubling over as she pillowed her forehead on her arms. The music seemed to fade away, her brain tuning out all sounds until she was only left with her thudding heartbeat in her ears.

It had been raining that night, too.

Lee startled and whirled when someone lightly touched her shoulder, slapping the hand away out of reflex.

Ariel drew his hand back, annoyance on his face as Lee pulled out her earbuds. The rain seemed unnaturally loud after she'd spent so long drowning it out.

"The hell do you think you're doing out here?" Ariel asked. "It's fucking freezing."

Lee shook her head, pressing her hands against her face. "Walking."

"Well, *walk* your scrawny ass back to the dorms before you get hypothermia," Ariel said, and strode off, gesturing impatiently for her to follow. His coat hung heavy with water, slapping loudly against the backs of his legs.

Not seeing any better options other than to remain by the railing and do just that, Lee followed him, suddenly very aware of the strain she'd put on her knee. "Ariel, wait," Lee called when she began to fall behind.

Ariel paused, glanced back at her, and groaned. He met Lee halfway, letting her wrap an arm around his waist for support, and he helped her limp to the bus stop.

They remained silent as they huddled, dripping, under the shelter, and still didn't speak even when they boarded the bus back to campus. Ariel mutely steered Lee to his dorm building, and Lee went along with it, too emotionally exhausted to do anything but lean on him as he navigated them up to his room.

Ariel shut the door behind them and shrugged out of his coat, letting it fall on the floor with a wet *splat*. "I've got clothes you can borrow," he said, peeling his sleeveless turtleneck off as well and throwing it atop his coat. He hit the quick release for the shoulder harness of his arm and removed the limb completely, tossing it haphazardly in the direction of its charging station as he toed off his boots. He squelched over to the dresser and pulled out a hoodie and sweatpants, tossing them onto the bed before retrieving a second set. "Unless you want to stand around cold and soaked through," he added, and Lee realised he was pulling off his jeans as well.

"Just—keep your face to that wall," Lee managed to say through chattering teeth, turning away from him as well. She peeled off her wet things, feeling some of the shivering subside when she pulled the borrowed clothes on.

"Here."

She turned, blinking in surprise when she saw Ariel was already dressed, and holding a towel out to her, his eyes squeezed shut. Lee laughed hoarsely and accepted the towel, attacking her hair to rid herself of the worst of the water. "I'm decent," she said, and Ariel opened his eyes. He took the towel back, dried his own hair, and dropped it on top of their pile of wet clothes.

"I've got whiskey, tequila, and vodka," he said, stooping to pull a plastic container full of contraband out from under his bed. "And smokes. Pick your poison."

"Honey whiskey?" Lee asked.

Ariel snorted. "Of course."

"Give."

They made themselves comfortable on the bed, leaning against the wall and drinking straight from their respective bottles.

"Alright," Ariel said, lifting his chin at Lee. "Now that we're out of the rain, you're gonna tell me why the hell I got a text from Maria at ten-fucking-o'clock at night to go find and drag your sodden, half-drowned rat-looking *butt* out of the freezing cold rain so you don't get turned feral like the others."

Lee squinted at him. "*Butt?*"

"Just answer the question, sheesh."

Lee shook her head. "You'd laugh."

"Yeah?" Ariel said. "Try me."

Lee sighed, and let her head fall back against the wall. It was a long moment before she answered, trying to gather her thoughts into a semblance of a response. "I didn't exactly ask to tag along on your patrols because I wanted to help with the load," she finally said. "I mean, I did, but that wasn't the main reason."

She glanced sidelong at Ariel, who was just watching her expectantly. He seemed content to let her speak, so she continued. "I think I always sort of knew that Tenebrous existed, even if I didn't know what it was called, or... even the full extent of what it was." Lee stared down at her bottle before taking a large gulp, relishing the sting of alcohol as it slid down her throat. "I grew up in the foster system because my parents were killed by Gloambeasts. I was four."

"I'm sorry," Ariel said, and Lee's head shot up in astonishment. "What?" Ariel said defensively. "I can be nice. I mean it. I'm sorry," he said again, much more petulantly this time.

Lee snorted and wiped her runny nose on her sleeve. "Bleh, sorry. I'll wash that."

"Don't worry about it." Ariel held his bottle between his feet as he busied himself lighting a joint one-handed. He took a drag, and when Lee motioned for him to pass it over, he did so, using the opportunity to sneak another sip.

"The thing is, when you're four, and... and you've been lost in the woods for three days," Lee said, her voice wavering, "and when you're finally found, you're babbling about shadow monsters that ate your parents, of course nobody's going to believe that. They tried to get the truth of what really happened to them out of me, and..." She sniffled, took another puff, and passed the joint back to Ariel.

Lee picked up her bottle again, swirling its contents without drinking. "Well, after too long, they're going to decide there's some deeper issue there, aren't they? So then it was shrinks, and meds, and more shrinks and more meds when nothing worked, and the whole time I was just being bounced from care home to care home because nobody wants an even slightly older kid, especially with a history of severe mental illness and trauma." She snorted, and took a long drink, putting a good dent in the bottle's contents before she stopped to breathe. "Thought, after so long, maybe it really was just something I'd made up as a kid to cope. I guess at some point you just... squash it down, or internalise what they're telling you. I don't know.

"Ran away, a few times," she continued, accepting the joint when Ariel offered it back to her. "Kept ending up in juvie. Court-ordered therapy and all that." She shook her head. "It was a fucking joke. They didn't care if you were actually better, just if you appeared well enough to no longer be classified as their problem. I basically finished up high school from a homeless shelter because I aged out of the system."

Ariel nodded to himself. "It's funny," he said, taking the joint back, "Bella and I *had* wondered at how readily you seemed to accept the night world."

Lee snorted, slumping back against the wall. "Either it meant I was crazier than I thought, or I wasn't crazy at all. So far I'd been leaning towards the latter, but... after today, I'm not so sure."

Ariel laughed hoarsely. "You ran out 'cause it felt good, didn't it?" he said. "Just shut the door on reality and pretend nobody else exists, and maybe for a while, you can convince yourself there's nothing left that can hurt you. S'what I did after my dad died."

"...Yeah." Lee slowly leaned sideways until she was pressed up against Ariel's side, swallowing hard. "You spend so long hiding that stuff from yourself, and then..." She giggled. "In comes the Big, Bad Wolf to blow the... foundations of reality down."

Ariel let out a bark of laughter. "I don't think that's how it goes."

They stayed like that for a long while, listening to the sounds of the rain, passing the joint between them as it burned lower.

"You know what the worst part is?" Lee said, her voice small.

She felt Ariel shift beside her. "What?"

Lee dropped the roach in Ariel's ashtray, and lifted up her nearly-empty bottle for examination, swirling the contents. "Now that I know the help I *actually* need, I don't know how to get it."

Ariel chuckled darkly, and clinked his own similarly empty bottle against hers. "Yeah. I'll drink to that."

Chapter 21

When Bella finally found them in the wee hours of the morning, it was only after being pulled away from her feeding by an alert from Augustus that sent her rushing home, only to find Lee's scent had long gone stale in their room. This sent her into a tailspin as she tried to follow the trail in the pouring rain, growing increasingly more frantic when she realised the water had washed away any hopes of tracking her roommate. She finally came to her senses and snuck into Ariel's building as a cloud of mist, creeping around the corners and up several flights of stairs to the hunter's room.

Really, Bella thought in annoyance, it was a wonder Ariel hadn't been busted for smoking in his room already. Then again, his family probably paid the university handsomely to look the other way. This did nothing to lessen her annoyance with the situation as she filtered under the door, past a sodden pile of clothing on the floor and empty alcohol bottles by the bed.

She reformed into her solid body and planted her hands on her hips, shaking her head as she took in the sleeping pair sprawled haphazardly across Ariel's bed. Lee was dressed in a pair of Ariel's sweats, hair plastered to the corner of her mouth with drool. After a quick glance around the room, Bella sighed, moving to set Ariel's arm on its charging stand, carrying it by gingerly picking the offending appendage up with her coat. She distastefully nudged the pile of clothes with her toe, glanced over at the pair on the bed, and decided to let them sleep for now. They could deal with that mess when they woke up.

Served them right for making her worry.

Bella sat at Ariel's desk chair, pulled her phone out and sent Augustus a message to let him know Lee was alright, and settled in to wait.

Ariel woke first, and if Bella hadn't heard him stirring earlier, she would have ended up having a significantly worse morning. Ariel stilled, and Bella glanced up from her phone, only to dive sideways to avoid the knife he hurled at her. It embedded itself in the wall, directly behind where her shoulder had been a moment before.

"It's me!" Bella yelled when Ariel leapt out of bed. "It's me, Ariel, Bella!"

He drew up short, rubbing his eyes as Lee sat up, peering blearily at the vampire on the floor.

"Fucking hell, Bella," Ariel said. "You're lucky I missed."

"Lucky *I* dodged," Bella sniffed, picking herself up and brushing herself off.

"You don't want knives thrown at you? Don't go around creeping on people when they sleep," Ariel growled, stalking past her to wrench his knife from the wall. He inspected the blade and snorted, setting it on his desk.

"You sure you don't sparkle?" Lee muttered, and Bella pouted.

"I wasn't *creeping* on anybody," she said, planting her hands on her hips. "There was another reported feral attack last night, and I was worried sick about Lee! I was running all over the place trying to find her because neither of you were answering your phones, and I finally think to check here only to find you two passed out drunk—!" She broke off, squeezing her eyes shut.

Ariel rubbed his hand over his face before carding his fingers through his hair. "Hell," he said. "Okay, sorry for scaring you, just..." He gestured at the door. "Next time, wait *outside?*"

"...Right," Bella said sheepishly. She still didn't open her eyes, but then she felt Lee pull her into a hug and she went willingly. "I'm sorry, too. It won't happen again."

"You were that worried about me?" Lee asked, smiling crookedly at her.

Bella pulled away, lightly smacking Lee's shoulder. "Don't give me that, after all the lengths I've gone to trying to keep you safe! Of course I was worried about you, you—you..." She trailed off, her breath hitching when Lee cupped her face.

"I'm sorry," Lee said softly.

Bella's eyes flickered, studying Lee from behind her sunglasses. "Lee," she said, her voice faint, "either you're sending very mixed signals right now, or I'm thinking you want to kiss me?"

She could have melted at the lopsided grin Lee gave her. "Depends. Do you want me to?"

Bella surged up to wrap her arms around Lee's neck, kissing her fiercely. Lee let out a muffled squeak of surprise before getting her arms around Bella's waist, lifting her up and into the kiss.

"It's about goddamn time," Ariel muttered, going to retrieve his arm.

Bella barely heard him, losing herself in Lee. The other woman's kiss was just like she'd imagined, lips slightly chapped, the piercings an unusual but not unpleasant contrast to the softness of her mouth. She tasted like sweet whiskey and smoke, her breath stale from sleep, and when they broke away, Lee smacked her lips, grimacing apologetically.

"Sorry," Lee said, her arms tightening around Bella's waist. "Haven't really had a chance to brush my teeth—"

"Shut up," Bella said, and kissed her again.

They only stopped when Ariel loudly cleared his throat. Lee grinned sheepishly and set Bella on her feet, and Bella reached up to tuck a strand of orange hair behind Lee's ear.

"That," Bella murmured, "was almost worth the scare."

Lee laughed nervously and stepped back, rubbing the back of her neck. Her smile faded as she glanced at Ariel, who was standing by the wall, arms crossed and tapping his foot impatiently. "Right," Lee said, sitting on the edge of Ariel's bed. "You said there was another attack..."

"And with the rain we got last night, tracking the werewolf back to where she came from will be impossible," Bella said.

"And I'm guessing there's still been nothing from the mages about that spell they've been working on," Ariel said grumpily.

"If there's been anything new on that front, I haven't heard anything," Bella said, shaking her head. "And I don't know what Augustus expects us to do—keep track of every single werewolf in the city? There's like two and a half million people in Chicago, probably a thousand werewolves alone—"

Lee spluttered. "A *thousand?*"

"Maybe less. That's still a tiny percentage of the population in a city this big," Ariel pointed out.

"And still way too many for the three of us to keep track of," Bella pointed out. "*And* not every one of them is known, even by the Lunar Delegation."

Lee frowned, gnawing on one of her lip rings. "But most of the ones who went feral were ID'd," she said slowly. "And they all went to the support group. There were maybe twenty people there—"

"Do you remember any of their names, what they looked like?" Bella cut in eagerly.

Lee looked up at her, nettled. "No," she said. "'Sides, I think one of them might kick my ass for breaking the 'anonymous'... thing."

"You even part of the group after your little tantrum last night?" Ariel pointed out. "Look, *someone* has knowledge of the members; there ain't no way it's a coincidence most of the ones gone feral were from the support group."

"Does Connor keep a list?" Lee asked, glancing up at him.

Ariel wrinkled his nose. "How am I supposed to know?"

Lee made a noise of frustration. "He's *your* brother's boyfriend!"

Bella cleared her throat. "Did Connor ever take his work to your house?" she asked delicately. "Notes, maybe a briefcase?"

Ariel glanced at her, his eyes narrowing slightly. "You're suggesting if he did, my mother stole the notes."

Bella shrugged helplessly. "Look, we need somewhere to start," she said. "And I know you don't want to think it's your mum, but Augustus made some good points..." She trailed off, biting her lip, fangs barely visible.

Ariel sighed, dragging a hand over his face. "Let me get this straight: You want me to drag my ass all the way back out to the house, just to bust into her office, on the *maybe* that Mom's got a copy of Connor's notes stashed away in there somewhere?"

"Well, ideally, we'd go, too," Bella said sheepishly. "But where else are we supposed to start? Leave Lee out on the street as bait? I thought we already agreed we weren't going to do that!"

"And there's no guarantee I'd even be targeted," Lee added, frowning. "I talked to Maria at the... meeting thing, and she said nothing weird happened at all."

Ariel let out a slow breath. "You think she was lying?"

Lee shook her head. "If she was, surely there'd be someone else who was in the safe house with her that could call her out on it. We'd know by now."

"So it's just you." Ariel began to pace, raking his fingers through his hair. "I don't know if there's gonna be stolen records at the house or not, but I *do* know Mo's got records of all the attacks. He's been working with the Lunar Delegation to try and find a connection, but maybe there's something they missed, something we could spot if we just took a look ourselves."

"What makes you think we're going to find something that they haven't?" Bella asked, frowning.

"*You're* the one who wanted to go snooping through my mother's stuff," Ariel shot back.

Lee held up a hand. "We *are* three new pairs of eyes," she pointed out. "And they don't know what we do, that we think there's someone behind this."

Ariel groaned and turned on his heel, still pacing. "I still hate we can't risk *saying* something without pointing fingers," he said, face screwed up in frustration. "Maybe if they knew what we did, something would be *done* sooner!"

Bella put a hand on his arm, and he drew up short, looking down at her. "We'll get to the bottom of this," she said, trying to smile reassuringly at him. "Hopefully *before* any more people get hurt."

Ariel sighed, patting Bella's hand briefly before letting his hand fall. "And before Tenebrous tears itself apart."

Chapter 22

C lasses seemed to go by far too slowly for Ariel's taste. Even his improv class, normally his favourite, dragged, and he caught himself checking his watch every few minutes before he forced himself to take it off and put it in his bag.

This just resulted in his glancing at the clocks in each classroom as the day dragged on, and when his last class of the afternoon was finally over, he bolted from the room without waiting to hear the announcements about dress rehearsals for the upcoming studio performance. He slung his backpack over his shoulder as he rushed to meet Bella and Lee out in the central quad on campus.

He paused in the doorway that led outside, swallowing when he saw them sitting on one of the benches under the clock tower, heads together. Bella's fingers were twined through Lee's, and as he watched, Bella lifted their joined hands to kiss the back of Lee's, drawing a giggle from the other woman.

Ariel shook himself and shoved down the unpleasant feeling that churned his stomach, pushing the door open. His long-legged stride carried him quickly to the bench, and he stopped before them, hand curled loosely around the strap of his bag. "Ready?" he asked loudly. "Or do you two lovebirds need another minute?"

Lee's face went a blotchy red and she jumped to her feet; Ariel nearly reached out to steady her when he caught her faint wince, but she straightened and nodded. "Ready."

"Let's blow this pop stand," Bella said, looping her arm through Ariel's.

He took a deep breath to calm his suddenly racing heart and pulled his arm free. "Kinda need that arm, Bells," he said, and twiddled the fingers of his prosthetic for emphasis. "Not so great gripping with this one."

Bella covered her mouth to hide her grin as she and Lee fell into step beside him. "You called me Bells," she said in a sing-song voice.

"Yeah, yeah, I'll call a press conference," Ariel said, heat creeping up his neck. "No need to make a big deal about it or whatever."

"Does this mean we're friends now?" Lee said teasingly, and Ariel groaned.

"*Yes*, fine, we're friends. Happy now?"

"Incredibly," Bella said, clapping her hands together. "Which will make up for you, seeing as you're never happy."

"Damn right."

Lee laughed, and Ariel's forced scowl softened. "I'm flattered," she said, putting a hand on her chest. "No, really, I'm touched."

"Go fuck yourself," Ariel said fondly.

"Fuck me yourself, coward," Lee shot back, and Ariel snorted, shaking his head as Bella covered her mouth to muffle her laughter.

"If this is the treatment I have to look forward to, I'm taking my friendship back," he threatened.

They made it out to the stadium parking lot, and Ariel slid into the driver's seat, Bella claiming shotgun again while Lee took the back, drumming her hands against her knees as Ariel turned the ignition. They pulled out to begin the long drive north, Ariel cranking up the radio's volume at Lee's request.

"Thought you liked alt rock," he said, glancing in the rear view mirror.

Lee shrugged. "I like lots of music," she said.

"Her 'Favourites' playlist is like Russian Roulette with music," Bella said, twisting in her seat to grin at Lee, who rolled her eyes. "Alt rock, thrash metal, pop, K-pop…"

"*I'm* not the one who has a hundred and nine hour playlist of classical music," Lee shot back, and Ariel raised an eyebrow, glancing over at Bella.

"*Some* of us have an appreciation for the classics," Bella said, imperiously fluffing her hair puff.

"They're classics for a reason," Ariel agreed.

Bella pulled her sunglasses down, peering at him over the rims. "Never would've taken you for a fan, Montgomery."

Ariel shrugged, his gloved fingers curling a little more tightly on the wheel as he turned onto the freeway. "Used to play piano 'fore I lost the arm," he said, keeping his eyes fixed on the road. "Never really bothered to relearn how to with the prosthetic; I had too many other things to figure out. Like fighting."

"I've seen you fight loads of times now," Lee said, and Ariel forced himself to not look. "You're pretty damn good at it. I... I guess it paid off."

"Got Mo to thank for that," Ariel said, the corner of his mouth quirking up in a faint smile. "He worked with me, figured out a style that I could use... Helped me relearn how to fight with my left hand, turn the prosthetic into an advantage instead of letting it hold me back."

Bella hung her sunglasses off the neck of her shirt and kicked her shoes off, tucking a foot up beneath her on the seat. "How old was he?" she asked quietly.

Ariel glanced up at the ceiling briefly while he thought. "Seventeen. Dad trained him himself, and he was a natural—it's a fucking waste, having him running radio when he oughta be out patrolling. He's the best damn hunter in the city, and he just spends his days training and nights coordinating everyone else." He chuckled darkly. "He'll never say it to me, but I know he worries about how much he drinks to deal with the stress. Neither of us wants to turn into Mom."

"Can't someone else help?" Bella asked. "I mean—is it *just* him coordinating the lot of you?"

"More or less," Ariel said, scowling at the road ahead. "I take over when he needs a break, but it's otherwise a three-sixty-five nights a year job. You've seen what Dearest Mother is like—she's paranoid, won't let anyone else do it, and while she's on the council..."

"What she says, goes," Lee finished.

Ariel nodded. "It's a fucking joke," he said, scowl deepening. "She's a Montgomery, yeah, but by marriage. Normally when someone marries into the family they learn how to fight, how to hunt same as us, and... I mean, she did, I think, but she's let herself go, hasn't picked up a weapon in years. Hasn't coordinated patrols since Dad died, either. It's all Mo, it's always been just Mo." He shook his head. "Jessie was just a baby, I was a mess, and Mom... fell apart. Morgan's the only thing that held the family together, and that's on top of all the other problems going on in his life before everything else; hell, he gave up a shot at college to raise us and look after the city because she couldn't do her fucking job."

"What about the other Montgomeries?" Bella said, but Ariel shook his head again.

"Don't get me wrong, we're a big family, and they were upset about Dad, too, but they have their own cities and towns to look after," he said. "Pop-Pop—"

He shot a look over his shoulder when he heard Lee bite back a snicker. "My *grandfather*," he said, and she struggled to compose her features before nodding. "Pop-Pop's the one who commissioned my arms as I outgrew them, but aside from that, he distanced himself. Mom kept her job with the company and all, and he pays her well enough to keep us more than comfortable, but we haven't seen anyone else in the family since the funeral 'cause nobody wants to deal with her." Ariel became uncomfortably aware of the lump in his throat, and he swallowed it down, ignoring the look Bella was giving him. "Family reunions from before, when I was a kid, used to get to well over a hundred. Now it's just us."

"Do you think your mum really could be... behind the attacks?" Bella said hesitantly. "If she thinks, maybe, if she thinks she could somehow avenge your dad—?"

"I don't know," Ariel snapped, and grit his teeth when he saw Bella's hurt look out of the corner of his eye. "Bella, she might as well be a stranger to me that just lived under the same roof the last six years," he said, forcing his voice to be more level. "Christ, Jessie never got the chance to know her *or* Dad. But we don't *know*, we just don't know, and *I* don't know my own mom well enough to wonder what or even *if* she's planning anything with Blanchard, I just don't fucking *know!*"

He fell silent, chest heaving as he took a deep breath, then another. Tears stung in his eyes, and he blinked hard in an attempt to clear his vision before he carefully closed his metal fingers on the wheel, holding the car steady while he used his sleeve to angrily wipe his eyes.

"I'm sorry," Lee said, and Ariel felt her hand settle on his shoulder, reaching around his seat.

"Me, too," Ariel muttered, hands settling on the wheel.

"Hey," Bella said, her own hand squeezing Ariel's leg, "look, we'll drop the thought for now, alright? Whatever Augustus thinks about her, we're just looking for answers about the werewolves right now. If that leads us to your mum, then we'll deal with that as it comes. Okay?"

Ariel glanced over at her, and Bella gave him a small, hopeful smile. Ariel looked away and nodded. "Okay."

Chapter 23

Night had long since fallen by the time they reached Ariel's house, and Bella began shifting nervously the closer they got to the turnoff.

"What if your mom's still up?" she asked nervously.

"Doubt it," Ariel said, his tone clipped. "She'll be two bottles in already; if she's not passed out on the floor of her room yet, she will be soon. Doesn't like anyone interrupting her," he added bitterly.

He pulled up in front of the house and killed the engine, and they piled out, Bella offering Lee a hand to help her up the steps in lieu of a railing.

"Might still want to stay close to us, just in case," Ariel said, glancing over his shoulder as he unlocked the front door.

They'd barely stepped inside before Jessie came running full-tilt from the next room, dressed in fluffy pink dinosaur pajamas. "ARIEL!" she squealed, and launched herself at Ariel to hug him around the knees. He laughed quietly, bending over to hug her back as Connor came into the entrance hall after her. He smiled at them, though the dark circles under his eyes gave away just how tired he really was.

"Heya, Jess," Ariel said, and glanced up, nodding at the werewolf. "Hey, Connor."

"Hey," Connor said; Ariel caught the look in his eye, and followed his gaze to see Lee staring at Connor, her jaw set defiantly. "Lee," Connor said by way of greeting. "Glad to see you're doing okay."

"More or less," Lee said shortly, looking away.

"Where's Mom?" Ariel asked, deciding it would be best to change the subject before it turned ugly.

"In her room," Connor said pointedly, and Ariel nodded, feeling Bella relax beside him. "I was just about to get this little monkey up to bed."

"Can't I stay up just a *little* longer, Uncle Connor?" Jessie wheedled. "Please? Pleeease? Ariel's here, please!"

"Ah, I can't play with you tonight, Jess, I'm sorry," Ariel said, gently peeling Jessie off his legs and crouching so he could look her in the eye. She pouted and pushed her purple glasses up her nose. "We've gotta do research, super boring work."

Jessie's pout only grew. "But I *like* research," she protested.

Ariel grinned. "I know, but this isn't the fun kind of research. It's just gonna be lots of comparing numbers and stuff. I'll play with you next time, okay? Pinkie promise." He held up his gloved hand, making a show of extending the pinkie with a quiet whirr of the motor.

Jessie giggled and locked pinkies with him. "Alright." She planted a sticky kiss on his cheek and went with some reluctance back to Connor, holding her arms out to him.

"Sweet dreams," Bella added as Connor scooped Jessie up, propping her on his hip.

"Night!" Jessie called, waving over Connor's shoulder as he carried her upstairs. "Luck with the research!"

"Soon, you're going to be too big to carry around like this," Connor said as they disappeared around a corner.

Ariel stood, wiping his cheek off and catching Lee's eye. "What."

She shook her head, glancing away. "Nothing. Just... it's good she's got you guys, even if your mom is..." She gestured vaguely.

Ariel sighed. "Yeah. Doesn't mean it should be like that, though." He jerked his head. "C'mon. Mo'll be in the command room already."

He headed up the stairs, moving more slowly than usual so Lee wouldn't have to hurry to keep up as she painstakingly hauled herself up by the bannister.

"So where's *your* bedroom?" Bella asked lightly when they reached the second floor.

Ariel jerked his thumb over his shoulder as he turned, leading them along a carpeted hall. "Back that way. If you're determined to be nosy, at least save it for after we're done."

"Careful," Bella said, lightly punching his arm. "I might just take you up on that."

Ariel rolled his eyes, stopping outside a pair of double doors, the both of them carved with the star and sword insignia of the Montgomery family. "Whatever, just don't touch anything in here." He rapped his knuckles against the wood before pushing the doors open.

"—Echo Bravo, copy that, over," Morgan said, looking up at them and grinning as they filed into the room.

It was a grand, open space, most of the floor taken up by a large electronic table displaying a live map of Chicago with a number of green dots marked on the streets. Papers were stacked haphazardly along one side of the table's wide frame, and Morgan had a laptop open beside his chair; he was half-risen from his seat, bent over the table's display as he zoomed in, marking a red dot before sitting back at the laptop and typing rapidly. A half-drunk mug of coffee sat by his elbow, and he paused to take a large gulp, waving them in with his free hand.

"Hello again, darlings," Morgan said as he set the mug back down. Along the wall to his left was a number of screens full of CCTV footage of city streets, the images looping between an untold number of cameras; a well-used coffee maker sat on the desk below, an eclectic collection of mugs strewn beside it. The wall on the right was nothing but floor-to-ceiling filing cabinets, their contents going back as far as the mid-twentieth century. "How was the drive?"

"It was fine," Ariel said, coming around the table to give Morgan a one-armed hug. "How's everything tonight so far?"

"Quiet, for the most part," Morgan said, giving him a tired smile. "Had to reroute Emily and Ling to help Jacob deal with a nasty pack of crawlers over on the south side, but they managed to handle it before there were any civilian casualties."

"Hunter?"

Morgan lifted one shoulder in a shrug. "Jacob took a nasty gash on the arm. Gina's on her way now." He lifted his chin towards Lee and Bella, who were lingering near the doors. "Lovely to see you two again. Coffee?"

"No, thank you," Bella said, smiling sweetly and flashing her fangs. "It doesn't exactly agree with me."

Morgan laughed at that. "Fair enough. Lee—? Hold on just a tick," he said, holding up a finger as he tapped his earpiece. "Copy that..." He stood again, tapping the table screen to back out to the map of the city before zooming in on another dot. He cocked his head as he listened, nodded, and drew a purple circle near one of the dots. "Sending a new route to you now. Over."

"I'm good on coffee, thanks," Lee said quietly.

"Well, if you change your mind, just bug Ariel," Morgan said, clapping Ariel's back. "He can show you how the machine works. Ariel, I pulled the records out for you; they're on the corner, there." He nodded at the stack of folders closest to the doors, and Ariel drew away to pick them up, leafing through the first one before re-straightening the folders against the tabletop.

"Holler if you need me," Ariel said, tucking the folders in the crook of his arm, but Morgan waved him off.

"I've got my job," he said. "You do yours. See if you can't put everyone's minds at ease."

Ariel nodded and turned to go, ushering Bella and Lee out of the room and closing the door behind him.

"He seems like he's got this well in hand," Bella remarked as she trotted after Ariel, Lee right behind them.

Ariel made a small noise of dissent. "Mo's great at what he does, but you heard him—it's a slow night tonight."

"Where are we taking those?" Lee asked, glancing at the folders.

"Sitting room just down here," Ariel said, taking them around the corner to yet another wood-panelled room with a large fireplace and soft rugs. They dropped their bags and settled on the large leather sofa, and Ariel set all but one of the folders out on the coffee table, making two stacks. "Left's files on the attackers, right's the victims."

"This is it?" Bella said in dismay as she stared down at the small stacks.

"There's only been six attacks so far," Ariel pointed out, opening the folder he'd held onto and pulling out a marked-up map of the city. "Two survivors, four dead victims, four dead werewolves. And for two of the incidents, the attacker—"

"Or attackers," Lee cut in.

"—is unaccounted for," Ariel said, glancing over at her. He set the map down, tapping it. "This shows the locations of the attacks..." He laid out another map, identical in street layout but differing with notes. "The locations of the attackers' homes." A third map. "The victims' homes."

"And they haven't found any pattern to them, have they?" Lee mused, and bit down on a knuckle as they studied the maps.

"None so far," Ariel said.

"Can't imagine why," Bella said, pursing her lips. She laced her fingers together and rested her chin on her hands. "These have been happening all over the place—it doesn't even really look like there's a central location, a, a patient zero this might be radiating out from."

She paused, considering. "Well, unless you count the centre of the city, but..."

"When this is happening all over the city, it doesn't necessarily mean anything," Ariel said heavily, and Bella nodded.

"What about the attackers?" Lee asked, reaching for one of the folders on the left stack. "Has there been anything linking them?"

Ariel sighed heavily. "At first, yes—they were all apparently regular, or somewhat regular, attendees of the support group." He picked up George Maclaren's folder, flipping it open; Bella snatched the case file off his lap as he read. "I mean, this guy was apparently pretty good friends with Connor," Ariel said. His thumb brushed over the file image, a smiling face of a young man with a mop of curly dark hair. "Figured out transforming pretty quickly, though nothing like what you can do," he said, nodding at Lee as he read. "Computer science major, did data analysis for a plastics manufacturing company. Used to be pretty active in the Lunar Delegation, too—helped Mrs Guadalupe manage things in his free time, offered informal classes on transformation for anyone who wanted them, stuff like that."

Lee had already finished leafing through Iris Cooper's folder and was reaching for the third on the stack. "Iris and Shayona weren't in these classes, were they?" she said, sliding off the sofa to sit on the floor.

"Doesn't look like it," Bella said. She held up a page covered in Morgan's untidy scrawl. "I mean, it's like I said—they've already covered all the obvious angles. These guys were from different parts of town, different social backgrounds, different races, ages, genders, sexualities... the only linking factor they had was the support group, until..."

"Brandon Steinbeck," Ariel said, picking up the folder. "But like I said, there's loads of Tenebrans that fly under the radar; we're good, but the Gloam Hunters can't be everywhere, and not everyone wants to get help."

"Or knows how," Lee murmured. "I mean, it's like in books, isn't it? You get attacked by a werewolf, don't know how you survived, but then weird things start happening, weird things you can't explain—so the protagonist tries to rationalise what's happening to them away until it's too late."

Ariel nodded, pursing his lips. "It's possible Brandon was just trying to muddle on with his life, or maybe he knew about Tenebrous and just wanted nothing to do with our world. Or any number of factors, really. But Mo's done a deep dive on the guy." He pulled out several printed pages, setting them out for Bella and Lee to see for themselves. "Bank statements, credit card withdrawals, that sort of thing. He rented a studio apartment, and hardly travelled anywhere except to work at a convenience store. No record of a car, consistent bus trips to work..."

"...But nowhere like the country where he might transform away from people?" Lee guessed, and Ariel tapped his nose.

"Morgan noted he stopped turning up to work a few months before, well," Bella said, and glanced at Lee, biting her lip. "Um. Well. Before he attacked Maria."

Lee stared down at the man smiling back up at them from the file image. Ariel noticed, and nudged her gently; she startled out of her reverie and shook herself, clearing her throat. "Was there a pattern to how long the others had been missing before they... attacked?" she asked.

"No pattern to how long they were *missing*," Bella said, rattling a page from the case file. "But they all went missing the day after a full moon, Brandon included."

Lee let her chin rest heavily on the coffee table. "There's got to be something else here," she said. "Just something not so obvious."

162

"Either that, or it really is just a freak mutation of the curse," Ariel said, but he wasn't so sure he believed it.

"No," Lee said, and Ariel and Bella looked over at her to see her sit up straighter, jaw set determinedly as she pulled her laptop out of her bag, flipping it open. "Let's forget the files for now. Fresh eyes, remember? Let's see what we can dig up on these guys without the other notes."

Ariel sighed and glanced at Bella, lifting one shoulder in a shrug. "It's worth a try," he said. "Lee, pass us our laptops, will you?"

They fell into silence as they worked, the only sound in the room the soft clacking of keys. Ariel started with social media before delving deeper, smiling wryly at the thought most parents would be dismayed to know their children were accessing strangers' confidential information. His father would have been proud to see his lessons being put to good use.

That was one of the darker sides of the Montgomeries and Silver Sword; hidden in the end user license agreement of their software was a note that confidential information could be accessed for security purposes at any time. Nowhere did it elaborate that these 'security purposes' provided a back door for hunters worldwide to investigate matters of Tenebrous.

They only took a quick break for Ariel and Lee to make cups of extra strong coffee, Morgan sighing in disappointment when Ariel shook his head in response to the question of how progress was coming.

"Like shit," Ariel said, and he and Lee re-joined Bella in the search.

"You know what we need?" Lee said into the silence of the room at one point, halfway into their second cups. She was lying on her stomach on the floor by now, foot kicked up behind her and jittering rapidly. "One of those boards with pins and strings connecting clues and all."

"I don't know if that's a *thing* outside of movies," Bella said sceptically.

"Yeah, but it looks cool."

"Trying to focus here," Ariel said testily.

They lapsed into silence once more.

Midnight came and went, and Ariel stifled a yawn as he turned his attention back to the folders, their independent searches turning up nothing.

He glanced over at Lee and frowned. "Oi, Ginger," he said, and Lee's head snapped around, her expression guilty. "What're you looking at?"

"Nothing," Lee said, face reddening as she hastily shut her laptop.

"We're trying to prevent modern society falling into chaos, if that ain't important enough for you," Ariel said, his patience wearing thin.

Lee's face flushed further. "I got distracted," she said, swallowing. "I'm sorry."

Bella put a hand on Ariel's arm. "I think we could use another quick break," she said. "We've been searching for hours, and it's been a long day. Night."

Ariel grunted and slumped back against the sofa, rubbing his itching eyes.

"What were you looking at?" Bella asked.

Lee tapped her fingers together. "Just... news articles," she said, biting her lip. "About my parents."

She quietly began telling Bella the story, and Ariel tuned them out, feeling his tired mind wander.

Strange she'd been able to see the monsters the night her parents had died; normally, it took an encounter with the Gloam like that one before people were able to see through its magic. He'd been well on his way to getting drunk and high that night, and the details were fuzzy in his memory; she'd been seeing monsters *after*, but...

"Lee," Ariel interrupted, opening his eyes. "How *exactly* did it happen? I need you to think back for me, if you really saw the Gloambeasts the night they died, or filled in the blanks after."

Lee bristled. "I *saw* them," she said insistently, but Ariel held up his hand.

"Calm the fuck down," he said, sitting forward. "I'm not one of your shrinks who doesn't believe you, so don't get pissy with me. This is important."

They eyed each other a moment before some of the tension went out of Lee's shoulders, and she nodded.

"What is it?" Bella asked, looking between them.

Ariel shook his head. "Don't want to influence the answer either way. Lee, did you see—?"

"I did," Lee said, and sat up. She twisted a lock of orange hair around her finger, untwisted, and re-twisted, her hands moving nervously as she spoke. "That wasn't my first time seeing Gloambeasts, either, just the first one that really stands out." She swallowed. "We were sitting around the campfire that night, singing songs, toasting marshmallows. You know, camping stuff. And my dad, he told a ghost story—I don't even remember the details, or what his voice sounded like, just that it was deep and he did the voices really well..."

She trailed off, and Bella slid down to the floor to sit beside Lee, putting a gentle arm around her shoulders. "Take your time," Bella said, rubbing Lee's back.

Ariel loosely folded his arms, eyes narrowed slightly as he waited.

"I started to cry, so they decided that was enough ghost stories and it was time to go to bed—they laughed about good timing because it was starting to rain anyway. I don't know how long we were inside b-before—" She broke off, leaning into Bella's hug, squeezing her eyes shut as she took a shuddering breath.

Bella glanced up at Ariel, giving him a death glare. "*Leave it,*" she mouthed, but Ariel shook his head.

Lee didn't lift her head from Bella's shoulder. "They tore the tent open. It fell over on me, but I could see—these *things*, they looked like dogs as big as people, but they walked on their back legs, and they had these evil glowing eyes, and they..."

She bit down on her knuckle in an attempt to muffle a sob; Bella's glare darkened as Ariel got up from the sofa to join them on the floor, but instead of reaching for Lee, he reached for her laptop, opening it up again to tab through the news articles she'd been browsing through.

His mouth felt dry as he read. Bear attack, they all reported, but left out the gruesome details; Accalia Lowell, aged four, missing, requests to come forward with any information. Articles of a hysterical child babbling about monsters, found days later, unharmed save for small cuts and bruises on her body and suffering from sleep deprivation.

One of the tabloid sites included a child's drawing of the monsters in question, which matched Lee's description as well as a four year old's artistic skills could convey.

"They ate your parents' intestines," he said quietly as he looked up. Lee's eyes squeezed more tightly shut as she nodded.

"I didn't move after they'd gone, not for ages," Lee said, her voice unsteady. "I didn't know if they had really left, because they just—they just disappeared behind trees too small to hide them, but—"

"Hidebehinds," Bella said in horror, and Ariel nodded grimly. "Hell, Lee, I'm so sorry..."

But Lee began to laugh, shaking her head. "No, it's—I'm just glad to finally have *answers,*" she said, lifting her head and wiping her

166

eyes. "To know I was right all along, I mean; I read so much about monsters from folklore, thinking it might make it less scary to know about them than to wonder what was out there in the dark..." She shivered.

"So you've always been Gloamtouched," Ariel mused. "Lowell... Lowell..." He passed Lee's laptop back to her, picking up his own again. "Your parents weren't werewolves, by any chance? Or—hunters?"

Lee snorted and shrugged. "Doubt they would have died like that if they were," she said bitterly.

"Hunters have died to less, before," Ariel said, opening a new tab. "What were their names, again?"

"Joseph and Marina," Lee said, and sniffled; Ariel grabbed the box of tissues off the end table and handed them to her, and she blew her nose gratefully.

"Name like Accalia, I would've expected something a little stranger," Bella said, and grinned when Lee laughed. It sounded strained, but she returned the smile.

Ariel's gaze dropped back to the screen, his brows drawing together.

"Why's it matter if I was Gloamtouched before, anyway?" Lee asked.

"Because we're hitting a dead end with the feral attacks, and I want to know why the hell you can control your transformations during the full moon," Ariel said, gesturing vaguely at her as he scrolled through results of countless news articles. "Because that ain't supposed to be possible, except for—"

Lee gasped, her eyes going wide as she practically yanked her laptop open again. "Blood moon," she said, as Ariel leaned over to see her searching for a list of full moons in 1997. "It's *why* they named me Accalia—they were on vacation in Rome when I was born, I was massively preemie, like sixteen weeks early—"

"Preemies aren't Gloamtouched without other factors," Bella said dubiously, but Lee flapped her hand at Bella, turning the screen around for both Bella and Ariel to see.

"That's my birthday," Lee said, pointing triumphantly. "September sixteenth."

"Total lunar eclipse," Bella breathed.

Ariel sat back, letting out a slow breath as he stared at the page.

"I mean, what are the chances?" Lee said, looking between them. "Being born under a total eclipse and later turning into a werewolf? If the lycan population's so tiny to begin with, that's gotta be a bigger than million-to-one odds."

"No kidding," Ariel said, shaking his head in disbelief. "This is... holy *shit*."

He startled when Lee suddenly lunged forward out of Bella's embrace, snatching up the folders of the attackers. She thumbed through them, and dived back to her laptop, searching different dates; Ariel picked up Iris' folder, glancing between it and Lee's screen, his eyebrow creeping up.

Page after page turned up the same results, a solid four for four. A stunned silence fell over the room as Lee mutely set her laptop back on the floor.

Bella spoke first. "They were all born during a full moon," she said, and Ariel slowly nodded.

"Different months and years, that's why they ruled it out as a connecting factor," he said. "What about the victims?"

Bella gathered up the folders, reading the birth dates out to Lee to look up.

"I guess I was the only one," Lee said, after the last search turned up nothing conclusive. "So the victims *don't* have that in connection, just the ones who went feral?"

"Ariel," Bella said slowly, "George, he had a knack for shifting, you said?"

"You think it had something to do with that?" Ariel said incredulously.

"The Gloam Hunters didn't know that already?" Lee asked. "I mean, if it's a thing—"

Ariel slowly shook his head; it felt like his brain was being squeezed in a vice. "As far as we know—*knew*—lycanthropy's just transmitted via bite," he said. "It's like with vamps; any kids werewolves have, they'll be human, too." He caught Bella's look and scowled. "So I did some reading lately, shut up."

"Those files in the command room," Lee said. "How far back do they go?"

"Only 1950s or so," Ariel said, "but there's more in the library in the basement, all the way back to 1815. We've also got an entire family archive dating back even to before the creation of the Night Treaty, all encrypted online, but only Mom's got access to that." He stood up, heading to the door. "But we kept notes on which werewolves had shifting come easy to them."

Morgan looked up when they hurried back into the command room; his blue hair was dishevelled from running his fingers through it, but the bleariness in his face vanished at their entrance. "Did you find something?"

"Think so," Ariel said, making a beeline to the cabinets. "Might've even solved an age-old mystery while we're at it, too."

Morgan blinked. "Do I get to hear this now, or—?"

Ariel had already yanked a drawer open, thumbing through it for the section on werewolves. "Not until we've got more data to back it up."

Morgan nodded and touched his earpiece, turning back to the table's display.

Ariel turned to the others, jerking his head impatiently for them to join him. "Drawers are labelled with years, each year's divided by types of Tenebran, types are subdivided by month." He reached into the drawer and pulled out the entire stack of folders for 1965, balancing them on his arm before setting them heavily on the floor.

"Why 1965?" Bella asked as she and Lee sat with him.

Ariel shrugged. "Far enough back we've got mostly different data, isn't it? Start looking."

Chapter 24

In the end, they came to the same conclusions as before. As the sun rose, and Morgan from his chair alongside it, Bella, Ariel, and Lee looked up at him as he blearily crossed the distance to the coffee machine, turning it on for the untold time that night.

"Coffee?" Morgan asked, looking around the room.

"*Please*," Ariel said, getting up, and Lee did the same with a quiet groan before Bella jumped to her feet to help Lee stand.

"I hope after you three flung those records all over the floor, you found something?" Morgan said, leaning back against the desk as he waited for the coffee to start brewing.

"We did," Ariel said. "All the werewolves who went feral were born on the nights of a full moon."

Morgan's eyebrows flew up at that, and he looked at the others, who nodded. "Well... I'll be," he said, dragging his fingers through his already-messy hair. "Though you didn't need the records to tell you *that*..." He trailed off meaningfully.

"It was Bella's idea," Ariel said, and Bella puffed up with pride when Ariel gave her one of his rare, genuine smiles. "I think it's time we told him."

Lee's eye widened, and she pointed curiously at herself. Ariel nodded, and Lee moved a little closer to him, gnawing nervously on one of her lip rings.

Ariel began to give Morgan the rundown of what they had learned about the effects the lunar cycle had, even for non-lycanthropes, and Bella drifted away to examine the table's display. Ariel had said not to touch, but it was sorely tempting to zoom in on the map, just to see what other details might pop up. Bella instead folded her hands behind her to resist temptation, leaning in until her nose almost touched the screen.

The green dots were travelling, some fast, others slower, and after a moment of studying, she realised it was the hunters heading home for the morning.

Fascinating, really. Bella wondered how the Gloam Hunters coordinated everything before modern technology. Sure, she had a vague idea, having met more than a few over the many decades of her life, but this was the first time she'd really had an in-depth look at the inner workings of the operation.

Which reminded her.

Bella glanced up at the hunters, still engrossed in going over Ariel's findings, and she swallowed, straightening and heading to the door.

"Where're you going?" Ariel asked, and Bella paused with her hand on the door before turning with a bright smile.

"You *did* say I was welcome to check out your room after we'd finished here," she said, raising her eyebrows at him.

Ariel groaned quietly, waving her off. "Fine, just make it quick."

Morgan began to laugh, clapping Ariel on the back. "You were saying, Ari?" he asked, and Lee gave Bella a tiny wave before turning back to the conversation. Bella gave Lee a tiny wave in return before slipping out the door, following the pervasive smell of wine gone sour to Ashley Montgomery's room.

She only had scant minutes before day broke; this would have to be quick.

Bella turned to mist to avoid making any noise and slipped under the door, reforming on the other side and taking a look around. The master bedroom was just as grand as the rest of the house, with a magnificent king sized bed against the far wall and a small sitting area with a table and comfortable armchairs. Ariel's mother was asleep in one of the armchairs, several bottles of wine in various levels of fullness on the tabletop, more empty bottles strewn about the floor around the chairs. Bella pursed her lips and stepped lightly

172

to one of the carved bookshelves set against the wall opposite, mindful of the creaking floorboards.

But if Augustus' intel had been right...

She began pawing at the blue-bound books, freezing when she heard a quiet *click* upon pulling one partly off its shelf. Ashley didn't so much as stir behind her, and Bella allowed herself to breathe as the bookshelf swung silently inwards on perfectly balanced hinges.

Knowing Ariel would probably come looking in his room soon—and the sensation of her powers waning as the sun rose serving as an urgent reminder to her time limit—Bella darted into the office, making full use of the blood she'd been overfeeding on to move far faster than she normally could.

Most of the records she found were largely concerned with stocks; it seemed, before meeting Ariel's father, Ashley had been a broker for Silver Sword, advancing her way through the ranks until she managed most of the East Coast branch's finances.

"Wonder how that's been pairing with the wine?" Bella muttered to herself, hastily replacing files and taking a moment to stop and *think*, really *think*, about where Ashley might be storing any information on nefarious plots if she was, indeed, plotting anything nefarious at all.

Bella's eyes fell on the framed photograph of Ariel's father sitting by the monitor, before her gaze flickered up to the folders above the desk. She selected the thin black one that was simply labelled *Jordan* and pulled it down.

"Oh my *goodness*," she breathed, her eyes going huge as she flipped through the pages detailing the sale of Jordan Montgomery's old office building to Blanchard—dated to a little over three months ago.

She heard a quiet snuffling from the main bedroom, and Bella hurriedly replaced the folder, beating a hasty retreat and closing the hidden entrance behind her.

It took some straining, but she managed to transform to mist just in time, reforming again in the hallway as the sun crept above the horizon. Bella panted, leaning against the wall, her mind reeling from the discovery. It wasn't conclusive proof, but it looked bad, either way.

Bella padded noiselessly along the hall to Ariel's room, taking a quick peek in. She made note of all the comic book posters plastered to the walls, before she ducked back out and turned, stifling a yelp when she realised he was right behind her.

"Like the room?" Ariel said, eyeing her in a way Bella wasn't entirely sure she liked at all.

"It was interesting," Bella said, her heart continuing its slow, languid beat despite the fright she'd just suffered. "I didn't realise you were such a comic book nerd."

"The posters are from when I was a kid," Ariel said, not taking his eyes off of her. "Got to be too much to keep up with outside of the movies. And even then, ain't seen any of the new ones, lately."

Bella laughed, rubbing the back of her neck. "Maybe we should have another movie night, then?" she suggested weakly. "One where Lee's not stuck watching a tiny phone screen from inside a cage?"

"Yeah," Ariel said. "Maybe."

They lapsed into silence for a long moment before Bella gave him a nervous smile. "What's Lee up to?"

"Getting our bags together," Ariel said, and inclined his head down the corridor. "Mo's gotta get Jessie up and ready for school, and Lee and I can still grab a few hours of sleep before classes if we get back into the city soon."

Bella cleared her throat. "What if I drove?" she asked, and hoped her look of innocence was enough for Ariel to believe. "I mean, I'm sure you two are exhausted, but I don't need to sleep; I could get you back while you napped in the car."

She had to bite back a sigh of relief when Ariel fished his keys out of his pocket and tossed them to her; Bella caught them deftly. "Fine," Ariel said shortly, and turned, lifting his chin. "We should finish putting the files back before we run off on Mo, though."

Bella laughed quietly, trying not to think too hard about the folder that lay tucked away on its shelf in the hidden office.

· · · ·

The drive back was uneventful; Ariel and Lee napped in the back seat, shoulders pressed together and heads knocking gently against each other. Bella wasn't sure if it was fondness or jealousy that curled in her stomach every time she glanced back at them, both of their faces relaxed in sleep in a way she never got to see while they were awake.

She loved Lee; of that much, she was certain. She'd latched onto this roommate of hers in a way she *knew* Lee would tease her endlessly about, but that was just one of the things she loved about her.

And, Bella realised with an unpleasant jolt, she loved Ariel, too. His acidly sharp tongue and dry humour could sometimes be a bit difficult to parse, but in him she saw a kindred soul: one who was just trying to do their best against a world full of monsters.

Bella had her medicine, and Ariel had his weapons.

Bella had her histories, Lee had her stories.

Opposites attracted, wasn't that what they said? Though, Bella thought, briefly closing her eyes before refocusing on the road, she wondered if they didn't have more in common than she'd previously believed.

She glanced back at the sleeping pair and sighed, twiddling the steering wheel to keep them on course.

Maybe...

Maybe, just this once...

Augustus didn't need to know what she'd found.

At least, not just yet. Not until she'd discussed it with the others. Ariel and Lee deserved that much.

Chapter 25

"**Y**ou *spied* on my *mom?*" Ariel all but shouted, and Bella winced, rubbing the back of her neck.

"Okay, I know, I know, I shouldn't have," Bella said as Ariel groaned, turning on his heel and angrily pacing the tiny length of his room. "But you *know* we've got reason to be suspicious of her, and this just seems to add to it!"

She swallowed, glancing at Lee who sat perched on the edge of Ariel's bed, looking nervously between vampire and hunter.

"All we know is that Blanchard disappeared from her old lab around the same time the feral attacks started up!" Ariel snapped, whirling on Bella. "Turns out, she was just moving office! The timing could've just been coincidence!"

"It could have, yes," Bella said desperately. "But Ariel, come on—we've got to at least consider the possibility!"

"What happened to dealing with it as it comes, huh?" Ariel demanded. "To dropping the thought? Was that just to get me to shut up while you went snooping?"

"*No!*" Bella protested. At Ariel's glare, and Lee's dubious look, she wilted slightly. "No. Maybe. A little."

Ariel's fingers gripped his hair and he sat heavily on the bed beside Lee. "Did you know about this?" he asked, turning his glare on her.

Lee took a deep breath, and squared her shoulders. "No," she said, "but I think Bella did the right thing, here."

"*She went snooping—!*"

"I know!" Lee said, her knuckles going white where she gripped her knees. "I know. And that wasn't exactly *great*," she added, side-eyeing Bella, who glanced away shamefacedly, "but it's given us a possible lead on the attacks, Ariel."

"So the ends justify the means, huh?" Ariel said bitterly.

Lee hesitated. "Well... not when you put it like that, no."

Bella swallowed and forced herself to meet Ariel's eyes as she stepped forward. "Ariel, I'm sorry," she said quietly. "I really am."

He snorted derisively.

"I *am*," Bella said, wringing her hands together. "Whether or not you believe me—no, it doesn't matter. I'm *scared*, Ariel! I'm scared for Lee, I'm scared for what's happening to the werewolves, I'm scared that maybe whatever is causing this *is* directed and isn't just a series of freak mutations! I have a family to think about—*siblings!* They're just Jessie's age, how do you think they're going to feel if one or *both* of our parents are next?!"

Some of the tension drained out of Ariel's shoulders, though the lines of his body were still taut. "Don't know," he muttered, pressing his hand to his face. "Still doesn't make what you did okay."

Bella nodded, rocking back on her heels. She swallowed. "I *am* sorry," she tried again, but Ariel lifted his head to glare at her.

"Sorry for what you did, or sorry that I'm pissed 'bout what you did?"

Bella hesitated. "...Both," she finally said.

Ariel let out a hoarse bark of laughter, looking away.

Lee's hand tentatively settled on Ariel's shoulder, and he reached up to squeeze it carefully, still not looking at either of them.

"Look," Lee finally said. "What's done is done. Be as mad as you want, but we've got to at least follow up on this, don't we? Or say something whenever the next council meeting is—"

Ariel's head shot up, and he stared at Lee. "The next meeting's *tomorrow*," he said incredulously. "So's the party. Don't tell me you forgot about it."

Lee blinked. "Uh. Tomorrow is Halloween?"

"*Yeah?*" Ariel said. "Christ, Lee, it's not like things have been so hectic you forgot what day it was. The full moon was only on the twenty-seventh."

"A lot's happened since then," Lee said defensively.

"Like running out on the support group and freezing half to death in the rain," Ariel said, arching an eyebrow.

Bella loudly cleared her throat. "Morgan's filled in Mrs Guadalupe on our discoveries about the full moon birthdays, right?" she said, and Ariel nodded. "So she'll almost certainly be bringing that up tomorrow," she said continued. "I'm sure the Gloam Hunters could arrange some sort of protection for the werewolves that meet the criteria; surely it can't be that many."

"The ones what were kidnapped were the only ones on record," Ariel said curtly. "So con-fucking-gratulations, we've hit yet another dead end."

"Not the only ones," Lee said after a long silence, and gestured feebly at herself.

"No," Bella said automatically. "No, I am *not* risking you, I am *not* using you as bait—"

"And why not?" Lee said, standing abruptly. She staggered slightly before righting herself again. "What's the worst that could happen? I *die?*"

"*Yes!*" Bella cried. "Yes, Lee, you could die, and you could very well die horribly and in pain and the rest of us would be left missing you forever!"

She sniffled, wiping away the tears that rolled down her cheeks, and when she blinked her vision clear, Ariel was nodding.

"Yeah, okay, fine, I'd miss you, too," he said, and Bella let out a slightly strangled laugh. "Look." Ariel hesitated, but took Lee's hand in his own, tracing the gloved fingers of his prosthetic over the back of Lee's wrist. "We bring this up at the council meeting tomorrow, we get folks to guard you until the next full moon—"

"And how long is that?" Lee demanded.

Ariel paused, then let go of her hand to check his watch. "Ehm. Day before Thanksgiving?"

"Oh, *fuck* that," Lee said, shaking her head. "I'm not having hunters guard me 'round the clock while I'm trying to deal with classes *and* enjoy my break."

"Well," Bella said, and paused.

Ariel jabbed a finger at her. "If you're gonna suggest we spy on my mother again—"

"No!" Bella took a deep breath to try and gather her thoughts. "No. Look," she hastened to add, when Ariel glared at her, "werewolves have always been disappearing the day after the full moon. Why don't you guys come stay with my family? It'll be Thanksgiving away from your mum," she said pointedly to Ariel, "and with the both of us there, *plus* my parents and their partners, I'm sure Lee will be protected enough from anything that might try to wolf-nap her."

Lee tilted her head. "...Partners?"

Bella hesitated briefly, but nodded, trying to squash down her growing unease. "It's, um, well—"

"Lotta vamps take multiple romantic partners," Ariel said shortly. "Or sexual. Mostly sexual."

"*That*," Bella said, folding her arms, "is stereotyping. You say that like most humans' partners aren't an overlap of both; don't try to make it out like vampires are any more so than you mortals who need sex to reproduce."

"I mean, there's test tube babies," Lee offered. "And don't vampires need humans to make more vampires, anyway—?"

"I think the point has gotten away from us," Bella said loudly as Ariel snickered. "Look, so what if my parents have other *partners*—" She glowered at Ariel. "—in their relationship? Nothing weird about it."

Ariel held up his hands. "Never said there was."

Chapter 26

Ariel was late getting to the council meeting, coming off of rehearsals for the last main stage performance of the year. He fended off Rose asking if he would be coming to the Halloween party later, promising he would be by with friends. He stopped by the props room to pick up his finished project and slipped it into his bag, then caught the bus downtown, heading for the closest entrance to the pedway system.

The hidden tunnel system deeper underground was deserted as Ariel walked to the council's meeting room; he supposed everyone was already there. Sure enough, when he slipped through the doors to find the meeting well underway, the room was even more crowded than it had been last time, with Tenebrans of all types standing around the edges of the room, shifting restlessly as they listened to Augustus drone on about zoning permits for a new nightclub.

Bella had turned around at his entrance and caught his eye, waving him over, and Ariel quietly made his way over to her and Lee.

"We saved you a seat," Bella whispered as Ariel took the chair between her and Lee, setting his bag on the floor by his feet. "How was rehearsal?"

"Long," he whispered back. "I haven't missed anything important?"

"Nah, just a lot of waffle so far."

"They're taking their sweet time," Lee whispered on his other side. Ariel wondered briefly if her leg had stopped bouncing once since she'd sat down, before snorting to himself. He knew full well it had not.

Though nobody in the crowd had been speaking, a deeper sort of hush fell over the room when Diana Guadalupe turned to the matter everyone had shown up for.

"At the council's last meeting," she said, adjusting her thick tortoise-rimmed glasses, her face grim, "we discussed the incidents of four confirmed feral werewolf attacks; since then, two more attacks happened, with two human deaths; the perpetrator—or perpetrators—were never caught or identified. I would like to observe another moment of silence at this time."

Heads bowed around the room; Lee bit down on her knuckle to stop an inopportune round of ticcing.

"Now then," Diana said, and heads lifted at her words, "I am pleased to report that some progress has been made in our investigation of the matter, though details will be announced in due time."

"As part of the investigation," Ashley Montgomery continued over the ripple of dissatisfied murmurs that sprang up, "the Gloam Hunters will be posting personal guards to certain select werewolves for the full moon of November 25th; those of you who will be receiving guards—"

"Only some? What about my son?!" a man yelled from the back, and shouts broke out from the werewolves in the room, wanting to know just why only some of them were to be afforded protection from the hunters while the rest would be left to fend for themselves.

Ariel slowly tugged his glove off, his other hand twitching toward his knife as the volume rose, and a few of the vampires joined in, adding their voices to the din. Beside him, Lee huddled in her seat, hands clamped over her ears and eyes squeezed shut. Ariel glanced worriedly at Bella, who was staring around at the scene, her mouth open in mute shock.

"What happens when one of those mutts attacks *us*, eh?" a vampire with dyed green hair bellowed, and the woman beside her hissed in agreement. "Not like the blonde bitch cares if any of us die! What's the sanctity of the Night Treaty mean if there's a few less vampires?!"

"What are the hunters doing for the rest of us, anyway?" a werewolf yelled, and the shouting rose.

Terry Nelson stood so fast he knocked his chair over, lifting his hands. Darkness gathered around him, the room filling with a palpable dread as the shouting became muffled, the volume dimming like someone turning the dial on a radio.

When the crowd realised their protestations were muted no matter how hard they shouted, the clamour gradually died down, though judging from the number of furious faces in the room, their anger had not died with the noise.

"Now then—" Ashley began, when a six-legged beast burst from the darkness surrounding Terry with a shriek and a chatter of dripping mandibles. Before Ariel or any of the other hunters could react, Ashley hurled a knife without looking; it embedded itself in one of the Gloambeast's many eyes, and it burst into shadows with one final shriek. Her knife fell to the floor with a clatter that rang out in the silence.

"*Now then*," Ashley said, glaring around the room and daring anyone to try to speak, even muted, "the Gloam Hunters are working as hard as they can to keep Tenebrous safe, but our resources are stretched thin. *Therefore*, we have identified several key individuals we believe to be most at-risk, and will be getting in contact soon to monitor them accordingly. In the meantime, any and all feral attacks will be responded to with nonlethal force. I can assure you we are doing everything we can to solve the issue, but releasing details to the public could put the investigation—and more people—at risk. The council will determine when it is safe to make a report, and will do so as soon as possible."

"In the meantime, though, we ask you to be patient," Augustus added as Ashley retrieved her knife, sliding it back into its hidden sheath. "And to my fellow vampires, I can assure you that I and the other Sanguine Lords want nothing more than our continued survival."

"If any werewolves have further concerns they wish to discuss," Diana said, "I'm in my office most days after five-thirty, and you can find my email posted on the door. Mr. O'Connor, who runs the local chapter of the support group, is also available to listen, with his office located in the community centre. I shall be posting his contact information on my door as well." She looked over at Terry, who was still standing with his arms raised, sweat beading on his forehead as he held the spell. "I think that concludes tonight's meeting. The next one will be in two weeks' time, on November 14th. Thank you."

Terry's arms dropped and the spell broke; the sound returned to the room at large, and Ariel realised Lee was quietly hyperventilating beside him, her eyes still squeezed shut.

He put a careful hand on her shoulder and she jumped, looking up at him. Her face was pale beneath her freckles.

"I think we'd better get out of here," Bella murmured, and Ariel nodded agreement, gathering his bag.

Up at the head table, Terry collapsed into his seat, his entire body wracked with tremors as Augustus bent to check him over. The vampire caught Ariel's eye before glancing at Ashley, who was steadfastly ignoring the room at large as she sorted through her papers.

Ariel's jaw set and he shook his head, then turned away to usher his friends to the door.

His heart stuttered when he realised that, at some point in the commotion, Madame Blanchard had arrived. She stood near the back, a literal cold spot in the room, warmed from all the close-pressed bodies that gave her a wide berth. Her ruby-red lips were turned up at the corners in an unpleasant smile, the gems at her throat like sparkling droplets of blood.

"Come on," Ariel said, his voice low. By unspoken agreement, he and Bella moved to flank Lee, shielding her on either side as they pushed their way to the doors.

He felt sick. In just two weeks, the Tenebrans of Chicago were losing faith in the people who were supposed to protect them. He knew his mother wasn't fit to lead, but Morgan, behind the scenes, had been working tirelessly to keep the hunters from falling apart even before all of this had started. That wasn't exactly reassuring to the general populace, though; who wanted to hear that the leader of the Gloam Hunters was foisting her responsibilities off on her son?

The Night Treaty had been in a delicate balance ever since it was first signed. If the hunters couldn't be trusted to do their jobs—if the werewolves couldn't be trusted to keep control—how many vampires would see this as an invitation to ignore the treaty's feeding constraints?

The mages, at least, he was sure would mostly keep to themselves. The price of magic tended to make its wielders cautious. Ariel briefly wondered how much strain Terry had put on himself, silencing the room.

"What *was* that?" Lee whispered into the silence of the empty corridor. "The monster appearing like that?"

Ariel sighed, glancing over at her. "Mages channel the Gloam to warp reality," he reminded her, and Lee nodded. "So when they do that, it's like opening a doorway—it can allow Gloambeasts to slip through into our world."

"Tensions were high in there," Bella murmured. "We're lucky it was only the one Gloambeast. It's like the things can smell malcontent."

"You know, that would've been *really* nice to know beforehand," Lee said, her eyes huge. "I thought mages just..." She twirled a finger around her temple and whistled like a cuckoo clock. "When they used magic."

"They do," Ariel said, pursing his lips as he opened one of the hidden doors that led back to the world above. "They also run the risk of inviting in Gloambeasts."

"Does all magic look like that?" Lee asked, her brow furrowed. "With the shadows all swirling and everything."

"Usually," Ariel said.

"Always," Bella said. "Well, except for—"

"Blanchard," the three said in unison.

"Because she's powerful?" Lee asked. "Because she's figured out some way to cast spells or whatever without the Gloam? Because—?"

"Whatever the reason," Ariel cut her off, "nobody knows, and she's not telling." He dragged a hand down his face, biting back a quiet sigh.

They caught the bus back to campus, Ariel tuning out Bella and Lee as he idly watched the passengers. Several of them were dressed up like they were heading to a costume party—or from one, judging by their drunken laughter.

His stomach turned over, and he shook his head, turning away to look out the window. He didn't want to entertain the possibility that Bella might be right after all.

Chapter 27

Bella glanced over at Lee as they got off the bus at the campus stop; the orange-haired werewolf had been growing more and more restless throughout the evening, and her agitation just seemed to grow as they approached the rec centre where the campus party would be held. Already, they could hear the music and chatter coming from the open doors, light flooding the quad.

"I keep telling you," Bella said with some amusement, "Halloween is just a bunch of human superstitious nonsense. Spirits *don't* walk around on the Earth, especially not on the same specific day each calendar year."

"I *know*," Lee muttered back, her fingers tapping restlessly against her arm. "Just. Still feels like something bad is going to happen. Especially at this party."

"Aw, come on, Lee," Bella said, placing a reassuring hand on her shoulder, "I've been around for centuries—"

"A hundred and eighty years is centuries?" Lee interrupted, and Bella laughed, Ariel biting back a snicker.

Bella gave Lee's shoulder a gentle squeeze and let her hand drop. "I know you're worried about the party, but after a council meeting like that, I think we all could use something a little more *normal* to take our minds off of everything."

"Normal," Lee muttered, hand drifting up to lightly touch her scarred cheek.

Ariel suddenly slung his bag around, unzipping it as they walked. "Actually, I got something for you," he said, and produced a *Phantom of the Opera* mask, mirrored to cover the left side of the face instead of the right. Lee's eye went huge as he pressed it into her hands.

"Did you... make this?" Lee asked, turning the mask over with a look of awe.

"Yeah," Ariel said, zipping his bag back up. "Don't make a big deal out of it or anything, alright?"

In response, Lee pulled him into a hug; Bella grinned as Ariel flailed for a moment before hugging her back, glaring at Bella over Lee's shoulder like he was daring her to comment.

"Would've given it to you earlier, but there's been a lot happening," Ariel muttered as Lee drew back. Her grin was infectious as she slipped the mask on, adjusting the thin elastic that held it in place.

"You're amazing, you are," Lee said, feeling around the mask. It melded to her face perfectly, the inside sanded smooth to lay as flat as possible against her skin. "I... I don't know what to say."

"Then don't," Ariel said, rolling his eyes even as his stomach fluttered at her words. "Just go have a nice night, yeah?"

Lee beamed at him, leaning up on tiptoes to kiss his cheek before disappearing into the building.

Ariel didn't realise he was staring after her until he became painfully aware of Bella standing far too close to him, grinning toothily. Her fangs glinted in the pulsing lights.

"Can I help you?" Ariel said irritably.

"That was a nice thing you did," Bella said, and Ariel groaned, dragging a hand over his face.

"Can we drop it already?" he said. "I've agreed you're my friends, I do nice things for my friends, call the presses."

"Don't let anyone else hear you say that you actually care about someone," Bella said, pulling her sunglasses down her nose to wink at him. "People will get the wrong idea."

"Whatever," Ariel said, rolling his eyes. "Do you want to do this party or not?"

"Well, someone has to be here in case Lee needs walking back to our dorm," Bella said cheerfully, pulling her sunglasses off entirely and perching them on the top of her head. "But are you offering to accompany me, Mr Montgomery?"

Ariel couldn't fight back the wry smile, so he just let it happen as he offered Bella his arm. "I believe I am, Miss Ward."

Bella snickered. "After you've already seen my ankles, even, the *scandal*," she said, looping her arm through his. "Never mind my legs."

"You mean all two feet of them?" Ariel said, and snickered when Bella scoffed and swatted his arm. "Okay, but seriously, was that actually a thing or something movies just exaggerate?"

"No, it was absolutely a thing," Bella said as they headed inside. "Believe you me, my mum and I were *very* glad when trousers came into fashion for women."

Inside was a press of bodies, students standing around with plastic cups and shouting to be heard over the music. Ariel and Bella were forced to let go of each other's arms, though Bella laced her fingers through Ariel's, which prompted him to look back at her in surprise, raising his eyebrows.

"Just so I don't lose you," she called over the din, and he raised an eyebrow but nodded. Together, they threaded their way through the crowd, spotting Lee dancing with abandon amidst a group of students dressed up like *Rocky Horror* refugees.

They snagged drinks, which Bella took a sniff of and confirmed that the punch was indeed spiked, and without prompting, Ariel led her upstairs, past the deejay, and to the much quieter balcony.

There were more partygoers at the various tables, which they avoided, going to the railing to look out over the city. Or, they would, if a skyscraper didn't block their view.

"Nice night," Ariel said, leaning against the railing on his flesh and blood arm, his prosthetic gripping his cup.

Bella hummed in agreement, leaning against the railing as well. "Thanks, by the way," she said.

Ariel glanced down at her, puzzled.

"For, uh, coming out here." Bella tapped the side of her head. "Sensitive. And, erm." She coughed delicately. "Not just because of the hearing."

Ariel nodded. "Figured," he said. "Reckon Lee'll be coming to find us soon enough, too."

"Coming to a party just to ignore everyone else," Bella said, and she and Ariel shared a laugh.

"You're the one to talk," Ariel said, glancing over at her. "I mean, she's *your* girlfriend."

Bella shook her head, prompting a questioning eyebrow raise from Ariel. "I mean, we've kissed a few times," she said. "And hold hands and things, but we're not..." She fluffed her hair puff as she thought. "I mean, we're not *dating*."

"Ah-*huh*," Ariel said. He hated the way his heart leapt in his chest—though which part of *that* particular bit of information excited him, Lee or Bella, he didn't know.

He wasn't sure he wanted to know.

Bella bumped him with her hip. "Seriously though, I'm glad you came out tonight. It can't be good for you, the whole 'I don't have friends' bit."

Ariel sighed, grimaced, looked away. "Just found it's easier," he said after a long moment. "Trying to be friends with people who ain't Gloamtouched gets difficult, and you make friends with the ones who are, you're just left wondering who's not coming back from patrol every night."

"I'm sorry," Bella said softly.

"Yeah," Ariel said. "Me too."

They lapsed into silence, Ariel slowly draining his drink. When it was gone, Bella mutely offered her cup to trade, and Ariel took that to drink, too.

"Does it ever bother you?" she asked. "The nights you're not on patrol, I mean?"

Ariel took a long time to respond, and for a moment, Bella thought he had either forgotten her question or was ignoring her. But then the motor in his wrist whirred, and he ducked his head to meet the cup as he brought it to his lips, drinking deeply. "Dunno," he said, and gave her a one-shouldered shrug. "It did when I was younger. Used to keep me up long past when I was supposed to be asleep, you know? Mo put my head on straight, though." He glanced at Bella out of the corner of his eye. "Said the whole bit about not setting yourself on fire to keep others warm, which sounds stupid, but it's true. People are gonna be dying anyway, and not even the best hunter in the world can stop that. But if I'm not keeping myself in as good shape as I can, even *more* people will be dying. So I go to class, do my homework, study for tests, go to parties like this. Normal college student." He snorted, then sighed, shaking his head. "Just gotta remember the others on patrol have the same training, same skills, same duty. If I can't trust them to have my back, who *can* I trust?"

Me, Bella wanted to say, but knew it wasn't what he wanted or needed to hear, and wouldn't go down well after she'd spied on his mother regardless. So she just put a hand on his shoulder, squeezing gently.

"I think it's very brave, what you do," she said softly. "Without you and the other hunters, god knows my kind wouldn't be able to thrive and flourish like we had. Which, uh," she said, wincing when Ariel snorted, "I guess sounds *really* bad, talking to a hunter, but for the vampires who've always had to live on the fringes of society, your family really set the scene for things to get better for everyone."

Ariel glanced over at Bella again, his brow furrowed. "Are you really only a hundred and eighty?" he asked.

Bella put a hand to her chest, mock-affronted. "Don't you know to never ask a lady her age?" At Ariel's glower, she relented. "Yeah."

"What was *that* like?" Ariel asked, and Bella could hear the weight of history contained in his question.

"It sucked," Bella said, grinning faintly when Ariel huffed out a laugh. "I mean, my parents and I largely stayed in England, so it wasn't nearly as bad as it was in America, but even so..." She shook her head, drumming her fingers nervously on the railing. "My mother was the daughter of Dragomir Ciobanu."

She heard the sharp inhale from Ariel. She didn't look at him.

"Shit," he finally said, and Bella laughed despite herself, nodding.

"My father was a servant in his home," she said, tracing a finger over the railing. "He and my mother fell in love, killed Dragomir after he'd turned my mother, ran away, and then my mother turned my father. And then I was born."

"Definitely not the sorts of vampires to lord it up in castles, then," Ariel said, though the sarcasm he'd been aiming for fell flat. "We'd always wondered what happened to him, but..." He shook his head and took another generous gulp of his drink.

"One more story to add to the archives," Bella suggested.

Ariel made a small noise in the back of his throat. "Guess so," he said. "Be nice to update that he's dead." He sighed. "Guess I'll be talking to your folks during Thanksgiving. Hope they don't mind."

Bella shrugged. "They might," she said, "but I think if you asked nicely—"

"Have you *met* me?" Ariel interrupted, and Bella laughed.

"*Okay*, but I've *also* met the very nice person who made Lee a custom mask just so she could enjoy a bit of normality for once." She tapped Ariel's shoulder. "Face it, Ariel Montgomery, you are a nice person."

"No need to sound so shocked," Ariel said dryly.

"I mean it," Bella said softly, turning and hopping up to sit on the railing. She swung her legs, smiling at him. Now that she was sitting on the railing, their faces were almost level with one another—and dangerously close.

Ariel's heart thudded, and he looked away.

Bella's smile faded. "Are you still mad at me about... what happened with your mum?" she asked, swallowing.

Ariel's shoulders hunched slightly before he drained his drink and turned to look at Bella straight on. "Still not best pleased about it, but it got us what we needed," he said at long last. "A lead. If we go check out the old office building, maybe it'll give us some answers."

• • • •

"Well, this looks..."

"Ominous?" Lee suggested.

"I was going to say promising," Bella said.

They stared up at the office building, on the outskirts of Chicago, which looked eerily abandoned. Maybe it was.

"Fuck it," Ariel said, locking the car and shoving the keys in his pocket. "Not like standing here gawping is gonna get us anywhere. Let's go."

They approached the front door, which swung open when they got close.

"I didn't realise Blanchard was accepting visitors," Lee said lightly.

"Or maybe she's expecting us," Ariel said, his brow furrowing in a scowl.

The front lobby was deserted, bits of trash blown in from the wind tucked away in the corners. The chairs in the waiting area were in fine enough condition, but had the distinct sense of not being used in a very long time. Lee brushed her fingers over the back of one as she passed, mouthing an apology to it.

"I'm actually starting to wonder if this is such a good idea," Bella said when Ariel tested the door leading deeper inside to find it locked.

"This was *your* idea," he said, patting his coat before fishing out a lockpicking kit and setting to work.

"Yes, but what if I'm wrong?" Bella said, wringing her hands. "Then we've got Blanchard bearing down on us for breaking into her building, accusing her of—"

The lock clicked open, and Ariel turned the knob.

"Well, there's clearly nothing to see here," Bella said, peering into the darkened depths of the rows of cubicles. A faint smell of mould hung in the air, nearly overpowered by the much stronger smell of bleach.

"Nothing to see *here*," Lee pointed out. "But there might be something further in..." She took a step forward, her form shimmering as she fell to all fours. She sniffed the air, and her ears flattened against her skull before she transformed back, coughing. "*Ow.*"

"Was it the bleach?" Bella asked, and Lee nodded, her eyes watering.

"Bleach?" Ariel said, sniffing as well. He shook his head. "I can't smell anything, so it's probably not recent." He tested the light switch, to no avail.

"It's all over, though," Bella said, helping Lee back to her feet. "I'm sure of it."

"Only one way to find out," Ariel said, and switched on a tiny pocket flashlight, grasping it with his silver hand as he moved in deeper. "Spread out, but stay close to each other," he added without glancing back.

They did so, Lee transforming back into a wolf and sniffing her way along, her eyes still watering from the stench of bleach. She paused to sniff at a doorknob that positively reeked of the scent, sneezed, and padded on.

"Either of you find anything?" Ariel called when he reached the end of the room.

"Just a lot of dust bunnies," Bella called back. "Lee?"

Lee hastily reverted back, making sure to end up standing rather than on all fours again. "Nothing here, either."

"We'll try the next row," Ariel said, waving them forward.

They scanned the entire room, but nothing appeared to be out of the ordinary. It was just another empty shell of a building.

"Maybe the bathrooms?" Lee suggested, wiping her hands on her jeans. She jumped when the lights flickered on with a buzz of electricity.

A cold chill filled the room, and they spun to see Madame Blanchard standing between them and the exit, snowflakes trailing from her arms and fading into the air.

"Well, well," she said, and goosebumps sprang up along Lee's arms at the languid, predatory smile she gave them. "I knew my building was infested with rats, but this *is* a surprise."

"Madame Blanchard," Ariel said, and gave her a shallow bow, not taking his eyes off her. "How fortunate. We were looking for you."

Lee remained frozen in place, her gaze darting between Ariel, Bella, and Blanchard. How Ariel could remain so calm, she didn't know.

Blanchard's smile widened. "Were you, now?"

"Yes, as a matter of fact," Ariel said, tucking his flashlight back in his pocket. "You're a difficult woman to find."

"Mmm," Blanchard said, examining her nails. "Yes, I suppose I am. Quit your stalling, boy, and tell me what you were really doing, sneak-sneaking around in the dark with your friends."

"We were hoping you could inform us of the progress being made with regards the werewolf monitoring spell research," Ariel said, and Lee had to force herself not to let out a sigh of relief. "Seeing as you so kindly offered your services, and you're the best magician for the task, it seemed prudent to check with you."

Blanchard laughed, a high, cold sound, and she smoothed back her immaculate, bone-white hair. "Oh, you're quite the flatterer, aren't you? I'll have to let your mother know what a shrewd child she raised."

"The spell report, please, Madame," Ariel said, undeterred.

Blanchard waved a hand. "Yes, yes, it's being worked on, but unfortunately it's rather at the point where, were any other magician to attempt to cast it, they would go stark raving mad."

"But not you?" Bella said, rather bravely, and Lee bit down on her knuckle when Blanchard's cold eyes slid sidelong to land on the vampire.

"My talents for magic surpass what others can only *dream* of," Blanchard said. "Others merely grasp at tendrils of power; I was born with it." She tilted her head, birdlike, and pressed her fingertips together, ruby-red lips curled in a smirk. "You could say it's in my blood."

"Is that supposed to be a vampire joke?" Bella said, her eyes narrowed.

"Blood is life, and life is power," Blanchard said, her pale gaze fixed unblinkingly on Bella's face. "What vampire doesn't thirst for more?"

"Some of us are content with what we have," Bella said, folding her arms.

Blanchard cackled at this. "Unless I'm sorely mistaken, aren't you the girl Augustus approved for extra feeding rights? That's *rich*, coming out of your mouth."

Bella's jaw set.

Lee's heart hammered in her chest, but she stepped forward, lifting her chin. "It's a temporary measure," she said, and even though her voice shook, she kept her head held high. "Which, I'm sure, you already knew."

"I'd watch your dog, if I were you," Blanchard said, her eyes narrowing. "Its barking is most tiresome."

Lee started forward, but Ariel held his arm out in front of her. "We'll take the dog outside, then, if that's alright with you," he said coolly, and though she knew he was just playing the part, Lee's stomach still twisted. "I'm sure my mother will be pleased to hear about the progress on the research."

"Do pass on my regards," Blanchard said, stepping aside and sweeping her arm towards the exit.

Ariel glanced at the others out of the corner of his eye and gave a slight jerk of his head. They approached the door cautiously, then passed through it, Blanchard's head slowly turning to watch them leave.

"Oh, and Ariel?" Blanchard called when they were almost across the lobby.

He paused, then turned, folding his arms. "Yes, Madame?"

"Tell your mother our plans are still on," she said, giving him a sickly-sweet smile.

"Your plans," Ariel said slowly.

Blanchard clapped her hands together, positively beaming; the tiny rubies in her jewellery glittered with the motion. "For cocktail night on Wednesday, of course. I don't know what silly, slanderous thoughts were running through that head of yours."

Ariel gave her a tight smile. "Mine is not to know the madness of mages," he said, and bowed. "Thank you for your report."

The walk back to the car felt like an eternity, Lee's skin crawling with the feeling of being watched.

They probably were.

It wasn't until they were what seemed a safe distance away that Ariel spoke. "Sorry about the dog comment," he muttered.

Lee slid down a little further in her seat. "It's alright."

"That was insane," Bella said, shivering and rubbing her arms. "*She's* insane."

"And bears shit in the woods," Ariel shot back. "We're lucky she let us go."

"We didn't even *find* anything," Lee lamented. "If we'd only had a little more time—"

"We're *not* going back there," Ariel said sharply. "If she catches us a second time, we're worse than dead."

Lee shuddered. "I wasn't going to suggest it anyway."

"We've got to be missing something," Bella said, and Ariel snorted. "No, I'm serious. Something big and obvious that we're somehow missing."

Lee gnawed on one of her lip rings as she thought. "The entire place smelled like bleach," she said slowly. "It might be because she didn't want us or anyone else smelling *something* if they ever came calling."

"Someone like Augustus or one of his underlings," Bella guessed.

"Bella," Ariel said in exasperation, "*we're* his underlings."

"You know what I meant."

"Either way, short of checking behind the toilets, we searched the whole building," Ariel said, shaking his head. "If there *was* anything there before, it's long gone now."

Chapter 28

November brought with it the cold and rain. The longer nights made for longer patrols, but Ariel found that they weren't quite so bad with Lee to accompany him. It became a regular occurrence to return to their dorms, soaking wet and freezing, to find Bella waiting for them with hot chocolate generously spiked with Bailey's.

"What *do* you do when we're out, anyway?" Ariel yawned, accepting the warm mug from her.

"Study," Bella said, like it should have been obvious. "There's a reason why they call it *practicing* medicine."

Ariel was starting to think Morgan had made the right call not going to college. Between the patrols and the rehearsals for the rapidly approaching main stage performance, he barely had time to study, himself. It was a small comfort there had been no new feral attacks, but the disappearances of humans born during a full moon had him worried they were being forcibly turned.

He'd informed Augustus of their encounter with Blanchard, to which the vampire could only sigh and pinch the bridge of his nose.

"Thank you for your update," Augustus said, letting his hand fall. "Take care this full moon; if Blanchard truly is the one behind these attacks, which I have no doubt she is..."

"Lee's gonna be a target," Ariel finished, and Augustus nodded.

"Aye," he said. "And the closer we draw to the winter solstice, well, you know as well as I do how thin the veil becomes. Be careful."

Ariel was already heading to the door. "Always am."

Lee had no rehearsals to worry about, but her classes piled on essay after essay, test after test, and with her already-short attention span taken up by the present mystery and the looming threat of the upcoming full moon, she was sufficiently overwhelmed long before she finally snapped, melting down at her desk in tears.

Bella looked up in alarm at Lee's sob, and she all but threw her book aside, hurrying over to wrap Lee in a hug.

"I'm sorry," Lee gasped out. "I'm sorry, I'm sorry, I'm sorry—"

Bella held her, stroking her hair and humming gently as Lee's sobs eventually slowed, then quieted. "Lee," she said gently. "I say this with all the love in my heart, but please give Connor a call."

She felt Lee stiffen, then go limp in her arms. "...Okay," Lee mumbled into Bella's shirt. "But when he tells me to get lost, I get to say 'I told you so.'"

• • • •

Connor O'Connor's office was a familiar sight to Lee; the safely boring beige of the walls, the shelf of toys and box of sand for children, the shelf full of books only a therapist would read. Connor sat at his desk, his chair turned so his back was to the computer and he was facing the squashy sofa opposite.

"I'm glad you decided to come in," Connor said when Lee shut the door behind her and sat, her leg jittering uncontrollably. "I'll be honest and say that considering the nature of our relationship, I shouldn't really be taking you on as a patient, but seeing as there's an unfortunate shortage of therapists who know about Tenebrous..." He smiled apologetically. "I'll still do my utmost best to help."

"...Right," Lee muttered.

"So," Connor said, crossing his legs and folding his hands on his knee. "What would you like to talk about today?"

Lee hesitated. "Where's your clipboard?" she said, frowning.

"I prefer to take notes after a one-on-one session," Connor said easily. "Right now, though, I'm here to have a dialogue with you about whatever it is that brought you in today."

"You know why I'm in here," Lee said, folding her arms tightly.

"I know what I was told when we scheduled the appointment," Connor corrected her. "You said you were feeling overwhelmed with school?" he prompted.

Lee snickered. "Yeah, no shit."

"What is it that has you feeling overwhelmed?"

Lee's gaze darted restlessly around the office, and she shrugged.

Connor smiled. "If you want something to fiddle with, the shelf—"

"I'm good," Lee said shortly.

"Well, if you change your mind, go right ahead," Connor said. "So: school."

Lee shrugged again.

Connor's smile faded, and he leaned forward. "I know you've had bad experiences with therapists in the past," he said softly. "And I'm genuinely sorry about that. I can't help you if you don't want to talk, but—"

"I do."

Lee's voice was tiny.

"I do want to talk, it's just..." She picked at her fingernails. "Hard, y'know?"

"I know," Connor said. "I know *very* well, believe me. Getting started is the hardest part." He studied her for a moment, and the jittering picked up the pace. "How about this? You tell me something about school that you like, and we'll see how it goes from there?"

"...Art history is cool," Lee said after a moment.

"Art history? That *does* sound cool," Connor said. "Is there something specific about it that you really like?"

"All of it," Lee said immediately, sitting up a little straighter. "Ancient Egyptian, Classical Greek, pre-Renaissance, Rococo, post-impressionism—ancient pottery and modern art, it's so fascinating to see how the styles changed with the world. It's like writing stories, or playing music, but with a paintbrush and canvas or a chisel and stone; imagining what the people were thinking during the process of creation and seeing it reflected in the final work..." She ducked her head. "Sorry," she mumbled.

"What for?" Connor asked, tilting his head.

"Going on about..." Lee shrugged.

"I asked," Connor pointed out. "And I was rather enjoying myself, too. It sounds like you have a lot of passion for the subject. Though if I remember right, you said English was your major?"

Lee glanced away. "Yeah."

"What is it about the subject that you're drawn to?" Connor asked.

Lee snickered. "Drawn to... 'cause I was just talking about art, and..." She bit her lip. "Sorry."

Connor shook his head. "You came in to talk to me, so please don't apologise for what we're here to do." His eyes crinkled in a smile.

"...Right."

"Why did you choose English for your major?" Connor asked again.

Lee glanced away. "It was kind of chosen for me," she said, tapping her fingers together. "I won a scholarship for a story I submitted. Full ride, so long as I majored in English."

"That sounds like it was an impressive story," Connor said. "What was it about?"

Lee's heart twisted in her chest. "It was about a kid who grew up in the foster system," she said quietly. "Whose parents were killed by monsters only he could see, so nobody believed him. So he killed himself."

Connor sat back. "I see," he said. "Lee, was this character based on you?"

"...Yeah."

"This character's suicide," Connor said, and Lee closed her eyes. "Was that based on thoughts you had?"

Lee nodded once, a sharp, jerky movement.

"Do you still experience these thoughts?" Connor asked, and Lee felt a bubble of laughter well up inside to burst from her lips.

"What do you think?" she said, opening her eyes to glare at him. She jabbed a finger at her face. "You heard me at the support group! It seemed like I had everything together, and then I got half my face ripped off and everything I thought I knew got turned on its head! Surprise, after being told your whole life you're insane, you actually aren't! The monsters that *ate your parents* are *real!*"

"It's a lot for anyone to handle," Connor said softly, reaching for the box of tissues on his desk and offering them to Lee. She took it, holding the box between her knees before blowing her nose, scowling at the floor. "It sounds like you have a lot of pain and anger which you've never been given the chance to process, because of being told you didn't actually experience that trauma."

"And then got an assload more added on top of that," Lee said thickly, and waved her hands. "Whee."

"I do have to ask you again, are you suicidal now?" Connor said.

Lee hesitated. "I... no? I don't know." She swallowed and blew her nose again. "I mean, I'm not going to go jump in front of a car or anything, but if a car hit me because I wasn't... paying attention or whatever..."

"I see." Connor cleared his throat. "Lee, I know I promised no clipboard, but I'd like to get it out so I can go through some questions with you."

"...Fine," Lee said, and sniffled.

· · · ·

"How did it go?" Ariel asked when Lee emerged from the office, a folder full of papers clutched to her chest.

"I, uh." Lee shrugged. "I'm going back to see him again after Thanksgiving."

"Sweet. You want burritos? I'm starving."

Lee grinned; if she was a little misty-eyed, Ariel didn't comment on it. "Sounds perfect."

Chapter 29

L ee's second full moon was spent in the dorms with Ariel and Bella, with popcorn and video games to pass the time. When the sun finally rose and the hunters assigned to guard their werewolves reported back that the night had passed without incident, they breathed a collective sigh of relief.

"Well, that's the first part of this test done," Ariel said, shoving his phone into his pocket. "I'm going to squeeze in a nap before we go to meet Bella's family. Least we can sleep easy now."

"You want to take my bed?" Bella asked. "It's not like I'm using it."

"Nah, arm's gotta recharge," Ariel said, twiddling the fingers of his prosthetic. "Thanks, though." He stood, stretching with a soft groan. "See you at the car."

They met up several hours later and piled into the car, Bella taking the passenger seat to give Ariel directions.

"I've got a GPS," he said with mild amusement as Bella pointed him to an off-ramp a moment before his phone did.

"Back in my day, we had to navigate by the *stars*," Bella said, sniffing haughtily. "You kids and your confounded technology."

"It's because you got lost on your way to get me donuts, isn't it," Lee said, and Bella flapped a hand at her to be quiet.

"It's not my fault the stupid phone was wrong!"

Bella's home was on the south side of the city, a three-story brick affair with a large backyard, the upper floors of a massive playset just visible over the top of the fence.

"Nice place," Ariel said. "Should I just park in front?"

"Yeah, just over there is fine..."

Ariel had barely removed his keys from the ignition when the front door flew open and Elena came rushing out, along with a little boy who looked to be slightly younger.

"Bella!" Elena yelled, and Bella laughed, jumping out of the car and holding her arms out for a hug. She was promptly bowled over by the children, laughing the whole time.

"Well, I'll be," Ariel said. "Someone is actually glad to see you."

"Shut up," Bella said happily. "Elena, Aaron, this is Ariel and Lee."

"Wow," Aaron said, staring up at Lee with wide blue eyes. "Mommy said not to stare at you 'cause it'd be rude."

"*You're* staring," Elena said, smacking his arm. "Stop it!"

Lee bit back a sigh, folding her arms uncomfortably as she studied the children. The two couldn't look more dissimilar; where Elena might have been a tiny version of Bella down to the sunglasses and fashion sense with her hair pulled up in a pair of afro puffs, Aaron's dark red hair hung loosely to his shoulders, his rocket ship T-shirt covered with a large stain that looked suspiciously like cranberry sauce.

"We heard shouting and just *knew* that meant Bella was home," a woman said from the doorway, and Bella lit up, running to hug her.

"Mum!" she cried, throwing her arms around her. "Bună ziua! Mi-a fost dor de tine!"

"Si tu mi-ai lipsit," Beatrice said, hugging her back tightly. If Bella was small, her mother was tiny in comparison; Lee doubted she reached five feet in height, though her most striking feature was her chestnut brown hair that fell well past her hips, held away from her face with a pair of clips. She, too, was wearing sunglasses, but it wasn't difficult to imagine the deep crimson colour of her eyes. "Oh, it's so good to have you home. Come in!" she called, waving the others inside. "Let's stop letting the cold air in."

She smiled at Ariel and Lee as they approached, Elena and Aaron running past her and back into the house. "Bella has told us so much about you both," she said. "I don't suppose she's told you about all of us?"

"She mentioned your partners would be here," Lee said uncertainly.

"That's because they live here," Beatrice laughed. "Henry and Lisa Zilberstein; Aaron is their son."

"*Zilberstein?*" Ariel said under his breath, stepping inside.

"It gave us quite the laugh when we met Lisa, I'll tell you that," Beatrice said, chuckling as she removed her sunglasses and set them on a rack beside the door.

The front hallway was filled with dozens of photographs of Elena and Aaron, as well as several beautifully-drawn portraits of a child that could only be Bella. The aroma of baking bread and frying foods immediately set Lee's mouth to watering.

"Is that you?" Ariel said, peering at one of the drawings.

"Yeah," Bella said, laughing faintly. "We don't exactly have any baby pictures of me."

Lee bumped her with her hip. "We don't have any baby pictures of me, either."

"Consider yourself lucky," Ariel said dryly. "First and only time I brought a date home, my mom got wasted and decided to pull out the photo album."

"Parents have a talent for embarrassing their kids," Beatrice said delicately, leading them deeper into the house. "Bill! Henric! Lisa!"

"We're in the kitchen where you left us, dearest!" a man's deep, distinctly British voice called back.

"I suppose we'd better go find them," Beatrice said.

Bella hurried on ahead, while Ariel moved at pace with Lee to make sure she didn't fall behind. "Alright, there?" he muttered.

Lee took a deep breath and nodded, glancing up at him. "Fine."

The kitchen was large, with a combined dining area that contained a massive table that was positively sagging under the weight of the dishes already on it. There was a large crystal bowl full of salad, mesclun greens, sliced pears, dried cherries, and candied walnuts; pumpkin spiced challah bread; latkes fresh from the fryer and spiced cranberry sauce; and, when a giant of a man who had to be William Graves set it on the table, a massive tray of honey-glazed corned beef.

"That's a lot of food for just four of us," Lee said, and went beet red when she realised that was hardly a proper greeting. "Uh... hello."

William laughed, pulling his daughter into a hug and waving at them over her shoulder. Bella was positively dwarfed by him, nearly disappearing into his hug. "We'll be eating a little bit too, don't you worry."

"Maybe *you'll* be eating a little bit," laughed a stout, muscular woman with a blonde plait draped over one shoulder—Lisa. "*I'm* going to eat so much there won't be any room left for dessert!"

"Aye, and you'll regret that when you have to make it come back up," Henric said. He was a beanpole of a man, with dark red hair like his son's, pulled up in a sloppy bun. Combined with his black turtleneck and small goatee, he looked like he'd wandered in from an art museum by mistake. "I apologise in advance for the inevitable retching noises," he added, bowing to Lee and Ariel. "The misfortunes of immortality."

"Henry and Lisa?" Lee guessed, and got a pair of fanged grins in return.

"Henric while it's just us," Henric said.

"Like how Mummy and Daddy have different names outside, too," Elena said as she perched in one of the chairs, tucking her feet under her. Even in the house, she refused to remove her sunglasses. "But not Mommy, because Mommy isn't old enough yet."

"Are you *really* a vampire killer?" Aaron asked loudly from his own seat.

Lee froze, glancing sidelong at Ariel, who just smirked. "Only if the vampires are being naughty."

"*Kinky,*" she saw Henric mouth, and he laughed as his wife swatted his arm.

"Please, have a seat," William said to the room at large. "No sense standing around letting the food go cold." He pulled out the chair at the head of the table for Beatrice, who sat and in a practiced motion, twisted her hair up into an elegant bun to keep it out of her face while she ate. William sat to her right, and she reached over to squeeze his hand briefly before beginning to dish small portions onto her plate.

"Here, sit with me," Bella said, taking a seat and motioning to the chairs on either side of her. So Ariel sat to her right, Lee to her left, which left her sitting across from Elena and next to Aaron, the mangled side of her face turned towards the boy.

"Did it hurt?" Aaron asked.

"I—"

She couldn't have been more relieved when Lisa stepped in. "It likely hurt very much, and makes her very unhappy to think about, so no more of that," she said firmly.

Aaron bobbed his head. "Okay, Mommy."

"What do you say to Lee?" Lisa prompted.

"Oh! Right." Aaron turned to Lee, putting on his best sombre face. "I'm sorry."

Despite herself, she couldn't help but grin. "It's alright," she said softly. "But thank yo—"

"Why's your name Lee and his name is Ariel?" Aaron said, leapfrogging to a new train of thought. "Ariel's a girl's name."

"Like the princess," Elena said, and gasped. "She sings really well! Can you sing like her?"

"Only with a kick in the—" Ariel cut himself off. "—motivation."

Henric snickered to himself as he began plating up, and jumped when Lisa elbowed him before he elbowed her back.

"No way you sing," Bella said to Ariel, turning to stare at him.

"I'm a fucking theatre major," Ariel said, and winced, glancing towards the children.

"Oh, go ahead and swear all you like, it's nothing they haven't heard before," William said. "They know better than to repeat it in public, though."

"Are you sure about that, Daddy?" Elena said innocently.

"I'd better be," William said sternly.

Elena giggled, reaching for the challah bread to tear off a chunk for herself. "Do you want any, Lee?" she asked.

"I would love some," Lee said, reaching across the table to take the offered tray.

"Your arms are *really* long," Aaron blurted out, and Lee spluttered with surprised laughter. "Are all werewolves like that? Do you have really long legs when you transform?"

"I mean, I'm bigger than a normal wolf?" Lee said uncertainly, glancing at Bella as she passed the bread down the table. "I could show you later, if you'd like."

The table went oddly quiet, and Lee got a *very* uneasy feeling in the pit of her stomach when she realised four pairs of red eyes were all looking at her.

"I, um, didn't tell them that bit," Bella whispered into the silence, as Ariel facepalmed.

"You must have quite the gift," Beatrice said, and Lee sighed with relief when that broke the tension. "Bella said you'd only been bitten... what was it, about two months ago?" She glanced at Bella, who nodded, picking at her tiny portion of salad.

"Impressive," Henric said, rubbing his jaw in thought. "In all my years, I've only ever met one other werewolf who claimed to be able to do that. No way of corroborating his claims, but he was an honest enough chap until he tried to rip my throat out."

Lee's eyes unwittingly went straight to the collar of his turtleneck.

"*Your* scars are way cooler than Papa's," Aaron informed her, and Lee turned to look at the boy in surprise.

"You think they're cool?" she asked, baffled.

"*All* the best heroes have scars," Aaron said, and Elena nodded enthusiastically, her mouth stuffed full of bread so she couldn't speak. "Except Wolverine, but he doesn't count 'cause he's got healing powers."

Lee laughed, genuinely laughed, and she nodded. "You make a very convincing argument."

"Also, all the best heroes are cyborgs," Aaron added, leaning forward in his seat to see Ariel seated at the other end. "Like Luke Skywalker!"

Ariel grinned. "Don't tell anyone," he stage-whispered, "but I'm actually from Tatooine."

Aaron's eyes went huge before they narrowed. "No you're not, 'cause Tattooine isn't *real.*"

"Oh no, you got me there," Ariel deadpanned.

"Can I see your arm after dinner?" Aaron asked eagerly.

"If you're asking me to take it off, hell no," Ariel said. "Wouldn't mind you looking at it while it's on me, though."

"Yes!" Aaron cheered, and took a bite of latkes covered in cranberry sauce that ended up more on his shirt than in his mouth.

"Smaller bites," Henric and Lisa said at once. Aaron mumbled something that sounded like an apology around his food before wiping his mouth on the back of his hand; Beatrice leaned over, not taking her eyes off the boy as she slowly and deliberately placed his napkin in front of him. Aaron just grinned and somehow managed to use the napkin to smear the cranberry sauce even more.

"You're *gross*," Elena informed him, wrinkling her nose. "You're worse than those vampire movies where they get blood all over their faces. Like a baby."

"I'm not a baby!" Aaron yelled.

"Indoor voices," William rumbled, and Aaron sulkily took another bite of latke.

"I'm not a baby," he muttered.

"So..." Lee looked around the table, inwardly marvelling at how *different* Bella's family was. "How did you guys, uh, meet?"

She didn't miss the glance that passed between William and Beatrice. Ariel lifted his head, looking curiously at the pair with a guarded expression.

"I was their surrogate for Elena," Lisa jumped in. "I was one of Henric's donors when he mentioned his partners were hoping to try for another child, and I didn't think twice, just got their numbers and a few months later, Elena joined our little family."

"'Little,'" Henric chuckled, shaking his head. "I met Bill and Bea when I fled France to escape the 1848 revolution; Bella was just a tiny thing, then," he added, grinning across the table at Bella, who gave him a lazy salute. "Ended up on the Isle of Thanet, and as it turns out is a very small place when you're part of the night world."

"Thanet?" Lee asked. "Like... Dover?"

"That's the one," William said. "We'd gone to Canterbury so I could find work on the railway line that was being developed at the time, and we'd figured it would be a large enough city we could blend in somewhat."

"You were doing human jobs?" Ariel said, blinking.

"Bella was still a child," Beatrice said. "Unturned. As much simpler as that would have been, she unfortunately couldn't survive on blood."

"I can't either," Elena said solemnly, and William put a hand on her shoulder, squeezing gently.

212

"One day, sunshine," he said. "And in the meantime you get to enjoy all the comforts of modern life." He gestured at the table. "The kings of old would turn green to see our feast here!"

"Which most of us are going to throw back up," Beatrice said. "It still feels like an awful waste."

"We're still enjoying the food, even if we can't live off of it," Lisa said, shrugging. "You want to guilt somebody about food waste, start with the supermarkets and restaurants."

Beatrice shook her head, rolling her eyes with a fondness that said they'd had this discussion many times. "I still remember when we would have to save every bit of food we could get our hands on," she said to Lee and Ariel. "Most of William's earnings went towards that, and the room we rented." She smiled humourlessly. "I sometimes found work washing clothes, but it would often disappear when my clients learned about my family."

"Still better than it would have been in America," Bella said, and Beatrice nodded.

"We made it work," William murmured, and he and Beatrice leaned their heads together briefly. "And now we have a lovely home and a beautiful family." He glanced up at Lee and Ariel. "And that includes the both of you, now."

"Oh, good," Bella said, relief obvious in her voice. "Because I told Ariel about Dragomir."

Elena and Aaron gasped quietly, both their heads snapping around to look at Beatrice.

Beatrice stilled, then set her fork down, dabbing delicately at her mouth with her napkin.

"Um," Lee said, glancing around and silently noting everyone's reactions. "Who's Dragomir?"

"The vampire that was the inspiration for Dracula," Ariel said bluntly, and Lee's eye went huge.

"My father," Beatrice said, a shadow passing over her face. "And may he rot in the deepest circle of Hell."

"You asked how we met," William said to Lee. "I was a porter in Dragomir's house, and Bea was his breathtakingly beautiful daughter."

"When Ariel says he was the inspiration for Dracula," Beatrice said, "what he ought to have said was how the literary character looks like a saint by comparison. We knew my father would never approve of a union between us, so we waited until he turned me when I came of age. The moment it was done, I drove a stake through his heart, William set the manor ablaze, and we fled. I turned William the moment we were safe." She smiled wryly. "It later turned out I was already pregnant with Bella at the time."

"And I was the best thing that ever happened to you," Bella chimed in, grinning toothily.

"What does that make the rest of us?" Lisa said, raising an eyebrow.

"Fine, fine," Bella said, flapping her hands. "*One* of the best things. Sorry, Lisa."

"Damn right you are," Lisa said, and winked.

"Sorry," Lee said, holding a hand up. "Why set the manor on fire? Instead of... staying?"

Beatrice shook her head. "Dragomir kept a circle of loyal vampires who were highly volatile," she said. "The Night Treaty had only recently been signed, and they were incredibly upset about the new restrictions they had to abide by or meet a Montgomery's blade."

"Like you," Aaron whispered down the table to Ariel, who lifted his shoulder in a shrug, not taking his eyes off Beatrice.

"If we burned the house down, it let us start a new life," William said softly. "They would suspect foul play, certainly, but without any bodies left as evidence, Bea was as good as dead."

"That, and Dragomir made it incredibly difficult to get silver into the house," Beatrice said, her voice dry.

"So the stake to the heart...?" Lee asked.

Every vampire in the room save Lisa winced.

"It paralyzes us completely until the damn thing is removed, but it's not *deadly*," Henric said. "Which is very, very lucky for us."

"You've been staked?" Lee asked Bella, horrified.

Bella shrugged. "Only like, twice. I got better."

Ariel snorted into his drink.

"I do sometimes worry that despite everything, he survived," Beatrice said.

William shook his head. "If he had, I doubt he would have stayed unnoticed for long."

"Well, until people start showing up on spikes again, I think we're safe," Henric said.

Lee hesitated. "So, uh, what about Vlad the Impaler...?"

"Who do you think gave him the idea?" Ariel said darkly.

Despite the warmth in the room, Lee shivered.

"Well," Lisa said, clearing her throat. "That was a cheerful bit of holiday chatter. Who wants spiced apple cakes?"

"Me!" Elena and Aaron both yelled, and Henric got up to retrieve the desserts.

. . . .

Ariel excused himself after dessert while everyone else was watching a wolfy Lee succumb to the petting hands of Elena's siblings. He slipped out the back door to the yard, nimbly scaling the play set and perching on the roof of its tallest tower.

Twilight was falling, casting long shadows over the lawn, and a light breeze ruffled his curls. He inhaled deeply, closing his eyes.

His mother would be long since passed out drunk, and Morgan would be taking Jessie to Connor's place for Thanksgiving supper before returning to the house to manage the patrols.

Just the house. Not a home. It hadn't felt like home since his father died.

The door opened and Bella stepped outside, peering up at him before turning into mist and flowing up the side of the tower to reform next to him.

"You okay out here?" she asked, letting her legs dangle over the edge. "You've got your brooding face on. Broodier than normal, I mean."

Ariel sighed, blowing a strand of hair off his forehead. It fell back into place, and he brushed it away. "Just thinking."

"About?"

"Stuff."

"Mm. Dangerous stuff, stuff." Bella glanced at him. "Is... is it about my grandfather...?"

Ariel blinked at her before shaking his head. "Nah, nothing so deep. Just..." He trailed off, listening to a burst of laughter from inside the house. "Being here—it's what my family was like, before. Everyone laughing and talking and *happy*. Just feels kind of messed up, everything that happened."

"I'm sorry," Bella said.

"Nah, don't be. Not your fault."

He felt Bella's small fingers creep into his, and she gave his hand a squeeze. After a moment, he squeezed back.

"For what it's worth," she said, "Dad meant it, that you and Lee are part of the family now."

"Just like that, huh?" Ariel said, raising an eyebrow. "He didn't misunderstand when you said you were bringing people over for dinner?"

Bella snickered, and Ariel laughed as well, feeling some of the heaviness lift from his heart.

"Just like that," Bella said. "It probably also didn't hurt that I told him I was falling very deeply in love with the both of you."

Ariel froze, his heart jackhammering in his chest. "*Uh.*"

"Oh, god, I've just gone and put my foot in it again," Bella said, pulling her hand away and hiding her face. "Look, just, forget I said anything, or say something sarcastic—"

Ariel pulled her hands away and put a finger under her chin. Bella's gaze flickered down to his lips, back up to his eyes, and she bit her lip.

"Well?" she said, and Ariel surged forward to kiss her.

A small part of his mind was screaming that this was a terrible idea, while the rest of him could only think of *Bella*, of the taste of the apple cakes and sweet, white wine still fresh on her breath, the softness of her sweater as his hands knotted in the fabric over her back, drawing her in closer. He nicked his tongue on one of her fangs by mistake, groaning when Bella's own tongue passed over the wound, sealing it shut with a rush of endorphins that just made him want *more*.

Because the longer this went on, the less he had to think about everything else.

His phone buzzed in his pocket, but he ignored it, shifting to pull Bella onto his lap, their hands roaming, exploring each other as the buzzing grew more insistent. Ariel finally pulled back with a groan. "That's probably important," he muttered, his irritation at being interrupted getting overridden by his ever-present duty as a hunter.

Ariel shifted, trying not to dump Bella off his lap to reach his phone, but when he pulled it out, the buzzing stopped.

His heart sank when he saw it was a missed call from Morgan, and he immediately hit the 'Call back' button.

"What is it?" Bella asked, her fingers curling on his shoulders.

"Mo," Ariel said, cursing when he got a busy tone. "Fucking hell, Morgan!"

The back door slid open with a loud *thunk*, and Lee came racing out with her odd, galloping run, phone to her ear. She skidded to a halt, staring up at Ariel and Bella, her horrified face starkly pale in the moonlight.

"Lee?" Bella called, and jumped down from the tower to land lightly beside her. "Lee, what's going on, what's the matter?"

Ariel's heart sank when he realised his mistake.

Bella might not have thought they were dating, but Lee's expression said she'd very much thought otherwise.

And he couldn't even worry about that now, because there were much bigger problems to deal with first.

Lee numbly held the phone up towards Ariel, and he saw her throat bob as she swallowed.

He grabbed hold of the fire pole and slid down to the lawn, snatching the phone from her. "Mo?" he asked, his eyes huge when he heard sniffling on the other end. "Shit, Mo, talk to me, what's happened?"

"We had the wrong marks," Morgan said, his voice thick. "The werewolves who were under guard are still fine, but everyone else—everyone else is *gone*."

"*Shit*," Ariel breathed, glancing up at Bella who was listening in, her eyes just as huge. "Connor?"

"That's how I found out," Morgan said, and Ariel heard him pause to sniffle again before there was the sound of the phone being set down, followed by the distant sound of a nose being blown. After a moment, he was back on the line. "Took Jess to his place for dinner, he didn't answer the door or his phone, we broke in, and dinner was half-cooked and cold." He paused, taking a deep breath. "And there was snow on the floor."

"Blanchard," Ariel growled.

"Jess and I are back at the house," Morgan said. "Every hunter's been rerouted from their patrols to search for the missing werewolves, but they could be anywhere by now..." He trailed off, clearing his throat. "I've called for an emergency council meeting. Get back to the city, it starts in two hours. I'm putting a folder together of all our confirmed missing wolves now. It's... it's long."

Ariel was already sprinting back into the house, past the worried faces of Bella's family, Bella right behind him and Lee taking up the rear. "We're already on our way," he said, tearing through the front door and across the lawn to his car. "Mom?"

"Drunk in the upstairs living room," Morgan said, and Ariel could hear the set of his jaw. "I'll try to get her sobered up enough to attend, but... God. With Diana gone, we're down two council members."

"Fucking figures," Ariel said as he started up the car; Bella climbed into the passenger seat, and Lee slid mutely into the back. "We'll be back as soon as we can."

He ended the call and tossed the phone over his shoulder at Lee, who caught it, tucking it back in her pocket. She turned her head to stare out the window, not speaking.

"It's going to be okay," Bella said, though it sounded like she was trying to reassure herself as much as them. "We'll get the council—or what's left of it—together, do some emergency protocols thing, it's going to be fine, they'll get Connor and the others back somehow—"

"Bella," Ariel said, "shut up."

Bella's mouth snapped shut, and she glanced back to Lee for reassurance, but Lee only shifted in her seat to further turn towards the window, away from them.

It was like a lightbulb went off in her head. Bella opened her mouth again, but at a sidelong glare from Ariel, she closed it again without another word.

The car sped through the darkness towards the city in silence.

Chapter 30

They arrived in the council's chambers to chaos. Morgan sat in Ashley's seat, both he and Terry Nelson fighting make themselves heard over the din, while Augustus was inhumanly still, his eyes fixed on Diana's empty chair.

"—no telling what that many werewolves could do—"

"—can't protect them, can't protect us—"

"—so irresponsible as to miss this—"

The crowd this time was mostly vampires; as Lee numbly scanned the sea of bodies clamouring at the front of the room, her heart sank when she realised there wasn't a single werewolf among them, and very few humans.

This became all the more apparent when a draft blew in behind them, carrying their scents into the room with it, and she suddenly found herself facing down a sea of crimson eyes.

"What's to say this one won't go feral and attack us, too?" one of the vampires yelled, and Lee froze in place when the crowd moved to advance on her.

Ariel planted himself firmly between her and the mass of vampires, stripping off his glove and flicking his wrist so a silver chain fell out of his sleeve and into his hand. "ANY ONE OF YOU WHO TOUCHES HER IS DEAD," he bellowed, bracing himself, and the vampires paused, the nervous energy thick in the air. "She ain't violated the Night Treaty, but any of you hurt her and your life is forfeit! Back the *fuck* off!"

Bella stepped up beside Ariel and hissed, narrowing her eyes as she looked around at the crowd, chin lifted in a challenge.

"He can't do that!" one of the vampires called, but Augustus finally seemed to break out of his trance.

"He speaks the truth," he said. He didn't need to shout for his voice to command the room, and the restless mutterings slowly died

221

down. "Now that you've all stopped your rioting, Morgan Montgomery, acting representative for the Gloam Hunters, has information to share."

"It's not much, I'm afraid," Morgan said, opening the very thick file in front of him and thumbing through it. "And reports are still coming in as we speak; I've rerouted the Gloam Hunters from their patrols to sweep the city for any signs of the missing werewolves." He sighed and looked up at the expectant faces. "It would seem as though we have made a grave error in judgement with regards to who the next targets would be, and for that I can only offer my sincerest apologies, and reassurances we're doing everything we can to save th—"

"Apologies won't bring my wife back!" a vampire yelled. "What are you going to do about Blanchard, huh? I saw the snow, we all did!"

"Or heard about it," another vampire shouted in agreement, and it seemed another riot was about to break out when Augustus stood, holding out a hand. When there was silence, he turned to Terry Nelson, giving him a nod.

Terry pulled his glasses off his nose, polishing them nervously on his shirt. "We're going to give the situation our full attention, but the Arcane Conclave's power is extremely limited as it is, and we are going to first focus our efforts on perfecting the tracking spell. If we can find our missing werewolves, we can almost certainly find whoever is responsible for their disappearances. If any more evidence comes to light, we will act on it, but Neve Blanchard is innocent until proven guilty, which is her right as laid out in the Night Treaty."

"You bring up an excellent point, Terry," Augustus said, and heads turned to look at him again. "Which is why I have been collecting intelligence of my own, and as fate or fortune would have it, my three key witnesses have just arrived."

With an unpleasant lurch, Lee realised he was talking about *them.*

Augustus opened his own folder and cleared his throat. "While I'm sure nobody here needs the reminder, for any who might be unaware, the relationship between Neve Blanchard and Ashley Montgomery, representative of the Gloam Hunters of Chicago and its surrounding areas, has been noted as 'most unusual' and 'highly irregular', especially now that the events of tonight have come to pass. Mrs Montgomery has made no secret of her dislike for our kind ever since the death of her husband, but in recent months she has displayed increasingly erratic and hostile behaviours towards vampirekind, with public comments such as, quote, 'Nobody ever said there weren't enough vampires in the world', unquote, at the council meeting of September 17th this year, or using silver to physically harm Arabella Ward, current alias Isabella Graves, while Miss Ward was an invited guest of Ariel Montgomery in his own home—"

A ripple of murmurs ran through the crowd as heads turned to stare at Bella. Her gaze darted between Ariel and Lee, wondering which one of them had told Augustus about that incident, before her eyes landed on Morgan, who was focused very hard on his file in front of him.

"And as any Gloam Hunter can tell you, it has been her son Morgan who has taken over her duties in all but title," Augustus continued, his voice rising. "She has been proven time and again to be unfit for her position, and now that her gross error of judgement has possibly cost the lives of werewolves under her protection, I would like to draw attention to one final point." He held up a piece of paper. "July 31st, the first recorded werewolf disappearance, happened a mere three days after Ashley Montgomery sold a disused Silver Sword office building to one Neve Blanchard, which was investigated by Ariel Montgomery, Arabella Ward, and Accalia

Lowell, who found evidence of heavy bleach use throughout the site before Neve Blanchard confronted them; her parting words to Ariel Montgomery were, quote, 'Tell your mother our plans are still on', unquote—"

There was another roar from the crowd, along with a chorus of hisses.

Ariel felt like he was going to be sick as he tried to think how Augustus could have possibly known that.

"Therefore," Augustus said over the din, "I move for an immediate review and investigation of Ashley Montgomery by the Tenebrous High Council!"

Morgan slowly lifted his head as the vampires cheered, and even from this distance Ariel could see his eyes were bloodshot and watery.

The world felt like it had slowed down as the jeers of the crowd continued, dimmed in the background. He knew Morgan was only human, only had human limits, but to Ariel, Morgan was always the one who held it together for the rest of the family's sake. Seeing his brother like this left his every breath a struggle to suck down air.

Callused fingers crept into his, and Ariel looked over to see Lee had taken his hand.

She gave him a fleeting, exhausted smile. "Come on, let's get you some fresh air."

They slipped from the room, and when Ariel glanced over his shoulder, equal parts relief and guilt gripped him when he saw Bella following. He focused on trying to steady his racing, uneven heartbeats, slowly inhaling through his nose and out through his mouth.

It didn't help much with the adrenaline surging through his body, but it did ease his breathing somewhat.

They slipped out of one of the hidden doors into the cold night air. The sting of it on Ariel's face cleared his mind a little further.

He took several steps towards the fountain in the middle of the square, then stopped, closing his eyes and tilting his head back to prevent the tears from falling.

Lee hugged him around the middle, resting her chin on his shoulder. His arms hung, leaden, at his sides, his body trembling slightly from the adrenaline.

"My mother," Ariel said at long last, "is many things. But she isn't responsible for the disappearances. Anyone else would've ordered the same."

"We know," Bella said gently. "Ariel, I'm so sorry my visit was used against her—"

Ariel let out a hoarse laugh, pushing Lee off of him. She stepped back, folding her arms against the cold. "She did that to herself," he said. "I just... god. I've been saying for years Morgan should've just taken her spot, but... not like this. Any other way."

Lee nodded, gnawing her lip. "The Tenebrous High Council," she said. "Is that, like...?"

"The head honchos," Bella said. "The big cheeses. The High Council is the top authority on enforcing the Night Treaty worldwide."

"And take a wild guess who represents the Gloam Hunters," Ariel said bitterly.

Lee had to think about it for a moment before her eye widened. "Not your grandfather?" she said.

Ariel's mouth set in a line. "Yeah," he said. "My Pop-Pop, Arthur Montgomery."

"You mean the guy who basically cut you guys out of the family after—?" Bella said.

"Yeah."

Bella let out a slow breath, beginning to pace in circles around them. "I know I was saying otherwise before, Ariel, but I think Blanchard is setting your mum up."

"No shit," Ariel said, but Bella flapped her hands at him.

"No, think about it," she said. "She sets up the perfect storm of too-guilty-to-be-believed-innocent circumstances, she doesn't care because she's a crazy mage who can't be easily tracked, so the blame falls on the much easier target—your mum—and so when people get scared and pissed off, they call for a council review—"

"All four council members in the same room," Ariel said, his eyes widening. "With a small army of werewolves that she could teleport in at any time, crazed out of their minds..."

"The Night Treaty would be dissolved," Lee said, and pressed her hands over her mouth.

"I see you've come to the same conclusions I have," Augustus said, and the three whirled to see him melding from the darkness to stand before them, his long black coat whipping in the wind. "At least now I won't have to walk you through my thought process."

"I hope you're pleased with yourself," Ariel said, just barely keeping himself from snapping at the vampire. "Even when—not *if*, *when* my mother is cleared, her reputation—"

"Died shortly after your father did," Augustus said, his voice cool.

The words were like a heavy blow to his chest. Ariel inhaled sharply, the motor in his wrist whirring as his fingers slowly clenched.

Augustus' crimson eyes glanced briefly at the prosthetic. "I've no doubt she'll be declared innocent through the simple fact that she's unfit to hatch so much as an egg, never mind any nefarious plots."

"You don't get to talk to him like that," Bella snapped.

"Mind your tongue," Augustus snapped back, before he took a deep breath, straightening up and turning his back on them, his fingers laced together behind him. After a moment, he turned to face them again. "I apologise for my outburst," he said. "It has been a very trying night for us all. I merely wished to tell you that the greatest

226

measures will be taken to ensure the High Council representatives have a safe visit, and that your mother will be afforded a fair trial."

"Okay," Ariel said curtly. "Good night."

Augustus hesitated a moment longer, then turned and walked away, his form melding with the darkness once more.

"What an utter *cunt*," Lee said, her lip curling. "Let's get out of here before he decides to come back."

· · · ·

Once the adrenaline wore off, though, Lee withdrew into herself again. She still joined Ariel on his patrols in an effort to distract herself from the countdown to when the High Council was due to arrive, but the patrols were now focused on scouring the city for any trace of the missing werewolves they could find, dispatching the night creatures they encountered along the way. She spent most of her time as a wolf so she didn't have to talk to Ariel.

She didn't think she could do it without breaking down crying, and god knows she'd done enough of that to last a lifetime.

Bella awkwardly asked Ariel one night when they returned from patrol how his mother was coping.

"Well, according to Mo, she's put the bottle down for now," he said. "Trying to make herself presentable for her review." He shook his head. "Bit late for that if you ask me."

To which Bella could only respond by gingerly patting his arm before he headed back to his dorm.

This was her fault. She still couldn't seem to learn that people were strange, and complex, and that she should have realised Lee would think sharing a few kisses now and then meant they were officially a couple.

Whatever happened to saying as such with words? Words were so much easier, so much clearer.

With the trial looming on the horizon, Bella decided that if she'd ruined things, then it was her job to set them right again.

The only lead they'd ever gotten was the abandoned building, and so, two nights before the trial was set, when Ariel and Lee headed out to patrol (in silence once more, she presumed), Bella transformed into a bat, winging her way over the city.

She did a perimeter loop several times, but couldn't see anything out of the ordinary from above, so she shifted forms again, and slipped inside as a cloud of mist.

Her senses were always strange, alien, when she didn't have a physical body, and that made it much more difficult to understand what she was 'seeing'. Even so, she felt vulnerable the moment she transformed back, alone in the dusty, dark, bleach-reeking room of cubicles.

She crept along the wall, brushing her fingers over its surface as she passed, idly noting a pair of strange ridges where the texture suddenly changed.

The wall burst open and a dark shape leapt through with a snarl, and as she flew backwards through the air, Bella realised with a new jolt of horror that she'd walked straight into an ambush.

She crashed down to the floor, and screamed when the werewolf's teeth sank into her shoulder. The saliva burned, her healing abilities trying and failing to work against it, and Bella thrashed and struggled before getting her feet beneath the werewolf's belly. She kicked with all her might, sending the beast flying over her head and through a row of cubicles with a *CRASH*.

Bella leapt after it, pressing the attack, but her hastiness cost her dearly. She couldn't quite get out of the way of a raking swipe of its paw, and white-hot pain seared her hip, parallel gashes dripping blood down her thigh.

Think, Bella, think—

The beast was crazed, feral, which meant it wouldn't be using any sort of strategy other than to attack, attack, attack like a rabid animal.

This was going to hurt.

Bella held her left arm out in front of her like a shield, and the werewolf latched on, snarling as it tried to rip her arm out of its socket. Bella punched it once, twice, three times in the ribs, horrific cracks echoing with each impact, before she brought her fist down on the werewolf's spine with a sickening wet *crunch*.

The werewolf howled, letting go of Bella's arm, as it tried to drag itself away by its front paws before it gave up from the pain to lay there, whining piteously.

Bella's knees gave out and she sat down hard on the floor, breathing heavily. She didn't think she could look at the state of her arm as she tore the bloody coat sleeve away, then peeled her coat off to wrap her arm in the fabric. She focused on the werewolf instead, whose breathing was coming in little pants.

Where had the creature come from? Bella could have sworn the wall exploded and hit her, but when she looked up, the wall was perfectly fine.

She was trembling all over as she fished around in her pocket for her phone, which had gotten horribly cracked in the fight.

"Please still work, please still work..."

It worked.

Bella put the phone to her ear. "Ariel. It's me. I... I've been hurt. Werewolf..."

"Bella?!" Ariel's voice sounded like it was coming from very far away. "Bella, where are you? We're coming!"

"Silver Sword," Bella said faintly, and her phone slipped from her fingers.

Chapter 31

Ariel radioed in to let Morgan know of the call as he and Lee raced back to the dorms. It was gut-wrenching, going the wrong direction however temporarily, but the abandoned building being on the other side of town meant the only real option was to drive.

And drive Ariel did, like a demon possessed, weaving through traffic, knuckles white on the steering wheel while Lee took over for the radio.

"I'm letting the other hunters know the situation," Morgan said, the too-familiar worried exhaustion heavy in his voice. *"But everyone's in the city proper at the moment after an umbral storm cropped up in the amphitheatre. Gina knows you're coming, she's prepping blood packs as we speak. Don't stick around to fight, just get in, get Bella, and get out of there. Over."*

"Copy that. Over." Lee looked over at Ariel. "Looks like we're on our own."

"Shocker."

"What's an umbral storm?" Lee asked after minute, and Ariel grimaced.

"Exactly what it sounds like. Giant cloud of darkness that spawns other Gloambeasts from within. That's the fun part about winter, longer nights and all, but with tensions being so high in Tenebrous, well, the Gloam feeds off that, thrives on it. Which is probably also what Blanchard wanted," he added bitterly.

"Shit's fucked."

"Shit's fucked."

Lee fell silent again, her fingers clenching and unclenching on her knees. "If she dies—"

"Nope."

"But—"

"Not gonna think about it," Ariel said.

The speedometer's dial crept higher.

The moment they reached the building and jumped from the car, Lee transformed again, galloping next to Ariel as they raced inside. Ariel barely paused as he kicked the door near the handle, snapping off the lock.

The pervasive smell of bleach was still there, but now there was a new smell: blood, and lots of it, both werewolf and vampire. Lee followed Bella's scent to the carnage, bracing herself for the worst.

Bella lay sprawled amidst the rubble of a cubicle, her phone just out of reach of her fingertips; for a horrible second, Lee thought she was dead before remembering that vampires didn't need to breathe.

"Lee," Ariel said, and Lee's ears perked up. "Any of this blood belong to the werewolf?"

Lee began sniffing around before stopping and pawing at a small puddle near the motionless, furry body. Ariel stooped to dip his finger in, and hurried back to Bella, holding his finger under her nose.

Bella gagged weakly, and Lee could have cried with relief.

But there was something about that blood... something...

Oh, no.

Lee reverted back to crouch on all fours beside the werewolf. She'd seen for herself that they turned human upon dying, which meant... "She's still alive, we have to take her with us."

"Yeah, no shit," Ariel said, already straightening with Bella in his arms.

"No, the werewolf too," Lee said, and after a moment of struggling, managed to get its body over her shoulders. She *really* didn't like how the back legs dangled. "It's Maria."

Ariel swore loudly and took off running to the exit. "Bella stays up front with me," he called as they ran, Lee with reflex tears in her eyes at the strain her knee was being put through. "You stay in the back with her, and if she wakes up, do *not* let her attack me, or I'll be really pissed off!"

"I'll get right on that," Lee said hysterically. They reached the car, and Ariel wrenched the passenger door open, setting Bella on the seat without regard to the blood getting everywhere. That done, he came to help Lee manoeuvre Maria's limp form into the backseat, Lee climbing in after and tugging the great furry head onto her lap. It at least seemed the easiest way to keep Maria's jaws shut, should she wake.

Ariel all but dived into the driver's seat, slamming on the gas and peeling out in a screech of tires.

"Radio in, let Mo know we've got them."

Lee put a shaky hand to her earpiece. "Extraction successful. Tell Gina we're going to need a second bed and a lot more sedatives." She paused, looking down at Maria, biting her lip. "We've got Maria, too."

. . . .

When they reached Gina's house, Ariel carried Bella inside while Gina helped Lee wrestle Maria up the steps and into the infirmary.

"What about her spine?" Lee asked unthinkingly.

"The way you had to stuff her in the car to get her to fit?" Gina shook her head. "If it's possible to somehow fix her brain and we can get her to transform back, I could re-align the spine and then we basically drip-feed her calories to accelerate healing, but if she's staying a wolf, well. I didn't exactly go to vet school."

Lee felt terrible about having to strap Maria down to her bed, even if it *was* just as a safety precaution while Gina worked on Bella.

"Never had to intubate a vampire before," she said, showing Lee how to hold Bella's head for easier access. "First time for everything, I suppose."

With that done and the contents of readied blood bags slowly being pumped into Bella's stomach, Gina had them help her clean out the wounds.

"Werewolf saliva is toxic to vampires, right?" Gina explained. "Seems about the stupidest thing you could do, leaving the nasty stuff in the wound. And look at that." She nodded at the gashes on Bella's hip, which were already starting to close up. "Claws? Nothing. Teeth? Whoooole other story."

It was at that point Maria's ear twitched as she started to wake up from her sedation.

"More," Gina barked to Ariel, who hastened to set up a new drip.

"I swear that much morphine would kill a person," Lee said.

"It would."

Bella's eyes flew wide, and she sat bolt upright, coughing uncontrollably around the tube in her throat before she ripped it out, blood dripping from the end of the tube.

"Jesus—!" Gina yelped before catching the tube. "I thought you were a doctor. You should know better."

Bella shuddered, coughing weakly. "Just gimme a straw, I'm alright," she said, and yelled when Lee threw her arms around her.

"I'm so sorry, Bella," Lee whispered. "I shouldn't have gotten mad at you, if you want to kiss Ariel or—or anyone else, I don't care, just that you're okay."

"No, *I'm* sorry," Bella said, leaning their foreheads together. Lee stayed very still, but Bella heard the way her heartbeat sped up. "Should've known better than to think something seemed obvious."

Lee sniffled, hugging her a little tighter. "You spend so much time with your foot in your mouth, I swear."

"Lucky I have small feet," Bella said, grinning weakly.

"Fangs."

"Touché."

233

Bella heard Ariel shift his weight, and she lifted her head, meeting his gaze. "You going to just stare at me, or do I get a hug, too?"

"You'll get a hug after you promise to never do anything so stupid as that again," Ariel said, folding his arms.

"I promise—"

"Even after me and Lee are long dead, you still have to promise," Ariel said.

"I *promise*," Bella said. She winced, rolling her shoulder when Lee let go to give Ariel space.

He briefly wrapped his arm around her, squeezing gently before letting go. "How's the shoulder?"

Bella considered before giving her arm another careful test. "Feels weirdly alright."

"Your shoulder injuries were a lot cleaner than your forearm," Gina said, going over to check on Maria. "I'm admittedly no vampire expert, but..." She shrugged.

"You brought her back from death's door," Lee said, swallowing as she looked up at Gina. "I'd say that makes you the expert."

Gina gave her a small smile. "You flatter me. Vampires are just humans with pointy teeth and an aversion to churches, though." She laid a hand on Maria's head, sighing. "Just wish I knew what to do for you."

"Well, I know what you can do for me," Bella said after a moment. "Could I get another blood pack?"

· · · ·

When it became obvious Gina no longer needed their assistance in the infirmary, Ariel, then Lee, took turns using the shower, changing into clean, blood-free clothes Gina loaned them.

"Oh, don't worry about that," she said when Lee apologetically mentioned she'd kept the lizard sweatshirt. "I raid charity shops all the time so my patients—or their helpers—don't have to walk around covered in blood and muck and god knows what else you hunter types get into."

Bella felt well enough to stand by the time Lee finished, so Gina helped her wrap her bandages in cling film and tape before she took her turn.

She let the hot water run over her skin, closing her eyes.

Talk to them.

Why did it feel like facing down Madame Blanchard again would be easier?

Snippets of that first encounter drifted through her mind. If it hadn't been for the extra feeding privileges, she would probably be dead right now, having the extra strength needed to take on a werewolf and (technically) win.

Hell, after a generous number of blood packs pumped into her, she felt like she could flip a tanker truck. Despite her brush with death, she was starting to realise just why some vampires had been so opposed to the limited feeding laws. She felt *powerful*.

Power...

"Blood is life, and life is power. What vampire doesn't thirst for more?"

"Blood is life and life is power."

"Blood is life..."

"Oh my god," Bella gasped, her eyes flying wide.

Ariel and Lee were sitting beside each other on the sofa, not quite cuddling with their sides pressed together, when Bella burst out of the shower, a towel hastily wrapped under her arms and shampoo still in her hair. "Lee, what's your blood type?!"

"I—what?"

"Your blood type, this is important! GINA!" Bella screamed, and Gina came running at once, her eyes wide. "Get ready for a blood transfusion, I think I know how to save Maria!"

"Wait, because of my—?" Lee began when Bella swung around to look expectantly at her. "Oh! O positive!"

"Maria's A pos," Gina said, and sprinted back to the infirmary. "I hope whatever you're planning works," she called over the sounds of her setting up the equipment. "Ariel, you find a diagram online or something. Bella, I'm going to need your nose for blood to help me find the actual vein. And then finish your shower when you're done."

"What about me?" Lee asked, practically vibrating as Ariel pulled his phone out to begin looking.

"You get to sit on the bed in here and look fluffy," Gina said, and Lee all but bounced off the sofa, transforming before trotting into the infirmary with her tail wagging excitedly. "I hope you're not afraid of needles."

· · · ·

"There's no way in hell I'd suggest this if it wasn't for your healing abilities," Bella said after they'd finished getting everything ready. Lee's tail thumped slowly on the bed; it was a strange sight, two massive wolves hooked up for a transfusion, which would involve replacing all of Maria's blood with Lee's. "I hope you're hungry, because you're going to need to eat a *lot* to keep up with the demand."

Lee *boof*ed and looked over towards Maria, her ears pricking forward.

"Well, it's not like we can just push a button and flush all her blood out and all of yours in," Bella said, planting her hands on her hips. "This is going to take a while."

"And now that we're all set, I can take it from here," Gina said, shooing Bella to the door. "Finish that shower!"

· · · ·

Pizza, it turned out, was a beloved food of humans and werewolves alike. Ariel deflected the delivery driver's inquiry about it being a bit late for a pizza party with a generous tip, closing and locking the door behind him as he balanced the boxes on his prosthetic.

The weight suddenly vanished, and he was briefly thrown off-balance before turning to see Bella holding the pizzas on the palm of her hand, her arm stretched out in front of her. "Huh."

Ariel blinked, then shivered, thinking about all the blood Bella had consumed earlier that evening. It was a sobering thought to imagine what a vampire whose feeding went unchecked could do. "Uh," he said, realising he was staring, "should probably take those in for Lee."

He heard a bark come from the infirmary, and he and Bella laughed as they headed in. Bella set the stack of pizzas on a chair, removing the top one and opening the box for Lee, setting it down in front of her. Lee promptly faceplanted in the pizza, her tail wagging as she scarfed her food like she was starving.

Then again, considering how much work her body was doing to keep replenishing the blood lost to the transfusion, she likely was.

"I hope there's one left for us," Gina remarked when Lee lifted her head from the empty box, her tongue sticking out as she looked eagerly towards the stack of boxes.

"Don't worry," Ariel said, swapping the empty box with a new one for Lee. "There's plenty more where that came from."

• • • •

Gina kept an eye on Lee's and Maria's vital signs, but when Bella asked what she was looking for, she admitted she wasn't sure.

"I could look it up for normal wolves," Gina said, "but that still leaves me wondering what a typical range is for a werewolf, so it's not exactly a great baseline comparison. I mean—" She glanced over at the growing stack of empty pizza boxes. "The metabolism alone is insane. How has she eaten *so* much and not had to poop yet?"

Lee's head shot up, her ears flattening as she whined.

237

"Or maybe it's just a more efficient metabolism in general?" Gina mused.

Bella nodded thoughtfully. "I've only ever bothered to learn about human anatomy," she said. "Small little squishy things that somehow keep working even when everything is breaking down. But... there really is a dearth of research on werewolf medical issues." She was quiet for a moment. "Maybe I could be the first."

Lee yipped, her tail wagging, and Bella smiled.

"All because of you, Lee."

· · · ·

Ariel decided to catch up on some much-needed rest while waiting to see if the transfusion worked, and crashed on Gina's sofa. It seemed like he'd barely closed his eyes when he heard Maria's scream. "I CAN'T FEEL MY LEGS!"

"SEDATIVES!" Gina bellowed, and Ariel sat up to see Bella go racing past him to assist. He tried to stand, got his legs tangled in the blanket someone had covered him with, and wasted precious seconds getting un-stuck before running after her.

"Don't transform back yet," Gina ordered to Lee, who was pawing at her blankets, whining anxiously. "I'm stopping the transfusion but if we need to keep going we won't have to hook you up again."

"That was Maria," Ariel said, dumbfounded. He realised Maria was human again and quite naked, and he hastily averted his eyes. "That's—it worked?"

"For now," Bella said as she undid the straps that had been restraining the werewolf. "Ariel, grow up and help me set her spine!"

"Oh, *fuck* me," Ariel whispered, but hurried to Bella's side, ready to assist however he could.

· · · ·

They found out it worked when the transfusion didn't.

Lee was startled awake by a sharp yank on her tubes as Maria thrashed, snarling, spittle flying from her teeth, her back legs kicking before Ariel sedated her again.

"Alright there?" he asked Lee, who yawned in return, her tongue lolling out. "Jesus, your teeth are massive."

Lee did her best attempt at a wolfish grin, and Ariel snorted, shoving her head away. "God, that looks awful. But, uh." He pointed gingerly at the tubes. "She didn't hurt you too bad?"

Lee rolled her eyes and very awkwardly used a paw to point at her face.

"Fair enough."

Lee put her nose back down on her paws, drifting off again.

Chapter 32

"Lee."

A hand ruffled the top of her head between her ears, and Lee yawned and flicked an ear in response.

"We're taking the tubes out. Have a look."

Lee peered up at Bella, who beamed at her and stepped aside with a flourish.

Maria was sitting up in bed, nursing a large cup of broth, looking quite exhausted—and quite human, wrapped in a fluffy grey bathrobe.

Lee transformed back and nearly fell onto the floor in her excitement. "It worked!" she cried. "Oh my god, it actually worked! Maria!"

Maria gave her a tired smile. "For now, anyway."

"Yet another problem of werewolf healing," Bella said, sitting beside Lee and throwing an arm around her shoulders. "But we don't need it to last long, just long enough for Maria to show us the secret door!"

Lee blinked. "Secret—? Oh. Oh *shit*. It was there the whole time, wasn't it? A Nevermind spell?"

Maria nodded. "And of course when the Arcane Conclave sent mages...?"

"Three days ago," Bella supplied helpfully.

"They didn't detect anything out of the ordinary because Blanchard is..." Maria shuddered. "It's like while they're playing checkers, she's playing four-dimensional chess. Her magic is almost completely different."

"Bella is brilliant," Ariel said from the doorway, folding his arms.

"Say that again, but to a microphone for me?" Bella asked sweetly.

"Fuck off," Ariel said, but there was no malice to it. "You figured out Lee's immunity to the full moon would fix this all by yourself."

Bella was very glad she couldn't blush. "I mean, Blanchard all but told me," she said. "But go on, Maria."

Maria took a shuddering breath. "I don't wholly understand it, myself," she said. "Being under her spell was like... a dream. Everything was fuzzy and sounded very far away. But there's a space under that building, a laboratory, a dungeon..." She shuddered. "She took my blood, took all of our blood, and did something with it. I don't know what. I sat in a cage for... ages... and then she made me follow her out, and there was this urge, a compulsion, to go out the door and attack the first thing I saw..." She shuddered. "I'm so sorry, Bella."

"Literally nothing to be sorry for," Bella said, shaking her head. "You weren't yourself. I'm only mad because of what she did to you."

Maria nodded, taking another tiny sip of broth.

"The High Council isn't meeting until sunset in an hour," Gina said, appearing in the doorway and gently but firmly elbowing Ariel out of her way. "But Ashley was brought in by hunters earlier today, something about security measures."

"We've got proof now, though, right?" Lee said, looking around the room. "That it was Blanchard this whole time?"

Ariel glanced away. "We know that she's involved, but nothing else. Not who else she's got under her control, or who might be in league with her but working of their own free will... we just don't know."

"Ariel and I have been coming up with a plan," Gina said, settling next to Maria and gently smoothing down the ex-hunter's hair. "They're opening the chamber up to the public audience ten minutes before they start the review."

"I'll take my car, try to talk to my mother beforehand to see if I can't get anything out of her before bringing what we've learned to the High Council's attention," Ariel said. "In the meantime, Bella will fly Maria and Lee to the old Silver Sword building. There's no telling what Blanchard—or any of her allies—might do once they realise the game is up."

"I'll be taking the shambulance ahead of time," Gina said, and Lee snorted before she could stop herself. "It'll be loaded with sedatives, so once Maria's got Bella and Lee into the dungeon, she comes back out to wait with me, and if she goes feral again..."

"Night-night," Maria said gloomily.

"What are we supposed to do if we find the missing werewolves down there?" Lee asked, biting her lip.

Ariel's face was grim. "Leave them," he said.

"But—"

"But what?" he said sharply. "You're just gonna set a bunch of mind-controlled werewolves loose in the city?"

Lee grit her teeth, hating that he was right. She nodded once, her leg beginning to jitter.

"Your main priority is intel," Ariel continued. "Bella's the heavy-hitter if things go south, and Lee... well, if she tries to do to you what she did to the others, play along until it's safe to escape. You're our secret weapon right now, and the last thing we want is for her to learn about you too early." His expression darkened. "Or start experimenting on you, too. There's no telling what sort of magic she might be able to do with your blood."

"Right," Lee said, and swallowed. "So we're trying to find notes on her research? If she even has any?"

Ariel spread his hands. "Anything. Everything. But don't sacrifice yourselves doing something stupid for the sake of the 'mission.'"

"Oh, please," Bella said, waving her still-bandaged arm. "When have I ever done anything like that before?"

"I'm deadass serious," Ariel said. His jaw set. "Last thing I want is to have to use my knife on either of you. The winters have enough funerals as it is."

"Believe me, it's the last thing we want, too," Lee said softly.

Gina cleared her throat to get their attention. "As cheerful as this conversation is, if I'm going to be in position in time to do my part, I have to leave, like... now." She patted Maria on the back and stood up. "Good luck, kids."

"I'm older than you," Bella said automatically, and Gina barked out a laugh, giving the room at large a lazy salute before grabbing her coat and heading off.

The room fell silent for another moment before Ariel grunted and pushed off from the wall. "I need to be going, too," he said, and strode off towards the front door.

Bella and Lee exchanged dismayed looks before Lee scrambled to her feet, the both of them hurrying after him. Ariel turned at the sound of their footsteps, blinking at them.

"Uh." Lee cleared her throat. "Look, just, if we die tonight..."

She yelped when Bella pulled her and Ariel into a crushing hug.

"Ow! Ribs!" Ariel wheezed. "Fuck me, Bella's going to kill me before Blanchard can."

"Sorry," Bella said sheepishly, relaxing her grip but not letting go. "I've never been this strong before. Still getting used to it."

"Oh, are we group hugging now? I guess?" Ariel said, and gingerly patted Lee's and Bella's backs a few times before letting his hands rest, one on each of them. He sighed. "I really can't dawdle doing the mushy stuff. So."

He let go and turned to Bella, cupping her face as he stooped to give her a gentle kiss that lasted far too briefly. Lee looked away, the tips of her ears red, before Ariel let go of Bella to turn to Lee. He cradled her unscarred cheek, his eyes flickering over her face.

Lee closed her eyes when his lips met hers. They were much closer in height, but even so she still had to lean up on tiptoes, nearly overbalancing when he pulled away before he steadied her.

"No more regrets," he said softly, and jogged down the front steps to his car.

They watched as he turned off at the intersection—and then was gone.

"So, uh," Lee said, and scratched the tip of her nose, "how do you reckon all the dried blood in there smells?"

Bella let out a strained laugh. "Awful," she said. "Absolutely horrid. I don't think there's a cleaning company in the world that could save those seats."

Lee laughed as well, though lost energy after only a few chuckles. She sighed and slipped an arm around Bella's waist.

"If we come out of this alive," Bella said, "then we are absolutely going to have a nice long talk about the future. Together."

"Together," Lee murmured, and Bella snuggled a little bit closer to her side.

Chapter 33

Maria raided Gina's stash of clothes and managed to come up with something that would at least be practical enough for acting as wayfinder to a dungeon full of mind-controlled werewolves.

"It actually looks alright," Lee said, and Maria laughed faintly. She looked pale, though, and kept playing with her ponytail, tightening and loosening the scrunchie almost on impulse.

Lee understood the urge all too well.

"I guess that's twice I owe you my life, now," Maria said, folding her arms.

Lee waved a hand. "Consider it me paying you back after I kicked up a fuss at the support group."

Maria gave her a crooked smile. "Yeah, I'll take that."

Lee hesitated, then cleared her throat. "I, uh. Talked to Connor. Like, made an appointment and everything... it wasn't too bad." She sighed and tucked her hair behind her ear. "Figures that as soon as I actually find a half-decent therapist he had to go get himself kidnapped."

Maria winced. "I suppose so," she said softly. "I still don't know how she did it; I was just sitting in my bedroom when everything went cold, and then my whole body sort of... seized up, and then I was in the dungeon."

Lee shivered, hugging herself. "You don't think she could just... do that whenever she likes, do you? To *who*ever?"

"God, I don't even want to think about that," Maria said. She slowly shook her head. "I... almost get the feeling the answer is no, though. Otherwise what's stopping her from just snatching the council members whenever she likes?"

"Now that's the kind of positive thinking I was sure they beat out of you in hunter training," Bella said as she approached them. "You guys ready? I promise I'll try not to crush you while we're flying."

"I'm more worried about you flying at all," Lee said as she and Maria stepped in close to Bella, who wrapped an arm around each of them.

"No, it's all very instinctive," Bella said, grinning. "Just because I've never done this before doesn't mean I can't!"

"Can I go back to the dungeon now?" Maria muttered.

"With pleasure!" Bella said, and leapt into the air.

Lee yelped and clung to Bella's neck as they shot up into the sky. There was only the faintest hint of orange on the horizon now, and the lights of the city below shone like a sea of stars.

"This is amazing!" Maria shouted over the wind from their passage, and Lee risked peering down.

"Wow," she whispered, her voice snatched away before Maria could hear it, but Bella turned her head to kiss her cheek.

"It's no magic carpet, but it's still pretty damn cool! Shame Ariel doesn't get to see this."

"He's got his job, we've got ours," Maria said. "And I've got a hell of a lot more faith in him than in us."

• • • •

Ariel had no faith that attempting to talk to his mother would even work, but he had to try.

He once again cursed the lack of signal in the council chambers, and resolved to raise hell to get Wifi put down there the moment this was all over.

As he drove, he found his thoughts kept turning to Lee and Bella, rather than the mission at hand. It didn't help that his heart was still going quite fast from their kisses.

246

"Should've known I'd get distracted," he muttered to himself, and reached for the volume dial, cranking it up.

If there'd ever been a mission he was more determined to survive, he couldn't think of it. All he had to do was hope the others would, too.

. . . .

Lee spotted the shambulance first, parked in a shadowy corner of the vacant building opposite their destination. She pointed it out to Maria, who peered down at it and nodded.

"Got it," she said, and Bella landed in front of the entrance to the Silver Sword building. She glanced down to see dried droplets of blood that grew thicker the deeper in they went.

Maria led them to the wall where she'd attacked Bella from, stopped, and pointed. "Right here."

Lee blinked and shook herself, staring at the door labelled *Janitor* that she could have sworn wasn't there a moment before. "How many times have we walked past this before? That's just... terrifying."

"Mages," Bella and Maria said together.

Maria swallowed, and Bella put a hand on her shoulder. "I guess this is it," Maria said. "Seriously, be careful down there."

"We will," Bella promised. "You get back to Gina and..."

"And wish us luck?" Lee suggested, and Maria laughed humourlessly.

"Yeah, I can do that," Maria said, turning to leave. "Good luck."

Bella tested the knob, finding it was unlocked. "I guess when nobody can see your entrance, there's no need to keep it locked," she whispered as the door swung open silently.

Lee's heart hammered in her chest as she peered down into the darkness; Bella stiffened at the noises that reached her ears. "Do you hear that?" Bella asked, though she realised that Lee probably couldn't without vampiric hearing. Sure enough, Lee shook her head.

Bella reached over to take her hand, squeezing carefully. "We've got this," she said, and Lee squeezed back.

"Let's go."

They descended into the darkness together.

• • • •

Ariel reached the council chambers when they were opened to the public, but it took far too long shoving his way through the crowd, to many disgruntled complaints, before he managed to squeeze out on the opposite side into the corridor that led to the holding rooms.

"I'm here to see my mom," Ariel said to the guards posted outside Ashley's room. When neither hunter budged—though they did exchange uncertain looks—Ariel felt his temper fray. "This is important," he snapped. "And it could make a difference between condemning an innocent woman and risking the Night Treaty and everything we've stood for! I'll take the fall for you if it comes to that, but I swear to god if you don't let me in—"

"Let him pass," came Augustus' voice behind him, and Ariel spun to see the Sanguine Lord gliding towards them, looking positively medieval in his high-necked collar and crimson robes. "The boy deserves a chance to speak to his mother."

"I'm still pissed at you," Ariel said as the guards stepped aside, "but thanks."

"Best make it quick," Augustus said, inclining his head.

Ariel needed no further urging and ducked inside, shutting the door behind him.

Ashley Montgomery stood near the back wall, studying a large oil painting on the wall, of Ariel's great-great-aunt Josephine Montgomery, looking every bit the resplendent hunter with her sword drawn, ready to strike an unseen foe. She was the most sober

Ariel had seen her in months, but that wasn't what he noticed when she turned to look at him.

Dangling from her ears, and hanging from her neck like droplets of blood, glittered a very familiar set of jewellery.

"Mom?" Ariel said, staring at the necklace, his heart hammering. "Is that... that necklace—?"

"Ah." Ashley's hand lifted slowly to touch the lattice of tiny rubies at her throat. "Yes, Neve gave them to me before this whole mess happened. She said to think of it as a token of her friendship... I hoped wearing it would bring me luck."

"Luck?" Ariel said incredulously. "This whole mess only started because of Blanchard, and you're wearing her jewellery for *luck?*"

"Neve has been nothing but a kind, supportive friend since your father died," Ashley said sharply, her hand dropping. "You could at least pretend to be happy someone has been there for me—"

"For the love of—shut the fuck up, *Mom*," Ariel snapped, his patience boiling over. "You go on and on about how you lost your husband that night, but you never even stopped to consider your kids lost both their parents!"

Ashley reeled back like she'd been slapped.

"So for once in your life you can at least pretend to be a parent and *listen* to me," Ariel continued, stalking forward. "Because whatever Blanchard is planning, she's been using you. We've found Maria, one of the missing werewolves, she was being held prisoner by Blanchard, the council will have to be put on hold when they learn this—"

"And you would trust the word of a werewolf who's gone missing?" Ashley said incredulously, her voice rising in pitch. "She could be feral, being made to say things—"

"There's no time to explain, I just—I need you to trust me—"

"Trust you..." Ashley said, and shook her head. "I don't even know you anymore. Neve was right. You've changed."

Blood roared in Ariel's ears, and he lunged for the necklace, hoping to rip it off, to destroy it *somehow*, because there was no way it wasn't part of Blanchard's plans at this point—

His vision went black, stars blinding him before he found himself flat on the floor, staring up at the ceiling with his mother crouched over him, strands of her hair falling out of its elegant bun.

"Guards!" Ashley yelled, and the doors burst open as Ariel struggled to suck down air. He was seized roughly by his arms, and hauled upright to his feet.

"I'm sorry, Ariel," Ashley said quietly. "But you don't know Neve like I do. I'll clear both of our names, and then—" She blinked away tears. "And then I'll do better. I promise, darling."

Ariel could have broken the grip, but not without severely hurting either of the guards, and panic shot through him. "It's her jewellery!" he yelled, hoping his voice would carry. "At least take the jewellery before she goes in!"

A second pair of guards appeared, one of them beckoning for Ashley to join them, and she walked out without a glance back at her son.

"I'm telling you, take the fucking jewellery!" Ariel bellowed, and tried to break free, injuries be damned. His heart sped up when he realised they were strong, far too strong to be human.

One of the guards tightened her grip on his prosthetic, and Ariel felt the metal groan under the pressure. "None of this, now," she said, and she and the other guard chuckled. "We wouldn't want anyone disrupting the meeting, after all."

· · · ·

Lee kept one hand braced against the wall as they made their way downstairs, shuddering at the feeling under her fingertips as brick gave way to stone, the rough-hewn rock covered with something wet and vaguely slimy. She hoped it was just mould.

The other hand, she kept on Bella's shoulder, relying on the vampire's keen senses to keep them moving forward through the darkness. Down, and down, and down some more, the stairs twisting this way and that as it followed the natural cracks, and Lee began imagining they were headed to the centre of the Earth.

"There," Bella said suddenly, still whispering. "Light, up ahead. And this place *reeks* of werewolf." Lee felt her turn under her fingertips, and she could hear the apologetic note in Bella's voice. "Not you."

"I got it." Lee's fingers tightened on her shoulder. "Can you tell how many?"

"No, but it's a lot. Blanchard's scent is everywhere, too, but it's not quite so recent."

They rounded the curve in the stairs, and gasped.

The dungeon, easily the size of three basketball courts, was low-ceilinged and dimly lit with witchlights encased in lanterns on the walls, damp with moss and slime of dubious origin. Lee wiped her hand on her jeans as they looked around, eyes wide in horror.

The left side of the cavern seemed to be an artificial greenhouse, a glass wall separating the main room from a secondary chamber full of all manner of strange plants.

In the middle of the main room was a trio of long wooden benches, each approximately fifty feet in length, covered with strange tools made of bronze and glass, beakers full of bubbling potions, vials full of what looked unnervingly like blood.

But the part that horrified them were the cages. Bars of silver set into hollowed out chambers barely the size of a walk-in closet lined the right side of the chamber, and werewolves of all manner of shapes and sizes and fur colours huddled within. There must have been fifty or so werewolves all together, a good number of them emaciated. There were some squashed three to a cage, the ones stuck pressed against the bars eerily silent, with festering wounds plastered against the silver, their fur long since burned away.

"Oh my god," Lee whispered, pressing her hand to her mouth. "*Bella...*"

Bella's face was grim. "I know," she said. She hesitated, before moving deeper into the room, swallowing. "But we need to find anything useful we can to break this spell, this curse, before we set them loose."

Lee limped after Bella, but she couldn't focus on the tables. Her gaze kept drifting back to the werewolves, horror coiling in her stomach. "They're suffering," she said desperately. "There's got to be something we can do, even if we can't free them..."

Bella shook her head, though she looked anguished. "Do what, exactly?" she said, examining the tables' contents. "If you can think of anything, I'm all ears, but we'll be helping them by doing our jobs."

Lee thought she was going to be sick, but she nodded. She decided to examine the greenhouses, partly to get as far away from the cages as possible, partly to see what sort of plants Blanchard was doubtless growing for her experiments. Glass cabinets lined the walls on either side of the greenhouse, full of dried bundles of plants and sprigs of herbs. Lee ran a finger over the labels, mouthing along as she read. *Belladonna. Stinging Nettle. Hogweed. Aconite...*

Lee paused, blinking at that last one.

"Bella?" she called over her shoulder. "Does wolfsbane have any effect on werewolves?"

No response.

The hairs on the back of Lee's neck rose, and she shifted into her lupine form, her hackles up.

The icy, sickly-sweet smell of Blanchard hit her nose immediately, and Lee whirled to see the magician kneeling at eye level with her, a chill filling the room to announce her presence.

"Let's find out!" Blanchard said, and blew a handful of powder at Lee's face.

The world wobbled and swayed, Lee's limbs growing heavy as she staggered on her paws, trying desperately to keep herself upright while Blanchard giggled at her.

She toppled sideways, asleep before she hit the floor.

· · · ·

Ariel's head snapped up when the door opened, and to his surprise, Augustus stepped in.

"What's all this I've been hearing about you, Ariel?" Augustus said, sounding disappointed as he approached. "You've been upsetting your poor mother before her trial?" He tapped his chin slowly, deliberately, and Ariel's gaze was drawn to the ruby ring on his finger.

The pieces clicked into place, and Ariel spat at him. "So this was what you were playing at, was it?" he snarled. "Set me up to help frame my own mother?"

"You were less easy to convince than I had hoped, if I'm being honest," Augustus said, stopping just outside of Ariel's reach were he to attempt a kick. "Though I suppose I might have gone a little overboard in nurturing her little grudge. Tell me," he added, and his grin widened, "how's the arm?"

Ariel froze, staring at him in horror. "No..."

Augustus brushed his thumb over the ring, and the illusion was dispelled. The vampire that stood before him was the spitting image of Beatrice, only with none of her warmth or charm.

"It was very kind of you to turn up to try and warn us, of course," Dragomir Ciobanu said, and his smile was that of a predatory snake. "I was beginning to think I would have to improvise. But now..."

One of his fingernails extended into a talon, and Ariel recoiled as the talon pressed against his neck, drawing blood. Dragomir held

253

his ring up to the wound, and Ariel struggled to see out of the corner of his eye as the droplet was absorbed into the gemstone. Darkness swirled around the vampire, and in his place stood a perfect replica of Ariel.

"*Fuck*," Ariel breathed as Dragomir began undoing the fastenings of his robes, dropping his clothing on the floor. Ariel spat and kicked when the vampires holding him down began peeling his clothes from his body, their gloves protecting them from his silver arm.

Dragomir's own arm looked like it was missing, but when he pulled on Ariel's clothes, he could see the way the sleeve filled out. All Dragomir needed was the glove to conceal his hand, and it really was the perfect disguise.

"I'm sure Arthur will understand when his darling grandson turns on him," Dragomir said, tugging the glove on and turning his hand this way and that to admire it. And then he winced, scratching at the back of his hand when the silver residue on the inside began to sting.

"You're not going to—!"

"Get away with this? Yes, yes, I've heard that one before." Dragomir turned to the guards with a cold smile that looked out of place on Ariel's face. "Feel free to eat this one, just save it until after I'm outside. I would hate for the screaming to disturb the proceedings."

Ariel knew he'd only get one shot at this, and his chest swelled like a bellows as he inhaled, preparing to yell a warning.

One of the guards punched him in the stomach, and the air wheezed its escape as Dragomir slipped outside, blue coat swishing behind him.

Chapter 34

L ee came to with a quiet groan. Her head pounded like the worst hangover of her life, and her limbs hurt so much it was like they'd gone numb. She forced her eyes open and terror shot through her when she realised she was strapped to an exam table, silver manacles clamped around her wrists and ankles. The skin around the edges was raw and weeping blood.

"Oh, good, you're awake," Blanchard said, and then she was hovering over Lee, grabbing Lee's jaw to turn her head. "I was beginning to wonder if I'd gotten the dosage wrong."

"Where's Bella?" Lee croaked.

"Oh," Blanchard said, giving an exaggerated pout. "How cute. You're *worried* about her! Very well, then," she said, stepping away with a sweep of her arm to show Lee Bella's prone form, face down on the grimy floor of one of the cages with a wooden stake in her back.

Lee's adrenaline spiked, and it was all she could do to keep calm, repeating to herself that Bella had been staked before, Bella was going to be okay, Bella had been staked before, Bella was going to be okay—

"Oh, she'll be *okay* for now," Blanchard said, and Lee realised she'd been mouthing it to herself. "But only because I promised someone that he would get the privilege of killing her himself. You, though, you *fascinate* me."

"Oh, yeah?" Lee asked, even as she tried to think how she could stall for time; Maria could show others to the entrance, when they didn't come back, there was still a chance they could be rescued...

Blanchard never broke her pace as she worked. "Oh, 'yeah,'" she repeated mockingly. "The Montgomery and the granddaughter of darling Dragomir, I could understand, but you? You're nothing. Unwanted, unloved, through no fault of your own..." She still didn't

255

pause as she glanced up at Lee. "We're not so different in that regard, you and I."

"Oh, god," Lee said, and began laughing, more than a little hysterically. "Are you *monologuing* at me?"

Blanchard matched her laughter before becoming icily serious again. "I find it soothing." She lifted the chalice with the potion to her lips, drinking deeply.

"Christ." Lee let her head fall back. "You ever consider keeping a journal or something? Seems like an easier way than kidnapping people and locking them up!"

"But nowhere near as much fun." Blanchard stepped forward, holding a long, thin tool that looked very much like a silvered ice pick.

"What're you gonna do with that, lobotomise me?" Lee asked lightly, though terror shot through her at the idea. "Trust me, you'd be doing me a favour."

"Nothing so barbaric." Blanchard plunged the pick into Lee's forearm between the bones of her wrist, and Lee screamed, her back arching off the table as she strained to get away, and her scream stretched on at the agony caused by the bindings.

The pick was jerked free and Blanchard pinched the tip with two fingers, slowly swiping upwards so the blood puddled on her fingertips.

Lee braced herself for the second stab in the other arm, pressing her lips together before the scream tore free.

Blanchard began chanting, and Lee felt her blood beginning to *move*, pumping around her body to flow from the wounds and float into the air, directed by Blanchard to wait as the mage coldly stabbed herself, first in the left arm, then in the right. Her own blood flowed out to mingle with Lee's in the air, and then darkness surrounded the blood, enveloping it.

And then, all at once, it vanished, and a tiny, sparkling ruby dropped into Blanchard's hand.

This was it. This *had* to be it.

Lee remembered Blanchard's necklace and flinched at the thought of how many rubies the thing contained.

"Still yourself," she purred to Lee, and Lee felt the brush of something cold against her mind at the order. She forced herself to hold still, hoping Blanchard couldn't hear her still-racing heart. "You'll have a part to play soon enough, my pet."

Lee struggled not to react to the feeling of the silver bindings snapping open, nor to the shadowy tendrils lifting her limp form off the table, carrying her toward the cages. She was thrown inside, and the door slammed shut.

"No more holding back," Blanchard said, and Lee felt that brush against her mind again, urging her to transform.

Lee only had a split second to consider if she wanted to risk faking being unable to control her transformations, but panicked and transformed as she normally did.

Blanchard clapped her hands together. "Another full mooner!" she said delightedly. "I was ever so sad to lose the others, you know. I hope you're proud of yourself. You can make it up to me by... eating your little friend."

Lee's bind went blank as she slowly approached Bella, trying to think how she was going to get out of this one—

Blanchard giggled to herself, turning and spinning on the spot. "I do like it when they fight it," she said to nobody in particular. "Here, I'll play nice: forget your friend, just throw yourself against the bars like the good little animal you are—"

Lee hurled herself at the bars, snarling, spittle flying from her mouth as the bars reacted to her touch with a sickening sizzle and the stench of burning fur and flesh.

"Stop that," Blanchard scolded, and actually swatted Lee across the nose. She yipped and fell back, tail tucked between her legs. "Bad dog!"

Lee didn't react, though she seethed inside.

When we get out of this, I'm tearing your throat out myself.

Blanchard crouched outside the bars, and there was a look that almost could have been... pity?

"Not much longer now," she said, and examined the ruby between her fingers before closing her hand in a fist. "Sit."

Lee sat.

"Stay."

Lee didn't move.

Blanchard's lips curled in that unpleasant smile of hers. "Good dog."

She disappeared in a flurry of snowflakes, and Lee reverted back, her hands fluttering anxiously over Bella. Her first instinct was to rip the stake out, but when—not if, *when* Blanchard returned, she might well decide to check up on them, and there was no way Lee was going to re-stake Bella for the sake of a ruse.

"I'll get that out of you before she teleports us out," Lee promised, her fingers lingering near the base of the stake, feeling like she was going to be sick. "Soon as she does, get out of here, go to the council chambers. It's the rubies, Bella. She mixed our blood, mine and hers, and made this ruby. Looked just like the ones in her necklace and everything. I'd bet we'll have to destroy them to free the werewolves..."

She sighed and shuddered, leaving her hand on Bella's back. "This can't be how it all ends for us," she said softly. "Not after everything that's happened."

Lee glanced down at Bella. "I love you," she said softly, and transformed back to wait, resting her nose on her paws.

She wondered if Bella would have said it back if she could.

Chapter 35

D ragomir had taken Ariel's weapons along with his clothes, but that was just an annoying setback. A very, very annoying setback.

"Hold onto his arm for me," one of the guards said as she sniffed at Ariel's neck.

"Why do you get to drink first?" the second guard whined. "Hunters always have the *best* blood."

"Because I called dibs," the first guard said, and sank her teeth into Ariel's neck.

This was hardly the first time he'd been bitten by a vampire, and though the pleasure crashed through his body like a hot, surging wave, Ariel still had enough presence of mind left to him when the vampire let go of his arm to tug his head further to the side for a better angle, wrapping her legs around his waist.

Ariel smacked the quick release for his prosthetic, and the second guard yelped and let go in surprise when he twisted, catching the arm before it hit the floor. He then proceeded to beat the one latched onto his neck about her head and face.

She shrieked and let go, falling to the floor as she threw her arms up to protect herself, angry silver burns swelling on her skin. The second guard recovered from his shock just in time for Ariel to lock the prosthetic back in place and lunge forward, plunging his fingers into the guard's eyes. The inhuman screech that tore from the guard's throat would not bring them any help; Dragomir, after all, had made well sure of that.

Ariel left that guard clutching at the bloody mess that had once been his eyeballs, turning just in time to block the first guard when she lunged at his back, turning her momentum against her as he flipped her over his shoulder.

She might have been inhumanly strong, but she was still light enough for Ariel to bodily hurl into a table with a loud crunching noise, and he dived on top of her, snatching up a splintered chunk of wood and driving it into her heart. He broke off a second piece and much more calmly staked the eyeless vampire, whose mouth locked open in a silent scream.

With the vampires sufficiently incapacitated, Ariel hooked the prosthetic's cables back up to his elbow before beginning to search them for the hunters' knives they'd doubtlessly stolen. Upon finding one, he made short work of finishing them off.

He snatched up one of the silver chains as he sprinted toward the council chambers, bare feet slapping against the cold stone.

• • • •

Lee had never been teleported before, but Maria's description gave her enough warning to lunge, grabbing the stake in her teeth and tearing it free as the cold overcame her.

She caught a glimpse of Bella's terrified face before the world went dark.

• • • •

Bella wasted no time in turning to mist, escaping through the bars and up the stairs, where she reverted to her human form, tucking her arms against her sides in the hopes of going faster as she flew across the city.

• • • •

There were all sorts of dramatic ways Ariel had envisioned stopping the High Council's proceedings, but bursting in, covered in blood and dressed only in his boxer briefs was not on the list.

Oh, well. Not like he hadn't done weirder things on stage.

"She's innocent!" he yelled, racing past the stunned audience members. "Blanchard and Dragomir are controlling the—!"

Ashley stumbled back, her jewellery thrumming with energy, a sinister red glow that seemed to radiate darkness rather than light, and Dragomir caught Ashley, steadying her.

"It's okay, Mom," he said, and smiled. "Neve is coming."

Snow filled the chamber and with it came the werewolves, and Ariel thought he'd be sick when he spotted a familiar flash of orange fur among them.

Everything was going wrong.

The assembled audience screamed, civilians making a break for the exit as the werewolves ripped into any nearby bystander—every werewolf but one.

Lee's lithe, coppery form fought against the crowd, snapping and snarling at anything that blocked the way between her and Blanchard, but it was like fighting back the tide itself.

Arthur, though far from the prime of his life, reacted first, likely thanks to decades of hunter training. His cane leapt into his hand, and he drew a sword from within, cutting down the first werewolf that lunged at him.

"Arthur!" Ashley screamed, falling back, and Ariel realised in horror that she would have been disarmed before her trial. He sprinted forward and got a running jump, chain cracking down on one of the werewolves' heads. It snarled as its chin hit the floor, and Ariel planted a foot on its broad, flat skull as it reared back, trying to shake him off. He used the momentum to leap on top of the writhing mass of bodies, racing over their backs towards the high table.

"LEE!" he bellowed over the din, and Lee met his eyes.

She was ready when he reached her, and she flung her head back, sending Ariel flying before continuing fighting her way towards Blanchard.

The Sanguine Lords' High Council representative was nowhere to be seen, likely fled in the chaos, and the Lunar Delegation's could have been any one of the writhing bodies for all Ariel knew. As for the Arcane Conclave, Terry Nelson and Agnes Blair pressed themselves against the wall, Terry's glasses half-hanging off his nose as Arthur cut down werewolf after werewolf that lunged at him.

Ariel cracked the chain whip at one of the werewolves that snapped at his ankle, and the werewolf yipped, falling back as Ariel landed on top of the council table in a crouch.

"Alright, Pop-Pop?" he panted, and grunted, rolling backwards to avoid a swipe of claws.

"You turn up at your mother's trial in your bloody underwear and that's all you have to say?" Arthur called, and turned to grin over his shoulder, his moustache twitching. "It's good to see you, my boy!"

"The werewolves are being controlled by Blanchard, they're not doing this willingly," Ariel said, and snapped the chain in a series of rapid cracks, driving another pair of wolves back.

"That would have been nice to know earlier!" Arthur said, and turned to slam the pommel of his cane sword down on another werewolf's head, causing it to go cross-eyed.

Ashley's scream made the both of them swing around, and Ariel's mouth went dry when he realised Dragomir had her in a tight grip, Ariel's own knife pressed to his mother's throat.

"Now then," Dragomir hissed, when a cloud of fog came flying into the room above the heads of the feral wolves.

Bella reformed and shot down to tackle her grandfather away from Ashley, and he dropped the knife as the two of them grappled with each other. Bella was strong from all the blood packs she'd had beforehand, but Dragomir had clearly not been following the feeding regulations he'd so meticulously laid out for his kin. He

262

snarled, his disguise falling away, and the pair went flying higher and higher towards the ceiling as they fought to gain the upper hand.

A scream pierced the battle.

For a moment, everything stopped when Lee sank her teeth into Blanchard's shoulder, snarling and hanging on for dear life.

The werewolves paused in their attack, frozen, twitching, fighting against Blanchard's control as she struggled to throw Lee off of her. The blood gem in Blanchard's fist slipped from between her fingers to roll across the floor, getting lost among the scattered, broken chairs.

Bella disengaged from the battle, shooting down towards Ashley, reaching for the blood rubies that hung around her throat.

Ariel and Arthur took a moment to catch their breaths, scratched but not bitten, and in that moment, the two shared a smile.

Dragomir appeared behind Arthur and punched through his spine, ripping out his heart.

Bella smashed the necklace between her hands, and as Ashley screamed, paralysed by the scene before her, Bella pulled the earrings off and crushed those, too, with her fingers.

The spell broke, and the werewolves shook themselves, panic sweeping the room as they realised what had happened. Panic—and fury.

"Dragomir, to me!" Blanchard shrieked, and Ariel watched, as if in slow motion, as Dragomir withdrew his hand, dripping with Arthur's blood.

The crushed heart fell to the floor, and Arthur's body crumpled.

Dragomir flew across the room and wrenched Lee's jaws open before he flung her aside, and he and Blanchard disappeared in a flurry of snow.

Chapter 36

L ee rolled the blood ruby between her fingers, her expression
pensive.

It would be time to leave soon, and she hadn't even packed so
much as a sock, let alone enough clothes for a trip overseas. For how
long, she didn't know.

Tenebrous was in an uproar. Dragomir returned from the dead,
Arthur Montgomery slain by his hand, Blanchard with the power to
turn werewolves feral, and who knew what else?

And now, Blanchard and Dragomir were on the run together.

The Night Treaty was still officially in place, but there was no
telling how much longer that would last. It seemed like war would be
breaking out any day, now.

There was a knock on the door, and Lee jumped off the bed,
snagging the suitcase Ariel had bought for her and beginning to
haphazardly throw in her clothes. "I'm almost done," she lied as Ariel
and Bella came inside.

"Bullshit," Ariel said, sitting beside her. "But, whatever. Flight
leaves whenever we do, after all."

"Ah, the perks of being rich," Bella added, setting Lee's new and
very hastily ordered passport on the bed next to the suitcase. "What
were you doing while we were out, anyway? Daydreaming?"

She still hadn't told them she'd gone back for the blood ruby,
her blood ruby, after the initial confusion was over and the council
rooms closed while everyone tried to figure out what to do next. She
knew she would have to, and certainly planned to, but it didn't seem
like now was the right time. Ariel and Bella had enough to worry
about.

"Something like that," Lee said, ducking her head to kiss Bella.
"Missing you guys."

She didn't kiss Ariel, though she did hug him tightly, resting her chin on his shoulder. "Been alright?"

"About as good as anyone planning a funeral can be," Ariel said quietly, hugging her back. "Not like Pop-Pop and I were really close after everything, it just..." He let out a slow breath. "Never mind. But thanks for asking, anyway." He drew back slightly, eyeing Lee's suitcase. "You, uh... want help with packing?"

Lee almost bristled before taking a deep breath and shrugging. "I mean, I wouldn't say no," she said. After a moment, she cleared her throat. "Never really had anything to pack that didn't fit in a garbage bag before, so..."

Ariel's fingers lightly brushed against the small of her back as he moved to help, and Bella hopped up to sit on the bed, her legs swinging slowly as she watched. "Are you *sure* it's such a good idea for me and Lee to go?" she asked, finally voicing the question she and Lee had both been too nervous to ask.

"No," Ariel said, handing Lee her flannel, which she tugged on. "But if the treaty's going to have any shot at staying in place, if we're going to have any chance at preventing all-out war, people need to see that we can still live in peace, and that's where we come in."

"You don't think they'll be upset that a Montgomery's got a vampire *and* a werewolf for... partners?" Lee asked, biting her lip. The word still felt strange to say, but not unpleasant. Definitely not unpleasant.

"Wouldn't be the first," Ariel said, and paused. "...Maybe the first at the same time, but it ain't exactly a new concept to anyone in Tenebrous, so they can get fucked if they have a problem with it."

"You're cute when you're grumpy at the world," Bella said, and Ariel snorted, though the tips of his ears slowly turned pink.

Bella leaned forward to press her forehead against Ariel's, and he closed his eyes, sighing softly when Lee leaned in as well.

"Right now, no more monsters, no more magic," Lee murmured. "Just a couple of college students... getting ready to go to a funeral."

"Out of all the ways to get a break from studying," Ariel muttered.

"Nothing says we have to keep studying," Lee pointed out, and Ariel and Bella drew away, Ariel raising an eyebrow. "Actually, I... I don't know that I want to. Not now that Blanchard and Dragomir are at large." She rubbed the back of her neck. "Just seems like there's more important things to be worrying about."

Bella opened her mouth, but Ariel, sensing a conversation they didn't have time for, held up his hand. "We'll talk about it on the plane," he said, and turned his attention back to the suitcase.

Lee tuned Bella and Ariel out as they discussed travel plans. Her mind wandered to the future, but over and over, her thoughts kept returning to the blood ruby that lay heavy in her pocket.

Winchmore Hill Village 1780 - 1

Contents

General

'Diary' Section

Sub Section on Edmonton Enclosure (E. E.) Act of 1800

Enclosure Maps Sub Section

Contents

Winchmore Hill Village 1780 - 1830
List of Illustrations and Plates

Front cover: St. Paul's Church, Church Hill sketched by Peter Brown.

Back cover: Cottages at the base of Church Hill sketched by Peter Brown.

Introduction

Twenty years have now elapsed since Regency Press published my small soft back *A History of Winchmore Hill.* This was the first known attempt at a chronological history of the old village, pieced together from numerous sources. For some of the eras covered I would have struggled to add much more detail, but for other periods I had already accumulated enough material to expand on what I wrote then. I was always hopeful that if my health held up I could return to certain periods and produce further books on these, and this volume of over two hundred larger sized pages shines the spotlight on the late Georgian period. We are particularly lucky here, because of the wonderfully detailed work that surrounded the Edmonton Enclosure Act of 1800.

Historically Winchmore Hill was in both the Manor and Parish of Edmonton. Pretty well every square foot, if not inch, of the area was mapped under the Act, and the ownership of each land holding indicated. We must be very grateful for the documentation of that map and schedule of ownership by William Robinson in his *History of Edmonton* in 1819, along with other historical information which he supplied. Without his comprehensive work our knowledge of the area would be considerably diminished.

The period 1780 – 1830 was an era of religious change. In 1780 the Test Act was still on the Statute Book, making the Church of England supreme, although at that time the only places of worship in the hamlet were a small Independent Chapel on The Green, and a late 17th century Quaker Meeting House at the top of what we now call Church Hill. In 1790 this failing structure was replaced by a new one. Then in the late 1820s St. Paul's Church, captured on the front cover, was built nearby. Both buildings, fortunately, have withstood the advances of the property developers, as have a few other old buildings, including the charming old cottages at the foot of Church Hill illustrated on the rear cover. By 1830 there was no longer a bar on Catholics sitting in Parliament, and the new University College London had opened its doors to people of all faiths.

Life then must have been quite hard, especially given the colder climate. We would consider that there was a lack of democracy, with severe restrictions on who could vote for an MP to sit in the House of Commons. However, in that respect it might be that the people then were not so much worse off as all that. Most people didn't pay the Westminster Government any Income Tax, for example.

Today much of our legislation emanates from our even more remote Government in Brussels, where only the unelected Commissioners, who meet in secret and whose accounts are mired in controversy, can propose new laws. These proposals are considered by a Council of Ministers, who also meet in secret, and a Brussels Parliament where members usually have only a short time to speak. In both the Council of Ministers and Parliament the British representation only amounts to about 8% of the total. Daniel Hannan, who sits in Brussels for the Conservatives, estimates that 84% of our laws are made in this manner, and a recent newsletter by the Southgate District Civic Trust explained that the way that benches on The Green at Winchmore Hill were being replaced was restricted partly by what had been decided in Brussels. (My octogenarian Uncle tells me that this is not what he thought he was fighting for on the Normandy beaches!)

Two hundred years ago those eligible might pay for the upkeep of the local poor, and pay national taxes of sorts, along with the Church's tithes. They might also be fined in the local Manor Courts, which were under the jurisdiction of the

Lord or Lady of the Manor. However, the villagers were well represented in these Courts, and affairs were conducted in open public gatherings, under well worn procedures. One wonders if the locals then would have felt any worse governed than we do now. Perhaps they felt that the 'decision making' most affecting their lives was actually more local, open and accountable than we do today! Although I certainly can't pretend to fully understand all the Manorial and other local documents I have unearthed from that era, I still think they make fascinating reading, and hope the reader does too.

Having said all that, even in a rural area like Winchmore Hill, where much was decided locally, people would still feel the affects of national and even international events. I have therefore tried to set local events in a broader context. The War with France, the Corn Laws, and such like, would have had some sort of impact on the villagers. Perhaps the best thing to do is to stop now, and invite the reader to enter the foreign land of two hundred years ago, by working his or her way through what is mainly a chronological account.

Before I finish the introduction, however, I should like to thank everyone who has aided me. This book has taken a number of years to research and write, so I couldn't possibly here acknowledge every person or organisation to have helped. I hope that no one out there will bear any kind of grudge if I list here only the 'major players'.

In the public domain my main sources have been the Friends Meeting House in Euston Road, the Guildhall Library, the London Metropolitan Archives (often abbreviated in this volume to LMA), the National Archives in Kew (often abbreviated to NA), and Enfield Library Service's Local History Unit (often abbreviated to LHU), where Graham Dalling and Kate Godfrey were the personnel who helped me. Graham has also kindly consented, as outgoing Local History Officer, to the publication of various items, and the use of the Unit's version of the Edmonton Enclosure Award Maps, which I copied and amended on my home computer to produce the maps in this volume (which are not to scale).

Ten years ago the then editor of *The Enfield Gazette* Aaron Gransby was good enough to let me go through the paper's archives, copy what I wanted, and publish as I saw fit. My thanks to Mr. Gransby and *The Gazette* for letting me quote from their articles, and publish their material. During the course of this book I sometimes abbreviate *The Palmers Green and Southgate Gazette* to *P.G. & S. Gazette*. The Southgate District Civic Trust, through the offices of Peter Hodge, have also been good enough to supply me with material for publication.

With regard to private individuals, Professor D. Olver long ago supplied me with valuable material on the local Friends. Earlier in the decade Sheila, widow of the late Alan Dumayne, invited me to use any papers I wanted from his archives. Nearly a year ago Pauline Holstius kindly offered me the excellent local material in her collection, whilst just before Christmas Stewart Christian was equally as generous in letting me use whatever I chose from the David Hicks archives, left in his custody following the sad death of that well known local figure. No one knew more about Winchmore Hill than David, so it was particularly sad that he should succumb to illness before he had the chance to write the comprehensive book he was capable of. Finally I should like to thank Peter Brown for his kindness in supplying his evocative sketches for publication.

Stuart Delvin
March 2009

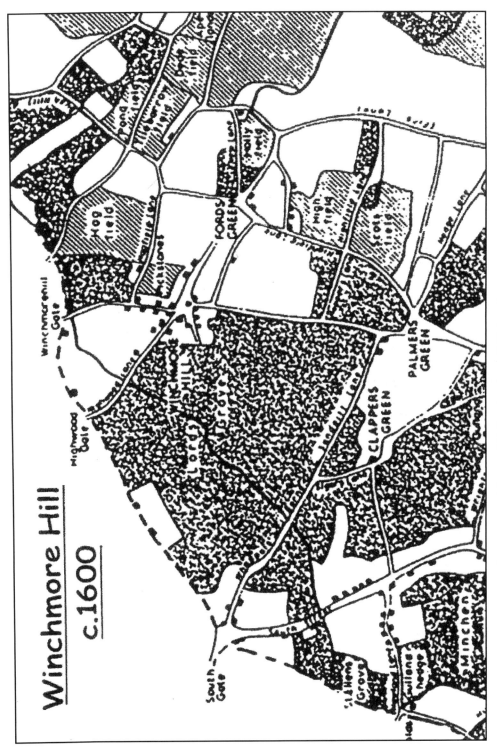

Winchmore Hill
c.1600

Figure 1. Map of Winchmore Hill in about 1600

Detail of the map 'Edmonton c. 1600', reproduced from A History of Middlesex, Vol. V (Oxford University Press 1976), p.132, by permission of the Executive Editor. The shaded areas with diagonal lines are the old common fields. The Green is near Pickstones field and the Broadway of today is near Fords Green. Sandpitt Lane is now Bourne Hill. Many of the lanes shown preceded today's roads.

1

General Section
Before 1780

My small 1989 softback entitled, *A History of Winchmore Hill* outlined the history of the old village from earliest times until the present day, so for more detail on the years prior to 1780, please see that book. The following is but a brief summary of events in those early years.

I am unaware of any finds from Roman times in Winchmore Hill itself, but there have been various successes in surrounding areas, and so it seems likely that there were people in what is now Winchmore Hill, two thousand years ago.

At the time of the Domesday Survey of 1086 the County of Middlesex was divided into hundreds for administrative purposes. Edmonton Hundred contained the manors of Enfield, Edmonton and Tottenham. Although there was no mention of Winchmore Hill in the Domesday Book, if the village existed it would have been included in the return for Edmonton Manor.

Noone knows the full story of the village's origins, but in 1319 it was known as Wynsemerhull, and the Vikers family had a house there in 1349. However, there is reference to a Yarildesfeld in the first half of the 13th century, when it was associated with a William de Forde, and we know from later references that the field was in the heart of the village. It could be that de Forde and Vikers have their names commemorated in the modern roads of Fords Grove and Vicars Moor Lane. There is also reference, in 13th century documents, to Hegfeld, which we shall see later, was one of the common fields, i.e. fields used in common by the villagers, rather than private property.

From those times, and no doubt many centuries before, Southgate, and the higher western portions of Winchmore Hill and Enfield, were given over to woodland, as part of the Forest of Middlesex. The stand of trees in Grovelands Park is a remnant of this forest. Part of the Forest was enclosed as a private hunting ground in, or around, 1136. The 8,000 acres lay entirely in the Manor of Enfield, but citizens of Edmonton retained the right to use this area to winter their pigs and take firewood. From at least 1322 the enclosed hunting ground was known as Enfield Chase.

By Elizabethan times the hamlet was based on a woodland economy. At Figure 1 is a map of the area in about 1600 from the Victoria County History (VCH) of Middlesex. This shows the local common fields of Hagfield, Pickstones, Tilebarrow (with Pondfield to its north), Dede Field, Holly Field, Highfield and Scotsfield. David Pam has additionally identified Broomfield, between 'Highfield Road' and 'Farm Road'. (At P5 of his 1819 book, Robinson says that only Hag Field, Dead Field, High Field and Scotch Field – as he calls them – remained at Enclosure 200 years later.)

From the VCH map it is clear how much of the area was wooded. Lords Grove, of which the stand of trees in Grovelands Park is a remnant, was in private hands. Much of it belonged to Queen Elizabeth's chief advisor Sir William Cecil, who she made Lord Burghley in 1571. He held about 230 acres. Apart from underpinning activities such as furniture making, the woods of Winchmore Hill allowed the villagers to produce charcoal, which supported the tanners of Edmonton. We don't know how long the local woodland industry thrived for. By the mid 18th century Lord's Grove estate was owned by the Third Duke of Chandos, who lived nearby at Minchenden House on Southgate Green (see Plate 58).

There was no physical Church of England presence in Winchmore Hill in 1780. There were, however, two religious places of worship that we are aware of at this 'starting point'. The Quakers had established a presence on the site of their current grounds on 'Church Hill' in the 1680s. The Independents were also worshiping in the village by the 1780s, reputedly, at The Green. Their prayers continue in the United Reformed Church in Compton Road.

In 1780 Winchmore Hill was a Middlesex hamlet, dominated by rich local landowners like the Teshmakers and Lakes, in which religion was important.

The Monarchy

George 111 was born on 4th June 1738, and crowned on 22nd September 1761, following the death of his grandfather, George 11, on 25th October 1760. He was the son of Frederick, Prince of Wales and, in contrast to his two Hanoverian predecessors, was English by birth. Initially sulky, idle and seemingly dim, by his late teens he had turned into a paragon of hard work and self discipline.

George 111 was a stubborn man, but also very religious. One of his first acts as king was to issue a proclamation against immorality. In this respect his only lapse seems to have been his rumoured 1757 marriage to a shoemaker's daughter named Hannah Lightfoot. He was musical, fluent in French and German, a competent draughtsman, and an avid reader, especially of history. He developed a great interest in farming and botany, earning him the nickname of 'Farmer George'. Following his marriage to Charlotte of Mecklenburg - Strelitz, eleven months after his accession, he fathered 15 children.

In 1788, George had his first attack of madness, which has since been ascribed to the blood disease porphyria. He recovered in 1789, and the execution of King Louis XVI of France on 21st January 1793, perhaps caused him some concern. English audiences demanded that the curtain be brought down in theatres, and performances abandoned. Every member of the House of Commons wore mourning dress, and crowds surrounded George's coach, crying 'War with France'. In the event, the French Republic took the initiative by declaring war on 1st February!

George, Prince of Wales, George 111's eldest son, was born on 12th August 1762, and became a dedicated follower of fashion. In his youth he was handsome, intelligent, charming, and a brilliant mimic. Unfortunately he thought his father mean and puritanical, whilst his father considered his son nothing better than a pampered layabout. The Prince led a faction of the radical opposition Whig Party into a coalition with the Tory Pitt, urging war as a Monarchist country against Republican France. This split the Whigs irretrievably, and condemned them to the political wilderness for a generation.

Despite his 'morality', like many of his Protestant subjects, George 111 was implacably opposed to the emancipation of Roman Catholics. When William Pitt the Younger, attempted to introduce a Catholic Emancipation Act in 1801, Pitt was forced to resign as Prime Minister. George III also represented other British qualities of that era - simplicity, sincerity, and commonsense. He undoubtedly had the common touch, and the Southgate writer Leigh Hunt called him, 'a royal John Bull'. His Golden Jubilee on 25th October 1810 was an astonishing success, with illuminations, fireworks, and dancing in the streets.

Unfortunately, that very day, George, who had already had two mysterious episodes of mental infirmity, began his tragic descent into a permanent world of madness, blindness and senility. He spent the rest of his life a prisoner in Windsor Castle while his eldest son ruled as Prince Regent, his powers being limited by Parliament. The Prince's expensive tastes were, however, undimmed, and it was at this time that the mock oriental Royal Pavilion in Brighton was created for him by John Nash, who had designed our own Grovelands.

George 111 died on 29th January 1820, and his eldest son ruled in his own right as George 1V. He was crowned on 19th July 1821, his coronation being the most lavish known to that date. He was uninterested in his public duties, preferring wine, women and song – and debt. In 1785 he had 'married' a widow, Maria Fitzherbert, and although he subsequently took mistresses, she was the abiding love of his life. It transpired that this marriage was illegal, and in 1795 George was forced into a disastrous marriage to his first cousin, Princess Caroline of Brunswick. However, the relationship was consummated, and a daughter, Princess Charlotte, was born nine months later (though she died in 1817). The couple were never divorced, but separated soon afterwards, and lived apart until Caroline's death in 1821. George attempted to keep Caroline out of England and tried to use Parliament to indict her for her many adulteries.

George IV's health declined as he washed down vast amounts of food with even larger quantities of alcohol, accompanied by laudanum. He died, unlamented, at Windsor on 26th June 1830, leaving his building project of Buckingham Palace still to be completed. He was succeeded by his eldest surviving brother, the 64 year old Duke of Clarence, who became William IV.

Governance

The way the country was Governed changed in the late 18th century. Decision making moved from the King having an important say, to the Prime Minister working with his Cabinet and answering to Parliament. Until the Reform Act of 1832, Middlesex was represented by two MPs, who were elected only by Freeholders whose estates were worth 40/- or more per annum.

David Pam and C. W. Whitaker, in his *History of Enfield,* explain that in England local Government evolved in something of a haphazard manner. A parish, such as Edmonton, would have its own priest, parson, or parish clergyman, to whom tithes (explained in a later section) and ecclesiastical dues were paid. The parish was initially governed by an "Open" Vestry and, for Poor Law purposes, by Overseers, appointed under an Act of 1601. The "Open" Vestry allowed any ratepayer to take part in the deliberations, but under an adoptive Act of 1819 Vestries became "Select", that is, composed of representatives duly elected by the ratepayers. The Vestry met under the presidency of the Vicar, with the Churchwardens as his principal officers.

Until the late 16th century local affairs were mainly managed by a meeting of tenants at the manor courts of the principal manors, Enfield and Edmonton. These were not religious in nature, but in the late 16th century many of the administrative functions of the manor came to be controlled by the Parish Church Vestries, their actions being sanctioned by Justices of the Peace. The system of local government by vestry lasted almost in tact until 1834, when the Board of Guardians of the Edmonton Union was set up to take over the care of the poor. In 1850 Select Vestries were replaced by Local Boards of Health, which in 1894 were in turn succeeded by Urban District Councils.

JFC Harrison in his *Early Victorian Britain 1832 – 51* tells us that ever since Elizabethan times the gentry, through the institution of the Justices of the Peace, had provided the crucial element in the government of rural England. Sitting on the local bench they dispensed rough and ready justice to their tenants and villagers. At the quarter sessions in the local county town they tried more serious cases, and dealt with administrative chores. At the Brewster Sessions they supervised the licensing of public houses. There could be wide differences in wealth and social prestige between the nobility and the 'squirearchy', but together they formed a group of privileged landowners – 'the gentlemen of England'.

In his *Middlesex* Michael Robbins says that in the towns standards sometimes dropped, and the 'trading justices' of Middlesex got a very bad reputation. The first effective measure to get rid of the 'trading justices' was the Middlesex and Surrey Justices Act of 1782, which established a stipendiary magistracy and regulated its relations with those responsible for enforcing the law.

The Gazette of 7th October 2004 contained an article by David Sanderson which told us that before Sir Robert Peel's Metropolitan Police Act of 1929, one *1829* unarmed, unpaid, able-bodied citizen would be responsible for patrolling his parish. The 1829 Act changed the face of policing, and created a structure which still serves the capital's people today. From the start they were dressed in civilian blue, and in their early years they wore top hats. (At this time Winchmore Hill was not yet under the Metropolitan Police.)

That is the general picture. However, as the reader works through the diary section, it becomes clear from local Manorial records that much of what happened in Winchmore Hill still involved the Manorial Courts during our era of interest.

Politics of the Era

The polling place for the County of Middlesex was removed from Hampstead Heath to Brentford at the end of the 17th century. The electorate was of freeholders whose estate had to exceed 40/- in value. The County returned two MPs, and during the century before the Reform Act of 1832, Middlesex had a reputation for returning radical MPs. In 1774 John Wilkes was elected Mayor of London, and returned unopposed as an MP for Middlesex, retaining his seat until 1790.

When George 111 succeeded his grandfather in 1760, Britain was held in great international esteem, and the American colonies were still devoted to the mother country. However, after the surrender of Cornwallis to Washington at Yorktown in October 1781, the war with America was virtually at an end. It also brought the system of personal government by the King to an end too. The House of Commons accepted, without a division, a strongly worded motion against the continuance of the war, and following Lord North's resignation as Tory Prime Minister, in March 1782, Britain has never been governed by a monarch's wishes. North was succeeded by Lord Rockingham, who in turn was replaced later in the year by the Earl of Shelbourne, both being Whigs (forerunners of the Liberals). The latter was instrumental in concluding peace with the new United States.

The first decade of Pitt the Younger's Tory Ministry (1783-93) established the Cabinet as a body answerable not to the king, but to the House of Commons. The Whigs had begun to demand civil rights for Roman Catholics. Pitt, in 1787, and again in 1789, opposed the abolition of the Test and Corporation Acts which debarred some Protestant as well as Catholic Dissenters from civil office. In 1790 the Whig George Byng of Wrotham Park was elected as an MP for the County, retaining his seat until 1847.

5

Thomas Paine started a democratic movement among a section of the working class. His 'Rights of Man' (1791-2) declared that all hereditary government, whether by King or Lords, was 'an imposition on mankind', and that all power was derived from the people. He demanded that a properly representative chamber should be established immediately. For years to come, Paine's unpopular Republicanism tarnished all liberal causes.

In January 1793 the French decapitated their monarch, and the following month declared war on England. The ruling class was so frightened that it over – reacted to the perceived threats. In 1794 a charge of High Treason was instituted against shoemaker Thomas Hardy, the founder of the Corresponding Society, and the principal leader of the constitutional movement amongst the working classes. Other innocuous and respectable people, like Thelwall and Home Tooke were similarly charged. The jury acquitted the accused on the capital charge, perhaps saving England from public turmoil.

However, the government managed to curtail political discussion for many years to come. The Corresponding and other Societies were suppressed by an Act of Parliament. *Habeas Corpus* was suspended in 1794, and many men against whom there was no evidence were kept in prison for years. Public meetings were prohibited, except for the anti-slave-trade movement, which for a time declined. Pitt's Combination Acts (1799-1800) were another manifestation of the repressive spirit of the times. These made Trade Unionism illegal, and punished all combinations of wage earners, effectively putting the employee into his master's hands. It was not until 1823 that they were repealed. The Tory Henry Addington succeeded Pitt as Prime Minister in 1801, until Pitt returned to that office for another two years in 1804.

In the General Election of 1802 the Whig George Byng of Wrotham Park retained his seat. Local people voted en masse for the free thinking, reforming, radical Independent candidate Francis Burdett, and he was returned as the County's second MP. Jubilant crowds ran through the streets after his apparent victory, and he had a celebratory dinner at *The Kings Head* in Enfield. However, the election was declared void in 1804 owing to irregularities in the election process, and in the 1804 re – run he lost by five votes. Later in life he became a Conservative MP for North Wiltshire. In 1806 the Tory William Mellish, who owned land locally, was returned alongside Byng, and sat in the Commons until 1820.

For a year immediately after Pitt's death, in his 40s, in 1806, there was a coalition Ministry of 'All the Talents', led by the Whig Lord Grenville, which included the dying Charles Fox. In 1807, with William Wilberforce as the driving force, the slave trade was abolished by an Act of Parliament. The purely Tory sub factions combined after 1807 to govern the country and fight Napoleon, and there wasn't another Whig Prime Minister until Earl Grey, who obtained office from 1830 – 34. The Tory Duke of Portland was Premier from 1807-9, and Spencer Perceval from 1809 – 12.

In 1812 Perceval was assassinated in the Lobby of the House of Commons by an insane merchant named Francis Bellingham (see Plate 61), to be succeeded by Lord Liverpool, who remained in office until 1827. Local author Tom Mason tells us that Woodside House on The Green was for a period let to various tenants. One of them was reputedly the son of the said Bellingham, though he assumed his mother's maiden name of Neville. Miss Cresswell says that Neville cut a sad, eccentric figure, and died sleeping in a room with a charcoal stove.

The Napoleonic struggle over 22 years led to a national death toll of about 100,000, along with economic suffering, though this was not evenly divided across society. The upper class thrived on enhanced rents, and paid too small a proportion of the war taxes, because revenue was largely raised by duties on articles of consumption, which hit the poor disproportionately hard. Pitt's Income Tax of 1798, which was continued with a very short break until the end of the war, did something, but not enough, to redress the balance. In 1815 £25 million was raised by direct, and £67 million by indirect, taxation.

Napoleon met his Waterloo on 18th June 1815. The ensuing Settlement of Vienna was characterised by comparative leniency towards the conquered, and it gave Europe 40 years of peace. The Corn Law of 1815 prevented the import of cheap grain from abroad. In 1816 Income Tax was abolished (to be revived by Peel in 1842).

William Cobbett led a working class movement, initiated by Thomas Paine, aimed at getting the ordinary man the vote. For a time the Habeus Corpus Act was suspended, whilst a tax of 4d was put on all periodicals, to cut the flow of communications. Public meetings were generally suppressed, though unfortunately on 16th August 1819 troops opened fire on those gathered to demand Parliamentary reform in Manchester – the so called Peterloo Massacre. The following year the Cato Street Conspiracy aimed to blow up the entire Cabinet.

The substitution of Robert Peel for Lord Sidmouth at the Home Office in 1822 soon brought an end to repressive Government. Peel abolished the death penalty for a hundred different crimes, and in 1829 established an efficient civilian Police force in London, the distinctively clad Constables still being referred to as Bobbies to this day, in honour of Robert.

The Earl of Liverpool was succeeded as Prime Minister by George Canning in 1827, and he in turn was followed later in that year by Viscount Goderich. In 1828 he was replaced by the Duke of Wellington, who became the last in a long line of Tory Premiers when he was replaced by the Whig Earl Grey in 1830. The Test Act, which for a long period had prevented Catholics and Protestant Non-conformists from holding State or Municipal office, was repealed on the motion of Lord John Russell in 1828. This was of great symbolic importance, but did not have a great practical effect until later reforms of the electoral system.

In 1830 the movement for Parliamentary Reform seemed to arise naturally with the return of bad times. The violence of the working class in town and country reflected its despair. All classes were united in their detestation of the 'rotten boroughs'. In November 1830 the Whig Lord Grey was called on by the popular new 'sailor King' William 1V, to form a ministry based on a programme of 'peace, retrenchment and reform'. Following 15 months of political agitation unparalleled in the history of Great Britain, the Reform Bill was carried in the face of the resistance of the Peers (March 1831 - May 1832). In 1833 Peel reconstructed a Conservative Party out of the Tory Party destroyed by the wrangling.

Taxation

The Universal Directory of Britain, 1791 states that the annual National Income for 1790 was £16,030,286, expenditure was £15,969,178, giving a surplus of £61,108. G.M. Trevelyan says that in 1815 £25 million was raised by direct, and £67 million by indirect, taxation.

The Window Tax Act of 1747 provided that households with between 10 and 14 windows paid 6d per window on top of the old basic 2/-, and those with between

15 and 19 paid 9d; those above that paid 1/- per window. In 1825 those with less than 8 windows were made exempt. The tax was abolished in 1851, when a glass palace was erected in Hyde Park for The Great Exhibition.

The Land Tax was collected between c 1692 and 1832 at the usual rate of 4 shillings in the £, by the county authorities. It was superseded by a similar tax until 1949. At P7 of his 1819 book on Edmonton, Robinson says that, 'In the year 1817, the sum assessed upon the Hundred of Edmonton to the Land Tax was £4,845 12s 1d which is at the rate of 2s in the pound. The quota charged on this parish was £1401. 19s. 9d. of which £957. 4s.1¾d. has been redeemed: the sum now raised amounts to £444. 15s. 7¼d. only.'

The County Rate Act 1739 allowed one general rate to be levied on the parishes to take the place of a number of miscellaneous payments. At Page 77 of his book Robinson tells us that, 'The quota of the county rate paid by the parish in September 1818 was £120. 18s. 6d, the like quota to February last was £117. 15s. 1d.' Robinson also tells us, 'Of the Rental and Rates of the parish, the Rental of the parish is about £22,515 p.a.....The sum raised last year for the relief of the poor, amounted to £5,107. 6s. 9d, which was raised by two half yearly payments: - the one at 3s and the other at 3s 6d in the pound. The poor's rate varies, sometimes 3s at others 1s 9d and 1s 6d in the pound. The church rate, from Lady-day, 1818, to Lady-day, 1819, was at 6d in the pound.

The highway rate is sometimes 1s and at others 9d in the pound, as circumstances require; from the produce of which the surveyors of the parish highways pay to the trustees of the Stamford Hill and Green Lanes turnpike roads, the sum of £110 per annum, under the provision in the act of parliament lately obtained by the trustees.' (This referred to the 1789 Act whereby responsibility for the portion of Green Lanes in Edmonton Parish passed to the turnpike trust already looking after Fore Street.)

John Richardson's *The Local Historian's Encyclopaedia* tells us of other financial impositions. A Male Servants Tax was levied from 1777 to 1852 on households employing such persons, and a Female Servants Tax was imposed from 1785 to 1792 on households employing female servants. A tax was even levied from 1784 to 1874 on the possession of horses! In an article in *The Daily Telegraph* of 2nd October 2007 Harry Wallop revealed that in 1795 Pitt the Younger introduced a tax on hair powder, followed, a year later, by an Inheritance Tax on estates over a certain value.

In 1798 Pitt announced an annual tax of 2/- in the pound on incomes over £60 p.a. In 1799 the new tax raised £6 million, £4 million short of its target. Peace ensued in 1802, which allowed the next PM, Henry Addington, to repeal this income tax, but it was promptly re – introduced the following year when war broke out again. The tax was repealed once more in 1816, the year after the Battle of Waterloo. And so the situation remained until 1842, when Sir Robert Peel re – introduced it. At about the time of Waterloo a tax of 4d a copy was put on all periodical publications, taking knowledge on all subjects out of the reach of the poor. Until 1836, 5d was the minimum price for a newspaper worth 1d.

Later in the section on The Edmonton Enclosure Act of 1800 I explain the system of tithes in operation, whereby taxes were paid to local Vicars, and others, based on what was produced on the land. In addition, manorial levies would have affected members of the local populace. For example, a Fine or Relief or Gressom was a money payment made by an incoming tenant to the Lord of the Manor, whilst a Grasson was a money payment made to the Lord on the transfer of a copyhold property. A Quit Rent was a fixed annual rent which released a tenant from feudal services to a manorial lord, and this features strongly in the manorial records reported in the diary section.

So the present day British citizen's concern about taxation is clearly nothing new.

The Post Office

In those far off days the Post Office was even more important for communications than it is today. In 1728 it ordered that all letter carriers should wear a brass 'ticket' with the King's Coat of Arms. Until 1784 mail was carried by horsemen and horse drawn carts. In that year the mail coach service was founded to provide a secure and efficient service between the main centres of population. The distinctive coaches, with their armed guards, had absolute priority over all other road users. In their early years the stage coaches departed from the General Post Office (GPO) in Lombard Street every week night between 8 and 8.20 p.m., the GPO HQ moving to St Martins Le Grand in 1829.

In 1792 a Money Order Office was opened, and the following year a uniform was introduced for London's 230 postmen, consisting of a beaver hat, with gold band and cockade; a cut away scarlet coat with blue lapels and cuffs; a blue waistcoat, with brass buttons and an identification number. Over the decades this was also gradually rolled out around the rest of the country.

The London Gazette of July, 1794 said, 'Two Deliveries of Letters are given to and from Southgate, Winchmore Hill, etc.' Papers in the public archives at Mt. Pleasant indicate that those deliveries were at 8.45 am and 3.45 pm. It was from 1794 that the Post Office, who have never had a monopoly in this field, treated Parcels as a different category of mail, and they suffered a penalty charge as 'heavy letters'. Carriers' wagons and stage coaches were used for their conveyance.

A Post Office fact sheet indicates that for many years the charging was complicated (though no more so than today). As an example, let's look at the year 1801, when the Penny Post for the 7 miles from Central London became the Two Penny Post. The more general 1796 tariffs, based on length of journey, were revised to – up to 15 miles = 3d; 15 – 30 miles = 4d; 30 – 50 miles = 5d; 50 to 80 miles= 6d; 80 – 120 miles = 7d; 120 – 170 = 8d; 170 to 230 miles = 9d; 230 to 300 miles = 10d, and then 1d for every further 100 miles.

At P57 of my 2001 *A Look at Old Winchmore Hill* I reproduced an 1811 poster which announced a change to the circulation of the 2d post in what are now 17 northern suburbs of London, whereby a letter posted in Southgate for Winchmore Hill, say, would go direct rather than via a central hub. The poster proclaimed that, 'By this Regulation, Letters put in at these Places in time for the Morning Dispatch are delivered at any of them about Noon, and such as are put in for the Afternoon Dispatch, the same Evening; Thus the Letters are delivered shortly after they are put into the Post.....This Bye Post to be considered an Experiment only, until further Notice ....'

Various other amendments were made to the tariffs over the years, the big change coming later in the 19th century with the Penny Postage Act of 17th August 1839. Further to that Act, on 10th January 1840 a uniform national tariff was introduced, based on weight rather than distance.

Pigot's 1826 local Directory contains the entry, 'POST OFFICE ...... Winchmore Hill receiving house at Wm. Board's, the *Green Dragon*, from whence letters are dispatched at half past eight morning, and at half past three afternoon.' Mail was first carried by rail on 11th November 1830, on the Liverpool – Manchester Railway. Rail effectively killed off the mail coach, the last London one running into the city on 6th

January 1848.

Albert Hill self published his *Seventy Two Years in Tottenham. Reminiscences* in 1899. He was a nephew of the famous Rowland Hill, owner of Bruce Castle and prime mover in the introduction of the uniform penny postage in 1840. Albert says, '....Tottenham being on one of the main roads to the North, was traversed by five mail coaches running to Cambridge, Louth, Lincoln, York, and Edinburgh. It was a very pretty sight to see them spanking through the village, drawn by four spirited horses, heralded by the guard's horn. The coaches left St. Martin's-le-Grand *(near King Edward Street)* at 8 p.m., and used to pass the Lancasterian Girls' School (now the Marlborough Mission) at 8.35 to the minute ......Before the Penny Postage, letters were few, and were conveyed to and from London on horse-back, contained in a leathern satchel strapped behind the rider. That mode of conveyance proving insufficient, the post-boys were replaced by mail carts, which were continued, I believe, until the opening of the extension of the Great Eastern Railway to Enfield in 1872 .....'

Agriculture

Our era of interest marks the start of the Industrial Revolution, and with it a growth in population. This growth was mainly fed, literally, by home production, owing to the effective efforts of three groups of people – the landowners, capitalist tenants and agricultural labourers. Nationally, arable replaced permanent pasture, and animal feeding was improved by the introduction of new fodder crops, such as clover and the easily hoed turnips. Low yielding rye was replaced by higher yielding cereals such as wheat or barley. The increased agricultural productivity of the period released manpower to fuel the burgeoning industrial sector. (By 1850 only 22% of the British workforce was in agriculture – the lowest percentage of any country in the world.)

Nationally, in the 1790s the condition of the poor became desperate when the harvests for the years 1794 and 1795 failed. Bread was the staple diet of the poor and its price doubled, so that even labourers in work were forced to apply for poor relief. The return of peace, following Wellington's triumph in 1815, ruined many farmers and business men. Although the price fall temporarily increased the purchasing power of wages, it threw many out of work. The Corn Law of 1815 seemed designed to ruin the poor, because it prevented the entry of cheap grain from abroad. However, against this grim general picture, Michael Robbins, in his *Middlesex*, says, 'The influence of London was already at work during the Napoleonic wars: from 1794 to 1824, when wages were falling in the south and south-east of England, they rose in Middlesex .... few of the Middlesex wages were supplemented from the rates.' (Under the Speenhamland System introduced from the mid 1790s, low wages could be supplemented by the poor rates.)

When I consulted a copy of Middleton's 1798 *View of the Agriculture of Middlesex* in the 1980s I could find no specific reference to Winchmore Hill in the text, but we know that Winchmore Hill and surrounds were then very much rural. I have therefore decided to quote extensively from Middleton's picture of country life in Middlesex, as some of it might have applied to our village.

'The wages most generally paid to ordinary labourers in husbandry in this county, is ten shillings a week during the winter half year, and twelve shillings a week during the summer half year; but on most farms, there is one handy, confidential workman, at twelve shillings a week all the year round. Those who are only employed during hay – time and harvest, are paid fifteen shillings a week; they are occasionally allowed beer, and sometimes a dinner, which makes it equal to their being paid twelve shillings a week the year round.

In summer, the hours of labour are from six o'clock in the morning, till six o'clock in the evening; and during the winter months, from light till dark: but half an hour of rest is always allowed at breakfast, and an hour at dinner.

A great deal of labour, perhaps a moiety (half) or more, of the whole, is done by the piece. Here follows some of the prices: Mowing grass for hay, from 3s to 6s – average 4s per acre. Mowing, making, stacking and thatching, teams and straw included, per acre 20s. Mowing clover the first crop, 3s per acre, the second crop 2s 6d per acre. Mowing barley and oats, from 2s 6d to 3s 6d – average 3s. Hooking peas, from 3s to 5s – average 4s. Ditto, or mowing tares, 5s. Reaping oats, 8s. Bagging wheat and rye, from 10s to 18s – average 12s. Ditto beans, from 6s to 9s – average 7s 6d.

The prices vary according to the bulk of the crop; whether it be standing or lying; and also in proportion to the distance from town. The said prices include the value of the usual allowance of beer, and also the labour of binding the crop into sheaves, and setting them into shocks, which two last operations are done in a very loose slovenly manner. By bagging, the straw is cut more closely to the ground, than is possible to be done by hand-reaping. It is performed in about the same time, and procures as much more straw as is worth about 7s per acre......Nurserymen are said to have their labour done cheaper than the farmers and gardeners..........

...........The number of *women* (mostly from North Wales) who are employed by the farmers and gardeners round London, during every summer season, in weeding and making hay, in gathering green peas and beans, in picking fruits, and carrying strawberries and other tender fruit to market, is astonishing. Their industry is unequalled in Britain, or perhaps in the world. The fruit-women will labour several hours in the garden, and go to and from the London markets twice a day, though at from four to seven miles distance. Their ordinary hours of labour are from eight till six, for which they are paid one shilling a day in summer; and from eight till dark for ten-pence in the winter. Their working so much in the open air, gives them a hale, brown complexion, the sure index of good health: just the reverse of which, are the complexions and health of those women in other counties, whose occupation is knitting, or lace-making.

Fruit is gathered by measure, and carried to London by the journey. *Green peas* are gathered at from 1s to 1s 6d per sack, according to the size of the pods, and the abundance of the crop. *Beans* at half the said price. On the whole, it cannot be said that the price of labour is high, for a county in which the metropolis of so great an empire is situated.

One great grievance which the industrious poor labour under, is, the imposition of *the lowest shop – keepers*, of whom they (the poor) are, from local situation, obliged to buy their provision. In the article of vegetables, such dealers *treble the market price*. Another great evil is, that many of this class of shop-keepers also deal in *spirituous liquors, scandal, and bad advice.*

The increasing number of public-houses is equally to be deplored. There the poor and thoughtless are irresistibly tempted to squander their money, in bad beer and spirits, to the manifest injury of their constitution; whereas a substantial meal at home, with a little good ale, would ensure that health and vigour so essential to persons who must earn their bread by the sweat of their brows.

I cannot here omit to mention, that *the increase of public-houses is*, in my opinion, *more ruinous to the lowest orders of society than all other evils put together.* The depravity of morals, and the frequent distress, of poor families, if traced to their true source, will be found, mostly, to originate in the public-house. On the contrary, where there is not such a house in the parish (and some such parishes there still are, though in distant counties), the wife and children of the labourer, generally speaking, enjoy happiness, compared with those where many public-houses are seen. They are also less disposed to deceive and pilfer; are better clothed, more cleanly, and less impudent and impertinent in their manners and deportment..............The low *inns on the road sides* are , in general, receiving – houses for the corn, hay, straw, poultry, eggs, &c which the farmer's men pilfer from their master.

Gentlemen's servants are mostly a bad set, and the great number of them kept in this county, is the means of the rural labourers acquiring a degree of idleness and insolence unknown in places more remote from the metropolis. The poor children who are brought up on the borders of commons and copses, are accustomed to little labour, but to much idleness and pilfering. Having grown up, and these latter qualities having become a part of their nature, they are then introduced to the farmers as servants or labourers, and very bad ones they make.

The children of small farmers, on the contrary, have the picture of industry, hard labour, and honesty, hourly before them, in the persons of their parents, and daily hear the complaints which *they* make against idle and pilfering servants, and comparisons drawn highly in favour of honesty. In this manner honesty and industry become, as it were, a part of the nature of such young folks. The father's property is small, and his means few; he is therefore unable to hire and stock a farm for each of his children; they consequently become servants on large farms, or in gentlemen's families, and in either situation are the most faithful part of such establishments......The number of these houses is wonderfully increased in this county, and in Surrey, by reasons of many of the brewers and distillers being in the commission of the peace.'

Middleton says that wages aren't that high, but there isn't an intimation of the grinding poverty indicated in comments earlier in this section. Certainly the workers seemed to have enough money left over for the ale house and, as we shall see later, Edmonton Fair. It could be, however, that the situation changed over the coming years, or was different in Winchmore Hill.

The Enclosure maps later in this book give the reader the impression that the area was predominantly agricultural. It therefore comes as something of a surprise when you turn to the Census returns for 1801 in the diary section. These indicate that Middlesex was the most populous county in England, though Yorkshire would have exceeded it if the three Ridings were combined. On the other hand, the County was amongst the lowest handful for numbers employed in agriculture. It was well in the lead for those classified as *not* being involved in agriculture, trade, manufacturing or handicraft. The Parish of Edmonton, which included Winchmore Hill, contained 5,093 inhabitants, of whom only 412 were involved in agriculture - only about one in twelve. However reference to the 1818 Diary section suggests that by then the proportion was greater.

The Poor

For this section I have particularly relied on John Richardson's *The Local Historian's Encyclopaedia*, J.F. Harrison's *Early Victorian Britain 1832 – 51* and David Avery's 1967 *Charity Begins at Home - Edmonton Workhouse Committee 1732 – 37*.

Even in Tudor times the authorities were concerned about the plight of the poor, and The Poor Law Act of 1597/8 established the post of Overseer of the Poor.

The Poor Law Relief Act of 1601 made the position compulsory in each Parish. In addition, under this Act at least two local persons were appointed annually by each Church vestry, subject to the approval of Justices of the Peace, to levy a Poor Rate, and supervise its distribution. These Overseers were unpaid, and it seems that they might include the local gentry. The poor receiving relief were divided into three main categories – the able bodied (who were to be found work), the incapable poor, and people who were unwilling to work. In 1691 it became mandatory to keep a register of those receiving Poor Relief.

Under the Settlement Act of 1697 strangers were allowed to settle in a new parish if they possessed a certificate from their home parish, guaranteeing to take them back if they became in need of Poor Relief. Paupers had to wear a 'P' on their clothing, followed by a letter indicating the name of their parish.

The next major development was Knatchbull's General Workhouse Act of 1723. This empowered single parishes to erect workhouses or, if they were small, to band together in unions for this purpose. The sheltering of vagrants outside the workhouse was forbidden, and those who were inside these could only leave on Sundays. The workhouses founded locally were at Tottenham (1726), Enfield (1729) and Edmonton, in 1731 – 2 , near to All Saints Church. By 1776 there were about 2,000 workhouses in England. David Avery says that by present standards the number caught in the welfare net was not large. Between 1732 and 1737, for when we have records, there were never more than twenty destitute families in a Parish of 7 – 800.

With the spread of enclosures after 1760 and the rise in food prices during the French wars, the number of poor to be relieved increased rapidly, and so, therefore, did the poor rates. In 1775 the poor rates nationally totalled less than £2 million, by 1801 they had doubled, and in 1831 they were nearly £7 million. For decades the problem of how to reduce the growing poor rates burden (which fell mainly on the farmers in the countryside and the middle classes in the towns) was debated. Edmonton Vestry met at Easter 1781 to discuss an extension of the workhouse.

Under Gilbert's Act of 1782, parishes were encouraged to combine in Unions, and independent inspectors were appointed. The able bodied were provided with work outside, only the incapable poor were kept inside. Children under seven were allowed to stay with their parents, and orphan children were boarded out. Paupers of good character were not obliged to wear the pauper's badge.

The mid 1790s was generally a time of high prices and low wages, and parishes tried to supplement the earnings of the poor with allowances related to the prevailing price of bread. The interpretation of this supplement varied from parish to parish, but it was known as the Speenhamland System (of c. 1795), deriving its name from a Berkshire village. Unfortunately the system only acted as an incentive for employers to reduce their wages further, putting yet more people on the Poor Relief.

Despite the gloomy picture just painted, it is possible that things were not as bad as all that for most local people. We have seen Middleton's account of agricultural life in Middlesex generally, as at 1798, and there is little there to make one think in terms of starvation, though things could have changed over the ensuing years. However, Robbins, in his *Middlesex*, says that from 1794 to 1824 when wages were falling in the south and south east of England, they rose in Middlesex, and few Middlesex workers had their income supplemented from the rates.

The Poor Law Amendment Act of 1834 minimized the provision of outdoor relief, making confinement in a workhouse the key measure, though as a deterrent, these places were made as unpleasant as possible. The old parish workhouses were abolished and the parishes grouped together in "Unions", each with one central workhouse. Boards of Guardians were elected by the ratepayers in each Poor Law Union.

Songs of the Era

The following are songs that were possibly popular in the village in the early 19th century. The first three are taken from the sleeve notes to the CD entitled, 'The Copper Family of Rottingdean', written by Steve Roud. He explains that these three were popular in SE England generally, and not just on the Sussex coast, where the Copper family have lived for hundreds of years. Perhaps one or more of these songs were sung in the alehouses of Winchmore Hill.

Good Ale

1. It is of good ale to you I'll sing
   And to good ale I'll always cling
   I like my mug filled to the brim
   And I'll drink all you'd like to bring

2. It is you that helps me with my work
   And from a task I'll never shirk
   While I can get a good home brew
   And better than one pint, I like two

Chorus: Oh Good Ale, though art my darling
Thou art my joy, both night and morning

3. I love you in the early morn
   I love you in daylight, dark or dawn
   And when I'm weary, worn or spent
   I'll turn the tap and ease the vent

4. It is you that makes my friends my foes
   It is you that makes me wear old clothes
   But, since you come so near my nose
   'At's up you come, and down you goes.

5. And if all my friends from Adam's race
   Was to meet me all here in this place
   I could part from all without one fear
   Before I'd part from my good beer

6. And if my wife should me despise
   How soon I'd give her two black eyes
   But, if she loved me, as I love thee
   What a happy couple we should be

7. You have caused me debts, and I have often sworn
   I never would drink strong ale anymore
   But you for all that I'll forgive
   And I'll drink strong ale as long as I live.

The Banks of the Sweet Primroses

1. As I walked out one mid-summer's morning
   For to view the fields and to take the air
   Down by the banks of the sweet prim-e-roses
   There I beheld a most lovely fair

2. Three long steps I stepp-ed up to her
   Not knowing her as she passed me by
   I stepp-ed up to her, thinking to view her
   She appeared to me like some virtuous bride

3. I said, "Fair maid where are you going
   Or what's the occasion for all your grief?
   I will make you as happy as any lady
   If you will grant me once more relief

4. She said, "Stand off! You are deceitful
   You are deceitful and a false young man
   It is you that has caused my poor heart to wander
   And to give me comfort lies all in vain"

14

5. I'll go down in some lonesome valley
   Where no man on earth shall there we find
   Where the pretty little small birds do change their voices
   And every moment blow blusterous wind

Mr. Roud says that this is one of the most popular old folk songs of England, being well documented through the 19th century, even though the full meaning of the words is not clear. Fairport Convention took a particular liking to it, having recorded it twice.

The Lark in the Morning

1. The lark in the morning, she arises from her nest
   And she ascends all in the air, with the dew upon her breast
   And with the pretty ploughboy, she'll whistle and she'll sing
   And at night she'll return to her own nest again

2. When his day's work is over, oh, what then will he do?
   Perhaps then in some rude country wake he'll go
   And with his pretty sweetheart he'll dance and he'll sing
   And at night he'll return with his love back again

3. And as they returned from the wake unto the town
   The meadows they are mowed, and the grass it is cut down
   The nightingale she whistles upon the hawthorn spray
   And the moon it is a-shining, upon the new mown hay

4. Good luck unto the ploughboys, wherever they may be,
   They will take a winsome lass, for to sit upon their knee
   And with a jug of beer, boys, they'll whistle and they'll sing
   And the ploughboy is as happy as a prince or a king

A Sailor's Life

1. A sailor's life, it is a merry life
   He robs young girls of their heart's delight
   Leaving them behind, to weep and moan
   They never know when he will return

2. Well there's four and twenty all in a row
   My true love he makes, the finest show
   He's proper tall, genteel and all
   And if I don't have him, I'll have no one at all

3. Oh father build for me, a bonny boat
   That on the wide ocean, I may float
   And every queen ship that we can find
   There I'll enquire of my sailor boy

4. We hung our sail for yonder
   When a queen ship we chanced to meet
   You sailors all pray tell me true
   Does my sweet William sail among your crew?

5. Oh no fair maiden he's not here
   For he is drowned we greatly fear
   On yon green island as we passed it by
   Then we lost sight of your sailor boy

6. Well she wrung her hands, and she tore her hair
   She was like an angry bird, in great despair
   And her little bird in her did rise
   How come my love, my sweet William, is gone?

This was taken from the Fairport Convention version sung by the late Sandy Denny in 1969.

15

Edmonton Manor

General

Apart from tithes and government taxes, citizens of the area were involved in payments associated with the ancient Manorial system. Understanding this today is difficult. The Crown owned the land and leased out a Manor for a fee for a period of time, and the Lord or Lady of the Manor was then responsible for what happened in their patch, raising fees by various means so that over time the enterprise was worth their while financially. Terms associated with the manorial system come up through this book, and are sometimes given different meanings by different authors, but I here rely mainly on John Richardson's *The Local Historian's Encyclopaedia*. He would have been faced with these sometimes conflicting interpretations and he came up with the following explanations.

A Tenement was a holding of land and a Hoppet was a small enclosure. A Quit Rent was a fixed annual rent which released a tenant from feudal services to a manorial lord. Some Edmonton Manor Quit Rent records survive, and I quote from them elsewhere.

A Freehold tenure was not subject to the customs of the manor or the will of the lord, and could be disposed of without restriction. The term alienation meant the transfer of property. Freehold tenures were conveyed by 'livery of seisure', sometimes called an indenture of (en)feoffment on the deed of conveyance. A Conveyance had to be recorded; it could not be carried out in secret. On entering the freehold the new owner paid the vendor a Relief. A freeholder could sub lease, or Demise, the land in a Release, holding for himself a future interest, called a Reversion.

For Copyhold property the tenant was protected not by national law, but by the title written on the manor court rolls, which he was provided with a copy of - hence the name. When transferring the property the tenant first *surrendered* it to the lord who held the fee-simple, and then the new tenant was admitted on payment of a fine. When a copyhold was mortgaged this was termed a 'conditional surrender'.

Borough English was the custom (abolished in 1922-5) whereby the youngest son was considered to be the legal heir. Where the deceased had no children his youngest brother inherited. Robinson tells us that this system applied in Edmonton Manor. Escheat was the term for the reversion of an estate to the lord or the Crown, for example where the tenant died without heirs or committed a serious offence.

The five ranks of peerage, in descending order of precedence are Duke, Marquess, Earl, Viscount and Baron (Lord). Esquire was the term originally given to an attendant to a knight or lord, responsible for carrying his shield and armour. Later on the term denoted a status above that of a Gentleman, but in the 19th century it became merely a courtesy title. Originally a Gentleman was a man born above the rank of yeoman who was entitled to bear a coat of arms, but by our era of interest it probably only meant that a man had money and did not earn it by the sweat of his brow.

A manorial Lord's jurisdiction, including his right to hold court, and to receive manorial profits and services, was referred to as sac and soc. Richardson identifies two types of manorial court – Court Baron and Court Leet. The first of these enforced the customs of the manor. The main business of this Court included escheats, surrenders, and transfers of land, dower administration, the agricultural management of commons and wastes, and the rights of lords and tenants. The Court appointed a reeve who represented the parish and collected the lord's dues, a hayward to look after fences and the common stock of animals, and other minor officials such as woodward and swineherd.

The Court Leet, which could also be a Hundred court, dealt with petty offences such as common nuisance or public affray, the breaking of the Assize of Bread and Ale, and with the maintenance of highways and ditches. It was presided over by the lord or his representative, and each male over the age of 12 or 16 (depending upon custom), was obliged to attend. The Court met at least twice a year and apart from the duties mentioned it appointed officials such as the constable, ale taster and pinder. In former times it was also responsible for the View of Frankpledge, which regulated the workings of the tithings.

The Frankpledge was an old system, thought to date back to Anglo Saxon England, whereby each little settlement was broken up into groups of ten or twelve households, known as tithings. These were responsible for keeping order within their jurisdiction, and for presenting anyone being charged with an offence to the Court Leet's View of Frankpledge.

Surviving records indicate that in Edmonton the Lord or Lady of the manor held 'The view of Frankpledge and general Court Baron'. Key dates in the year for the management process were Lady Day on 25th March, and Michaelmas on 29th September.

Edmonton Manor Itself

Winchmore Hill was in Edmonton Manor. Most of the following is from documents referenced CRES 2/578 at the National Archives, Kew.

James Gould was Lord of the Manor upon his death at the age of 67 on the 8th Feb. 1767. In his Will of 13th January 1767 he left the manor to his nephew Thomas Teshmaker (son of Merry). Thomas, 'of Fords Green' died on 9th November 1771 aged just 34, and made a last Will dated 17th October 1771, by which he left his wife 'Sara' all his land, so that at the start of our era of interest in 1780, she was the Lady of the Manor. There is a document titled, 'Manor of Edmonton. Case and opinion of Mr. Sey. Bond on Edmonton Statute' (no date given). I reproduce the first two sheets here, rather than in the Diary section. The Edmonton Statute Fair mentioned has a separate section devoted to it.

'Mrs. Sarah Teshmaker is Lady of the Manor of Edmonton in the County of Middlesex as Lessee from the Crown, and bound by Covt. to assert support maintain & preserve all the Perogs. Rights and Royalties appertaining to this Manor during the Term of the Lease and intitled to receive All Profits arising from the Manor.

During all the time she has been Possed of the Manor and for many years before a Statute has been held in Edmonton within the Manor for Hiring of Servants - and For a considerable length of time past sundry persons have Erected Booths & Stages upon the Waste of the Manor for Puppet Shews and for Selling sundry Sorts of Goods, Exhibitions of Curiosities etc.

In September 1778 Mr. Flockton applied to the Lady of the Manor for leave to Erect his Booth on the Waste for Exhibiting Puppet Shews. She referred him to Mr. Smart the Steward, who settled with him for one Guinea a year – which he regularly paid to Mr. Smart till the year 1786. When the Lady of the Manor being informed that the High Constable annually recd. a considerable Sum for the Standing of Booths, which it was supposed she had a right to, she therefore laid a claim to a fine for every Booth Built on the Waste; and in order to establish it peaceably, agreed with the High Constable to allow him half the Profits gave him the underwritten Authority which he Exercised by her Consent for two Years vizt. 1786 & 1787 and paid her according to her Agreement.

To all and singular High Constables Constables Head boroughs and other officers and to all others to whom these Presents shall come Greeting Know ye that I Sarah Teshmaker Lady of the said Manor of Edelmeton otherwise Edelington otherwise Edmonton in the County of Middlesex for divers good Causes and Considerations me hereunto moving have made Order and appointed John Erwood of Edmonton in the County of Middlesex my Receiver the Year 1786 of all Terrage Tallage Pesage and Pitage to be arising under accruing and become due to me for the Erection Building or Standing of any Booth Stall Carriage or other Erection Building or Standing at the Fair or Statute called Edmonton Statute on the Waste of the said Manor Given under my hand and dated this 11th September 1786.

In the year 1788 Another man who had acted as High Constable for the Hundred & had recd. money as afsd. by Agreement with the Lady of the Manr., having behaved to her in a very ungenteel manner, She recalled her Authority & prohibited him from receiving any more money for her, & appointed another person under a Similar Authority; but notwithstanding such Prohibition the Constable did demand in her Name, & reced. money of several persons who attended the Statute & Erected Booths and Stalls upon the Waste of the Manor, & would not suffer the person she had Employed, to receive anything. Some time after the Fair was over the Constable sent an Acct. of what he thought fit to Mrs. Teshmaker offering to pay her half the Amount which she refused to receive;

As of late Years the Number of Booths have increased very Considerably. Another person was Sworn into the office of High Constable – And some time …. For to the Day on which the Statute is usually held The Lady of the Manor caused following Notice to be Printed and Stuck up in many places in the Parish Vizt.

Edmonton Statute

August 17th 1789. Will be held on Monday the 14th, Tuesday the 15th, and Wednesday the 16th, of September next according to Annual Custom. "All persons desirous of Erecting or having Booths Stands yea must approach William Skelton of Lower Edmonton, who is appointed by the Lady of the Manor to settle and agree for the same on her Behalf – And Notice is thus given that all Booths Stands etc. erected without Application, and Satisfaction being made to the said William Skelton will be pulled down immediately."

The latter Clause of pulling down Booths and Stands without permission was intended merely to prevent improper people from Erecting Tipling Booths but not proposed to be put in Execution. In Consequence of the above Note being printed and stuck up. On the 28th Augt. The High Constable caused the following Notice to be Stuck up all round the Parish & Neighbourhood.

Edmonton Statute

Begins Sept. the 14th 1789. Any Persons who are desirous to Erect Halls or Booths, must apply for License for that purpose, to William Wright High Constable at Edmonton, and person or persons shall presume to Erect any Booth or Hall without such the same will be Pulled down and the person or persons so Erecting it will be taken into Custody and Dealt with according to Law. Dated this 28th day of August 1789. William Wright High Constable."

In Consequence of which the people who wanted Booths to be Erected apply to him for leave to Erect Booths and paid the Sums he demanded for such Licenses before he would permit them to Erect Booths, and forbid them to any thing to the person appointed by the Lady of the Manor. And by of his Authority Booths, Shops, Roundabouts, Pens and other Inclosures for the Exhibition of Wild beasts yea were Erected on the Waste of the Manor without Consent of the Lady of the Manor on both sides of the High Road. Complaints made to the Justices at the Quarter Sessns. held at Hick's Hall before the day that was held of the misbehaviour of the Constable, he was ordd. to attend them when he was told, that it was his Duty to attend to preserve the Peace without Money, ...'

The National Archives papers Crest 39/153 contain the following, 'Land Revenue Office, Scotland Yard. The Commissioners appointed by an Act of Parliament, intituled, "An Act for appointing Commissioners to enquire into the State and Condition of the Woods, Forests, and Land Revenues belonging to the Crown, and to sell or alienate Fee Farm or other unimprovable Rents;" do, in Pursuance of the Said Act, hereby require that you will transmit to them, under your hand, a Rental of the Quit Rents payable by the Freeholders and Copyholders of the Manor or Lordship under mentioned together with an answer to the several enquiries following, on or before the Tenth day of October next. Given under our Hands and Seals this Fourth day of September 1792. To The Steward of the Manor of Edmonton Middlesex. Signed – Indecipherable' There is then a series of questions and answers which are too extensive to reproduce in full here, but a feel for the document can be gained from the following,

'1. *What Courts are held for the said Manor, and at what times?* There is one general Court Leet and Court Baron holden on the Tuesday next after Whit Sunday in every year. *2. What number of the Messuages and Cottages, and what quantity of Land by computation; of Copyhold or Customary Tenure, are held of the said Manor?* The number of Copyhold messuages & Cottages are supposed by the Bayliff to amount to about 120. The quantity of Land of Copyhold tenure the Bayliff cannot ascertain The no. of Copyholders about 200 Freeholders 40.....

.... *4. What Fines are payable to His Majesty or His Lessee, as Lord of the said Manor, on the Descent or Alienation of the said Customary Estates, or the Granting or Exchanging of Lives, or otherwise, and by what rate are they assessed at?* A Fine Certain of one Shilling for the site of a Messuage or Cottage. For Copyhold pasture 6/8d per acre (allowing 1/0 quit rent) mat (?) 5/- per acre For Marsh Land 10/- per acre (allowing 3/4d quit rent) (on every admission on Death or Alienation is due by Custom) neat 6/8d per acre, and for Arable Land 2/8d net per acre.....

.... *7. Whether the Timber or other Trees growing on the said Copyhold or Customary Estates, or any and what part thereof belong to the Lord of the said Manor?* All Timber & other Trees growing on the Copyhold Estate within this Manor belong the owners thereof, paying to the Lord or Lady 2d per Tree for every Timber Tree cut down and not used for Repairing Building. The Timber Trees growing on the Wastes at a distance from any houses may be felled by the Lord for repairing Bridges or any other use except such ornamental Trees as grow near to the dwelling or Buildings of the Copyhold Tenants.

8. What is the reported extent of the said Manor? The reported extent of this manor comprises the whole Parish of Edmonton.

9. Whether the said Manor is subordinate to, or dependant on any other Manor, or comprises any subordinate or dependent Manor or Manors, and their names, and the names of the reputed owners thereof? The Manor is not subordinate to or dependent on any other Manor. There are two Manors within this Manor belonging to the Dean & Chapter of the Cathedral Church of St. Pauls London viz. Willoughby's & Diphams (?) but they are not dependent on or subordinate to this Manor ....

..... 10th October 1792. Wm. Briggs Stewd. of the Courts of the Manor of Edmonton. Midlx. (Footnote) The lease of this Manor is made subject to a Rent of £6 13s 4d pa net £5. 7s 10d also to the repair of Seven Bridges within the Manor which were very old & have most of them been lately Rebuilt by Mrs. Teshmaker, who is bound to support the Rights of the Manor, and has disbursed for her Expenses in supporting the rights of the Manor about £90. Court Dinners for the Leet Jury & Homage about £8 per ann. Bayliffs Salary for collecting Quit Rents 5 Guineas p. ann.'

The Land Revenue Office in Scotland Yard sent a further questionnaire to the Manor on the 26th November 1792. However, Mrs. Teshmaker's days as Lady of the Manor were drawing to a close. From the time of the Edmonton Enclosure Act in 1800 we have the following documents.

'Edmonton Manor. Mrs. Teshmaker 4th Aug. 1800. Offering £3,150 for the Purchase thereof. Recd. 5th Will Harrison. Esq. Land Revenue Office.' Then overleaf, 'Sir, I take the earliest opportunity to offer Three Thousand one Hundred & Fifty Pounds for the Purchase of the Manor of Edmonton. I am Sirs your able Servant. S. Teshmaker.'

'Old South Seaton Broad Street. Monday 4th August 1800. Sir, In reply to the letter I had the honor of receiving from Mr. Harrison Esq. I beg leave to state to you. I am willing to give Four Thousand pounds for the Manor of Edmonton including the right to the allotment to be made to his Majesty under the late Act for the Edmonton Inclosure, together with the Right to the Timber & Trees on the Waste and all other Rights, Royalties, Members & appurtenances that now do, or ever did, belong to the said Manor. I have the honor to subscribe myself. Yours faithfully & Obd. Serv. W. Curtis. John Fordyce Esq. Surveyor General.'

'Edmonton Manor. To Mr. Thompson 13th Aug. 1800 to acquaint him that any further offer from Mrs. Teshmaker or him will be in time – if recd. tomorrow or Friday.'

'Mrs. Teshmakers Acct. of Disbursement on acct. of Edmonton Manr. to be submitted to the Surveyor Genl. in reduct of amount of Arrears Claimed since the Expiratn. of Mr. Gould's Lease of Edmonton manor. Recd. 26th Aug. 1800.' Overleaf was, 'Payments made by Mrs. Teshmaker in supporting the Rights of the Manor of Edmonton – Mr. Smart's Bill – The Expenses of a Law Suit for some Cottages at Southgate in right of the manor £78. 3s. 0d: Mr. Biggs's Bill Expenses & Opinions respecting the right of the Fair £5. 8s 10d: Mr. Smart ditto £3. 4s. 0d: Mr. Hargrave's Opinion and other Expenses & Mr. Biggs's Bill respecting Land Tax for the Manor £6. 0s. 0d: Land Tax for 1795 - £12. 2s. 2d: 1796 - £11. 11s. 2d: 1797 - £9.18s 2d.: 1798 - £9. 18s 2d: 1799 - £9. 18s 2d; 1800 - £8. 18s 2d; Case & Opinion of Mr. Seyr. Hill on an Escheat £2. 12s 6d; The Bayliffs Salary deducted from the Quit Rents – 5 Guis. £26. 5s. & Ann. 5 years - £183. 17s 4d.

Mrs. Teshmaker observes that the Claim is made for 5 Years Rent instead of 4 up to Lady day 1800. The Current Rents will not be due at Michas. next, but at Lady day 1801. She does not understand in what way the proportion of a Fine for 5 Years can amount to £410 according that rate 30 years would amount to £2500. Mr. Gould's Fine was £1,050 for 30 years. One 6th of this sum is only £175. 4 Years Int. of £875 would amount to £175. Together £350. Allow for expenses of Law Suits & amount of Land tax paid as account £183. 17s. 4d. Balce. £166. 2s 8d. Would leave a Balance of the above Sum only £166. 2s 8d.'

'Edmonton Manor. Mem. on of things desired on the part of Mrs. Teshmaker 30 Oct. 1800' Overleaf was, 'An Authority from the Surveyor General to deliver the Manor Book & Rolls etc. to Mr. Curtis or his agent. A Memorandum Declaration that Mrs. Teshmaker is entitled to the Rents of Arrears up to the time of Mr. Curtis's purchase at Michaelmas. An Allowance to Mrs. Teshmaker ? of the sum claimed for arrears for the Disbursements & Expenses incurred by her in relation to the Manor.'

'31st Oct.1800. To Mrs. Teshmaker notifying the Sale of Edmonton Manor from Mich.Last Or.'

Headed, 'William Harrison Esq.' Overleaf, 'Sir, I shall be very ready to Deliver the Rolls Books & writings in my possession relating to the Manor of Edmonton agreeably to the request in your letter of the 31st Oct. as soon as the Rents & profits now in arrears and owing to me are received or due provision is made for reserving to me Power to recover them and when a full Discharge is given me for all Demands on the Part of the Crown. I am Sir Your Able Servant S. Teshmaker. Fords Grove. Nov. 6th 1800.'

Papers referenced CRGS 2/579 contain a document which reads, 'Guildford Street Oct. 13th 1821. Gentlemen, On the rect. of your former letter enclosing Mr. King's I write to him to say that the Manor of Edmonton was sold to Mr. Curtis between the passing of the Act and the allotting; in consequence of which no Allotment was made to His Majesty. I am Gentlemen Your obed. S. Tho. Bainbridge.' Presumably this was addressed to a Government Office.

There is, of course, the question as to where the Manor Court was held during Sir William's tenure as Lord. A fact sheet given out at the Salisbury House open day in September 2006 suggested that the most likely candidate was Bury Hall. This lay immediately east of where the A10 intersects Bury Street, and was demolished in 1920. At the LMA is a book of Manorial records referenced ACC/695/40 which incorporates the minutes of Curtis's Special Court Baron of 26th November 1830, which was held at 'the Angel Inn Edmonton.'

Another file at the LMA is entitled 'Book of Manor Procedures and Precedents' and this incorporates the paragraph, 'Edmonton Manor. Upon searching the Court Rolls it appears that no second Court Leet was held for the re appointment of Constable or other Parish offices for upwards of 100 years previous to 3rd Dec. 1823. Book M p340 when Robt. Long was apptd. to serve in consequence of death of Thomas Manning .....' This implies that for periods the Manor Court rather than the Vestry was responsible for appointing Parish officers, which might relate to the fact that the Manor and Parish, as noted at 8 in the 1792 Questionnaire above, were coextensive.

Documents ACC 727/128 at the LMA record that in his Will of 9th April 1828 Sir William Curtis left Edmonton Manor, 'unto his Nephew Thos. Curtis and Charles Stephens their heirs and assigns. To the use of his eldest Wm. Curtis and his assigns during his life without impeachment of waste rem. To the use of his Grandson William Curtis the eldest son of said William Curtis and his assigns during his life .....' The documents further record that Sir William died on 18th Jan. 1829. His son Sir William died on 16th March 1847. There is more on Sir William in the section on Pigot's 1826 Directory. He is pictured at Plate 1.

Also at the London Metropolitan Archives are papers (Ref. ACC 1016/224

– 232) which document Southgate Urban District Council's 1926 purchase, for £50, of The Pound, and associated triangle of grass, in Bourne Hill, from the Lord of the Manor, Sir E. F. Curtis. So a hundred years on a member of the Curtis family was still the local Lord.

Plate 1. William Curtis Esq. by Bromley & Drummond in 1799

Ownership of Edmonton Manor passed from James Gould to his nephew Thomas Teshmaker, and thence to Thomas's widow Sarah. William Curtis purchased the lease to the Manor in August 1800. By the time he died in 1829 he had been knighted. This illustration has been reproduced courtesy of L. B. Enfield Library Service.

Edmonton Fairs

In 1926 Crushing & Son Ltd. published H.J. Griffin's *Historical Articles on Old Tottenham and Edmonton from the 'Tottenham and Edmonton Weekly Herald'*. He tells us quite a bit about Edmonton Statute fair, which was held at Winchmore Hill in the early 18th century, and it was obviously such a big event that it must also have featured strongly in the lives of villagers when hosted elsewhere in the surrounding area. The following are extracts from Griffin's book;

'A turning off Fore-street, Edmonton, opposite to, and a little beyond, the Angel Hotel, bears the name of Fairfield-road (Plate 2), a name which recalls the memory of the pranks which Edmonton indulged in at its annual statute Fair. Lyson's, in 1810, described it as "A holiday fair of great resort, held in the high road in the town of Edmonton, on the 14th September and the two following days. It is called Edmonton Statute Fair, and was formerly held for the purpose of hiring servants, but that practice has for some time discontinued." Fairs, a great many of them, had their beginnings in remote antiquity, and as they were established at the convergence of great roads or waterways they usually brought together huge gatherings of buyers and sellers to traffic in merchandise not otherwise procurable in the district where the fair was held.....

Plate 2. Fairfield Road, Edmonton in 2004

I took this picture of The Crown and Anchor on 8th June 2004. The pub is on the corner of Fore Street and Fairfield Road, the latter being written on the street sign two feet above the pavement. The road is named after the old fair.

.... No fair could be held without a Royal grant or its equivalent, and "if His Majesty grant power to hold a fair or market in a particular place, the liege can resort to no other even though it be inconvenient. But if no place be appointed the grantees may keep the fair or market where they please, or rather where they can most conveniently." Besides being appointed for the distribution of merchandise, they were used as a medium of exchange for the hiring of servants and labourers, and because such a concourse of people usually gathered on these occasions there was added a pleasure fair .... Until the practice was prohibited, it was customary in England to hold those fairs in or as close to the churchyard as possible; the Church field on the south side of Edmonton old parish churchyard is perhaps, a witness to this ancient custom.

Edmonton, it appears, enjoyed the privilege of three annual fairs. Two of them were of unknown antiquity, but it was not improbable that they superseded the local fair held in Saxon times, for the statute fairs of Northaw and Waltham Abbey would seem to have deflected local interest, although Edmonton already gave its name to the Shire division.....But when James 1 acquired Theobalds he enlarged the park and enclosed it with a wall ten miles in circumference......This, however, took in the ground where the fairs were held. These fairs were probably never very crowded gatherings, but somebody's rights had been infringed. As compensation for this aggression the King granted a patent to the holder of the fair rights of a piece of ground on the common land outside the park walls. This in turn was disputed by those who held Common rights; so the King granted a new patent which fixed the locality of the fairs near Southgate, close to a clump of trees and forest undergrowth known as Bush, or Bush Hill; it appears to have given its name to the neighbourhood, and it does not seem to have been a reputable locality.

Anyhow, the public interest in these fairs was but languid and, owing probably to the institution of a third fair later on, what popularity these Bush Fairs had originally was ultimately transferred; they had sunk so low, and the class of vendors became so mean that they acquired the name of Beggars Bush Fair. There are records of the sale of the fair rights on several occasions during the 18th century in the auction rooms of the City, but they dwindled away for the lack of patronage.

There was, however, another Fair held in Edmonton, as hinted at already, and in the 17th and 18th centuries it was reckoned among the great pleasure fairs of the country: it was know as Edmonton Statty Fair, the local way of naming the Statute or Hiring Fair. It came into existence because Edmonton was growing and it wanted a Statute Fair of its own for the hiring of servants and agricultural labourers. On request, such a fair was proclaimed by the High Constable on September 14th, 1680, and as it was not a royal patent no exact geographical fixture of its locality was made. Consequently it was moved about from place to place to suit the convenience of the township. According to Robinson's "History", between 1680 and 1819 it made many moves; it originated in the grounds of the "George and Vulture Inn", thence it migrated to "The Cross Keys" across the road; thence to the "King's Head", at Winchmore Hill; from thence to "The Cock", at Bowes Park ......

.... The popularity of Edmonton Statty Fair in its heigh-day, was enormous, second only to that of Bartholomew's and Fairlop. The area it sprawled over was almost incredible. It is said it was remarkable as being a combination of three fairs held at once for three days. Huge concourses of people from all parts were attracted to this gigantic pleasure fair daily, as many as 30,000, a tremendous crowd when you think of the population of the Metropolis at the time and the difficulty of moving about. It was known as "one of the greatest of fairs" because it was possible for papa and mamma to drive in the chaise in the early morning hours to take little Sophie and dear little Freddy to see the wild beasts and freaks of Nature, and the gypsies' camps without hustling and jostling as it would be later in the day. It is said that the stream of carriages, with their genteel occupants, stretched from Stamford Hill to "The Bell" at Edmonton.

The fair ground really began at "The Bell", where, in Kennington's

Fields behind it, the first fair was being held, and this may account for Robinson's term used as above "The Angel and Bell". All along the High-road to the "Angel" were rows of stalls selling all sorts of cheap sweets, toys, trinkets. There were "Aunt Sallies", cockshies, acrobats and organ-grinders, a terrible din. On the open green in front of the "Angel", to these attractions were crowded all sorts of shows; strong men, giants and dwarfs, fat boys and girls, tattooed ladies, living skeletons, mummies, mermaids, learned pigs, working fleas, glass blowers: horrors and delights galore, all providing a happy hunting ground for the pickpocket and beggar among a gaping, bewildered multitude of delighted sightseers. In the Whittington's Fields behind the "Angel", and in the "Angel" yard, to the general confusion of sound was added the roar of lions and other wild beasts in Polito's Managerie (afterwards known as Wombwell's): this was the second fair, and across the high road, beyond the bridge, by the "Crown and Anchor", where Fairfield-road now is, (see Plate 2) was the entrance of the third fair, held in Biglay's Fields. Here was pitched Richardson's theatre and Gyngell's Circus, with the wonderful "young" horseman, Master Saunders; Richardson's Theatre, wherein Edmund Kean and other stars first rose in the theatrical firmament. Stretching away in all directions were the camps and caravans of this great gathering of travelling showmen and stall-keepers, all to make this pleasure fair as memorable to our ancestors as a jaunt to the Derby on Epsom Downs was sixty years ago and perhaps still is.

Mr. Farmborough, Edmonton's chief librarian, lights on some fortunate "finds" occasionally. He has recently obtained possession of a copy of a MS account of this fair made by a former resident of his boyhood recollections in the early years of the last century, and from this account Mr. Farmborough has kindly permitted me to take a few of the above details .... This pleasure fair was extinguished by the power of public opinion, but of its popularity a hundred years or so ago there can be little doubt .....'

In 1947 George Sturges brought out *An Edmonton Heritage, being an anthology of verse and prose relating to Edmonton.* This also contained a section on Edmonton Statute Fair. Sturges quotes descriptions from contemporaneous newspaper articles of 1805 and 1813. The following is from 1813.

'This Statute Fair commenced on Tuesday, and attracted, as usual, a vast body of folks from London and the villages contiguous. The wonders exhibited were in the greater part those seen recently at Bartholomew Fair. Several recruiting parties picked up a number of fine fellows, well disposed to become soldiers. The men parading with ribbons, while the drum and fife playing "How happy's the soldier who lives on his pay And spends half-a-crown out of sixpence a day" produced a gay effect, and gave the fair an interesting martial character. This is the only statute near London where men and women servants attend to be hired. Many rustics, assembled for that purpose, brought to recollection the scene in Bickerstaff s Opera of "Love in a Village". The females appeared peculiarly clean and neat, while the carters, ploughmen, &c., flourished their whips to the best style.'

Robbins, in his *Middlesex*, says, 'Hiring fairs, where the country people came up and were hired for yearly engagements as domestic or farm servants, were still held at Enfield and Edmonton in September about 1825. Edmonton also had the 'Beggars' Bush Fair[1], granted under James 1, which fell into abeyance about 1870 after being "an inconsiderable holiday fair" for some years.'

Sturges's 1813 account, and Robbins words seem to indicate that Lysons was wrong in saying the hiring aspects of the fair had died out by 1810.

In the 1980s Ralph Mc Tell wrote a romantic song called 'The Hiring Fair', which is also part of Fairport Convention's stage repertoire. Although not a contemporaneous old folk song, this seems to conjure up a believable image of one of these old gatherings. The fact that there was such a large annual gathering in the nearby Angel area suggests that Robbins may have been correct in his assessment that Middlesex wasn't as badly hit by recession as other counties. (See also the section on Edmonton Manor.)

The New River

Running north – south through the length of Winchmore Hill is the man made New River. A Thames Water information board near the source of the River in Hertfordshire, tells us that in 1606 Parliament granted power to the Corporation of London 'for the bringing in a fresh Stream of Running Water to the North parts of the City of London.' The Act provided powers to construct a 'New River for bringing water to London from Chadwell and Amwell in Hertfordshire.' The City gave this task to merchant adventurer Hugh Myddelton, and he started the work on 21st April 1609 at Chadwell Spring.

The course of the River was constructed along the 100-foot contour for a total distance of nearly 40 miles to its, then, final distribution point by Saddlers Wells in Islington. Its fall over this distance was, incredibly, a mere 8 feet. In his *Exploring the New River,* Michael Essex-Lopresti informs us that the New River was ceremoniously opened on 29th September, 1613, by the Lord Mayor of London, Sir John Swinnerton, in the presence of the Lord Mayor elect, Sir Thomas Myddelton - Hugh's brother.

In July 2007 I visited the southern end of Bush Hill, and noted the content of the Thames Water information board, where Salmons Brook passes under the New River, through the Clarendon Arch. Thames Water explain that Salmons Brook was originally spanned by a bridge and an aqueduct. In 1682 the bridge was replaced by an arch named after the Earl of Clarendon, who was Governor of The New River Company at the time. It was rebuilt in 1725, and is now a Grade 11 listed structure.

The Bush Hill Frame was a wooden aqueduct exactly a furlong (1/8th mile) in length. It carried the New River in a 6' wide, 5' deep lead lined trough. The wooden arches were 24' above the Brook, and locally the New River was, apparently, referred to as 'Myddelton's boarded river'. The wooden aqueduct is featured in the diary section at 1784, 1786 and 1788. The last carries an entry in *The Gentleman's Magazine* which reports that in May 1788 the old frame had been completely removed, the lead being sold off at 18/- a ton to plumbers, 'the water having continued near 12 months in its new bed of earth and clay'.

The Thames Water information board at Bush Hill is slightly at odds with the details on this, and states that the old Frame was replaced by the present clay embankment in 1786, as commemorated by a nearby stone tablet of that year.

A Thames Water display board in Hertfordshire tells us that over the years the route of the River has changed, many of the original bends having been straightened, leaving some sections, such as the Enfield Loop, redundant. Today the river's southern termination is at Stoke Newington. It still rises in the same area, near the River Lea, and a spring, nearly 160 feet across, known locally as 'the banjo', can yield up to a million gallons of water a day. The water comes up through cracks in the underlying chalk rock, though in dry weather the flow can stop.

Life in Those Times

In this section I attempt to draw together some of the various strands in previous sections. Perhaps the first thing to remember is that between about 1400 and 1850 A.D. Northern Europe suffered what became known as the 'Little Ice Age'. The famous winter Frost Fairs were held on the Thames when it froze over, the last one being held in 1814. John Adams, master at Latymer School, noted a temperature of minus six and a half degrees *Fahrenheit* in December 1796. So life must have sometimes felt physically uncomfortable.

White bread and tea, previously luxuries of the upper class, were by the 1830s staple fare of the labouring poor throughout the south of England. The universal use of the potato was also relatively new. Home baking and brewing decayed rapidly in the south after 1815, because white bread could be had from the baker for a few pence. There is plenty of evidence from vicars in agricultural areas that most of the brides whom they married were pregnant on their wedding day.

In his 1899 book on Tottenham, Albert Hill helped paint for us, a picture of how things were at this time. He says, ' ...... Leaving Birmingham, my native place, at about 5 p.m., I reached Bruce Castle at noon the following day, April 23rd, 1827 (Shakespeare's birthday), after a tedious coach journey of nineteen-hours ...... What a boon in my boyhood would have been the Lucifer matches and vestas which one is now pestered to buy by children in the streets and at railway stations! The only way to procure a light at the time I speak of was by use of the flint and steel - a process which occupied some minutes ...... Our large sitting room at Bruce Castle (34 x 18 ft) was lighted, I remember, by two mould candles, which needed frequent use of the snuffers, an instrument long rendered obsolete by the composite candle, which snuffs itself .....The only light carried from room to room was the tallow dip, now all but universally superseded by the paraffin lamp ...... For several years after coming to Bruce Castle, our only light was that of the murky oil lamp and the murky dip candle ....

.... Although then but a lad of ten, I have a vivid recollection of the Reform (Act) agitation of 1831, when the country was on the brink of revolution, and when Birmingham threatened to march 100,000 men on London to enforce the passing of Lord Grey's Bill, which became law in 1832. ...... At the time I speak of, before the introduction of railways, the poor used to travel by large hooded waggons, which constantly passed through Tottenham on their way to the North. The families would be seen sitting on straw and dangling their feet behind the large wains with their broad-tired wheels, travelling from two to three miles an hour. The humble passenger looked very comfortable, albeit their progress was very slow .... The High Road I remember as a gravel road, and after a long spell of bad weather I have seen the coaches and other vehicles sink through the gravel into the clay, and so stick fast. In times of flood I have seen the coaches up to their axle-trees in water; and, on rare occasions, I have seen boats plying in the High Road to convey persons from house to house. The side roads, which are now curbed and drained, used in bad weather to be quagmires all but impassable.'

Earlier in our period governments seemed somewhat repressive. Remember that in 1794 a charge of High Treason was instituted against the shoemaker Thomas Hardy, one of the leaders of a campaign to extend the rights of the working man. Though the jury acquitted him of this charge, the Corresponding and other Societies were suppressed by an Act of Parliament. *Habeas Corpus* was suspended, and many men against whom there was no evidence were kept in prison for years. Public meetings were mainly prohibited, whilst Pitt's Combination Acts (1799-1800) prevented the formation of Trade Unions. Against this generally repressive background it is, perhaps, surprising to find that there was a growing dissatisfaction with the slave trade.

Britain was at one time a world leader in this trade in human misery. By ruthlessly exploiting the poorest people in Africa, people in this country were able to have tobacco, coffee, tea and sugar on every table. The Quakers were prominent in their opposition to the trade, and the long campaign to curtail it was led by the physically slight William Wilberforce. In 1789 he spoke out on the subject for three hours in the Commons. His group of activists managed to get two thirds of the male population of Manchester to sign a petition calling for an ethical foreign policy, involving an end to slavery. The Slave Trade Abolition Act came into effect in 1807, having been passed in the teeth of vehement opposition from most of the moneyed classes in Britain. After the 1807 Act Britain pressurized other countries to halt the trade, so that by the 1830s, only the Brazilians continued to ship slaves in any number. It is fitting that Wilberforce was buried with solemn honours in Westminster Abbey in 1833.

Our era of interest saw the start of The Industrial Revolution in Britain, and indeed the world. New businesses sprang up all over the country, many helped by some adaptation of James Watt's steam engine. Workers from the impoverished countryside flocked to the newly industrialising cities, as did the poor of Ireland. The Irish tended to undercut the English workman's pitiful wage, and there were frequent riots against them in London and among the farm hands. The concentration of machinery in town factories also led to the destruction of home based activities such as spinning, weaving, clock-making, basket weaving, carriage and wagon building, tanning, milling and brewing, saddlery, cobbling and tailoring. The decline of this craftsmanship left many villages dependent on the wages paid by the local farmers.

The enclosure movement was a way of improving land utilisation, and thus feeding more mouths in the rapidly increasing population. Unfortunately, the enclosure movement helped to remove much land which had been used by the poor man to graze his stock, gather firewood, and similar life supporting activities. Arthur Young had been a leader of the enclosure movement, but in 1801 he wrote 'By 19 out of 20 Enclosure Bills the poor are injured and most grossly.' The poor were not helped by the decline in the cottage industries just discussed. The 'Speenhamland system' of subsidised poor relief kept down wages, and militated against self respect. On the other hand, enclosure increased the wealth of the landlords and the large tenant farmers. The Houses of Parliament which passed the Enclosure Acts were largely composed of land owners, and these same people were the rural Justices of the Peace. England was effectively controlled by a comparatively small group of 'great landed families'.

The Corn Law of 1815 was designed to prevent the import of cheap grain, and this upset not only the poor, but also the manufacturing middle class, who needed the working man to have money left over to buy goods. The hard times in Britain after the Napoleonic wars, in the days before the welfare state, drove settlers to the Colonies in their hundreds of thousands. However, the poor that remained could see an ever increasing gap between themselves and members of the landed 'gentry', and the newly rich industrialists.

The famous Luddites demonstrated the sort of unrest that was sweeping through the country. From 1811 to 1816 they attacked machinery, which they believed was taking away their employment, particularly in the North. The authorities became frightened, and public meetings were generally prohibited. However, on 16th August 1819 a vast but orderly crowd of working people assembled on St. Peter's Fields, Manchester, to demand reform of the Parliamentary system that excluded them. In a panic soldiers killed a dozen, and seriously injured hundreds of both sexes. This became known as 'The Peterloo Massacre' and must have caused huge resentment. The following February, in the so called Cato Street Conspiracy, a set of Radicals sought to murder the Cabinet as it sat at supper. The hard times led to formally organised mutual aid, and the popular Friendly societies started in the late 18th century.

Despite the hardships of the time, and not withstanding the Swing Riots of 1830-1, in the 1820s and 1830s there did seem to be a gradual a mellowing by those in power, and a desire for improvement and reform. For example, Trade Union activity increased rapidly after the repeal of the Combination Acts. Then, in 1829, The Test Act, which prevented Catholics and Non-conformists from holding public office, was repealed. The electoral reforms of 1832 were a step forward.

The enclosure maps for Winchmore Hill show that much of the area was under grass, being either pasture or meadow. There were some arable fields too. You are therefore left with the impression that the area was predominantly agricultural. In his 1819 book Robinson says that 43.3% of households in Bury Street Ward, containing Winchmore Hill, were engaged in Agriculture, 26.38% in Trade, and 30.31% in other occupations. This tends to bear out that impression.

It therefore comes as something of a surprise when you turn to the Census returns for 1801 in the Diary section. In Edmonton Parish only about 1 in 12 workers were employed in agriculture. Of the Parish's 5,093 employed, 4,124 were in occupations other than agriculture, trade, manufacturing, or handicraft. Much of the land was in the hands of wealthy people who had made their money in various ways. They would employ servants in their houses. Life was obviously not too hard for the wealthy, and Middleton's account of Middlesex agriculture in 1898 suggests that the ordinary man probably earned enough to buy a regular pint of beer and spend at Edmonton Fair each year.

Diary Section
1780

General

In January in the Battle of Cape St. Vincent Admiral Rodney destroyed all but four ships of the Spanish fleet, temporarily lifting the siege of Gibraltar. Russia, Denmark and Sweden entered an alliance, called the Armed Neutrality, to prevent the British exercising their old 'right' to search vessels at sea. Britain declared war on Holland because of its support for the American Colonies (ending in a British victory in 1784). A petitioning movement against high taxes, and government waste, began in Yorkshire and spread across the whole country. In March the first Sunday newspaper *The British Gazette and Sunday Monitor* appeared, whilst in May the first Epsom Derby was run over 1½ miles. The Irish MP Henry Grattan demanded Home Rule for Ireland.

Local

The First Test Act of 1673 excluded Roman Catholics from civil and military office, the Second, of 1678, from Parliament. The Catholic Relief Act of 1778 made provision for Catholics to own land, which sparked off a series of disorders, culminating in the Gordon Riots of 1780. These were named after their instigator, Lord George Gordon, who had made himself head of the Protestant Association, whose aim was to abolish the 1778 Act. He and his supporters marched on Parliament carrying their petition against the reform and, in June, rioting was quashed by 12,000 troops. There were 700 fatalities and 25 executions.

In his 1948 *A Southgate Scrapbook* Tom Mason relates that there were repercussions locally because the rioters threatened to destroy the aqueduct that then carried the New River over Salmons Brook at Bush Hill, thus cutting off London's water supply. The New River Company appealed to the Government for military protection, and two regiments of infantry were sent - the 32nd Foot, and the 60th Foot (the Cambridgeshire Regiment). Although the London riots were brought under control in 14 days, the soldiers remained in the area for more than three months.

The letter book of the New River Company for the year contains correspondence between their local surveyor at Bush Hill, and the Officers Commanding the two Regiments. The first letter is dated July 6th and is addressed to the Officer in Charge of the 60th Foot notifying him of the arrangements made for food and accommodation for his officers and men. This seems to have crossed with a letter from the Commanding Officer to the New River Company, in which he asks for a special food allowance for the men, on account of their strenuous work! The Company replied that they would arrange for an additional allowance of 4 ounces of meat per day for each man.

By the end of July 1780 the Riots were all over, but the soldiers showed no signs of moving. After some ineffectual attempts to see the back of them, the New River Company appealed direct to Field-Marshal Lord Amherst, Commander-in-Chief of the Forces, and asked for the troops to be withdrawn. The Company stated that no further danger was to be expected, and added a tribute to the behaviour of officers and men, but the appeal was to no avail, and the troops were still at Bush Hill in October, for reasons that are not apparent from the correspondence. On October 19th the Company wrote a strongly worded letter to their Deputy Surveyor at Bush Hill, ordering him not to admit or receive any more soldiers, and the following day the soldiers left!

Mason argues, rightly or wrongly, that the soldiers must have been billeted in Winchmore Hill. It must have been as a consequence of the riots that the wooden aqueduct was replaced, in 1786, with the current clay and earth embankment, which would be less prone to acts of terrorism.

Staying with Tom Mason a little longer, we note his article in the July 1934 edition of *The Gazette* on *The Green Dragon* (see Plate 3). In it he repeats a local legend whereby in 1780 a highwayman of evil repute was arrested in the bar of *The Green Dragon*, which in those days was situated approximately where Lloyds pharmacy is today at Mason's Corner. As an example to others he was reputedly hung on a gallows erected just outside the front entrance to the Inn. This was bad for trade, but for some reason the landlord was unable to remove the gallows, so he transferred to very near the current site at the Green Lanes end of Vicars Moor Lane, a little to the east of the present Inn. This new Inn retained its name from its earlier proximity to Green Dragon Lane, being replaced by the existing structure in 1893. (See Pages 55-6 of my *A Look at Old Winchmore Hill.*)

Mason's *Gazette* article informs us that when the premises of the original Inn were vacated they were taken over by John Blackburn of Bush Hill House (later known as *Halliwick*). He converted the old Inn into a lodge to his estate and it stayed essentially unaltered, it appears, until Ridge Road was made up in 1907. The building was then pulled down, when extensive cellarage was found under it.

I have covered this little story under 1780 in line with Mason's account, but a glance at the map titled 'From "Vicars Moor Lane" to Green Dragon Lane and beyond' shows that even in the first years of the 19th century there were no signs of the 'new' *Green Dragon* in or near what is now Vicars Moor Lane. This legend must have come from somewhere, but if it is true, perhaps the timescales are wrong.

In his *A to Z of Enfield's Pubs Pt. 2,* Gary Boudier tells us that the licensee for *The Green Dragon* from 1775 to 1784 was Margaret White, for *The Orange Tree* from 1777 to 1787 it was Henry Butcher, whilst the licensee of *The King's Head* from 1772 to 1789 was Samuel Patrick.

In a Friends Journal of 1938 we learn that 'John Fothergill, the founder of Ackworth School, who died in 1780, was buried at (Church Hill) Winchmore Hill, it is said for the sake of privacy, but 70 coaches and chaises followed his funeral procession.' A paper by Archibald King adds that he was Physician to both George 11 and George 111.

At the London Metropolitan Archives (LMA) are papers MJ/SP/1780/09/006, for which the public can only see a synopsis. This reads, 'Daniel Williams, labourer, of Edmonton, releases Francis Lawrence, shopkeeper, of Highfield Row, Winchmore Hill, from a charge of assault. John Howson witnesses the release 1780 Sep 11.'

Also at the LMA is document ACC/695/49, which has a list of Edmonton Manor Quit Rents for 1780 – 1. This indicates that a Captain Richard Morrison had a holding in the village at a Quit Rent of 3d. Tom Mason's notes at the Local HistoryUnit (LHU) record his death at Winchmore Hill, in June 1780, indicating that he was, 'late of the Duke Kingston Indiaman'. Rather than list all the entries of the Quit Rents of 1780 - 1 here, I have generally entered them against individuals in the Edmonton Enclosure Schedule.

1781

General

It was in this year that the first noticeable effects of the Industrial Revolution were felt, with the growth of the cotton industry. William Pitt the Younger entered Parliament.

The Treaty of Paris had brought the Seven Years War to an end in 1763, and an attempt to recoup the costs of the conflict imposed harsh taxes on the 13 colonies in North America. In 1774 the first American Congress passed the Declaration of Rights. In April the following year General Gage, aiming to seize rebel munitions and agitators in Lexington, sparked off the first battle and by 4th July 1776 Congress was able to proclaim the Declaration of Independence. With the French fleet blockading the harbour, Lord Cornwallis and his 7,000 men surrendered to General Washington in Yorktown, Virginia on 19th October 1781, marking the end of the War of Independence. In 1783 Britain recognised the former colonies as an independent nation.

Local

It was in 1781 that Martha Richardson Tugwell, daughter of John Tugwell and Martha Richardson, was born. She later married the third Jacob Yallowley and became a prominent member of the local Independent Church community (now the United Reformed Church). In her later years she was known as 'Old Grandma Yallowley', before passing away in 1844. (See Figure 4.)

The list of Edmonton Manor Quit Rents for 1780 – 1 indicates that a John Taylor (possibly of the brewing family) had 'a messuage at Vickors (stet) Well' with a Quit Rent of 6d.

Edmonton Vestry met at Easter 1781 to discuss an extension to the workhouse.

1782

General

On 27th March the Whig Marquis of Rockingham succeeded the Tory Lord North as Prime Minister, but died on 4th July to be replaced by the Whig Marquis of Lansdowne. Henry Grattan announced his Irish Declaration of Rights demanding Ireland legislative independence, and Fox introduced the Repeal of Ireland Bill to grant Ireland legislative independence.

Under Gilbert's Act 1782 for the poor, parishes were encouraged to combine with others to form unions, and independent inspectors were appointed. The able bodied poor were to be given work outside England's 2,000 or so workhouses, which were to be devoted to the upkeep of the incapable. Children below seven were allowed to stay with their parents, and orphan children were boarded out. The poor of good character were to be freed of the obligation to wear a pauper's badge. The next development in the treatment of the poor was the introduction of the Speenhamland System in about 1795.

James Watt introduced the double rotary steam engine, a much more powerful machine than his previous invention, and Josiah Wedgwood became the first manufacturer to install a steam engine.

C. W. Radcliffe, in his *Middlesex, The Jubilee of the County Council 1889-1939*, tells us that little is known of where the County justices convened before the mid 16th century, but from then the records give a continuous story. Before 1613 the Court assembled at *The Castle*, a tavern in St. John Street, Clerkenwell. Then in that year Sir Baptist Hicks, a wealthy mercer and a justice of the County, built a hall near *The Castle* for the use of the justices. This came to be known as Hicks Hall, and was continued as a place of Sessions until its closure in 1782. A new Sessions House was built on Clerkenwell Green and opened in the same year with great pomp. The new building continued to be used until the year 1892, when the justices moved to the Guildhall at Westminster, as a result of the arrangements made under the Local Government Act of 1888.

In his *Middlesex* Robbins says, 'The first effective measure to get rid of the 'trading justices' was the Middlesex and Surrey Justices Act of 1782, which established a stipendiary magistracy and regulated its relations with those charged with enforcing the law.'

Local

Sir Atwell's eldest son, Sir James Winter Lake, was the man in occupation at The Firs at the time of Enclosure. In 1782 he was appointed Deputy Governor of the Hudson's Bay Company. He held this position until he succeeded Samuel Wegg as Governor in 1799, remaining in post until his death in 1807.

1783

General

In April the Whig Marquis of Lansdowne (Earl of Shelburne) was replaced as Prime Minister by the Duke of Portland, at the head of a coalition. On 7th December Pitt the Younger became Britain's youngest PM at the age of 24, at the head of a Tory Government. The first decade of Pitt's Ministry established the Cabinet as a body answerable not to the king, but to the House of Commons. The heated air balloon was first used for flight in 1783.

With the surrender of Cornwallis to Washington at Yorktown in October 1781, the war in America was virtually at an end. On 3rd September 1783 The Treaty of Versailles was signed, and American Independence was formally recognised. Britain had to pay a war indemnity of £10 million and, amongst other colonial 'transactions', relinquished Florida and Minorca to Spain in exchange for Providence, the Bahamas and Gibraltar.

Local

The Gazette and Observer for Fri. 16th March 1923 contained an article on Gibraltar Cottages which put forward a theory that they could have been built during the 3 ½ years of the great siege of Gibraltar 1779 – 1783, when General Elliott, afterwards created Lord Heathfield, successfully held it against combined French and Spanish force.

On 27th April 1987 I noted a group of headstones in the Friends Burial Ground, Church Hill denoting the resting places of the Hoare family. One read, 'Sarah Wife of Samuel Hoare. Hampstead. Died 1783. Aged 36 Yrs.'

At the LHU are Tom Mason's handwritten notes. In them he records the death at Winchmore Hill, in August 1783, of Mr. Delarive, 'a policy broker, whose death was accelerated by a run of ill success in the alley, a heavy loss in a large cargo of Irish provisions returned upon his hands from France, & the dangerous illness of a young woman who lived with him and of whom he was dotingly fond. She survived him but a day or two and they were both buried in one grave at Edmonton'.

1784

General

In 1784 Pitt reduced the duties on teas and spirits. A tax on horses, discontinued in 1874, was started in this year. The Window Tax was reduced in 1784 (being again increased in 1797). The Anglo Dutch War of 1780 - 84 culminated in the Dutch defeat off Ostend in June 1784, their fleet being completely destroyed, with the loss of over 2,000 men. On 13th August the East India Act placed the Company under a Board of Control to manage its revenues and administration.

Until 1784 mail was carried by horsemen and horse drawn carts. On 2nd August the first specially constructed secure Royal Mail coach ran from Bristol to London. Letters were charged by weight and distance. With the mail coach came a full uniform for the armed guards, who were the only Post Office employees on board. They wore black hats with gold bands, scarlet coats with blue lapels and trimmed in gold.

Local

It will be recalled that the Gordon Riots of 1780 had alerted the authorities to the security risk posed by the wooden aqueduct at Bush Hill. In September 1784 a correspondent's description of the Bush Hill Frame was published in the *Gentleman's Magazine:*

'The annexed plate' (Plate 3) 'exhibits a view of the wooden aqueduct near Bush Hill, in the Parish of Edmonton, made 1608 for the conveyance of the New River, where the natural level of the ground was unfavourable. This being the only one now remaining (for a similar aqueduct at Highbury, near Islington, was taken away and replaced by a bed of clay, about six years ago); I thought a representation of it would not be disagreeable to your readers, especially as preparations for removing this also are now actually going forward under the direction of Mr. Mylne, Surveyor to the New River Company. The length of this wooden trough is 660 feet; its height and depth five'. It adds: 'The house seen at the right corner is the *Green Dragon* public house, where penny-post letters are received.'

1785

General

In 1785 George IV, as he became in 1820, married a widow named Maria Fitzherbert, though it then transpired that this was illegal under the Royal Marriage Act of 1772. Supported by Fox, Pitt proposed Parliamentary Reform, but was defeated by the Commons. In 1785 a Female Servants Tax came into effect for those households employing female servants, though it only lasted until 1792.

Edmund Cartwright invented the power loom, which mechanized weaving, and paved the way for mass production in the textile industry. The English Channel was successfully crossed by balloon for the first time, and James Hutton's 'The Theory of the Earth' laid the foundations of modern geology and geomorphology.

Local

Mary White took on the licence to *The Green Dragon* in 1775, and was replaced by James Halliday in 1785. Boudier lists the licensees of *The Bull* at Tanners End (now the western end of Silver Street in Edmonton). Robert Peverill is listed for 1764, and the next licensee shown is Mary Peverill, in 1785, followed by Lawrence Allen in 1788.

Robert Barclay Jnr., of Leyton, son of Robert Barclay (1758 – 1816) of Clapham, was born in 1785. He died in 1853, and was buried in the local Friends' burial ground.

The middle of the three clapperboard cottages at the foot of Church Hill, illustrated on the back cover, bears a plaque stating, 'The Old School House c 1785'. An estate agent's brochure of recent years stated that there are two upstairs bedrooms and two downstairs reception rooms. Miss Cresswell said that in its schoolroom days it took, 'some fifty children if they sat close together.' These premises were the sole or main one for such use until the late 1850s.

At the Guildhall Library is a book entitled, 'Charges and Orders for the Several Officers of Christ's Hospital; revised by the Committee of Almoners at Several Meetings; And approved and confirmed by General Courts Held in the said Hospital on Monday the 29th Day of November 1784, and on Friday the 11th Day of February 1785'.

At the back of the book are 48 pages c. 7" x 5" headed, 'Christ's Hospital and the Parish of Edmonton. A Letter to William Mellish Esq. M.P. on a Late Dispute in the Parish of Edmonton and the Alleged Abuses in Christ's hospital, by the Reverend Dawson Warren, A.M. Vicar of Edmonton'. The letter starts, 'My Dear Sir, As I now publicly address you, without your consent or even knowledge, I ought to begin with an apology for the liberty I am taking. I have received from your hands a most valuable favour, the presentation of my son to Christ's Hospital. Your kindness to my family in this instance, has been most scandalously misrepresented, and every exertion has been made that malice and falsehood could suggest, in order to draw a public odium on us both ....' by a Mr. Waithman.

Gent Mag. Sep.r 1784.

View of the New River, as conveyed through the Frame at Bush Hill.

The Green Dragon Inn is in the right corner.

Plate 3. The New River and Green Dragon Inn in 1784

See the Diary entries for 1784, 1786 & 1788. This illustration has been reproduced by courtesy of L. B. Enfield's Library service.

36

1786

General

An economic boom began, based on the growth of the coal mining and cotton industries. An Anglo French commercial treaty was signed and duty was reduced on English clothes, cotton and iron goods, and on French soap, wine and olive oils.

Local

In his book of 1819 Robinson records the following two inscriptions for burials at All Saints, Edmonton, 'John Blackburn, Esq. Died October 12th 1798, aged 67 years' and 'Ann the Wife of John Blackburn, Esq. Died June 26th 1786, aged 44 years.'

The Clarendon Arch carries Salmons Brook beneath Bush Hill. Part of the explanatory plaque there tells us, 'In 1786 the "Bush Hill Frame" was replaced by the present clay embankment that carries the New River; this feature is clearly evident by the New River Path on the opposite side of Bush Hill. These embankment works were commemorated by the adjacent plinth with inset stone tablet which bears the inscription, "This Bank of Earth was raised and formed to support the channel of the New River. And the Frame of Timber and Lead which served that purpose 173 years was removed and taken away. MDCCLXXXV1. Peter Holford Esquire Governor". To this day the New River under the operation of Thames Water continues to supply London with drinking water as well as providing a long distance footpath.'

Until the late 19th century Rowantree and Woodside on the Green were one house. In his 1948 *A Southgate Scrapbook*, Tom Mason tells us that the earliest deed to Rowantree is dated 1786, but mentions six previous owners or tenants, including a surgeon named Richard Guy. Mason says, 'The 1786 deed describes the property as a messuage in Windsmore Hill, Edelmeton, including a cottage, an orchard and a field of 1½ acres. The place was sold by William Cobb to Jacob Dore of Windsmore Hill, and at that time the cottage (now Mably's shop) was in the occupation of Mary Taylor.' The price of the property in 1786 appears to have been £250. Jacob died in 1790 and in 1801 the house was in the hands of his widow.

In 1786 the surveyor Launcelot Dowbiggin prepared three plans and an elevation for John Gray, which led to the construction of what became known as Beaulieu Mansion, covered in the map section. (See Plate 43)

1787

General

In May 1787 the First Fleet set off from Portsmouth for Botany Bay on the Eastern coast of Australia, with 1,400 people in 11 ships. The convicts on board started the settlement of Australia. Meanwhile the Association for the Abolition of the Slave Trade was founded, mainly by Quakers.

Local

Robert Barnes (d. 1862) was born in 1787. He went on to marry Martha Yallowley Jnr., daughter of Martha (nee Richardson Tugwell) and the third Jacob Yallowley.

It was in 1787 that a report condemned the premises and walls of the Friends' burial ground as being in a ruinous condition. It recommended that they should be rebuilt. The Church Hill burial ground includes a tombstone that reads, 'John Barclay (Son of D. Barclay) Born 1728. Died 1787'. He was known as John Barclay of Cambridge Heath, and his wife Susannah was also buried in the grounds.

1788

General

On 26th January the first consignment of English convicts arrived at Botany Bay and Sydney in Australia. Sierra Leone became a British refuge settlement for Black waifs and ex-slaves. At home Andrew Meikle patented the threshing machine. This was the year that George 111 had his first attack of madness, since ascribed to the blood disease porphyria. He recovered the following year.

Local

Sir James Lake of The Firs, in 'Firs Lane', employed John Smith as art master to his daughters. Smith was also the author of "A Book for a Rainy Day", containing local references. At 314 Firs Lane is a blue plaque stating, 'London Borough of Enfield. John Thomas Smith 1766 – 1833. Artist and Engraver. Lived at Myrtle Cottage on this site 1788 – 1795.' (See Plate 8).

In 1784 there was as an article in *The Gentleman's Magazine* about the then impending replacement of the Bush Hill New River wooden aqueduct by the earth embankment we see today. In May, 1788, we read in the same magazine: 'In the course of this month, the frame or trough in which the New River runs near Bush-hill Edmonton as described in our Vol. LIV pp 643 723 was completely removed, the water having continued near 12 months in its new bed of earth and clay. The old lead, amounting to near 50 tons, was sold at 18s per ton to five plumbers.......' However, the 1786 diary entry quotes a Thames Water information board that casts doubt on the accuracy of this.

The Quaker Monthly Meeting held at Epping on the '29th of the 4th month 1789' tells us that, 'Taken 17th of 4 mo. 1788 from John Decka of Winchmoor hill by John Scott , Constable, with warrant, for three years. Church Rate (so called) said to be due to Joseph Brown, Warden of the Parish of Enfield – One mare, value £6. 6s; Demand 31/4d. Chas. 8/- Left at his house 54/-. £4. 13s 4d. Taken more than demanded £1 12s 8d.

Taken 18th of 11 mo. 1788 from John Decka, by Wm. Wright & Wm. Jones, Constables, with two warrants, for two years great tithes said to be due to Samuel Platt, Tithe farmer – Seven ? & seven baskets wheat and one Heifer, value £21. 4s; Demand 178. 5 wa? L. & Chas. 36/6 £19. 4s. 11d. Taken more than demanded £1. 19s 1d' (There is more about John Decka of Roseville in the section on the E.E. Ownership Schedule.)

Elizabeth Butcher took over the licence of *The Orange Tree* from Henry Butcher, who had held it since 1777.

At the LMA is a document referenced ACC 2558/NR13/277. It is titled, '13th May 1788 Manor of Edmonton. Surrender of Matthew Cooke to the New River Company – and John Bowe's admission Trust for them.' It reads, 'Manor of Edelmeton otherwise Edelington otherwise Edmonton in the County of Middlesex. The View of Frank Pledge with the General Court Baron of Sarah Tesmaker (stet) widow Lady of the said Manor held in and for the said Manor on Tuesday in Whitsun week being the thirteenth day of May in the year of our Lord one thousand seven hundred and eighty eight and from thence adjourned to Wednesday the fourteenth day of the same month Before John Lucas Smart Gentleman Steward there.

At this Court came Matthew Cooke a customary tenant of this Manor in his own proper person and in full and open court surrendered into the hands of the Lady of the said Manor by the Rod by the hands and acceptance of the said Steward and according to the custom of the said manor all that triangular part of Land and containing by estimation one rood as the same is now divided and separated from a piece or parcel of pasture land situate near Green Dragon Lane near Winchmore Hill and now the Estate of John Blackburn with all and singular its appurtenances to the use and behoof of John Rowe of the New River Office London Gentleman his heirs and assigns for ever in trust for the Governor and Company of the New River brought from Chadwell and Amwell to London their successors and assigns for ever according the custom of the said Manor under the yearly apportioned Rent of six pound.

And now at this Court comes the said John Rowe in his own proper person and prays of the Lady of the said Manor to be admitted tenant to the said premises so surrendered to him by the said Matthew Cooke as aforesaid to whom the Lady of the said Manor by her said Steward granted seizin (i.e. possession) thereof by the Rod according to have and to hold the said piece or parcel of Land hereditaments and premises with the appurtenances unto the said John Rowe his heirs and assigns for ever on the trust mentioned in the aforesaid surrender of the Lady of the said Manor by the Rod by copy of Court Roll at the Will of the Lady according to the custom of the said Manor under the yearly appointed Rent of six pounds ffealty (oath of allegiance to the Crown) sint of Court and all other customs and services therefore due and of Right accustomed and he gave to the Lady a fine for his Estate and Entry into the promised as appears in the margin did ffealty and was admitted Tenat accordingly.

Appointed Rent 6d. Fine 1s 3d.　　Ext. John Lucas Smart.'

1789

General

The average British male stood 5' 5" tall, as against today's 5' 9". George 111 recovered from his first fit of madness, which had begun in 1788. The summer was particularly wet, and so crops failed. The price of a loaf of bread rose by 88%, and some people starved. It was probably no coincidence that the French Revolution broke out on 14th July, sending shock waves through Britain.

Local

At this time the Grovelands acres were still part of the Minchenden Estate. James Brydges, the 3rd Duke of Chandos, of Minchenden died in 1789.

Under an Act of 1789 the portion of Green Lanes in Edmonton Parish came under the turnpike trust looking after Fore Street. Improvements were made by the Trust, but in 1826 responsibility for Green Lanes passed to the Commissioners for Metropolitan Turnpike Roads.

1790

General

An election saw Pitt returned to Government with an increased majority. George Byng, of Wrotham Park, sat for the county as a Whig MP from 1790 to 1847. In 1790 Crompton's Mule was harnessed to water power by Walter Kelly, Manager of the New Lanark Mills, and the machine's use spread very rapidly. Turner exhibited his first water colours at The Royal Academy.

Local

Minutes lodged at the Quaker HQ in Euston Road tell us that, "At a Monthly Meeting, held at Tottenham 25th of 2 mo: 1790. The compleating the meeting House at Winchmoor hill is continued to the Friends appointed." This new building is the current Meeting House, the plaque over the front reading, 'Friends Meeting House Built 1688 Rebuilt 1790' (Plate 22) While it was being rebuilt Friends held their Meetings in Baker Street Meeting House, Enfield. The School Room, Lobby and upstairs room were added in 1796, a Washhouse, now the kitchen, was built in 1809. Since that date there have been no major alterations to the main building. Of the 39 Friends who subscribed to the re-building in 1790, 27 are buried there. There is more on the rebuilding in the Quaker minutes of 1791.

Thomas Goodfellow was the licensee of *The King's Head* in 1790, succeeding Samuel Patrick, who had held the lease since 1772. In his *Southgate and Edmonton Past*, Graham Dalling informs us that Millfield House was probably constructed in about 1790. Isaac Walker was Hayward of the Manor.

At the National Archives in Kew are documents PROB/780 containing a paper labelled, 'Will Jacob Dore Dec. Propounded 5th May 1790. Pronounced against.' The Will is in a clear hand and reads, 'In the Name of God. Amen. I Jacob Dore of Winchmore Hill in the parish of Edmonton in the County of Middlesex. Gent. (Formerly of Cock Lane in the parish of St. Mathius Bethnal Green) being sick and weak in the Body but of sound mind, perfect memory and understanding do make and Ordain this my last Will and Testament in Manner as follows.

First. I do Will and Bequeath to my Wife Magdalin Theresa Dore all my Freehold Estates Situated at Winchmore Hill aforesaid together with all the Household Furniture belonging to the same and my wearing apparell During the Term of her Natural Life the above said Bequest being Subject that the said Estate shall be upheld and kept in good Tenantable Repair by my Wife aforesaid and after the Decease of my Wife aforesaid I do will and Bequeath the above said Estate to John Levesque of Hoxton in the County of Middlesex Stock Broker, his Heirs, Executors or Assigns. I do likewise will and Bequeath to my Aforesaid Wife the sum of One Thousand Pounds Sterling Subjected to the payment of all my just and lawful Debts.

I do likewise Bequeath to Peter Levesque of Hoxton the sum of twenty pounds. I do likewise Bequeath to Magdalin Levesque the wife of the above said John Levesque the sum of Ten pounds, and all the rest of my Property whatsoever and wheresoever I do give and Bequeath to my Cousin John Levesque aforesaid whom I do hereby appoint my Executor to this my last will and Testament, hereby revoking all former Wills and Testaments made by me, in Witness whereof I have hereunto Subscribed my Hand and Seal in the presence of the subscribing witnesses this fourteenth Day of February in the Year of our Lord One Thousand Seven Hundred and Ninety. (signed) Jacob Dore. Witnesses William Jones, James Bedzeville, William Bayley.'

40

There is a rather less clear document, reference PROB 18/99/24, titled 'Levesque against Dore and Hammond Allegation dated 5th May 1790'. This records a challenge to the Will, but I am unable to say for certain what the conclusion was. We do know, however, that 'Doree, Magdalene Teresa' was shown in the 1801 Edmonton Enclosure Schedule as being the owner of Rowantree - Woodside House on The Green. The notes with the Enclosure listing quote Tom Mason's understanding of the history of the house's descent, and this is consistent with the terms of the Will quoted above. In those days it seemed to be the practice to sometimes leave property to one relation but stipulate that another relative could have tenure for the length of their life. This seems to have helped females in the days before emancipation.

1791

General

In 1791 Roman Catholics were granted freedom of worship. William Wilberforce proposed a Parliamentary motion for the abolition of slavery, which was carried. Joseph Priestley's house was burnt down by a Birmingham mob, protesting at his support for the French Revolution. On 2nd March John Wesley, founder of the Methodist movement, died in London, aged 87. Thomas Paine's 'The Rights of Man' was published. The Universal Directory of Great Britain 1791 contained the following.

'OF THE CONSTITUTION AND PARLIAMENT OF GREAT BRITAIN

In almost all the states of Europe, the will of the prince holds the place of law; but it is the singular happiness of this country, that the legislative power is vested solely in the parliament; the constituent parts of which are the king; the house of lords, and the house of commons....

....The counties are therefore represented by knights, elected by the proprietors of lands; the cities and boroughs are represented by citizens and burgesses, chosen by the mercantile part, or supposed trading interest of the nation. The number of English representatives is 513, and of Scots 45; in all 558. And every member, though chosen by one particular district, when elected and returned, serves for the whole realm....

....The annual taxes are 1. The land tax, or the ancient subsidy raised upon a new assessment 2. The malt tax, being an annual excise on malt, mum (stet), cyder, and perry The perpetual taxes are 1. The customs, or tonnage and poundage of all merchandise exported or imported 2 The excise duty, or inland imposition, on a great variety of commodities 3. The salt duty 4. The post-office, or duty for the carriage of letters 5. The stamp duty on paper, parchment & co. 6. The duty on houses and windows 7. The duty on licences for hackney coaches and chairs 8. The duty on offices and pensions, with a variety of new taxes since imposed. The clear neat produce of these several branches of the revenue, old and new taxes, after all charges of collecting and management paid, is called the annual revenue of the nation, out of which is paid the interest of the different stocks composing the national debt, the civil list, the navy, ordnance, and army expenditures, and every other species of claim that can be made upon the public.

To illustrate this subject more extensively, we have subjoined the following correct statement of the annual income and expenditure of the nation, calculated from the average of the last five years receipts and disbursements, as delivered in by the Select Committee of Finance, to the House of Commons, on the 10th of May, 1791.

The INCOME, or net Produce of the Permanent Taxes, (exclusive of land and malt) for each of the five years, from the 6th of January 1786, to the 5th of January, 1791, both inclusive, was as follows:

In the year	1786	£11,867,055
	1787	£12,923,132
	1788	£13,007,642
	1789	£13,433,068
	1790	£14,072,978

The produce of the Annual Taxes, which are those on Land and Malt, may be taken upon an average of the years 1786, 1787, and 1788, (which is as far as those accounts are made up:)

The Land Tax, at	£1,972,000
The Malt Duty, at	£586,000

The total average thus arsing from the Permanent and Annual Taxes for those years, evidently proves the annual revenue or income of the nation to be £16,030,286 viz.

Permanent Taxes	£13,472,286
Land Tax	£1,972,000
Malt Duty	£586,000
	£16,030,286

.......The national EXPENDITURE, during the last five years, under the heads of Interest and Charges of the National Debt – Interest of Exchequer Bills – Civil List – Charges on the Aggregate and Consolidated Funds – Navy - Army – Ordnance – Militia – Miscellaneous Services – and Appropriated Duties, was as follows:

For the year	1786	£15,720,543
	1787	£15,620,783
	1788	£15,800,796
	1789	£16,030,204
	1790	£15,912,597

The annual interest and other charges on the public debts, as they stood on the 5th January, 1791, was, £9,289,110, from which must be deducted £14,000, interest on short annuities otherwise provided; and to which, on the other hand, must be added £42,862, one year's interest on the Tontine, which will be due in September 1791, and the whole of the charges will then be £9,317,972

The annual expense incurred by Exchequer Bills, upon the Land Tax, the Malt Duty, and the Supplies, is	£260,000
The sum this year charged upon the consolidated fund, for the support of his majesty's household, is	£898,000
The remaining charges upon this fund in the last year	£105,385
Annual expence (stet) for the Navy	£2,000,000
Ditto for the Army	£1,748,842
Ditto for the Ordnance	£375,000
The annual charge of the Militia, is	£95,311
Miscellaneous Services	£128,416
Appropriations not included under any of the preceding heads of charge	£40,252
The sum issued in each year, for the reduction of the national debt	£1,000,000
Amount of the sums above as stated	£15,969,178

Total ANNUAL REVENUE of the Nation.

Permanent Taxes	£13,472,286
Land and Malt	£2,558,000
	£16,030,286

Total ANNUAL EXPENDITURE

Interest and charges of the Public Debt	£9,317,972
Exchequer Bills	£260,000
Civil List	£898,000
Further charges on Consolidated Fund for ditto	£105,385
Navy	£2,000,000
Army	£1,748,842
Ordnance	£375,000
Militia	£95,311
Miscellaneous Services	£128,416
Appropriated Duties	£40,252
Annual million for reducing the debt	£1,000,000
	£15,969,178
Balance of the Revenue, over and above all expenditures	£61,108

Hence it is evident, that some of the present taxes will, in a few years, cease; and, that there is no necessity for any new ones. May 10, 1791.'

The above figures can be compared and contrasted with the present day by looking at a breakdown of the finances of the United Kingdom (which, of course, includes Northern Ireland) as given in *The Daily Mail* of 7th December 2006. The millions have now become billions.

Total ANNUAL REVENUE of the Nation.	£ billion.
Income Tax	146
National Insurance	89
VAT	76
Other	75
Corporation Tax	48
Excise Duties	40
Borrowing	37
Council tax	23
Business Rates	21
	555

Total ANNUAL EXPENDITURE	£ billion.
Social protection	153
Health	96
Education	71
Other expenditure	53
Public order and safety	32
Defence	32
Debt interest	28
Personal Social Services	27
Transport	21

Local

The Universal Directory of Great Britain 1791 also lists the members of the Livery Companies of London. Amongst those listed is Moses Adam, Tiler and Bricklayer of Winchmore Hill. Thomas Yates was the licensee of *The King's Head* in 1791.

Turning again to the minutes of local Quaker meetings we have, 'At a Quarterly Meeting held at Devonshire House the 10th of 1st month 1791. John Deck (stet) reports that he has received from C. Bartholomew £1. 16s 9d being one year three quarters rent of a field at Winchmoor Hill due 25th of 12th mo. last. List of the Trustees for the Meeting Houses and Burial Grounds belonging to Tottenham Monthly Meeting – Winchmore hill – David Barclay, Daniel Bell, Michael Phillips, John Phillips, Benj. Head, Tho. Coar, Thos. Shillito, Wm. Forster, Benj. Fincham Jnr., Benj. Doubleday.'

'At a Monthly Meeting held at Tottenham 11th of 8 mth. 1791. The following Report was brought in and read, from Friends appointed respecting the new Meeting House at Winchmoor hill, "We your Committee report that the rebuilding the Meeting House at Winchmoor hill is compleated; and also a Tenement for a doorkeeper, and a considerable Addition of the Wall for the Burial Ground, the total Amount of which is £710. 2s. 6d which has been paid by the kind Subscription of Friends agreeable to Account Sent herewith. Tottenham 30th of 6 mo 1791 James Healey, John Decka, Thos Phillips, Wm. Forsters.

Subscription & Expenses in rebuilding the meeting house at Winchmoorhill - Samuel Hoar £50, Samuel Hoar junr. £50, Isaac Walton £50, David Barclay £50, Abraham Gray £50, Isaac Smith £50, Josph. Osgood Freame £30, John Gray £30, Jn. Vickris Taylor £25, Hannah Plumstead £25, Ann Fothergill £21, Thomas Weston £21, Jonathan Bell £20, Nathl. Newbury £10 10s, Richard Chester £16 15s 6d, Thos. Broadbank £10 10s, Robert Barclay £10 10s, Elizabeth Welch £10 Mary Steny £10, John Chorley £5 5s, Thos. Home £5 5s, Rachel Marshall £5 5s, Thomas Phillips £5 5s, John Goad £5 5s, Joseph Woods £5 5s, Thomas Smith £5 5s, Nathl West £5 5s, Priscilla Bevan £5 5s, Mary Vaston £5 5s, John Decka £5 5s, Richard Hillary £5 5s, John Eliott £3 3s, William Forster £1 2s, John Decka Jun. Trus. £2 2s. £710 2s 6d" '.

The expenditure outlined in the minutes adds up to this same £710. 2s 6d, but is not so clearly put. Professor A. David Olver, in his *A History of Quakerism at Winchmore Hill* of 2002 tells us that it reads,

		£	s	d
30.4.1790	C. Bartholomew for loss of a Cow	6	6	-
03.07.1790	John Bevan his contract for Meeting House	401	14	6
26.08.1790	William Hobson for Wall of Burial Ground	191	3	-
02.11.1790	H. Draper, Carpenter	14	1	-
02.11.1790	N. Skiklethorpe, Glazier	2	10	-
04.04.1791	John Bevan extra for Tenement	85	13	-
04.04.1791	John Decka and W. Forster, Sundries	8	15	-
		710	2	6

The '8 mth. 1791' minutes conclude by saying, 'John Decka, John Chorley and Thomas Phillips are desired to enquire for a suitable Family to occupy the Dwelling adjoining Winchmoorhill Meeting house and report.' The minutes for the next month read,

'At a Monthly Meeting held at Epping, 8th of 9 mo. 1791. The Friends appointed are continued to enquire for a suitable family to occupy the Dwelling at Winchmoor hill Meeting House and report. There being now only two Trustees left for our Meeting Houses and Burial Grounds at Enfield & Winchmoor - hill William Forster is desired to prepare new writings, & provide Transfers to be made to the following Friends as Trustees viz. Michael Phillips, John Phillips, Benj. Fincham Jnr., Benj. Head, Benj. Doubleday, Thos. Coar, Wm. Forster, and Thomas Shillito.'

At the London Metropolitan Archives are papers MJ/SP/1791/10/029 for which the public can only see a synopsis. This reads, 'William Hunt and (-) Oram, accused of assault; Forster, farmer (?), of Winchmore Hill, and (-) Wilson, of Newcastle Court, Temple Bar, stand bail. 1791 Oct.' One wonders if this Forster is the Quaker William Forster.

1792

General

In 1792 coal gas was first used for lighting. The London Corresponding Society was formed by artisans to campaign for electoral reform. The tax imposed in 1785 on employing female servants was repealed. In his budget speech to the House of Commons in February 1792 Pitt the Younger said, 'Unquestionably there never was a time in the history of the country when from the situation of Europe we might more reasonably expect fifteen years of peace, than we may at the present moment.' In the light of the French Revolution of 1792 he halted his programmes of reform for fear of stirring up unrest at home. This was especially so, given a French Government statement of 19th November that it offered help, 'to all those nations who desire to overthrow their kings.'

Local

Quaker Minutes archived at Euston Road read,

'At a Monthly Meeting held at Tottenham 8th of 3 mo. 1792. John Decka, John Chorley & Thomas Phillips are continued to enquire for a suitable Family to occupy the Dwelling at Winchmoorhill. Thomas Coar and William Forster are continued to prepare new writings for Enfield & Winchmoorhill Meeting Houses.'

'At a Monthly Meeting held at Tottenham 9th of 8 mo. 1792. This Meeting appoints Richard Carter to be Grave maker to our Burial Grounds at Winchmoorhill & Waltham abby.'

Tom Mason's handwritten notes at the LHU tell us, '1792 June 12. Died, in her 49th year, universally lamented, Mrs. Rachel Barclay, wife of Mr. David Barclay, of Youngbury co. Hertford. On the 19th her remains were interred in the burial ground of the Society of the Quakers at Winchmore – hill.' They also tell us, 'Winchmore Hill. Mary Ann Peverell (daughter of Mr. Callow) born in London 17 July 1792. Married in parish church of St. Mary Whitechapel 17 April 1814. John Peverell lived for many years at Winchmore Hill, near Edmonton, died at Winchmore Hill 6 January 1896 aged 103 buried Edmonton Parish Churchyard Jan. 10.'

In 1792, Samuel Patrick, who had held the licence from 1772 to 1789, again became licensee of *The King's Head* for a further year. Sarah Huxley was Hayward of the Manor.

1793

General

France declared war on Britain on the 1st February, and there wasn't a permanent peace until 1815. The British economy entered a depression. Parliament passed an Act which permitted the punishment of masters found guilty of ill treatment of servants and apprentices. The first £5- notes were issued and Lord George Gordon, who was behind the 1780 riots, died in Newgate Prison. In 1793 a uniform was introduced for the 230 London postmen. As the London Penny Post ran out to Winchmore Hill it is likely that the new uniform was seen in our village.

Local

In 1793 Martha Newman became the licensee of *The King's Head*, whilst George Hallsey took over the licence of *The Orange Tree* from Elizabeth Butcher, who had held it since 1788.

The Friends' Minutes at Euston Road read, 'At a Monthly Meeting held at Epping 11th of 4 mo. 1793. The Friends appointed report they have placed a family in the Dwelling at Winchmoorhill they are desired to prepare an Agreement thereon and bring to another meeting.'

1794

General

In 1794 a charge of High Treason was instituted against shoemaker Thomas Hardy, the founder of the Corresponding Society, and other innocuous people, but the jury acquitted them. However, the same year the Habeas Corpus Act was suspended. On 1st June Lord Howe achieved a great victory over the French at the Battle of Brest. In 1794-5 landscaper Humphry Repton (Plate 5) entered into a partnership with John Nash. It lasted only until 1799, but fortunately resulted in what is now Grovelands Park. The harvests for the years 1794 and 1795 failed. The price of bread doubled, so that even labourers in work were forced to apply for poor relief. However, in his *Middlesex* Robbins says, 'The influence of London was already at work during the Napoleonic wars: from 1794 to 1824, when wages were falling in the south and south-east of England, they rose in Middlesex...'

Local

It was from 1794 that the Post Office treated Parcels as a different category of mail. *The PGS Gazette* of 13th January 1939 featured a small article, presumably by the ubiquitous 'Memorabilia', on the London mails the year after the new uniform had been introduced. It was headed, 'Southgate Penny Post in 1794. First Notice of Daily Delivery.' It ran, 'Mr. A. G. Smith, of 15, Chelmsford Road, Southgate, who recently retired after 45 years' service with the Post Office as Overseer of Southgate's Postmen's Sorting Office, has been delving among some old papers. He has discovered, among many other interesting 'relics' a copy of the first notice of the daily delivery of letters to Southgate. It is from the *London Gazette* of July, 1794, and reads as under,

"General Post Office, June 27, 1794. NOTICE is hereby given that a Ride, for the Conveyance of Letters to be delivered by the Penny Post, is established between

London and Edmonton, by which letters are now dispatched to and from Town three times a day to and from the following places, via, Hackney, Homerton, Clapton, Shackelwell, Dalston, Kingsland, Stoke Newington, Tottenham and Edmonton, and the intermediate places; and Two Deliveries of Letters are given to and from Southgate, Winchmore Hill, etc. On Monday next the Penny Post will be extended to the Town and Neighbourhood of Enfield; the number of posts daily to and from which will be Two. By command of the Postmaster-General, ANTH. TODD, sec."

Mr. Smith adds that, as is generally known, it was not until 1836 that Rowland Hill was successful in extending the penny post over the whole of the British Isles. Shackelwell, he added, lies between Hackney Downs and Stoke Newington Road. "But," he concluded to our representative, "you will note that in those days letters were delivered to just plain 'Southgate'. There were no 'trimmings' – such as 'Old' – in those days!'''

In the years following the division of the Chase, the Edmonton vestry became concerned at the continued activities of those who took away wood, turf, loam and gravel from the part allocated to the parish. In 1794 the vestry ordered the printing of a thousand handbills warning would be offenders.

Elizabeth Butcher took over the licence for *The Orange Tree* again, George Hallsey having taken it on the previous year. The VCH tells us that in 1794 *The Green Dragon*, was the meeting place of a benefit society. Susanna Salmon was the Manor's Hayward.

It was in 1794 that the Friends Monthly Meetings ended in Enfield, owing to lack of demand, and Winchmore Hill became part of the Tottenham Monthly Meetings.

John and Rebecca Walker had a daughter named Rebecca, who, with her husband Abraham Gray of Tottenham, produced sons John (owner of Beaulieu) and Walker Gray (owner of Grovelands). Abraham and his wife both died in 1794. Tom Mason records another local death in his notes at the LHU as follows, '1794 Oct. 16. At Winchmore – hill, in her 93rd year, Mrs. Sarah Woods, formerly of Bartholomew – lane, & one of the people called Quakers. She sank quietly into the arms of Death after a short illness, her frame being apparently worn out by the action of its own machinery.'

Edmonton Manor Minutes for 12th June 1810 tell us that on the same date in 1794 John Acott was admitted as a tenant to four cottages on the Bourne under the Will of his father William.

In the extensive archives of the late David Hicks is a copy of the Will of William Wilson of Hoxton Square, in the Parish of St Leonard, Shoreditch, dated 4th November 1794. It was extracted from the Registry of the Prerogative Court of Canterbury and proved at London on 1st June 1801. After covering his funeral expenses and discharging his debts he left, 'unto my dear wife Mary Wilson my household furniture plate linen and the house she now lives in with the adjoining house let to Mr. Stay both situated in Hoxton Square in the Parish aforesaid together with my leasehold estate situated in Kingsland Road and known by the name of Pleasant Row let on lease to Mrs. John White for and during her natural life. Fourthly I give and bequeath unto my son James Wilson his heirs executors and assigns for ever my freehold estate situate at Winchmore Hill in the parish of Edmonton already in the possession of my said son James Wilson ...' He also left property in East London to his other sons William and Benjamin, who were nominated as Executors of the Will. The holding in Winchmore Hill was almost certainly Plot 101 in the Edmonton Enclosure Award, towards the western end of 'Vicars Moor Lane'.

1795

General

Following his abortive illegal marriage of 1785, in 1795 Prince George (later George 1V) legally married his first cousin Princess Caroline of Brunswick, the union producing Princess Charlotte. From 1795 – 8 Pitt the Younger ran a duty and licensing system on the use of hair powder. On the war front Holland joined France. Overseas, Britain took Ceylon (now Sri Lanka) from the Dutch, and secured The Cape of Good Hope.

Under Gilbert's Act of 1782 the able bodied poor were given work outside England's 2,000 or so workhouses, which were used for the keep of the incapable. Under the Speenhamland System, introduced in about 1795 (devised in the Berkshire village of that name) parishes were to top up the low wages prevailing at that time to enable workers to meet the high cost of living, the main barometer being the price of bread. This was rising steeply as the harvests for 1794 and 1795 both failed. Unfortunately the parish supplement only encouraged employers to reduce wages still further, leading to ever more people on the 'poor relief'. The next major development was the Poor Law Amendment Act of 1834.

Local

The only local Quaker Meeting Minutes from the era read, 'At a Monthly Meeting held at Waltham abby 8th of 1 mo. 1795 - John Decka reports he has received from C. Bartholomew, one pound, being one Year's Rent of the small field at Winchmoor hill to 25th of 3 mo. last which he now paid our Cashier – John Chorley is desired to pay as follow – To John Decka land at Winchmoor hill £6. 11s. 4d. Various others – blank space; Total £14. 16s 1d.' 'At a Monthly Meeting held at Tottenham 5th of 3 mo. 1795. No new meeting settled, one meeting discontinued at Enfield, the meeting formerly held there being held at Winchmoorhill.'

Tom Mason's handwritten notes at the LHU record the death of 'Mrs. Judith Teshmaker, spinster, sister of the late Justice T.' at her house in Church Street on 27th March. Thomas's widow, Sarah, was Hayward for the Manor.

The Palmers Green Gazette of 18th October 1940 carried an article headed 'Charles Pole of Southgate' by 'Memorabilia'. It continued, 'From the "Obituary, with anecdotes of remarkable Persons" in 'The Gentlemen's Magazine', 1795, 12th September,.....' I quote from the article under Samuel Pole in the EE Ownership Schedule.

The Lake family is also covered in detail under that Schedule, along with their friend John Thomas "Rainy Day" Smith. He moved into Myrtle Cottage in Firs Lane in 1788, and left in 1795. The Lakes were strongly associated with the Hudson's Bay Company, and it was in 1795 that the Company established a fort on the North Saskatchewan River. The name given to it was Edmonton House, from Lake's home in that parish, and it was then applied to the city in Alberta, established 20 miles upstream from the fort.

Robinson tells us that amongst the commemorative stones that were in the grounds of All Saints in 1819 was one which read, 'On the 15th October, 1795, in the 80th year of his age, ceased to be mortal, Dr. Henry Owen, many years vicar of this parish. Manet post funeral virtus.' At Plate 4 is J.T. Smith's likeness of the Vicar in 1795.

In 1795 Thomas Yates was again licensee of *The King's Head*, having previously held the licence in 1791, whilst John Biggs became the licensee of *The Orange Tree*, succeeding Elizabeth Butcher. She was the last Butcher listed as licensee after the name seems to have dominated in this role since 1764.

Painted & Engraved by J. T. Smith.

Plate 4. The Rev. Henry Owen M. D. in 1795

I am grateful to the L.B. Enfield Library Services for permission to reproduce this 1795 sketch by John Smith. Owen was born at Merionethshire in 1716, and obtained his Master of Divinity degree at Jesus College, Oxford, after which he started his life in the church. He was Vicar of Edmonton from 1776 until his death on 15th October 1795. One of his publications was titled, 'Remarks on the Four Gospels'.

In the Local History Unit is a sale catalogue concerning *The Green Dragon*, which the Enclosure Map drawn up in 1801/2 reveals was still on its old site on what is today Mason's Corner, approximately where Lloyds Chemist is. It refers to James Halliday, or Holliday, who had held the licence from 1785, as a bankrupt, yet it seems he remained as licensee (Gary Boudier tells us), until William Boards took over in 1799. The catalogue reads as follows,

'To be SOLD by AUCTION, By Wm. MATTHEWS, (By Order of the Assignees,) The GREEN DRAGON, Winchmore – Hill, Edmonton, Middlesex, On MONDAY, December 28, 1795, and following Day, at Eleven o' Clock, all the neat and genuine **Household – Furniture**, Linen; China; Glass; Live and Dead Stock; Six Horses and Colts; Two Heifers; Cow and Calf; Market Cart and Harness; Hay Cart; Large Quantity of Potatoes; Cucumber Frames; Quantity of Dung; and other Effects, of Mr. JAMES HOLLIDAY, a BANKRUPT. The furniture consists of FOUR-POST and other Bedsteads, with striped Manchester and other Furniture; eleven good Feather Beds and Bedding; Chests of Drawers; Mahogany dining, card and drinking Tables; Leather Jack; Chairs; Pier and other Glasses; a good eight Day Clock; Carpets; Bath and other Stoves; Pewter Pots, and Measures; Settles; Benches, and all Sorts of useful Kitchen Requisites, & c.

May be view'd on Saturday preceding the Sale, and Catalogues had at the WHITE HART, Tottenham; GOLDEN LYON, Edmonton; BLACK HORSE, Enfield – Highway; COCK, Waltham – Abbey; CHERRY TREE, Southgate; the Place of Sale, and of Mr. MATTHEWS, Auctioneer, Enfield. At the same Time will be sold, the Lease of the above Inn and Premises, eight Years unexpired at Lady Day next, at the very low Rent of Twelve Pounds per Annum, unless sold by private Contract previous to the Sale.'

1796

General

On the 14th May, Edward Jenner proved the vaccination theory, laying the foundations for modern immunisation. In December France's attempt at an invasion of Ireland, under General Hoche, failed when the fleet was scattered by a storm.

Local

In 1796 Millfield House was occupied by the Russian ambassador. Latymer schoolmaster John Adams recorded a temperature of minus six and a half degrees *Fahrenheit* in December. John Blackburn was Hayward for Edmonton Manor.

In 1736 John Nicoll acquired the Minchenden estate, and in 1753 his only daughter, and heiress, Margaret married James Brydges, the Third Duke of Chandos, who came to live in the mansion. Margaret died childless in 1768, and in 1777 the Duke married Anne Eliza Gamon. Their daughter Anna Elizabeth, married Richard, Marquis of Buckingham, in 1796, and the family appears to have sold what became the Grovelands estate to Walker Gray shortly after this.

In 1796, when Quaker Samuel Hoare was buried locally, Church Hill was described as "the Westminster Abbey of Friends in Middlesex". The same year the Monthly Meeting paid £20 towards the construction of a new dwelling house and lobby. This was added next to the main Meeting Room. Professor Olver says, 'Observation of the exterior of the building will show that the east section is an addition to the main building. It was used as the caretaker's accommodation until the cottage was constructed in the early part of the 20th century. Then it was called the School Room and is now called the Small

Meeting Room.' It was also in 1796 that David Barclay, Isaac Smith, Samuel Hoare, jun and Joseph Osgood, gave £100 each to be invested in a fund, the interest for which was to be applied for the upkeep of the premises. One shilling a week was to be given to the resident doorkeeper, in addition to the Monthly Meeting allowance for taking care of the building and keeping the ground in decent order. The remainder was to be used for repairs as needed.

At the National Archives is the following, 'This is the last Will and Testament of Mr. William Batty of Winchmore Hill in the County of Middlesex Gentleman. I Give Devise and Bequeath all my Real and personal Estate to whatsoever and wheresoever and of what nature or kind so ever which shall be it seized or possessed of and cutched to or in any way interested in unto my dear wife Mary Batty her Executors Administrators and all equis to and for her and their own proper use and benefit absolutely forever and I hereby nominate and appoint my said wife and my Brother John Batty joint Executors of this my Will and Guardians of my Son during his Minority. So witness when of I have ....the sixth day of February in the year of our Lord one thousand seven hundred and ninety six. W. Batty .....'

In 1786 the surveyor Launcelot Dowbiggin had prepared three plans and an elevation for John Gray which led to the construction of what became known as Beaulieu Mansion, covered in the map section. (See Plate 43) In 1796 Sir John Soane added minor outbuildings to the Mansion, and some of his work is documented in his Day Book for the last nine months of that year, at the Sir John Soane's Museum, along with an elevation. The entries I recorded are –

'Wednesday April 13th John Gray Esq. drawing Plan and Elevation of Lodge. Laing.' 'Wednesday August 31st Mr. J. Gray Winchmore Hill. Went in Heels (?) chaise fix'd situation of Lodge etc. and returned to Dinner.' 'Friday Sept. 2 1796. Gray Esq. About working drawings for a Cottage Provis. ¾ Day ..... John Gray Esq. About Plans of Lodge Steward. John Gray Esq. About Perspective Plan of a Lodge.' 'Saturday Sept. 3rd 1796. John Gray Esq. About Copies of Drawings of the Lodge. Savard. John Gray Esq. Waiting on him at his House in Water Lane about the Lodge. Provis. ½ Day.' 'Monday September 5th 1796. Jn. Gray Esq. At Winchmore Hill setting out the Gardeners House. Provis. ½ Day. Food & Expenses 5/6d.' 'Monday Sept. 12th 1796. Jn. Gray Esq. Attending the work at the new Gentlemen's House Winchmore Hill. Provis. 1 Day.' 'Monday September 26th. Mr. Gray Attending the work at Winchmore Hill Provis. 1 Day Coach & Expences (stet.) 5/3d.'

1797

General

The window tax, which had been reduced in 1784, was increased again in 1797. It was in this year that the first £1 notes and the first copper pennies were issued by the Bank of England. 1797 also saw an invasion of Britain when 1400 troops under the command of the Irish American General Tate landed in Dyfed, later surrendering to British soldiers. At the Battle of Cape St. Vincent British forces under General Sir John Jervis, and Commodore Nelson, defeated the Spanish Fleet. In October at the Battle of Camperdown off the Dutch coast, the British fleet under Admiral Duncan triumphed over the Dutch.

Local

In 1797 John Glover became the licensee of *The King's Head*. Douglas Haigh, in his *Old Park in the Manor of Enfield*, of 1977, says that Samuel Clayton died on the 20th May 1797, aged 66. Haigh suggests that the estate passed to his brother John.

Plate 5. Portrait of Humphry Repton in 1802

Repton (1752 – 1818) landscaped the surrounds of The Grove. His work, including the picturesque lake, remains to this day in Grovelands Park. He is commemorated in the name of the flats overlooking The Green.

The Brewer Jacob Yallowley (2) came to Winchmore Hill in about 1797, and bought the Leasehold Independent Meeting House, next to property owned by John Radford on The Green, sometime before he died in 1801.

In 1797 Walker Gray commissioned John Nash to design The Grove mansion. Grovelands, as we now know it, still overlooks the grounds that were simultaneously laid out by the eminent landscape gardener Humphry Repton.

Plate 6. Portrait of J.D. Taylor in the Birdcage Room of his Grovelands in 1880

John Donnithorne (1798 – 1885) married Elizabeth Henrietta Thompson on 13th January 1830. He pursued his own Victorian 'Greenbelt Policy', so that the area didn't become urbanised until the 20th century. It would be nice to have a likeness of J.D. from our era of interest, but my thanks to Sheila, widow of the late Alan Dumayne, for kindly supplying this picture of him in his latter years, from her late husband's archives.

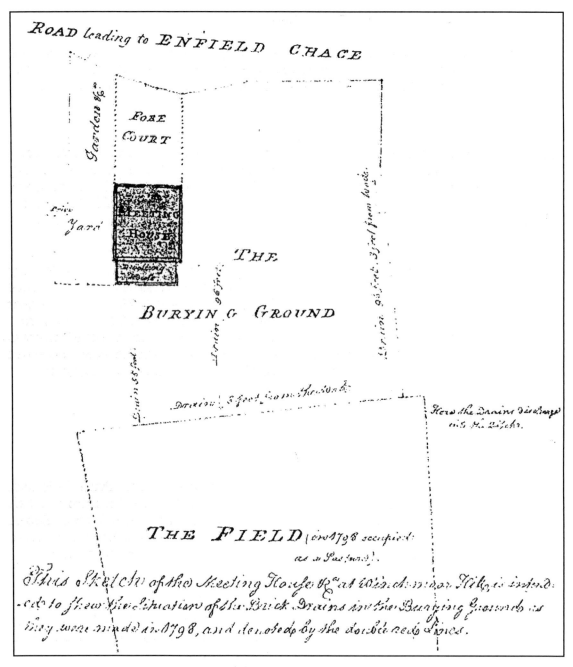

Figure 2. Layout of the Friends Burial Grounds in 1798

This drawing of the Friends' Burial Ground in 1798 was kindly supplied by Professor A. David Olver, and reproduced by courtesy of the Friends.

1798

General

The scientist Henry Cavendish determined the mean density of the earth. It was in 1798 that Pitt increased the tax on newspapers and the Government formed an alliance with Russia against France. On 1st August Nelson sank 11 out of the 13 French battleships in the Battle of the Nile, so effectively trapping Napoleon's Army in the Middle East.

Local

In 1798 Macmillan published *View of the Agriculture of Middlesex* by J. Middleton, which makes no specific reference to Winchmore Hill in the text. However, as our surrounds at that time were very much rural I have quoted extensively from that book in the section on Agriculture.

The Palmers Green Gazette of 1st November 1940 contained a Memorabilia article which reported that, 'In the *Gentleman's Magazine* dated 23rd March, 1798, I read: "At Howsfield Grove, Palmers Green, Edmonton, in his 82nd year, Isaac Smith, esq. many years partner in the house of Freance and Barclay, bankers, Lombard Street, and one of the people called Quakers."' It will be recalled that Smith gave £50 towards the rebuilding of the local Meeting House in 1790, and £100 towards its upkeep in 1796. There is a drawing of the burial grounds at Figure 2.

John Vickris Taylor moved to our area in about 1770, his second wife being Sophia Donnithorne. Their son John Donnithorne Taylor, who was to be such an influential owner of Grovelands in Victorian times, was born on 23rd August 1798. Later in the year John Blackburn Junior inherited Bush Hill House (Halliwick in the 20th century) from his father John Blackburn senior, who died on the 12th October at the age of 67, and was buried at Edmonton Church on the 20th. Also in this year, Francis Newman succeeded John Glover as licensee of *The King's Head*. Isaac Walker was the Manor Hayward.

1799

General

Pitt's Combination Acts (1799-1800) essentially made Trade Unionism illegal (until repealed in 1823-4). To pay for the War against France Pitt introduced an income tax at 2/- in the pound on incomes over £200 p.a. Britain and Austria rejected a French offer of peace. The Duke of York, commanding the British Army in Holland, surrendered to the French at Alkmaar, although an Irish rebellion was suppressed.

Local

At the Poultry, by Bank station, is a Blue Plaque which reads, 'In a house on this site Thomas Hood was born 23rd May 1799'. This famous poet moved to what became known as Hood's Cottage in Vicars Moor Lane in 1829.

In 1799 Martha Newman, who held the licence to *The King's Head*, in 1793-4, again became the licensee. This was also the year that William Boards replaced James Halliday as licensee of *The Green Dragon*.

In the Guildhall Library the front cover to one of the documents filed under Ms. 14, 365 says, "County of Middlesex. The Master Wardens and Commonalty of the Mystery or Cordwainers. Certificate of the Contract for the Redemption of Land Tax. Duly Registered the 25th day of July 1799.' I have extracted details from that document in the notes with the Enclosure map of The Green.

William Radley became a copyhold tenant of the Manor of Edmonton in 1799, when he took over various pieces of land in Winchmore Hill which had previously been in the occupation of William Skilton. Together with subsequent additions, this land formed the nucleus of the later Highfield House estate. We meet Radley again in the Enclosure Ownership Schedule.

Sir James Winter Lake of The Firs succeeded Samuel Wegg as Governor of the Hudson's Bay Company in 1799, remaining in post until his death in 1807. (The local Council appear to have missed this promotion off their Blue Plaque at 335, Firs Lane.)

1800

General

James Hatfield attempted to assassinate King George 111 at a theatre in Drury Lane. The Royal College of Surgeons was founded in London, whose population now exceeded one million. The Armed Neutrality of the North alliance was forged between Russia, Denmark, Sweden and Prussia to counter the British right of search on the high seas, and to keep the British out of the Baltic.

Local

For many years David Pam wrote a weekly article for *The Enfield Gazette*. Two of these in August 2001 featured the dramatic events surrounding the Balaams in March 1800, the family being remembered in Balaams Lane near Southgate Green. Joe was herdsman and common driver to the Parish of Edmonton, and his domain was the Parish Common of about a thousand acres. Pam says that he lived in a cottage standing just inside the gate to the common, about where today Wades Hill meets Houndsden Road, though neither a gate, nor a suitable cottage appear to be marked on the Enclosure Map.

Many wealthy Londoners chose to house their offspring out in the country air of the district, so Joe's wife Sarah earned money as a nurse or child minder. One afternoon in March 1800 a Mrs. James, her companion Miss Clark, and her friend Captain Owen, of the Royal Artillery, came by post-chaise, to visit her infants of one and two years of age at Mrs. Balaam's. The visit finished with the chaise moving off through what on the Enclosure Map is marked as Winchmore Hill Gate (at the foot of 'Church Hill'), when it was stopped by a masked horseman brandishing a small pistol. The Captain was forced to hand over £4.11s in cash and his watch, worth £10, for fear of his life. Then incredibly, according to Mrs. Balaam, the highwayman walked his horse to within three yards of where she was standing, removed his mask, tucked it in the crown of his hat, and then rode off at a gallop towards Enfield!

A reward of £40 was offered for his capture and Sarah claimed to have seen him twice in the following fortnight. On a subsequent third occasion her husband appeared not long afterwards, and she asked him to help her give chase. Accordingly he took up his bill and stick and they followed the suspect as he jogged along on his horse. A man with a cart load of dung approached him from the opposite direction and Joe waved to the driver frantically, in an effort to have the suspect's path blocked, but there was a misunderstanding, so that it was not until the horseman had reached the gate into the Common that Joe was able to grab the horse's bridle and shout, 'It's your life or mine'.

The man slipped off from his horse and tried to make a run for it, but Joe grabbed the man by the skirt of his coat and held him back. They struggled into a muddy ditch and Joe managed to get on top of the other man, with his hand round his throat and knee in his groin, whence he was able to remove the man's pistol from his waistcoat pocket. By now Joe's son, also named Joe, had appeared, and together they bundled the captive off to the son's nearby cottage. However, after he had cleaned himself up, the prisoner made a rush for the door, only to be thwarted by the older Balaam. Both Balaams then tied his hands behind his back, put him in a cart and took him off to see Mr. Nathaniel Gundry, the nearest magistrate, at South Lodge.

Gundry committed the prisoner and asked the Balaams to take him to Bow Street, stopping at *The Cock Tavern* (latterly the *Faltering Fullback*) near Bowes Farm, where the captive treated himself to a shilling's worth of brandy and water. The prisoner, who it transpired was named Richard Franklyn, went for trial at The Old Bailey, where he received a good character witness from his landlord, who had never seen him ride a horse. Further, the post-chaise driver at the scene of the robbery said that Franklyn's horse was not like the one used that day.

The case was dismissed, but the saga wasn't yet over. Only a few days after the robbery of Captain Owen a highwayman had robbed Gundry's wife Emma, the thief then riding off to Edmonton through the gate to the Common near Balaam's house. Franklyn was tried for this crime immediately after the Owen trial, and this time a stable keeper identified Franklyn as the hirer of the horse identified in the hold up of Mrs. Gundry and party. Franklyn was also identified by Mrs. Gundry's coachman and butler, both present at the robbery. This time he was found guilty and hanged.

In August 1800 Sir William Curtis submitted the winning bid to replace Sarah Teshmaker of Fords Grove as Lessee from the Crown of Edmonton Manor. The following month her daughter Sarah Thomasine married Edward Busk. This was the year that Mary Newman took over the licence to *The King's Head* from Martha Newman. John Radford, the first recorded deacon of what is now the Winchmore Hill United Reformed Church, was appointed, and served until 31st October 1849. Sarah Huxley was Hayward for Edmonton Manor.

Richardson says that in the last forty years of the 18th century about 1500 private Enclosure Acts were passed by Parliament. Enclosure Acts were passed for Cheshunt in 1799, Enfield in 1803, Finchley in 1810 and Hornsey in 1812. We are concerned, of course, with the Edmonton Enclosure Act of 1800, which takes up a significant portion of this book. Before the section devoted to it, we go back in time a few years to the enclosure of Enfield Chase, in order to have a better understanding of the 1800 Act.

Section on Edmonton Enclosure
(E. E.) Act of 1800
Enfield Chase Enclosure Act 1777

It will be recalled from an earlier section that Geoffrey de Mandeville had converted this part of the ancient Forest of Middlesex into a private hunting ground in about 1136. The Manor of Enfield consisted of over 15,000 acres, of which about 8,000 at the western end were enclosed in the Chase, but citizens of some of the surrounding villages in the manors of Enfield and Edmonton retained their 'common rights' to use the grounds for such basic things as wintering their pigs and taking firewood. Oliver Cromwell's administration mapped the Chase from 1656 - 8, and this showed the Winchmore Hill Gate also shown on the E.E. Enclosure map.

In 1770 Arthur Young, a farmer of nearby North Mimms, wrote critically of the uneconomic use of Enfield Chase; 'so large a tract of wasteland, so near to the capital, within reach of London as a market and as a dung hill, (it) is a real nuisance to the public ...... If this tract of useless land was enclosed, with farm houses and proper offices built, it would let at once at 15s an acre.' Proposals for the Chase's enclosure were first made at a Duchy of Lancaster (i.e. Crown) court on 5th July 1775. The Crown and ratepayers of the local parishes stood to benefit, whilst the small farmers and the poor might suffer, but the whole thing slipped quietly through the Duchy court, vestry committees, House of Commons, and into the statute book, in 1777, without much contention.

The Crown had resurveyed the Chase in 1776, and allotted sections to each of the local parishes involved. Newby in his *"Old" Souhgate* reports the allocation of the Chase's (then) 8,349 acres as follows - To the King 3218 acres; the Lodges 313 acres; Enfranchised 6 acres; Manor of Old Ford 36 a; Manor of Old Park 30 a; South Mimms Parish 1026 a.; Hadley Parish 240 a.; Enfield Parish 1732; Edmonton 1231 a.; Tithe Owners 519 acres. The rights of the Edmonton commoners were transferred from the whole Chase, to the Edmonton allotment. The Lodges had been involved in the running of the Chase, and West Lodge today survives as a Country Hotel at the corner of Hadley Road and Cockfosters Road. South Lodge's position was commemorated in the name of part of what was Highlands Hospital, off of 'Worlds End Lane'. Let's now look at the 1777 Act, as quoted in Robinson's book of 1819.

'By the Act of Parliament 17th George III. chap. 17. intituled "An Act for dividing the Chase of Enfield, in the County of Middlesex, and for other purposes therein mentioned."

Reciting, that the King was seized to himself, his heirs and successors, in fee-simple of the Chase of Enfield, lying within the parish of Enfield, in the County of Middlesex, being parcel of the estates and possessions of the Duchy of Lancaster, subject to such right of common and other rights, as the freeholders and copyholders of messuages, lands and tenements, situate and being within the several parishes of Enfield, Edmonton, South Minims, and Monken Hadley, in the said County of Middlesex, or the tenants and occupiers thereof for the time being, are entitled unto, within and upon the said Chase.

And that the said Chase, in its present state, yielded very little profit or advantage, either to the King's Majesty, or to the said freeholders and copyholders, or their tenants, in comparison of what it might do, if the same was divided and improved.   And with a view to such division, an accurate survey, admeasurement, and plan of the said Chase, with a table of references thereto, have been lately made and taken, whereby it appeared, that the said Chase contained 8349 A. 1 R. 30 P. or thereabouts, including the several lodges and incroachments thereon.

As to the Allotment to Edmonton.

It was (amongst other things) enacted, "That all that portion or allotment of land within, and part of, and set out upon the said Chase, and described and distinguished on the said survey or plan thereof by words and green lines from the residue of the said Chase, as *the Edmonton Allotment*, containing 1231 A. 2 R. 6 P. abutting on the north and west parts thereof upon the King's allotment; further north upon *the Louth (stet) Lodge Farm*, the tythe allotments and *Enfield* allotment, further west upon inclosures in the Parish of *East Barnet* on the south part thereof, upon the township or village of *Southgate*, and divers inclosures in the said parish of *Edmonton*; and on the east part thereof upon *Enfield Old Park*, and upon the allotment hereinafter assigned to the owner of the said park, and all incroachments thereon, and also all timber trees, woods, and underwoods standing on the several parts of the said allotment hereinafter described," (that is to say) on that part which lyeth south and south-west of *Hounsden* Gutter, and on those parts of the said allotment which abut westward on a visto, or line cut or staked out from *Winchmore Hill* gate to the *Louth (stet) Lodge* inclosure; eastward on *Enfield Old Park*, and northward on the *Enfield* allotment, shall, from and after the passing of this act become, and the same shall from thenceforth be and remain vested in the churchwardens of the said parish of *Edmonton* for the time being, and their successors for ever, in trust for the sole benefit of the owners and proprietors of freehold and copyhold messuages, lands, and tenements within the said parish of *Edmonton*, their heirs and assigns, and their lessees, tenants and undertenants for the time being, intitled to a right of common, or other rights within the said Chase, according to their several estates and interests therein." sect 102.

As to making a Road by Enfield Old Park.

......., it has been agreed between the owner or proprietor of the said *Enfield Old Park*, and the parishioners of the said parish of *Edmonton*, that a public way of forty feet WIDE SHALL BE FENCED OUT OF THEIR SAID ALLOTMENT, next to the fence of the said *Enfield Old Park*, from *Filcap's Gate to the Enfield Old Park* allotment, and be for ever maintained by the parishioners of the said parish of *Edmonton*; and the said way shall be considered as a public way, belonging to the said parish of *Edmonton*; and, in consideration thereof, the said owner and proprietor of *Enfield Old Park* hath agreed to pay to the parish of Edmonton, a clear yearly rent charge of £5. a year for ever, free and clear of all taxes, reprisals and deductions whatsoever, in manner hereinafter mentioned......

.......As to Allotments being accepted in Lieu of other Rights.

That the said allotment herein before aforesaid, for the benefit of the owners and proprietors of the messuages, lands, and tenements in the said parish of Edmonton, shall be taken, and accepted in full compensation, satisfaction, and discharge of all their rights, claims, and privileges whatsoever, in, over, and upon all the residue of the said Chase : and that the said allotment shall, from and after the passing of this Act, be, become and remain freed, exonerated, and for ever absolutely discharged of and from all rights of Chase, right of soil, and right of common, of the King's Majesty, his heirs and successors, and his and their tenants and lessees, within or upon the same." Sec. 13.

As to Edmonton Allotment annexed to that Parish.

That the portion or allotment of the said Chase hereby assigned to or for the benefit of the Parish of *Edmonton*, and all incroachments which shall become vested in the churchwardens of that parish, (save and except in respect of the tythes of the said allotment, or of lands which may be set apart in lieu of such tythes,) and all messuages, buildings, and inclosures whatsoever within the circuit or limits of the allotments, which are now part of the parish of Enfield, shall be for ever hereafter annexed to and become part of the said parish of *Edmonton.....'*

The Duchy of Lancaster was the Crown. The new road from Filcap's Gate to the Enfield Old Park allotment is now the western end of Green Dragon Lane.

The clearing and sale of great numbers of trees in the years following the enclosure, depressed prices (excepting oak). The local colliers, who had had a number of hearths in the vicinity for charcoal, had now exhausted the wood available. Much devastation occurred in the early 1780s, and in his 1984 book on the Chase Pam cites particular cases. For example, he tells us of Aaron Patrick, landlord of *The King's Arms* in Green Street, and his greed, in 1783, in coming in a cart with four horses to cut down young oaks at Crews Hill. When his house was searched 29 trees were found stored on the premises.

Middleton in 1798 tells us that, 'Three fourths of Edmonton allotment is covered with bushes and has about one solitary, unthrifty, and unsightly tree to an acre. And as these are deficient in side-branches, they look like may-poles encumbered with ivy. The live stock, of course, is proportioned to the scantiness and poverty of the pasture.' So the pressure for enclosure continued, culminating in the Edmonton Enclosure Act of 1800.

Robbins asserts that after enclosure the former wasteland began to assume a prosperous appearance, as arable field or parkland. He says that the best land was constantly improved with London manure, which made a convenient return load for the carts that took the local produce to market. London manure was reckoned to cost 6s a load at Hendon, 10s at the more distant South Mimms.

Tithes

Taxation is not, of course, a modern concept, and in the period covered by this book there were still agriculturally based levies known as tithes. These feature in the 1800 Enclosure Act, so a few words of explanation seem in order. I have relied mainly on two sources – John Richardson's *The Local Historian's Encyclopaedia*, and *Tithe Surveys for Historians* by Kain & Prince, though the two sources occasionally seem to be in conflict.

There were three types of tithes. The first of these was called a Pr(a)edial tithe, and was calculated on produce from the soil, such as corn, oats, wood etc. The second type was the Mixed or Agistment Tithe, calculated on income from stock, such as pigs, lambs and milk. The third tithe was Personal, assessed on income derived from labour, and generally levied on milling and fishing. Kain and Prince say that after 1549 Personal tithes were not significant.

Income from barren heath, waste woodland, and glebe land, was exempt. The tithes were intended for the support of the incumbent of the local Parish Church. Richardson says that they were the equivalent to a tenth part of the income, whereas Kain and Price say that they represented a tenth part of the annual *increase* in value of produce. Until the mid 17th century Praedial tithes were commonly taken as actual produce, and were stored in tithe barns, many of which still survive around the country. After that time locally negotiated monetary equivalents gradually replaced actual produce.

Richardson explains that in medieval times where monasteries were involved in the appointment of a local vicar, the tithes were divided between the monastery and the vicar. The monastery received the Great or Rectorial Tithes, the vicar received the Small or Vicarial Tithes. Things became complicated following Henry V111's Reformation as many monastic buildings fell into the hands of the Crown, and then lay hands. This led to lay people and organisations claiming the Great or Rectorial Tithes. Kain and Prince say that generally speaking the Great Tithes consisted of grain, hay and wood – the Praedial tithes of the earlier definitions. The Small Tithes constituted everything else that remained. Kain and Prince say that generally under Enclosure Acts the tithes were extinguished in exchange for allotments of land.

In the agricultural depression that followed the Napoleonic Wars tithes were seen as an intolerable burden by the small farmer, and the labourer who relied on him for his wage. This wasn't helped by the fact that many payments were fixed when the corn prices had recently been high. On the recommendation of a Select Committee on Tithes in 1816, many such charges were made binding upon the parties concerned, and their successors, by leases entered into for a period of up to 14 years. The same money still had to be found from reduced incomes. Feeling eventually ran so high in the early 1830s that there were rick burning riots in parts of SE England much, no doubt, like the incident witnessed by Charles Lamb in Enfield in the diary section for 1830.

The sore feelings were directed not only at the tithes themselves, but also at the Church of England, and there was even grim talk of disestablishing it. Many Quakers had long objected to the payment of tithes to the C of E. We can see that locally in the diary entry for 1788, when John Decka had wheat and animals taken for non – payment of tithes.

Finally Parliament acted. Under the Tithe Commutation Act of 1836, tithes could be commuted to a rent charge, and Commissioners were appointed to negotiate fair land values with the inhabitants. The Tithe Act of 1936 extinguished tithes altogether.

Before proceeding to the section on the Enclosure Act it might also be as well to briefly explain the acre, rood and perch used in the Ownership Schedule. The acre is an ancient measurement that was derived from multiplying a furlong (1/8th of a mile = 220 yards) by a chain of 22 yards, which was long used in surveying on both sides of the Atlantic (and incidentally, internationally defines the distance between the wickets in cricket). The acre, which is still in common use today, is 4840 square yards. The rood, which died out some years ago, was ¼ acre, and the perch, at 16 ½' x 16 ½', was 1/40th of the rood. The perch also died out some time ago here, but surprisingly, in the officially metric country of Sri Lanka, it is still *the* common unit for describing property!

Edmonton Enclosure (E. E.) Act of 1800

Robinson says, 'By an act of Parliament, 40 Geo. 3. (1800,) intituled *"An Act for Dividing and Inclosing the Common, Common Fields, Common Marshes, and Waste Land, within the Parish of Edmonton, in the County of Middlesex; and for other purposes therein mentioned."*

Reciting that, by an Act made and passed in the seventeenth year of the reign of his present Majesty King George the Third, intituled, "An Act for dividing the Chase of *Enfield*, in the county of *Middlesex*, and for other purposes therein mentioned," it was (amongst other things) enacted, that a certain portion of land, therein particularly mentioned and described as the Edmonton allotment, containing one thousand two hundred and thirty-one acres two roods and six perches, should, from the passing of the said act, become vested in the churchwardens of the said Parish of *Edmonton* for the time being, in trust for the freeholders and copyholders of the said parish having right of common within the said chase.

That there were in the said parish of *Edmonton* divers large quantities of open or common fields; and also a large quantity of common marshes and wastes. That the King, in right of his crown, was seised to himself, his heirs and successors, of, in, and to the manor and manorial rights of *Edmonton,* otherwise *Edelmeton,* in the said county;

Plate 7. Harvesting in an enclosed field

By Thomas Berwick (1753 – 1828) who worked in the north of England, but one presumes that this scene bears some resemblance to one which might have prevailed locally.

and also in right of his duchy of *Lancaster,* of the manor and manorial rights of *Enfield,* in the said county, whereof the said *Edmonton* allotment is part and parcel, and whereof her grace *Anna Eliza* Duchess of *Chandos* is lessee.

That the master, fellows, and scholars of Trinity College, in the University of *Cambridge,* were patrons of the Vicarage of *Enfield* aforesaid, and also owners of the impropriate and rectorial tythes arising within the same parish, and as such were entitled to all great tythes arising or to arise within the said allotment called Edmonton allotment of Enfield Chase. That the Rev. *Richard Newbon,* Clerk, Batchelor in Divinity, was the present Vicar of the said parish of *Enfield,* and by virtue thereof was entitled to all vicarial tythes and dues arising within the said allotment.

That the Dean and Chapter of the cathedral church *of Saint Paul,* in the city of *London,* were patrons of the Vicarage of *Edmonton* aforesaid, and also owners of all impropriate and rectorial tythes arising within the same parish (except to such as arise within the said allotment called the Edmonton allotment of Enfield Chase;) and as such were entitled to all great tythes arising or to arise within the said Parish. That the Reverend *Dawson Warren,* Clerk, was the then Vicar of the said Parish of *Edmonton,* and by virtue thereof was entitled to all vicarial tythes and dues within the said Parish of *Edmonton* (except to such as arise within the said allotment:)

And that the said common, common fields, marshes, and waste lands, in their present state yielded very little profit or advantage, in comparison with what they might do if the same were divided, allotted, and inclosed. But as such division, allotment, and inclosure cannot be effectually made and established without the aid of parliament,

It was, amongst other things enacted, "That *Thomas Bainbridge,* of Upper Guildford-street, in the County of Middlesex, *William Young,* of Chancery-lane, in the same county, and *Francis Wilshaw* of Thavies-inn, Holborn, London, gentlemen, and their successors, to be elected in the manner hereinafter mentioned, shall be and they are hereby appointed Commissioners for dividing, allotting, and inclosing the said Edmonton allotment of Enfield Chase, and the said open and common fields, common marshes, and waste lands and grounds, within the said parish of *Edmonton,* and for putting this act into execution, in the manner, and subject to the rules, orders, directions, and exceptions, hereinafter contained."

As to the Survey.

"That a true and correct survey and admeasurement shall be made of the said common, common fields, common marshes, and waste lands, and also of all the present inclosed grounds and lands of the said parish, and a plan shall be drawn thereof."

As to Allotments to the Lords of the Manors.

"That the said Commissioners shall, and they are hereby required to set out, allot, and award unto the King, in right of his crown, as Lord of the said Manor of *Edmonton* otherwise *Edelmeton,* one sixteenth part of all the said waste lands, lying within the aforesaid Manor of *Edmonton,* in lieu of his right as Lord of the said Manor of *Edmonton* otherwise *Edelmeton,* in and to the soil of all the commons and wastes hereby intended to be divided and inclosed, lying and being within the Manor of *Edmonton* otherwise *Edelmeton;*

and also to set out, allot, and award unto the said Dean and Chapter, Lords of the Manor of *Edmonton, Bowes, Ford, Paul House,* and *Darnford,* within the said parish, one sixteenth part of all the waste lands lying within the said last mentioned Manor, in lieu of their rights as Lords thereof in and to the soil of all the commons and wastes lying within the same."

As to Allotment in lieu of Tythes of the Chase Allotment,

"That the said Commissioners, ... allot, unto and for the said master, fellows, and scholars of Trinity College in *Cambridge,* and their lessee, and the said Reverend *Richard Newbott,* Vicar of *Enfield* aforesaid, such plot or plots, allotment or allotments, of the said common or parcel of waste land called the Edmonton Allotment of Enfield Chase, as shall be, in the judgment of the said Commissioners, quantity quality, and situation considered, equivalent to one ninth part of the said Chase Allotment; ...... in lieu of all tythes, payments, and compositions in lieu of tythes, due or payable to them or either of them respectively, ...

As to the Allotment of Land, in lieu of the Tythes of the Common fields and Common Marshes, and of Land to the Vicar of Edmonton.

"That the said Commissioners shall ...... to set out, from the then residue of the lands and grounds hereby intended to be inclosed (except from the said allotment of Enfield Chase) such plots or allotments of land as shall, in the judgment of the said Commissioners, be equal in value to one fifth part of all the arable parts of the said common fields, and to one ninth part of all the grass or greensward ground in the said common fields and common marshes, and waste lands (except glebe land) lying and being within the said Parish of *Edmonton,* subject or liable to the payment of tythes in kind, or to any composition in lieu thereof; and that out of the same lands so to be set out in lieu of the tythes of the said common fields and common marshes

the said Commissioners shall, and they are hereby required *to allot unto the said Dawson Warren, and his successors, Vicars of Edmonton as aforesaid, one plot or allotment of land containing twenty acres, which shall be situate in a certain common field, called the Hyde, adjoining to or as near the vicarage house in Edmonton aforesaid as will conveniently permit;* and all the residue of the said plots or allotments of land in lieu of the tythes of the said common fields and common marshes, shall be allotted to the said Dean and Chapter of the cathedral church of *Saint Paul,* in the City of *London,* and their lessee, his executors, administrators, and assigns, for the residue of his term and interest therein."

As to Corn Rents or Yearly Money Payments in lieu of the Tythes of Old Inclosures, and Corn Rents to be allotted to the Vicar.

"That the said Commisoners (stet) shall and they are hereby required in the next place to set out, determine, and fix such corn rents or yearly tythe rents, or money payments in lieu of tythes........ and the said Vicar shall have and be entitled, as well to the said twenty acres of land hereinbefore directed to be allotted to him, as to the corn rents so ascertained and directed by the said Commissioners to be paid to the said Vicar of *Edmonton in lieu of his vicarial tythes ;* and the said Dean and Chapter, and their said lessee, shall have and be entitled, as well to the said plots or allotments of land hereinbefore directed to be made to them, as to the corn rents or yearly tythe rents, or money payments in lieu of tythes, so directed to be paid to the said Dean and Chapter, and their said lessee, *in lieu of their great or impropriate tythes;*.........

.... and the said Commissioners shall, from the London Gazette, ascertain what hath been the average price of good marketable wheat in the County of *Middlesex,* during the term of twenty one years next preceding the passing of this act, and shall in and by the schedule hereinafter directed to be made and annexed to their award, ascertain and set forth what respective quantities of wheat shall, according to such average price as aforesaid be equal to each of the said respective corn rents or yearly tythe rents, or payments in lieu of tythes, so charged upon the old inclosures within the said parish of *Edmonton,* in lieu of Tythes as aforesaid. .... That immediately after the expiration of twenty one years from the execution of the said award, the average price of wheat as aforesaid shall be again ascertained;......

For regulating the Corn Rents.

"And in order to prevent any difficulty to the said Dean and Chapter, or their said lessee or lessees, or the said Vicar or his successors, by the division of any estate, by sale or otherwise, and to facilitate the future regulating the said corn rents or yearly tythe rents, or money payments in lieu of tythes; it was further enacted, that the said Commissioners shall, and they are hereby required to make, or cause to be made, two complete schedules or descriptions of each and every parcel of ancient inclosure, with the name of the owner thereof, the exact measure in acres, roods, and perches, the corn rent or yearly tythe rent, or payments in lieu of tythes, issuing out of each respectively, and the quantity of wheat which is to govern each of the said future yearly rents payable to the said Dean and Chapter, their said lessee or lessees, and Vicar, and the rate by the acre by which the said corn rent shall be charged as aforesaid, ...

Respecting the Allotments to Houses.

"That in the making of such allotments, the said Commissioners shall consider all houses, messuages, tenements, and cottages, which have been erected and built and used as dwelling houses twenty five years and upwards, as entitled to right of common, and shall allot unto and amongst the owners of all such houses,

64

messuages, tenements, and cottages, such part or proportion of the said lands and grounds hereby intended to be divided and inclosed as in their judgment shall be fair and reasonable -.....'

As to Sale of Lands for defraying Expenses.

"And in order to raise a sufficient sum of money to defray the charges and expences (stet) of obtaining and passing this Act; .... That it shall and may be lawful to and for the said Commissioners, as soon after the passing of this Act as they shall think proper, and so from time to time as often as they shall think necessary, to sell by private contract, or by public sale by auction, unto any person or persons, such part or parts of the said common or allotment of Enfield Chase, and the said common fields, common marshes, and waste lands and grounds, as they shall deem sufficient for the purposes aforesaid; .....'

E. E. Act Land Ownership Schedule – Appendix 1

Robinson says, 'Of the several parts of the Common or Allotment of Enfield Chase, Common Marshes, Waste Lands, and Grounds, sold by the Commissioners, to raise a sufficient sum of Money to defray the Charges and Expenses of obtaining and passing an Act intituled "An Act for dividing the Common, Common Fields, Common Marshes, and Waste Land, within the Parish of Edmonton, in the County of Middlesex, and for other purposes therein mentioned" and of surveying, admeasuring, planning, valuing, dividing, and allotting the Lands and Ground, by the said Act, intended to be divided and inclosed, and of forming, making, and putting into good and sufficient repair the Roads and Highways, and of preparing the Award, & c.'

There then follows a table from which I have here tried to extract the entries for Winchmore Hill and immediate surrounds (remember A = Acre, R = Rood, P = Perch) -

To whom sold	No. on Map	No. of Lots	Quantity A.R.P.			Quality	Where Situate	Purchase Money £. s. d.
Tho. Lewis	1343	2			28p.	Waste	Palmer's Green	£223 – for both
	1348		1a.	3r.	33p.	Waste		
J. Walker Esq.	1349	1		3r.	23p.	Waste	Palmer's Green	£91-
	1353	2	1a.	2r.	6p.	Waste	Dog & Duck Lane	£130 for both
	1363		1a.	0r	6p.		In another Lane	
S. Pole (his	1406	1	5a.	2r.	12p.	Waste	At Bourne	£420 -
Executers)	1407	1	1a.			Waste	The Green, near Southgate	£105-
W. Gray Esq.	1354	1	1a.			Waste	Dog & Duck Lane	£40-
	1533				8p		Chase – side	
	1532			1r.	0p.		Chase – side	
	1402	1533 -			4p.	Waste	Winchmore – hill lane	1533 -
	1401	1356			4p.	Waste	Winchmore – hill lane	1356
	1400	= 8			3p.	Waste	Winchmore – hill lane	= £42-
	1359				12p.	Waste	Hopper's lane	
	1358				22p.	Waste	Hopper's lane	
	1356			1r.	37p.	Waste	Hopper's lane	
Wm. Eaton	1362	1362 -		2r.	0p.	Waste	In a private lane	
	1360	1361			25p.	Waste	Hopper's lane	£40 for 3 Eaton
	1361	= 3			8p.	Waste	Near Hopper's lane	

To whom sold	No. on Map	No. of Lots	Quantity A.R.P.			Quality	Where Situate	Purchase Money £. s. d.
J. Merrington	1392	1	1a.	0r.	0p.	Arable	In Hag Field	£100-
John Davis	1589	1	1a.	0r.	0p.		On the Chase Allot-	£105-
							ments near Filcap's Gate	
R. Marshall	1578	1	1a.	0r.	0p.		Ditto near Winchmore Hill	£105-
Philip Godsal	1535	2	1a.	0r.	32p.		Chase Side, lately inclosed	£120-
	1536		2a.	0r.	20p.		from the Chase	
	1517	1	6a.	0r.	0p.		Ditto, part of the Chase Allot.	£480-
	1522	1	3a.	3r.	0p.		Adjoining Ditto	£285-
H. Thompson Esq.	1569	1	3a.	0r.	0p.		Old Park Corner, part of	£240-
							Chase Allotment	
	1403				16p.		Near Winchmore - hill	
Wm. Radley	1376	1	1a.	0r.	24p.		In High Field	£125-
John Decker	1390	1			23p.	Waste	At Winchmore Hill	£12-
John Hobbs	1357	1		1r.	32p.	Waste	Hopper's - lane	£22-
S. Teshmaker	147	1		1r.	20p.	Waste	In a Lane near Ford's Green	£20-

E.E. Act Land Ownership Schedule – Appendix 11

Robinson says, 'The corn rents set forth in the following schedule, amounting to the sum of £1263 12s. 7d. per ann. and are equal in value to one-fifth part of all the arable lands already inclosed, and one-ninth part of all the pasture, meadow, grass, and green sward lands in the Parish of Edmonton, and are payable by the occupiers of such lands for the time being out of the same, from the 10th of October, 1801, by equal half yearly payments on the 5th of April and 10th of October in every year, free and clear of all manner of parochial taxes whatsoever now imposed.

The several corn rents or yearly tythe rents, or money payments in lieu of tythes, which are set forth in the eighth column of the following schedule as payable to the Vicar of Edmonton, amounting to the sum of £829 4s. per annum, are to be paid to the Vicar of Edmonton, and his successors, vicars, for ever: and which together with the allotment of twenty acres in the Hyde Field as a compensation for all the vicarial tythes, and other payments in lieu of tythes, arising and payable within the Parish of Edmonton, (except the payment after mentioned). And the several corn rents or yearly tythe rents, or money payments in lieu of tythes, which are set forth in the ninth column of the following schedule, as payable to the Dean and Chapter of St. Paul's, amounting to the sum of £434 8s 7d. by the year, are for ever hereafter to be payable and paid to the said Dean and Chapter, and their Lessees, and are with the six allotments (4) awarded to them and their lessees in lieu of tythes, as a compensation for all the great or impropriate tythes and compositions, or money payments in lieu thereof, within the said parish of Edmonton, (except the Edmonton allotment of Enfield Chase) which said plots or allotments of lands and corn rents, awarded to the said Dean and Chapter, and the lessee or lessees, and to the said Vicar, are by the act 40 Geo. III. before mentioned, directed to be deemed, taken and considered as equal to the value of, and accepted in full bar, satisfaction and compensation, of and for all the tythes both great and small, and all compositions and payments in lieu of tythes, arising, renewing or payable within the said Parish of Edmonton, (Easter offerings, mortuaries, arid other surplice fees to the said Vicar of Edmonton only excepted) and also except the accustomed yearly payment of £20. from the said Dean and Chapter and their lessee to the said Vicar of Edmonton, which is to continue due and payable as heretofore. (See the Award of the Commissioners under the Act 40 Geo. III.)

(4) The allotments are as follow:

Fo.		No.	A.	R.	P.		
22 in the award	1259 in plan;	37	0	31	of Arable in	Hound's Field.
23	"	1367	16	1	20	"	Scotch Field
	"	1270	11	2	22	"	Nest Field
	"	1285	112	3	10	"	Hyde Field
24	"	1257	15	1	0	"	Barrow Field
25	"	1236	83	1	32	"	Meadow or Marsh land in Edmonton Marsh

A. Schedule

Of each and every parcel of ancient inclosure within the Parish of Edmonton, with the name of the owner thereof alphabetically arranged; the exact measure in acres, roods, and perches, the corn rents or yearly tythe rents, or payments in lieu of tythes issuing out of each respectively; and the quantity of wheat which is to govern each of the future yearly rents payable to the Dean and Chapter of St. Paul's, as the impropriators and their lessees, and to the Vicar, and the rate per acre, by which the said corn rent is charged. – To which is added a schedule of the several allotments which are freed and discharged from the payment of tythes.

And after setting out the public highways, private roads, and foot paths, and allotting out certain portions of the Edmonton allotment of Enfield Chase for public gravel pits, for digging gravel and other materials for repairing the roads and highways within the Parish of Edmonton; the residue of the common or allotment of Enfield Chase, and the open and common fields, marshes, and waste lands was allotted to the several persons, & c. and in manner set forth in the following schedule.'

In the first column in Robinson's reproduction of the Ownership Schedule he has used the term 'Proprietors', but I have put the owners' names as separate sub headings, thus removing them from the columns. So my first column for each listing is actually Robinson's second column. Robinson has a column titled 'Corn Rent payable to the Vicar', followed by one titled 'Corn Rent payable to the Impropriators', though only one of these is ever filled in for each Plot. I have amended the table to show just one column headed 'Corn Rent' being the rent payable to the Vicar unless otherwise shown. The final column shows the Bushels (Bus.) of wheat equivalent.

E. E. Land Ownership Schedule for Winchmore Hill

A

Acott, Christopher

No.on Map	Premises	Tenure	State in 1801	Quantity A.R.P	Per Acre	Corn Rent	O'tv Bus.Decim.
Pt. 172	Several houses			Pt.172+173			
173	and yards			= 0a 1r 25p			

Acott, John

No.on Map	Premises	Tenure	State in 1801	Quantity A.R.P	Per Acre	Corn Rent	O'tv Bus.Decim.
Pt. 172	Four tenements, & c			-37p			

Plots 172 and 173 are in the small cluster of cottages near the junction of The Bourne and 'Fox Lane' (see Figure 11).

67

At the LMA is document ACC/695/49, which records the Edmonton Manor Quit Rents for 1780 – 1, and often tells us when tenants were admitted. There are three entries for a William Acott who, the Edmonton Manor Minutes for 12th June 1810 list as one of the Jurors, and record that, 'John Acott late a customary Tenant is dead and he died seized of all those four cottages or tenements situate at the Bourne .....', which in that diary section I suggest were not on Plot 172. He was admitted as tenant upon the death of his father William in 1794, and upon his own death, the cottages passed to his younger brother Joseph. Joseph is mentioned in the Manor minutes for the Dean of St. Paul's in 1817.

A William Acott is also listed as a Juror in the Manor minutes for 16th May 1826, and in that year's Pigot's Directory as a Carpenter and Builder in the village of Southgate. So there was clearly more than one William Acott. The William Acott in the Quit Rent schedule for 1780/1 paid 1/- for a Copyhold cottage at the Bourne (for which he was admitted on 2nd July 1770), 2/6d for a Copyhold cottage at the Bourne (also admitted 2nd July 1770) and 1/- for a Copyhold holding adjoining his home in Southgate (admitted 9th June 1770).

Adams, M. (his executors)

No.on Map	Premises	Tenure	State in 1801	Quantity A.R.P	Per Acre	Corn Rent	O'tv Bus.Decim.
1583	Allotment on the Chase	Copyhold		1a 1r 3p			
99	Two houses and garden			0a 2r 0p	5/6d	2/9d	0B 423d
96	One house and garden			- 16p	4/-	4d	51d

Plot 1583 is on the map of the 'Eversley Crescent' area (Figure 8), being in the angle between 'Wades Hill' and Green Dragon Lane. Plots 99 and 96 are on the northern side of what is now Vicars Moor Lane. 99 is on the corner with 'Wades Hill', whilst 96 is about half way along.

The Universal Directory for Great Britain of 1791 gives a 'List of the Livery of London' that shows a Moses Adams living in Winchmore - hill and working for the Tiler and Bricklayer's Company. This must surely be the M. Adams listed in the schedule. The LMA document ACC/695/49 mentioned entries for Moses Adams. The first is for a Copy hold premise 'by Winchmore Hill' with a Quit Rent of 6d, for which he was admitted in 1770. The second was for 'Copy a Cottage Barn.', for which he was admitted in 1776. The third was for, 'Copy a Piece of Land in front of his house, at Winchmore Hill' with a Quit Rent of 8d, for which he was admitted in 1777.

Allison, Ann

No.on Map	Premises	Tenure	State in 1801	Quantity A.R.P	Per Acre	Corn Rent	O'tv Bus.Decim.
177	House and garden			0a 0r 12p			

Plot 177 is near the plots of the Acott family at The Bourne.

The records of the Edmonton Manor Quit Rents for 1780 – 1 list a Henry, Thomas and John Allason, which might be a variant of Allison. Each had a cottage at the Bourne, and each paid a Quit Rent of 1/-.

B

Barnes, John

No. on Map	Premises	Tenure	State in 1801	Quantity A.R.P	Per Acre	Corn Rent	O'tv Bus.Decim.
167	Two houses and gardens			37p	5/-	1s 1d	167d
194	A field		Meadow	3a 0r 7p	5/6d	16s 8d	2B 565d
			Total	3a 1r 4p		17s 9d	2B 732d

Plot 167 is in the vicinity of the modern *Salisbury Arms*. In the notes accompanying the map of The Green area (Figure 14), I surmise that the 'old' *Salisbury Arms,* which served its last pint on 14th February 1936, was a butcher's shop in the early 19th century. Plot 194 was in the vicinity of the modern day Arundel Gardens (Figure 13). Plot 194 must be the Kitchen Croft pastureland in the following section relating to John Barnes.

The Palmers Green and Southgate Gazette of 31st January 1936 tells us that Mr. W.H. Pratt, a curator at Southgate Museum, had recently received three Manorial documents relating to land in Hoppers Lane from a Mr. J.W. Harris. The earliest of the three deeds was dated 9th June 1772 and records that at the View of Frankpledge and General Court Baron of the Manor of Edmonton, John Barnes (a minor) by Hannah Barnes, his mother and guardian, was admitted as a tenant of three messuages and land, on the death of his father, Robert Barnes, who had died intestate. The 1772 deed read as follows,

'Manor of Edelmeton, otherwise Edelington, otherwise Edmonton, in the County of Middlesex. The View of Frankpledge with the General Court Baron of Sarah Teshmaker, Lady of the said Manor, held in and for the said Manor, on the Tuesday in Whitsun week, being the ninth day of June one thousand seven hundred and seventy two, John Stuart, Gentleman, Steward.

At this Court the homage find and present that Robert Barnes, late a customary tenant of this Manor, is dead, intestate, and that he died seized of one piece or parcel of pastureland called Kitchen Croft containing by estimation three acres lying nigh to Hoppers Lane.... and also three acres land in Highfield abutting Hoppers Grove and Stottfield ...... and also of that messuage or tenement situate at Winsmore Hill within the said Manor, and also of another messuage there, and also of two cottages with the appurtenances lately erected upon the waste of this Manor situate lying and being at Winsmore Hill aforesaid to which said premises the said Robert Barnes was admitted at a Court held in and for the said Manor on the sixteenth day of May, one thousand and seven hundred and forty nine, under the will of his uncle, Robert Barnes, deceased, and that John Barnes now an infant is his youngest son and heir at law ......

.... And because the said John Barnes is under the age of twenty one years so that he cannot govern himself or his estate therefore the Lady of the said Manor by her said steward aforesaid granted the custody as well of the body of the said John Barnes as the estate of him the said John Barnes to the said Hannah Barnes, his mother, until the said John Barnes shall attain his full age of twenty one years and then to render a just and true account of the rents and profits of the said premises to the said John Barnes and she was admitted guardian accordingly.
Exd. JNO. STUART (Steward) The fine 5s. 3d'

The second document cited in the 1936 *Gazette* article recites that at a Court held on the 4th June 1816, Jane Barnes (the widow of John Barnes) was admitted as tenant and, at the same Court and in the same deed, her three children were admitted as tenants in reversion. In her paper on Highfield House, Ms. Griffith – Williams informs us that it was in 1816 that William Radley purchased Kitchen Croft from the representatives of the deceased John Barnes, to add to what became the Highfield House Estate.

The third document sets out that at a Court held on the 4th June, 1819, the three children of Jane Barnes, who had by then entered into possession on the death of their mother, sold, out of Court, the three messuages or cottages to John Brown for £300, and that the said John Brown had been admitted as tenant.

The Lady of the Manor, Sarah Teshmaker, is covered in the Busk-Teshmaker notes. It seems worth pointing out that in the family account of the Tugwells and Yallowleys later in this schedule, they are shown to have intermarried with a Barnes family, though there is no evidence to suggest that it was the same Barnes family as John's.

Bartholomew. Charles

No. on Map	Premises	Tenure	State in 1801	Quantity A.R.P	Per Acre	Corn Rent	O'tv Bus.Decim.
71	House and field adjoining		Pasture	2a 2r 27p	6/-	16s 0d	2B 463d
1541	Allotment on the Chase	Copyhold		0a 1r 23p			

Plot 71 is in the vicinity of the modern day Hill House Close. Plot 1541 is in the vicinity of the 'The Glade' (see Figure 8 for both).

Mr. Bartholomew is mentioned as renting a field from the local Friends in the Monthly Meeting Minutes of the 1790s, but little else is known of this man.

Beale, Daniel Esq.

No. on Map	Premises	Tenure	State in 1801	QuantityA.R.P	Per Acre	Corn Rent	O'tv Bus.Decim.
1347	Allotment on waste at Palmer's Green			1r 27p			
1364	Allotment on lane (stopped up)			1r 37p			
1366	Allotment on Barrow's Well Green	Copyhold		31p			
353	Field		Meadow	4a 2r 37p	5/6d	£1 5s 11d	3B 987d
354	Ditto next ditto		Meadow	1a 3r 37p	4/6d	8s 10d	1B 359d
355			Meadow	5a 3r 35p	5/1d	£1 10s 3d	4B 653d
356			Arable	5a 0r 28p	8/-	£2 1s 4d	6B 359d
357			Meadow	6a 0r 35p	5/4d	£1 13s 1d	5B 91d
358			Pasture	2a 2r 23p	5/1d	£0 13s 4d	2B 52d
359			Meadow	3a 2r 12p	5/4d	£0 19s 0d	2B 925d
360			Arable	5a 3r 23p	10/-	£2 18s 11d	9B 66d
352	House, outbuildings and yards			0a 3r 32p	5/6d	£0 5s 2d	0B 795d
343			Meadow	4a 2r 27p	5/-	£1 3s 4d	3B 590d
344			Meadow	4a 1r 26p	5/6d	£1 4s 2d	3B 718d
345			Meadow	6a 0r 17p	5/-	£1 10s 6d	4B 692d
346			Arable	5a 2r 3p	9/7d	£2 12s 10d	8B 129d
347			Pasture	0a 3r 29p	5/3d	4s 9d	730d
348	Barn Close		Meadow	3a 3r 1p	5/3d	£0 19s 8d	3B 27d
349			Meadow	2a 3r 5p	5/-	£0 13s 10d	2B 129d
350			Meadow	2a 1r 4p	5/3d	£0 11s 10d	1B 821
351			Meadow	3a 0r 8p	4/6d	£0 13s 8d	2B 103d
134	Cottage & garden			0a 1r 25p	5/-	2s	0B 308d
161	Pightle		Pasture	2a 1r 28p	>5/9d	14s 11d	2B 296d
162	Cottage & stable			0a 0r 20p			

See Figure 18. Plot 1347 is nearly opposite what would today be St. John's Church in Green Lanes. Plot 1366 is opposite what is today the refuse tip in Barrow's Well Green. Plots 353/4/5/6/7/8/9 and 360 are in Palmer's Green, on the southern side of 'Hedge Lane'. Plot 352 is, just north of Plot 1347. Plots 343 and 1364 are on Green Lanes, approximately opposite what is now St. Monica's Church. Plots 344 and 5 are in the vicinity of modem day Farndale Avenue. Plot 346/7/8/9/350/351 constitute a stretch of land just north of 'Hedge Lane'. Plot 134 is on the northern side of 'Station Road'. 161 and 162 are just west of Woodside/Rowantree on The Green.

Millfield House (Plate 54)was probably constructed in about 1790, and is now an Arts Centre. In 1801 it was the home of Daniel Barbot Beale, whose family came from St. Pancras, where they continued to own property.

Beckett & Ostliffe

No.on Map	Premises	Tenure	State in 1801	Quantity A.R.P	Per Acre	Corn Rent	O'tv Bus.Decim.
80	King's Head public house & yards			1r 4p	6d		

Plot 80 is shown at the corner of what are now Church Hill and Wades Hill on the map of The Green area (Figure 14).

In 1801 *The King's Arms* and *The Cock* (now *The Faltering Full Back)* in Palmers Green, and *The King's Head* were all owned by the Enfield brewers, Beckett and Ostliffe. The landladies listed for the Inn from 1799 to 1803 inclusive were a Martha and Mary Newman.

Mr. Kent of Edwards Estates (recently owners of Devon House) kindly supplied me with information about a deed dated 1839 between Wm. Tyall and John Ostliffe Beckett (declared bankrupt), son of deceased brewer Wm. Beckett, along with his wife Mary. There is, apparently, a long list of properties in Enfield, Edmonton and Winchmore Hill, which had been bequeathed by Wm Beckett to John Ostliffe Beckett. They were mainly public houses, and included *The King's Head*.

Edwards Estates also followed up the ownership and occupation of the Devon House/Kings Head 'complex' throughout the 19th century. Their research tells us that members of the Beckett family were still known to be owners (though not necessarily occupants) of *The Kings Head* in 1825, 1852 and 1884.

Blackburn, John

No. on Map	Premises	Tenure	State in 1801	Quantity A.R.P	Per Acre	Corn Rent	O'tv Bus.Decim.
773	House, lawn & co.		Pasture	3a 0r 39p			
776	Gardens			2a 1r 14p	>5/6d	£10 12s 9d	32B 731d
777	Park		3/4 mead. ¼ pasture	33a 0r 17p			
	Ponds in ditto			2a 0r 0p			
739	Sluice Field		Meadow	2a. 0r. 8p	6/-	12/3d	1B 885d
740	Green Dragon Garden & co.			0a. 2r. 4p	6/-	3/1d	475d
737	Field adjoining (got in Exchange from Thos. Oliver)			12p		7d	0B 90d
	Ditto		Arable	1a 0r 4p	9/7d	9s 9d	1B 500d
741			Arable	2a 1r 12p	5/6d	12/8d	1B 949d
770	Houses, yards, gardens & co. called Quaker's Row		Pasture	7a 3r 12p	7/-	£2 14s 9d	8B 424d

71

1275	Allotment in Dead Field and in lane adjoining	Copyhold		28p			
1276	Ditto in ditto, ditto			23a 3r 10p			
1277	Ditto in Ditto, ditto	Freehold		5a 0r 0p			
			Totals	83a 2r 0p		£15 5s 10d	47B 54d

See Figure 16. Plots 90, 91, 92 and 93, constituting Gibraltar Fields, form a block of over 13 acres bounded by Green Dragon Lane, 'Vicars Moor Lane' and Green Lanes. Plots 742, 747 and 748 cover much of the land in the angle between the eastern end of Green Dragon Lane and the southern stretch of Bush Hill.

See Figure 17 for the location of Plots 735, 736 and 737 on the north eastern side of 'Firs Lane', near The New River. There is further discussion of these early in the map section entitled, 'Highfield Road' to top of 'Firs Lane'.

John Blackburn lived at Bush Hill House (later known as Halliwick), which was established in the early 17th century. He had inherited the property in 1798 from his father, John Blackburn senior, a former army contractor who had made a good profit supplying the Gibraltar garrison during the great siege of 1779-83. Blackburn is not listed in the 1826 Pigot's Directory.

In his book of 1819 Robinson records the following two inscriptions for burials at All Saints, Edmonton: 'John Blackburn, Esq. Died October 12th 1798, aged 67 years' and 'Ann the wife of John Blackburn, esq. Died June 26th 1786, aged 44 years'. One presumes that this was John's first wife, because Tom Mason's notes at the LHU tell us, 'Obituary. Southgate & c.1803. Feb. 17. Aged 76 at Bush hill, Edmonton, Mrs. Blackburn, relict of John B. esq. who died 1798. She was D. of – Small esq. of St. Helena, married, first to Felix Baker esq. captain of an East Indiaman who brought her from thence secondly to John Berens esq. of Southgate, who died 1787, and lastly to Mr. Blackburn. She was interred on the 24th in the chapel of Southgate with her second husband....'

Bond, Edward Esq.

No.on Map	Premises	Tenure	State in 1801	Quantity A.R.P	Per Acre	Corn Rent	O'tv Bus.Decim.
1546	Allotment on the Chase	Freehold		1a 3r 24p			

Plot 1546 is roughly where Willow Walk is today on the map of the Eversley Crescent area (Figure 8).

A Captain Bond is referred to as a tenant of Lot 1 of the sale documented at 1824 in the diary section, and also of Lot 2 in the sale catalogue documented in the 1826 diary section. The Captain is listed for Winchmore Hill in the 1826 Pigot's Directory. Is that Edward, or a relative of his?

Bosden, Charles

No.on Map	Premises	Tenure	State in 1801	Quantity A.R.P	Per Acre	Corn Rent	O'tv Bus.Decim.
50	House, & c.	Freehold		0a 0r 35p	5/-	1/1d	167d

In the map section (Figure 9) I suggest that Plot 50 contains the two uppermost (easterly) clapperboard cottages that still stand at the foot of Winchmore Hill – lane ('Church Hill'), illustrated on the back cover.

Bradford, Mary

No.on Map	Premises	Tenure	State in 1801	Quantity A.R.P	Per Acre	Corn Rent	O'tv Bus.Decim.
175	Three tenements and gardens			0a 0r 26p	5/-	9d	OB 115d

This Plot is in the small cluster of cottages at The Bourne (Figure 11).

Brazen - nose College

No. on Map	Premises	Tenure	State in 1801	Ot'itv A.R.P	Per Acre	Corn Rent	O'tv Bus. Decim.
130	The Two Acres		Meadow	2a 0r 30p	5/6d	12/-	1B 847d
131	The One Acre		Meadow	1a 0r 4p			
132	The Two Acres		Meadow	2a 0r 16p	>5/6d	£2 8s 9d	7B 500d
133	The Five Acres		Meadow	5a 3r 1p			
165	Three cottages and gardens			0a 3r 6p	5/-	3s 11d	0B 603d
1483	Allotment on Chase			2a 1r 17p			
			Totals	14a 0r 34p		£3 4s 8d	9B 950d

Plots 130, 131, 132 and 133 are in the vicinity of 'Radcliffe Road' (Figure 15). Plot 165 is up on The Green. Plot 1483 is on the Chase near 'Southgate Circus'.

In *Winchmore Hill Bowling Club 1932 - 1982* the unlisted author(s) tells us that, 'Dr. Samuel Radcliffe (1580 - 1648) was Principal of Brazenose College, Oxford from 14th December 1641 until he was ejected by the Parliamentary Committee of the Cromwellian period in 1647/8. He was also Rector of Steeple Aston from 1617 until 1646, and he built a school there in the early 1630s. In 1640 he gave two closes at Winchmore Hill in trust for his school, with a power to the Bursar of Brazenose to receive the rents and pay the schoolmaster. In his will of 1648 there is a note that he had "already endowed Steeple Aston School with £10 yearly charged on his property at Winchmore Hill and had arranged the rent-charge to the College in trust." 'The booklet tells us that Winchmore Hill deeds begin in 1548, with the early documents all being entered under Edmonton, whereas the deeds from 1591 refer specifically to 'a close at Wynsemore Hill of 10 acres' - which is, of course, approximately the total acreage of the four meadows listed above.

In September 1931 the Broadfields and Roseneath Estates were put up for auction by E.J. Westoby, whose family ran a successful Estate Agent business locally for many years. The Roseneath Estate also included land off of Radcliffe Road then being leased to Sir William Paulin by the Radcliffe School Estate - presumably the one started at Steeple Aston by Dr. Radcliffe in the early 1630s. The maps in the sale booklet indicate these were remnants of the 1801 Plots 130 and 132. In 1932 E.J. Westoby and others formed a new Bowling Club as a breakaway element from the one that played in Grovelands Park, and on 12th December 1932 local builder George Ingram, who had bought most of the Roseneath Estate, leased the Club all the freehold land on which the green and clubhouse were to be constructed, together with part of the land he held on a 48 year lease from the Dr. Radcliffe School Estate. He sub let more of the School's land from 29th September 1937.

After the Club's lease ran out new housing was put in, erected in the angle in Radcliffe Road, and the Club now inhabits smaller grounds compared to when I moved into the road in 1972. The road's name obviously comes from the learned man who had connections with the area nearly 400 years ago.

Mrs. Burrell

No. on Map	Premises	Tenure	State in 1801	Quantity A.R.P	Per Acre	Corn Rent	O'tv Bus.Decim.
95	House & garden			15p	5/-	5d	0B 64d
1391	Allotment in Hagfield	Freehold		2a 2r 5p.			

These Plots are about halfway along the north side of what is now Vicars Moor Lane. Mrs. Burrell had been allocated land in the enclosed common field of Hagfield, which had existed in some form, of varying size, since at least the 13th century.

Busk, Edward Esq. and his wife Sarah Tomason (stet)

No. on Map	Premises	Tenure	State in 1801	Ot'titv A.R.P	Per Acre	Corn Rent	O'tv Bus.Decim.
			JOINTLY				
142	Old Orchard (part incroachment)	Copyhold	Meadow	1a 1r 28p	6-	8/6d	1B 308d
156	Cottage & garden			1r 17p	6/-	2/1 d	0B 321d
157	Small meadow		Meadow	3r 11p	6/-	4/10d	0B 743d
1563	Allotment on the Chase	Freehold		1a 1r 30p			
1564	Allotment on the Chase	Copyhold		3r 16p			
1565	Allotment on the Chase	Copyhold		1a 0r 32p			

Plot 142 is in the angle between 'Fords Grove' and 'Farm Road', just east of the footbridges. Plot 157 is in the vicinity of the grounds to modern day Highfield Road School, whilst 156 is diagonally opposite on that old lane (Figure 17). Plots 1563/4/5 are near the junction of what are now Worlds End Lane and Eversley Park Road (Figure 7). The plots were part of the common allotments awarded to Edmonton Parish when Enfield Chase was disaforested in 1777.

No. on Map	TESHMAKER, Mrs - ONLY	Tenure	State in 1801	(In Robinson these are listed under the letter 't') Ot'titv A.R.P	Per Acre	Corn Rent	Ot'tv Bus.Decim.
143	Houses, yards, and orchard			1a 1r 0p	6/-	7s 6d	1B 154d
144	Two acres		Meadow	2a 0r 18p	6-	12s 8d	1B 949d
145	Cottage and yard			0a 0r 23p	5/-	8d	0B 102d
146	Five acres		Meadow	5a 1r 9p	6/1d	£1 12s 3d	4B 962d
147	Three acres		Arable	3a 1r 1p	10/-	£1 12s 6d	5B 1d
148	Farm - house, barns,& yard			0a 3r 9p	6/-	4s 10d	0B 743d
149	Field adjoining		Meadow	1a 0r 19p	6/-	£0 6s 8d	1B 25d
158	Wood Rooffe		Meadow	5a 0r 30p	5/-	£1 5s 11d	3B 987d
159	Wood Rooffe		Meadow	5a 2r 12p	4/10d	£1 6s 10d	4B 128d
160	Wood Rooffe		Arable	5a 1r 14p	7/-	£1 17s 4d	5B 745d
150	Mr. Radley's Meadow		Meadow	3a 1r 11p	6/1d	£1 0s 1d	3B 90d
151	One acre		Meadow	1a 1r 30p			
152	One acre		Meadow	1a 2r 31p			
153	One acre		Meadow	1a 3r 0p			
154	Orchard		Meadow	0a 1r 18p			
155	Fellmonger's office and yard			1r 26p			
			151 – 155	inclusive	6/1d	£1 14s 11d	5B 373d
129	Two acres		Meadow	2a 3r 35p	5/7d	16s 6d	2B 540d
107	Two acres		Meadow	2a 0r 22p	5/4d	11s 4d	1B 744d
106	Three roods		Pasture	0a 3r 7p	5/4d	4s 2d	0B 641d
89	Three acres		Meadow	3a 2r 3p	5/-	17s 7d	2B 707d
73	Field		Meadow	2a 0r 0p	5/10d	11s 8d	1B 795d
74	House and garden			0a 2r 21p.	5/-	3s 1d	475d
98	House and garden			0a 1r 32p.	5/-	2s 3d	0B 346d.

136			Meadow	1a 3r 11p	6/-	10s 11d	1B 679d
137	Plantations		Wood	0a 1r 33p.	2/6d	1/-	154d.
138	Two acres		Pasture	2a 2r 22p	5/6d	14s 5d	2B 219d
139	Seventeen acres		Meadow	17a 3r 28p.	6/1d	£5 8s 11d	10B 756d
140	House and garden			1a 3r 4p.	6/1d	£0 10s 8d	1B 640d
141	Long Walk			1r 22p			
1397	Allotment in Hag - field	Copyhold		8a 3r 22p			
1555	Allotment on the Chase	Copyhold		48a 3r 27p			
	Grand Total for Mrs. Teshmaker (in & out of village)			274a 1r 29p		£31 1s 6d	147B 144d

(See Figure 17) Plots 143/4/5/6/7 are all the land between what are now called Fords Grove and Farm Road east of The New River, opposite Plots 158 and 159 (and 160 to their SE). References to the VCH Map of c. 1600 at Figure 1 will show that these five holdings at one time constituted Holly Field common field, the small orchard to the west (Plot 142) being owned by the Busks. Plots 158, 159 and 160 (off map) are east of 'Firs Lane' in the vicinity of modern day Hyde Park Avenue. Plots 148/9/150/1/2/3/4/5 are all in the triangle of land between what we now call Green Lanes, Farm Road and Highfield Road.

Plot 129 is in the vicinity of today's Shrubbery Gardens, off of Green Lanes. 106 and 107 are adjoining pieces of land on the south side of 'Vicars Moor Lane', west of where the rail line now runs. Plots 98 and 1397 are diagonally opposite on the north side of the lane. Plot 89 is in the vicinity of Myddelton Gardens. Plots 73 and 74 are to the west of Wades Hill near The Green. Plots 136/7/9 are the Paulin's Playing Fields of today, Plot 138 being just west of these. Plot 140 is Fords Grove Mansion (now the site of Capitol House) and its grounds. 141 – the Long Walk – is the thin strip of land to the east of the New River adjoining 140. Plot 1555 was an allotment given to the people of Edmonton Parish (of which Winchmore Hill was then a part) upon the disafforestation of Enfield Chase in 1777. The land is now part of the Highlands Village development, and traversed by Pennington Drive (Figure 7).

The LMA document ACC/695/49 has a list of Edmonton Manor Quit Rents for 1780 – 1 which indicates that a John Tatham and George Gosling held Copyhold land or property in Trust for Mrs. Teshmaker and her children. One such plot attracting a Quit Rent of 4/- was 'near the Farm & House at Fords Green formerly Felix Clarke'. There was a further 2 acres near the mansion attracting a Quit Rent of 4/-. Also in Trust was a messuage with three acres near Hag Field formerly belonging to Elizabeth Goddard, with a Quit Rent of 3/6d, and 1 acre in Hag Field at 6d Quit Rent which had belonged to Edward Addison, his wife and Elizabeth Brown. There was a further plot in Hag Field, with a Quit Rent of 2/-, which had belonged to Jacob Harvey.

Fords Grove Mansion (Plot 140) and The Goulds - Busks - Teshmakers

The VCH says that there was a mansion at this location in 1605, which was possibly the house where pioneering Quaker George Fox visited the London haberdasher Edward Mann in the 1680s, and as Fords Grove it was the home of the Goulds and Teshmakers in the 18th century. If the 1605 date is correct, then it would seem to have been a very recent addition at that time, because in the LHU is a sketch map of the vicinity which dates, I believe, from 1599. This shows that in the angle between what we now call Green Lanes and Fords Grove was 6 acres 3 roods and 36 perches of woodland called 'Fords Grene Grove'. In the angle between what are now called Fords Grove and Farm Road was a smaller patch of wood, consisting of 1 acre 1 rood, called 'Foords Hill Grove'. To the east of that Grove was 'Holly Fielde', and to the Grove's west was the foot of a lane that we now call Station Road, this stretch then being called 'Foords Grene'.

The Baths, in their history of Winchmore Hill Cricket Club, say that Mr. Merry Teshmaker purchased Ford's Grove in about 1720. However, *The Gazette* of 4th September 1925 tells us that William Gould lived at Fords Grove. Robinson says that William purchased the lease to the Manor of Edmonton in about 1720, holding his first Court in 1723. Upon his death, aged 65, on 12th April 1733, he was succeeded at Fords Grove by his son James Gould, who Robinson notes was granted the lease for the Manor of Edmonton for 29 years from 13th September 1766.

On a black marble slab on the pavement under the West Gallery in All Saints is a commemorative stone reading, 'William Gould Esq. Citizen & Merchant of London. Died the 12th April, 1733, Aged 65 years. Elizth Gould, daughter of the above Wm. Gould Esq. Obt. April, 20th 1766, AEt. 67 Jas Gould, Esq. son of Wm. Gould Esq., of Fords Grove, in this parish, Died the 8th Feb. 1767, Aged 67 years. Also Thomas Teshmaker, Esq. of Fords Grove, Nephew and Heir of James Gould, Esq. Died 9th Nov. 1771. Aged 34 years.' Thomas was a Justice of the Peace. His widow Sarah, listed above, passed away on 16th June 1832, aged 82. Thomas's spinster sister, Judith, died aged 76 on 27th March 1795, at her house in Church Street, Edmonton.

Thomas Teshmaker inherited Edmonton Manor from James Gould, and when he died it passed to Sarah, who retained it until William Curtis's successful bid for it in August 1800. In September 1800 Sarah's only surviving daughter Sarah Thomasine (this name having a variety of spellings) Teshmaker married Barrister-at - law Edward Busk, of Bedford Row, just in time for them both to be featured in the Enclosure land ownership schedule alongside Mrs. Teshmaker.

What of the Busk family? Tom Mason tells us that according to Mr. Walford's 'County Families' the family was of Norman extraction and could be traced back to Richard de Busc, who was born in 1315. His descendant, Hans Busk, was naturalized by an Act of Parliament in 1721. In contrast the Baths say that the Busk family originated in Scandinavia, but was established in England as merchants and lawyers by 1700.

Edward Busk was called to the Bar on 28th November 1806, and died at 'Ford's – grove', aged 72, on 20th September 1838, 'a bencher of the Society of the Middle Temple'. Sarah Thomasina died at Fords Grove on 8th June 1824, at the age of just 52. In 1805 Edward and Sarah Thomasine had their eldest son Edward Thomas, who was educated at St. John's College, Cambridge and was called to the Bar at the Middle Temple in 1832. In fact at the LMA is a document referenced MJP/R/028, dated 23rd October 1834, concerning Edward Busk Esq. (obviously meaning Edward Thomas). It tells us that his residence was Fords Grove, Winchmore Hill, Edmonton and his date of appointment to the Bench was 1831, following retirement from Business or Trade. He was qualified in Conveyancing, his jurisdiction as a Justice extending through Westminster, London and Edmonton, though he normally sat in the last named without payment, and without a nominated deputy. The document was signed by a Joseph Jolsopp in the Name of the Clerk.

Edward Thomas Busk, J.P. 'Gentleman of Fords Grove' was Chairman of the Edmonton Local Board of Health from 1850 – 60, and Chairman of the Edmonton Union (which helped the poor) from 1849 – 1860. Turning to his private life we note that in 1851 he married Susan, daughter of Thomas Benson Pease esq., by whom he fathered five children, the first of these being Thomas Teshmaker in 1852. He died on 19th January 1868, Fords Grove, at the age of 62.

In 1880 eldest son Thomas Teshmaker was elected President of the newly formed Winchmore Hill Cricket Club, a position he held until his premature death aged

42 in 1894, and the family were the Club's landlords for its first 40 years. He married Miss Mary Ackworth in 1885, and it is said she did not like her new home. They left after a few years, after which Fords Grove was tenanted by several people who were 'incomers' to the district. Then, for many years it remained unoccupied, and so fell into ruination. The mansion was finally demolished and sold off for development in 1920. The Capitol Cinema opened on the site in 1929, and closed in 1959. It was succeeded, in the early 1960s, by the current block of Inland Revenue offices and the corner building, which for many years saw service as a NatWest Bank.

G.M. Trevelyan's *History of England* tells us that the Justices of the Peace held their commissions from the Crown, through the selection of the Lord Chancellor, but they were not paid by the Crown, and their wealth and local influence came to them from their landed estates which the Government could not touch. They tended to be Tory rather than Whig. In England in our era of interest there were only two MPs to represent the whole of Middlesex, whilst elected County Councils were set up by Lord Salisbury's Government as late as 1888. Justices of the Peace ruled much of Middlesex, making the Teshmakers and Busks powerful men in their times.

Butcher, Matthias

No. on Map	Premises	Tenure	State in 1801	Quantity A.R.P	Per Acre	Corn Rent	O'tv Bus.Decim.
214	Orange Tree public house			0a. 1r. 10p	5/6d	1/8d	0B 256d

The Orange Tree - albeit in a different physical guise - still exists today in Highfield Road. Butcher is also mentioned in the Award to Henry Thompson.

In 1764 Matthias Butcher became the licensee for *The Orange Tree*. In 1773 the licence passed to Mary Butcher, in 1777 to Henry Butcher, in 1788 to Elizabeth Butcher, in 1793 to George Halsey, and in 1794 to Elizabeth Butcher. She is the last Butcher listed. In 1795 John Biggs took on the licence, to be succeeded, in 1818 by James Lawford. We will see in the map section, where I say more on *The Orange Tree*, that it is possible that the Butchers were shady characters.

One of the documents in a box referenced J90 at the National Archives, Kew is labelled, 'Dated 27th May 1802. Edmonton Inclosure. Mr. Mathius Butcher to William Mellish Esq. Grant of Freehold Common Rights.' The Indenture indicates that Butcher was, 'of the parish of Saint James, Clerkenwell in the County of Middlesex Victualler...' The Indenture stated that the Commissioners, 'have not yet executed their award.' My understanding of the document is that Butcher sold some Winchmore Hill properties to Mellish for £6 16s 0d in anticipation of being awarded them under the Enclosure award. I am not aware as to where these premises were.

C

Chandos, the Dutchess of (her Committee)

No. on Map	Premises	Tenure	State in 1801	Quantity A.R.P	Per Acre	Corn Rent	O'tv Bus.Decim.
311			Meadow	5a 1r 8p	5/4d	£1 8s 3d	4B 346d
312			Meadow	2a 0r 7p	5/6d	£0 11s 2d	1B 719d

Plots 311 and 312 are at the eastern end of Dog and Duck Lane (now Bourne Hill), on the south side of that lane (see Figure 12).

The Victoria County History of Middlesex (VCH) tells us that Grovelands was first mentioned in the 15th century as the woodlands of Lords Grove. By the late 17th century Sir Thomas Wolstenholme owned Lords Grove, and it was part of the Minchenden Estate. In 1736 Minchenden was purchased by John Nicoll, a wealthy London merchant, and in 1753 Margaret, his only daughter and heiress, married James Brydges, the Marquess of Carnarvon, who later became the 3rd Duke of Chandos. Thus the Duke came to live on Southgate Green. (See Plate 58.)

Margaret died childless in 1768 and, in 1777, the Duke remarried, this time to Anne Eliza Gamon. The Duke died in 1789, and she became mentally deranged. Leigh Hunt suggested this was because she held herself responsible. Being fond of practical jokes, she had thrust aside his chair just as he was about to sit on it, with apparently fatal consequences. The VCH says that Lord's Grove followed the descent of Minchenden until Anna Elizabeth, daughter and heir of the Duke of Chandos inherited it.

Anna Elizabeth married Richard, Marquis of Buckingham, in 1796, though he seems to have been known by a range of titles. The VCH says that at the time he was known as Richard Nugent – Temple – Grenville, Earl Temple. David Starkey tells us that Earl Temple was the brother - in - law of Pitt the Elder. He was created Duke of Buckingham and Chandos in 1822.

The VCH says that in 1799 Temple sold the Lords Grove estate to Walker Gray, but it must have been in 1796 or 7, upon marriage, as Gray had Grovelands Mansion (as we now call it) built in 1797/8. Minchenden was sold to Isaac Walker in 1853, and he demolished it, the park being incorporated into the grounds of Arnos Grove.

So, although it is not well publicized, the Chandos family was a key one in the history of Winchmore Hill. It was also involved, in the 18th century, with the management of the Chase, and we may note the following paragraph from the 1800 Enclosure Act in relation to the Manor of Enfield, 'That the King, in right of his crown, was seised to himself, his heirs and successors, of, in, and to the manor and manorial rights of *Edmonton,* otherwise *Edelmeton,* in the said county; and also in right of his duchy of *Lancaster,* of the manor and manorial rights of *Enfield,* in the said county, whereof the said *Edmonton* allotment is part and parcel, and whereof her grace *Anna Eliza* Duchess of *Chandos* is lessee.'

Clayton, John Esq. (his executors)

No. on Map	Premises	Tenure	State in 1801	Quantity A.R.P	Per Acre	Corn Rent	O'tv Bus. Decima
743			Meadow	2a 0r 16p	3/4d	6/11d	IB 64d
744			Meadow	4a 3r 11p	4/6d	£1 1s 7d	3B 321d
745			Meadow	3a 3r 36p	4/-	£0 15s 10d	2B 437d
746			Meadow	6a 0r 7p	4/-	£1 4s 2d	3B 718d
752			Pasture	2a 1r 31p	2/4d	£0 5s 7d	0B 859d
753			Arable	4a 0r 10p	6/-	£1 4s 4d	3B 743d
754			Meadow	8a 0r 27p	3/6d	£1 8s 7d	4B 398d
755	Wood		Wood	5a 3r 34p	1/2d	6s 10d	IB 51d
756			Pasture	13a 3r 38p	2/4d	£1 12s 6d	5B 1d
757			Pasture	9a 2r 20p	2/4d	£1 2s 5d	3B 449d
758			Pasture	4a 2r 11p	3/4d	£0 15s 2d	2B 335d
			Total	65a 3r 1p		£10 3s 11d	3IB 376d

In my previous books I have defined the northern border of the old village of Winchmore Hill as Green Dragon Lane. The above gives all John Clayton's land listed in the schedule, and it is all north of Green Dragon Lane, constituting, today, the area around Bush Hill Park Golf Course (Figure 16). It is possible that Old Park is 'a park' mentioned in the Domesday Book of 1086 for the Manor of Enfield.

Douglas Haigh, in his *Old Park in the Manor of Enfield*, of 1977, says that Samuel Clayton died on the 20th May 1797, aged 66. Haigh suggests that the estate passed to his brother John. It was eventually inherited, he says, by another John Clayton, who lived in Market Harborough, though his relationship to Samuel and the other John is not known. In the early 1800s most of the estate was on lease to various people.

In 1811 the Clayton family sold a large portion of the Old Park Estate to a Mr. Thomas Cotton. It was put up for sale on Thursday 6th May 1825. By 1826 it had grown to 181 acres, and was purchased by Mrs. Elizabeth Lewis for £23,997 - 8s - 0d. In December 1827, she sold a portion, now known as Grange Park, to Isaac Currie. She also sold 56 acres between what is now Carrs Lane and the New River to William Carr. In 1832 Carr bought part of the land previously held by Thomas Cotton, so giving him, in total, the estate of Chase Park.

Clowes, Joseph

No. on Map	Premises	Tenure	State in 1801	Quantity A.R.P	Per Acre	Corn Rent	O'tv Bus. Decima
224	House and garden			0a 2r 4p	5/-	£0 2s 7d	0B 398d
220	Three acres		Meadow	3a 3r 15p	5/10d	£1 2s 4d	3B 436d
221	Five acres		Meadow	5a 1r 36p	5/10d	£1 11s 10d	4B 898d
222	Three acres		Meadow	3a 1r 18p	6/-	£1 0s 2d	3B 103d
223	Seven acres		Meadow	7a 1r 28p	5/6d	£2 0s 9d	6B 269d
225	Orchard			1a 0r 0p	5/6d	£0 5s 6d	0B 846d
226	Two acres		Meadow	2a 3r 22p	6/-	£0 17s 3d	2B 655d
		Total		24a 2r 3p		£7 0s 5d	21B 605d

Joseph Clowes owned plots 220 to 226 inclusive, and today the aptly named Clowes sports ground, north of Barrow's Well Green, occupies much of these. In 1801 most of the estate was meadow, though Plot 224 was a 'House and garden', (now the site of the Council rubbish tip) with the adjoining field to the east being an orchard (see Figure 18).

The Palmers Green and Southgate Gazette of 6th August 1934 ran an article by 'Memorabilia' concerned with The Firs in Barrowell Green (as we now call it), as opposed to The Firs of the Lake family, off of Firs Lane. The Firs were believed to be the 'house and garden' of Plot 224, and there is more on it in the map section. In the article 'Memorabilia' says that the estate had been owned by the Clowes family for over 300 years by the time that Southgate Borough Council purchased it in 1935, subject to Carter Page and Co's lease as a nursery, of which some eleven or twelve years were then unexpired. Unfortunately I have been unable to ascertain anything about the influential local family, except to note that Joseph is mentioned in Manorial records quoted in the 1817 diary. It is not listed in the 1826 Pigot's Directory, so perhaps the family didn't actually live on the estate.

Cobb, Thomas Esq.

No. on Map	Premises	Tenure	State in 1801	Quantity A.R.P	Per Acre	Corn Rent	O'tv Bus. Decim.
86			Pasture	3r 9p	5/-	4s 3d	653d
105			Meadow	1a 1r 14p		7s 9d	1B 192d
1587	Allotment on the Chase	Freehold		32p			
			Total	2a 1r 15p		12s	1B 845d

Plot 86 is an oddity. John Richardson owned a 'House & c.' on Plot 86a about half way along the south side of Green Dragon Lane, whilst Thomas Cobb owned the ¾ acre of pasture behind Richardson's house. Cobb's Plot 105 was on the south side of 'Vicars Moor Lane', by its junction with 'Wades Hill'. Plot 1587 was an allotment on what had formerly been part of Enfield Chase, approximately where Hadley Way is today.

I have no information on Thomas Cobb. He is not listed in the 1826 Pigot's Directory. In his *Gazette* article of 30th April 1948 Tom Mason tells us that in the late 18th century Jacob Doree purchased Rowantree on The Green from a William Cobb. Was he related to Thomas?

Cobley, Sarah and Mary Price

No. on Map	Premises	Tenure	State in 1801	Quantity A.R.P	Per Acre	Corn Rent	O'tv Bus.Decim.
1525	Allotment on the Chase	Freehold		1a 3r 14p			

Plot 1525 ran off of Chase Side Road, west of where The Glade is today (see Figure 8).

The Cordwainers' Company

No. on Map	Premises	Tenure	State in 1801	Quantity A.R.P	Per Acre	Corn Rent	O'tv Bus. Decim.
57	Three houses, and orchard & c		Pasture	1a 3r 32p	6/-	11/8d	1B 795d
56	Field adjoining		Meadow	1a 1r 12p	6/-	7/11d	1B 218d
1551	Allotment on Chase	Freehold		3a 0r 36p			

Plots 56 and 57 are on the Upper Green, in the vicinity of where Uplands Court flats are today. Plot 1551 is just off the western side of 'Eversley Park Road', in the vicinity of today's Holly Hill and Willow Walk. It had, until recently, been part of the Edmonton Allotment of Enfield Chase. In the 1804 Diary we see that the Company then let the plot to farmer William Baker.

Jennifer Lang's 1980 book entitled *The Cordwainers of London* informs us that the story of the Cordwainers' Company may have started even before 1272 - the year it was given its first Ordinances. She says that the forerunners of the present livery companies of London were nearly all religious fraternities.

By the eleventh century there were one hundred parish churches in London, and the transformation from religious fraternity into craft or 'mistery' was gradual, haphazard and largely undocumented. (The word 'mistery', incidentally, is derived from the French 'metier' which meant an art or a craft.) The freemen belonged to the guilds, each being duly admitted after serving his apprenticeship, and proving his knowledge of his craft or trade. Each guild was under the supervision of two masters, who ensured that the standard of work was kept up. The oldest guild is that of the Weavers, who obtained their charter from Henry 11 in 1184.

The name 'cordwainer' is derived from 'cordwan', which is a fine, soft, durable, goatskin leather which came from Cordova in Spain. Gradually it became the material most in demand for top quality footwear throughout Europe. Ms. Lang tells us that by the eleventh century the shoe wright was making ankle leathers, shoes, leather hose, bottles, bridle thongs, trappings, flasks, boiling vessels, leather neck pieces, halters, wallets and pouches. The Cordwainers formed an association at a very early date, which was located approximately where the Royal Exchange is now. In the thirteenth century they moved to Cordwanestrate and when the City was divided into Wards, the Cordwainers were the first group of craftsmen to have a Ward named after them.

The crown relied on the guilds for money and a degree of stability. The guilds paid their dues, and in return won some very far-reaching legal concessions. They had the power of search and the control of wages and prices. The most important concession, in the long term, was the right to hold land and property in perpetuity. By Elizabeth's time the Cordwainers had settled their differences with the Cobblers and merged with them. Throughout her reign they acted as the champion of the small, shoemaker and cobbler.

For centuries our local woods had been worked for economic purposes. One such use was that timber had been processed to produce charcoal for the tanners of Edmonton. Once hides had been tanned, of course, the leather could be used in the shoe industry. Perhaps the Cordwainers' Company had bought land in the village because it was some sort of centre for shoe making? There is more on the Company's actual holdings in the notes that accompany the map of The Green.

Creed, Sarah

No. on Map	Premises	Tenure	State in 1801	Quantity A.R.P	Per Acre	Corn Rent	O'tv Bus.Decim.
178	House and garden			12p		4d	51d

Plot 178 is a cottage that is possibly seen behind *The Woodman* in the lower picture at Page 31 of my *A Look at Old Winchmore Hill,* if it had survived for about another hundred years. (See Figure 11.)

Cressee, David senior

No. on Map	Premises	Tenure	State in 1801	Quantity A.R.P	Per Acre	Corn Rent	O'tv Bus.Decim.
102	Two tenements and orchard			2r 18p	5/-	3/-	462d

Plot 102 was just west of where the modern Broadfield Court development is on Wades Hill (see Figure 14).

Crowder, Jacob

No. on Map	Premises	Tenure	State in 1801	Quantity A.R.P	Per Acre	Corn Rent	O'tv Bus.Decim.
215				0a 0r 34p	5/-	1/-	154d

Although no premises are listed in the schedule, the Enclosure map shows a small building on this Plot, which was the next one east of Butcher's 214 - *The Orange Tree Inn* (see Figure 18).

D

Dale, Michael (Trustee for Ann Dale)

No. on Map	Premises	Tenure	State in 1801	Quantity A.R.P	Per Acre	Corn Rent	O'tv Bus. Decima
191			Pasture	0a 3r 5p.	5/6d	4s 2d	641d
193			Pasture	3a 3r 28p.			
195	House and yard			0a 0r 34p.			
196			Pasture	3a 0r 39p.	193-166	inclusive -	
197	House and Garden			0a 0r 38p.	= 5/6d	£4 0s 10d	12B 436d
198			Meadow	2a 3r 19p			
199			Meadow	4a 0r 26p.			
166	House and Yard			0a 0r 10p			
			Dale Totals	15a 1r 39p		£4 5s 0d	13B 77d

Plot 166 was a little away from the others, today being occupied by Repton Court, overlooking The Green, and covered in the notes with that map. The remaining plots are adjoining strips in the angle between Hoppers Lane and 'Compton Road'. Within a few decades they had become part of the Highfield House Estate, as summarised in the notes accompanying the map for that area (Figure 13). I know nothing of the Dale family.

Davis, John

No. on Map	Premises	Tenure	State in 1801	Quantity A.R.P	Per Acre	Corn Rent	O'tv Bus. Decim.
1588	Allotment on the Chase	Freehold		1a 2r 24p			
1590	Allotment on the Chase	Freehold		0a 2r 18p			

Plots 1588 and 1590 were formerly part of the Edmonton Award under the disafforestation of Enfield Chase, and correspond fairly well to the line of today's Hadley Way (Figure 8). The Schedule tells us that 1590 was 'purchased of Caesar Andrews'. In his handwritten notes at the LHU Tom Mason records the death of a 'John Davies of Winchmore – hill' on 11th November 1810.

Davis, Robert

No. on Map	Premises	Tenure	State in 1801	Quantity A.R.P	Per Acre	Corn Rent	O'tv Bus. Decim.
125	Cottage and field adjoining		Meadow	1a 0r 5p	6/-	6/2d	949d

Plot 125 is at the SE end of 'Vicars Moor Lane', just west of the comer plot (Figure 15). Was Robert related to John? Neither are listed in the 1826 Pigot's Directory, but Robert is mentioned in the Edmonton Manor records for 1801.

Dean and Chapter of St Paul's – As tithe owners.

No. on Map	Premises	Tenure	State in 1801	Quantity A.R.P	Per Acre	Corn Rent	O'tv Bus. Decim.
1367	Allotment in Scotch field	Freehold		16a 1r 20p			

Plot 1367 is a large tract of land in the angle made between the eastern bank of The New River and Barrow's Well Green, to the south of the latter (Figure 19). Some of this land is still given over to allotments, even to this day, as pictured at Plate 50.

The Dean and Chapter of St. Paul's, in the City of London, had been the owners of all impropriate and rectorial tythes arising within the Parish of Edmonton, excepting for the Edmonton allotment of Enfield Chase, and as such had been entitled to all great tythes arising.

Dean and Chapter of St. Paul's – J. English, Lessee

No. on Map	Premises	Tenure	State in 1801	Quantity A.R.P	Per Acre	Corn Rent	O'tv Bus. Decim.
1530	Allotment on the Chase	Freehold		0a 3r 32p			

This Plot on the old grounds of the Chase was on Chase Side Road (now Winchmore Hill Road), near where *The Winchmore Arms* now is (Figure 8). William English, listed a little further on, held Plot 1369 at the time of Enclosure. Possibly the two were related.

Dean and Chapter of St. Paul's (late Tho. Sharpless lessee, now John Erwood)

No. on Map	Premises	Tenure	State in 1801	Quantity A.R.P	Per Acre	Corn Rent	O'tv Bus. Decim.
1550	Allotment on the Chase	Freehold		2a 2r 38p			

Plot 1550 was a strip off of 'Eversley Park Road', roughly where Willow Walk is today (see Figure 8).

I know nothing of Tho. Sharpless. The LMA document ACC/695/49 has a list of Edmonton Manor Quit Rents for 1780 - 1 which indicates that John Erwood was admitted as a Copy tenant in 1781 for 3 acres in 'High Ffield' and ½ acre in the Hide. His Quit Rent for these was 1/3d. It is not obvious as to where the 3 acres were.

In his 1984 book on Enfield Chase David Pam tells us something of John Erwood. He was a local builder and surveyor who sat on the Edmonton vestry. He had been responsible for the drastic (and possibly illegal) alterations to All Saints in 1772. His accounts for 1783 reveal that he had auctioned off Chase stackwood for £993, bark for £81, and 1,200 oaks for £245. He received 4% of the £1,240 total, and the following year claimed 4% on total sales of £1,476.

In 1786 Lady of Edmonton Manor Mrs. Teshmaker appointed Erwood as her collector of revenues owing to her from booth proprietors at the September Statute Fair. The Manor Court Minutes for 16th May 1826 record the then recent death of this man.

Dean and Chapter of St. Paul's - Edmund Whitbread, Lessee

No. on Map	Premises	Tenure	State in 1801	Quantity A.R.P	Per Acre	Corn Rent	O'tv Bus. Decim.
1585	Allotment on the Chase	Freehold		1a 0r 10p			

Plot 1585 was a strip in the angle between Green Dragon Lane and 'Wades Hill' (Figure 8). I have no details on Mr. Whitbread.

Dean and Chapter of St. Paul's - Sold to W. Eaton.

No. on Map	Premises	Tenure	State in 1801	Quantity A.R.P	Per Acre	Corn Rent	O'tv Bus. Decim.
331			Meadow	8a 1r 32p	5/6d	£2 6s 5d	7B 141d
332			Meadow	4a 2r 39p	5/6d	£1 6s 0d	4B 0d
333			Arable	4a 2r 27p	9/7d	£2 4s 8d	6B 871d
334			Meadow	5a 1r 21p	5/6d	£1 9s 6d	4B 539d
335			Meadow	3a 0r 0p	5/6d	16s 6d	2B 540d
	Barn and Yard			0a 0r 16p			
	Incroachment on Waste			0a 0r 22p			
			Totals	26a 1r 37p		£8 3s 1d	25B 91d

William Eaton possessed other land in the Parish of Edmonton including the following, in what I consider to be Winchmore Hill -

No. on Map	Premises	Tenure	State in 1801	Quantity A.R.P	Per Acre	Corn Rent	O'tv Bus. Decim.
337	House + garden at Palmer's green			0a 1r 23p	6/-	2/4d	0B 359d

(See Figures 12 and 19) Today a road off of Green Lanes, not far north of the Intimate Theatre, is named Eaton Park Road, and it seems reasonable to assume that the name derives from the former land holdings of William Eaton. In 1801 he already owned the house and garden on Plot 337, and perhaps bought the adjoining strips to farm them, using his house as a farmstead. He also bought the adjoining strips of waste at 1360/1/2.

We do not seem to know much about William Eaton, but he is mentioned by Gary Boudier in relation to *The Woolpack* Inn, Southgate in his books on the borough's pubs. He tells us that in 1832 an Edward Sewart held the freehold to the property and put it up for sale. William Eaton made an unsuccessful bid to purchase it, but in 1833 Sewart sold it to a Henry Eaton, who was presumably a relative of William's. Then, on 2nd December 1886, an agreement was drawn up between Caroline Eaton and Henry Mobbs for the latter's rental of the Inn and adjoining cottage. Mr. Boudier lists Henry Eaton as licensee of the nearby *Cherry Tree* in 1834 and 1839, John Eaton being the licensee in 1838. He further informs us that Henry was the son of John, and that he also ran the Southgate posting shop and farmed the fields of Osidge. After he retired Henry and his son Charles went to Whitehouse Farm in Waterfall Road, before occupying other houses in Southgate.

The Edmonton Manor Minutes of 16th May 1815 mention the death of a George Eaton, who left three copyhold cottages in Winchmore Hill to his wife Sarah.

Dean and Chapter of St. Paul's - Sold to Robert Williamson

I have shown the three Plots listed here against the later entry for Williamson.

Decka, John

No. on Map	Premises	Tenure	State in 1801	Quantity A.R.P	Per Acre	Corn Rent	O'tv Bus. Decim.
186	Two houses and field		Meadow & Pasture	5a 1r 4p	5/6d	£1 18s 11d	4B 449d
1581	Allotment on the Chase	Copyhold		2a 0r 20p			

Plot 186 contained Roseville Mansion, off 'Station Road', and now commemorated in a 1960s block of flats. Decka also bought a small strip of waste, Plot 1390, adjoining Roseville. Plot 1581 is a strip in the former Chase that runs west of 'Wades Hill', just north of 'Houndsden Road' (Figure 8). It was bought by William Good in 1825.

I have covered the story of Roseville in the map section (Highfield House Estate), where we learn, courtesy of Tom Mason, that the mansion was built for John Decka in the mid 18th century, and that he sold the copyhold to a William John Reeves in 1809. There is more on Friend Decka in the diary section, and the reader may wish to consult those entries, guided by the following brief summaries.

In early 1788 John Decka had problems with the authorities over his apparent withholding of payments of Church Rates and tithes (presumably owing to religious reasons). At a Quarterly Meeting in early 1791, Decka reported that he had received rental for part of the Quaker grounds from Charles Bartholomew. Minutes from later in 1791 have Decka as one of the Friends' Committee reporting that the rebuilding of the Meeting House was completed. Amongst the smaller donations to the cost were John Decka's £5 5s and the Trustees of John Decka Junior's £2. 2s. However, John Decka also received payment for his contribution to the building project. In the same year John Decka and two other Friends were asked to find *a* suitable family to be live in caretakers at the new building. They were still being urged to fill this vacancy in 1792. The minutes from a Monthly Meeting of 1795 reported that Decka had received Charles Bartholomew's annual payment of £1 for his rental of a field. In this year Decka received £6 11s 4d from John Chorley for land in the village.

According to Tom Mason's handwritten notes at the LHU, '1807. May 20. On Winchmore – hill, Mrs. Decker (presumably Decka), wife of Mr. J.D. one of the people called Quakers. She was blind and having been left a few minutes by the servant, in endeavouring to find her way into another room, she fell into the cellar, fracturing her skull, and died within an hour.' We see in the diary section for 1820 that Decka made a Will in November 1807, presumably prompted by his wife's death, and that his nephew John Catchpool was a major beneficiary of it upon John's death in 1820.

Doree, Magdalene Teresa (stet)

No. on Map	Premises	Tenure	State in 1801	Quantity A.R.P	Per Acre	Corn Rent	O'tv Bus. Decim.
164	House and garden		Pasture	1a 1r 34p	5/6d	7/1 1d	IB 218d
1584	Allotment on the Chase	Freehold		0a 3r 22p			
			Total	2a 1r 16p			

Plot 164 contained Rowantree/Woodside on The Green, when it was still one building. Plot 1584 is a slice of land on what had been the Chase, in the angle between 'Wades Hill' and Green Dragon Lane (Figure 8). I have covered the history of Rowantree in the section relating to The Green. What of Magdalene Teresa Doree?

A 1948 article by Tom Mason in *The Gazette* explains that Rowantree belonged to Magdalene and her husband Jacob Doree, though it is listed only in her name in 1801. The article said that Jacob left the property to his cousin, whose surname was Levesque. He in turn left the property to his three daughters. Two of them were married, and their surnames were Gosselin and Dupray. All these French names suggest that the family was of French Huguenot extraction. Magdelen (stet) Theresa Doree is listed by Robinson as having reached 80 in 1812.

In the 1790 Diary section I reproduce the content of a disputed Will Jacob Dore is said to have made not long before his death. This is consistent with what Mason says, the house being left to his wife 'Magdalin Theresa' for her lifetime, to pass to Jacob's cousin John Lévesque of Hoxton upon her death.

Eaton, William

See relevant entry above under Dean and Chapter of St. Paul's.

English, William

No. on Map	Premises	Tenure	State in 1801	Quantity A.R.P	Per Acre	Corn Rent	O'tv Bus. Decim.
1369	Allotment in Scotch field	Copyhold	Arable	3a 0r 22p			

This Plot is in the angle between Green Lanes, The New River, and the south side of Barrow's Well Green (Figure 19). Was William a relative of the I. English who leased land from The Dean and Chapter of St. Paul's?

Fox, William

No. on Map	Premises	Tenure	State in 1801	Quantity A.R.P	Per Acre	Corn Rent	O'tv Bus. Decim.
79	Three houses at Winchmore Hill			0a 0r 16p			

Plot 79, near *The King's Head,* is discussed on the section on The Green.

Girdler, J. Sandford

No. on Map	Premises	Tenure	State in 1801	Quantity A.R.P	Per Acre	Corn Rent	O'tv Bus. Decim.
1523	Allotment on the Chase	Freehold		1a 3r 33p			

Plot 1523 is in the vicinity of 'Elm Bank' just off of 'The Vale' (Figure 8).

Godsall, Phillip Esq.

No. on Map	Premises	Tenure	State in 1801	QuantityA.R.P.	Per Acre	Corn Rent	O'ty Bus. Decim.
45	House and garden			0a 3r 32p			
46	Site of a house, & co.		Pasture	0a 1r 31p			
				1a 1r 23p	6/-	8/4d	1B 282d

At Pages 10,11 and 12 of my 2001 *A Look at Old Winchmore Hill* I mention Hope House in 'Winchmore Hill Road'. A *Gazette* article dated 23rd April 1937 by 'Memorabilia' infers that it had then recently been demolished. 'Memorabilia' says that although he had been informed that Hope House had been built in 1798 with Grovelands, he had examined the house internally and externally in about 1905, and had concluded that it was of early to mid 18th century in origin, and identified it as being Walker Gray's 'Farm – house and garden' at Plot 20 in the Enclosure Schedule, though I am not so sure (Figure 5). Descriptions of Hope House seem to suggest it overlooked the road, whilst the Farm House of Plot 20 was set back some way from the road. The old field systems can, to a certain extent, be identified in the 1865 and 1895 Ordnance Surveys, and Hope House on both is shown overlooking the road in the same position as Godsall's House on Plot 45. Godsal (stet) is also listed in Appendix 1 as having bought Plots of land, numbered 1517 and 1522 on the opposite side of Chase Side Road (now Winchmore Hill Road), as well as Plot 1536 – now the site of *The Winchmore Hill Arms.*

Goslee, Thomas

No. on Map	Premises	Tenure	State in 1801	Quantity A.R.P	Per Acre	Corn Rent	O'tv Bns.Decim.
336	Tenements	Copyhold	Meadow	0a 0r 23p	5/-	8d	102d
1540	Allotment on the Chase	Copyhold		0a 1r 31p			

Plot 336 is at the southern end of Hopper's Lane (Figure 12). Plot 1540 is where we today find Meadow Bank, off of 'Eversley Park Road' (Figure 8).

At the National Archives in Kew is an Insurance (Ref. 11936/537/1148233) which gives Thomas Goslee's address as 16, Golden Lane, Cripplegate, and indicates that he was a broker and carpenter.

Gosling, William Esq.

No. on Map	Premises	Tenure	State in 1801	QuantityA.R.P.	Per Acre	Corn Rent	O'ty Bus. Decim.
1526	Allotment on the Chase	Freehold		1a 0r 26p			
1527	Allotment on the Chase	Freehold		0a 2r 8p			
1528	Allotment on the Chase	Copyhold		1a 0r 0p			

These are three adjoining strips off of Chase Side Road ('Winchmore

Hill Road'), approximately where 'The Glade' now runs. 1527 was 'purchased of W. Whittingstall', and 1528 'purchased of Wm. B. Naylor' (Figure 8).

The Edmonton Manor Court minutes of 16th May 1826 record the death of William Goslin (stet).

Gray, John Esq.

No. on Map	Premises	Tenure	State in 1801	Quantity A. R.P	Per Acre	Corn Rent	Q'ty Bus. Decim.
135	Two houses, lawn, and pleasure ground		¼ Pasture ¾ Meadow	10a 1r 25p	6/3d	3/5d	10B 0d
1378	Allotment in High field	Freehold		1a 1r 25p			
1379	Allotment in High field	Copyhold		7a 0r 30p			
		Totals		19a 0r 0p	3/5d		10B 0d

Plot 135 is the Beaulieu Estate, with the main mansion where Beaulieu Gardens is today. The Allotments in High field were near today's 'Carpenter Gardens'. Beaulieu is covered in detail in the map section ('Highfield Road' to top of 'Firs Lane').

Gray, Walker Esq.

No. on Map	Premises	Tenure	State in 1801	Quantity A.R.P	Per Acre	Corn Rent	Q'ty Bus.Decim.
18	Well close		Meadow	5a 2r 32p	5/1d	£1 8s 11d	4B 449d
19	Home field		Meadow	3a 3r 10p	5/1d	19s 5d	2B 989d
20	Farm - house and garden			1a 0r 9p			
21	Garden			0a 3r 27p	6/1d	12s 4d	1B 898d
22	Home pasture		Pasture	2a 1r 20p	4/8d	11s 1d	1B 706d
23	Chase field		Meadow	7a 1r 38p	5/1d	£1 18s 0d	5B 848d
24	Wood field		Meadow	3a 0r 31p	5/4d	16s 11d	2B 604d
25	Wood field		Meadow	5a 0r 12p	5/1d	£1 5s 9d	3B 961d
26	Wood field		Meadow	4a 2r 19p	4/8d	£1 1s 5d	3B 295d
27	Wood field		Meadow	4a 1r 38p	4/6d	£1 0s 1d	3B 90d
28	Wood field		Meadow	4a 1r 35p	4/3d		2B 912d
29	Pond and waste			0a 2r 29p			
30	Great Pond		Water	4a 0r 35p			
31	Slip next to Great Pond		Pasture	1a 2r 22p	29 – 32 inc.	29 – 32 inc	29 – 32 inc
32	The Grove		Pasture	27a 2r 31p	= 3/-	£5 11s 9d	17B 192d
32	Garden			1a 2r 6p			
52	Wood	Freehold	Wood	47a 1r 19p			
53	Wood		Wood	62a 1r 27p	1/3d	£6 17s 2d	21B 104d
51	Wood (late cleared)		Pasture	13a 3r 32p	2/6d	£1 14s 9d	5B 347d
170	Wood (late cleared)		Pasture	11a 2r 10p	2/6d	£1 8s 10d	4B 436d
1514	Allotment on the Chase			6a 2r 28p			
1518	Allotment on the Chase	Copyhold		4a 2r 4p			
1520	Allotment on the Chase	Copyhold		0a 3r 4p			
1521	Allotment on the Chase	Freehold		3a 2r 16p			
		Total 18	To 1521 inc.	231a 1r 14p		£26 5s 4d	80B 831d
17	Three acres next the Chase		Meadow	3a 1r 27p	5/-	£0 17s 1d	2B 630d

Most of these holdings are in the vicinity of today's Grovelands Park. The Map of the western half of the area in 1801 (Figure 5) shows how the Plots are laid out. Plots 1518, 1520 and 1521 are shown as having been, 'purchased of Philip Godsal, Esq.' in the Ownership Schedule, whilst Plot 17 is shown as, 'exchanged with P. Pole Esq.' Later in the Schedule are entries for the executors of Samuel Pole Esq. which indicate that part of his Plots 33 and 34, and all of his Plots 35 and 36, were, 'sold and exchanged to Walker Gray Esq.'.

Walker Gray also bought waste land, as listed at Appendix 1 of the Enclosure Schedule. Plot 1354 was towards the eastern end of Dog and Duck Lane (Bourne Hill). Plots 1532 and 1533 were listed as being in Chase – side (though I can not locate them on the maps). Plots 1400, 1401 and 1402 were on the south side of Winchmore Hill – lane (now Church Hill) (Figure 9). Plots 1356, 1358 and 1359 were along the western edge of Hopper's – lane (Figure 13).

The Grays. Walkers and Taylors

The main sources of information for the following are: *The Palmers Green and Southgate Gazette* article by Tom Mason of 17th August 1951 entitled, 'The Taylors and their local estates'; Herbert Newby's 1949 book *"Old" Southgate*; the Taylor family's personal papers viewed on 21st March 1987; the family tree in Ruby Galili's Arnos *Grove and the Walker Family*; Alan Dumayne's 1993 *Southgate - A Glimpse Into the Past* ; Horace Regnart's *Memories of Winchmore Hill*; Pam's *Southgate and Winchmore Hill, A Short History 1982*; Ptolemy Dean's *Sir John Soane and London*.

The Walkers, Grays and Taylors were intermarried families who were major local land owners. The Taylor - Walker relationship was famous nationwide, until comparatively recently being commemorated in the name of the family brewery.

Robert Taylor, a descendent of the 16th century John Vickris, of Worcestershire, had a son by the name of John Vickris Taylor (1747 - 1828) in Doncaster. John Vickris Taylor moved to our area in about 1770, and gave £25 towards the rebuilding of the Quaker Meeting House in Church Hill. He is listed in the Ownership Schedule of 1801 as having a house set in grounds approximately where Selbome Road now cuts Fox Lane. He married an Elizabeth Gray, by whom he had two children, both of whom, unfortunately, died young. His second wife was Sophia Donnithorne. Their son John Donnithorne Taylor (1798 - 1885), pictured in later life at Plate 6, married Elizabeth Henrietta Thompson in 1830 at Edmonton Parish Church, and they went on to become owners of Grovelands Estate. On 29th June 1801, John Vickris and Sophia had a daughter named Sophia.

In 1710 John Walker of Cockermouth Castle (1658 – 1739) married Rebecca Bell (1683 – 1738-9). Their daughter Rebecca married Abraham Gray of Tottenham. Their son John Gray married the daughter of Bank of England Director Thomas Lewis, who lived at the Lodge in Palmers Green. John had Beaulieu built by the New River, based on drawings made by the Surveyor Lancelot Dowbiggin in 1786. Another son, Walker Gray had The Grove (what we now call Grovelands) built to the design of John Nash in 1797-8, J.D. Taylor assuming ownership in 1839, after Walker's death. Like John Vickris Taylor, Abraham and John Gray gave towards the rebuilding of the Quaker Meeting House in Church Hill.

John and Rebecca Walker also had a son named Isaac (1725 - 1804), who was a prosperous linen merchant, and was buried in the local Friends' burial ground. Isaac married Elizabeth Hill in 1764, and purchased Arnos Grove in 1777. Isaac and Elizabeth had a daughter named Elizabeth (who married the Rev. Thomas Winchester Lewis of the Old Park Estate), and a son named John (1766 - 1824), who married Sarah Chorley (1774 - 1852).

John and Sarah's son Isaac Junior (1794 - 1853) married Sophia Taylor, daughter of John Vickris Taylor and Sophia Donnithorne. Isaac and Sophia Walker produced five daughters and the famous seven cricketing bachelor brothers of Southgate, remembered in the cricket ground in Waterfall Road. I have tried to represent this complicated story diagrammatically at Figure 3. The Walker - Gray - Taylor dynasty owned much of the land in Southgate and Winchmore Hill, and in the 19th century tried to keep the area sheltered from the clutches of the urbanisers.

As well as family links, there were also business associations. Robert Taylor, and his son John Vickris, were the main owners of a brewery at Limehouse, in the East End. The firm, established in 1730, was originally Harford and Taylor, but on the entrance of the Walkers in 1816, the name was changed to Taylor Walker and Co. John Donnithorne succeeded his father in the brewery in 1827, but in about 1843 he sold out the family's entire interest to the Walker family. He then led the life of a country gentleman at the estate he re- named Grovelands, which he acquired in about 1839, following the death of Walker Gray in 1834. By the time he died, in 1885, the 230 + acres of estate had mushroomed to about 600 acres – Taylor's own 'Green Belt'.

Green, George – an infant (his Guardian)

No. on Map	Premises	Tenure	State in 1801	QuantityA.R.11	Per Acre	Corn Rent	O'ty Bus.Deeim.
113	Thoroughfare close		Meadow	1a 2r 32p	5/3d	8s 11d	1B 372d
118	Thoroughfare close		Meadow	4a 2r 12p	5/4d	£1 4s 4d	3B 743d
119			Pasture	2a 0r 37p	5/7d	12s 4d	1B 898d
1394	Allotment in Hag field	Copyhold		7a 1r 30p			
			Totals	15a 3r 31p		£2 5s 7d	7B 13d

(See Figure 15) Plots 113, 118 and 119 form a continuous area of land between 'Station Road' and 'Vicars Moor Lane' towards The Green end. The railway line, opened in 1871, seems to have been driven bang through the centre of the north - south line of field 113. Plot 1394 is in the southern vicinity of what is now Green Moor Link.

The Edmonton Manor Court Minutes of 12th June 1810 tell us that all this land was then surrendered by George Green, Plots 113, 118 & 119 at the time being known as Whitlocks. There is no Green family in the 1826 Directory.

Grover, Jos (in right of his wife)

No. on Map	Premises	Tenure	State in 1801	Quantity A.R.P	Per Acre	Corn Rent	O'tv Bns.Decim.
176	Messuage and garden	Freehold		0a 0r 13p	5/-	4d	51d

Grover's cottage is the north most of the four cottages that lay behind where *The Woodman* later appeared, on what even in those days was called The Bourne (see Figure 11).

H

Hall, Francis

No. on Map	Premises	Tenure	State in 1801	Quantity A.R.P	Per Acre	Corn Rent	O'tv Bns.Decim.
59	Cottage and garden			0a 0r 11p	4s	0s 3d	38d

59 is a tiny plot by what is marked as Winchmore Hill Gate on the Enclosure Map (see Figure 8). This is probably the cottage that Hall Surrendered to allow Henry Thompson's possession in 1804.

Figure 3. The Taylors and Walkers and Grays

A Diagrammatic Representation of Family Relationships

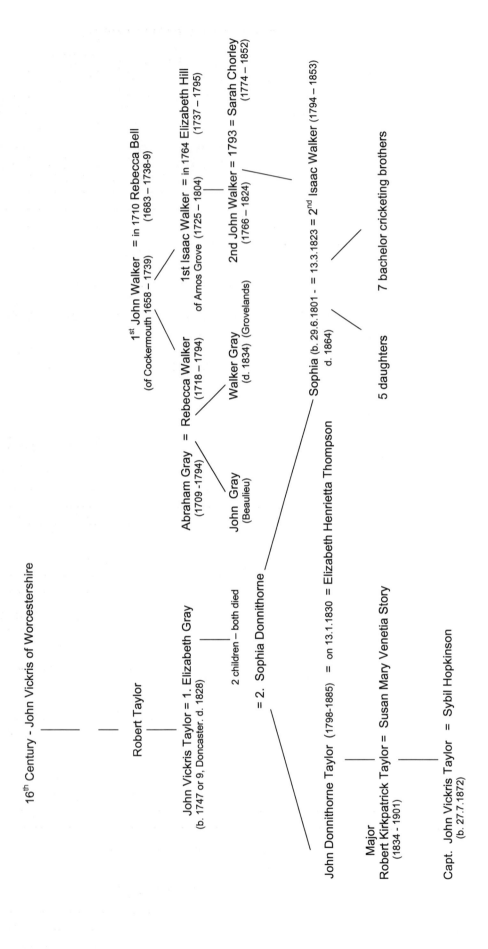

90

Harrison, a minor (his Trustees)

No. on Map	Premises	Tenure	State in 1801	Quantity A.R.P	Per Acre	Corn Rent	O'tv Bus. Decim.
288	Messuage, garden & yards			2a 2r 6p	5/7d	14s 1d	2B 168d
289	The thirteen acres		Meadow	13a 0r 20p	5/3d	£3 8s 10d	10B 590d
290	Cottages and gardens			0a 1r 22p	5/-	1s 11d	0B 295d
291	Cherry tree field		Meadow	8a 2r 23p	5/3d	£2 3s 6d	6B 693d
180	The Grove		Pasture	15a 0r 38p	4/6d	8s 6d	10B 539d
181	Wood Pightle		Meadow	1a 3r 36p	4/6d	7s 11d	1B 218d
182	Wood			1a 3r 32p	1/3d	2s 4d	0B 359d
1405	Allotment on waste at the Bourn	Freehold		0a 1r 32p			
1510	Allotment on the Chase	Freehold		3a 0r 0p			
1509	Allotment on the Chase	Copyhold		0a 3r 28p			
			Totals	48a 0r 17p		£10 7s 1d	31B 862d

Plots 288, 289, 290 and 291 are a set of adjoining holdings in the region of today's Mall, off Fox Lane. Plots 180, 181 and 182 are just north of Dog and Duck Lane in the vicinity of where Oaklands now runs. Plot 1405 is approximately where today's Bourne entrance to Grovelands Park is. Plots 1509 and 1510 are on the north side of Chase Side Road (now Winchmore Hill Road), in Southgate, rather than Winchmore Hill, but I have shown the entries to complete the list of John Harrison's holdings. There is no Harrison in the 1826 Directory.

Harvey, Jacob

No. on Map	Premises	Tenure	State in 1801	Quantity A.R.P	Per Acre	Corn Rent	O'tv Bus. Decim.
94			Meadow	2a 1r 30p	4/8d	11s 4d	1B 744d
122			Meadow	2a 3r 2p.	5/6d	15s 1d	2B 322d
114	Barn and Yard			0a 1r 22p			
115	Garden and house			0a 0r 4p.	5/6d	12s 1d	1B 860d
116	Yard			0a 2r 23p			
117	Garden			0a 2r 23p			
1395	Allotment in Hag field	Copyhold		3a 2r 16p			
				11a 0r 0p		£1 18s 6d	5B 926d

See Figure 15. Plot 94 is just north of 'Vicars Moor Lane', approximately where Drayton Gardens now runs. 1395 borders Plot 94 on the latter's western boundary. Plot 122 is opposite these on the south side of 'Vicars Moor Lane'. West of 122, but separated from it by John Merrington's 123 and 124, is the square block of land comprised of Plots 114, 115, 116 and 117.

In the diary for 1820 I quote the 1807 Will of John Decka, who therein refers to his late sister Lydia Harvey. Perhaps she had been married to Jacob.

Harvey, Jacob – sold to H. Thompson Esq

No. on Map	Premises	Tenure	State in 1801	Quantity A.R.P	Per Acre	Corn Rent	O'tv Bus. Decim.
97	Two cottages and garden			0a 1r 19p	5s	1s 10d	282d

Plot 97 is opposite the block of 114/5/6/7.

Harvey, Jacob – exchanged to Jos. Osborne

No. on Map	Premises	Tenure	State in 1801	Quantity A.R.P	Per Acre	Corn Rent	O'tv Bus. Decim.
121	Green man field		Pasture	1a 0r 0p	5/6d	5s 6d	846d

Plot 121 is approximately where Winchmore Hill Station is now situated.

Huxley, Miss Sarah (her Executors)

No. on Map	Premises	Tenure	State in 1801	Quantity A.R.P	Per Acre	Corn Rent	Q'ty Bus. Decim
378	Six Acres		Meadow	6a 1r 28p	6s 1d	£1 19s 0d	6B 2d
379	Four Acres		Meadow	5a 1r 20p	6s 1d	£1 12s 8d	5B 26d
381	Farm-house and yard			1a 1r 12p			
382	Garden			1a 1r 35p	6s 1d	£1 0s 3d	3B 115d
383	Yard			0a 2r 1p			
391	Four acres and cross ways		Arable	4a 3r 4p	9s 2d	£2 3s 8d	6B 718d
392	Six acres		Meadow	7a 0r 17p	5s 9d	£2 0s 9d	6B 269d
393	Three acres		Arable	3r 0r 2p	9s 7d	£1 8s 10d	4B 436d
394	Three acres		Arable	2a 3r 20p	10/-	£1 8s 9d	4B 423d
395			Arable	6a 0r 0p	10/-	£3 0s 0d	9B 231d
396			Pasture	2a 3r 7p	5/6d	15s 3d	2B 347d
397			Meadow	2a 3r 39p	5/7d	16s 7d	2B 553d
398			Meadow	2a 3r 33p	5/7d	16s 4d	2B 514d
375	Little six acres		Meadow	6a 0r 29p	5/10d	£1 15s 11d	5B 27d
376	Great six acres		Arable	6a 1r 30p	10/5d	£3 7s 0d	10B 308d
384	Nine acres		Arable	9a 2r 37p	10/10d	£5 5s 4d	16B 204d

See Figure 19. Plots 378, 379, 381, 382 and 383 constituted Huxley's Farm in the angle between Hedge Lane and 'Firs Lane'. Plots 375, 376 and 384 are today near to, or actually the site of, Tatem Park, to the west of the 'Great Cambridge Road'. The remainder of the Plots were on the south side of Hedge Lane, opposite the farm, or nearly so.

On 25th May 1934 *The Enfield Gazette* ran a story by 'Memorabilia' that was headed 'The Gravel Pit in Hedge Lane'. It ran as follows, 'A gratifying piece of news to me is that published in your issue of April 27th that the Gravel Pit in Hedge Lane, generously offered to the Edmonton and Southgate Councils by the owners, the Misses Harman, subject to it being used as an open space and recreation ground, and to the family name of their uncle, Mr. J.G. Tatem, being associated with it, has been accepted by the two Councils concerned. No difficulty should arise in devising a scheme for the lay-out, maintenance and management of the ten acres long before Southgate's lease expires seven year's hence.

The land formed part of the Wyerhalle, Wyralls, or Goodesters estate. Robinson says it probably took its name from the family Wyrehalle, who had considerable property in Edmonton in the time of Edward 111,1340. About 1581 it was the property of Jasper Leeke Esq., who inherited it from his father. On June 12th, 1609, George Huxley, citizen and haberdasher, of London, bought the estate from Sir John Leeke and Ann, his wife, and it continued in the direct male line of the Huxley family until the death in 1743 of Thomas Huxley, who bequeathed his estates to his two daughters, to which on the partition in 1752 Wyer Hall was apportioned to Sarah, the younger, who died unmarried in 1801. Sarah devised Wyer Hall, with her lands in Edmonton, unto her five cousins, from whom it descended to James George Tatem, a collateral relative.

So far as a I can trace it, the modern Weir Hall must not be confused with the Wyer Hall of which I am writing, which was demolished in 1818, the site of which appears to have joined the gravel pit and will be found on the Ordnance Map 1897 marked Wyerhall Nursery and Millfield Nursery......... In the old parish church of All Saints', Edmonton, may be found numerous memorials of the Huxleys and

Tatems from 1613 onwards (see Plate 52), perhaps the most interesting for the present occasion being;-

"In a vault under this inscription lies inter'd Elizabeth, The eldest daughter of John Huxley, late of Wyer Hall, Esq, and wife of Samuel Tatem, of London, Merchant, by whom she had issue eleven children, three of which are deposited in the same Vault, and eight survived her. She constantly Practized the Virtues of a well-spent Life, in her duty to God, her affection to her husband and a tender care to her Children. This life she exchanged for a better the 4th day of April, Anno Domini 1730, in the 47th year of her age. To the Memory of her so dear to him when living, her Husband has caus'd this Monument to be erected."

Also in the same Vault are Interred the Remains of the above Samuel Tatem, Esquire, who died the 29th Anno Domini, 1756, in the 82nd year of his age. To six other members of the Tatem family is a memorial which concludes: - "This Monument is erected as a tribute of fraternal affection By the desire of George Tatem, Esq., late of St. George's, Bloomsbury, who at an early age was appointed, and for many years resided His Majesty's consul general in the island of Sicily. When returning to his native Country, He was elected a director of the Honourable United East India Company, the duties of which station He fulfill'd with ability, diligence and fidelity, upwards of XXX, years. He died the XXV, July MDCCCV11 in the LXXXV1 year of his age."

The Misses Harman are following an honourable tradition of their forbears because another memorial (at Plate 52) is inscribed: - "To the Memory of Mrs. Sarah Huxley, the last surviving Daughter of Thomas Huxley, Esqr. Of Wyer Hall, who departed this life on the 6th May, 1801, aged 73. Whilst living she was a Benefactress to the poor and at her decease bequeathed the following Charitable Legacies, Viz; To the Charity Schools in the Parish of St. Sepulchre, commonly call'd the Ladies Charity School £50-0-0d. To the poor of the Parish of Edmonton £100 – 0 - 0d. To the Fifteen Alms Houses, called Styles and Latimer £1,000 – 0 - 0d. To the Girls Charity School in the Parish of Edmonton £200 – 0 - 0d. Also lies interred the Body of the afore-said Thomas Huxley, who died the 18th of June, 1743. Also Meliora Shaw, eldest daughter of the aforesaid Thomas Huxley, who died the 12th of April 1788."

Although the inscription on this tomb is Mrs. Sarah Huxley she was the unmarried lady previously referred to, it being in her lifetime the custom to designate such ladies 'mistress'. The name Huxley will probably be connected with the district for centuries and it is fitting that the Tatem family shall always be commemorated. I welcome alike Alderman Joy's manner of acceptance of the gift and Mr. Arthur Ingram's assistance in securing it. Probably some people will demur to the Borough of Southgate spending money on it because the gravel pit is in Edmonton, but it is only about 460 yards outside the boundary. Such boundaries become the more arbitrary as the population increases.

The late Mr. V.E. Walker set an excellent precedent by his gift of 15 acres as the New Southgate Recreation Ground, and the Children's Boundary Playground, which is partly in Southgate, Edmonton and Wood Green, is a co-operative effort by adjoining communities whose aim it should ever be to be good neighbours."

At Page 78 of his 1819 book Robinson gives a table of local longevity, which includes George Tatem at age 86 in 1807, and Catherine Tatem at 92 in 1812. The Tatem – Huxley family are not only remembered in the name of Tatem Park, just off the Great Cambridge Road, but also in Huxley Place (off Hedge Lane), Huxley Parade (just south of Cambridge Circus), and Huxley Road (north of Millfield House).

J

Jackson, James

No. on Map	Premises	Tenure	State in 1801	Quantity A.R.P	Per Acre	Corn Rent	O'ty Bus. Decim
126	House and Garden			0a 2r 19p			
127	House and Garden			0a 1r 25p			
128	Field adjoining		Meadow	2a 1r 7p	None of	the Plots	given
340	Little Pightle		Pasture	1a 0r 0p		separately	
241	House and yard			0a 1r 39p			
342	Great Pightle		Meadow	2a 2r 34p			
			Total =	7a 2r 4p	5/7d	£2 1s 11d	6B 440d

Plots 126/7/8 are in the angle of 'Vicars Moor Lane' and Green Lanes (Figure 15). I believe the 241 is a misprint for 341, in which case the adjoining Plots 340/341/342 are on the south side of Barrow's Well Green, about half way between Green Lanes and 'Firs Lane' (Figure 19). It is possible that the House on Plot 341 was the Highfield House marked in this vicinity on the 1822 OS Map (Figure 21).

One wonders if James Jackson is any relation to the Mary Jackson - William Tash family of Broomfield House.

Jauncey, George

No. on Map	Premises	Tenure	State in 1801	Quantity A.R.P	Per Acre	Corn Rent	O'ty Bus. Decim
49	House and garden			0a 0r 20p	5s	7d	90d

I believe that the House on Plot 49 still remains as the lowest (i.e. most westerly) of the old clapperboard cottages on Church Hill, shown on the back cover (Figure 9).

The LMA document ACC/695/49 has a list of Edmonton Manor Quit Rents for 1780-1which indicates that George and Sarah Jauncey were admitted to a cottage at 'Winchmore Hill' (presumably this one) in 1779, at a Quit Rent of 2/6d.

Jauncey, John

No. on Map	Premises	Tenure	State in 1801	Quantity A.R.P	Per Acre	Corn Rent	O'ty Bus. Decim
112	Three tenements and gardens			0a 0r 9p			

This Plot, John Jauncey's only one in the Award, is today occupied by shops overlooking The Green.

Jauncey is an unusual name, so one assumes that George and John must have been related. The LMA document ACC/695/49 indicates that John Jauncey was admitted to 'a cottage at Winchmore Hill' in 1772, for which the Quit Rent was 6d. In his 1984 book on Enfield Chase David Pam tells us, from documents at the National Archives, that on the night of 18th/19th October 1784, 'one black man, the property of John Jauncey' was on Edmonton common.

Joachim, Mary

No. on Map	Premises	Tenure	State in 1801	Quantity A.R.P	Per Acre	Corn Rent	O'ty Bus. Decim
78	House and land			0a 0r 16p	5s	6d	77d

Plot 78 is just to the east of Friends' Meeting House on 'Church Hill'.

Jones, William and Jane

No. on Map	Premises	Tenure	State in 1801	Quantity A.R.P	Per Acre	Corn Rent	O'ty Bus. Decim
108	Two tenements & field	adjoining	Meadow	1a 3r 20p	5/10d	£0 10s l0d	1B 666d

Plot 108 is on the eastern side of 'Wades Hill' near The Green. Are one, or both, of the tenements represented in the Georgian terrace that exists there today?

At the National Archives in Kew is the last Will of Jane Jones, as reported in the 1814 diary section. In it she left her estate to her sister Mary Jones, 'the wife of William Jones'.

L

Lake, Sir James Bart.

No. on Map	Premises	Tenure	State in 1801	Quantity A.R.P1	Per Acre	Corn Rent	O'ty Bus. Decim.
367	Mansion – house & c.		½ meadow	14a 2r 30p	6/-	£4 8s 1d	13B 552d
			½ pasture				
368	Three cornered Pightle		Pasture	1a 1r 29p	5/6d	£0 7s 9d	1B 192d
369			Meadow	6a 3r 0p	6/1d	£0 2s 1d	6B 308d
370			Meadow	5a 2r 27p	6/1d	£1 14s 5d	5B 296d
371			Meadow	5a 1r 8p	5/7d	£1 9s 7d	4B 552d
380	Two orchards		Pasture	2a 1r 17p	6/1d	£0 14s 3d	2B 193d
1374	Allotment in High - field	Copyhold		1a 1r 16p			
1373	Allotment in High - field	Freehold		1a 1r 15p			
1365	Allotment of a lane near	Copyhold		0a 2r 17p			
	his dwelling house		Totals	39a 1r 39p		£10 15s 1d	33B 93d

Plots 367 – 380 (inc.) listed above are either side of the southern stretch of 'Firs Lane', Plot 367 containing The Firs mansion (which is pictured at P28 of *A Look at Old Winchmore Hill*). The location of Plots 1373, 1374 and 1365 are given in the schedule itself.

The main sources for the following account relating to the Lakes, and John Smith, are – Tom Mason's 1948 *A Southgate Scrapbook*; Alan Dumayne's *Once Upon a Time in Palmers Green*; George Sturgess's 1947 *An Edmonton Heritage*; *The Hudson's Bay Record Society Saskatchewan Journals and Correspondence – Edmonton House 1795 – 1800. Chesterfield House 1800 – 02*, edited by Alice Johnson in 1967; Professor D. M. Cruden's article in *Alberta History – Winter 2004*; William Robinson's 1819 *History of Edmonton*.

Mason tells us that records of the Lake family go back to the reign of Queen Elizabeth 1, the earliest known members residing in Lincolnshire. Edward Lake was born in 1598, and in his later years he became an ardent Royalist. Charles 1 rewarded him with a baronetcy, but when he died in 1674 he left no children, so the baronetcy fell into disuse. Edward's estates passed to his nephew, Thomas Lake, who was a Bencher of the Middle Temple, and the first of the Lake family to be a stock holder in the Hudson's Bay Company, being Deputy Governor, 1710 - 11.

The estates then passed to Thomas's son Bibye, the unusual first name coming from the maiden name of Edward Lake's wife, Anne Bibye. Bibye was the first Lake to live in Firs Lane, and he approached the Lord Treasurer to renew the lapsed baronetcy, which Queen Anne duly approved in 1711. Sir Bibye was a sub Governor of the Africa Company, a Bencher of the MiddleTemple, and was Governor of the Hudson's Bay Company from 1712 until his death in 1743. Sir Bibye's eldest son, Sir Atwell, was Governor from 1750 until he in turn died in 1760, being buried at the Parish Church, Edmonton on 28th April. Sir Bibye's second son, Bibye Jnr. (another Bencher of the Middle Temple) was Governor 1770 – 82.

Sir Atwell's eldest son, Sir James Winter Lake, was born in Edmonton, no doubt at The Firs, and lived there all his life, being the man in occupation of The Firs at the time of Enclosure. His wife's name was Jessy, and they had four sons and three daughters, whose names were James, Willoughby, Atwill, Andrew, Mary, Charlotte and Anne. Sir James was elected to the Committee of the Hudson's Bay Company each year from 1762 – 81 inclusive, and in 1782 was appointed Deputy Governor. He held this position until he succeeded Samuel Wegg as Governor in 1799, remaining in post until his death in 1807. In 1794 the Company's capital stood at £103,950 with about 100 accounts, including the then Deputy Governor Sir James's £1,817.

It was in 1795 that the Company established a fort on the North Saskatchewan River. The name given to it was Edmonton House, from Lake's home in the Parish of Edmonton, and that was then applied to the city in Alberta, 20 miles upstream from the fort. Edmonton in Canada now has a population of over half a million.

Sir James studied classical languages at Trinity College, Cambridge, and was a Fellow of both the Royal Society and the Society of Antiquaries. His love of the Arts can be gauged by the Sale Catalogue of his collection at Piccadilly on 31st March 1808, following his death. The 1,135 lots cover 56 pages. More details are given in an article by 'Memorabilia' in *The Palmers Green and Southgate Gazette* of 27th December 1935, for anyone wishing to learn more.

Sir James Winter's final promotion is not reflected in the Council's commemorative Blue Plaque. This is on the front of the house numbered 335, Firs Lane. On 29th May 1989 I noted that it read, 'London Borough of Enfield. Site of Firs Hall where lived Sir James Winter Lake 1742 – 1807. Deputy Governor of the Hudson's Bay Company. Edmonton Alberta was named from his place of residence.' Sir James was buried at the Parish Church, Edmonton on 4th May 1807.

Sir James employed John Thomas Smith (1766 – 1833), as art master to his daughters for seven years from 1788. Smith stayed at Myrtle Cottage 'over the lane' from The Firs (at Plot 371 upon Enclosure). He is sometimes referred to as 'Rainy Day Smith', after he produced his *Book for a Rainy Day* (published posthumously in 1864), which contained some local references. In his book Smith tells us that whilst he was at Myrtle Cottage, Sir James Winter's wife Jessy retained much of her youthful beauty, was very affable with all she met, and was benevolent to the local poor.

Sir James and Lady Lake provided Smith with a reference when he applied for the post of drawing master at Christ's Hospital, a London charity school, in 1798. They wrote, 'We have known Mr. Smith for upwards of 14 years, and found him an able drawing master to our daughter, whose drawings he has never touched upon, a practice too often followed by drawing masters in general; and we believe him to be a truly valuable member of society, as a husband, father and good man.' Smith later became a print seller in St. Martin's Lane and, in 1816, was made Keeper of Prints in the British Museum, retaining this position until his death. There is a Blue Plaque commemorating his stay in the District, captured at Plate 8. Plate 55 portrays Myrtle Cottage.

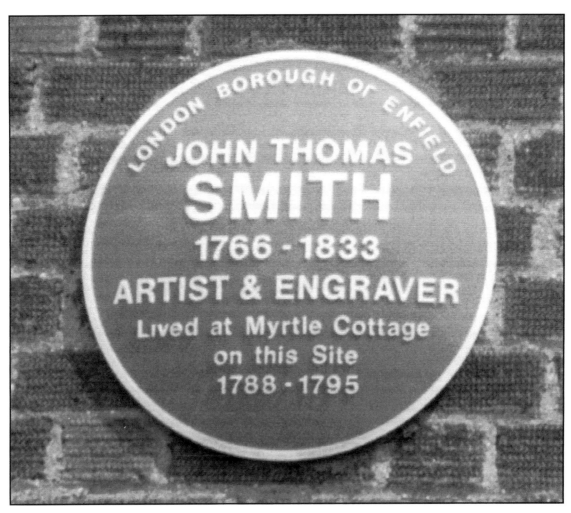

Plate 8. Blue Plaque to J.T. Smith in Firs Lane

At Plate 55 is a sketch of Myrtle Cottage, home to the artist John Smith, whose likeness of the Rev. Henry Owen is at Plate 4. On 29th May 1989 I took this photograph of the Blue Plaque on the wall of No. 314, Firs Lane, a Newsagent in a parade of shops.

In his *History of Edmonton* Robinson tells us that in his Will of 12th April 1662 John Wild of Edmonton bequeathed some land to various people. On the 25th October 1731 the then trustees leased Sir Bibye Lake some of that land, which included, 'five acres of arable land in Hag Field, for 999 years from Michaelmas 1732, at £9 per annum. This was increased to £12 1s by the Commissioners of Inclosures. This lease having been considered an improvident one, a Bill in Chancery was filed by order of the vestry of the parish of Edmonton, in the year 1814, to set the same aside; and by a decree, dated July, 1818, the said lease was ordered to be given up to the trustees to be cancelled, and the premises (as far as they could be ascertained) restored to their possession. The premises now consist of eight acres three roods and thirty perches, allotted by the Commissioner of Inclosures, in lieu of the common field lands, and one rood, twenty - two perches, at the north - west of the estate, formerly called "'The Firs", and are at present in the occupation of – Gable, at a rent fixed by the Court of Chancery of £20 per annum.'

Obviously this leased land wasn't included in the schedule relating to Lake's ownership. In 1801 Mrs. Teshmaker was awarded Plot 1397's 8 acres 3 roods and 22 perches in Hagfield. However, it is difficult to tie this in with the above. In the land ownership under John Wild's Charity, later on, we see that the Charity leased 8 acres 3 roods and 30 perches of allotment in High Field, and I suspect that Robinson made a 'clerical error' in his book by printing Hag Field, when he meant High Field. (See also the later entry for Sir John Wild's Charity).

Leathersellers Company

No. on Map	Premises	Tenure	State in 1801	Quantity A.R.P	Per Acre	Corn Rent	O'ty Bus. Decim
1524	Allotment in the Chase	Freehold		1a 0r 26p			

Plot 1524 is near Winchmore Hill Gate at the foot of Chase Side Road (now Winchmore Hill Road). (See Figure 8).

Legrew, Thomas (his Executors)

No. on Map	Premises	Tenure	State in 1801	Quantity A.R.P	Per Acre	Corn Rent	O'ty Bus. Decim
1529	Allotment on the Chase	Freehold		0a 3r 35p			

Plot 1529 is near Winchmore Hill Gate at the foot of Chase Side Road (now Winchmore Hill Road). (See Figure 8).

Lewis, Thomas

No. on Map	Premises	Tenure	State in 1801	Quantity A.R.P1	Per Acre	Corn Rent	O'ty Bus. Decim.
313	Meadow		Meadow	3a 3r 27p	5/1d	19s 10d	3B 53d
314	Meadow		Meadow	3a 2r 4p	5/4d	18s 9d	2B 886d
315	Meadow			3a 2r 34p	5/4d	19s 8d	3B 27d
316	Meadow			3a 3r 14p	5/7d	£1 1s 5d	3B 295d

These Plots are on the west side of Green Lanes SW of 'St. John's Church'. (See Figure 12).

Whilst following up David Hicks's lead on Beaulieu I came across some information on Thomas Lewis in Ptolemy Dean's *Sir John Soane and London*. Dean tells us that John Gray was married to the daughter of Bank of England Director Thomas Lewis, who owned The Lodge in Green Lanes. In his *Once Upon a Time in Palmers Green*, Alan Dumayne tells us about Ye Olde Thatched Cottage, that stood on Green Lanes near The Triangle until 1938. Alan reports that it was built about 1790 by Thomas Lewis, as an outhouse to a mansion called 'The Lodge', which must be Plot 523 on the 1801/2 Enclosure Map.

Lloyd, Richard, W. and others

No. on Map	Premises	Tenure	State in 1801	Quantity A.R.P	Per Acre	Corn Rent	O'ty Bus. Decim
771	Field adjoining garden	Copyhold	Meadow	3a 2r 26p			
772	House, garden and yards			2a 1r 15p			
			Total	6a 0r 1p	6/-	£1 16s 0d	5B 540d

These were in the vicinity of today's Quaker Walk. (See Figure 16).

Lowen, Robert

No. on Map	Premises	Tenure	State in 1801	Quantity A.R.P	Per Acre	Corn Rent	O'ty Bus. Decim.
179	Cottage, &c.			0a 0r 17p	5/-	6d	77d

This appears to be the most southerly cottage in a terrace which is behind where *The Woodman* later opened. It is therefore probably captured in the picture of that Inn reproduced at the base of Page 31 of *A Look at Old Winchmore Hill*. (See Figure 11).

I know nothing of Robert, but the 1826 Pigot's lists a John Lowens as a general dealer in Winchmore Hill – perhaps a relation? (Even today people are quite careless about the spelling of names.)

At Page 19 of her *Memories of a Lost Village*, Miss Cresswell tells us that, 'Near the *Salisbury Arms* was a tiny shop kept by the ancient spinsters, the Misses Lowen. One of them was quite deaf, and as bald as an egg – a rather forbidding old lady from whom to make purchases. The other had no legs!' Miss Cresswell was talking of her early childhood c 1860, so we may well be hearing from her of two old villagers who were children in 1801. Robert Lowen's daughters?

Lucas, Nathaniel

No. on Map	Premises	Tenure	State in 1801	Quantity A.R.P	Per Acre	Corn Rent	O'ty Bus. Decim.
168	A house and garden			0a 0r 25p	5/-	£0 0s 9d	115d

Plot 168 is sited near to where the *Salisbury Arms* is today (Figure 14).

The LMA document ACC/695/49 has a list of Edmonton Manor Quit Rents for 1780-1 which indicates that Nathaniel Lucas was admitted to a Copy (hold) 'Piece of Ground adjoining his house at Winchmore Hill' in 1770. The Quit Rent was 6d.

Lumbess, James

No. on Map	Premises	Tenure	State in 1801	Quantity A.R.P1	Per Acre	Corn Rent	O'ty Bus. Decim.
174	Cottage and garden			0a 0r 17p	5/-	6d	0B 77d
1404	Allotments - On the waste at the Bourne	Copyhold		0a 0r 23p			

Plot 174 was in the set of cottages near where *The Woodman* is today. Plot 1404 adjoined 174. (See Figure 11).

M

Marshall, Rachael

No. on Map	Premises	Tenure	State in 1801	Quantity A.R.P1	Per Acre	Corn Rent	O'ty Bus. Decim.
104	House and Garden			0a 1r 25p	5/6d	2s 2d	0B 334d
103	Cottage and garden			0a 0r 26p	5/-	9d	115d
1579	Allotment on the Chase			1a 2r 36p			

Plot 104 is at the SW corner of 'Vicars Moor Lane', where it meets 'Wades Hill'. Plot 103 is opposite, on the west side of 'Wades Hill'. (See Figure 14). Plot 1579 is further north on 'Wades Hill', on the western side, approximately where Houndsden Road runs today. Rachael bought the acre of adjoining land on Plot 1578 for £105. (See Figure 8).

Quaker Meeting Minutes indicate that Rachael gave five guineas towards the rebuilding of the local Meeting House in 1790. I examined documents in a box referenced J90 at the National Archives, Kew. Two of these were dated 19th December

1801, regarding Mrs. Marshall and 'Edmonton Inclosure'. One involved an agreement between The Trustees of the Quakers Meeting of Tottenham and Mrs. Rachael Marshall, who was shown as being a widow of Castle Street, Hertford. The parchment seems to indicate that for £21. 14s Mrs. Marshall bought the 'Freehold Common Rights' to land the Quakers would have obtained under the Enclosure Award. The other similar document shows Mr. Richard Caleb Morrison paying Rachael £37. 2s 0d for the 'Freehold Common Rights' for two tenements in Winchmore Hill then in the occupation of Mrs. Sarah Morrison. Could these be the ones at Plots 103 and 104 one wonders. (Sarah Morrison appears later in the schedule)

Mellish, William Esq.

No. on Map	Premises	Tenure	State in 1801	Quantity A.R.P	Per Acre	Corn Rent	O'ty Bus. Decim.
60			Pasture	1a 3r 28p			
61	Farm – house, and yards			2r 31p			
62	Orchard		Pasture	1a 1r 10p	60 – 64 inc.		
63			Pasture	2a 3r 30p	= 5/7d	=£2 19s 8d	= 9B 181d
64			Meadow	3a 3r 13p			
65			Meadow	4a 2r 35p	5/1d	£1 3s 11d	3B 680d
66			Meadow	1a 3r 7p	66 + 67		
67			Meadow	3a 0r 26p	= 5/7d	=£1 7s 7d	= 4B 244d
68			Meadow	6a 3r 11p	5/1d	£1 14s 7d	5B 322d
81			Meadow	4a 2r 8p	5/3d	£1 3s 10d	3B 667d
82			Meadow	9a 1r 36p	4/8d	£2 4s 1d	6B 782d
83			Meadow	6a 1r 28p	4/9d	£1 10s 5d	4B 679d
188			Meadow	2a 3r 24p	4/8d	11s 6d	1B 770d
189			Meadow	4a 1r 7p	5/7d	£1 3s 11d	3B 680d
1388/9	Allotments on waste near	Copyhold		24p			
	Winchmore - hill	Copyhold		1r 20p			

(See Figure 8). Plots 60 – 68 inclusive comprised the bulk of the land between 'Church Hill' and 'Wades Hill' south of today's Houndsden Road. Plots 81/2/3 are in the angle between 'Wades Hill' and Green Dragon Lane. Plots 188 and 189 form the eastern two thirds of the land between 'Station Road' and 'Compton Road'. Plots 1388 and 1389 formed thin strips that adjoined Plot 189, the former to its north, the latter to its south. (See Figure 13).

Mellish lived at Bush Hill Park Mansion (not to be confused with John Blackburn's Bush Hill House), which was later known as Clock House, prior to its demolition in 1927. This is clearly shown, just north of our area, on the 1895 O.S. Map of South Enfield, being on the northern leg of Bush Hill, near where Ringmer Place is today. Mellish owned much land in this area to the north of Winchmore Hill. He was Tory MP for Grimsby, then for Middlesex from 1806 to 1820, when he sat alongside the Whig George Byng. Mellish was also a Magistrate, Chairman of the Royal Exchange, and a Director of the Bank of England for nearly 50 years. He died in 1838 after catching a chill whilst watching the Royal Exchange burn down, and was buried at All Saints, Edmonton. In his book *Middlesex* Michael Robbins says Mellish had been described, in his day, as, 'a thick and thin man for the government and a jolly, comely, hereditary protestant'. See the 1785 diary section regarding a letter from the Rev. Warren to this local 'land baron'.

Merrington, John

No. on Map	Premises	Tenure	State in 1801	Quantity A.R.P	Per Acre	Corn Rent	O'ty Bus. Decim.
123	House and garden			0a 2r 6p	5/6d	2s 11d	449d
124	Field adjoining		Arable	3a 3r 2p	7/2d	£1 6s 11d	4B 141d
1393	Allotment in Hag Field	Freehold		1a 0r 0p			
1560	Allotment on the Chase	Freehold		1a 3r 24p			
1559	Allotment on the Chase	Copyhold		2a 2r 32p			
			Total	9a 3r 24p		£1 9s 10d	4B 590d

Plots 123 and 124 were in the vicinity of 'Ringwood Way' (See Figure 15). Plots 1559 and 1560 were at the northern end of 'Worlds End Lane'. Merrington also purchased Plot 1561, which was described as Galliard's Thick, adjacent to Plot 1560. (See Figure 7). Plot 1393 was in Hag Field, running off of 'Vicars Moor Lane', and he purchased Arable Plot 1392 adjoining it to the west. (See Figure 16).

In the diary section for 1820 mention is made of the proving of John Decka's Will. One of the witnesses verifying its authenticity was John Merrington, 'of Union Court Old Broad Street in the City of London'.

Mordaunt, George

No. on Map	Premises	Tenure	State in 1801	Quantity A.R.P	Per Acre	Corn Rent	O'ty Bus. Decim.
210	House and garden			0a 1r 28p	5/-	2s 1d	321d
1383	Allotment on waste in front	Freehold		0a 0r 6p			

These two Plots are sited in the vicinity of today's Duncan Court on the eastern side of Green Lanes, near 'The Broadway'. (See Figure 17).

Morrison, Sarah

No. on Map	Premises	Tenure	State in 1801	Quantity A.R.P	Per Acre	Corn Rent	O'ty Bus. Decim.
58	Houses and garden			0a 3r 1p	5/9d	4s 3d	653d

Plot 58 overlooks The Green at what would today be the start of Broad Walk, on the Park side. (See Figure 14).

Sarah Morrison is mentioned above under the entry for Rachael Marshall. Was she related to the 'Morrison' who in 1798 was shown to be occupying a cottage owned by the Cordwainers Company, which was probably situated on the nearby Plot 57 on The Green. The LMA document ACC/695/49 has a list of Edmonton Manor Quit Rents for 1780-1 which indicates that a Captain Richard Morrison had a holding in the village at a Quit Rent of 3d. At the LHU are Tom Mason's handwritten notes in which he records the death at Winchmore Hill, in June 1780 of Captain Richard Morrison, 'late of the Duke Kingston Indiaman'.

N

Nailor, William Baker

No. on Map	Premises	Tenure	State in 1801	Quantity A.R.P	Per Acre	Corn Rent	O'ty Bus. Decim.
216			Arable	3a 2r 20p	9/7d	£1 14s 9d	5B 347d
217	Half acre arable		Meadow	2a 0r 17p	5/4d	11s 2d	1B 719d
218	House, yards & homestead			1a 1r 38p	6/1d	9s 0d	1B 385d

No. on Map			Meadow	4a 0r 4p	6/1d	£1 4s 5d	3B 756d
219		Total		11a 0r 39p		£3 19s 4d	12B 207d

Nailor's 11 ¼ acres were in the vicinity of modern day Laburnum Grove. (See Figure 18).

The *PGS Gazette* of 31ˢᵗ May 1935 contains an article on Pickering's Cottage. The illustration with that article is reproduced at Plate 49, with kind permission of *The Gazette*. The article surmises that William Baker Nailor's Plot 218, of 'House, yards and homestead', could well be Pickering's Cottage, which it says, had been demolished, and replaced by houses, about three years previously. The Edmonton Manor Court minutes of 16ᵗʰ May 1826 record the death of William Baker Naylor, brother of Thomas.

New River Company

No. on Map	Premises	Tenure	State in 1801	Quantity A.R.P.	Per Acre	Corn Rent *	O'ty Bus. Decim.
751	House and garden	Freehold		0a 1r 8p	5/-	5/3d	0B 807d
768	Two tenements + gardens			0a 0r 37p	5/-	1/1d	0B 167d
774	Next Mr. Blackburn's park			1a 3r 21p	5/4d	9/11d	1B 526d
775	Next Mr. Blackburn's park			1a 3r 36p	5/4d	10/4d	1B 589d
750	Field			5a 0r 37p	3/4d	17/4d	2B 668d
749	Slip and bank			1a 0r 29p	2/9d	3/2d	0B 489d
	New River within the parish			18a 3r 6p			
1371	Allotment on the Waste	Copyhold		0a 0r 3p			
	next High - field						
1370	Ditto	Copyhold		0a 0r 23p			
1372	Allotment on High - field	Freehold		0a 3r 30p			
			Totals	31a 1r 30p		£2 7s 1d	7B 245d

* For this company the Corn Rent isn't payable to the Vicar, but to the Impropriators. (See the sections on the actual Enclosure Act and on tithes.) The first six Plots listed are in the vicinity of 'Bush Hill' and 'Bush Hill Road' (see Figure 16). Plots 1370/1/2 skirt the eastern side of Green Lanes between 'Highfield Road' and Barrow's Well Green (See Figure 18).

I have very little information on this Company, and its history. One presumes that it is the same company, incorporated in 1619, which built the New River under the direction of Sir Hugh Myddelton in the early 17th century.

Oliver, Thomas

No. on Map	Premises	Tenure	State in 1801	Quantity A.R.P.	Per Acre	Corn Rent	O'ty Bus. Decim.
90	Gibraltar field		Meadow	2a 3r 22p	5/1d	14s 7d	2B 245d
91	Gibraltar field		Arable	3a 3r 12p	9/7d	£1 16s 7d	5B 630d
92	Gibraltar field		Pasture	4a 0r 3p	5/-	£1 0s 1d	3B 90d
93	Gibraltar field			2a 3r 30p	5/7d	£0 16s 4d	2B 514d
735	Home field			3a 0r 21p	6/-	£0 18s 9d	2B 886d
736	House, yard, garden, & c.			0a 3r 38p	5/9d	£0 5s 7d	0B 859d
737	Tile Barrow field		Arable	1a 1r 11p	9/7d	£0 12s 8d	1B 949d
	Part of a close got in exchange		Pit	1a 0r 4p		£3 0s 10d	
	from John Blackburn Esq.		Meadow	0a 2r 36p	6/-	4s 4d	0B 666d

742	Meadow		Meadow	12a 0r 27p	5/-	£3 0s 10d	0B 359d
747			Meadow	6a 2r 31p	5/1d	£1 13s 11d	5B 219d
748			Meadow	5a 2r 35p	4/-	£1 2s 10d	3B 513d
	Allotment in exchange from			0a 2r 2p			
	J. Blackburn Esq		Totals	45a 0r 32p	32/-	£12 6s 6d	37B 930d

See Figure 16. Plots 90, 91, 92 and 93, constituting Gibraltar Fields, form a block of over 13 acres bounded by Green Dragon Lane, 'Vicars Moor Lane' and Green Lanes. Plots 742, 747 and 748 cover much of the land in the angle between the eastern end of Green Dragon Lane and the southern stretch of Bush Hill.

See Figure 17 for the location of Plots 735, 736 and 737 on the north eastern side of 'Firs Lane', near The New River. There is further discussion of these early in the map section entitled, 'Highfield Road' to top of 'Firs Lane'.

The Edmonton Manor Minutes of 14th May 1817 tell us that, 'At this Court the Homage find and present that Thomas Oliver late a Customary Tenant of this Manor is dead .....' See the diary section for 1817 for more of the minutes.

Osborne, Ann

No. on Map	Premises	Tenure	State in 1801	Quantity A.R.P	Per Acre	Corn Rent	O'ty Bus. Decim.
1151	Allotment on waste in	Freehold		0a 0r 11p			
	Dog and Duck Lane						

The 1151 would seem to be a misprint for 1351. An 11 perch Plot is marked on the Enclosure Map immediately west of Joseph Osborne's 310 at the foot of 'Bourne Hill' (see Figure 12).

Osborne, Joseph

No. on Map	Premises	Tenure	State in 1801	Quantity A.R.P	Per Acre	Corn Rent	O'ty Bus. Decim.
47	Tenements and garden			0a 1r 6p	4/-	1s 1d	167d
187	Tenements and garden			0a 0r 27p	4/-	8d	0B 102d
310	Tenements and garden			0a 0r 30p	4/-	9d	0B 115d
87	Tenements and garden			0a 0r 20p	4/-	6d	0B 77d
120	Tenements and garden			0a 0r 15p	4/-	4d	0B 57d
738	House and Garden	Freehold		0a 0r 19p	4/-	5d	0B 64d
192	Late Mr. Thompson and	Mr. Busk		0a 2r 4p	5/7d	2s 10d	436d
1368	Allotment in Scotch field	Copyhold		3a 0r 5p			
1586	Allotment on the Chase	Freehold		4a 2r 25p			
	(purchased of John Clayton Esq.)						
88	Cottage and garden			0a 0r 14p	4/-	4d	0B 51d
	Sold to H. Thompson Esq.						

See Figure 15. Plot 187 is near today's *Queen's Head*. Plot 120 was diagonally opposite on the north side of 'Station Road', approximately where Milton Court is today. It was alongside the one acre Green Man Field of Plot 121, which had belonged to Jacob Harvey, but was 'exchanged to Jos. Osborne' as listed under Harvey's entry. Plot 47 is at the foot of Church Hill.

Plot 310 is at the foot of Dog and Duck Lane, and contains the cottages inhabited by the Downes family (see Plate 14). Plot 87 was on the south side of Green Dragon Lane, between 'Green Moor Link' and 'Myddelton Gardens'. Plot 88 is a little east of 87. (See Figure 16).

Plot 738 (top of Figure 17) possibly housed Gibraltar Cottages, pictured at Plate 41. Plot 192 (Figure 13) is at the western end of 'Arlow Road'. Plot 1368 (Figure 19) is where 'Greenwood Gardens' is today. Plot 1586 is in the angle between Green Dragon Lane and 'Wades Hill', later to be assimilated into the grounds of *The Chase*, featured on the front cover of *A Look at Old Winchmore Hill*. (See Figure 8).

One presumes that Joseph was a relative of Ann Osborne. Gary Boudier tells us that the earliest reference he could find for *The Dog and Duck* was a surrender of lease document dated 30th August 1802, when Joseph Osborne surrendered the house to Christopher Idle. In the map section I suggest that Osborne's cottages on Plot 310, at the eastern foot of Dog and Duck Lane, contained an early version of the beer house. This theory must be taken seriously as in the Edmonton Manor Court Baron minutes of 12th May 1818 the death of Joseph Osborne was announced, and his Will of 1815 included *The Dog and Duck*.

ℙ

Parker, James

No. on Map	Premises	Tenure	State in 1801	Quantity A.R.P	Per Acre	Corn Rent	O'ty Bus. Decim.
1544	Allotment on the Chase	Freehold		1a 0r 13p			

Plot 1544 is a narrow strip running west off 'Eversley Park Road', approximately where 'Springbank' now is (see Figure 8).

Patrick, Samuel

No. on Map	Premises	Tenure	State in 1801	Quantity A.R.P1	Per Acre	Corn Rent	O'ty Bus. Decim.
190	House and garden			0a 1r 27p	5/6d	2s 3d	346d

Plot 190 is on the corner of 'Compton Road' (south) and Hopper's Lane (Figure 13) and is pictured at Plate 19.

Thomas Goodfellow was the licensee of *The King's Head* in 1790, succeeding Samuel Patrick, who had held the lease since 1772. In 1792 Patrick again became licensee for a further year.

In the diary section, under 1819 and 1821, I record documents in the LMA which relate to the leasing of property by a John Parkinson from Aaron Patrick (of Enfield Highway) and Miss Mary Peverell (of Hackney Road, Bethnal Green), both of whom seem to have come into it by way of the Will of the (then) late Samuel Patrick, listed above. In 1821 it seems that all agreed to let the property to a John Radford of White Conduit Street, Pentonville. One presumes that he was the Radford who was so prominent in the local Independent Movement.

In the Edmonton Court minutes for 16th May 1826 it is recorded that Mary Hudson, formerly Peverell, and Aaron Patrick had died. Samuel is revealed to be the brother of Aaron, and father of Mary Peverell. In his Will of 1808 Samuel mentions his grandson Henry Peverell and his granddaughter Frances Peverell.

Tom Mason's handwritten notes record, 'Winchmore Hill. Mary Ann Peverell (daughter of Mr. Callow) born in London 17 July 1792. Married in parish church of St. Mary Whitechapel 17 April 1814. John Peverell lived for many years at Winchmore Hill, near Edmonton, died at Winchmore Hill 6 January 1896 aged 103 buried Edmonton Parish Churchyard Jan. 10.'

In his books on Enfield's pubs Gary Boudier lists the licensees of *The Kings Head* on Edmonton Green. He shows Henry Peverell as assuming the licence in 1793, followed by Mary Peverell in 1802, and John Hudson in 1810.

In his 1984 book on Enfield Chase David Pam tells us that Aaron Patrick was landlord of *The King's Arms* in Green Street. Pam describes his greed, in 1783, in coming to the recently disaforested Chase with four horses to cut down young oaks at Crews Hill. When his house was searched 29 trees were found stored on the premises.

Peverill, Mary, widow, (late Henry Peverill)

No. on Map	Premises	Tenure	State in 1801	Quantity A.R.P	Per Acre	Corn Rent	O'ty Bus. Decim.
163	Hoppet at Winchmore - hill			0a 1r 32p	5/6d	£0 2s 5d	0B 372d
163a	Allotment on the waste in	Freehold		0a 0r 3p			
	front of her Paddock		Total	0a 1r 35p		£0 2s 5d	0B 372d

Plot 163 is where the first houses in Broad Walk now stand, adjacent to Woodside/Rowantree. 163a would now be the pavement in front.

In his books on Enfield's pubs Gary Boudier lists the licensees of *The Bull* at Tanners End (now the western end of Silver Street in Edmonton). Robert Peverill is listed for 1764, and the next licensee shown is Mary Peverill, in 1785, followed by Lawrence Allen in 1788.

So there were two families with the similar names of Peverell and Peverill working in the same manor as each other, and for a while I thought they were one and the same family, though it seems that they were probably two separate families.

Phillips, William

No. on Map	Premises	Tenure	State in 1801	Quantity A.R.P	Per Acre	Corn Rent	O'ty Bus. Decim.
169	House, and c.			0a 1r 3p	5/-	1/4d	205d

Plot 169 is on the western side of Hopper's Lane, approximately where the start of Downes Court is today (see Figure 14).

Pole, Samuel Esq. (his Executors)
(sold and exchanged to Walker Gray Esq.)

No. on Map	Premises	Tenure	State in 1801	Quantity A.R.P	Per Acre	Corn Rent	Q'ty Bus. Decim.
Pt. 33	Part of the nine acres	Freehold	Meadow	3a 1r 24p	4/9d	16s 2d	2B 489d
Pt. 34	Part of Woolpack Field		Meadow	3a 0r 22p	5/4d	16s 8d	2B 565d
35	Site of the Wool – pack & garden			1a 1r 35p	5/-	7s 4d	1B 128d
36	Lodge field		Meadow	3a 1r 14p	4/8d	15s 6d	2B 386d

All these are in the vicinity of what is today Queen Elizabeth's Drive (see Figure 11). Pole is also listed as having purchased the 5 ½ acres of waste in Plot 1406 'At Bourne' for £420.

The Palmers Green Gazette of 18th October 1940 carried an article headed 'Charles Pole of Southgate' by *Memorabilia*. It continued, 'From the "Obituary, with anecdotes of remarkable Persons" in *The Gentleman's Magazine*, 1795, 12th September,

I extract: "Of an inflammation in his bowels, Charles Pole, Esq., of Southgate. He was possessed of £300,000, half of which he left between his four sisters; one married, 1788, to W.C. Shaw Esq. Of Youngsbury, Herts.; another to Mr. Vannotten (nephew to Mr. V. an eminent Dutch merchant) who took the name of Pole, and was created baronet 1791; a third 1791, to Cousin Manley of the royal navy; and a fourth single. All these ladies had £10,000 from their father, and are to have only the interest of their brother's legacies. To his first cousin, the Rev. Mr. Blundell, £50 pa, to cease when he gets a living worth £100 pa; to his housekeeper £100 pa; and several other legacies of inconsiderable amount."

In 1801 the Pole Trustees' estate contained 71 a 0r 26p. The mansion was Southgate House (now Minchenden School) or on the site therof. The frontage commenced about where the Church House stands in High Street and continued north to Bourne Hill where it turned in a SE direction to a point about opposite the lodge and drive into Grovelands Hospital, then the recently built (1798) Nash designed mansion, Southgate Grove, of Walker Gray, and included therein were 4a 1r 32p on what is now the Grovelands Hospital Estate at present occupied by tennis courts on the left of the drive as the hospital is approached from Bourne Hill; and 11a 1r 13p of the land adjoining on the west which the schedule described as "sold and exchanged to Walker Gray Esq." ..... The Van Notten – Pole baronetcy still exists .....'

The article does not explain how Charles Pole came to be called Samuel Pole in the schedule. We should also remember that at P56 of his 1819 book, Robinson tells us of 'The Manors of Bowes, Dernford, Pauls House and Fordes'. There is no obvious link, but he says, 'These manors are now in the possession of the Dean and Chapter of St. Paul's, for all of which they hold a court baron and view of frankpledge. The family of Forde was settled at Edmonton, in the reign of Henry 111. The name of Roger Dernford is found in a record relating to the parish of Enfield, in the time of Edward 111. Pauls House should be Pole House, by which name it is described in most ancient deeds, as having been the property of John Atte Pole, or de la Pole, who purchased a house in Edmonton, called Gysors Place, of William Gysors, and some lands and tenements of Robert de Munden, in the time of Edward 111......Dorothy Burrough was the lessee of the manor of Pauls House and Fordes, in 1694; before that time Adam Fulwood; and 1701 Mr. Skinner. The present lessee is Thomas Smith Esq., who lately purchased the lease of Thomas Vere Esq. and Mrs. Judith Teshmaker. The reserved rent of these manors is £10 p.a.'

Quakers' Society

No. on Map	Premises	Tenure	State in 1801	Quantity A.R.P	Per Acre	Corn Rent	O'tv Bus.Decim.
75	Field behind meeting - house		Meadow	0a 2r 4p	5/9d	2s 11d	0B 449d
76	Meeting – house and yard			0a 2r 7p	4/-	2s 2d	0B 334d
1580	Allotment on the Chase	Freehold		3a 12r 0p			

Plot 76 contains the Meeting House still standing at the top of Winchmore Hill – lane (Church Hill), 75 houses the burial grounds, and Plot 1580 is a strip near to where the eastern end of Houndsden Road is now situated. Plot 1580 is shown on the Enclosure Map as being owned by the Quakers' Poor, rather than the Quakers' Society itself (see Figure 8).

The LMA document ACC/695/49 has a list of Edmonton Manor Quit Rents for 1780 - 1 which indicates that the Quakers paid a Quit Rent of 8d for their Meeting House. (i.e. they paid 8d p.a. to the Lord or Lady of the Manor rather than perform services for him or her).

A document in a box referenced J90 at the National Archives, Kew is labelled, 'Dated 19th December 1801 Edmonton Inclosure. The Trustees of the Quakers Meeting of Tottenham to Mrs. Rachael Marshall. Grant and Appointment of Freehold Common Rights.' The parchment seems to indicate that for £21. 14s Ms. Marshall bought the rights to land the Quakers would have obtained under the Enclosure Award. I am unable to tie it in with the Award Schedule.

I have written quite a bit about the local Quakers in the section on the properties around The Green (Plots 75 and 76). There is no point in repeating that here. As the Society is small (there being only about 20,000 Friends in c. 400 Meetings nationally), what they stand for is probably not as well known as for many other religious groups. I therefore thought it an idea to say a little more about them, based on the writings of the Friends themselves, including Professor Oliver.

Quakerism started in the middle of the 17th century in NW England. George Fox assumed the leadership of the new sect, and was only 23 when, in 1647, he went through a period of spiritual turmoil that led to his adopting a new vision of Christianity. In 1652 he preached on the top of Pendle Hill in Lancashire, and this is generally taken as the start of the Quaker movement.

Friends believe that there is something of God in all of us. They start their meetings in silence and are not led by an appointed person, but allow anyone present to do this. Quakers accept the life and teachings of Jesus, and that we should love one another. War is therefore frowned upon. Two hundred years ago the movement was a prime mover in the abolition of the slave trade. More details are available from local Quakers, or Friends House, Euston Road, London, NW1 2BJ.

R

Radley, William

No. on Map	Premises	Tenure	State in 1801	Quantity A.R.P	Per Acre	Corn Rent	O'tv Bus.Decim.
203			Meadow	4a 1r 33p	5/1d	£1 2s 7d	3B 475d
202	Home field		Meadow	6a 3r 32p	5/6d	£1 18s 2d	5B 874d
205			Meadow	2a 0r 12p	5/1d	£0 10s 6d	1B 615d
206			Meadow	2a 2r 4p	5/1d	£0 12s 9d	1B 962d
201	Cottage and garden			0a 2r 33p	5/6d	£0 3s 10d	0B 590d
204	Field		Meadow	5a 1r 15p	5/4d	£1 8s 5d	4B 372d
1375	Allotment in High field	Copyhold		1a 3r 20p			
			Total	23a 3r 29p		£5 16s 3d	17B 888d

Guidelines for locating these Plots, using today's roads as landmarks, are: Plot 203 - Arundel Gardens; Plots 202 and 201 – Coombe Corner; 205, 206, 204 – Fernleigh Road; 1375 – S. of Cedars Road. Next door to this he bought Plot 1376 for £125. (See Figure 13).

William Radley was born in about 1750, and became a distiller (i.e. wine merchant) of Fleet Street, where he continued to own a house after moving to Winchmore Hill. He became a copyhold tenant of the Manor of Edmonton in 1799, when he took over various pieces of land in Winchmore Hill which had previously been in the occupation of William Skilton – presumably at least some of the above.

Radley gained a small piece of waste land in Hoppers Lane, adjacent to his existing holdings, in 1811, and in 1816 he acquired a further piece of pasture land, of about three acres, near Hoppers Lane (Plot 194 I believe), known as Kitchen Croft, from the representatives of the deceased John Barnes. The Highfields estate was now largely formed, and Highfield House was certainly in existence by 11th November 1818, when Radley made a will leaving "all my dwelling house commonly called Highfield House in the parish of Edmonton" to his wife, Margaret, for her lifetime.

William Radley died suddenly at Highfield House, aged 72, in January 1821. A brief notice in *The Times*, observed that he had been "sincerely respected by all who knew him". He was buried in Edmonton churchyard on 6th February, and his death was reported to the Court Baron of the Manor of Edmonton on 12th June 1821, when his widow, represented at the court hearing by her son, John Radley, was formally admitted as tenant. City merchant Peter Pope Firth bought the Highfield House estate from Margaret Radley and her son, John, on 1st June 1830.

Redhead, William

No. on Map	Premises	Tenure	State in 1801	Quantity A.R.P	Per Acre	Corn Rent	O'tv Bus.Decim.
1589	Allotment on the Chase	Freehold		0a 1r 34p			

A strip in the angle between Green Dragon Lane and 'Wades Hill' close to modern day Hadley Way (see Figure 8).

Richardson, John

No. on Map	Premises	Tenure	State in 1801	Quantity A.R.P	Per Acre	Corn Rent	O'tv Bus.Decim.
86 a	House & c.			0a 1r 36p	5/6d	£0 2s 6d	0B 385d

Plot 86a is on the south side of Green Dragon Lane, near where, today, 'Green Moor Link' meets it. Under a strange arrangement that seemed to have prevailed, Thomas Cobb owned the ¾ acre of pasture behind Richardson's house (See Figure 16).

According to two handwritten sheets by a member of the Barnes family in Alan Dumayne's archives, James Carpenter, a cooper of Wormwood Street, built a cottage in Winchmore Hill at an unspecified time. It initially comprised four rooms, but was enlarged by later members of the family to 25 (stet) rooms, with a coach house and stables. His daughter (or a later descendent) was Martha Carpenter (1722 – 1792). She married William Richardson (1714 – 1772), who was the son of John Richardson and Isabella (nee Nash). Martha and William RIchardson were known to have had a daughter, also called Martha Richardson (1750 – 1824). Perhaps Martha and William also had a son named John, or maybe there was some other family link?

Rookby, Lord

No. on Map	Premises	Tenure	State in 1801	Quantity A.R.P	Per Acre	Corn Rent	O'tv Bus. Decim.
211	Meadow		Meadow	0a 3r 15p	6/6d	£0 5s 4d	0B 820d
212	Meadow		Meadow	1a 2r 12p	6/-	£0 9s 5d	1B 449d
213	Seven houses and gardens			1a 0r 29p	6/-	£0 7s 1d	1B 90d
1377	Allotment in High field	Freehold		0a 2r 32p			
1382	Ditto – on the waste near	Freehold		0a 0r 26p			
	High field						
1545	Ditto on the Chase	Freehold		1a 0r 25p			
			Total	5a 2r 19p		£1 1s 10d	3B 359d

Plot 1545 is in the vicinity of today's 'The Vale', near 'Eversley Park Road'. The remaining Plots are in the 'Highfield Road' – 'Cedars Road' area (see Figure 18).

Lord Rookby is remembered in the street name Rookby Court, off of Carpenter Gardens. I have been unable to find any information on this gentleman. (He is not listed in the local 1826 Directory).

S

Smith, Edward Esq.

No. on Map	Premises	Tenure	State in 1801	Quantity A.R.P	Per Acre	Corn Rent	O'tv Bus. Decim.
1480	Allotment on the Chase	Copyhold		34a			
1481	Allotment on the Chase	Freehold		36a 1r 5p			
1553	Allotment on the Chase	Freehold		1a 1r 12p			
				71a 2r 17p			

Plots 1480/1 were 'purchased of Mrs. Bowles'. Plot 1553 was 'purchased of Mrs. States'. All three were in the 'Eversley Park Road' – 'Oakwood Crescent' area (see Figure 8).

Snelson

No. on Map	Premises	Tenure	State in 1801	Quantity A.R.P	Per Acre	Corn Rent	O'tv Bus. Decim.
48	Two cottages and gardens			0a 0r 24p	4/-	7d	90 dec

Plot 48's two cottages were in the vicinity of the cottages currently situated by the park gates at the foot of 'Church Hill' (see Figure 9).

The LMA document ACC/695/49 has a list of Edmonton Manor Quit Rents for 1780 - 1 which indicates that a John Snolson was admitted to a holding in 'Winchmore Hill' in 1774, the Quit Rent being 1/-. In the same year he was admitted for a 'messuage adjoining' with a Quit Rent of 2/6d. The minutes of the Court Baron of 1st June 1819 tell us that John Tugwell had died in possession of the 2r. 34p of what had been Plot 1542 at the time of Enclosure. Although the Award showed Tugwell as owner in 1801, the Court minutes record that it was purchased from Thomas Snelson, the previous Copyholder, in 1805.

T

Tash, William (both sold to Mr. Thompson)

No. on Map	Premises	Tenure	State in 1801	Quantity A.R.P	Per Acre	Corn Rent	O'tv Bus.Decim.
69	The nine acres		Meadow	8a 2r 24p	6/-	£2 11s 10d	7B 975d
70	Hoppet		Pasture	0a 1r 37p	6/6d	3s 0d	0B 462d

These Plots are in the 'Broadfields Avenue', 'Paulin Drive' area (see Figure 8). In addition Tash owned a large Plot to the NW of 'Highlands Village' which was not included in the settlement.

The Jackson family held the Broomfield House Estate in Palmers Green for nearly two hundred years, until Mary Jackson married William Tash, who therefore became its owner. After his death in 1816 it was bought by Phillip Lybbe Powys. Plates 56 & 57 show Tash's home.

Taylor, Elizabeth (her Trustees)

No. on Map	Premises	Tenure	State in 1801	Quantity A.R.P	Per Acre	Corn Rent	O'tv Bus.Decim.
77	Houses and orchard			1a 2r 3p	5/10d	8s 10d	1B 359d
109	Garden before the King's Head			0a 1r 39p	5/7d	2s 8d	0B 410d
110	Four houses and gardens			31p	5/7d	1s	0B 154d
			Total	2a 0r 33p		12s 6d	1B 923d

Plot 77 was diagonally behind Devon House. Plots 109 and 110 were opposite *The King's Head* on the corner of 'Wades Hill' (see Figure 14).

The LMA document ACC/695/49 has a list of Edmonton Manor Quit Rents for 1780 - 1 which indicates that Elizabeth Taylor was admitted to a Copy holding of 3 roods (3/4 acre) in 'Winchmore Hill' with a Quit Rent of 9d in 1771. Was Elizabeth a member of the Taylor – Walker brewing clan?

Mrs. Teshmaker

I have listed Mrs. Teshmaker's holdings with the Busks, as the two families were intermarried.

Thompson, Henry Esq. (late Tash)

No. on Map	Premises	Tenure	State in 1801	Quantity A.R.P	Per Acre	Corn Rent *	O'tv. Bus. Decim.
1398	Allotment in Hag - field (purchased of Joseph Osborne)	Copyhold		2a 1r 8p			
1571	Allotment on the Chase	Copyhold		10a 0r 18p			
1570	Allotment on the Chase	Freehold		25a 0r 14p			
1554	Ditto (purchased of Matthew Salisbury)	Copyhold		3a 2r 7p			
1577	Ditto on the Chase (purchased of William Mellish Esq.)	Freehold		6a 1r 25p			
1575	Ditto on the Chase (purchased of Matthew Butcher)	Freehold		0a 1r 2p			
1574	Allotment on the Chase (purchased of ditto, late Richard Davis)	Freehold		0a 0r 38p		£9 17s 6d.	30B 388d
1576	Allotment on the Chase (purchased of ditto, late Joseph Dawson's)	Freehold		0a 0r 38p			
1572	Ditto on the Chase (purchased of ditto, late Mary Joachim)	Copyhold		0a 1r 0p			
1573	Ditto on the Chase (purchased of ditto, late Nathaniel Lucas, since William Bowman)	Copyhold		0a 0r 38p			
			Total	81a 2r 12p		£9 17s 6d	30B 388d
	Below = with his wife Judith						
1567	Allotment on the Chase	Copyhold		1a 1r 30p			
1566	Allotment on the Chase	Copyhold		1a 0r 32p			
			Total	2a 2r 22p			

*Corn rent for all these payable to Impropriators (not Vicar) as set out in the 1800 Act. Plot 1398 runs north off of 'Vicars Moor Lane' towards its western end (see Figure 15). Plots 1570 – 1577 inclusive constitute a large tract in the angle between 'Eversley Park Road', Green Dragon Lane and 'Wades Hill', which later formed the basis of the Eversley Park Estate. Plot 1554 is in the vicinity of Oakwood Crescent. 1566 and 1567 are at the junction of 'Eversley Park Road' and 'Worlds End Lane'. Most of these holdings were situated in lands which, until the 1777 Act of disafforestation, had been part of Enfield

Chase. (See Figure 8.)

Thompson is also listed as having purchased the 3 acres of Chase allotment in Plot 1569 for £240. It was situated on the southern junction of 'Eversley Park Road' and Green Dragon Lane. Thompson is also listed as buying Plots 1399 and 1403 for £28. I can't locate either Plots on the Enclosure Map, but it seems likely that 1399 would be next to Thompson's Plot 1398 running off of 'Vicars Moor Lane'. Plot 1399 is indicated as being in Middle Chase – lane in the waste schedule, so indicating that this may have been an earlier name for Vicars Moor Lane.

The Diary for 1806 indicates that Henry Thompson was of Tottenham Green. I have examined documents in a box referenced J90 at the National Archives, Kew. One of these, dated 20th May 1804, said that Henry Thompson gained possession of a cottage near Chase Gate. I believe this was Francis Hall's Plot 59. The minutes of the Court Baron held on 24th May 1825 announced the death of Henry Thompson.

Thurkle, Mrs. Jane.

No. on Map	Premises	Tenure	State in 1801	Quantity A.R.P	Per Acre	Corn Rent *	O'tv. Bus. Decim.
1531	Allotment on the Chase	Freehold		0a 2r 21p			

Plot 1531 is in the vicinity of 'The Glade' (see Figure 8).

Tingey, John (purchased of George Mordaunt)

No. on Map	Premises	Tenure	State in 1801	Quantity A.R.P	Per Acre	Corn Rent *	O'tv. Bus. Decim.
1537	Allotment on the Chase	Freehold		0a 0r 34p			

Plot 1537 is in the vicinity of *'The Winchmore Hill Arms'* (see Figure 8).

Trinity College in Cambridge (for great Tythes)

No. on Map	Premises	Tenure	State in 1801	Quantity A.R.P	Per Acre	Corn Rent *	O'tv. Bus. Decim.
1558	Allotment on the Chase			56a 2r 14p			

This Plot forms the section of Highlands Village nearest to 'Worlds End Lane' (see Figure 7).

Paragraph 3 of the 1800 Enclosure Act reads, 'That the master, fellows, and scholars of Trinity College, in the University of *Cambridge,* were Patrons of the Vicarage of *Enfield* aforesaid, and also owners of the impropriate and rectorial tythes arising within the same parish, and as such were entitled to all great tythes arising or to arise within the said allotment called Edmonton Allotment of Enfield Chase.'

Kain and Prince, in their *Tithe Surveys* explain that, 'The small, or vicarial, tithes included all the tithes, except those of grain, hay and wood, which constituted the great tithes, generally reserved for the rector. But the division between the great and small tithes was by no means fixed and unalterable...'

Tugwell, John

No. on Map	Premises	Tenure	State in 1801	Ot'itv A.R.P	Per Acre	Corn Rent	O'tv Bus. Decim.
54	House and orchard			1a 0r 36p	54+55+72	54+55+72	54+55+72
55	Cottage			0a 0r 15p	= 5s 10d	= 16/-	= 2B 463d

72	House and field		Pasture	1a 1r 29p			
1543	Allotment on the Chase	Freehold		0a 3r 14p			
1542	Allotment on the Chase	Copyhold		0a 2r 34p			
			Totals	4a 1r 8p		16/-	2B 463d

Plots 54 and 55 were opposite Friends' Meeting House, on Winchmore Hill – lane (Church Hill), Plot 72 was the next Plot down (NW) from The Meeting House (see Figure 14). Plots 1542 and 1543 were in the vicinity of 'Spring Bank', off the western side of 'Eversley Park Road' (see Figure 8).

The Edmonton Manor Court minutes for 12th June 1810 show that John was then the Foreman of the Jury responsible for the upkeep of the local fields. The minutes of the Court Baron of 1st June 1819 report that John Tugwell had died in possession of the 2r. 34p that had been Plot 1542 at the time of Enclosure. The minutes say that he was awarded this Plot under the Enclosure Act, but they then appear to contradict this by saying that it was purchased from Thomas Snelson, the previous Copyholder, in 1805. The minutes say that under his Will of 20th February 1806 he left the Plot to his wife Martha Tugwell for her life, whence it would pass to his daughter Martha Richardson Yallowley. At the N.A. is a copy of the last Will of Martha Tugwell nee Richardson, wife of John Tugwell which was made in 1818, but I have reproduced it in the diary section in the year 1824, when it was proved in London. The Tugwells were related to local families the Barnes, Yallowleys, Carpenters and Richardsons, as summarised at Figure 4.

V

Vevers, F.

No. on Map	Premises	Tenure	State in 1801	O'titv A.R.P	Per Acre	Corn Rent	Ot'tv Bus. Decim.
1538	House & yard			0a 0r 7p			
1538	Allotment on the Chase	Freehold		0a 0r 36p			

I can't locate Plot 1538 on the Enclosure Map, but Plots with adjacent numbers are in the vicinity of 'The Winchmore Arms' (Figure 8).

Vicar of Enfield, (for Vicarial Tythes)

No. on Map	Premises	Tenure	State in 1801	O'titv A.R.P	Per Acre	Corn Rent	Ot'tv Bus. Decim.
1557	Allotment on the Chase			34a 1r 11p			
1547	Allotment on the Chase			8a 2r 24p			
			Total	42a 3r 35p			

Plot 1557 is a large tract to the north of what is now Highlands Village, just north of the South Lodge allotment belonging to George 111 (see Figure 7). Plot 1547 is a strip running west off 'Eversley Park Road', approximately where Willow Walk runs today (see Figure 8).

Paragraph 3 of the 1800 Enclosure Act states, 'That the Reverend Richard Newbon, Clerk, Batchelor in Divinity, is the present Vicar of the said Parish of Enfield, and by virtue thereof is entitled to all vicarial tythes and dues arising within the said (Edmonton) allotment.'

Figure 4. The Barnes, Yallowley, Tugwell, Carpenter and Richarsdson families

The following is mainly taken from papers in the archives of the late Alan Dumayne, kindly loaned by his widow Sheila. It diagrammatically shows the relationship of various old village families. The papers were apparently drawn up by members of the Barnes family in 1912.

Barnes

Barnes b 1670
Samuel Barnes (1695 - 1737)
Joseph Barnes Snr. (1727 - 1795) Floor cloth manufacturer of City Ro.
Joseph Barnes Jnr. (1753 - 1814) (City Road)
Robert Barnes (1787 - 1862) = m. Martha Yallowley

Yallowley

Yallowley, Farmer of North Shields
Jacob Yallowley (1) 1717 - Farmer
Jacob Yallowley (2) (1736 - 1801) Whitbreads brewer
Jacob Yallowley (3) (1769 - 1823) Brickmaker of Whitecross Street = m. Martha Richardson Tugwell
Martha Yallowley

Tugwell

John Tugwell (1741 - 1818) = m. Martha Richardson
Martha Richardson Tugwell (1781 - 1844) 'Old Grandma Yallowley' prominent with the Independent Chapel

Carpenter

James Carpenter, Cooper of Wormwood St. - Built cottage at Winchmore Hill
Martha Carpenter (1722 - 1792) = m. William Richardson

Richardson

John Richardson = m. Isabella Nash
William Richardson (1714 - 1772)
Martha Richardson (1750 - 1824)

Robert and Martha had 10 children, of whom one was Anna (1826 - 1901).
She stayed single, and lived in the old family home, which was sold off upon her death.

Notes: The papers state that, 'James Carpenter bought land & built cottage at W. Hill – 4 rooms – gradually enlarged by later members of family to 25 rooms – coach house, stables etc.' They also say, 'Jacob Yallowley (2) came to Winchmore Hill and "bought the Meeting" = Leasehold Property on which 1st Independent Hall was built, next to property owned by John Radford, who was a Deacon & (probably) a Trustee. He pulled it down later. 1848. It was situated where Woodside Cottages now stand (1912).' (Radford is not listed in the Edmonton Enclosure Schedule of 1801-2.)

W

Waddle, William

No. on Map	Premises	Tenure	State in 1801	O'titv A.R.P	Per Acre	Corn Rent	Ot'tv Bus. Decim.
338	Cottage and garden			35p	6/-	1/3d	0B 192d.

Plot 338 is on the northern corner of what we would call Bourne Hill and Green Lanes (see Figure 12).

Walker, Isaac Esq.

No. on Map	Premises	Tenure	State in 1801	Ot'titv A.R.P	Per Acre	Corn Rent	O'tv Bus.Decim.
37	House and yards			2a 2r 1p	6/-	15/-	2B 309d
38			Pasture	3a 1r 29p	4/6d	15/4d	2B 360d
39			Meadow	6a 0r 1p	4/3d	£1 5s 6d	3B 923d
40			Pasture	1a 1r 21p	4/6d	6s 2d	0B 949d
41	Loak (an avenue)			0a 0r 36p			
42			Pasture	3a 3r 25p	4/6d	17s 6d	2B 694d
43			Pasture	4a 0r 25p	4/6d	18s 7d	2B 861d
44			Meadow	6a 2r 0p	4/6d	£1 9s 3d	4B 500d

These Plots form a block of land to the south side of Chase Side Road which might have constituted a farm worked by Isaac Walker, independently of his nephew Walker Gray, who owned much of the surrounding land (see Figure 5).

It will be recalled from the section on Walker Gray that John and Rebecca Walker had a son named Isaac (1725 - 1804), who became a prosperous linen merchant. Isaac married Elizabeth Hill (1737 - 1795) in 1764, and purchased Amos Grove in 1777. Isaac and Elizabeth had a daughter named Elizabeth (who married the Rev. Thomas Winchester Lewis), and a son named John (1766 - 1824), who married Sarah Chorley (1774 - 1852). The following entry must be for father and son.

Walker, Isaac Esq. and John Walker, Esq.

No. on Map	Premises	Tenure	State in 1801	O'titv A.R.P	Per Acre	Corn Rent	Ot'tv Bus. Decim.
1516	Allotment on the Chase	Copyhold		3a 3r 5p.			
1515	Allotment on the Chase	Freehold		23a 0r 0p.			
1515	Allotment on the Chase	Copyhold		2a 0r 0p			
	(Yes, two 1515s)		Total	28a 3r 5p			

These Plots are on the north side of Chase Side Road, in the vicinity of modern day Oakwood Park Road (see Figure 5).

Walker, John Esq.

No. on Map	Premises	Tenure	State in 1801	Ot'titv A.R.P	Per Acre	Corn Rent	Ot'tv Bus.Decim.
111	Two tenements			0a 0r 5p			
300	Farm – house and yards			0a 1r 8p	5/6d	1s 7d	0B 244d
298			Meadow	7a 2r 30p	5/1d	298 + 299 =	298 + 299 =
299	Orchard			0a 3r 3p	5/1d	£2 2s 11d	6B 603d
301			Meadow	2a 3r 4p	5/-	13s 10d	2B 129d
302			Meadow	3a 1r 3p	5/-	16s 4d	2B 514d

303		Copyhold	Meadow	7a 3r 37p	5/-	£1 19s 10d	6B 130d
304			Meadow	2a 3r 15p	5/6d	15s 7d	2B 399d
306			Meadow	1a 2r 16p	5/-	8s 0d	1B 231d
307			Meadow	2a 1r 6p	4/6d	10s 2d	1B 564d
308			Meadow	2a 2r 10p	5/-	12s 11d	1B 988d
305	Tenements and garden			0a 2r 10p	5/-	2s 9d	0B 423d
171	Several small tenements			0a 0r 10p			
309	Late woodland		Arable	10a 0r 29p	6/-	£3 1s 1d	9B 398d
450	Field adjoining gravel pits		Meadow	4a 0r 30p	4/6d	18s 10d	2B 899d
324	House and garden			1a 0r 7p	5/6d	5s 8d	0B 871d
207			Meadow	4a 2r 2p	5/4d	£1 4s 0d	3B 692d
208			Meadow	4a 1r 11p	5/7d	£1 4s 1d	3B 705d
209			Meadow	3a 2r 25p	5/4d	19s 5d	2B 989d
Total for in and out of Winchmore Hill =				60a 2r 21p		£15 17s 0d	48B 779d

Plot 111 is on the north face of The Green (see Figure 14). Plots 207/8/9 are in the vicinity of 'Woodberry Avenue' (see Figure 13). John had much land just south of Dog and Duck Lane (see Figure 5).

I have covered the link between the Walker – Gray – Taylor families under the section on Walker Gray. The following extra information specifically on John Walker is mainly based on an article by Ruby Galili in the Bulletin *Oakleaves* No. 3. Isaac Walker Senior and John Walker were local Quakers who were both buried in Winchmore Hill – lane. As a non Anglican John was barred from Oxford and Cambridge, but studied law at the Inns of Court. He went on to develop a keen interest in science, and was elected to the Royal Society, the Society of Antiquaries, the Linnaean Society and the Royal Institution.

In the Borough's Local History Unit is *The Commonplace Book* of John Walker, which he began in 1794, soon after being elected a member of the Royal Society. This leather bound book contains his handwritten notes on the lectures he had attended with the learned societies. For example, he tells us that on 2nd March 1796 he went with a Mr. Ford to see the telegraph that had been erected over the Admiralty. He also tells of a lecture by Professor Volta of Padua describing the electric battery he had invented. In addition, the book also contains the text of John's correspondence with diverse luminaries of the time.

John lived in Lincoln's Inn until his marriage to Sarah Chorley in 1793, when her father John – a prosperous Quaker merchant from Liverpool – gave them a house in Bedford Square. He was an admirer of Robert Owen, and in 1815 invested in the latter's new model factory in New Lanark, where workers were treated as people rather than production robots. It was in 1816 that John also invested in a partnership with the Taylors regarding their brewery at Limehouse, which thus became the famous Taylor Walker concern. John's benevolent nature drove him to open Southgate village school, sometime between 1810 and 1814, which was free to all local boys.

Were, Ellis Esq.

No. on Map	Premises	Tenure	State in 1801	Quantity A.R.P.	Per Acre	Corn Rent	O'tv Bus.Decim.
1549	Allotment on the Chase			0a 1r 6p			
1548	Allotment on the Chase			1a 2r 16p			

These Plots are in the vicinity of 'Willow Walk' (see Figure 8).

Whitehead, Edmund

No. on Map	Premises	Tenure	State in 1801	Quantity A.R.P	Per Acre	Corn Rent	O'tv Bus. Decim.
100	Tenements and garden			0a 0r 9p			

Plot 100 is at the western end of the northern side of 'Vicars Moor Lane', between Plots 99 and 101 (see Figure 14).

The LMA document ACC/695/49 has a list of Edmonton Manor Quit Rents for 1780 - 1 which indicates that Edmund Whitehead had a Copy cottage 'at Winchmore Hill' with a Quit Rent of 6d.

John Wild's Charity (Sir J. Lake, Lessee)

No. on Map	Premises	Tenure	State in 1801	Quantity A.R.P.	Per Acre	Corn Rent	O'tv Bus.Decim.
1380	Allotment in High field	Copyhold		6a 0r 30p			
1381	Allotment in High field	Freehold		2a 3r 0p			

These Plots, totalling 8 acres 3 roods 30 perches, are west of what is now the rubbish tip on the north side of Barrow's Well Green (see Figure 18).

Robinson devotes several pages to this Charity. Please see the comments under the entry for Sir James Winter Lake.

Williams, William

No. on Map	Premises	Tenure	State in 1801	Quantity A.R.P	Per Acre	Corn Rent	O'tv Bus. Decim.
1552	Allotment on the Chase	Freehold		0a 2r 13p			

Plot 1552 is in the vicinity of 'Holly Hill', off of 'Eversley Park Road' (see Figure 8).

Williamson, R.T.

No. on Map	Premises	Tenure	State in 1801	Quantity A.R.P	Per Acre	Corn Rent	O'tv Bus. Decim.
507	Fox public house, &c.			0a 1r 10p	5/6d	1/7d	0B 244d
339	House and garden			0a 1r 16p	5/6d	1/9d	0B 269d
84	Field and Green Dragon lane			1a 3r 0p	6/6d	11/4d	1B 744d
85	House, yards, & c.			0a 2r 20p	5/6d	3/4d	0B 513d
			Total	3a 0r 6p		18/-	2B 770d

Dean and Chapter of St. Paul's - Sold to Robert Williamson

No. on Map	Premises	Tenure	State in 1801	Quantity A.R.P	Per Acre	Corn Rent	O'tv Bus. Decim.
183		Freehold	Arable	5a 0r 24p	5/-	£1 5s 9d	3B 961d
184			Arable	7a 0r 21p	5/-	£1 15s 7d	5B 476d
185				7a 0r 36p	5/-	£1 16s 1d	5B 553d

Plot 339 is on the northern corner of Green Lanes and 'Bourne Hill' (see Figure 12). Plots 84 & 85 are near where 'Green Moor Link' meets Green Dragon Lane (see Figure 16). Plots 183, 184 and 185, totalling about 21 acres, are in the vicinity of modem day Brackendale off of 'Broad Walk'. In the Ownership schedule these last three are actually entered against The Dean and Chapter of St. Paul's.

Wilson, James

No. on Map	Premises	Tenure	State in 1801	Quantity A.R.P	Per Acre	Corn Rent	O'tv Bus. Decim.
101	House, barn, and garden			0a 3r 17p	5/6d	4/8d	0B 717d

Plot 101 is next door to Whitehead's 100, near the NW corner of 'Vicars Moor Lane'.

      The Wilson family were based in Shoreditch, as revealed in the Will of James's father in the 1794 diary section. James also features in the 1822 diary section, and at Plate 40, which reproduces the sale agreement between him and John Udall for Plot 101.

Section on Edmonton Enclosure Act
Map Section

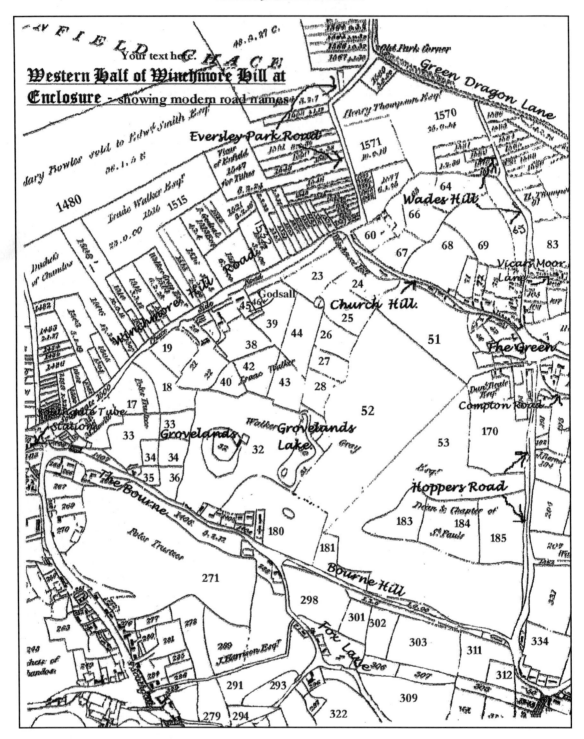

Figure 5. Western half of Winchmore Hill at Enclosure

This is the Edmonton Enclosure Map (not reproduced to scale), upon which I have marked the modern names of roads that follow the lines of former country lanes.

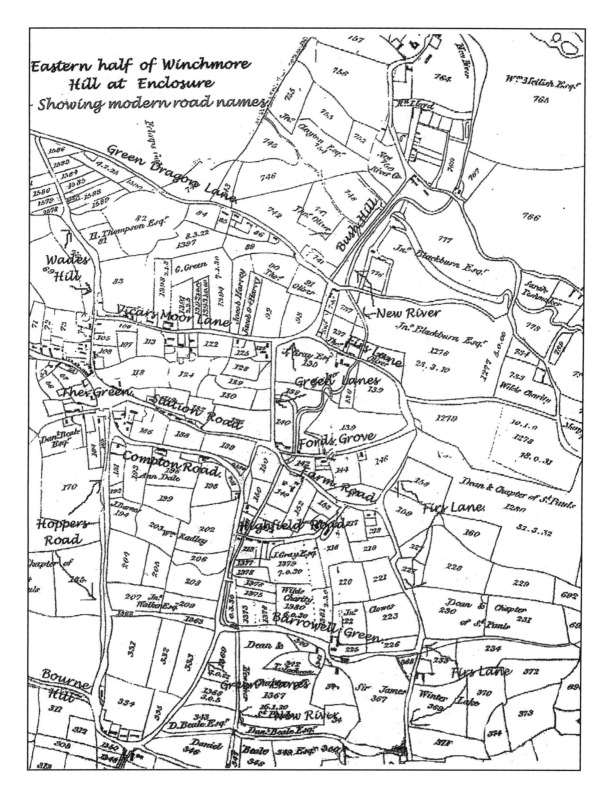

Figure 6. Eastern half of Winchmore Hill at Enclosure.

This is the Edmonton Enclosure Map (not reproduced to scale), upon which I have marked the modern names of roads that follow the lines of former country lanes.

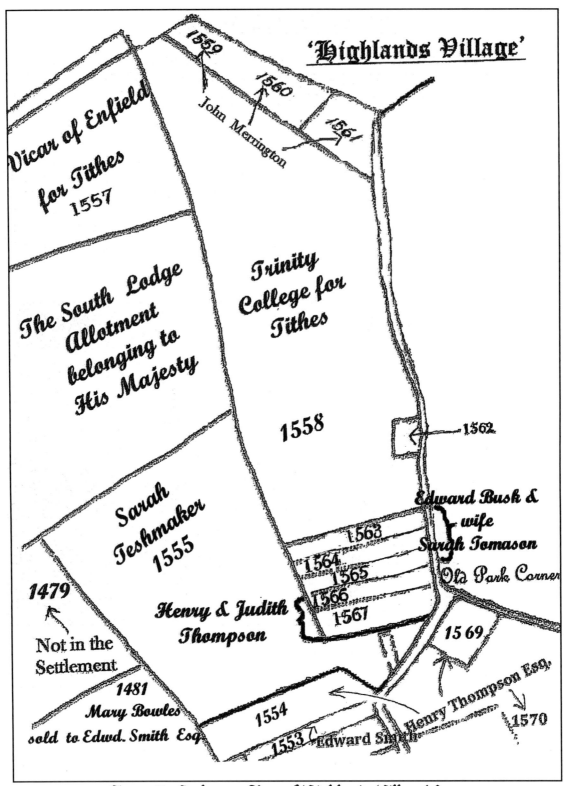

Figure 7. Enclosure Map of 'Highlands Village' Area

The main north – south lane is the forerunner of 'Worlds End Lane'. There are no properties in this area, the numbered plots having been part of Enfield Chase until its disafforestation by an Act of 1777. I cannot locate the owner of Plot 1562.

'Highlands Village' Map

South Lodge Allotment takes its title from a former Lodge on the Chase, and the name lived on for many years in South Lodge hospital, which became part of the larger Highlands Hospital. The history of the hospital is covered in my *A look at Old Winchmore Hill* and *More Winchmore Hill Lives*. (West Lodge is now a private hotel on the outskirts of Cockfosters.)

At Plate 9 is a recent photograph of Oakwood Park, in the southern regions of this map, which probably reflects a scene relatively unchanged from hundreds of years ago. At Plate 10 is a shot taken in May 1989 looking north up the footpath on the eastern edge of Worlds End Lane. Audrey Goodchild and Dr. Curley have told me that this path is actually the old country lane that preceded the road, now running alongside it. So again, the view is probably reasonably similar to that prevailing at the time of Enclosure along the main north – south lane shown in the map.

Plate 9. Enfield Chase

I took this photograph of Oakwood Park, in the southern regions of the 'Highlands Village' Enclosure Map, on 20th June 2003. It reflects a scene relatively unchanged from hundreds of years ago, going back to the time when the land was part of Enfield Chase.

121

Plate 10. Ye Olde Worlds End Lane

*This shot was taken in May 1989 looking north up the footpath on the eastern edge of Worlds End Lane,
nearly opposite Roundhill Drive.   Both Dr. Curley and the late Audrey Goodchild have told me that this path
is actually the old country lane that preceded the road, now running alongside it.*

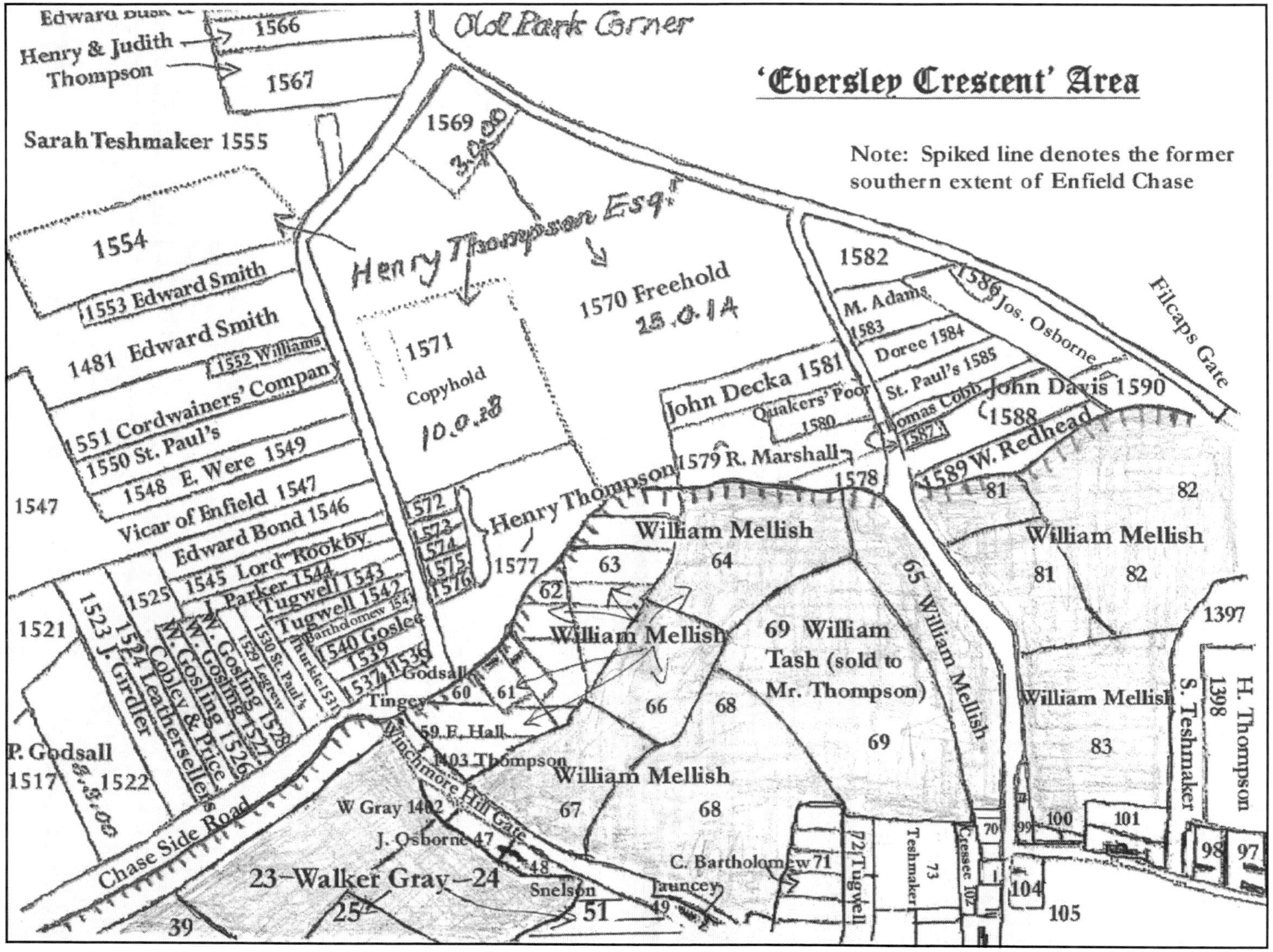

Figure 8. Enclosure Map of 'Eversley Crescent' Area

The text section accompanying this map explains the layout of the lanes in relation to today's roads. The shaded fields were meadow, those with horizontal lines were pasture.

'Eversley Crescent' Area

Note: Spiked line denotes the former southern extent of Enfield Chase

Old Park Corner

Edward Bush — 1566
Henry & Judith Thompson — 1567
Sarah Teshmaker 1555

1554

1569
Henry Thompson Esq.ʳ

1553 Edward Smith
1481 Edward Smith
1552 Williams
551 Cordwainers' Company
1550 St. Paul's
1548 E. Were 1549
Vicar of Enfield 1546
Edward Bond 1546
1545 Lord Rookby
Parker 1544 1543
1525 W. Tugwell 1542 Bartholomew 1541
1540 Gosling
1539 1538
1537 Godsall
Thurkle 1531 1530 St. Paul's
1529 Legrew
W. Gosling 1528
W. Gosling 1527
W. Gosling 1526
Cobley & Price
1524 Leathersellers
1523 J. Girdler
1521
1522
R. Godsall 1517

1547

1570 Freehold 25.0.1A

1571 Copyhold 10.0.33

572 573 574 575 576
Henry Thompson
1577

1582
1586 Jos. Osborne
John Davis 1590
M. Adams 1583
Doree 1584
St. Paul's 1585
Thomas Cob 1587
1588
1589 W. Redhead
Quakers' Poor 1580
St. Paul's 1581
John Decka 1581
579 R. Marshall
578

82
William Mellish 81
82
81
William Mellish 83
1397
H. Thompson 1398
S. Teshmaker

97
98
101
100
99
104 105
70
Cressee 102
73 Teshmaker
72 Tugwell
71
49
Bartholomew
51
Pauncey

65 William Mellish
William Mellish 64
69 William Tash (sold to Mr. Thompson) 69
68
66
William Mellish 63
William Mellish 67
68
William Mellish
62
61
60
59 F. Hall
Tingey
Winchmore Hill Gate
N.º3 Thompson
J. Osborne
48
47
Snelson
W Gray 1402
23—Walker Gray—24
25
39

Chase Side Road

'Eversley Crescent' Area Map

The small stretch of lane running north from Old Park Corner is the forerunner of modern day World's End Lane. The lane branching south east from Old Park Corner was, even in those days (see entry for R.T. Williamson's Plot 84) known as Green Dragon Lane. The lane branching south west from Old Park Corner, and then turning SSE by Plot 1553, is the line of what is today Eversley Park Road. The lane running SSE off of Green Dragon Lane at Plot 1582, has today been built up into Wades Hill. It meets what we now call Vicars Moor Lane at Plot 99.

The lane turning SW off of 'Eversley Park Road' at Plot 1577, is marked on the Enclosure Map as Chase Side Road, and is today known as Winchmore Hill Road. The track leading SE off of that lane at Winchmore Hill Gate is Winchmore Hill – lane (what is now Church Hill). Chase Side Road trends approximately SW - NE, and its line could be projected more or less along the northern borders of William Mellish's land. That line marks the former extent of Enfield Chase, until the disafforestation under the 1777 Act of Parliament. At the intersection of Chase Side Road and Winchmore Hill – lane is Winchmore Hill Gate, a former entrance to the Chase. The bulk of the area that had been formerly been the Chase had been given to Edmonton Parish under the 1777 arrangement, and was divided, under the 1800 Enclosure Act, into many allotments, making it difficult to show the ownership clearly on the map. The following listings attempt to help the reader further.

West of 'Eversley Park Road', and north of Chase Side Road

Plot No.	Owner	Plot No.	Owner
1565	Edward Busk & wife	1542/3	J. Tugwell
1566/7	Henry & Judith Thompson	1541	C. Bartholomew
1554	Henry Thompson·	1540	T. Goslee
1555	Sarah Teshmaker	1539	?
1481 + 1553	Edward Smith	1537	J. Tingey
1552	William Williams	1531	J. Thurkle
1551	Cordwainers' Company	1530	St. Paul's
1550	St. Paul's	1529	Thomas Legrew
1548/9	E. Were	1526/7/8	W. Gosling
1547	Vicar of Enfield	1525	Sarah Cobley & Mary Price
1546	Edward Bond	1524	Leather Sellers
1545	Lord Rookby	1523	J.S. Girdler
1544	James Parker	1517/1522/1536	Phillip Godsall

Bounded by Winchmore Hill – lane, 'Eversley Park Road', Green Dragon Lane and 'Wades Hill'

Plot No.	Owner	Plot No.	Owner
1569 – 1577 (inc.)	Henry Thompson	1578/9	Rachael Marshall
1580	Quakers' Poor	1581	John Decka

124

Plot No.	Owner	Plot No.	Owner
1582	?	1583	M. Adams
1584	Magdalene Teresa Doree	1585	St. Paul's
1586	Jos. Osborne	1587	Thomas Cobb
1588 + 1590	John Davis	1589	William Redhead

There are a few properties marked on the map, but I have covered these in the text accompanying other maps.

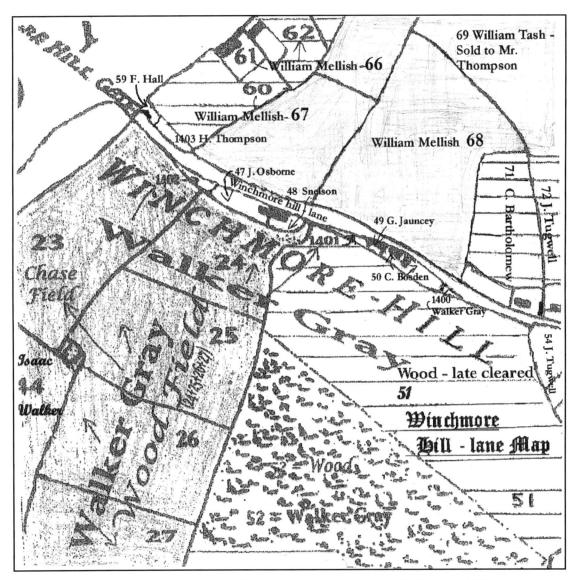

Figure 9. Enclosure Map of Winchmore hill – lane ('Church Hill') Area

The shaded fields were meadow, those with horizontal lines were pasture. See text for explanation of the layout.

Winchmore Hill – lane ('Church Hill') Map

At the NW corner of the map is Winchmore Hill Gate, leading into what, prior to disafforestation, had been Enfield Chase. This gate was approximately where *The Winchmore Arms* is today. The lane leading from the gate, running ESE across the map, is Winchmore Hill – lane, the rural forerunner of today's Church Hill. We know of the older name because of the way that Plot 1400, and others belonging to Walker Gray, were listed at Appendix 1 in the Enclosure Schedule. The eastern extremity is covered in the text with the map of The Green area. The bulk of the land owned by Walker Gray to the south of Winchmore Hill – lane is now in Grovelands Park, and some of the stand of trees in the Woods of Plot 52 remains to this day.

Woodside Cottages

I have compared the Enclosure Award Map with the 1895 OS Map to get a better feel for the properties shown, and I do not believe that there are any remaining from the Enclosure Map on the south side of Winchmore Hill – lane other than those in Plots 49 and 50 physically near the base of the hill. The Enclosure Ownership Schedule tells us that George Jauncey's Plot 49 contained a 'House and garden', Charles Bosden's Plot 50 a 'House & c.'.

These buildings are illustrated on the back cover. The sketch reveals three old clapperboard buildings, as opposed to the two listed. However, the Enclosure map indicates two (detached) premises on Plot 50. The middle one has for many years featured a plaque in the porch saying, 'The Old School House c. 1785', and it differs from the premises on either side in being a single storied bungalow. So my suggestion is that the top and lower most buildings were listed in the Schedule as houses, but for some reason the middle bungalow was omitted.

In her delightful *Memories of a Lost Village* Miss Cresswell described how she went for a walk down Church Hill one warm April day in about 1860. She says that, 'Below the (St. Paul's) church were the New Schools and a pretty house with a jessamine covered verandah, in which lived a Quaker lady, Mirah N-, who took life very seriously ..... The low cottage, standing high above the road, next door, was till 1859 the Village School, and later was used as a night school. It appears as if it might have accommodated some fifty children, if they sat close together, and it is not surprising it was deemed insufficient for the needs of the neighbourhood ....'. The roof to the old verandah in the top cottage appears to be fully in tact in Peter Brown's sketch.

According to a Mc Kenzie & Co.'s. brochure of the early 21st century, Woodside Cottage (the top cottage) was built in 1785. The brochure stated that the first floor contained two front facing bedrooms, sized 14' 6" x 12' and 14'6" x 8'1", along with a WC. Downstairs were two Reception Rooms. One of these was 15' x 14' with an original sash window to the front, whilst the second was 14'2" x 12'. There was also a 6'5" x 5' Utility Room, Bathroom/WC and a 13' 7" x 10' Conservatory leading to the rear patio garden with its direct access to Grovelands Park. The Freehold Cottage was Grade 11 listed and priced at £425,000.

'Park Gate' Cottages

Miss Cresswell says that, 'At the bottom of Church Hill there were more small houses with gardens of wallflowers, irises, and white and purple stocks. The first house by the brook had a wealth of double yellow daffodowndillys....' These were probably (though not certainly) the properties at Plots 47 (Jos. Osborne) and 48 (Snelson).

Francis Hall's Plot 59

Hall's 'cottage and garden' is on a tiny plot by what is marked as Winchmore Hill Gate on the Enclosure Map, though a document relating to this Plot in the 1804 diary section suggests that this was also known locally as Chase Gate (meaning, perhaps, the gate to the Chase). The 1804 document says that Hall took possession of the plot in 1774, and surrendered it in 1804, to be replaced by Henry Thompson, who had bought the adjoining 16 perches of wasteland at Plot 1403.

Charles Bartholomew's Plot 71

In the section on The Green I suggest that John Tugwell's Plot 72 ('House and field') is what became known as Hill House. After all, at P79 of her *Memories of a Lost Village*, Miss Cresswell tells us that Hill House was the next building on the right past the Friends Meeting House. This is confirmed in the listing of the two in the 1899-1900 Kelly's Directory.

In 1801/2 Bartholomew had a house in a field of 2a 2r 27p, which exactly corresponds to the property portrayed at Lot 1 of the Sale Catalogue at 1826 in the diary section. It is described as a Cottage, but has four upstair bedrooms and two coach houses. There is a property on the site of Bartholomew's house on both the 1865 and 1895 OS Maps, opposite St. Paul's Church. Laurel Lodge is captured from a distance on what seems to be this site in the photograph at P55 of my 1991 *Winchmore Hill Lives*.

In a *Gazette* article of 16th September 1927 entitled 'Winchmore Hill Fifty Years ago', Horace Regnart says that in Church Hill, 'On the site of Laurel Lodge was a long low house with a verandah, occupied by a Mr. Wright. He died a couple of years after we came, i.e. about 1880, and the house was pulled down and Laurel Lodge built.' The mention of a verandah ties in with the mention of a 'Handsome Veranda extending along the Front and one end of the Cottage' in the advert for Lot 1 in the sale of 1826. Regnart also describes the property as a house (rather than cottage), consistent with the two stories portrayed in the catalogue.

The Palmers Green Gazette of 31st December 1937 carried an article entitled, 'Stones of Old Blackfriars Bridge' by 'Memorabilia'. It ran, 'Miss Cresswell (P80) tells us that "opposite the church was a low-roofed cottage of gentility, with gardens and fields reaching to the brook in the valley. Stone Hall was built later in these fields, the building material being the stones of Old Blackfriars Bridge" ..... The "low roofed cottage of gentility" which Miss Cresswell wrote of was at one time the residence of Mr. Francis Wyatt Truscott, who became Alderman Sir Francis Wyatt Truscott, Lord Mayor of London 1879-80, whose custom it was to walk daily to and from Wood Green Station (the Wood Green-Enfield line had not been constructed). He was father of Sir George Wyatt Truscott, Bart., Lord Mayor 1908-9. The cottage was demolished about 1881 and Laurel Lodge was built on the site by Mr. Thomas Mann, father of Sir Edward Mann, Bart., and later it was purchased by Mr. Charles Morgan of Grove Lodge, who resided there until his death .....' Stone Hall was built much later in the 19th century, in the field which in 1801 had been William Mellish's Plot 68

'Winchmore Hill Wood' Map

The north - south trending track on the eastern edge of the map at Figure 10 is Hopper's Lane (now Road). The Plots to the east of the Lane, as well as in and around The Green, are covered in other sections. The bulk of the land to the west of the Lane formed part of the Walker Gray *Grove* estate. Today much of this land forms Grovelands Park, although the portion close to Hopper's Lane has been built over to provide the housing of Woodland Way, and nearby roads. The woodland was, for many years, known as Winchmore Hill Wood.

Figure 10.
Enclosure Map
of 'Winchmore
Hill Wood'.

The north - south trending track on the eastern edge of the map is Hopper's Lane (now Road). Today much of the land to the western side of the map forms Grovelands Park. The shaded fields were meadow, those with horizontal lines were pasture. Wood fills much of the map.

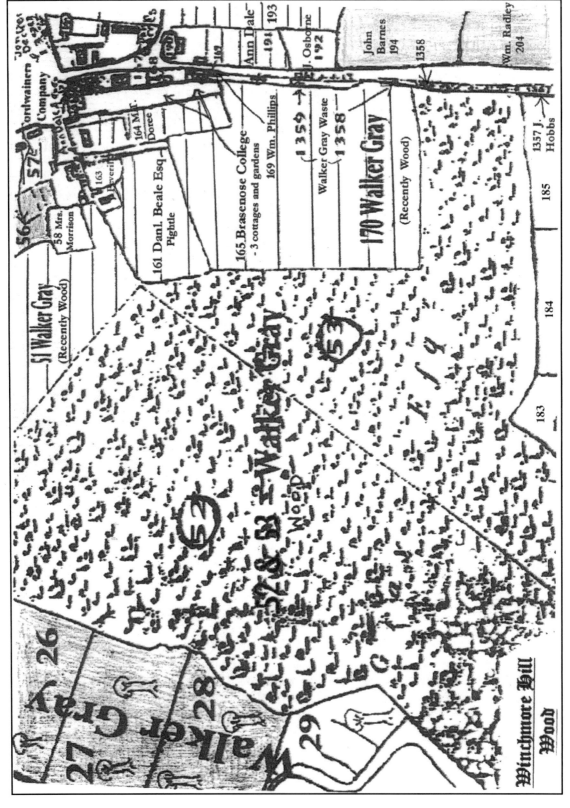

128

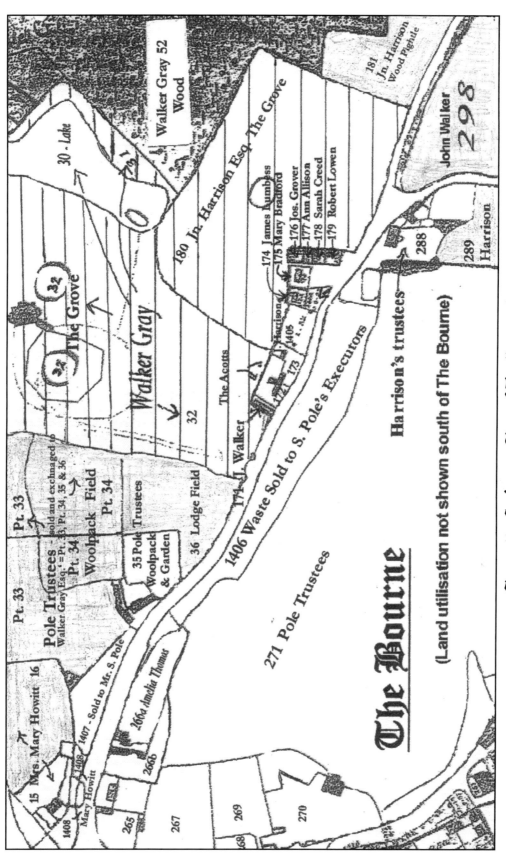

Figure 11. Enclosure Map of The Bourne Area

The lane running from the NW corner of the map to the SE corner is now what we call The Bourne (to the NW end) and Bourne Hill (to the SE end). The spur off of the lane is what we now call Fox Lane. The shaded fields were meadow, those with horizontal lines were pasture.

The Bourne Area Map

At Appendix 1 to the Enclosure Schedule, the 5½ acres of waste of Plot 1406 is indicated as having been sold to Pole's Executors, and it is described as being 'At Bourne'. In that same Appendix Walker Gray is shown as having purchased the acre of waste at Plot 1354, which is just off the map, not far east of Plot 181. Gray's purchase is indicated as being in 'Dog and Duck Lane'. So with these two entries we have the then current names of local roads. The map of the 1865 Ordnance Survey shows the western extremity of the lane as being called Bourneside, the hamlet around *The Woodman* (as it now is) as Bournehill, and the eastern length as (still) Dog and Duck Lane. These are also the names used on the 1895 O.S. map.

Plate 11. Grovelands Mansion Exterior

I took this snap of John Nash's fine 1797 building in 1987. Now a Grade 1 listed building, it was built for Walker Gray upon his purchasing the local estate from Earl Temple, not long after the latter had married into the Chandos family, which also owned the nearby Minchenden. For many years the mansion was the home of the Taylor brewing family, whilst for long periods of the 20th century it acted as a hospital. It functions today as a private psychiatric hospital.

Grovelands Estate

North of The Bourne the appearance of some of the land in 1801 was probably not too different to that of today. Plot 32 was 28 acres of pasture, that contained what we now call Grovelands Mansion, then known as *The Grove*. To its east, at Plot 30, was the lake that we continue to admire today, and to its east, in turn, at Plot 52, was woodland, some, of which still overlooks the lake. These Plots, including the mansion, were owned by Walker Gray. The ownership schedule indicates that Plots 33, 34, 35 and

36 were owned, at the time of Enclosure, by the executors of Samuel Pole, but later 35, 36, and Parts of 33 and 34, were 'sold and exchanged to' Gray, to add to his great estate. Plates 11,12 & 13 portray aspects of Grovelands.

It is interesting to note that Plot 35 is shown in the Ownership Schedule as being the 'Site of Wool-pack and garden'. I have consulted Gary Boudier's extensively researched, *A – Z of Enfield Pubs Pt. 2* and his coverage of *The Woolpack Inn* makes no mention of it having ever been other than in The High Street, Southgate. The 1801/2 *Woolpack* seems, on the 1865 OS Map, to have been replaced by a Lodge to what by then was Grovelands. The site is now the start of Queen Elizabeth's Drive. The reader is referred to the section on William Eaton in the Ownership Schedule.

It is not the place of this book to trace the full history of the Grovelands estate, but a brief resume is in order. *The Victoria County History* tells us that Grovelands, or Southgate Grove, was first mentioned in the 15th century as Lords Grove - woodland treated as a demesne of Edmonton Manor i.e. farmed by the Lord of the Manor. It descended with the manor until 1571, when the Queen granted it to Lord Burley. By the late 17th century it was in the hands of Sir Thomas Wolstenholme (d 1691), and was part of the Minchenden Estate. Lord's Grove followed the descent of Minchenden until it was inherited by Anna Elisabeth, daughter and heir of the Duke of Chandos (d 1789) and after 1796 wife of Richard Nugent-Temple-Grenville, Earl Temple, later Duke of Buckingham and Chandos. Starkey informs us that Earl Temple was William Pitt the Elder's brother in law.

In his 1997 2nd edition of *The Story of Grovelands* Matthew Eccleston tells us that in about 1796 the Duke sold the estate to Walker Gray, the wealthy brandy merchant from Tottenham, who had inherited a large fortune from his father Abraham. Eccleston says that, 'Grovelands consists of a Grade 1 listed country villa built in 1797 to the designs of John Nash - the celebrated architect, planner and builder of the superb classical Regent's Park terraces and the sumptuous orientally inspired Brighton Pavilion. It stands on elevated ground overlooking around 90 acres of undulating parkland and woodland laid out by the eminent landscape gardener Humphry Repton, boasting a fine, tree girthed ornamental lake as its centrepiece.' Repton is pictured at Plate 5.

Enfield's Local History Unit (LHU) has a copy of the Winstanley and Sons Catalogue for the sale of The Grove Estate on 4th July 1834, further to the death, earlier in that year, of Walker Gray. There were 260 acres in the surrounding grounds. Details from the Catalogue are given at Pages 52-5 of my 1989 *A History of Winchmore Hill*. Matthew Eccleston says, 'Soon after he acquired Southgate Grove in 1834, John Donnithorne Taylor retired from the Taylor Walker brewery to live the life of a country squire ..... One of the first improvements to be carried out at Grovelands was the enlargement of the lake .....' The Taylor family pursued a Green Belt policy in relation to their land in our area for the remainder of the 19th century.

The 1902 prospectus for the sale of over 600 acres in the neighbourhood, upon the death of Major Robert Kirkpatrick Taylor, J.P., incorporated the Grovelands Estate of over 314 acres, including a Deer Park of about seven acres. Eccleston tells us that the Grovelands part of the family estates remained unsold and continued in the ownership of the Major's son, Captain John Vickris, when he moved to Oxfordshire.

The Taylor personal papers indicate that 63 ¾ acres of land were sold to Southgate UDC for £22,500 on 5th September 1910. Copies of legal papers confirming this sale are to be found in the Local History Unit, being dated 1st December 1911. Grovelands Park was opened by the Lord Mayor of London, Sir David Burnett, on 12th April 1913. The 20th century history of the Mansion, which was retained by the Taylors at that time, is beyond the scope of this book. Suffice is to say that at one time it fell into a very sad state, being saved when The Priory Hospitals Group took it over in 1985. The Group restored the mansion and opened it as a private psychiatric hospital, its most famous patient probably being the former Argentinean dictator General Pinochet.

Plate 12. Inside the Birdcage Room at Grovelands

In June 1999 the management of Priory Hospital, as Grovelands now is, kindly gave me a tour of the premises and allowed me to take this photograph of the famous Birdcage Room, with its octagonal shape and umbrella vaulted ceiling.

132

Grovelands Mansion has generally been well described, and its history well documented, in other publications, such as Matthew Eccleston's, and I see no merit in repeating all that detail here. However, one aspect that I would like to dwell on is of particular interest to the era covered by this book. I am talking of the walled garden. Amongst the many informative small soft backs by Shire Books is the 1998 *Walled Kitchen Gardens* by Susan Campbell. In it she tells us that virtually every cottage and country house once had their own kitchen garden, but those of the middle and upper classes were usually separate enclosures contained by high walls. These walled gardens, she says, were at the top of their productivity between 1800 and 1939.

Plate 13. The walled garden at Grovelands

Today exotic fruit is flown into our supermarkets from all over the world. Incredible as it may now seem, two hundred years ago, during the 'Little Ice Age', Gray's The Grove, like many other country mansions of the time, would have produced its own pineapples, mangos and the like by heating walls and carefully protecting the developing produce. I took this photograph, showing the area where all this was once carried on, during an open day in September 1998.

Each acre was expected to supply enough produce for twelve people, and required the attention of two to three gardeners. They provided the family, its servants, and sometimes the estate staff, with fruit and vegetables all the year round, in addition to flowers for the house. Hardy crops grew on the open quarters; fruit trees were trained up the walls, and heated glasshouses supplied tender or exotic delicacies.

Walls were usually at least 10' high, but could be twice that. They not only protected the kitchen garden from thieves, but also provided shelter from the wind and rain, as well offering support for trained fruit trees and lean to structures, such as glasshouses and sheds. The walls were usually of brick, and they could contain flues to improve their heating effect. A further way of engendering warmth was by fixing glass casements and panes to the walls by means of brackets

Incredibly, given that England was still in 'The Little Ice Age', by training trees against these warm, high walls, using glass, pits, manure and coverings, the most exotic of fruits were grown. These included peaches, nectarines, apricots, figs, nectarines, apricots, cherries, plums and grapes, melon, mango and pineapple (a favourite), as well as the more expected pears and apples.

In Southgate Civic Trust's *Oakleaves No.1* of 1987 there was an article by Reg Martin specifically on the heated wall in the kitchen garden at Grovelands, which survives to this day. It is of irregular shape and lies roughly west of the house, with grilled openings in the south wall which look towards the lake. I believe the photograph at Plate 13 captures at least a part of it.

We do not know when the heated wall at Grovelands dates from. The 1802 description in *New Vitruvius Britannicus* by G. Richardson mentions a connection from the conservatory through the hot-houses to the stables at the back of the kitchen garden, which perhaps suggests that the garden wall was installed with the construction of the mansion in 1797. The design was, apparently, based on Millar's pattern of flue system, which was divided into sections, so that no fire was of excessive length. The flues are fronted with thin bricks laid vertically. Larger, square bricks are laid at the U bends and could easily be taken out to remove ash deposited in these areas of slower gas flow. We don't know where the heating stove was - possibly in the centre of the garden?

The Woodman

The Palmers Green and Southgate Gazette of 28th December 1945 contained an article by Tom Mason entitled 'Where Beer is Sold by the Pound' (which would imply an American pint of 16 fluid ounces, as opposed to the British 20). It informed us that *The Woodman* was formerly a cottage, dating back to 1727. A licence was only obtained as late as 1868, by retired police sergeant Henry Wale, who remained there until 1893. At that date it was taken over by retired lock maker Henry Reed, and the inn was still with his family at the time of the article.

The inn is captured in its rural days at Page 31 of my *A Look at Old Winchmore Hill*. From those pictures it is clear that the building's longer side ran parallel to the lane, cottages behind running at right angles. Cottages 176/7/8/9 on the Enclosure map are positioned such that they might be those pictured, but there is no structure on the map that looks as though it could be the one later occupied by the Inn. Possibly the conventional wisdom is wrong, and it was not built until after Enclosure.

The Pound

There is an old colour picture of the Pound on the rear cover of my *A Look at Old Winchmore Hill*. Tom Mason's 1945 article explained that village Pounds had been in use from the earliest times. Acts of Parliament passed in 1847 and 1864 gave the local authorities of those days power to purchase a site and erect a Pound, but he considered it likely that the Southgate Pound existed prior to those dates. There were two kinds of Pounds. One was a Pound Covert, which was a covered Pound, used for goods impounded by the Sheriff's Officer under authority of the Court. The other, such as the one near *The Woodman,* was a Pound Overt (i.e. Open Pound), used for straying animals.

If the animals were impounded, they could not be released until the fine was paid, along with the expense of feeding the animals. The keeper of the cattle was called a Pinner, and the man who looked after the pound was called a Pinder. The Southgate Pound was officially closed in December 1904, and in 1926 Southgate Urban District Council purchased it from the Lord of Edmonton Manor, Sir E. F. Curtis, for £50.

Again we are faced with the question as to where, if at all, the Pound was in 1801. It is possible that it is the rectangular structure in Plot 288, belonging to the Trustees of Master Harrison. This is listed as 'Messuage, garden and yards'.

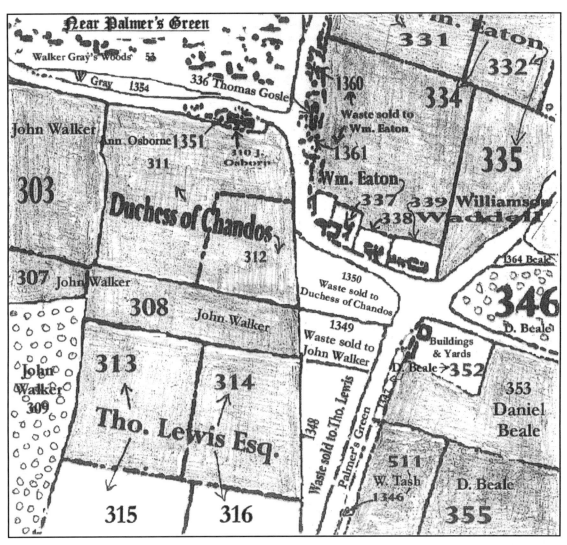

Figure 12. Enclosure Map of near Palmer's Green

At the top of the map the N-S trending Hopper's Lane (now Road) meets Dog and Duck Lane (now Bourne Hill), running in from the west. The lane then continues south for a few yards, before swinging south east to cross Green Lanes, continuing as 'Hedge Lane' between Plots 346 and 353. The shaded fields were meadow, those with horizontal lines were pasture, and those with small circles in were used for arable.

Near Palmer's Green Map

Osborne's Cottages at Plot 310

We know something of Joseph Osborne's cottages at Plot 310. The ownership schedule describes the Plot as 'Tenements and garden', occupying nearly a quarter acre of land. My *More Winchmore Hill Lives* of 2004 contains an account of Valerie Darvell and her family, many of whom bear the surname Downes. At Plate 10 in that publication there is a likeness, made by a member of the Downes family in 1860, of the family home in 1800. It was one of the six cottages on Plot 310, the upper of the two storeys, at least, clearly being clapperboard in style. They were demolished in 1868 to make way for the (then) new railway through Winchmore Hill. In an effort to show a link between the Enclosure era and the present, at Plate 14 I have published a photograph I took of the Downes brothers at a family get together in Bounds Green in August 2005. (See my comments at the foot of the next section.)

Plate 14. The Downes family

I took this photograph at a Downes family gathering in Bounds Green in August 2005. It captures three Downes brothers from then, and I reproduce it as they are a link to the old village that this book is about. Eric is standing, whilst Don is looking at the copy of More Winchmore Hill Lives that his twin Les is holding. The family gave its name to Downes Court.

Thomas Goslee's 'Tenements' at Plot 336

At Page 18 of my *More Winchmore Hill Lives* of 2004 I quote a conversation with a Mr. Lindsay regarding his old cottage (now No. 80 Hoppers Road), in the terrace that includes *The Dog and Duck*. He said that he can trace his property back to at least 1760. Mr. Lindsay said that the property has no foundations, and there are the remains of a well in the back garden. He believes the adjoining cottages are of a similar age, and also had wells. The terrace is pictured at Pages 15 and 16 of that book, and P29 of the original *Winchmore Hill Lives* of 1991. The only conceivable location for these cottages on the map of 1801 is Thomas Goslee's Plot 336, described as 'Tenements'.

The lower (eastern) end of Bourne Hill (as we now know it) has moved slightly south since the time of Enclosure, so the cottages are now some yards up from the Hoppers Road/Bourne Hill junction. Alan Dumayne explains, with the aid of a photograph at P54 of his *Old Borough of Southgate*, that this change came about in 1971, when the current skew bridge over the railway was constructed.

In his book on the local pubs, Gary Boudier indicates that the first licensee of *The Dog and Duck* that he can find is Joseph Osborne, in 1802, followed in 1803 by Christopher Idle. What we now call Bourne Hill was, in the land ownership schedule of 1801, known as Dog and Duck Lane. It has long been believed that this name derives from the old alehouse, and it has always been assumed that this was on the site of the current establishment. Of course the row of 'tenements' at Plot 336 might have included the Inn, but as Joseph Osborne was the owner of the 'Tenements and garden' of Plot 310, and that was actually in the so called Dog and Duck Lane, perhaps the original Inn was in the six cottages there, moving to one of the cottages in Hoppers Road at some later stage. This theory must be taken seriously as in the Edmonton Manor Court Baron minutes of 12th May 1818 the death of Joseph Osborne was announced, and his Will included *The Dog and Duck*.

William Eaton's Plot 337, Waddell's Plot 338 and R.T. Williamson's Plot 339

Today a road off of Green Lanes, not far north of the Intimate Theatre, is named Eaton Park Road, and it seems reasonable to assume that the name derives from the nearby land holdings of William Eaton. In 1801 he already owned a 'House and garden at Palmer's green' on Plot 337. The meadowland of Plots 331, 332, 334 and 335, and the arable strip of 333, had been owned by the Dean and Chapter of St. Paul's, but were sold to William Eaton. On the map the name of the owner of Plot 338 is spelt Waddell, but in the ownership schedule it is spelt Waddle. He owned a 'Cottage and garden'. Next door to him was R.T. Williamson's 'House and garden' on Plot 339. (Williamson also owned *The Fox* public house).

At P54 of my *A Look at Old Winchmore Hill* I wrote about this particular stretch. I quoted Miss Cresswell as saying that in about 1860, 'On the right, as Hoppers Road was entered, stood a row of cottages with long gardens. Next to them was Eaton Farm with old barns roofed with antique mossy tiles... ' These words accompanied a sketch made by her father at about that time, where he stood by the bend in the road by Plot 337, looking towards Green Lanes. The description of 'antique mossy tiles' suggests that the sketch captures Eaton's 1801 'House and garden at Palmer's green', and that he used it as his Farmhouse after buying the adjoining land.

Palmer's Green

In *Once Upon a Time in Palmers Green* Alan Dumayne tells us that in 'Place Names of Middlesex' by JEB Gover the earliest known documented reference to that locality is in 1205, when it was called Palmeresfeld, feld being old Saxon for an area of cleared trees. It was situated between what we now call Fox Lane and St. John's Church. Alan goes on to tell us that in 1228 Radulfum Palmer is listed as holding a messuage and 4 acres of land in Edelmeton (i.e. Edmonton). He also says that the name Palmer is further mentioned in deeds dated during the 14th, 15th and 16th centuries. The first recorded mention of 'Palmers Grene', as such, is in 1608.

On the Enclosure map the stretch of Green Lanes that runs from about the southern boundary of today's St. John's Church, to Fox Lane, has, on its western edge, Plot 1348 - Waste sold to Thomas Lewis. This part of Green Lanes is actually marked 'Palmer's Green' on the map, so one presumes that Plot 1348 was an ancient stretch of green verge that gave the hamlet its name in the dim distant past, when it was under different ownership. The stretch, as it was in July 2007, is shown at Plate 15.

Plate 15. Palmer's Green today

In July 2007 I took this photograph as I thought that readers might want to contrast the scene today with the rural one that must have prevailed at the time of enclosure. This stretch of Green Lanes pavement, south of St. John's Church (seen in the distance), was at one time probably the ancient 'Palmer's Green'.

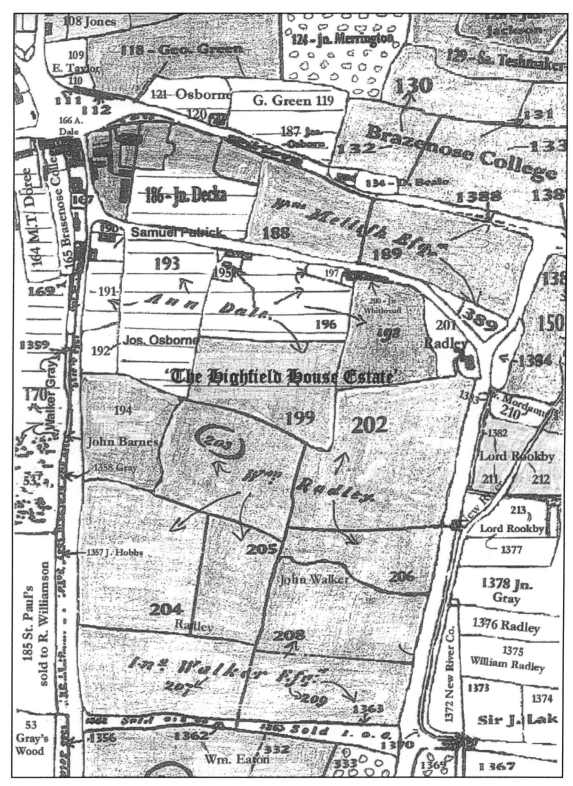

Figure 13. Enclosure Map of 'The Highfield House Estate'

The map shows The Green at the NW corner, with 'Station Road' running east from it, and Hopper's Lane (now Road) leading off south, at right angles to the former. Parallel to 'Station Road', and just to its south, is 'Compton Road'. At their eastern extremities both 'Station Road' and 'Compton Road' meet the N-S trending Green Lanes. Towards the south of the map Green Lanes is met by Barrow's Well Green running in from the east. In those days it continued west to Hopper's Lane as a path, which upon enclosure was sold off as wasteland. The shaded fields were meadow, those with horizontal lines were pasture, and those with small circles in were used for arable.

139

The Highfield House Estate Map

The map shows The Green at the NW corner, with 'Station Road' running east from it, and Hopper's Lane (now Road) leading off south, at right angles to the former. In the notes that follow I consider only that part of the map south of 'Station Road' between Hopper's Lane and Green Lanes. The remaining parts of the map are considered in other sections.

Plate 16. Chalkley's Bakery, Hoppers Road

The Southgate District Council Guide for 1922 had an advert for, 'Ye Olde Village Bakerie' which claimed that it, 'is reputed to be about eight hundred years old, the heavy hewn, irregular oaken beams of the frame - work are fastened together with stout oak pins; not a nail has been used in that portion of its construction.' Despite the 1801 in the photograph, there is no evidence of the Chalkleys being in our village in late Georgian times.

Plot 186 - The Bakery in Hoppers Road ('Chalkley's')

The Southgate District Council Guide for 1922 has an advert at Page 68 headed, 'Ye Olde Village Bakerie' which contained the following,

'There are few who realise how the very ancient and very modern are blended at Mr. Chalkley's Bakery in Hoppers Rd. Winchmore Hill, which is undoubtedly the oldest in the Village, and though a wooden structure, possibly has a future power of endurance surpassing that of any other house and shop near by. The building is reputed to be about eight hundred years old, the heavy hewn, irregular oaken beams of the frame - work are fastened together with stout oak pins; not a nail has been used in that portion of its construction. The oak is so hard that on the few occasions when an attempt has been made to drive a nail therein for use as a coat hook, nail after nail has turned up at the point and the task has been abandoned ...... There are evidences of interior alterations at different periods, and also that at one time it was used as a farm house. Doubtless the exterior boards have been renewed more than once, but the main fabric seems to be as firm and substantial as ever. W.F. Chalkley, Baker and Pastrycook, Winchmore Hill, N21 . Phone Palmers Green 863.'

The foregoing ties in with local builder Ewan Lewis's comments to me on 22nd November 1986 that the bakery, 'is probably very ancient'. Alan Dumayne also covers the history of the bakery in his *Fond Memories of Winchmore Hill (1990)*, in which he reports that he was lucky enough to be shown around the premises by the then owner. He confirms that the main beam and joists are made of oak. The bakehouse, he says, ceased to operate from about 1945, and for some years served as an antiques shop. The associated corner baker's shop continued to trade into the 1960s. Alan tells us that he saw evidence of the old original oven, with its curved and domed walls, and that there is a more recent oven bearing the clear inscription of 'J.C. 1822'. In the basement is a well with pure water where the level rarely deviates from a few inches below the basement floor. At the rear are the old stables and straw house.

The bakery is pictured at Plate 16 in what is thought to be the 1920s. The sign says that Chalkley's business was established in 1801, but I have not seen the family name in any old documents of that era, nor is it mentioned in the 1826 Pigot's Directory. So who was the 'J.C. of 1822' if it wasn't Chalkley? My bet is 'Catchpool, John, baker & corn dealer, Winchmore hill', who was listed in the 1826 Directory. There is a write up on the Catchpools in the section on that Directory.

Plate 17. Front view of Roseville Mansion on The Lower Green

This photograph was kindly supplied for publication by Pauline Holstius. The mansion was built in the second half of the 18th century for Quaker John Decka, owner of Plot 186 at Enclosure. In 1801 the bakery and Roseville were both part of this Plot. In this view from The Green the building looks like a cohesive structure.

Plot 186 - Roseville

The old bakery is at the top of Hoppers Road, just around the corner from where *Roseville* mansion used to overlook the Lower Green, until replaced by the current flats bearing the same name. In 1801 the bakery was part of the same plot (No.

186) as *Roseville*, belonging to John Decka. This was listed in the Enclosure schedule as, 'Two houses and field' occupying about 5 ¼ acres. There is a front view of Roseville at Plate 17, but the rear view at Plate 18 makes it appear that the building is probably an agglomeration from different eras.

The Palmers Green and Southgate Gazette of 16th June 1950 carried an article by Tom Mason headed, 'Story of "Roseville" at Winchmore Hill Green' and contained the following, 'By the kindness of Dr. Gordon Simpson I have been allowed a sight of the ancient documents and deeds relating to the large house called *Roseville*, standing on the south side of Winchmore Hill Green .... Apparently, *Roseville* was built nearly 200 years ago for a man named John Decka. The land came into his possession in 1768, on which date he was admitted at a Court held for the Manor of Edmonton. He was a Copyholder, the freehold being in the hands of the Lord of the Manor. Decka sold the copyhold in 1809 to William John Reeves, who immediately proceeded to get the land released and enfranchised, by the payment of £31. 10s to Sir William Curtis, the Lord of the Manor. .... In 1830 the house and the surrounding land came into possession of John Radford, and it remained with him and his heirs for 91 years. During that time it was let to various tenants ..... after the railway came in 1871, the owner of *Roseville* still retained the land on the east side of the cutting ....' One presumes that this John Radford was the prominent member of the local Independent Church community referred to elsewhere.

Plate 18. Rear view of Roseville Mansion

This is another photograph that Pauline Holstius has been good enough to supply and, as you can see, the rear view makes it look as though Roseville was actually an agglomeration from different periods. A hundred years ago the mansion was home to Dr. Vivian, who brought my friend Mrs. Lucy Pettifer into the world in 1901, and was later occupied by the colourful Dr. 'Simbo' Simpson.

In his *Fond Memories of Winchmore Hill* Alan Dumayne says that the house was demolished in the late 1950s, to be replaced by flats of the same name, which are still there today. The *1958 Southgate Borough Street Directory* in the LHU makes no mention of *Roseville,* either as a house or flats. The 1966 Electoral Register, compiled in October 1965, also stored in the LHU, lists the occupants of the new flats.

The minutes of the Court Baron of 8th June 1821, at the LMA, tell us that, 'At this Court the Homage find and present that John Decka formerly of Winchmore Hill in the County of Middlesex Farmer late a Customary Tenant of this Manor is dead and that he died seized of all that Messuage or Tenement with the Appurtenances together with the Orchard Stable and Garden to the same belonging containing by estimation One Acre together with two Cottages or Tenements thereon lately erected and built by the said John Decka (being part and parcel of the Hereditaments and Premises to which he was at a general Court Baron holden in and for this Manor on the Twenty fourth day of May One Thousand and seven hundred and sixty eight admitted Tenant on a Surrender to him thereof made by Benjamin Young ....' Presumably we are here talking of *Roseville* and grounds.

At the National Archives is a copy of the last Will of John Decka. The first or original part was made out in 1807, probably just after his wife died, but was amended a number of times afterwards, and these papers refer to his nephew John Catchpool. A late amendment stated, 'C: In order that my nephew John Catchpool may remain in the business in Winchmorehill in which he is now engaged it is my desire that he may have the refusal of my estate at Winchmorehill consisting of my dwelling house and premises thereunto belonging two cottages a Barn with the land and gardens ......' The Will was proved in 1820.

At P34 of my 1991 *Winchmore Hill Lives* regarding *Roseville* I recorded that, 'However, a part of the old grounds remain in the form of the wall and "shed" on the western boundary to the flats. The wall bears a plaque inscribed, "J.R. 1830", the "J.R." presumably denoting John Radford. At the south end of the wall the "shed" bears a plaque inscribed "J.C. B.G. 1831".' One assumes that the J.C. is the same J.C. - John Catchpool - as for the bakery oven in 1822. Could the B.G. be the William Gates listed as a plasterer in the 1826 Pigot's Directory?

At the LMA is a set of papers (ACC 1016/224 – 232) concerning, 'Edmonton Manor. 1 -12, Compton Terrace and 1 – 3, Devonshire Place, Winchmore Hill.' Devonshire Terrace is the small parade of shops on The Green as you turn right out of Hoppers Road. The papers explain that the properties had formed the estate of the late Miss Catchpool, who had died in 1926 at the age of 84, and she had left them to her nieces Grace Mary Young and Francis Maud Young.

The Enclosure map indicates that *Roseville,* the bakery and other premises occupied Decka's land. These were presumably all left to nephew John Catchpool in 1820, but in 1830 Radford bought *Roseville* and grounds from him, or a successor, with Catchpool retaining the bakery and adoining strip along Hopper's Lane, a wall being erected between the two men's holdings. The Catchpool family retained at least some of their plot for over a hundred years.

The Queen's Head

There is no mention of *The Queen's Head* in the ownership schedule of 1801. Plot 187, of around a quarter of an acre, belonged to Joseph Osborne, and was described as 'Tenements and garden'. The first landlord Gary Boudier cites for *The Queen's Head* is William King in 1855. There may not have been an ale house in our era of interest, but perhaps the actual building was in existence in the form of one of the 'tenements'.

The Queen's Head was built in its current guise in the mid 1930s. The late Keith Surtees (b.1916) contributed to my 1991 *Winchmore Hill Lives*. His father was born in the village in 1883. On 28th February 1990 he told me that earlier in that century, when *The Queen's Head* was being rebuilt, the architect and surveyor had considered that the old cellar dated from the 16th century! He further informed me that his grandmother had told him that there had been a concealed passage under 'Station Road', linking the Inn to Mummery/Udall's on The Green.

Holly Lodge

Plot 190, on the corner of Hopper's Lane and what is now Compton Road was a 'house and garden' belonging to Samuel Patrick, who for some years was licensee of *The King's Head*. At Plate 19 is a drawing of Holly Lodge by Peter Brown. The Southgate Civic Trust described it as, 'A small but architecturally interesting 18th century house in a fine landscaped garden, it was demolished in 1972.' The diary for 1826 includes Manorial minutes which almost certainly make reference to this plot.

Plate 19. Holly Lodge, as seen from the Compton Road Bridge

My thanks to Peter A.J. Brown for supplying another of his charming sketches for publication. As with Roseville the viewer is left with the impression that the property was in fact possibly an agglomeration, with the clapperboard part probably being the older section. In 1972 the house was replaced by flats bearing the same name.

Highfield House Estate

In this section I rely heavily on the detailed research brought into the public domain by Brenda Griffith-Williams in the EHHS Occasional Paper No. 61 entitled, *Highfield House, c.1818-1952.* The house is pictured at Plate 20.

The 1865 O.S. map shows Highfield House about where the boundary between Mr. Radley's fields 204 and 205 meet his field 203. The estate is bounded by Hopper's Lane, 'Compton Road', Green Lanes and, to the south, apparently, the line of the 1801 boundary between the land of Radley and John Walker. However, there is no indication of this grand house on either the 1822 OS map, or the 1801 land schedule map. At the time of Enclosure, land in the future estate was in the hands of various people, including William Radley, John Barnes and the Trustees for Ann Dale.

The Pigot's Directory of 1826 makes no reference to a Dale family, but it does list a SI. Compton Esq. amongst the Gentry. Henrietta Cresswell was presumably thinking of him when she said that 'lawyer Compton' lived about half way along the road now bearing his name, on the south side. However, in her paper, Ms. Griffith-Williams tells us that Samuel Compton was formerly of Hackney, and associated with the Whitechapel firm of Compton and Sharp, plumbers and glaziers. There was, thus, no obvious connection with the legal profession. Perhaps Pigot listed him amongst the Gentry, rather than Tradesmen, because he was a man of money?

Wm RADLEY'S ESQ^E NEAR WINCHMORE HILL.

Plate 20. Highfield House

The 1865 O.S. map shows Highfield House as having been located about where the boundary between Mr. Radley's fields 204 and 205 met his field 203 in the Enclosure map. I am indebted to Stewart Christian for allowing me to publish this sketch from the archives of the late David Hicks, of which he is custodian. Highfield House is not shown on the 1822 OS Map, but after detailed research Brenda Griffith-Williams concluded that it was in existence by 11th November 1818.

Ms. Griffith-Williams says that the house Samuel occupied, with its eleven acres of land, was owned by Joseph Compton, a ship and insurance broker of Hackney who later moved to Manchester. Presumably, given the family name, and the Hackney link, Samuel and Joseph were related. It seems that Compton's land is shown allocated to Ann Dale's Trustees on the 1801 map, and he acquired it from her successors in two purchases, in 1820 and 1826. The Compton house which Miss Cresswell mentions must, at Enclosure, have been either the one at Ann Dale's Plot 195, or on her Plot 197. But what became of the land owned, in 1801, by Barnes and Radley?

William Radley was born about 1750, and was a wine merchant of Fleet Street, where he continued to own a house after moving to Winchmore Hill. He became a copyhold tenant of the Manor of Edmonton in 1799, when he took over various pieces of land in Winchmore Hill which had previously been in the occupation of William Skilton. He acquired a small piece of waste land in Hopper's Lane, adjacent to his existing holding, in 1811. In 1816 he purchased Plot 194, which was known as Kitchen Croft, from the representatives of John Barnes, who by then had passed away. It seems that although Highfield House is not shown on the 1822 OS Map, it was in existence by 11th November 1818, because on that day Radley made a will leaving 'all my dwelling house commonly called Highfield House in the parish of Edmonton' to his wife, Margaret, for her lifetime.

The exact date of construction for the early 19th century house is not known. The official Borough of Southgate brochure for the Highfield House flats, opened by the Mayor of Southgate on 25th September 1954, included a contribution by Ernest P. Wilkinson in which he says that the original house was 'about 80 years old' when his father bought it 'in or about the year 1895'. This is probably a reasonable approximation, although in fact Samuel Wilkinson did not buy the house until 1898.

It is interesting, here, to ponder on the house's name, because, of course, High Field had long been a common field on the eastern side of Green Lanes, with Highfield Row running along its northern edge. If you refer to the VCH reconstruction of the area in about 1600 at Figure 1, you will see that the stretch of Green Lanes to the field's west was called Highfield Lane, as was 'Barrowell Green' to the field's south. Perhaps the proximity of this lane gives us a clue as to why Radley should opt for the name Highfield. On the other hand, maybe it was simply that the house was on a high field that allowed a view over lower land to the east?

Anyway, continuing our story, William Radley died suddenly at Highfield House, aged 72, in January 1821 . A brief notice in *The Times* said he had been "sincerely respected by all who knew him". He was buried in Edmonton churchyard on 6th February, and his death was reported to the Court Baron of the Manor of Edmonton on 12th June 1821. His widow was represented at the Court hearing by her son, John Radley, who was formally admitted as tenant. He is listed amongst the local Gentry in the Pigot's of 1826.

Well-to-do City merchant Peter Pope Firth bought the Highfield House estate from Margaret Radley and her son, John, on 1st June 1830. On 2nd August 1830 he also bought the adjacent piece of freehold land previously belonging to Joseph Compton, and occupied by Samuel Compton, so significantly enlarging the original Highfield House estate. The freehold of all this land was granted to Firth on 26th January 1831 .

Ms. Griffith-Williams explains that some of the land fronting Hoppers Road, near the junction with Compton Road, remained outside the Highfield estate. This included the site of Trois Vase House (later the home of the Cresswells), and that of the Independent Chapel, immediately to the north of that house, opened in 1844. I have compared the 1865 O.S. map with the 1801 Enclosure one, and it looks as though the Independent Chapel was erected on what had been Plot 191. This had belonged to Ann Dale in 1801.

On 13th September 1842 a Captain Clark purchased the estate from Frith, and upon his death in 1848 it passed to his wife Elizabeth. She lived at the house until her own death in 1862. The grounds of the estate at that time were later described by Miss Cresswell (born 1855). The Clarks had no children, so upon Elizabeth's death the estate passed to a relative by the name of George Bartlett. He was shown as Head of Household in the 1871 Census. Ms. Griffith -Williams says that in 1898 (rather than the popularly believed 1895) the estate was bought by Samuel Wilkinson. He sold off much of the estate for housing, but retained the mansion. In the 1920s it was rented out for use as a Girls' school, but was sold to Southgate Council in 1947, being demolished, then replaced by the existing flats in the mid 1950s.

At the base of 'Compton Road', Mellish's Plot 1389 is a piece of waste that seems to have survived to the present era as a triangle of land. Plot 201, which overlooked this waste in 1801, contained a 'Cottage and garden' belonging to William Radley. A similar set of premises appears on the 1865 O.S. Map, marked as 'Highfield Lodge', with a 'Pine Lodge' now appearing just to its north. The 1895 Survey still shows a similar structure for Highfield Lodge to that in the previous maps. There are also premises where Pine Lodge had previously been shown.

The Green Area Map

Plots east of 'Wades Hill' and Hopper's Lane are covered in other map sections. Let's now start our look at the hub of our area by completing our examination of Winchmore Hill – lane as it approaches The Green.

John Tugwell's Plots 72, 54, 55

Miss Barnes's Laurel Cottage

At Page 79 of her *Memories of a Lost Village*, Miss Cresswell talks of a walk she took out of the village as a small child, one warm April day in about 1860. She says, in relation to Church Hill, 'Next came the Friends' Meeting House, which was very holy ground, as George Fox had once preached there. On the left was Miss Barnes' house, which claimed to be the oldest in the village, and to have been standing long before Enfield Chase was enclosed. It had a large old-fashioned garden and small fields marching with the Wood ..... '

At Figure 4 I have shown the relationships between various old village families according to information held in the late Alan Dumayne's archives. James Carpenter, a cooper of Wormwood Street, came to Winchmore Hill, presumably in about 1700, and built a cottage. It initially comprised four rooms, but was later enlarged by the family to 25 (stet) rooms, with a coach house and stables. By a series of intermarriages, summarised in Figure 4, the 'old family home' came into the possession of lifelong spinster Anna Barnes (1826 to 1901), and it was sold off upon her death.

At Pages 54/5 of his *Memories of Winchmore Hill*, Regnart tells us that in the late 19th century, past Uplands on The Green, 'came an old house also enclosed by a brick wall. The grounds included an orchard bounded by a tarred wooden fence and a row of lime trees which extended as far as the (St. Paul's) Church. I saw the lime trees being lopped from my nursery window (at Hill House). Miss Barnes lived here. A man and his wife lived in a cottage adjoining the house and between them they looked after Miss Barnes and also the grounds. Miss Barnes also owned Hill House where her father, Robert Barnes, had lived. She belonged to a sect that had a chapel somewhere in London and she used to go there every Sunday. She died about 1904. My mother and I went to the sale of the furniture.'

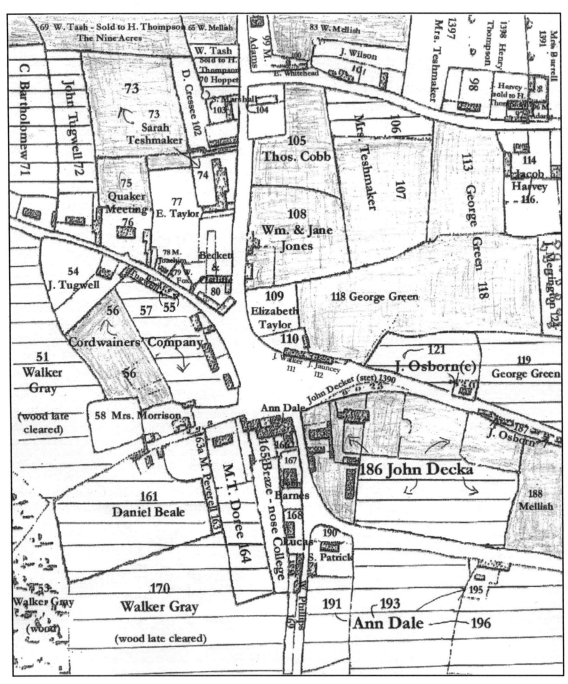

Figure 14. Enclosure Map of The Green Area

The lane running ESE from the western (left) edge of the map is Winchmore hill – lane (the forerunner of modern day Church Hill). It meets the ancestor of the north - south trending 'Wades Hill' at The Green. Near the top of the map 'Wades Hill' intersects with what we now call Vicars Moor Lane. The lane that became Station Road runs off ESE from The Green, whilst Hopper's Lane (now Road) runs southwards from the village's nucleus. Parallel to 'Station Road', running east from Hopper's Lane, is what we call Compton Road. The shaded fields were meadow, those with horizontal lines were pasture, and those with small circles in were used for arable.

148

The 1899-1900 Street Directory for 'Church Hill' - then confusingly known as Winchmore Hill Road - indicates that the first property on the west side of the road, above St. Paul's Church, was Laurel Cottage, occupied by a Miss A. Barnes. She must be the great granddaughter of John Tugwell, owner of Plot 54 in 1801. At that time the house was surrounded by an orchard. Tugwell also owned Plot 55, the next one up towards the Green. This is described as a cottage in the 1801 schedule, and could well be the cottage inhabited by the couple who tended Anna Barnes.

Hill House
has the simplicity of
to-day's building - but it was
made in the days of Queen Anne.

Rutherford.

Plate 21. Hill House in the 1930s

Tugwell's Plot 72 in Winchmore hill-lane, at the time of Enclosure, was almost certainly Hill House, which was inherited by his great granddaughter Anna Barnes. Later in the 19th century Horace Regnart and family lived there. Horace dated the bulk of the house as being early 18th century in origin, though he hints that parts might have been much older. The property was demolished in 1960, to be replaced by flats bearing the same name. My thanks to The Gazette for allowing the use of this sketch by Rutherford.

Plot 72 – Hill House

Plot 72, on the north side of the lane, contained a house and pasture adjoining The Friends Burial Ground. We have just noted that in the late 19th century Horace Regnart cited Anna Barnes as being the owner of Hill House, which his own family occupied for a time. It seems reasonable to suppose that the house of Plot 72 was the ancient Hill House, and that Miss Barnes inherited the property as John Tugwell's great granddaughter. This would seem consistent with the Will of his widow Martha Tugwell in the 1824 diary. The 1825 Edmonton Rate Book shows Martha Yallowley, her granddaughter, living at the property along with the Independent's Rev. Henry Pawling.

The diary section for 1826 records a land sale catalogue where Lot 3 would seem to be a description of Hill House – 'Also pleasantly situate at Winchmore Hill, and adjoining Lot 1, comprising A Residence, with Veranda in Front, Garden Pleasure Grounds and Paddock, containing on the whole about Two Acres. The house consists of a Dining-room, Drawing-room, Four Bed-chambers and a Dressing-room. The Domestic Offices comprise Kitchen, Washhouse, pantry, Cellar, &c, with Coach-house and Stable.'

That description was from our era of interest. *The Palmers Green and Southgate Gazette* of 6th January 1939 contained the sketch of the building by Mr. Rutherford reproduced at Plate 21   It also had a brief description of the interior, but there was a better one in Regnart's *Memories of Winchmore Hill*. Regnart says, 'We went to Hill House in 1878. The kitchen and scullery were originally a pair of cottages. The tiled roof which I had to replace a few years ago showed that they were from four to five hundred years old. In the reign of Queen Anne (1702 – 14), or soon after, the house was added on to them …… On the lawn is a well, hidden away by shrubs. All the occupants previous to us got all the water required for the house from this well. The staircase went out of the dining room ....'

There is a photograph of Hill House in the mid 20th century, kindly supplied by the late Ewan Lewis, at Page 55 of my 1991 *Winchmore Hill Lives*. There is another picture at Page 63 of Alan Dumayne's *Fond Memories of Winchmore Hill*. In that book Alan tells us that the house was demolished in 1960.

Quaker Meeting House and Grounds – Plots 75 and 76

Main sources: A letter from Barclays Bank Archive of 20th Feb. 1987; a paper entitled, *Two Hundred and Fifty Years of Winchmore Hill Meeting* from The Journal of Friends Historical Society of 1938; *Essentials of Quakerism* by George H. Gorman and *An Account of Winchmore Hill Meeting* by Archibald King 1938; some pages (presumably from a book) headed *Tottenham Monthly Meeting etc.*; Professor A. David Olver's *Quakerism at Winchmore Hill over 300 years* and *A History of Quakerism at Winchmore Hill*. Peter Brown has kindly supplied the attractive sketch at Plate 22.

Origins: The grounds were originally given to the Friends by John and Elizabeth Oakeley in about 1682. John died two years afterwards and upon the death of Elizabeth, in 1686, a part of the already existing structure was adapted to be a meeting house. The building work was finally completed in 1688. The village was an ideal wooded, out of the way place for the Quakers to have chosen, because at the time they were being persecuted in London.

There is a rich further Quaker history in the area prior to the timespan upon which this book focuses, including the presence of prominent Friends such as the Barclays, of banking fame. I don't intend to dwell on that here, and would refer the reader to my small *A History of Winchmore Hill* (1989), which contains a fair amount of detail, as well as Professor Olver's softbacks.

Plate 22. Peter Brown's sketch of the local Quaker Meeting House

The Meeting House grounds were originally given to the Friends by John and Elizabeth Oakeley in about 1682, with the original building being completed in 1688. That structure was replaced by the current one in 1790, and Peter has captured it well in this sketch he has been kind enough to supply.

The general Quaker situation in our era of interest: Professor Olver tells us that Quakerism might well have withered away as other sects such as the Ranters did, had it not been for the strong organisational structure bequeathed by George Fox (who was no stranger to Winchmore Hill in the late 17th century). This consisted of the Monthly, Quarterly, and Yearly Meetings together with the Meeting for Sufferings. There were also rules of discipline, which became increasingly strict, and led to many disownments, dramatically reducing the membership of the Society. These disownments were for a variety of reasons. Between 1785 and 1789 there were 180 in the London area, of which 91 were for marriages by a priest (i.e. "marrying out"); 17 were for bankruptcy and fraud; 29 were for drinking, gaming or disorderly conduct, and 19 were for immorality. Twenty four were for taking oaths or paying tithes - the tax paid to the local Church of England.

By 1800 there were only about 15,000 Quakers! The community at Winchmore Hill was small. In 1819 there were fewer than 15 families associated with the Meeting, although official returns show that the Meeting House could accommodate 250 persons - presumably because a gallery existed. I have reproduced Friends' Epping Meeting Minutes for 1789 in the diary section of this volume. These show that the local people were being chased hard for not paying Rates, or Tithes to the local Church. Local landowner John Decka of Roseville features prominently in those accounts.

Recently the LB Enfield Museum Service has brought out a small paperback to commemorate the 1807 Act which made it illegal for British ships to be involved in the Slave Trade. This highlighted the role of some of the local Friends in the abolitionist movement of the time, four of the campaigners being buried on Church Hill. These four are John Fothergill (1712 – 1780), Joseph Woods (1738 – 1812), John Barclay Junior (1729 – 1809) and Samuel Hoare Jnr. (1751 – 1825).

Building Developments: Let's return to the subject of the original building. This was rustic, if not barn like, in character, for as late as 1757 there was a charge for 'straw and thatch' of 19s 4d. In 1758 the ground was properly drained at a cost of £18, which was defrayed by both David Barclay senior and junior, Joseph Freame, and Jonathan Bell. In 1787 a report was made that the premises and the walls of the burial ground were in a ruinous condition, and so they decided on a rebuild. The new Meeting House was completed in the Seventh Month, 1790, at a cost of about £700, which was raised by special subscription. Of the 39 Friends who subscribed to the building of the present Meeting House in 1790, 27 are buried there, and their graves are listed in the existing records.

A caretaker's cottage, now the Small Meeting Room, Lobby and upstairs room were added in 1796; a Washhouse, now the kitchen, was built in 1809. It was also in 1796 that a special fund for the care and maintenance of Winchmore Hill Meeting House was set up. David Barclay, Isaac Smith, Samuel Hoare, junior and Joseph Osgood, gave £100 each to be invested, the interest to be used to pay a shilling a week to the resident doorkeeper (in addition to the Monthly Meeting allowance for taking care of the building and keeping the ground in decent order), with the remainder to be used for repairs as needed. This fund was further increased in 1830 by £100 from Robert Barclay, in 1838 by an extra £100 from John Osgood Freame, and in 1858 by £100 from Lydia Catchpool.

The Burial Grounds: By 1821 the upper part of the Burial Ground, near the road, was full and so they started to use the lower part, which had previously been used for grazing. Until then the lower part of the Burial Ground was let as an allotment to a number of tenants, including Charles Bartholomew, who owned Enclosure Plot 71 a few yards down 'Church Hill'. At Figure 2 is a plan of the grounds in 1798.

There are records of some 450 burials in the lower ground and of at least 1,000 in the whole area since 1684. In 1796, when Friend Samuel Hoare was laid to rest in this then rural spot, James Jenkins wrote in his Diary that "Winchmore Hill is the Westminster Abbey of the Friends of Middlesex where our Kings, Statesmen & Poets repose".

The Barclays are conspicuously represented in the old grounds. A group of four headstones is preserved near the Church Hill entrance. The oldest is that of David Barclay and reads *David Barclay of Cheapside. Son of Apologist. Born 1682. Died 1769.* The Apologist was the name given to Robert Barclay of Ury in Scotland because he had written a major book, published in 1676, called *An Apology for the True Christian Divinity, at the same time is held forth and preached by the people called in scorn Quakers.*

A second headstone reads *John Barclay (son of D. Barclay), Born 1728. Died 1787.* He was known as John Barclay of Cambridge Heath, and was connected to the banking firm. A third tombstone nearby reads *Susannah Barclay (wife of Jn. Barclay). Born 1739. Died 1805.* The fourth headstone reads *David Barclay. Son of D. Barclay. Born 1729. Died 1809.* He was known as David Barclay of Walthamstow and Youngsbury, and was a partner in the Bank.

Robert Barclay (1758 - 1816), as well as his son of the same name (1785-1853) are also buried in the grounds. So too is Robert Barclay of Bury Hill (1751-1830) who was the nephew of David Barclay of Cheapside. However, he did not come into the bank, but instead became the co-owner of the *Anchor Brewery* in Southwark, later to be known as Courage Brewery.

Other worthies buried there in this era include John Fothergill (1780) a leading doctor of his time, being Physician to George II and III, and founder of Ackworth School. He was buried at Winchmore Hill, it is said for the sake of privacy, but 70 coaches and chaises followed his funeral procession! As previously noted, Samuel Hoare, a city merchant and ancestor of Viscount Templewood, was buried in Church Hill in 1796 There is also the record of the burial of two Frenchmen in 1790 - Marquis of Longchamp and Joseph Peter Le Bretham, who was a teacher of languages at Tottenham. They could well have been refugees from the French Revolution.

In 1823 prison reformer Elizabeth Fry recorded in her Journal, "Since I last wrote I have attended Winchmore Hill Meeting to my satisfaction together with my dear Sister Elizabeth, Wm. Allen and my Brother Samuel whose company I enjoyed." Her family, the Gurneys, were interrelated with the Barclays, who long had country residences in the area, presumably mainly in Quaker's Row, off Bush Hill.

We have noted earlier that in the early 19th century there was a dip in Quaker membership both nationally and locally, but one couple who were local stalwarts for a number of years were John and Lydia Catchpool, faithful members from 1803-58. The Monthly Meeting testimony to John Catchpool describes him as a corn chandler and baker at Winchmore Hill and says, 'he was a constant attender of the small Meeting held in that village'. Lydia left £100 to the Trustees of Winchmore Hill Meeting. John is listed in the 1826 Pigot's Directory, and there is more on his family in that section. There is more on the Monthly Meetings in the diary section, including the rebuilding of the Meeting House.

Plots 56 + 57 - The Cordwainers' Company

I have covered the Cordwainers' Company in the section on the land ownership schedule. The name 'cordwainer' is derived from 'cordwan', which is a fine, soft, durable, goatskin leather which came from Cordova in Spain. This leather was much in demand, and in due course shoemakers became known as Cordwainers. By Elizabethan times the rich woodland round the village had been used, amongst other things, to provide charcoal for the tanners of Edmonton, who would no doubt have supplied the shoe industry. So perhaps it is not too great a surprise to see that the shoe makers had land in the heart of the old village.

Plot 57 consisted of three houses and an orchard, classified as pasture in the 1801 Schedule. We appear to have more information regarding the three houses at this time. In the Guildhall Library one of the documents filed under Ms. 14, 365 has a front cover which says, "County of Middlesex. The Master Wardens and Commonalty of the Mystery of Cordwainers. Certificate of the Contract for the Redemption of Land Tax. Duly Registered the 25th day of July 1799.' I have extracted the following from the document,

'Tax Office - Know all men that we Rici Davies Esquire Thomas Bennett Clarke two of the commissioners appointed for the purposes of an Act, intituled An Act for making perpetual, subject to Redemption and Purchase in the Manner therein stated, the several sums of money now charged in Great Britain as a Land Tax for one Year, from the Twenty-fifth Day of March One Thousand Seven Hundred and Ninety - eight, for the County of Middlesex do hereby certify, that in the Execution of the said Act, and of two other Acts for extending the Powers of said Act, and for explaining and

153

amending the same, we have contracted with the Master Wardens and Commonalty of the Mystery of Cordwainers of London ??? for the Redemption by them of Four Pounds Four Shillings and three pence & three farthings Land Tax, being the Land Tax charged upon the several messuages or tenements and premises, with the Appurtenances, herein after described, and assessed as follows viz .....

..... The Messuage or Tenement, Outhouses, Garden, a Close of Pasture, with the Appurtances, situate at Winchmore Hill, in the Parish of Edmonton aforesaid, in the occupation of Weathman .... £0.16s.10¼ d; The Messuage or Tenement and Garden with the Appurtances, situate at Winchmore Hill, in the Parish of Edmonton aforesaid, in the occupation of Kent .... £0. 5s. 7½ d; The Messuage or Tenement, Garden and Close of Meadow or Pasture, with the Appurtances, situate at Winchmore Hill, in the Parish of Edmonton aforesaid, in the occupation of Morrison .... £0. 5s. 7$^1/_2$ d ....
.... The Consideration for the Redemption is declared to be so much of lawful Money of Great Britain to be paid to the Receiver - General, or his Deputy, for the said County of Middlesex as according to the Current Price of Stock, transmitted to such Receiver-General, will be sufficient to purchase One Hundred and Fifty Four Pounds Eleven Shillings and 5¾ Capital Stock in the Three Pounds per Centum Consolidated Bank Annuities, on the Twelfth Day of June Instant such Price to be estimated according to the Current Price of Stock transferred in the Week preceding the Above Day.

Dated at the Session House Clerkenwell Green this First Day of June 1799. Witness our Hands and Seals, R. Davies and Thomas Bennett.'

These must be the three cottages on The Green, as the only other land owned by the Cordwainers in Winchmore Hill was an allotment on what had been the Chase, and this isn't shown as having any property on. We can only surmise as to whether the Morrison in the third property was related to the Mrs Morrison who owned Plot 58 adjoining the Cordwainers' Plot 56.

Mrs. Morrison's Plot 58

The ownership schedule indicates that Sarah Morrison's ¾ acre consisted of 'houses and garden'. We know little else about this Plot from literature of the time, but it is possible to speculate about the nature of the buildings from various sources.

At page 64 of my *A History of Winchmore Hill* is a picture of Mummery's on The Green, prior to its demolition in 1912. There is another picture at Page 38 of Alan Dumayne's *Fond Memories of Winchmore Hill*. This shop, a hundred years ago, faced onto The Green at right angles to Woodside and Rowantree House. The shop was formerly known as 'Udall's' or 'Udall & Childs'. Pigot's 1826 Directory lists, 'Udall John, draper. haberdasher, grocer, & tea dir.'

The Recorder for Palmers Green, Winchmore Hill and Southgate of 13th February 1913 contained an article by Henrietta Cresswell, headed 'Udall & Childs – A Reminiscence'. It reads, 'When my father John Cresswell, came to Winchmore Hill, in 1842, Udall's shop was not in the house recently pulled down, but opposite to 'Woodside' or 'Rowantree House', on the site of the present stables of 'The Limes', but before he married, in 1853, the business had been removed to the larger premises. All this property belonged to a family named Ostcliffe, and no doubt they were as deeply engaged in the smuggling trade as their neighbours, as it was in secret places at the side of the skylight in Mummery's shop that the hoard of lace and silk was found some time in the late sixties.

When the Udalls moved to the large shop they gave up the grocery, which (as in many a country village) had been carried on in one side of their small premises, and retained only the more important linen drapery. Ostcliffe had the grocery business in the shop at the Wood Corner, afterwards kept by Mr. Adams, and I have often heard that all the cellarage and some passages really communicated with Child's shop, though doors were papered over or hidden. It was all an old rabbit warren of a place. The portico and flagged pathway no doubt belonged to the old house behind, and a shop front was added.

Mr. and Mrs. Udall died before I can remember anything …… Some time ago it was stated in the *Recorder* that Charles Lamb (see Plate 64) frequently visited Udall's. This must have been the little old shop long since demolished, as he died in 1834, years before the business was removed to Mummery's.'

We know that later in the 19th century, Wood Corner was the area behind Mummery's. The premises are shown on the 1895 OS Map. On that map are the main buildings of The Limes opposite Woodside/Rowantree, but far removed from the path between them. However, two much smaller structures are shown in the grounds of The Limes by the pathway, near where a small building is shown on the Enclosure map where Plots 57 and 58 meet. Presumably one or both of these were the stables to The Limes in 1895, and the small 1801 building was the site of the original Udall smuggling operation. Possibly the horse shoe shaped premises of Plot 58, just north of Plot 163, could be the larger premises to which the Udalls later moved.

One assumes that the Ostcliffe Miss Cresswell mentions might be a relation to the similarly named Ostliffe, who in 1801 was a co – owner of the nearby *King's Head*. In an era when names were even more loosely spelt than today, the possibility can't be discounted.

The front page of *The Recorder for Palmers Green, Winchmore Hill and Southgate* of 21st December 1911 featured a photograph of Mummery's and an article headed, 'An Old Landmark Going'. The article ran,

'One by one the things which make this district so different from that which the suburban builder is engaged in obliterating are disappearing, to the sorrow and regret of most of us. One of the things of which we are all so proud is the ancient houses in this district, standing amid all that is so new and garish ….. Winchmore Hill is about to lose one of its venerable and historically interesting houses ….. Prominent at Wood Corner stands Mr. Mummery's house and shop ….. This old house has stood the changes and chances of three centuries at least ….. Beyond the evidence of some part of the interior, there is no proof of such a great age ….. At the back of the (Mummery's) old house and shop are some cottages, which are also coming down. Part of these cottages was once a Baptist and Methodist chapel, and in one of them the old pulpit steps are still preserved'

These cottages were 19th century structures known as Woodside Cottages, and in her *Memories of a Lost Village* Miss Cresswell says, 'Before 1842 there was an Independent Chapel where Woodside Cottages now stand, and from the numbers of bones found of persons who had been buried in or near it, it is probable it stood there for a long period.'

The Barnes family notes on old families of the village say that Jacob Yallowley (2) came to Winchmore Hill in about 1797, and bought the Leasehold Independent Meeting, next to property owned by John Radford, sometime before Yallowley's death in 1801. (Radford doesn't feature in the Enclosure Ownership Schedule.) The Barnes family say it was situated where Woodside Cottages later stood.

This must mean that it was one of the buildings shown on the south side of plot 58, on what would now be the north side to the start to Broad Walk.

The first Independent Chapel in Winchmore Hill is pictured at Plate 23 We are not sure when that sketch was made, but it looks too large to be the small western most premises on Plot 58, so one must presume it is the larger more easterly ones. Were Yallowley and Radford just sub - tenants of Mrs. Morrison? Perhaps they were not well publicised because non Conformists didn't want to draw attention to themselves as far as 'the authorities' were concerned, the Test Act still being in force.

In their *History of Winchmore Hill United Reformed Church 1742 – 1991* Jacob's daughter – in law, 'Old Grandma Yallowley' (1781 – 1844) is quoted by Ramsbotham et al as remembering the Conventicle as being old when she knew it as a child in 1785. She later wrote that it was subject to a lease that ended in 1841. Leases were conventionally for 99 years, so tentatively fixing the date of origin for the Conventicle at 1742.

Plate 23. The old Independent Chapel on The Green

We don't know when this sketch dates from, but during the period 1780 – 1830 it is believed that the old Independent Chapel was situated on The Green. Unfortunately there is no sign of such a chapel anywhere in Winchmore Hill on the Enclosure maps, or in the associated ownership schedule. Perhaps it was on Mrs. Morrison's Plot 58, to it's SE corner. The building to the viewer's right might therefore be what became Mummery's

Just to briefly cover the Independent's subsequent local history, the church moved a couple of times. On 13th August 1844 The New Independent Chapel was opened 30′ back from the east side of Hopper's Lane, just north of where the skew railway bridge now stands. It was, apparently, a large white brick building with pinnacles of the Gothic variety. Somehow the old Conventicle must have come into John Radford's possession because in 1848 he pulled it down! The current structure, in Compton Road, came into use in 1874 under the ministry of the Rev. John Mark, because the land the Hoppers Lane Chapel was on was needed for the new railway (opened 1871). In 1972 it became known as the United Reformed Church.

Plate 24. Ye olde view looking south on The Upper Green

This old snap looking south on the Upper Green, kindly supplied by Pauline Holstius, captures, Rowantree and Woodside, to the viewer's extreme right, which today stand at the start of Broad Walk. (See Plate 26) The building just to the left of these, partly shielding them from the observer, is today a Dentist. (See Plates 25 & 26) These were all on the Doree family's Plot 164 at Enclosure. The row of cottages to the east of these, set back from the road, were also quite possibly in existence at Enclosure. Ann Dale's Plot 166 contained the next property to the viewer's left, a later view, not long before its demise, being at Plate 27.

I would put forward, then, a theory that Udall's business in the early 19th century was in the small building at the junction of Plots 57 and 58. The larger premises on Plot 58, which are horse shoe shaped in plan, were at that time partly used as the Independent Chapel, being in a sub lease. The old Chapel moved to Hopper's Lane in 1844, the old building being demolished by Radford in 1848, pieces being preserved in the then new Woodside Cottages. It was probably then that the Udalls moved to the adjoining part of the old horse shoe building, fronting the Green. The land perviously occupied by the Chapel became the site of the shop and cottages known as Wood Corner.

Plot 164 – Rowantree/Woodside and The Dentist on The Green

At Plate 24 is an old view of the Upper Green from the north which to the west (the viewer's right) captures Rowantree, Woodside and the associated premises (now used as a dentist's). The rear of the latter, which were probably in existence at the time of Enclosure, are shown from the south, at Plate 25, in a snap the occupiers kindly let me take in 1990. Plate 26 is a photograph I took of the buildings in February 2006.

Plate 25. Rear view of the Dentist on The Upper Green

I took this rear view of the Dentist in September 1990 by kind permission of the owners. It was probably in existence at the time of Enclosure, at the NE corner of Magdalene Teresa Doree's Plot 164.

The house and garden at Plot 164 is listed in the Enclosure ownership schedule as belonging to Magdalene Teresa Doree. The grounds of about 1½ acres were indicated as being used for pasture. There is no mention of the little erection at the NE corner of the Plot. For the rest of this section I have relied heavily on the writing of Tom Mason. *The Gazette* of 30th April 1948 featured an article by him on the property, whilst in that same year he also covered it in his book entitled, *A Southgate Scrapbook.*

Plate 26. Front view of the Dentist, plus the adjoining Rowantree and Woodside

that I took in 2006.

Mason explains that because his son at that time owned Rowantree, he had been given the chance to examine the deeds to that property, which in its earlier years was joined with the neighbouring Woodside (furthest from The Green) as one property. In its early days the deeds also included the nucleus of the premises next door (now part of the dentist's). The earliest deed was dated 1786, but that deed made mention of six previous owners or tenants, one of whom bore the name Richard Guy. The cost of the property in 1786 was £250.

A William Cobb sold the property to Jacob Doree of 'Windsmore Hill', and at that time the cottage (now part of the dentist's) was occupied by Mary Taylor (possibly a relative of the Elizabeth Taylor listed in the Enclosure Ownership Schedule). By the time of the disafforestation of Enfield Chase, by the Act of 1777, the property was officially in the hands of Magdalene Teresa Doree and, as a freeholder, she had a right of common on the Chase. She thus received an allotment as compensation for the loss of her rights. This was Plot 1584 in the angle between Green Dragon Lane and 'Wades Hill'.

The house then seems to have gone back into the ownership of husband Jacob Dore(e), who made the Will of 1790, quoted in the diary section for that year. He left the property to a cousin with the surname of Levesque, who in turn bequeathed it to his three daughters. Two of them married, their names becoming Gosselin and Dupray. All these names sound typical of Huguenots. None of the Levesques lived at 'Rowantree', and it was let to various tenants. One of them was the son of the man who assassinated Prime Minister Spencer Perceval in the lobby of the House of Commons in 1812 (see Plate 61). The son changed his name from Bellingham to his mother's maiden name of Neville, and came to live at this house in Winchmore Hill. (See, also, the diary section for 1812.)

By 1883 the main house was in the hands of John James Butson, the builder who erected Compton Terrace in Hoppers Road. He divided the house into two sometime between 1883 and 1889. The part nearest The Green he named 'Rowantree House', and the other retained the original name of 'Woodside'. The adjoining shop

159

and cottage became vacant, and he let then to Mr. G. Richards, a draper of Shepherds Bush, for £40 per annum on a lease of 21 years.

Since Butson, who seems to have occupied 'Rowantree' until 1894, the houses have had various owners, and during the latter part of the Second World War Rowantree was used as HQ by 'D' Coy. of the 26th Batt, Middlesex Regiment, Home Guard for over two years.

In October 1999 I picked up a brochure on the five bedroomed Grade 11 Rowantree House from Anthony Pepe & Co. It was being offered at £725,000 Freehold. The entrance hall had a coved ceiling, with a door to a wine cellar, and another to an inner lobby, leading to a garden. There was a downstairs cloakroom, with a hand basin to go with a low flush WC. There were two Reception Rooms, front and rear, both exceeding 13' x 15'. They each had sach windows, coved ceilings and open fireplaces. The Kitchen/Diner was 18' 10" x 10' 10" with a sash window. The downstairs Utility Room was 8' 2" x 7'.

The first floor landing had a 13' 6" x 12' 6" bedroom with sash windows, an original fireplace, and en suite bathroom. On the first floor were a bathroom and two bedrooms. One was 13' 6" x 13' 2", with sash windows and original fireplace. The second was 10' 7" x 8' 11" with sash windows. The second floor landing boasted two bedrooms as well. One was 12' 8" x 12' 7" with sash windows, and the other was 14' x 12' 8" with sash windows, a roof window and an original fireplace. The south facing rear garden was approximately 150' x 42'.

Braze Nose College's Plot 165

The area's link with Brazenose College is outlined in the land ownership section of this book. This Plot, of about three quarters of an acre, is indicated as containing three cottages and gardens. Today to the immediate east of the dental surgery is Cookley House, which was built by the father of the late Lucy Pettifer (nee Maynard) in the late 1920s, the first Kelly's Directory listing being in the 1929 edition. This replaced a row of old cottages, which must be the ones set back from the Upper Green in the old photograph at Plate 24. One suspects that these remained from the Enclosure period.

Plot 166 - Michael Dale (Trustee for Ann Dale) - 'Aldridge's'

The corner where The Upper Green meets Hopper's Lane, is marked as Ann Dale's 166 - 'House and yard'. (The bulk of her land in Winchmore Hill was the area just south of the lane that became Compton Road, forming the basis of what became the Highfield House Estate.)

At Page 49 of my *More Winchmore Hill Lives* is a 1938 sketch by a Mr. Rutherford of Aldridge's greengrocer on The Green. 'Memorabilia', writing in the 4th November 1938 edition of *The Palmers Green and Southgate Gazette*, says, 'The weatherboard cottage is considerably older than the shop, which is quite old enough to be venerable for a building of that description, and was built on the forecourt, which is quite obviously shown on the sketch .....' *The Palmers Green and Southgate Gazette* of 16th June 1938 carried an article by 'Memorabilia' that concentrated on the area towards the top of Eversley Park Road and the *Chase Side Tavern*. However, it also says that, ' .... About that time I mentioned to Mr. F. Aldridge that weaving had been carried on in his premises about seventy years previously. He at once said "Quite right, I own this place now and it is recorded in the deeds which go back for a period of about 180 years".....'

Plate 27. Anthony Cope Ltd. on The Green

At one time this had been Aldridge's the greengrocer, as featured at Page 49 of my More Winchmore Hill Lives, but by the time I took this snap in 1989 it had clearly had a 'makeover'. Mr. Aldridge once told The Gazette that the old deeds suggested an origin in about 1760, and so it would have been one of the buildings marked at Plot 166 at the time of Enclosure. The Old Bakery in Hoppers Road, featured at Plate 16, is in the background.

As the building dated from about 1760, Plot 166 must have contained 'Aldridge's'. It can be seen at Plate 24, being the first building flush with the street to the left (east) of the old cottages set back from The Green. The houses to its east, flush with it, were probably built after Enclosure. Plate 27 'kills two birds with one stone', being a view of 'Plot 166' on 29th July 1989, which also managed to capture the old bakery (Plot 186) in the background.

John Barnes's Plot 167 – The Salisbury Arms?

Plot 167, of about a quarter of an acre, is described in the ownership schedule as 'two houses and gardens'. At Plate 28 is a picture of 'the old *Salisbury Arms*', which was replaced by the current building, slightly to its south, in the mid 1930s. In my 1991 *Winchmore Hill Lives* Mr. Harry Finch (b. 1907) says that in about 1920 it, 'was only a small wooden country pub with one bar and a billiard room.' In the same book Mrs. Nancy Hicks (nee Andrew) describes it as, 'an old "spit and sawdust" establishment with a billiard table.'

The *Palmers Green and Southgate Gazette* of 31st January 1936 contained a photograph of Hoppers Road looking north, up the west side, from the triangle of grass at the top of Compton Road. This followed the then recent rebuilding of *The Salisbury Arms*. 'Memorabilia's' accompanying article told us that, 'On the left of our picture is part of the Hoppers Road front of the new *Salisbury Arms*, and Mr. Stockton's new premises. Thence towards the Green are the old *Salisbury Arms*. Mr. Stockton's (old) butcher's shop, Nos. 1 and 2 Esther Cottages .... Even the old *Salisbury Arms* is almost double its original size and it has the peculiarity that its cellars are not below the house but under Mr. Stockton's (old) butcher's shop, at the rear of which, and in whose yard, is the flap and slope down which barrels are lowered. The property is old and has obviously been built at different periods, some of the upper rooms are lofty, others low, and there are variations in floor levels. Mr. Stockton courteously showed me over his

161

premises of which (an aged villager some 35 years or more ago informed me) the shop and cellars were once the *Salisbury Arms*. That would account for the tenancy of the cellars still pertaining to the public house.'

Ḥoppers Road, Winchmore Ḥill.

Plate 28. Ye olde Salisbury Arms

This picture is taken from an undated postcard. This is the old 'spit and sawdust' version of the pub before its rebuilding in the mid 1930s. In early 1936 The Gazette received a letter from a descendent of the first landlord of this Inn who said that it was originally a butcher's shop until about 1852, when the writer's grandfather built a new one just to its north, and converted the old one into a pub. It seems likely that the Horsey family was the one involved, and that the premises were on John Barnes's' Plot 167 at Enclosure.

The *P.G. & S. Gazette* of 27th February 1936 contained a follow up article by 'Memorabilia' which reported, 'We have received from one of the five counties bordering Middlesex a letter from a descendent of the first landlord of the old *Salisbury Arms* ...... (it) was originally a butcher's shop until about 1852, when my grandfather built a new butcher's shop, now occupied by Mr. Stockton, and converted the old into a public house. Why it was called the *Salisbury Arms* I cannot tell you ... .'.

The minutes of the Court Baron of 12th June 1821 tell us that at the Court of 13th Oct. 1803 John Decka had been admitted as a Copyhold tenant upon his purchase of 'Hereditaments' from John Barnes – presumably Plot 167. In his books on the Borough's pubs Gary Boudier lists the first landlord of the Inn as being William Horsey in 1855. The 1826 Pigot's Directory lists a Charles Horsey as butcher in the village. So it seems likely that the Horsey family started the Inn, quite possibly in the premises which were owned by John Barnes in 1801.

In May 2009, with the book at the printers, I came across file ACC/1016/219 at the London Metropolitan Archives. This is titled, 'Correspondence concerning the extinguishing of manorial incidents on the *Salisbury Arms* and the adjoining butcher's shop in Hopper's Road, Winchmore Hill, held by the Misses Francis and Maria Horsey and Mr. Edward Horsey.' One letter on the file, addressed to Messrs H. Seymour Couchman & Son, 520 High Road, Tottenham N17 reads,

'Golding, Hargrave & Golding, 99 Cannon St., London EC4, 27th April

1931. Dear Sirs, (Re:) Edmonton Manor. Butchers Shop & Public House, Winchmore Hill. We wrote to Miss E. Horsey to ask if she would wish to enter into a voluntary agreement for the extinguishment of the Manorial incidents in respect of the above property, and today Messrs. Marson & Toulmin, Solicitors of 1, Southwark Bridge Road, SE called upon us representing the Misses Frances Ellen Horsey and Maria Horsey, and Mr. Edward William Horsey, the tenants on the Court Rolls, inquiring what would be the cost of extinguishing the Manorial incidents by a voluntary agreement.

We asked them if they could supply us with the ages of the tenants, and they estimated that the average of the three tenants would be 85. Based on these ages will you kindly inform us the amount which would be payable as Lord's compensation to extinguish the Manorial incidents, and your fees in the matter, and then, of course, we can add the compensation payable to the Steward, and the costs. Yours faithfully - Golding, Hargrove & Golding.'

In later papers it became clear that at least one Miss Horsey lived in Hatfield, and that Messrs. H. Seymour Couchman & Son were the Lord of the Manor's agents, Steward and Solicitors. The sum needed to extinguish the Copyhold Manorial incidents was £50. 12s. 6d. Everything seems to have been resolved by Christmas 1931.

Plate 29. Belmont House, Hoppers Road

On the viewer's far right are Salisbury Cottages, which were demolished in the mid 1930s to make way for the rebuilding of The Salisbury Arms. The next building along, bearing a resemblance to Devon House (in Church Hill), was Belmont House which, the Victoria County History (VCH) says, was built in the 18th century. This must therefore have been the house listed for William Phillips's Plot 169 at the time of Enclosure.

In a letter of 2nd July 1931 the butcher's shop is described as, 'of similar construction to the Salisbury Arms, and possesses a frontage of about 36' to Hoppers Road. 1st Floor = 3 bedrooms + 1 sitting room, bathroom with geyser. Ground Floor = Shop, living room, kitchen with range, scullery, outside W.C. Outbuildings inc. slaughter house, 2 sheep pens, refrig. room with 2 lofts over. Inn = 3 beds, 1 sitting room, 1st floor 4 + 1 Attic. Ground Floor = Public Bottle & Saloon Bars, Billiard Room, Living Room,

Scullery with bath, sink & copper, Beer store and a large cellar which extends under the adjoining Butcher's shop. Outside urinal, separate W.C., very small yard.'

Nathaniel Lucas's Plot 168

Plot 168 is listed as a house and garden. At Plate 29 is a view, from a bygone age, of 'Hoppers Road' looking south from just north of the Chestnut tree at the top of 'Compton Road'. The first buildings on the right, with a pale exterior, look very much like Salisbury Cottages captured at Page 48 of my *A Look at Old Winchmore Hill*. They are physically positioned where Lucas's house is, but their design, with two front doors, is not that of a converted house, so it seems likely that they were built later.

William Phillips's Plot 169

This is listed as 'House & c.', and is a site of about a quarter of an acre, stretching south of Plot 168. The position of the house appears to approximate to that of the brick house south of Salisbury Cottages at Plate 29. Regnart, in his *Memories of Winchmore Hill*, tells us that late in the 19th century, 'Opposite the junction with Compton Road was a very picturesque old red brick house, Belmont House, which was once a girls' school kept by Miss Tebb. Then came half a dozen cottages and finally Eaton's yard....' The pictured house is surely old Belmont House. To me it bears a slight resemblance to Devon House, so it does not surprise me that the VCH says that it was built in the 18th century. This must have been Mr. Phillips's 1801 abode.

As previously stated, Plots east of 'Wades Hill' and Hopper's Lane are covered in other map sections. So I will now look at the west side of 'Wades Hill', starting towards its northern end. Immediately to the south of Tash's *Hoppet* at Plot 70 was a small Plot (103) owned by Rachael Marshall, described as a 'cottage and garden'. Plot 102 to the west and south of Marshall's Plot 103 was owned by David Cressee Snr., and consisted of two tenements (on the southern leg) and an orchard. There are a number of old cottages remaining in this stretch of Wades Hill, but I don't know whether any of these might be Ms. Marshall's and Cressee's former properties.

Plot 74 – Mrs. Teshmaker's 'house and garden' – Glenwood House?

Peter Hodge says in his 'Winchmore Hill; Historic Walks in Conservation Area No. 1', written for L.B. Enfield Libraries in 1973, that Glenwood House (Plate 30) dates from the 18th century. He confirmed this century of origin in his notes on the rear of the 1987 Southgate Civic Trust's reprint of the 1865 OS Map of the village, saying that it was from early in that century. However, the VCH puts its origins in the early 19th century. The house was used for a while as St. Paul's Vicarage in that century.

Mr. D. Grammer was born at Glenwood House in 1925 and was kind enough to contribute to my 1991 *Winchmore Hill Lives*. In it he says that there were two cusps in the lead in the roof of Glenwood from which it was possible to survey the neighbourhood. One of these cups bore the inscribed date of 1842, though that, of course, is not necessarily indicative of when the whole structure was built.

In his account Mr. Grammer goes on to tell us a bit more about the building's interior, saying, 'Glenwood consists of a three-roomed attic and three other storeys (the ground, first and second floors). Each of these storeys has but two rooms, one facing to the front, the other to the rear. In my day these all had extensive pine panelling which had been painted over. Below the ground floor was a large cellar, next to which was a coal cellar, and a large "walk-in" pantry. The rear garden backed onto the Quaker burial ground. I did not have to go far to attend my preparatory school. Keble

House School, as you know, stands next door, and in those days the school building was closer to the roadway. It was demolished in the mid 1930s and the present structure was erected behind it. Miss Harper started the school in 1929....'

Plate 30. Glenwood House, Wades Hill

I took this photograph on a fine July afternoon in 2006. Keble House School stands next door to your right. Peter Hodge of the Southgate Civic Trust dates Glenwood House to the 18th century, though the Victoria County History says that it was built in the 19th century.

The *Palmers Green and Southgate Gazette* of 6th January 1939 contained an article on Hill House which also touched on Keble House School. The article featured a drawing by Rutherford showing the old building, which had previously been known as *The Elms*. This is reproduced at Plate 31. The shape of Mrs. Teshmaker's 'House and garden' at Plot 74 can be traced to the 1865 O.S. Map, where it seems to have been broken into two properties, and the situation remained unchanged at the time of the 1895 O.S. Map. I think Peter Hodge is probably right with his 18th century dating.

Plot 80 – The King's Head – and Devon House?

In his *Enfield Pubs Part 2* Gary Boudier tells us that the earliest licensee he could find for *The King's* Head was Abraham Jones in 1722, but at the time of the land ownership schedule the landlady was an M. Newman. He tells us that on 5th May 1766 *The King's Head* was to be sold by auction, the advertisement for which contained, '..... There has been built within these few years an additional modern building to the said dwelling - house, and finished in the present taste: whereof there are one room which will dine about 80 people, lodging rooms for about 20 beds, stabling for 20 horses. The whole premises put into thorough repair and made very convenient. Also to be sold are the leases for two messuages adjoining the property, and a large garden, presently occupied by Mr. Cox, gents and others.'

The land ownership schedule indicates that Plot 80, of about a quarter of an acre, was owned by Beckett and Ostliffe, who also owned *The Cock* (now a Polish pub) and *The King's Arms* - two other pubs south of the old village. This version of *The King's Head* was illustrated at page 6 to my *A Look at Old Winchmore Hill* and was demolished in May 1898, being rebuilt at a cost of £8,000. The elegant new building was pictured in colour on the front cover to my 1989 paperback *A History of Winchmore Hill*.

plate 31. keble house in the 1930s

These drawings by Rutherford are reproduced by kind permission of The Gazette. Glenwood can just be seen to the viewer's left in the upper drawing. The old building was known as The Elms, and was demolished in the mid 1930s, with the current Keble House School having been erected behind it.

166

Plate 32. 1989 photograph of Devon House

The newly refurbished Devon House is clearly within only a few yards of The King's Head. Even allowing for the fact that this incarnation of the pub replaced the one in existence in 1801/2, this suggests that Devon House was probably part of the Beckett and Ostliffe Plot 80 at the time of Enclosure.

The recent photograph at Plate 32 shows clearly that Devon House is within only a few yards of *The King's Head*. Even allowing for the fact that the latter building replaced the one in existence in 1801/2, this suggests that Devon House was possibly part of the Beckett and Ostliffe Plot 80 at the time of Enclosure. William Fox's Plot 79 is too far away. Devon House must be in the 'dog's leg' along Winchmore Hill – lane. So I now think some of my notes at P7 of *A Look at Old Winchmore Hill,* alongside a picture of Devon House from 1933, are in error.

I was fortunate that nearly 20 years ago Mr. D. Kent of Edwards Estates not only gave me a guided tour of Devon House, but also a copy of the research notes his Company had recently compiled at the time of the building's extensive refurbishment. I have used these as the basis of the following, and the bit in the 1819 diary section relating to an inquest held at the Inn. It was on the guided tour that I was able to take the photograph of the old stabling area at Plate 33.

There is actually no mention of a Devon House by name earlier than 1900. The House's porch is considered to be early 18th century in style, as are some of the other architectural features, perhaps dating its origins to somewhere around 1720. The windows in the 1933 photograph are, however, probably Victorian replacements to the originals. In its early days it was possibly structurally connected, by single storey outhouses, to the old Inn.

There is a deed dated 1839 between Wm.Tyall and John Ostliffe Beckett (the bankrupt son of the late brewer Wm. Beckett), and Mary his wife. There is, apparently, a long list of properties (mostly public houses) in Enfield, Edmonton and Winchmore Hill, bequeathed by Wm Beckett dec. to John Ostliffe Beckett including, 'also, of and in all those two freehold messuages or tenements formerly one messuages or tenement one of which is now used as a public house and called, known or distinguished by the name or sign of the *King's Head* with barns, stables, outbuildings, garden and orchards and appurtances to the same messuages belonging or holden therewith situate lying

167

and being in Winchmore Hill parish of Edmonton, county of Middlesex, and abutting upon the Queen's highway ..... ' In 1839 Edward Flowerday was the landlord of the inn.

Plate 33. Old stabling area of Devon House following the 1980s refurbishment

Devon House is thought to possibly date back to 1720. I took this photograph when Mr. Kent of Edwards Estate was good enough to give me a guided tour of the newly refurbished premises in April 1990.

Was the second freehold building what we now call Devon House? From the middle of the 19th century, to the mid 1930s the premises were mainly occupied by butchers and it has been a Grade 2 listed building since 1950. Plate 34 shows Devon House from a Postcard franked 25th April 1903.

Plate 34. Photograph of Devon House from postcard franked 25th April 1903

One wonders if some of the other buildings featured also date back to late Georgian times – or earlier.

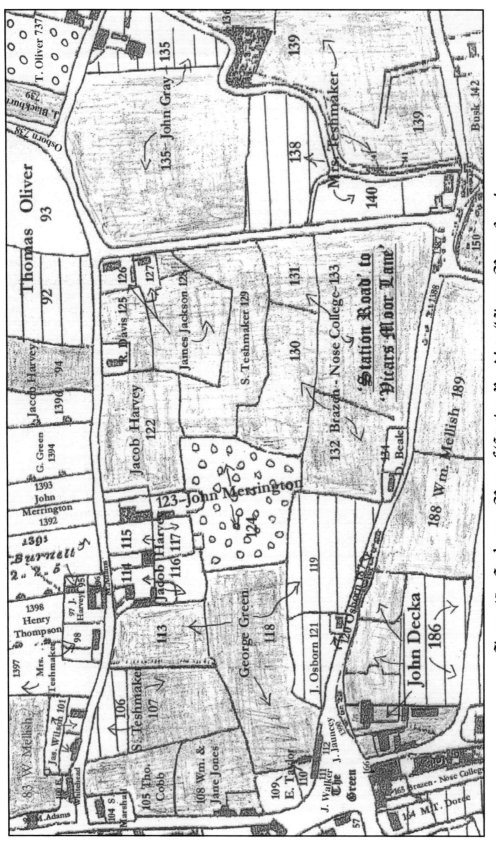

Figure 15. Enclosure Map of 'Station Road' to 'Vicars Moor Lane'

The lane leading off east from The Green is the forerunner of modern day Station Road. Parallel to it, at the north of the map, is the lane which preceded Vicars Moor Lane. Linking these to their west is the north – south trending 'Wades Hill', whilst to their east they are linked by Green Lanes. The shaded fields were meadow, those with horizontal lines were pasture, and those with small circles in were used for arable.

170

'Station Rd.' to 'Vicars Moor Lane' map

In this section I will concentrate on the rectangle defined by the south side (only) of 'Vicars Moor Lane', the west side of Green Lanes, the north side of 'Station Road', and the east side of 'Wades Hill'. The remainder of the area shown in this map I have covered in the notes accompanying other maps.

Plot 104 – Rachael Marshall

This Plot was over a quarter of an acre, consisting of a 'house and garden' on the corner of 'Wades Hill' and 'Vicars Moor Lane'. Percy Lodge stood on this site for many years, until demolished in the early 1930s, and was at one time the home of Sharon Turner (1768 – 1847), a noted historian and friend of the Disraeli family. It is possible that Ms. Marshall's house was, or formed the nucleus of, Percy Lodge.

Roseneath?

Jacob Harvey held the four plots 114/5/6/7 east along 'Vicars Moor Lane'. Plot 115 contained a house with a garden. At the London Metropolitan Archives is document B/MMN/6/39 which states, 'E. Harvey Esq. and Thomas Mann Esq. Deed of Covenant for production of Deeds relating to a Messuage or Cottage pieces of Land and Heredits at Edmonton Middlesex. Dated 13th July 1853.' However the document contains records dating back to 1770. The following is an extract.

'The Schedule to which the foregoing Indenture refers. As to part of hereditments comprised in recited Indenture of even date herewith. 1770 June 5th. Steward's Copy. Court Roll of the Manor of Edmonton of Admission in Court of Samuel Clay Harvey under Surrender and will of Jacob Harvey and do Surrender by him at same Court to the use of his Will.- 1791 Jany. 27th Official Extract of the Will of the said Samuel Clay Harvey-. 1795 May 21st. Attested Copy Court Roll of the same maner (stet) of Admission in Court of Joseph Cooper for his life under Surrender and Will of the said Samuel Clay Harvey. 1798 Nov. 10th. Attested Copy Court Roll of same maner of Admission in Court of Jacob Harvey under the same last mentioned Surrender and Will-. 1803 Oct. 13th Stewards Copy Court Roll of same Maner of Admission out of Court of John Merrington on Surrender of said Jacob Harvey and Surrender of said John Merrington to use of his will. 1807 May 28th. Conditional Surrender out of Court by said John Merrington to the use of Jonathan Bugg. ....'

The last entry is, '1853 May 26th Indenture between Thomas Curtis and Charles Stephen of the first part Sir William Curtis Baronet of the second part and Ebenezer Harvey of the third part ..... Burial certificates of Lady Curtis and Sir William Curtis her son and Declaration of verification annexed.'

At Page 9 of their book on Winchmore Hill Cricket Club Tony and Jennifer Bath say that Thomas Mann purchased Roseneath and its eleven acres of land in 1867. It is possible that the house of Plot 115 formed the nucleus of what became *Roseneath* mansion. It was demolished in 1936.

Plate 35. Exterior view of Hood's Cottage

Also known as Rose Cottage, the premises were occupied by the poet Thomas Hood from 1829 to 1832, though Miss Cresswell suggests that the cottage dates back, at least in part, to the 17th century, or beyond. At the time of Enclosure this was probably John Merrington's house on Plot 123. The bulk of the property was destroyed by a German V2 rocket in 1944.

Plot 123 - John Merrington – Hood's Cottage

John Merrington's half acre Plot contains a 'House and garden'. It is backed by his 3¾ acre field (124) behind, which was given over (unusually in the district at the time) to arable crops. The map indicated a small circle of some kind in the field, which can be traced through to similar features on the 1865 and 1895 O.S. maps. This helps identify Merrington's house as Rose Cottage, home of the poet Thomas Hood from 1829 to 1832 (see Diary section) and illustrated at Plate 35. At Plate 36 is an unusual view of the cottage's rear garden wall, which, unlike the cottage itself, survived the blast from a German V2 rocket that landed in Ringwood Way in November 1944, described in Miss Bowman's account in the 1991 *Winchmore Hill Lives*. The current house bears a Blue Plaque on the front.

Miss Cresswell wrote of the cottage, 'A part of this house is very old, and a vague tradition asserts that Henry Cromwell, son of the Lord Protector, lived here for a time ...... Tom Hood's house, a dear old place, grey fronted and bow windowed, and roofed with shingle tiles red, brown, and mossy. The house still stands, but the east front, which was its oldest part, has been altered. In those days it had long dark passages, unexpected stairs, and mysterious cupboards disguised with wallpaper. There were two enormous pollard elms by the carriage gate, and a large cherry tree in full blossom made a white mass against the after glow in the south eastern sky ..... '

Plate 36. Surviving rear garden wall of Hood's Cottage

Colin and Maureen Clark kindly allowed me to take this photograph of the rear garden wall to their rebuilt version of Hood's Cottage in July 1995. It is one of the small bits of the property to survive the Nazi attack of 1944.

Vicar's Well

Writing in 1819 William Robinson says, 'In the lane leading from Bush Hill, near a little thatched cottage, is a well, called "Vicar's Well", so called from having been enclosed by a vicar of this parish. It is of antiquity, but what was the vicar's name, and in what year he enclosed it, is not at this day known. The water is very pure, always flowing, and was formerly in great estimation among the inhabitants of the adjacent villages.' Miss Cresswell confirms that in Victorian times Vicarsmoor Well was still a major source of the villagers' water supply. The well was marked on the 1865 OS Map as being at the NW corner of the acre field which in 1801 was Plot 125 owned by Robert Davis. Plot 125 housed a cottage. (Alan Dumayne says that in terms of modern geography, the well was located where there is a gulley in the forecourt of the garage to No. 41 Vicars Moor Lane.)

The late David Hicks spent some hours investigating the history of Vicar's Well, and obtained an extract from *A History of Hammersmith based upon that of Thomas Faulkner in 1839* edited by P.D. Whitting in 1965. Thanks to Stewart Christian I have a copy of the extract, which runs, 'In 1645 Thomas Collop left to his niece, Elizabeth Hemmings, two tenements and one acre, called Vicarswell in Edmonton, on condition that she should pay a yearly rent charge of 26/- to be distributed, 6d each Sunday, in bread by the overseers of the Hammersmith Chapel. Later this was incorporated as part of a general fund ...'.

The VCH tells us that the Vikers family had a house in the village in 1349 and David concluded, without giving all his reasoning, that it was this family, rather than a Vicar, who gave the road and the old well their names. This seems credible, and I have no better theory to advance.

Green Lanes

I have no information relating to James Jackson's properties (Plots 126/7) at the corner of 'Vicars Moor Lane' and 'Green Lanes', which today would be opposite *The Green Dragon*. Today's busy Green Lanes was then, of course, but a rural track, which at one time had probably been used as a drove road for cattle from Wales, and other far flung places, to the meat market at Smithfield. Under an Act of 1789 the portion of Green Lanes in Edmonton Parish had been put under the Turnpike Trust looking after Fore Street. Improvements were made by the Trust, but in 1826 responsibility for Green Lanes passed to the Commissioners for Metropolitan Turnpike Roads.

The north side of 'Station Road'

I am unable to shed any light on Daniel Beale's cottage at Plot 134 or Joseph Osborn(e)'s tenements at Plot 120 on the north side of 'Station Road'. With regard to Plots 130/1/2/3 owned by Braze Nose College, I have covered their role in the history of the area, including the naming of modern day Radcliffe Road, in the notes in the ownership schedule. However, I can say a few words about two Plots overlooking The Green.

Plate 37. Old drains to the rear of 14, The Green

The late David Hicks told me of the carefully researched history of his antiques shop, and he invited me to take this picture in June 1996, when he was digging up his rear yard. David believed that his shop and the adjoining Elizabeth on the Green were once part of a single house built in the late 18th century, which had become split into John Walker's two cottages at Plot 111 by the time of Enclosure. These drains were believed to date from the late 18th century.

North Eastern Corner of The Green

In 1801 the Trustees of Elizabeth Taylor owned Plot 109 described as 'Garden before the *King's Head*'. This was opposite the Inn and later in the century was used for its beer garden, which even at this early stage might have been its function.

Plot 110 also belonged to the Trustees of Elizabeth Taylor in 1801 and consisted of 'Four houses and gardens'. These houses are the small, barely discernable, terrace along the eastern edge of the Plot. Plot 111 was owned by John Walker and described as 'Two tenements'. Plot 112 was owned by John Jauncey and described as 'Three tenements and gardens'.

The 'two tenements' of Plot 111 were, I believe, at one time a single residential property that had been split up by the time of the Enclosure Map. Shop fronts were added much later, and in the 1990s the lower 'tenement' was 'Winchmore Antiques' (14, The Green), and the upper was 'Elizabeth of the Green' (No. 16). Parts of these premises are captured at Plates 37 and 38.

One might just add here that in his 1996 *Enfield - Portrait of a London Borough*, Matthew Eccleston says that, 'A remnant of another (probably 18th century) cottage, joined to, but never part of the other two, survives at the back of No.12; and the passageway between it and No.14 (which Miss Cresswell mentions in her book) once provided the access to the village blacksmith's forge, which formerly stood behind these buildings.' Possibly that remnant is part of the row of cottages on the eastern boundary of Elizabeth Taylor's field number 110?

Plot 108 - William and Jane Jones

This Plot of nearly 2 acres, in 1801, was listed as having 'Two tenements and field adjoining'. There is, today, a small row of terraced Georgian houses just north of the shops on the eastern side of Wades Hill, as you leave The Green. Do these appear on the map?

Plate 38. Old cottage face at 16, The Green

At the time of the 1865 O.S. Survey the two cottages that had been John Walker's in 1801 still retained their front gardens. However, the 1895 O.S. Survey showed that the gardens had disappeared, and the cottages now fronted directly onto The Green. In July 2000 the Bowens, who ran the florist shop at No. 16, let me take this view of the front part of the premises. The lower level in the foreground was where there was once garden, the higher level at the rear represents the original floor level of the cottages.

175

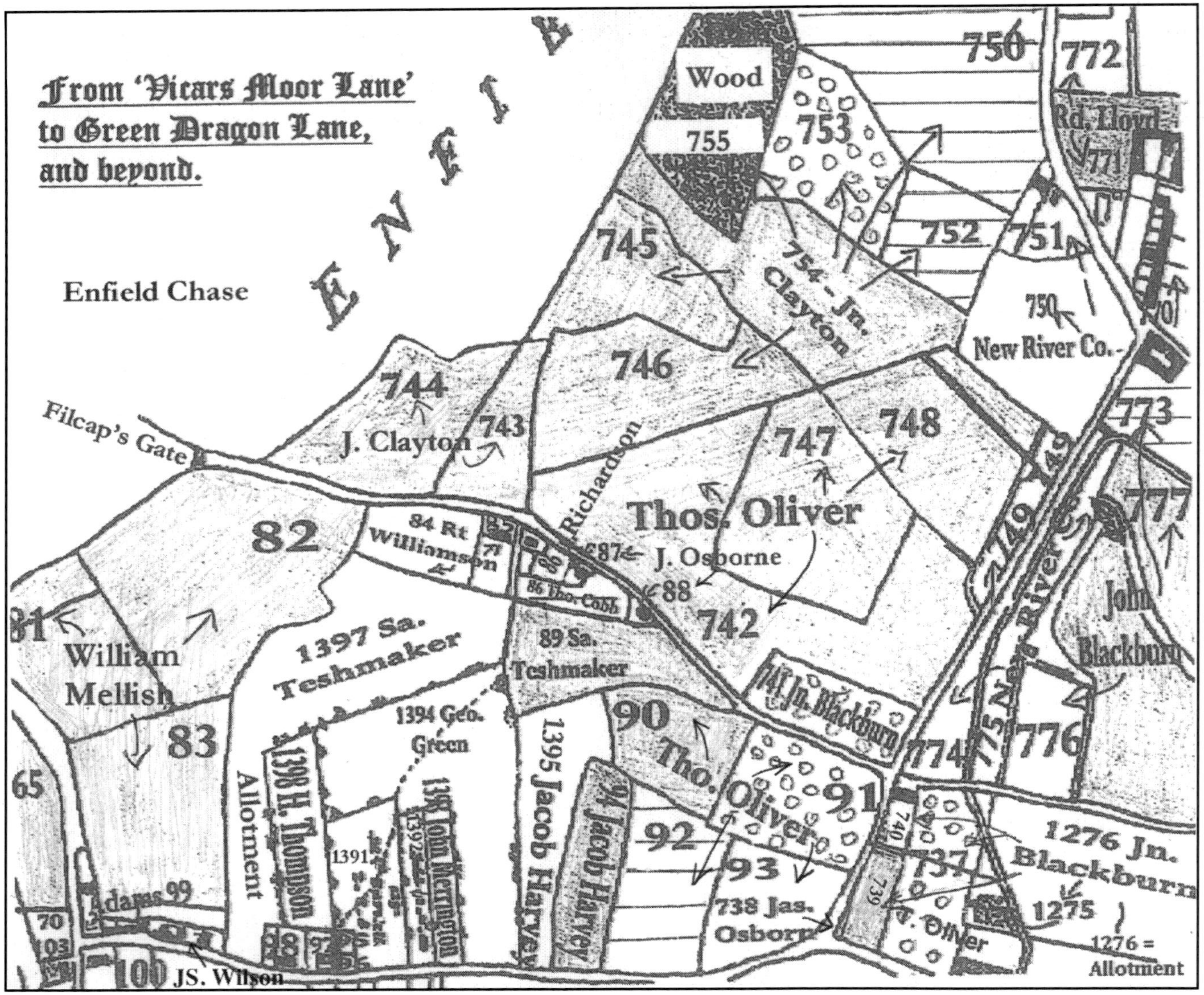

Figure 16. Enclosure Map from 'Vicars Moor Lane' to Green Dragon Lane, and beyond

The track running ESE in the centre of the map is Green Dragon Lane. It meets the NNE trending Bush Hill at Plots 741 and 774, and then continues east along a line similar to the modern day Ridge Avenue. Filcap's Gate, to Enfield Chase, is approximately where today Viga Road meets Green Dragon Lane. Bush Hill, south of its intersection with Green Dragon Lane, is today called Green Lanes. At its southern extremity on this map Green Lanes meets 'Firs Lane' (by Plot 739) and the west running 'Vicars Moor Lane' (by Plot 93). That lane runs all the way up to Plot 99, where it meets with what we now call Wades Hill. The shaded fields were meadow, those with horizontal lines were pasture, and those with small circles in were used for arable.

From 'Vicars Moor Lane' to Green Dragon Lane, and beyond

Quaker's Row

One of the Plots John Blackburn owned, at the top of Bush Hill, was 770 'Houses, yards, gardens, & co. called Quaker's Row', the line of which is followed today by Quakers Walk. Alan Dumayne tells us that the premises were demolished in about 1825 by that other big local landowner, Squire Mellish.

In their extensive book on the Barclay family HF Barclay and A. Wilson – Fox tell us that, 'David Barclay of Cheapside died at his country house, Bush Hill, Winchmore Hill, Middlesex, on March 18th 1769, and was buried in the graveyard attached to the Quaker Meeting House there ..... It is interesting to record that Bush Hill, ... he left to his second surviving son, David (of Walthamstow) .... At his death (30th May 1809) his large fortune, including his interest in the Brewery of Barclay, Perkins & Co., went to his daughter, Agatha, and her husband, Richard Gurney ....'

Although we know from the local Friends Meeting Minutes that various prominent members of the Barclay family lived locally, none are listed in the Land Ownership schedule. Perhaps the Blackburns had bought out the Barclays.

Bush Hill House

John Blackburn lived at Bush Hill House, as it was called for many years. It is shown at Plot 773 at the bend in the line of Bush Hill. In 1798 he had inherited the property from his father, John Blackburn senior, a former army contractor who had made his fortune supplying the Gibraltar garrison during the great siege of 1779 - 83. The mansion was on the site of a previous one that had been owned by Sir Hugh Myddelton, of New River fame. In the mid 1850s the house was briefly the home of Sir Samuel Cunard, the Canadian born shipping magnate. In the 20th century it was used for many years as a home and school for disabled children, and known as Halliwick House. (See, for example, Mrs. Dougal's account in my *More Winchmore Hill Lives*.) The property was demolished in 1993, and replaced by blocks of flats. The grand mansion is captured at P23 of Graham Dalling's, *Southgate and Edmonton Past*. All that now remains is the plaque at Plate 39.

Bush Hill Embankment

The Enclosure map encompasses the Clarendon Arch, which was built in 1682 (and rebuilt in 1725) to enable Salmons Brook to pass under what was then a lead lined wooden aqueduct that ran for a furlong. In 1786 this wooden aqueduct was replaced by the still extant clay embankment, situated principally in Plots 774 and 775, owned by The New River Company. See the section on The New River, as well as the 1784, 1786 and 1788 Diaries.

The Green Dragon Inn

The Victoria County History tells us that a *Green Dragon Inn* had been established by 1750, and Gary Boudier has found record of a James Hound as licensee as early as 1726.

Plate 39. Blue Plaque to Sir Hugh Myddelton at what was Bush Hill House

The Blackburn family lived at Bush Hill House for many years. It is shown at Plot 773 on the Enclosure Map. The mansion was on the site of a previous one that had been owned by Sir Hugh Myddelton, of New River fame. In the 20th century it was a home and school for disabled children, and known as Halliwick House. The property was demolished in 1993, and replaced by blocks of flats. Sadly, all that now remains is this Blue Plaque

In July 1934 *The Gazette* ran an article on *The Green Dragon* by Tom Mason. In it he repeats a local legend whereby in 1780 a highwayman of evil repute was arrested in the bar of *The Green Dragon,* which in those days was situated approximately where Lloyd's Pharmacy is today, at Mason's Corner. As an example to others, the story goes, he was hung on a gallows erected just outside the front entrance to the inn. This was bad for trade, but the landlord was unable to remove the gallows, and so he transferred to very near the current site at the Green Lanes end of 'Vicars Moor Lane'. The '1780 built inn', retained its name from the earlier proximity to Green Dragon Lane, being replaced by the existing structure in 1894. There is a section on this second incarnation of the Inn at Pages 55/6 of my *A Look at Old Winchmore Hill.*

Mason's *Gazette* article informs us that when the premises to the original building were vacated 'in 1780' they were taken over by John Blackburn. He converted the old Inn into a lodge to his estate, and it stayed essentially unaltered, it appears, until Ridge Road was made up in 1907, and the building pulled down, extensive cellarage being found under it.

The site of the old Inn was obviously the building shown at what is now Mason's Corner, on John Blackburn's Plot 740. In the ownership schedule this is described as 'Green Dragon Garden, & co.', implying, in fact, some sort of continued existence here for the pub, whilst the entries for Lots 94, 92 and 93, which by now should be housing the then reputedly new pub, are devoid of any premises, both on the map and in the Schedule. So it might be that a false legend has grown up around the old pub, or more likely, it was something that actually occurred, but some time early in the 19th century. The 1822 O. S. Map at Figure 21 shows the Inn in it's new location.

Hagfield

In his *The Hungry Years,* David Pam tells us that Hagfield, or Hegfield, Common Field existed from at least the 13th century. It is marked on the Victoria County History's 1600 reconstruction (at Figure 1) as still being quite extensive. By the time of the 1801 Enclosure it would seem to have been reduced to the Plots bounded by (and inclusive of) Sarah Teshmaker's 1397 and Jacob Harvey's 1395.

The Retreat Inn

At Page 23 of my *A Look at Old Winchmore Hill* is a small section on *The Retreat* Inn, including a sketch of the building by Dr. Cresswell sometime around 1865 - 1870. The building looks a substantial one of two floors, very much as if, in style, it had originally been a house. The inn was on the junction of the ancient Hagfields footpath, which ran from 'Vicars Moor Lane' to Green Dragon Lane. Close examination of the top copy of the Enclosure Map at the library reveals that this followed the line of the boundary between Plots 1394 (Green) and 1395 (Harvey). On the Enclosure map the building occupying the site of *The Retreat* is marked as being John Richardson's 'House & co.', at Plot 86a. It is quite possible that Dr. Cresswell captured Richardson's premises.

At the time of the sketch the inn was owned by a man named Pomfret, and in the foreground Dr. Cresswell showed a barn like building, which was used by Pomfret as his pigsty. This would appear to be on the site of the, 'House, yards, & co.' on Plot 85, owned in 1801 by R.T. Williamson, though there is no reason to suppose the shed was a remnant from 1801. Williamson also owned the adjoining 1¾ acres Plot 84, to the west of 85, which was listed in the Schedule as, 'Field and Green Dragon lane'. Though the phrasing is a little awkward, it does at least allow us to know that the current road name was in use two hundred years ago.

James Wilson's Plot 101

Wilson's Plot 101 of over ¾ acres, at the western end of 'Vicars Moor Lane' contained a 'House, barn, and garden'. The late David Hicks's archives include his notes on the history of this Plot, though these don't necessarily quote the sources of his information. His notes say that in March 1766 John Hurdle, a farmer of Palmers Green, sold this Plot to Philip Jarvis. In June 1769 Philip, and his wife Mary, sold it for £90 to James Morgan. At that time it contained a messuage that had formerly been two houses, along with associated farm buildings and an orchard. In March 1770 James and his wife Ann sold the Plot to William Wilson for £100.

The Hicks archives include a copy of the Will of William Wilson of Hoxton Square, Shoreditch, dated 4th November 1794, proved in London on 1st June 1801. In this Will he appears to have left his son James Plot 101. In his notes David indicates that he is aware of documents which suggest that James built several cottages on the land soon after inheriting it. David also had an official document dated 11th June 1806 which shows James Wilson as the owner of various adjoining Winchmore Hill properties that were exonerated from Land Tax as from 25th March of that year (Lady Day), for reasons that are not explained. This refers to two newly erected cottages.

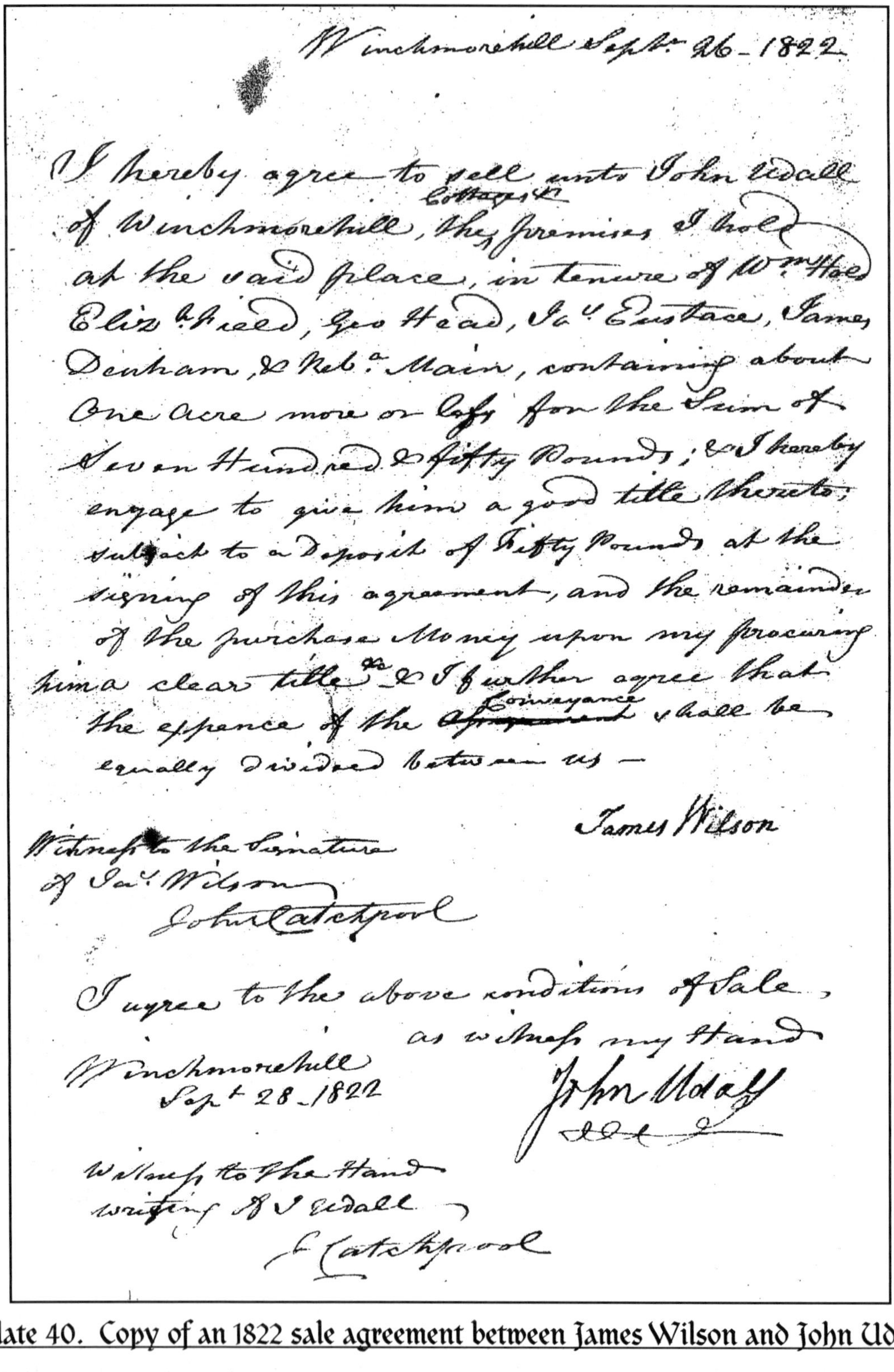

Winchmorehill Septr. 26 – 1822.

I hereby agree to sell unto John Udall of Winchmorehill, the premises I hold [Cottages &c] at the said place, in tenure of Wm. Hoe Elizh. Field, Geo. Head, Jas. Eustace, James Denham, & Reba. Main, containing about One Acre more or less, for the Sum of Seven Hundred & fifty Pounds; & I hereby engage to give him a good title thereto; subject to a Deposit of fifty Pounds at the signing of this agreement, and the remainder of the purchase Money upon my procuring him a clear title &c & I further agree that the expence of the [Conveyance] shall be equally divided between us —

James Wilson

Witness to the Signature of Jas. Wilson
John Catchpool

I agree to the above conditions of Sale, as witness my Hand

Winchmorehill Sept 28 – 1822

John Udall

Witness to the Hand writing of J Udall
J. Catchpool

Plate 40. Copy of an 1822 sale agreement between James Wilson and John Udall

My thanks to Stewart Christian, custodian of the late David Hicks's archives, for kind permission to publish this document, which relates to what had been Plot 101 at the time of Enclosure. Udall was responsible for building Providence Chapel on the land in 1825, though it was rebuilt in the 1880s. The last service was held in the building in 1982, but the listed façade still remains in Vicars Moor Lane, marking the site of Udall's original construction.

David's notes say that in August 1808 James borrowed £373 to build six cottages by his house. The notes hint that the house might be North Villa, which still stands in Vicars Moor Lane, and which might date back to at least 1702. A further document of David's, reproduced at Plate 40, is an agreement of September 1822 whereby James Wilson sold the Plot to John Udall for £750.

Pauline Holstius's many papers include Page 192 out of *A History of Middlesex,* of undisclosed authorship. It contained the following, 'Providence chapel was erected in 1825 in Vicar's Moor Lane by John Udall the elder, a member of a Winchmore Hill family which used its grocer's shop as a front for contraband goods. The chapel was registered by Independents (according to documents in the Guildhall), and the Udallite sect which worshipped there called itself Independent in 1851, and (Regnart says) Calvinistic in 1866 ...... The chapel was rebuilt in 1888 in yellow brick with red brick dressings in the Gothic style ....' A handwritten document in the possession of Miss Holstius, again of unknown authorship, tells us that the foundation for the second Chapel was actually laid on 23rd August 1883 (not 1888), and that the last sermon was held in August 1982. The premises are now a private residence retaining the listed Victorian façade.

Pauline's papers also include typed documents of unknown authorship, which are obviously based on someone's copying of old documents. An Indenture of 27th October 1835, 'between John Udall the elder of Wlnchmore Hill in the Parish of Edmonton Draper and Grocer Thomas Ostcliff of the same place Grocer John Wade of the same place baker John Mitchell of the same place Baker and William Binsted of the same place Draper Trustees for the purposes mentioned in the Indenture,' record Udall's sale to these men, for 5/-, 'all that piece or parcel of freehold ground situate on the Northernmost side of a certain lane called Vicars Lane at Winchmore Hill containing ..... together with that brick building thereon situated standing and being used and intended to be used as a place of public worship and called or known and registered by the name of Providence Chapel together the pulpit pews seats and fittings up of the same .... '

The field system to the north of 'Vicars Moor Lane' can be made out on the 1895 O.S. Map, and it is clear that the 1871 railway line was driven through where Sarah Teshmaker's Plot 1397 met the lane in 1801. Plot 101 was therefore the only one which could conceivably have harboured any of the properties now lying on the north side of Vicars Moor Lane between the railway line and 'Udall's Chapel'.

My 2004 *More Winchmore Hill Lives* features an account by the late Mrs. Netherclift (nee Aldous) in which I noted that there is a row of high terraced brick houses numbered 86, 88 and 90 Vicars Moor Lane, which all bear the name of Compton Villas over their doors. On the brickwork above the doorways to Nos.86 and 88 there is a matt black plaque, only a few inches across, which gives the date of 1710. From the foregoing it would seem unlikely that this denotes the date of their construction.

Beaumont Lodge

Later in the 19th century a wealthy John Wade – who gave his name to two local roads – lived at the northern corner of 'Wades Hill' and 'Vicars Moor Lane' in a great mansion called Beaumont Lodge. This is pictured at P53 of my *A History of Winchmore Hill.* It was near where Moses Adams (Plot 99) and Edmund Whitehead (Plot 100) had properties. Whether one or both of these helped form the nucleus of Wade's later home is impossible to say. (We can note the presence of local baker John Wade in the 1835 agreement recounted a few paragraphs previous to this one).

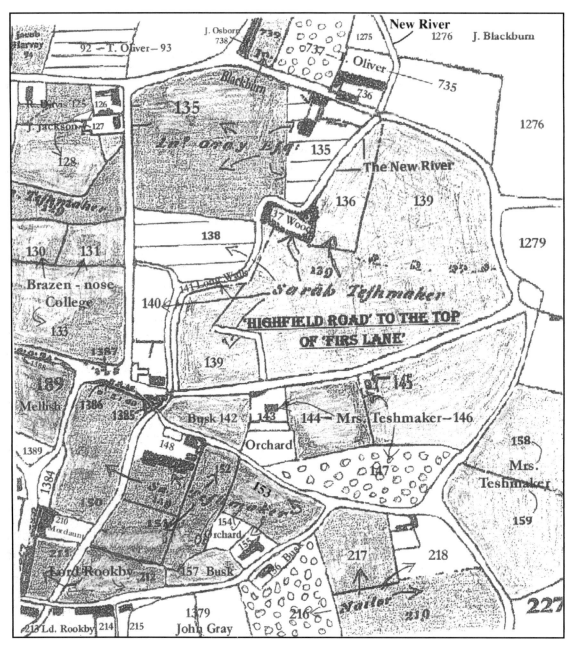

Figure 17. Enclosure Map of 'Highfield Road' to top of 'Firs Lane'

The shaded fields were meadow, those with horizontal lines were pasture, and those with small circles in were used for arable.

'Highfield Road' to top of 'Firs Lane' map

The New River runs from near the centre of the top of the map to its SW corner. The lane starting at the top just to its west, and running down to the bottom SW corner, is what we now call Green Lanes. The lane-forking west off it at the top of the map (by Plot 92) is the start of 'Vicars Moor Lane'. The lane at the top of the map forking off it to the east (by Plot 739) is 'Firs Lane', which curves around to run south and leave the map near its SE corner. The lane running to the northern edges of Plots 142, 144 and 146 is 'Fords Grove'. The lane running along the southern edges of Plots 142 and 147 to meet 'Firs Lane' is what we now call Farm Road, and it intersects with 'Highfield Road' coming up from the SW corner of the map. The following notes cover only the land east of 'Green Lanes', and north of 'Highfield Road'.

Gibraltar Cottages

In 1801 Freehold Plot 738, at the north of the map, was a 'House and Garden' belonging to Joseph Osborn(e). This is where you would expect to find Gibraltar Cottages, featured at Plate 41. They were on the site of the telephone exchange which replaced them on the corner of 'Firs Lane' and Green Lanes, which bears the plaque, 'EVIIIR1936'. An article in *The Enfield Gazette and Observer* gives us some theories.

The first line of thinking is that the cottages were built in the first twenty years of the 18th century, either after the British and Dutch captured Gibraltar in 1704, or after its permanent cessation to Great Britain by the Treaty of Utrecht in 1713. The wood screws used were apparently consistent with constructions of this era. The other proposition is that they were built in the 1780s by local landowner John Blackburn.

Plate 41. Gibraltar Cottages at the junction of 'Firs Lane' and Green Lanes

Gibraltar Cottages were replaced by the current telephone exchange on the corner of Firs Lane and Green Lanes in 1936. In this photograph, kindly supplied by the late Keith Surtees, Green Lanes runs to the viewer's left, Firs Lane runs off to the right.

Thomas Oliver's Plots

Oliver's land is also shown on the map titled "'Vicars Moor Lane' to Green Dragon Lane, and beyond". Plots 90,91,92 and 93 were known as Gibraltar Fields. Oliver's Plot 735, of a little over 3 acres, is called 'Home field' in the land ownership schedule. Plot 736, of an acre, is described as, 'House, yard, garden & c.'

Arable Plot 737 is confusingly shown against John Blackburn's name in the Schedule as, 'got in exchange from Thomas Oliver'. Under Oliver's name it consists of about 1¼ acres and is known as 'Tile Barrow field'. Beneath the Plot in the Ownership Schedule, without any numbering against them, are two more lines of entries against Mr. Oliver's name. These are described as, 'Part of a close got in exchange from John Blackburn Esq.'. The first of these extra two lines lists a 'Pit' of an acre; whilst the second line is a meadow of approximately 3/4 acre. In the ownership schedule the triangle of 1275 is listed as part of John Blackburn's estate, in Dead Field, but on the map it is shown as half an acre belonging to Oliver. 1276 and 1277 are also listed as being allotments in Dead Field under Blackburn's ownership.

Tile Barrow Field is shown on the VCH Map of the district of c1600 at Figure 1 as extending over a far greater area than it did in 1801, with 'Dede (Dead) Field' adjoining it to the east, though by 1801 Field 1275 was, it seems, part of Dead Field. The latter was so named because it was used to bury the dead in the earlier times of plague. 'Barrow' is sometimes taken to mean an ancient mound for the burial of the dead, and being just next door to Dead Field, perhaps we can consider such a history for this field? The Tile' part of the name suggests that it, or part of it, was used as a pit where clay was mined for making tiles (see, also, my comments below).

In an article in *The Palmers Green and Southgate Gazette* of 13th August 1937 'A.W.' (who I take to be Arthur Willis) wrote a piece headed, 'Story of Riverbank'. It told us, amongst other things, that Riverbank was originally a small cottage built around 1760, but had been enlarged on two or three occasions to become an imposing house, set in grounds abounding in trees of numerous varieties. It was, apparently, originally known as Butt's Farm, which was enlarged in 1808, converted into a 'gentlemen's residence' and renamed 'Riverbank'. This 'Butt's Farm was surely the 'House, yard, garden & c.' of Plot 736 in the ownership schedule, the 'house' perhaps being a farmhouse.

Plate 42. Riverbank in Firs Lane

This photograph is reproduced by courtesy of L.B. Enfield Library Service. See the section on Thomas Oliver's Plots for more information.

In the London Metropolitan Archives (LMA) are papers relating to Butt's Farm, coded ACC/241/15 and dated the 1st August 1658. The handwriting and sense are not always clear but the document is an agreement between, on the one hand, William Stand, and his wife Jamario, and on the other, John Aylot, and his wife Mary (all of Essex). They appear to be selling the property to a John Bathurst, a fishmonger of London, for five shillings. The land was then currently occupied by Robert Gregory, and was even then known as 'Butts' farme', apparently because it had been built by a John Butt on land, '...... known by the name of Tyleborow otherwise Dead Field, att on now obtains land my from Winsmore hill to Edmonton Church towards ..... ' The deal was witnessed by a John Jackson. Perhaps he was a member of the Jackson family of Broomfield House? The VCH says that Butts Farm stood by 1591.

It is clear that the original farm was very old indeed, much older than the *Gazette* article's 'built around 1760' suggests. It is also interesting that the document refers to Tile Barrow and Dead Field being one and the same, which would certainly make my earlier comments about the 'Barrow' part of the name plausible.

The *Gazette* article indicates that during the last 20 years of the 19th century the "Riverbank" property was 'one of the choicest little residential estates in the neighbourhood', and was at that time tenanted by Mr. Bresano, who manufactured artificial flowers in a factory in the City. He and his wife occupied the 'rural retreat' for many years. Riverbank mansion was demolished in 1935, but its name lives on in the set of flats where it stood. See Plate 42.

John Gray's Plot 135 - Beaulieu

Much of what follows is based on David Pam's 1982 publication *Southgate and Winchmore Hill - A Short History*, an article by Peter Hodge in The Southgate Civic Trust's *Oakleaves* No. 1, Alan Dumayne's *Fond Memories of Winchmore Hill*, and, further to a David Hicks initiative, the Sir John Soane's Museum.

In 1786 the surveyor Launcelot Dowbiggin of Paternoster Row (adjacent to St. Paul's Cathedral) prepared three plans and an elevation for John Gray who, in his *Sir John Soane and London*, Ptolemy Dean says had, 'a counting house at Water Lane in the City.' John was the brother of Walker, owner of The Grove (Grovelands). His building became known as *Beaulieu*, and the Dowbiggin paperwork is stored today at the Sir John Soane's Museum, Lincoln's Inn Fields under reference Drawer 46, set 9, No. 17. The front elevation features a two storey building with a door at the centre, mirrored by a window on the floor above. There were two windows shown on either side of the door (i.e. four in total), which were also mirrored in the higher of the two floors, giving a symmetrical appearance. There is a picture of the old mansion at Page 58 of my *A Look at Old Winchmore Hill*, which looks very much like the Dowbiggin design, except that there appears to be an extra, third, floor, with windows mirroring those in the lower two floors.

Also at the Sir John Soane's Museum (archive reference drawer 62, set 8, No. 24) are two elevations for a Lodge to the main building by Soane himself, drawn in 1796. Dean says that in 1796 Soane also added a 'rustic gardener's house'. In 1801 the estate was over 10 acres. Gray sold out to a Thomas Nisbett, who we know little about. However, we do know more of the Cass family which followed. In 1806, William Cass purchased the estate for £4,750, which, on his death, was handed down to his son Frederick. He was a well respected man, who was later to be appointed High Sherrif for Hertfordshire. He married Martha Dell in 1823. The Reverend Frederick Charles Cass, son of Frederick Snr., was born at *Beaulieu* in 1824 and moved to Little Grove, in nearby Cat Hill, with his parents in 1827. The Reverend was the author of three learned local histories, covering Monken Hadley, South Mimms and East Barnet. Despite their move of 1827, the Cass's retained *Beaulieu* until 1832.

John Buonarotti Papworth (1775 - 1847) was a prolific architect and garden designer, being responsible for much of early 19th century Cheltenham. One of his schemes was at Little Grove, and some time between 1823 and 1832 Papworth was engaged in 'laying out grounds' at *Beaulieu* for Frederick Cass (the elder). We do not have any account of what *Beaulieu* looked like at the time of Gray, Nisbett and the Cass family, but we do have Miss Cresswell's account of the grounds later in the 19th century to persuade us that they were quite beautiful. We also know that it was the home, at least later on, of many bird species. There is an old picture showing The Rookery in the grounds of *Beaulieu*, opposite *The Green Dragon* at P56 of my *A Look at Old Winchmore Hill*.

Plate 43. Remnant of Beaulieu Mansion

I took this snap of an old arch left over from the grounds of Beaulieu on 12th February 1999 by courtesy of the owner of 10, Beaulieu Gardens. These, and a few other fragments in the back garden, by the New River, are all that remains of John Gray's estate.

We are now moving out of this book's era of interest, so I will only briefly outline *Beaulieu's* further history. At the London Metropolitan Archives I located papers reference ACC/1292 about the Johnston family. From these I believe that they lived at *Beaulieu* in the middle of the 19th century. The brewer Thomas Paulin, of Mann, Crossman & Paulin fame, moved into *Beaulieu* with his family in 1865, for a stay of 8 years, possibly as direct successors to the Johnstons. The Paulins left after building *Broadfields* in Wades Hill, and were followed by the Phillips family.

Towards the end of the 19th century, *Beaulieu* was purchased by Mr. Foster of Palfreyman, Foster & Co., timber merchants. He cut Elm Park Road through the estate in 1898/9 and it was developed soon after. In the first part of the 20th century running a large house like *Beaulieu* was not an economic proposition, and the house was finally demolished in 1937. However, it is commemorated in the name of the road that was laid over the building site - Beaulieu Gardens.

At Plate 43 is a photograph of a remnant of the old estate in the back garden of No.10 Beaulieu Gardens, whilst at Plate 44 is a recent picture capturing a timeless nearby view of the New River.

Plate 44. New River near Beaulieu Gardens

This photograph was taken on 14th May 2001, but the scene depicted could easily date from 200 years before.

Pot 140 - Fords Grove Mansion

See section under Busk in Enclosure Land Ownership Schedule.

Plot 143 - Fords Grove Cottage

A glance at the VCH reconstruction for c 1600 shows that much of the Busk – Teshmaker land in the 'Farm Road', 'Firs Lane', 'Fords Grove' triangle was once the common field known as Holly Field. It had presumably been enclosed long before 1801. Widow Sarah Teshmaker's Plot 143 is shown in the ownership schedule as being 1¼ acres containing 'Houses, yards, and orchard'. This was Fords Grove Cottage.

Miss Cresswell wrote of the old country lane of 'Fords Grove', and the cottage, in the days of her childhood in about 1860. At the time of which she was writing the cottage was occupied by Captain Tills, who had served at Trafalgar, and his wife. The scene had probably altered little since the early 19th century, in what was then still a 'remote' Middlesex village. Some of her 'pictures in words' are reproduced at Pages 46 and 47 of my *A Look at Old Winchmore Hill,* alongside old photographs of what she was describing.

By 1871 only the Captain's daughter Charlotte remained of the Tills family, and she moved that year to The Green. The cottage was taken over by Mortiboy 'the cow-keeper', who appears to have let the old premises decay, as outlined in the following from an *Enfield Gazette and Observer* article of 31st October 1924, '.....Twenty five years ago Ford's grove was better known as Mortiboy's Lane, owing to the land on both sides being farmed by the late Mr. Mortiboy, who about the year 1870 became tenant of the old cottage which was demolished a year ago. The cottage had stood for 400 years, during which it had undergone various alterations. Up to about 1909 it possessed an old Jacobean chimney corner, and in one of its tiny, quaint rooms there was a horn window, and Mr. Mortiboy had stored upstairs the old leaden frames which were at one time used as window casings. In 1911 the Southgate Council issued a closing order for the cottage because its ivy clad roof and its floors were in very bad condition. It stood on the south side of the lane and was very picturesque, most of its ancient walls remaining to the end; little of the building, however, was visible owing to the whole of it being overgrown with creepers .....'

Plate 45. Fords Grove Cottage, Fords Grove

Widow Sarah Teshmaker's Plot 143 is shown in the ownership schedule as being 1¼ acres containing 'Houses, yards, and orchard'. This was Fords Grove Cottage. This illustration is from the front page of the local Recorder of May 11th 1911.

The presence of a horn window, used before the introduction of glass, certainly suggests an old age for the structure. A 1933 *Gazette* article said that the Cottage had occupied the site of 14 – 20 Fords Grove. See Plate 45 for an idea of how the cottage looked in its later years.

Plots 148/149 - Fords Grove Farm

Plot 148 - another of Sarah Teshmaker's numerous holdings - is nearly an acre of land housing 'Farm - house, barns & yard', whilst her adjoining Plot 149 contained over an acre of meadow. The farmhouse must have served all the surrounding land that she held.

The field system in the triangle bounded by The New River, 'Farm Road' and 'Highfield Road' remains much the same in the 1865 O.S. map, where farm buildings are shown in similar positions to 1801, and are labelled 'Ford's Grove Farm'. The buildings bear a similar title on the 1895 O.S. map, though there has been some change in their surrounds. At Plate 46 I reproduce, by kind permission of *The Gazette*, a sketch of The Broadway by a Miss Ewing as it was in 1897. I believe that it could well portray the farmstead at Plot 148 on the Enclosure Map.

Plate 46. Fords Grove Farm

I reproduce, by kind permission of The Gazette, a sketch of The Broadway by a Miss Ewing as it was in 1897. I believe that it could well portray the farmstead at Mrs. Teshmaer's Plot 148 on the Enclosure Map.

George Mordaunt's Plots 210 and 1383

Plot 210 is listed as 'House and garden', whilst 1383 is an 'Allotment on waste in front'. The fields in this vicinity do not change form by the time of the 1865 OS map, where a house is shown on what had been Plot 210. The 1895 OS map indicates a similar shaped building (in plan view), but this time with a new building on what had been Plot 211 to the south. The 1899-1900 Kelly's Directory lists this as The Chestnuts, occupied by John Reed. The building on what had been Plot 210 was called The Grange, and was occupied by a Mrs. Seymour.

In his *Memories of Winchmore Hill*, Horace Regnart, harks back to the village of about 1880 onwards. He must be referring to this building when he says, '...on the site of Duncan Court was Highfield Grange, an old red brick house. The house had been a workhouse, and later a medical home. Charles Lamb and his sister Mary lived at different times both in Enfield and Edmonton. Mary was liable to temporary fits of insanity and, when these were coming on, her brother used to take her to

189

Highfield Grange .... There was a beautiful garden at the back which stretched down to the New River ....'

In the 1830 Diary there is reference to a local Mental Institution being run by a Jane Holmes. It seems unlikely that there would be more than one Asylum in so small a community, so it would presumably be the one to which Regnart refers. The Institution was housed in what became known as The Grange, but in 1801 it seems it would have been Mordaunt's property.

THE LITTLE HOUSE IN HIGHFIELD ROAD

F. Rutherford 1937

"The little house with four slender pine trees in front which stands next to Winchmore School," mentioned in last week's interesting history by "Memorabilia." It still has a picturesque rural aspect.

Plate 47. The Fellmonger's Office in Highfield Road in 1937

Mr. Rutherford's sketch reproduced by kind permission of The Gazette.

Highfield Road – Plot 155 – The Fellmonger's Office

On 31st December 1937 *The P.G & S Gazette* published a story by 'Memorabilia' headed, 'The Rookery and Highfield Road of Old'. It said, '.... In 1800 there were not any houses at all on the northern side of Highfield Road with the exception of the little house with the four slender pine trees in front, which still stands next to Winchmore School - or an earlier house which stood on the same site, described in the official schedule as a "Fellmonger's office and yard 1r 26p" which was owned by

Mrs. Teshmaker and ultimately became by marriage part of the estate of Squire Busk, of Ford's Grove. That cottage and two old buildings next *The Orange Tree* are the only buildings now left standing that were existing 136 years ago......' The Fellmonger's office was captured by F. Rutherford in a sketch in *The Gazette* of 7th January 1938, reproduced with the paper's kind permission, at Plate 47.

I can add a little to what 'Memorabilia' says of the "Fellmonger's office and Yard 1r. 26p' (Plot 155) owned by Mrs. Teshmaker at Enclosure. Both the 1865 and 1895 OS Maps portray buildings where the ones are shown at Plot 155, and opposite at Plot 156, in 1801. The 1899-1900 Kelly's Directory indicates that the 'Plot 155' premises were occupied by Isaac Solomon, florist. My *More Winchmore Hill Lives* of 2004 featured an account by the Everett sisters, who were born in Edwardian times. In it they say, 'Our mother's father was Isaac Solomon who, with our Uncle Joe, owned the famous nurseries on the site now occupied by the school playing fields on the north side of the road. His father (our Great Grandfather) Isaac Gerald owned "The White House", a grand old building past the nurseries near the end of the Road - or Row as it was called in those days. Eventually his son (grandfather) moved there also.' This does suggest that Mrs. Teshmaker's 'Fellmonger's office' persisted into the last century. Local man Terry Teer remembers the ruined old cottage being replaced by an air raid shelter in the Second World War.

'Highfield Road' to Barrow's Well Green Map

Highfield Road – Plot 213

Lord Rookby's Plot 213 is listed in the Ownership Schedule as, 'Seven houses and gardens'. On 31st December 1937 *The Palmers Green and Southgate Gazette* published a story by 'Memorabilia' headed, 'The Rookery and Highfield Road of Old', accompanied by the illustration at Plate 48. The article ran, 'We reproduce from water-colours of the late Dr. John Cresswell "Back View of Highfield Row, Winchmore Hill, about 1858" ...... We believe (it) represents Lord Rookby's "Seven houses" which are represented on the plan as a row - miserable little cottages they seem to have been ....'

At Page 26 of Miss Cresswell's *Memories of a Lost Village* she tells us that, 'Winifred and the Doctor went down Highfield Row for him to visit a sick child in "the Rookery" at the back of *The Orange Tree*. It was a house where the stair was steep, and the ceiling so low that the Doctor invariably broke the top of his chimney pot hat when he went there. He kept a little wooden trumpet in that hat which was rather a mystery ....'

The LB Enfield let me reproduce a sketch Dr. Cresswell made of Highfield Road, looking east from near the footbridge, in about 1860, at P25 of *More Winchmore Hill Lives*, to accompany the account of the Everett sisters, who were born in Edwardian times. The sketch shows the building that their mother Ada Solomon was born in, being the fourth premises west of *The Orange Tree*. It is possible that the sketch captures the front of some of Lord Rookby's 'Seven Houses'. As 'Memorabilia' hints, perhaps this row of old buildings led to the Victorian street name of Highfield Row.

Figure 18. Enclosure Map of 'Highfield Road' to Barrow's Well Green

What we now call Green Lanes runs N-S down the left (west) side of the map. The lane intersecting it from the east, towards the top of the map, is the rural predecessor to modern day Highfield Road, which for many years was known as Highfield Row. 'Firs Lane' runs in a SSE direction down the east side of the map. At the bottom (south) Barrow's Well Green joins Green Lanes and 'Firs Lane' together. High Field common field is shown on the VCH reconstruction for c.1600 as approximating to the land between Green Lanes and Plots 1379 and 1381 (inclusive of both). The shaded fields were meadow, those with horizontal lines were pasture, and those with small circles in were used for arable

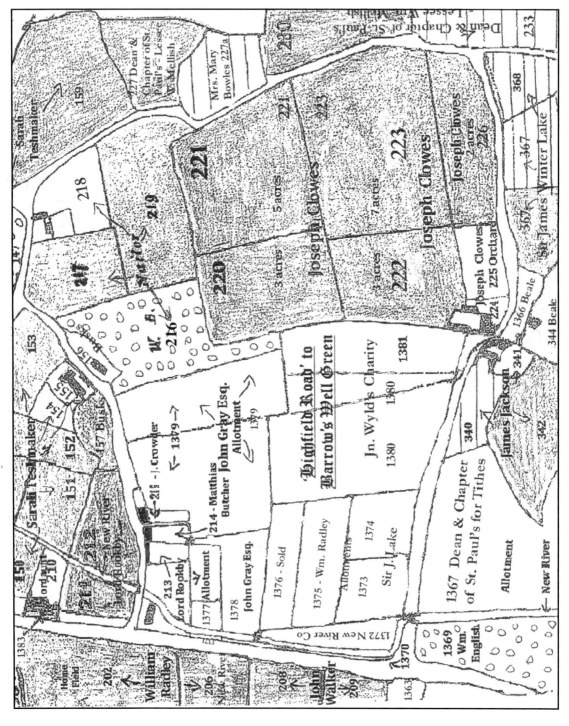

192

The building on Plot 213, in the triangle bounded by 'Highfield Road', The New River and Green Lanes, occupies the same site as the recently remodelled Cedars House. The Enfield Archaeological Society's News No. 180 of March 2006 contained an article by Mike Dewbrey, which started, 'It is my sad duty to begin the year by reporting the demise of one of Winchmore Hill's most attractive early Victorian villas, "Cedar House", to make way for yet another development of flats.' He finishes, 'Why Cedar House was allowed to be bulldozed beggars belief.' It seems only the original front facade remains in the current building.

Plate 48. Lord Rookby's (?) Highfield Row

My thanks to The Gazette for permission to publish this sketch by Dr. John Cresswell entitled "Back View of Highfield Row, Winchmore Hill, about 1858". It appeared in the P.G. & S. Gazette of 31st December 1937.

So Cedars House was probably not in existence in 1801. Presumably, if it had, it would have been individually mentioned. On the other hand, the premises on the Enclosure Map indicate the building was about the same size as the demolished building, so it is possible that until 2006 we were able to see the house that existed in 1801, perhaps with modifications.

Highfield Road – The Orange Tree

The VCH says that there was an Inn, possibly a precursor of *The Orange Tree*, at Highfield in 1611. In his extensive research on the pubs of the LB of Enfield, Gary Boudier established that Richard Barrett was the licensee of *The Orange Tree* in 1726, though of course there may well have been others before him of whom we are unaware. With regard to the 1780 – 1830 timespan, Mr. Boudier lists the passing of the Licence as follows: 1777 - Henry Butcher; 1788 - Elizabeth Butcher; 1793 - George Hallsey; 1794 - Elizabeth Butcher; 1795 -John Biggs; 1818 - James Lawford; 1820 - Thomas Clarke.

A paper in Pauline Holstius's collection is a snippet from an undisclosed magazine (but probably *The Recorder* c. 1910) titled, 'Smugglers in Highfield Row!'. It ran, 'Smugglers, who journeyed on horse back and on foot, used the "Orange Tree" as a stopping place. The old inn was raided times out of number by revenue officers, who

193

tried to discover the goal of these vendors of French lace, brandy, schnapps, gloves, silk, tea and tobacco. Later, in the earliest part of the 19th century it was discovered that a busy "clearing-house" for smuggled goods was run by a man and his wife named Udall. Their premises represented the village stores on the site of the present stables of "The Limes." Contraband trade was carried on quite openly. The ultimate end of the "Udalls" is not known.

The Hostelry of Highfield Row was rather picturesque with a round bow window of small panes, and with benches in the porch. The swinging signboard opposite stood on the edge of a running brook full of water–cress and forget–me–nots, with a golden border of flea bane on the bank. The rushes were long and green, and it was possible to get fine lengths of their velvety-white pith.'

At Page 167 of *Fond Memories of Winchmore Hill,* Alan Dumayne published a picture of the Inn before its replacement by the current structure in 1912. I am unable to say whether that incarnation is the same one as the one that existed in 1801, when the plot of land on which it stood (214) was owned by Matthias Butcher.

Pickering's Cottage, at the southern corner of Farm Road and Firs Lane, Winchmore Hill. Note, the lane in the immediate foreground is Firs Lane, which turns to the left in the picture; the lane turning right passing the front of the house is Farm Road.

Plate 49. Pickering's Cottage

Reproduced from The Palmers Green and Southgate Gazette of 31st May 1935 by kind permission of The Gazette

Plot 218 – Pickering's Cottage

In his *Fond Memories of Winchmore Hill,* Alan Dumayne tells us that No. 83, Farm Road was built in 1933 on the site of Pickering's Cottage. His father bought it in that year, when Alan was four, for the princely sum of about £900 freehold. Alan relates how the cottage gained its name from a Mrs. Pickering, who lived there at one time, and took in washing. At P156 of his book he reproduces a photo' of the cottage from 1926.

The Palmers Green and Southgate Gazette of 31st May 1935 contains an article on Pickering's Cottage. The illustration with that article is reproduced at Plate 49, with kind permission of *The Gazette*. The article surmises that William Baker Nailor's Plot 218, of 'House, yards and homestead', could well be Pickering's Cottage, which it says, had been demolished, and replaced by houses, about three years previously.

Che Clowes Estate

Joseph Clowes owned plots 220 to 226 inclusive, and today the aptly named Clowes Sports Ground occupies much of these. In 1801 most of the estate was meadow, though Plot 224 was a 'House and garden', with the adjoining field to the east (Plot 225) being an orchard.

The Palmers Green and Southgate Gazette of 6th August 1937 ran an article by 'Memorabilia' concerned with The Firs in Barrowell Green, as opposed to The Firs of the Lake family, which was off Firs Lane, and dealt with in another section. The OS Maps of 1865 and 1895 both show The Firs on the site of Clowes's house at Plot 224.

'Memorabilia' had little doubt that the house then known as "The Firs", in Barrowell Green, was built in the days of the window tax, but that was enacted, he said, in 1694, and repealed in 1851 - a span of 157 years! The number of blank or blind windows suggested to 'Memorabilia' that it was built in the years between the first increase in the window tax, in 1746, and the first reduction in 1784. From its appearance he surmised that it wasn't built as a farm-house, fitting in with the ownership schedule's description of the 'House and garden 2r 4p' at Plot 224. The article tells us that in the 19th century The Firs was let and sub let to many tenants.

'Memorabilia' says that, 'The whole estate in 1800, comprising 24a 2r 3p had been owned by the Clowes family for over 300 years, when it was purchased by the Southgate Borough Council in 1935, subject to Messrs. Carter Page and Co.'s lease as a nursery of which some eleven or twelve years are unexpired; therefore, it is unlikely to become a public open space until about 1948.' 'Memorabilia' adds that the Clowes estate was originally copyhold and held under the Manors of Bowes, Dernford, Pauls House, and Fordes. The Dean and Chapter of St. Paul's were the proprietors in 1800, and many years thereafter.

In the Local History Unit is a document that reads, 'Deed No. 793. Plan No. 18. By a Conveyance of the 31st January, 1936 Arthur Frederick Clowes conveyed to the Southgate Borough Council, for the sum of £19,800, all that messuage or tenement known as *The Firs*, Barrowell Green and adjoining lands, containing in the whole approximately 24.038 acres.' There was a restriction letting land on it to Carter Page Nurseries on a 21 year lease from 29th September 1926, but this was surrendered later in the year.

I cover the south side of Barrowell Green in the section on the map titled 'Hedge Lane' to Barrow's Well Green.

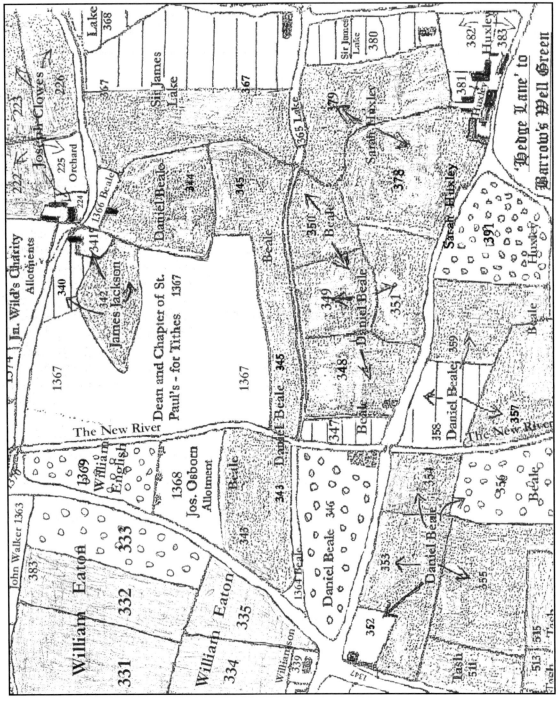

Figure 19. Enclosure Map of 'Hedge Lane' to Barrow's Well Green

The main lane running ESE across the lower part of the map is the forerunner of modern day Hedge Lane. At its eastern extremity it meets the N-S running 'Firs Lane', whilst at its western end it meets Green Lanes as it comes down from the north of the map, the New River running N-S just to that lane's east. Parallel to 'Hedge Lane', towards the north of the map, is the rural ancestor of today's Barrowell Green, whilst between them is another lane that has long since disappeared. The shaded fields were meadow, those with horizontal lines were pasture, and those with small circles in were used for arable.

'Hedge Lane' to Barrow's Well Green Map

The main lane running ESE across the lower part of the map is the forerunner of modern day Hedge Lane. The VCH reconstruction of c. 1600 indicates that this was the name even then, and it occurs to me that it might have been so called because it led in the direction of Lang*hedge* Common field, Edmonton. I do not cover the land west of Green Lanes in this section, nor the land on the north side of Barrow's Well Green.

Scots Field

Please see the VCH reconstruction of c. 1600 (Figure 1). The ancient Scots common field was, following the Enclosure Act, in the hands of James Jackson, the Dean and Chapter of St. Paul's, William English, and Joseph Osborn(e). Today part of this land has still not been built upon, being covered by allotments, pictured at Plate 50.

Plate 50. Allotments south of Barrowell Green, in what had been Scots Field

I took this photograph looking south from Barrowell Green in December 2004. For centuries this had been Scots Common Field, and it occurs to me that this small patch of suburban London has never been built upon.

The only plot of these to house a property in 1801 was Jackson's 341 (obviously wrongly listed as 241) – a 'House and yard' set in half an acre. A glance at the 1822 O.S. map (Figure 21) shows Highfield marked against what very much looks like this house. In this respect it is interesting to note that the VCH says that a Highfield House known in 1677 and 1703 was probably sited in Highfield Road.

Daniele Beale's Estate

Daniel Barbot Beale lived at what is now Millfield House, Edmonton.

(Plate 54.) He possessed a large acreage locally, and even the briefest of glances at the bottom end of the map reveals that he owned much of the land on either side of 'Hedge Lane'. Through his land, and beyond, ran the lost lane that connected the 'Hedge Lane/ Green Lanes' junction to 'Firs Lane', at a point near to what is today No. 335 in that road. This might have been the 13th century Scottes Lane. The western part was allotted to Beale under the Enclosure Act (1364), whilst the eastern part was allotted to Sir James Lake (1365). No doubt the transfer into private ownership led to the demise of the lane, as it became assimilated into the surrounding land. By the time of the 1822 OS Survey (Figure 21) it had disappeared.

Sir James Lake's Estate

Sir James was another local land owner whose estate extended beyond the confines of the old village. Plot 367, just west of Firs Lane, was about 14 ¾ acres in extent, being half meadow and half pasture (shown thus, only diagrammatically, in the map). It also contained a 'Mansion - house & c.' This was The Firs, now commemorated with a Blue Plaque on the face of No. 335, Firs Lane.

Much seems to be known about the Lake family, and I would refer the reader to the ownership schedule section in that respect. It is sufficient here to summarise by saying that Sir Bibye Lake was created a Baronet in 1711 and he was, according to author Tom Mason, the first of the family to live at Firs Lane. He was followed by his son, Sir. Atwell Lake, Bart, (died 1760), who in turn was succeeded by his own son, Sir James Winter Lake, owner at the time of enclosure. He died on 4th May 1807, aged 65. All three Lakes just mentioned held senior positions with the Hudson's Bay Company.

Given that so much is known about the family, it is curious that so little is known of the mansion, especially as we know that Sir James employed the artist John Smith to teach his daughters. In his article in *The Palmers Green and Southgate Gazette* of 6th August 1937 'Memorabilia' tells us that, 'From Hedge Lane to Sir James Winter Lake's mansion, Firs Lane was an avenue of Scots pines (pinus sylvestris), commonly, but incorrectly, called Scotch firs, hence the name of the house and Firs Lane.' The great mansion is caught in a sketch at Page 28 of my *A Look at Old Winchmore Hill.*

'Memorabilia' says the mansion was demolished in about 1815. On the other hand, Tom Mason tells us that Sir James Winter's son sold The Firs, and that the house was demolished sometime between 1820 and 1830. It still seems to be marked on the 1822 O.S. Map. at Figure 21. However, in his book of 1819 Robinson says, 'it has been some years pulled down. The estate has been sold, and is now the property of John Grant Esq.'

Although there is no such structure on the Enclosure map, the 1822 OS map shows a Barrow at the SW corner of what was Plot 367 in 1801. The site, in terms of today's geography, would have been very approximately where the eastern end of Crawford Gardens meets Farndale Avenue. This seems, therefore, a good point to consider the Barrow, and the name of the nearby lane.

Barrow's Well Green

In the LHU is a map of the area in 1599 which indicates that there was a Grove to the north of Scotts Field, in what looks to be the crook of the bend in the (then unnamed) Barrow's Well Green lane, about where Plot 341 was in 1801. This stand of trees was 3 acres 3 roods 22 perches in extent, and was called 'Barrowes Well Grove', so the name was old even at the time of Enclosure.

The *Palmers Green and Southgate Gazette* of 10th April 1936 contained another article by 'Memorabilia' which ran, ' .... Presumably Mr. (Charles H.) Agate is a member of the family who at one time occupied Firs Nursery, which was on the Southgate or western side of Firs Lane, near its southern end, quite close to the site of 'Bunce's Farm Cottages'......I have in my possession a sepia sketch of the Barrow Well or Barrow's Well, which gave the name of Barrowell Green. It was copied from a rather badly damaged water-colour painted by Dr. John Cresswell ..... on the spot in the late 1840s or early 1850s .... In a letter dated December 21st 1927, Miss Cresswell wrote to me, "My father always instructed me that the great mound at Barrow Well was not a barrow proper but only a mound and not a burial place. Barrow's Well is probably correct." Her meaning was the name of a person by whom at one time the well was owned. It is rendered "Barrow's Well Green" in the schedule of properties in Edmonton attached to Act 40 George 111,1800, and is not in any sense to be confused with Barrow Field, which abutted the main road through Tottenham and Edmonton close to the Enfield boundary ......

.... In the letter before mentioned Miss Cresswell informed me that "the mound" was quite near to the Barrow Well and her indication of the position of the latter is, "Going along Barrow Well Green from the 8 milestone (which is on the Green Lanes flank of No. 1 Woodberry Avenue, near the Methodist Church) and over the bridge which spans the New River, there was on the left old Jolly's cottage, demolished about 40 years ago, and beyond it the stile and the footpath, between the Southgate Council's dust destructor *(in 2009 Cosgrove Close)* and the old gravel pit playground *(just to the west of today's Cosgrove Close)*, which leads to Highfield Row. Opposite the stile (which disappeared about 1910) was a farm, now Heath's nurseries, with a pond in the rear of it, and an accommodation road or lane with a ditch like running stream beside it, it was a cul-de-sac and led to a pool with a fence at the back. This was the dipping well, the Barrow's Well ...... It is highly improbable that it was the burial place of victims of the plague for which deep pits were dug. Edmonton's plague pits seem to have been in the Dead Field through the site of which Ridge Avenue now runs" ....'

Sarah Huxley's Estate

The *Palmers Green and Southgate Gazette* of 25th May 1934 relates that Sarah Huxley, of Wyer Hall, died on the 6th May, 1801, aged 73, and so the land ownership schedule lists Sarah Huxley's extensive estate against her executors. Again we are looking at someone whose holdings extended beyond the old village. The Plots we are now concerned with are those at the SE corner of the map. Plot 381 is shown in the ownership schedule as being a 'Farm-house and yard'.

We know quite a bit about the Huxley family, but less about the property she had in our area. Alan Dumayne, in his Once *Upon a Time in Palmers Green,* tells us that by 1850 the running of Huxley Farm, as the land we are concerned with was called, had been taken over by a Richard Smith. He then employed 20 men, 8 women and 2 boys to work land that ran to a massive 350 acres. John Smith - presumably a relative - took over in the 1880s, to be followed by William Watson in 1905. In its later years, it was often referred to as Watson's Farm. Alan says that it survived longer than most of the local farms, finally yielding to the developers in 1931.

Huxley's Farm is marked as such on the 1822 OS Map at Figure 21 and the 1912 Survey, published in 1914, where the lay out of the premises looks very similar to that on the Enclosure map. There is a picture of the farmyard, taken in 1930, at Page 98 of my 1991 *Winchmore Hill Lives*. There is also a fine photo' of the main farm building, taken in 1929, at P54 of Mr. Dumayne's book. It could well be that in these we are looking at the farmhouse of 1801.

Outside of Winchmore Hill - Edmonton

There are many properties outside of Winchmore Hill which would have been familiar to the old villagers. In this section I cover some of those in the Edmonton area.

All Saints Church, Edmonton.

See Plates 51 & 52. I have based the following on a 'Memorabilia' (Colonel Willis) article in *The Enfield Gazette* of 25th October 1935, and David Pam's recent *Edmonton: Ancient Village to Working Class Suburb.*

Plate 51. Ye olde external view of All Saints Church, Edmonton

This card has no writing or postmark on its reverse, but seems to be very much in the style of Edwardian cards that I have. The church dates back many centuries, but its current appearance owes much to a refurbishment carried out in 1772.

The Church of All Saint's was originally built of hewn stone and flints in the ornate style of the late 12th century, abounding in beakheads and chevron ornament. Willis says that, 'The first resident Vicar of Edmonton of whom there is a record, was John ab. Greene, in 1335, but there is very good reason for believing that long prior to that date the monks of Walden (Saffron Walden), ministered in a small chapel or church, or perhaps a chantry, at Edmonton; the name of which village is deemed to be derived most probably from Adelm, or Athelm, who was the first bishop of Wells, translated to Canterbury in 915 and died 924, or possibly from Eadhelm, who was Bishop of Selsey in 970. Domesday gives the name Edelmton and it is spelt in later records as Edelmeston, Edelmeton, Aedelmton and other variations. The present name with the then common slight variations in spelling appears to have come into use in the late 15th or the 16th century.'

At that time All Saint's was the only church in the parish, and it was not until 1828 that Winchmore Hill had its own Established place of worship, when St.

200

Paul's was opened as a Chapel – of - Ease to the Edmonton Church. So for centuries it would have acted as a focal point for the lives of the locals, even though it was physically situated outside the hamlet.

The building retained almost all its original form until 1772, when the outer walls were encased in brick. With the exception of the chancel windows, the stone mullions were removed, and replaced with wooden frames, apparently relating to the fact that the church wardens at that time were a bricklayer and a carpenter. However, they were restrained before they could alter the chancel windows, which are the chief relics of the original structure still on view.

Pam tells us that the main concern of those who governed the parish throughout the 18th century was the care of the poor. All the institutions concerned were situated near the church. Church Street boasted Latymer School for boys and the Girls Charity School, both of which were involved in the education of poor children. It was also the home of the almshouses for the old and infirm. From 1731, the Parish Workhouse stood just off of Church Street, on the site where All Saint's School was subsequently built.

Some of the people I have mentioned in relation to this era were buried at All Saints. There is a tablet inscribed, 'In memory of Charles Lamb, "the gentle Elia" and author of "Tales from Shakespeare" etc, born in the Inner Temple, 1775, educated at Christ's Hospital, died at Bay Tree College, Edmonton, 1834, and buried beside his sister Mary, in the adjoining churchyard." Underneath is a quotation from Wordsworth. Charles and Mary, it will be remembered, were customers at Udall's on The Green, and Mary was periodically an inmate of the mental institution at Highfield Grange, where Duncan Court now stands.

One of the chancel windows is a memorial to 'Edward Busk of Ford's Grove, Esq. (Winchmore Hill), the offering of many who knew his worth, AD1868.' He was the Justice Busk and Squire Busk of Miss Cresswell's *Winchmore Hill, Memories of a Lost Village*. The church or the churchyard contain the remains of some of the Goulds and Teshmakers (who intermarried with the Busks) of Fords Grove - families who were, at various times, Lords of the Manor.

Also buried there, in 1838, was local worthy William Mellish of The Clock House in Bush Hill Park. The registers record the death of Sir Attwell Lake in 1760, and Sir James Winter Lake, Bart., in 1807. Though they were a little before our era of interest, we can note that the church bears the remains of some of the children and grandchildren of Sir Hugh Myddelton, of New River fame, who lived at Bush Hill House (known as Halliwick in the 20th century).

The Church also contains many members of the Huxley family (commencing in 1613) and Tatem family, both of Wyer Hall fame; John Blackburn,1798 (and his wife), of Bush Hill House; Joseph Salmon, 1790, from whose family Salmons Brook derived its name, and the Rev. Dawson Warren, MA, 1838, for forty-three years Vicar of Edmonton, whose successful legal action of 1815 secured the patronage of the Weld Chapel (and therefore its successor, Christ Church), Southgate, to the Vicars of Edmonton.

Salisbury House

See Plate 53. I attended an open day at Salisbury House in Bury Street in September 2006, the preceding lane giving its name to the Ward to which Winchmore Hill was formerly allocated. The following is based on the handout I obtained at the time.

Plate 52. Memorial to Sarah Huxley in Edmonton Church

I took this photograph on 21st September 2002 during an Open Day. Read more about the Huxleys in the Land Ownership Schedule.

The House is the only survivor of the former hamlet of Bury Street, the most northerly settlement in Edmonton in the 16th Century. There is, unfortunately, relatively little documentary evidence relating to its history. The style of the house suggests it was built as a timber framed town house between 1600 and 1620, and the VCH records what it believes to be a reference to Salisbury House dated 1605. It was then described as a two-storied mansion house. It is the finest piece of late Elizabethan - early Jacobean architecture left in the Borough.

The original entrance to the building would have been where the back door now is, the present porch and front entrance dating from the 19th century. The unusually high quality panelling in the Edinburgh Room dates from the 1620s. Other interesting features in the building include the Tudor hinges still to be seen on some doors, and a concealed priest hole in the cellar, which used a false chimney for ventilation. This presumably indicates that one, at least, of the early owners secretly worshiped as a Catholic.

Plate 53. View of Salisbury House, Edmonton in September 2006

I took this photograph during an 'open day' visit. The building was already quite old at the time of the 1800 Edmonton Enclosure Act.

The name *Salisbury House* first appears in the 1861 census, although on a map of 1867 it is called Bury Lodge, with the section we now call Salisbury House marked as farm buildings. It is thought that the Lodge was a late medieval or early Tudor timber-framed house, with the upper floor jetted out over the ground floor. When Salisbury House was added, it seems likely that Bury Lodge became the service wing of the property, as this would explain the lack of service rooms in Salisbury House itself.

The joining building was demolished in the late 19th century, and Bury Lodge itself was demolished in 1936, upon acquisition of the complex by the former Edmonton UDC. The grounds were then laid out as Bury Street Lodge Recreation Ground. In 1957, after a period of extensive restoration, Salisbury House opened as Edmonton Arts Centre, which still remains in the building today.

The name of the house suggests a link with the Cecil family, as the title Earl of Salisbury, later Marques of Salisbury, has been held by this family since 1605. At one time the Cecil family owned a substantial amount of land in Edmonton, but there is no surviving evidence to suggest that the Cecils ever owned Salisbury House.

Possibly the name comes from Sayesbury, as this is what the Manor of Edmonton was known as in the 15th Century. The De Say family owned the Manor for four generations, and the word 'bury' was sometimes used as a suffix to denote a Manor, which suggests that Salisbury House may originally have been known as Sayesbury House, i.e. the Manor House of the Manor of Sayesbury (Edmonton). Unfortunately for this theory, the surviving evidence links Sayesbury with Bury Hall. This lay immediately east of where the A10 intersects Bury Street, and was demolished in 1920.

Wyer Hall

On 25th May 1934 *The Enfield Gazette* ran a story by 'Memorabilia' that was headed 'The Gravel Pit in Hedge Lane'. It celebrated the, then recently announced, news that the Harman sisters had offered their ten acre gravel pit in Hedge Lane to Edmonton and Southgate Councils, for use as a public recreational area. There was a condition that the family name of their uncle, Mr. J.G. Tatem, should be associated with it, so explaining the still existing name of Tatem Recreational Ground, situated in the angle between Hedge Lane and The Great Cambridge Road.

'Memorabilia' explained that the land formed part of the Wyerhalle, Wyralls, or Goodesters estate. Robinson says it probably took its name from the family Wyrehalle, who had considerable property in Edmonton in about 1340, during the reign of Edward 111. In about 1581 it was the property of Jaspar Leeke Esq., who inherited it from his father. On June 12th, 1609, George Huxley, 'citizen and haberdasher of London', bought the estate from Sir John Leeke and Ann, his wife, and it continued in the direct male line of the Huxley family until the death of Thomas Huxley in 1743, who bequeathed his estates to his two daughters. In 1752 Wyer Hall was apportioned to Sarah, the younger girl, who died unmarried in 1801. Sarah devised Wyer Hall, with her lands in Edmonton, unto her five cousins, from whom it descended to James George Tatem, a collateral relative.

'Memorabilia¹ cautions against confusing 'Weir Hall' with the Harmans' old Wyer Hall, which was demolished in 1818. He fixes the latter's position as being adjacent to the Tatem Park gravel pit in the OS Survey of 1894, the land then being given over to Wyerhall and Millfield Nurseries. The former nursery would today be occupied by Kendal Parade, the latter by Bromley Road.

In his *Southgate and Edmonton Past,* Graham Dalling confirms this location and says that the mansion was clearly of Tudor origin. Robinson tells us that it was repaired in 1611 by George Huxley, and his wife Katherine. He says, 'Their united arms carved in oak was placed over the chimney piece in the great hall; and their initials also appeared on the cistern heads of the water pipes ...... On the demolition of the Mansion - house in 1818, it was evident that it had been partly rebuilt at some period, since old mortice holes were formed in many of the larger girders. Musket shot of small size, or pistol balls, were found in many parts of the walls; and from this circumstance we might be induced to form a conjecture, that, during the civil wars, this house had been attacked.

Among the coins found, there were none of antiquity, being chiefly those of the reigns of Elizabeth, and Charles the First. The only article found, worthy of notice, was a silver spoon with a hexagonal stem, surmounted by a crest; a lion in a sitting posture; the crest was gilt. This spoon, the bowl of which is much shattered, is in the possession of James George Tatem Esq., and appears to be of the date of Elizabeth.

The house was built of bricks, and of lofty and spacious dimensions. The principal entrance was through a porch, which formed the lower part of a central projecting turret. The upper divisions of the building were ornamented with pediments of scroll work, among which appeared the rose and pomegranate, the devices of England and Arragon. The interior experienced only a few alterations, and did not contain any particular of unusual interest. In the hall were some good family portraits. In an upper room were the arms of the Merchant Adventurers, to which Company Mr. Huxley belonged.

This house had for many years been inhabited by different persons, and was once occupied as a boarding house. Mr. James George Tatum, the present owner of the estate, experiencing much difficulty in getting a tenant from the very dilapidated state, into which the house had fallen, caused the whole to be pulled down, and the materials to be sold by auction. The site of the house, out offices, gardens, and an orchard, together about seven acres, is now let to Mr. Robert Warner, the possessor of the unique cottage opposite, the site of which with the grounds, was formerly the fish ponds attached to, and part of, the ancient domain of Wyer-halle'. There is a picture of Wyer Hall in 1685 at P23 of Robinson, which is reproduced at P22 of Graham Dalling's book.

Millfield House

See Plate 54. EHHS Chronicle 1 of October 1978 contained an article entitled, 'Millfield House: New Arts Centre'. It told us that the property originally formed part of the Wyer Hall Estate, just discussed above. The house was built about 1760 by the famous Adams brothers. The facts surrounding the earliest known residents are a little cloudy, but it is certain that from 1796, till after the turn of that century, the ambassador of either Imperial Russia or Austria stayed there. Sometime after 1800 the Mushet family owned the property. Robert Mushet was first clerk to the master melter and refiner at the Royal Mint. In 1842 the house was put up for auction, and described as follows,

'For sale, one very excellent mansion standing upon an extensive lawn, perfectly secluded and retired.' The mansion included a drawing room, two morning rooms, a circular hall, three wine cellars and a well "with a never – failing supply of excellent spring water." The lake was, "a beautiful sheet of water, flowing through the lawn and pleasure grounds into a constantly – flowing stream which, passing through the grounds, refreshes the banks, walks and plantations." (The stream is now called Pymmes Brook.)

The Chronicle tells us that the estate later became the property of the Strand Vestry and was used as a Poor Law orphanage in the early 1900s. Belgian refugees stayed there briefly during the First World War, and afterwards it became St. David's Hospital, and was run by the Metropolitan Asylums Board, mainly to house epileptics. St. David's closed in 1972, whence it became an Arts Centre.

The VCH confirms that Millfield House was built in the late 18th century, and was occupied in 1796 by the Russian Ambassador. In his *Southgate and Edmonton Past,* Graham Dalling tells us that Millfield House was probably constructed c 1790, and that in 1801 was owned by Daniel Barbot Beale, whose family came from St. Pancras, where they continued to own property. Beale also owned much land in this area (see Enclosure Ownership Schedule).

Plate 54. Millfield House, Edmonton in July 2004

The House was built in the late 18th century, and at the time of Enclosure was owned by Daniel Barbot Beale, who also possessed much land in the area.

Myrtle Cottage

The Palmers Green and Southgate Gazette of 8th October 1948 contained an article headed 'Myrtle Cottage, Firs Lane, Doomed'. The accompanying sketch of it is at Plate 55. The article went on to explain, ' .... The last parcel of the Heath lands has been purchased by Edmonton Borough Council. This is Myrtle Cottage and the ground attached in Firs Lane, on a dividing line between Southgate and Edmonton. This charming rural scene had been preserved in its serene aspect by Mr. Heath, son of the late Mr. Heath, who vacates the cottage and grounds this month, after disposing of the greenhouses and the saleable produce. It is gathered that the deeds of Myrtle Cottage date back to the year 1710, and the low ceilings are some indication of its age ..... the tall figure of Mr. Heath nearly links up ceiling and floor. The inside is typical of an old country cottage as also is the front garden...' The first name of the tall Mr. Heath, Junior was Stanley.

Myrtle Cottage was on the east side of Firs Lane, opposite Firs Mansion, as shown on the enlargement of the Enclosure Map of a stretch of Firs Lane at Figure 20. In the section on the Lake family there is an account of John Thomas Smith (1766 -1833), an artist, engraver and author of distinction. He came to live at Myrtle Cottage, aged 22, in 1788 to teach art to Sir James Winter Lake's daughters, and he stayed for seven years. The cottage, and the land on which it stood, were owned by Sir James. Today it is commemorated by a Blue Plaque on one of the shops that now sits on its site in the modern parade of shops, photographed at Plate 8.

Myrtle Cottage, Firs Lane, Doomed

Plate 55. Myrtle Cottage, Firs Lane in 1948

My thanks to The Gazette for letting me reproduce this 1948 sketch by Mr. Rutherford. The Cottage was believed to date back to 1710, and is shown on the Enclosure Map at Figure 20. From 1788 – 1795 it was the home of the artist John Smith, whose likeness of the Rev. Henry Owen is at Plate 4. The Blue Plaque to Smith, on the site of what had been Myrtle Cottage, is at Plate 8.

Firs Farm

In 1801 Plots 232 and 233 (shown at Figure 20) were owned by the Dean and Chapter of St. Paul's, but leased to William Mellish. Plot 232 was described as 'Farmhouse and yards', and 233 as 'Home field'. The Farmhouse was on the opposite side of 'Firs Lane' to Barrow's Well Green, and just south of where those two lanes intersected.

Alan Dumayne, in his *Once Upon a Time in Palmers Green,* tells us that Firs Farm is thought to have been built about 1720 on the instructions of Mrs. Childs, of the well-known local family (who later inter - married with the Udalls). For some years the equally well known Bunce family ran the farm. Alan tells us that the local Council purchased the farm from the Dean and Chapter of St. Paul's, and it was demolished in 1927. Part of the land was later used for housing developments, the remainder being converted into the sports grounds we see today. There is a photograph of the old farmhouse at Page 27 of my *A Look at Old Winchmore Hill.*

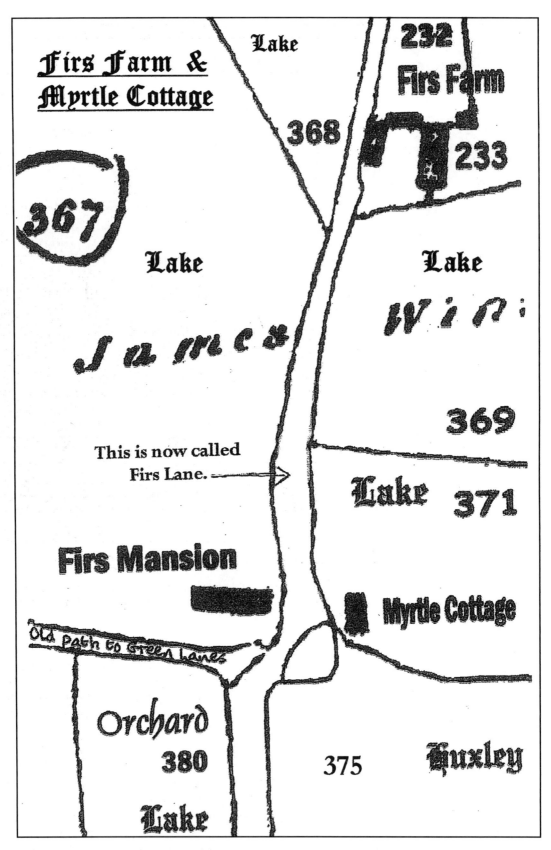

Figure 20. Firs Farm and Myrtle Cottage at the time of Enclosure

The main lane running from north to south is what we call Firs Lane. Firs Mansion was the home of the Lake family, and Myrtle Cottage, where artist John Smith lived for some time, was on the other side of the lane. Both sites now bear Blue Plaques commemorating their famous former residents. Firs Farm to the north gives its name to the present day playing fields. (I have not marked the land utilisation on this map.)

Outside of Winchmore Hill – Palmers Green & Southgate Areas

Broomfield

At Plates 56 & 57 are two photographs of the old mansion from before the first catastrophic fire of 1984. Before that fire I periodically visited Broomfield House, when it was a museum. For this section I rely heavily on the official booklet of that era - *Broomfield in Southgate - A Souvenir Guide* by David Pam.

Plate 56. Ye Olde picture of Broomfield House, Palmers Green

This picture is taken from a Postcard bearing a Postmark of 16th July 1906. The Mansion is shown on the earliest maps of Edmonton parish, dating from Elizabethan times. William Tash owned it at the time of Enclosure.

The booklet tells us that the house is shown on the earliest maps of Edmonton parish, dating from Elizabethan times. Its name of *Brumfeld* was written in the hand of Lord Burghley himself! Geoffrey Walkaden was the owner at that time, having bought the house from John Broomfield. Walkaden sold it to Richard Skevington. By the end of Elizabeth's reign it was the property of Alderman Sir John Spencer, and he sold it to Joseph Jackson early in the 17th century.

The Jackson family held the estate for nearly 200 years until Mary Jackson married William Tash. After William's death in 1816 it was bought by Phillip Lybbe Powys. The Powys family remained owners until 1903, and their influence is commemorated in the name of one of the nearby major roads. However, the family seldom lived at Broomfield, but let the house to tenants, the most famous of these being Sir Ralph Littler, who played an important part in securing Southgate's independence from Edmonton in the 1880s.

William Tash features strongly in the Edmonton Enclosure Schedule of Ownership, and he is shown as the owner of Broomfield at the time. There is also a James Jackson in the Schedule, and one wonders if he is a relation of William's wife Mary.

Plate 57. Broomfield House in the 1970s

When I first moved to the Borough I sometimes used to visit the Museum there. This 1976 photograph is a reminder of what we have all lost.

Minchenden

In 1801 the Duchess of Chandos owned Minchenden, on the south side of Southgate Green (see Plate 58). It was listed in the Enclosure Schedule at Plot 411 as 'Mansion, yards and lawn'. In his 1982 softback, *Southgate and Winchmore Hill – A Short History,* David Pam tells us that at the time of the Restoration of Charles 11, in 1660, Minchenden was in the possession of Sir Thomas Stringer. Sir Thomas Wolstenholme bought the mansion from him. *The Victoria County History* tells us that by the late 17th century Grovelands, or Southgate Grove, was also in his hands, and part of the Minchenden estate. Sir Thomas Wolstenholme died in 1691, and Pam says that early in the 18th century, Sir Nicholas Wolstenholme sold the house to Sir David Heckstetter, who in turn sold it, in 1736, to John Nicoll, a wealthy London merchant.

In 1753 Nicholl's only daughter, and heiress, Margaret married James Brydges, the Third Duke of Chandos, who came to live in the House. Regrettably, Margaret died childless in 1768, and the Duke married Anne Eliza Gamon in 1777. She became mentally deranged after his death in 1789, and that is presumably why the Ownership Schedule actually lists 'her Committee', rather than her, as the owner of Minchenden. Anne's daughter, Anna Elizabeth, married Richard, Marquis of Buckingham, in 1796, and he was created Duke of Buckingham and Chandos in 1822. The family appear to have sold what we now call the Grovelands estate to Walker Gray shortly after the marriage.

In his small 1906 paperback titled *The Story of Winchmore Hill and Southgate,* Walker Round tells us that, '....Minchenden House, a spacious and commanding old mansion which occupied a site east of the church (in Waterfall Road), and between that edifice and Duchess' pond. Immediately opposite the vicarage, in the grounds of Arno's Grove, will be noticed two magnificent cedar trees; these stood in front of the old house.

It was a square red brick structure of the early Georgian period, and contained so many windows that the village folk used to say there was one for every

210

week in the year. The house was shut out from the road by a high brick wall and heavy wooden gates. It was built by Mr. John Nichol, a wealthy citizen of London, who, however, died very soon after its completion (1747). His daughter and sole heiress, Margaret, became the wife of James, third Duke of Chandos.

A View of the Marquis of Caernarvon's Seat at Southgate.

Plate 58. Ye olde view of Minchenden on Southgate Green

My thanks to Southgate District Civic Trust for supplying this old illustration for publication. The estate we came to know as Grovelands was associated with Minchenden for some while before Walker Gray bought it just prior to Enclosure. Early in the 19th century Minchenden mansion was acquired by Isaac Walker who, in 1853, demolished it and added the grounds to those of Arnold's Grove. The bland rectangular building seems to have been lacking in any architectural merit.

The grounds of Minchenden House, which ran down to Pymme's Brook, and were bounded by Betts Stile Wood, contained much fine timber. The residence of the Duke and Duchess of Chandos at Minchenden House must have conferred quite a considerable importance upon Southgate. His Grace, who was very wealthy, was fond of pomp and ceremony, and he always travelled about in great state. So many horses did the Duke possess that the stabling attached to the mansion, extensive though it was, was insufficient for their accommodation, and another large range of stables was erected on the opposite side of the road, the site of these being where the vicarage now stands.

The property passed to the Marquis of Buckingham, in right of his wife, second daughter and sole heiress of the Duke of Chandos. Early in the last (19th) century the estate was acquired by Mr. Isaac Walker who, in 1853, demolished the mansion and added the grounds to those of Arno's Grove. George 11 was an occasional visitor to the Duke at Minchenden House ....'

Arnos Grove

In the summer of 2006 I visited 'Southgate Beaumont' home for the elderly (once known as Arnold's Grove), just south of Southgate Green, and photographed it as at Plate 59 . Plate 60 shows it in its former glory. The home kindly gave me a brochure, from which I have extracted the following information. I give more detail beyond the book's time frame than for other properties, as it is not likely to appear again in any book that I am responsible for.

211

Plate 59. 'Arnos Grove Mansion' in 2006

I took this picture in the summer of 2006. The nucleus of the current building was constructed by James Colebrook, in 1721, with the help of architect Sir Richard Naylor, though it has seen many modifications over the years.

In 1610 Sir John Weld sold the estate, then known as 'Arnolds', to Mr. (later Sir) William Acton. His family subsequently sold it to Mr. James Colebrook, in 1719. In 1721, with the help of architect Sir Richard Naylor, he set about replacing the old smaller house in Waterfall Road. This included the construction of the centre portion of the existing building. Dominating the entrance hall of today are frescoes painted in 1723 by Gerard Lanscroon, a pupil of Verrio. They depict Julius Caesar's triumphant entrance into Rome, and are considered important examples of English Baroque wall painting. On the ceiling are the arms of James Colebrook and his wife Mary Hudson.

On James's death his son George, who later became Sir George Colebrook, completed the work. The house was built without a basement, or the extensions on the north and south, or the front and rear porches. It would appear that Sir George built the North Wing to designs closely resembling the, then new, offices of the Bank of England, under the direction of Sir Robert Taylor. This Wing housed an 'eating room' 35' by 24' and 20' high. There was also a library of 25' by 20', again 20' in height.

Sir William Mayne, also known as Lord Newhaven, was the next owner, and he changed the name to Arnos Grove. He added the South Wing, which reputedly contained an 'Eating Room' 25 by 20 feet and 20 feet in height, although later alterations have obliterated any trace. He also added the porch on the West Side of the drawing room, together with a very large entry portico on the northern side, and the smaller portico at the front of the house.

After Lord Newhaven, a gentleman named James Brown owned the property for a short time. In 1777 the house passed into the possession of Mr. Isaac Walker. He created three miles of pleasure walks, along with a 'new river', that winds for nearly a mile through the grounds. The Walker family owned the house for four generations and was responsible for buying much of the surrounding land in an effort to stop urbanisation. In 1884 the house was said to command 'a view of several rich valleys, with hills towards Finchley and Muswell Hill'. The Walker family is covered in the ownership schedule, under the entry for Walker Gray.

Plate 60. Ye olde view of Arno's Grove

My thanks to The Southgate District Civic Trust for supplying this 1784 sketch of Arno's Grove.

In 1918 the property was purchased by the shipping magnate Andrew Weir (Lord Inverforth). In 1928 he sold the estate as building land, and the mansion was bought by the North Metropolitan Power Supply company, who renamed it Northmet House. In 1935 the grand entrance portico was demolished when the first section of the newer South Wing was constructed. It was about this time that Sir George Colebrook's original library was altered into the existing art-deco room, with period ceiling and walnut panelling. Unfortunately, this alteration included a new door from the main staircase at first floor level, which obliterated Lanscroon's Julius Caesar!

In 1975 Legal and General Insurance acquired the property. They extensively altered and restored the interior, and added the second section of the new North Wing. In 1995, after standing unused for some two years, PPP Beaumont bought the property, and they sold the entire South Wing for conversion to private apartments. The central portion and the North Wing were renovated and converted into a care home, which was opened in June 1997, the same month that its current owners, Westminster Health Care, acquired the property. It now offers a good home for the care of older and frail residents. The old name of Arnos Grove has been enshrined in a nearby tube station.

Diary Section continued
1801

General

On 1st January 1801 the Act of Union of Great Britain and Ireland came into effect under the name of the United Kingdom, and Ireland sent 100 members to the Commons in Westminster. This was the year that the Health and Morals of Apprentices Act was passed, forbidding children under nine from working, and restricting the working day of older children to 'only' twelve daytime hours. The General Enclosure Act of 1801 obviated the need, in most cases, for private Enclosure Acts such as the 1800 one for Edmonton, which were costly and time consuming.

Pitt proposed to extend religious tolerance in his Catholic Emancipation Act, but King George 111 objected, and Pitt was forced to resign after 17 years in office. He was succeeded as Prime Minister by the Tory Henry Addington, Viscount Sidmouth, only to return to office for a further two years in 1804. At the Battle of Copenhagen the Danish fleet was destroyed by Nelson, and the Northern League shattered.

1801 saw Richard Trevithick's steam carriage being given a run out on a road, though it blew up whilst he was in the pub! It was also the year that the London Penny Post became the Two Penny Post. This was a time when an income of £300 pa was sufficient to support a Gentleman of leisure in some style, with his own house, servants, carriage and horse. The first British census was published in 1801. It indicated that in addition to England's 7,492,484 people, there were 255,889 in Wales and 469,188 in the armed forces, giving a grand total of 8,217,561 – probably less than the numbers living in Greater London today.

Local

The Census returns for 1801 are available at the Guildhall Library. At the time, remember, Winchmore Hill was in the Parish of Edmonton. I have extracted the following –

'Abstract of the Answers and Returns made pursuant to an ACT, passed in the Forty-first Year of His Majesty King GEORGE the Third, intituled "AN ACT for taking an Account of the Population of Great Britain, and of the Increase or Diminution thereof", - in so far as such Answers, and Returns, have transmitted to His Majesty's Principal Secretary of State for the Home Department; up to the Twenty-Sixth Day of June 1801.

Unit	Inhabited	By no. families	Uninhabited	Males	Females	Persons chiefly in agriculture	Trade, Manufact – uring, Handicraft	All Others	Total
Edmonton Parish	901	950	47	2,438	2,655	412	557	4,124	5,093
Edmonton Hundred	2,831	3,475	172	8,285	8,600	1,357	1,528	14,000	16,885
Middlesex County	112,755	209,786	5,158	373,327	444,383	13,417	162,218	619,911	817,710

Of the Hundred's other Parishes of South Mimms, Monken Hadley, Tottenham and Enfield, only the last named boasted a greater population, with 5,881.

Middlesex was the most populous County of England, though Yorkshire would have exceeded it if it had not sent in three separate returns for the East, North and West Ridings. These three between them had about 125,000 engaged in Agriculture, which therefore could be deemed to push Devon into second place with 95,208. These were obviously greatly in excess of Middlesex. Only Surrey, Rutland, Huntingdon and Westmoreland had fewer engaged in this pursuit. Only 'Lancaster' (i.e. Lancashire) and the three Yorkshire Ridings combined boasted more employed in 'Trade, Manufactures or Handicraft'. Middlesex was way out in front in the 'All Other Persons' category. Even with the three Ridings combined Yorkshire's total 'only' amounted to about 464,000.

On 25th May 1934 *The Enfield Gazette* ran a story by 'Memorabilia' that was headed 'The Gravel Pit in Hedge Lane'. It told us that on June 12th, 1609, George Huxley bought the Wyer Hall estate from the Leeke family, and it continued in the direct male line of the Huxley family until the death of Thomas Huxley in 1743. His younger daughter Sarah inherited it, but she died unmarried in 1801, and her lands in Edmonton went to her five cousins, and by that route Wyer Hall descended to James George Tatem. (See also the section on Sarah Huxley in the ownership Schedule, and on Wyer Hall in the map section covering Edmonton.)

The VCH tells us that in the early 19th century the discovery of a well with Epsom salts brought Winchmore Hill the reputation of a Spa. At Page 82 of her masterpiece Miss Cresswell explains that it was situated in the vicinity of what we now call Eversley Park Road.

John Vickris Taylor first of all married an Elizabeth Gray, and then Sophia Donnithorne. On 29th June 1801, John Vickris and Sophia had a daughter named Sophia, younger sister of the John Donnithorne who later owned Grovelands. She went on to marry the second Isaac Walker. (See Figure 3.) In the Friends' graveyard is a tombstone which reads, 'Ann Barclay (Wife of R. Barclay, Clapham) Born 1763 Died 1801' This was also the year in which the 2nd Jacob Yallowley, who had bought the Independent Chapel on the Green, died.

Box J90 at the National Archives contains a document labelled, 'Dated 19th December 1801 Edmonton Inclosure. The Trustees of the Quakers meeting of Tottenham to Mrs. Rachael Marshall. Grant and Appointment of Freehold Common Rights.' The parchment seems to indicate that for £21. 14s Mrs. Marshall bought the rights to land the Quakers would have obtained under the Award in lieu of common rights. She paid the money to David Barclay of Walthamstow, Danl. Bell, Michael Phillips, John Phillips, Thomas Coar, Thomas Shillitoe, Wm. Forster and two others whose signatures are faint. The document was witnessed by a Josiah Forster of Tottenham. Rachael Marshall was shown as being a widow of Castle Street, Hertford.

J90 contains another document labelled, 'Dated 19th December 1801. Edmonton Inclosure. Mr. Richard Caleb Morrison to Mrs. Rachael Marshall. Grant and Appointment of Freehold Common Rights.' Morrison receipts £37. 2s 0d. from Rachael Marshall for two tenements in Winchmore Hill that the parchment indicates were in the occupation of Mrs. Sarah Morrison. Could these be the ones shown for Ms. Marshall in the Award Schedule at Plots 103 and 104 one wonders?

At the LMA is document ACC/0695, which contains the Edmonton Manor Minutes for the period 1801 to 1832. One excerpt is, '26th May 1801 Received by Mr. Hardy the then Steward, but assumed by Mr. Wadeson the following Fines viz. On the Admission of Robert Davis 7s 6d; Thomas Oliver £6. 5s. 0d; Robert Davis £1.16s 0d'

1802

General

Income tax, which had been introduced in 1799, was abolished in 1802. Under the Peace of Amiens, between Britain and France, Britain returned most of the gains made in the Revolutionary Wars. Ceylon and Trinidad became British colonies, and Malta was returned to the Knights of St. John. Madam Tussaud arrived in Britain.

Local

In the General Election of 1802 the Whig George Byng of Wrotham Park retained his Middlesex seat. Local people voted en masse for the radical Independent candidate Francis Burdett, and he was returned as the County's second MP, though the election was declared void in 1804 owing to irregularities in the election process, and in the 1804 re – run he lost by five votes.

In a document of 30th August 1802 Joseph Osborne surrendered the lease of *The Dog and Duck* to Christopher Idle. Martha Newman again took over the licence to *The King's Head,* from Mary Newman. In 1802 Mathias Butcher, former licensee of *The Orange Tree*, was involved in a land transaction with William Mellish, as detailed under Butcher's name in the E.E. Ownership Schedule section.

The Palmers Green Gazette of 1st November 1940 contained a Memorabilia article headed 'A Winchmore Hill Burying Ground'. It ran, 'Here's a snippet from *The Gentleman's Magazine* dated 9th July, 1802: - "In Great Russell Street, Bloomsbury, aged upwards of 90, Mrs. Anne Fothergill, sister of the late Dr. John F.: and on the 14th, her remains were interred by those of her brother in the Quakers' burying ground in Winchmore-hill, a very numerous train of coaches attending."

She was a maiden lady, it being then the custom to speak of, address and write of the elder spinsters as "mistress". "Mr. Urban", editor of the magazine, was not quite accurately informed, because if you go into the Friends' Burial Ground, Church Hill, Winchmore Hill, walk almost to the door of the Meeting House, turn sharply left and again bear left, you will see two of the usual small headstones standing a few feet apart, by themselves, near to, but at a right angle to the Church Hill boundary wall. One of them is inscribed: "John Fothergill, M.D. Died 12 Mo. 26 1780, aged 68" and on the other is "Ann Fothergill. Died 7 mo. 8, 1802, aged 84". '

Tom Mason's notes at the LHU state, 'Winchmore Hill 1802 Oct. 19. At Stamford Hill in his 77th year Mr. Daniel Bell, an eminent coal merch. & one of the people called Quakers. His remains were deposited in the Quakers' burying ground at Winchmore – hill.'

At the LMA is document ACC/0695, which contains the Edmonton Manor Minutes for the period 1801 to 1832. The following is an extract -

	£.	s.	d.
'Debit William Curtis Esq. Lord of the Manor. 1801			
Oct. Paid Bill for General Court on 26th May last	23.	3.	9
1802 Paid for Sundries as Bill	59.	14.	8
June 8th. Paid expenses of General Court (your proportion)	12.	12.	0
Carried over	95.	10.	5

On the opposite page is the statement, 'Edmonton in account with

Samuel Wigman Wadeson his Steward – 1801.' There then follows a list of fines paid on admission to the Manor, and we know that some of the names are associated with the old village. On 8th June 1802 George Jauncey paid £1. 0s 0d., William Davies paid 1/- on the surrender of Robt. Davies., Isaac English paid 1s., George Jauncey (again) paid 1s., and Thos. Oliver 1s. On 30th December 1802 James Gosling paid 1s, whilst Danl. Beale paid two fines – 1s and £29. 15s. 8d.

1803

General

In 1803 John Dalton introduced his atomic theory, whilst John Horrocks introduced the first power looms made entirely of metal – a decisive development in the mechanisation of the textile industry. Napoleon assembled a huge fleet at Boulogne and an army of 150,000 at Dunkirk in preparation for an invasion of Britain. To fund the military the Government re started Income Tax.

Local

Tom Mason's notes at the LHU state, 'Obituary (continued). Southgate & c.1803. Feb. 17. Aged 76 at Bush hill, Edmonton, Mrs. Blackburn, relict of John B. esq. who died 1798 …'.

In 1803 Mary Newman took over *The King's Head* licence, again, from Martha Newman. Meanwhile Christopher Idle replaced Joseph Osborne as licensee at *The Dog and Duck*.

At the LMA is document ACC/0695, which contains the Edmonton Manor Minutes for the period 1801 to 1832. I have extracted some pieces for this book -

'1st May 1803 Received of Mr. Blackburn for Heriot £50. 0s 0d; Received of Jn. Merrington for Admission 30th 1802 1s.' '31st May 1803 Received at the General Court on the Admission of William Eaton 10s.' '8th August 1803. Of George Tatem Esqre. Fine on his Admission to 3/18th of the late Sarah Huxley's Estates on Dec. 30th 1802. £2. 14s 7½ d - Relief 7s 3d. Of Ditto fine on his admission to 1/5th of another 1/18th on the 31st May 1803 3s. 7¾d. Of Catherine Tatem – the like fines £3. 9s. 2d.'

1804

General

Richard Trevithick built the first steam train to successfully haul a load. The Tory Henry Addington had succeeded Pitt as Prime Minister in 1801, but in 1804 Pitt returned to that office for another two years. Urged on by France, Spain declared war on Britain.

Local

In the General Election of 1802 the franchise of Middlesex elected the Independent radical Francis Burdett as one of its two MPs. In 1804, owing to irregularities in the election process, the election was re – run, and he lost by five votes.

Tom Mason's handwritten notes at the LHU tell us that the actor John

Reeve (1799 – 1838) was born in Ludgate Hill, but attended Mr. Thompson's preparatory school in Winchmore Hill, this being represented in the 1826 Pigot's Directory by the entry, 'Thompson Francis, (gent's bdg.)'. One of his school mates was a Frederick Yates. 1804 would be the sort of time that someone born in 1799 would start Prep. School. It seems Reeve shone in comedy and played at the Adelphi and Haymarket in London. Unfortunately he died young through his addiction to alcohol and it seems that in his last appearance in 1837 he was, 'conspicuously imperfect'. Yates (1797 – 1842) was a versatile actor, and in 1825 he co – purchased the Adelphi Theatre in London for £25,000, becoming the sole owner in 1836.

Isaac Walker of Arnos Grove died aged 79 on 6th December 1804 and was buried in the Friends Meeting Ground in Church Hill. It was also in this year that Francis Newman (previously licensee in 1798) again took on the licence to *The King's Head*, until succeeded by John Smith in 1815. 1804 saw the award of land under the 1800 E.E. Act published.

One of the documents at The Guildhall Library is an Indenture of 2nd May 1804 between 'the Master Warden's and Commonalty of the Mystery of Cordwainers of the City of London of the one part and William Baker of Winchmore Hill in the County of a Middlesex Farmer of the other part.....do demise leave and to farm let unto the said William Baker that piece or parcel of Land situate on Enfield Chase in the County of Middlesex late part of the Edmonton Allotment of the said Chase containing by admeasurement three acres three roods and nine perches now in the tenure or occupation of him the said William Baker abutting on the East on a new made road and on the west on Land belonging to the Vicar of Enfield on the North on Land belonging to Mr. Smith and on the South on Land belonging to the Dean of Chapter of St. Pauls.... every year during the said term of twenty one years....the Yearly Rent or sum of four pounds four shillings of lawful money....' The facts given indicate that this plot of land was numbered 1551 on the 1801 Enclosure Map, off of the lane that is now Eversley Park Road.

Various documents at the National Archives, Kew are referenced J90. One of these is labelled, 'Dated 20th Day of May 1804. Sir William Curtis Bart. Lord of the Manor to Henry Thompson Esq. Release in fee and enfranchisement of a Copyhold Cottage parcel of the manor of Edmonton otherwise Edington otherwise Edmonton County Middlesex.' The Winchmore Hill cottage, with garden, is said to be near Chase Gate.

A parchment referenced J90/980 at Kew reads, 'Manor of Edelmeton, otherwise Edelington, otherwise Edmonton in the County of Middlesex. The View of Frankpledge and General Court Baron of Sir William Curtis Baronet Lord of the said Manor holden in and for the same Manor on Tuesday in Whitsun Week being the Twenty second day of May One thousand eight hundred and four before Samuel Weyman Wadeson Gentleman Steward there.

At this Court comes Francis Hall a Customary Tenant of this Manor in his own proper person and in full and open Court surrenders into the hands of the Lord by the hands and acceptance of his Steward by the Rod according to the Custom of this manor All that Cottage or Tenement with the Garden and appurtenances thereto belonging & situate by the Chase gate at Winchmore Hill within this Manor and in the occupation of the said Francis Hall which said premises were at the General Court Baron holden in and for this Manor on the Twenty fourth day of May One thousand seven hundred and seventy four granted by the then Lady of this Manor To the said Francis Hall for his Life and all the Estate right Title interest must(?) possession property profit benefit claim and demand whatsoever as Lord and in Equity of him the said Francis

Hall of in to and one of the said premises and every or any part and parcel thereof To the use of Henry Thompson of Tottenham in the County of Middlesex Esquire his heirs and assigns for and during the natural life of the said Francis Hall at the Will of the Lord according to the Custom of this manor.

And thereupon the Lord by his Steward with the consent of the Homage according to the Custom of this manor Grants the said premises to the said Henry Thompson by Gilbert Grosvenor his Attorney duly authorized and by the rod delivers seizin (i.e. possession) there of to have and to hold the said premises with the appurtenances unto the said Henry Thompson his Heirs and assigns for and during the natural life of the said Francis Hall at the Will of the Lord according to the Custom of this Manor of the Lord by the Rod by Copy of Court Roll by the yearly Rent of Two Shillings and the yearly Rent charge of Two Shillings and six pence to the Church Wardens of the parish of Edmonton for the time being to be by them distributed amongst the poor of the said parish Fealty suit of Court and all other Customs and Services therefore are and of right accustomed and the Lord demands no Fine upon this occasion and he is admitted Tenant accordingly but his Fealty is respired because & c. Examined by me SW Wadeson Steward'

Presumably this is the same cottage and land as was granted to Thompson on the 20th May, now formally being confirmed at the Manorial Courts. Hall only has Plot 59 listed against his name in the Enclosure Schedule, and this is by what is marked as Winchmore Hill Gate on the Enclosure Map. The Gate was obviously also known as Chase Gate locally.

1805

General

On the morning of 21st October Admiral Nelson was fatally wounded in winning the battle with the Franco - Spanish fleet that took place off Cape Trafalgar on the southern coast of Spain. This convincing victory ended Napoleon's plans to invade England.

Local

At the LMA is document ACC/0695, which contains the Edmonton Manor Minutes for the period 1801 to 1832. An entry for 1805 reads, 'May 8th Of John Blackburn on admission on the death of Catherine Blackburn £13. 19s. 0d.' In 1805 Edward and Sarah Thomasine Busk had their eldest son Edward Thomas. Friends Burial Ground contains a headstone which reads, 'Susannah Barclay (wife of Jn. Barclay). Born 1739. Died 1805'. She had been the wife of the John Barclay who was known as 'of Cambridge Heath and Lombard Street', and who was a key figure in the early history of Barclay's Bank.

1806

General

The great engineer Isambard Kingdom Brunel was born at Portsmouth. Ralph Wedgwood secured a patent for carbon paper. Food prices rose and the textile industry declined as a result of Napolean's economic blockade. Prime Minister William Pitt the Younger died at Putney, to be succeeded by William Lord Grenville as leader of a Whig dominated coalition. The Dutch colony at the Cape in South Africa ceded to the British.

Local

Local land baron William Mellish became Tory MP for Middlesex, and retained his seat until 1820. On 28th November 1806, Edward Busk of Fords Grove was called to the Bar. This was also the year William Cass purchased the Beaulieu estate from Thomas Nisbett for £4,750. The Cass family lived at Beaulieu until 1827, when they moved to Little Grove at Cat Hill in East Barnet. However, Frederick, son of William, retained the property until 1832. At the LMA is document ACC/0695, which contains the Edmonton Manor Minutes for the period 1801 to 1832. An entry for 1806 reads, 'Nov. 25th 1806. On the admission of Danl. Beale on Surrender of Eaton. 19s 4d.'

Other LMA documents referenced ACC/0386/002, bear the Library's synopsis, 'Lease for 9 ½ years. Farm house with farmyard, barn, stable, outhouses and other buildings on Chase Side; with 27 fields of arable and grass land containing 124a. 3r. 3p., being part of Edmonton allotment of Enfield Chase. Yearly rent - £327. 10s. 4d. 8th Mar. 1806.' I reproduce the start of one of the documents here – 'Sold by W. and G.D. Witherby Birch in London. This Indenture made the eight day of March in the forty sixth year of the Reign of our Sovereign Lord George the Third by the Grace of God of the United Kingdom of Great Britain and Ireland King Defender of the faith and in the year of our Lord one thousand eight hundred and six between Henry Thompson of Tottenham Green in the parish of Tottenham in the County of Middlesex Esquire of the one part and John Karmock of Hermitage Street in the Parish of St. George in the East in the said County of Middlesex Painter of the other part ...' The file gives a breakdown of the large acreage as follows,

	A. R. P.		A. R. P.		A. R. P.
No. 1	0. 2. 31.	No. 6	2. 3. 30.	No. 11	7. 2. 21.
No. 2	1. 3. 28.	No. 7	3. 3. 13.	No. 12	32. 2. 15.
No. 3	3. 0. 27.	No. 8	0. 2. 0.	No. 13	25. 3. 39.
No. 4	1. 1. 11.	No. 9	3. 2. 4.	No. 14	38. 1. 14.
No. 5	1. 3. 7.	No. 10	0. 2. 3.	Total	124. 3. 3.

I am unable to pinpoint where these plots are, or say more about Karmock.

1807

General

The Geological Society of London was founded in 1807, and Lord Byron had a volume of poetry published. Gas lighting was first introduced into London, and by 1820 much of the City was gas lit. In Parliament William Wilberforce was the driving force behind the passing of the Slave Trade Abolition Act, which abolished the Slave trade throughout the British Empire. Whig Lord Grenville rejected Catholic emancipation and his ministry fell. Grenville was succeeded as Prime Minister by the Tory, The Duke of Portland.

Local

At the London Metropolitan Archives is a report of the 1807 Middlesex Court Sessions (MJ/SP/1807/01/011). It reads, 'James George Young agt. An Order of Edward Rowe Mores Esq. for payment of Labourers wages. Granted 17 Jany. 1807.

Lodge ...... To move to enter & ? this appeal to the next Sept. on the within Petition ½ Qua. Wm. S. Jessop. W. Smith (for Cater) 15, Bedford St. Bedford Row.

To the Worshipful his Majesty's Justices of the Peace acting in and for the County of Middlesex in General Quarter Sessions of the Peace of the said County assembled. The humble Petition and appeal of James George Young of Winchmore Hill in the County of Middlesex. Builder Theweth, that by a certain order or conviction under the hand of Edward Rowe Mores Esquire one of his Majesty's Justices of the Peace for the said County of Middlesex bearing date the fifteenth day of January instant your Petitioner was convicted as herein alledged (stet) on the oaths of Henry Luxton and Robert Slight of Winchmore Hill aforesaid Labourers for that they were duly hired by your Petitioner to be his Handicraftsmen for the term of one week to wit from the fifth to the tenth day of January both days included in the year 1807 for the wages of Thirty one shillings and that they duly performed the said service and that your Petitioner was summoned and appeared thereto and after being examined into the premises and duly investigated the matter on both sides it was the determination of the said Justice that the said wages were justly due. And the said Justice did hereby adjudge determine and order that your Petitioner should pay to the said Henry Luxton and Robert Slight the sum of Thirty one shillings each for their wages aforesaid as also the further sum of Six Shillings for the costs incurred in recovering the same.

That your Petitioner thinks himself aggrieved by the judgment of the said Justice and therefore Your Petitioner doth appeal to your Worships at the present general Quarter Sessions of the Peace against the judgment of the said Justice and doth pray such relief in the premises as to your worships shall seem (?) meet. James G. Young.'

The Governor of the Hudson's Bay Company Sir James Winter Lake of Firs Hall died, aged 65, and was buried at the Parish Church in Edmonton on 4th May. Following his death his books took 14 days to sell, engravings 11 days, and the paintings took seven days. One of the headstones at All Saints reads, 'This Monument is erected as a tribute of fraternal affection by the desire of George Tatem, Esq. He died the XXV, July MDCCCV11 in the LXXXV1 year of his age.'

Tom Mason's handwritten notes at the LHU include the entry, '1807. May 20. On Winchmore – hill, Mrs. Decker (presumably Decka), wife of Mr. J.D. one of the people called Quakers. She was blind and having been left a few minutes by the servant, in endeavouring to find her way into another room, she fell into the cellar, fracturing her skull, and died within an hour.'

The first recorded Minister of the Independent Church, now the United Reformed Church, was the Rev. Robert Little, who served from 1st September 1807 to 30th November 1809.

1808

General

France occupied Spain, where there was an uprising. Work was undertaken on the Dome, Brighton and the Bank of England was completed.

Local

On 13th August 1937 The P. G. & S. Gazette ran a story about 'Riverbank', which was originally known as Butt's Farm. The author, Arthur Willis, tells us that the name 'Riverbank' was bestowed in 1808, after the then existing smaller premises had been enlarged and converted into a gentlemen's residence.

1809

General

Humphry Davy invented the arc lamp, and Arthur Wellesley was made Duke of Wellington. The Tory Prime Minister the Duke of Portland resigned owing to poor health, to be succeeded by the Tory Spencer Perceval. William Gladstone, who was to be one of the key politicians during Victoria's reign, was born.

Local

The first recorded Minister of the local Independent Church (now URC) was the Rev. Robert Little, who served from 1st September 1807 to 30th November 1809. He was succeeded by the Rev. Thomas Humpage, who served from 6th December 1809 to 30th June 1821.

Turning to the Quakers, in 1809 a washroom (now a kitchen) was built, and the Meeting House has remained much the same since. The detached keeper's cottage was constructed in 1911, and a toilet block has been added to the rear of the main building. The Meeting House became a listed Grade 11 building in 1973.

David Barclay of Walthamstow and Youngsbury in Hertfordshire was the second son of David Barclay of Cheapside by his second wife, Priscilla Freame. For many years he was a merchant in London, and became a partner in the Bank in Lombard Street in 1776. He died on Tuesday, May 30th at Walthamstow, age 81, and was buried near his father at Church Hill. The rear cover of my 1989 book *A History of Winchmore Hill* contains a colour photo' of his tombstone, which bears the inscription, 'David Barclay, son of D. Barclay. Born 1729, died 1809'.

It was in 1809 that local Friend John Decka sold the copyhold of *Roseville* to William John Reeves, who immediately proceeded to get the land released and enfranchised, by the payment of £31 10s to Sir William Curtis, the Lord of the Manor. This same year the Rev. T. Winchester Lewis married Elizabeth, the daughter of Isaac Walker of Arnos Grove.

1810

General

The popular 'Farmer George' 111 celebrated his Golden Jubilee on 25th October 1810. There were illuminations, fireworks, dancing in the streets and a laudatory poem. Unfortunately the King, who had already experienced two episodes of unusual behaviour, began his final decline into insanity, senility and blindness. This was also the year that Waterloo Bridge was built.

Local

At the LMA is the, 'Manor of Edmonton Middx. Court Book Commencing 12th June 1810' (document ACC 695/26). The minutes of the first Court recorded in the book open, 'Manor of Edelmeton otherwise Edelington otherwise Edmonton in the

County of Middlesex. The View of Frankpledge and General Court Baron of Sir William Curtis Baronet Lord of the said Manor holden in and for the same Manor on Tuesday in Whitsun Week being the 12th day of June 1810 before Samuel Hayman Wadeson Gentleman Chief Steward there.

Jurors for our Lord the King. John Tugwell Foreman. William Eaton; William Cobbett; Joseph Etheridge; George Robinson; George Panton Carr; Samuel Woodward; John Rowley; John Whitbread; James Henry Pierce; William Acott; William Linwood; James Burden; Thomas Leach; George White; Daniel Hayward; George Corker; William John Clinker; Edward Skittlethorpe; George Young. Who being sworn present as follows. First the Common Fine Ten Shillings. Also the following persons to serve the undermentioned offices for the Year ensuing.

Ward	Markers of Cattle & Field Drivers	Aleconners	Constable	Headboroughs
Church Street	Thomas King	George Young	George Austin	Edward Pratt
Bury Street	William Goddard	William Cobbett	Aistebie	John Grimby
Fore Street	John Carter	John Whitbread	Harry Wilson	Booker
South Street	Thomas Lucas	Thomas Leach	Joseph Peele	Andrew Bolster

Thomas Richards Constable of the whole Parish; Edward Gardner William Tuck Pound Keeper. Also they present that the several Constables Headboroughs and other Officers by them named do take their respectful Oaths for the Execution of their Several Offices on or before the twenty fourth day of June instance.

And now for the Court Baron. Homage James Pierce and John Merrington Sworn. At this Court came George Green a customary Tenant of this Manor in his own proper person and surrenders into the hands of the Lord of this Manor by the hands and acceptance of his Steward according to the Custom of this Manor by the rod. All those three closes of pasture ground called Whitlocks lying and being at Winchmore Hill containing by estimation six acre be the same more or less but also all that Attachment or parcel of land situate in Hag field containing seven acres one rood and thirty perches bounded on the north by the Allotment of Sarah Teshmaker on the South by the allotment of Mr. Burrnell and John Merrington and a lane on the east by the allotment of Jacob Harvey and the ancient inclosure of Sarah Teshmaker and on the west by the allotment of John Merrington Mr. Burnell and Henry Thompson Esq. and which is allotted and awarded unto the same George Green by the Commissioners appointed in the Act of Parliament passed in the fortieth year of the reign of the present Majesty inhabited .....

...... At this Court the Homage find and present that John Acott late a customary Tenant is dead and he died seized of all those four cottages or tenements situate at the Bourne within this manor formerly in the respective occupation of Allison Simmons Lowen and Barber and now in the respective occupations of Allison and Lowen and Ball and Reading with the Appurts whereof the said John Acott was admitted Tenant at a Court holden in and for this Manor on the tenth day of June one thousand seven hundred and ninety four and under the will his Father William Acott. And that the said John Acott died without ? and that Joseph Acott Master of His Majesty Ship Monarch (?) is his younger brother and Heir according the custom of the Manor ....'

George Green's plots are clearly those shown as his in the E.E. Ownership Schedule. A glance at the Enclosure Map for The Bourne (Figure 11) suggests that these four cottages belonging to Acott were not on Plots 172 and 173, but those shown as under different ownerships at Plots 176/7/8/9.

In his handwritten notes at the LHU Tom Mason records the death of a 'Mr. John Davies of Winchmore – hill' on 11th November 1810. One presumes he is the John Davis listed in the E.E. Ownership Schedule.

1811

General

George 111 was declared insane and the Prince of Wales ruled as Prince Regent in his place. Between 1811 and 1816 protesters, known as Luddites, organised sabotage attacks to destroy machinery that threatened their livelihoods, particularly in the cotton and wool mills of northern England. Two new music-publishing houses were founded in London - Novello and Chappell. Jane Austen's *Sense and Sensibility* was published, whilst the poet Shelley was sent down from Oxford for publishing *The Necessity of Atheism.*

Local

In his *The History and Antiquities of Edmonton in the County of Middlesex,* William Robinson gives the following tables for the Parish of Edmonton –

Edmonton Parish Population (Winchmore Hill was in Bury Street Ward)

	Inhabited houses 1801	Inhabited houses 1811	Uninhabited houses 1801	Uninhabited Houses 1811	Males 1801	Males 1811	Females 1801	Females 1811
Church - street Ward	200	210	7	12	541	639	647	513
Fore - street Ward	253	268	17	11	677	1,053	769	1,258
Burv - street Ward	189	339	14	13	390	582	494	724
South - street Ward	259	340	9	12	830	1,065	745	990
	901	1,157	47	48	2,438	3,329	2,655	3,485
Total Population 1801	5,093							
Total Population 1811	6,824	(+1,731)						
Estimated Population 1818	7,500							

At the time of Enclosure William Radley was a major land owner in the village, and in 1811 he acquired a further piece of land that would form part of the Highfield House Estate.

In 1801 the Penny Post became the Two Penny Post and at P57 of my 2001 *A Look at Old Winchmore Hill* I reproduced an 1811 poster which announced a change to circulation in what are now 17 northern suburbs of London, whereby a letter posted in Southgate for Winchmore Hill, say, would go direct rather than via a central hub. The poster proclaimed that, 'By this Regulation, Letters put in at these Places in time for the Morning Dispatch are delivered at any of them about Noon, and such as are put in for the Afternoon Dispatch, the same Evening; Thus the Letters are delivered shortly after they are put into the Post..... This Bye Post to be considered an Experiment only, until further Notice ....'

1812

General

Tory PM Spencer Perceval was assassinated in the House of Commons lobby by a mad merchant named John Bellingham, as captured at Plate 61. Tory Lord Liverpool succeeded him, and remained in office until 1827. Two more Regiments were called out to quell the ongoing Luddite rebellions. Food canning was invented by Bryan Donkin of London, and the first meat cannery was set up in Bermondsey – though the tins had to be opened with a hammer and chisel! The Waltz was introduced into Britain. 1812 marked the birth of Edward Lear, and Charles Dickens (in Portsmouth).

Plate 61.
The murder of the PM Spencer Perceval at the House of Commons in 1812

This old sketch captures the assassination of the Tory Prime Minister in the Commons lobby on 11th May 1812 by a merchant named John Bellingham.

Local

The Palmers Green Gazette of 19th September 1941 carried a 'Memorabilia' article headed 'Centenarian's Death'. It included the following, 'The passing of Miss Alice Frederica Percival of Royal Avenue, Chelsea, at the age of 105, is announced. She was the grand-daughter of the Right Hon. Spencer Percival (sic), the Prime Minister who was shot dead in the lobby of the House of Commons in 1812, by Bellingham, who is now generally believed to have been insane at the time, owing to financial loss, for which Mr. Percival (sic) was not personally responsible, and in no way connected.

Appeal was made against the capital sentence on the ground of insanity at the time, but, was rejected, and the culprit was hanged about a fortnight after the assassination. Bellingham's son shortly afterwards assumed his mother's maiden name, Neville, and came to live at Winchmore Hill in Woodside House on the Green ...... Poor Neville lived a solitary life of melancholy and eccentricity, and died through sleeping in a room in which a charcoal fire was burning; presumably the weather was cold and the windows closed, but I have no reliable information on that point.'

At the LHU are Tom Mason's notes which tell us that, on 27th April 1812 Esther Barbara Lane, 'relict of Revd. T. Lane, late rector of Hampworth co Stafford & d. of Sir J. Birch, last formerly a Judge of the Common Pleas' died at 'Winchmore – hill, aged 76'. At Page 78 of his 1819 book Robinson gives a table of local longevity, which includes George Tatem at the age of 86 in 1807, and Catherine Tatem at 92 in 1812.

1813

General

Wellington defeated the French at Vitoria. The Fourth Coalition of Britain, Russia, Sweden, Prussia and Austria closed in on Napoleon and forced him back to Leipzig, where he was defeated at the Battle of the Nations. The last gold guineas were minted, and The East India Company's monopoly in India was abolished. Jane Austen's *Pride and Prejudice* was published.

Local

Earlier in the book I have devoted a section to Edmonton Fairs, and that contains an eye witness account of the 1813 Statute Fair gathering.

At the Guildhall Library is document MS 14,367 titled, 'Mr. John Millard on behalf of the Cordwainers Company and Mr. Wm. Pitcher, Agreement for a Building Lease of Premises at Winchmore Hill'. In the document John Millard is shown as Clerk of the Cordwainers at Distiff Lane, whilst William Pitcher is of, 'Dorset Street Salisbury Square Fleet Street in the said City of London Carpenter and Builder of the other part'. The document, which is dated 21st July 1813, outlines an agreement to lease shopkeeper John Udall a cottage, outhouse and garden, then currently occupied by Udall, for 21 years from Lady Day 1814 at £20 p.a., paid quarterly. There is also a 59 ¼ year lease for Pilcher from 24th June 1813 at £8 p.a. It seems that the Cordwainers (who had land on the Upper Green) were to pay Pitcher £200 to put up a new brick building on the site, but the document is quite confusing. There are various other similar documents from this era.

1814

General

The allied forces defeated Napoleon at the Battle of Laon. Wellington captured Bordeaux and the Allies then marched victorious into Paris, whence Napoleon abdicated and the Congress of Vienna began. This conference, which lasted until June 1815, was to negotiate the Resettlement of Europe. The first cricket match was played at Lord's in St. John's Wood. Jane Austen published *Mansfield Park*. The last winter Frost Fair on the frozen Thames was held in 1814.

Local

In his *History of Edmonton* Robinson says that in his Will of 12th April 1662, John Wild of Edmonton bequeathed some land to various people. On the 25th October 1731 the then trustees leased Sir Bybye Lake some of that land, which included five acres of arable land in Hag Field, for 999 years from Michaelmas 1732. In 1814 a Bill in Chancery was filed by the Edmonton vestry, 'to set the same aside; and by a decree, dated July, 1818, the said lease was ordered to be given up to the trustees to be cancelled, and the premises (as far as they could be ascertained) restored to their possession.....' (Hag Field is probably a misprint for High Field.)

Tom Mason's handwritten notes at the LHU record, 'Winchmore Hill. Mary Ann Peverell (daughter of Mr. Callow) born in London 17 July 1792. Married in parish church of St. Mary Whitechapel 17 April 1814. John Peverell lived for many years at Winchmore Hill, near Edmonton, died at Winchmore Hill 6 January 1896 aged 103 buried Edmonton Parish Churchyard Jan. 10.' See the entry for Samuel Patrick in the E.E. Ownership Schedule.

At the National Archives in Kew is the last Will of Jane Jones. The document reads, 'Proved at London with a Codisil of September 1814 before the Judge by the Oaths of Susanna Jackson (?) Widow of Robert William ..... This is the last Will and Testament of Jane Jones of Winchmore Hill in the County of Middlesex. I give and bequeath all my Estate property and Efforts whatsoever and wheresoever unto my Sister Mary Jones the wife of William Jones for her own absolute use and benefit and I appoint my said Sister the sole Executrix of this my Will ...... as set my hand this 23rd day of February 1807 Jane Jones Witness to the signing hereof by the said Jane Jones – John Konison (?) John Udall.' A William and Jane Jones are listed in the E.E. Ownership Schedule.

1815

General

In 1815 £25 million was raised by direct, and £67 million by indirect, taxation. Napoleon escaped from Elba, but was defeated by Blucher and Wellington at Waterloo on 18th June. Under the second Peace of Paris France returned to her 1790 frontiers. The Quadruple Alliance, between Britain, Russia, Austria and Prussia, was renewed. At the end of the Napoleonic Wars, Lord Liverpool's government introduced The Corn Law. It prohibited the import of any foreign corn until the domestic price reached 80 shillings a quarter (2 stone) – in effect a famine price. This made the price of the working man's loaf much higher than it needed to be. The law was modified in 1828 and 1842, before being abolished by Sir Robert Peel's government in 1846.

Sir Humphry Davy invented the miners' safety lamp and William Smith published the first geological map of England and Wales. John Loudon Mc Adam improved road making with his use of crushed stone and tarmac, whilst John Nash (of Grovelands fame) began his Royal Pavilion in Brighton. By 1815 there were an estimated 4,000 gas lights in London.

Local

Tom Mason's handwritten notes at the LHU report the death, on 14th March 1815, of, 'Mrs. Pullen, relict of the late J. Pullen esq., of Winchmore – hill'. In 1815 John Smith took over the licence to *The King's Head*, in succession to Francis Newman, being succeeded himself by Edward Flowerday in 1834.

At the LMA is the, 'Manor of Edmonton Middx. Court Book Commencing 12th June 1810' (document ACC 695/26). The minutes of the meeting of 16th May 1815 include the following entry, 'At this Court the Homage find and present that George Eaton late a customary Tenant of this Manor is dead and that by his Will bearing date the twenty sixth day of January One thousand eight hundred and fifteen the probate where of under the seal of the Perogative Court of the Archbishop of Canterbury dated the sixth day of May one thousand eight hundred and fifteen is now presented in Court and unrolled he devised as follows "I give and bequeath unto my wife, Sarah Eaton three copyhold Cottages and garden with outbuildings adjoining situate at Winchmore Hill now let unto Mr. Billings, Mr. Bailey and Mr. Baker Tenants at Will for her life".' One presumes that George was a relative of the William listed in the E.E. Ownership Schedule.

The National Archives in Kew contain papers referenced PROB 31 1104 – 351 relating to the death of a John Hudson. They are dated 21st October 1815 and run thus, 'A Declaration instead of a true and perfect Inventory of all and singular the Goods, Chattels and ? of John Hudson late of Winchmore Hill in the County of Middlesex deceased which have come to the Hands possession or knowledge of John Hudson the Grandfather and Curator or Guardian lawfully assigned to John Hudson an Infant the natural and lawful and only Child of the said deceased for the use and benefit of the said Infant and until he shall obtain the age of twenty one years follows to wit

First this Declarant doth declare that the said deceased was possessed of a Leasehold House and premises situate at Winchmore Hill aforesaid together with the Fixtures of the same and also sundry Household Goods Furniture ? Linen and China together with the good will for the same which have been valued and appraized at the sum of Four Hundred and forty two pounds and three pence.

Also this Declarant doth declare that the said deceased died possessed of a Silver and Metal watches which were valued at the sum of Four pounds and no more. Also this Declarant doth declare that the said deceased was also possessed at the Time of his death of a Chaise which was sold and provided the sum of Five pounds. Also this Declarant doth declare that the said deceased was possessed at the time of his death of a Horse and Cart and Harness, which were valued and appraised the sum of Ten pounds.

Also this Declarant doth declare that the deceased died possessed of cash in the House and wearing apparol (stet) which produced Twenty five pounds. Also this Declarant doth declare that the said deceased was possessed at the time of his death of Spirits and other Liquors amounting to the sum of Thirteen pounds eight shillings. Also this Declarant doth declare that the said deceased was at the time of his death to four small Cottages which he held upon Lease for an unexpired Term which were valued at ten pounds and no more.

Also this Declarant doth declare that the said deceased was possessed at the time of his death to sundry Articles in his Garden which have been valued and appraized at the Sum of five pounds. Also this Declarant doth declare that the said deceased was also possessed of a Leasehold House at Winchmore Hill aforesaid the unexpired term has been valued at the sum of Forty Pounds. (There is then a grand totalling of all the previous sums, which came to £554. 8s 3d.)

Lastly this Declarant doth declare that no Goods Chattels or ? of or belonging to the Personal Estate and Effects of the said deceased have at any time since his death come to the Hands possession or knowledge of this Declarant other than what are set forth in this Declaration. On the 17th day of October 1815 the said John Hudson was duly sworn to the truth of this Declaration. Before me (there are then three signatures – John Hudson, an illegible one and one that seems to read John Curtis).'

1816

General

Even by the standards of The Little Ice Age 1816 was a particularly severe year – 'the year without a summer'. This was at the worst possible time, because Britain went into a depression. The War had left the people of Europe poor, and so unable to afford British manufactures. Thus thousands were thrown out of work, swelled by the 400,000 discharged from the armed forces. To try and stimulate the economy

Income Tax was abolished (until 1842), but it was replaced by duties, so raising prices. The poverty and distress led to increased emigration to North America. British forces defeated the King of Kandy, and so Ceylon becomes a British colony. Jane Austen published *Emma*.

Local

We have touched on the discharge of soldiers from the Napoleonic Wars above. At the National Archives is a Microfilm file WO121/189 (46) which tells us, 'His Majesty's Eighth Royal Veteran Battalion whereof Alexander Muir is Colonel. These (papers) are to certify that Thomas Goodwin in ? Captain Adam..? Company, in the Battalion aforesaid, born in the Parish of Winchmore Hill, in or near the Town of Edmonton in the County of Edmonton (stet) was enlisted at the age of Nineteen Years; and hath served in the said Regiment for the space of one year and - days, as well as in other corps, after the age of eighteen, according to the following Statement, but in consequence of the Battalion being ordered to be disbanded is rendered unfit for further Service and is hereby discharged; having first received all just demands of Pay, Clothing & c. from his entry into the said Regiment, to the date of this Discharge, as appears by the receipt on the back hereof.

And to prevent any improper use being made of this Discharge, by its falling into other hands, the following is a Description of the said Drumr. Thomas Goodwin he is of about Thirty two years of age, is Five feet Four ¾ inches in height, Dark hair Hazle (stet) eyes, Dark complexion, by trade a labourer. Statement of Service: .... (Difficult to read) ..... Total length of service = 8 years 198 days. Given under my Hand, and Seal of the Battalion, at Portsmouth the 3d day of June 1816, (Illegible signature).

I Thomas Goodwin do acknowledge that I have received all my clothing, Pay, arrears of Pay, and all just Demands whatsoever, from the time of my entry in the Regiment mentioned on the other side, to this day of my Discharge. As Witness my Hand, this third day of June 1816. Witness J. Perritt, Thos. Goodwin.

I do hereby Certify that the cause which has rendered it necessary to discharge the within mentioned Thomas Goodwin as stated on the opposite side, has not arisen from Vice or Misconduct, and that he is not (to my knowledge) incapacitated by the Sentence of a General Court Martial from receiving his Pension. ...... (Illegible) ..... Surgeon ...... (Illegible) ....Commanding

I Certify that Thomas Goodwin served in the 8th Royal Victoria Battalion, for the period of One year during which time he behaved himself as a good Soldier. I do therefore recommend him as a fit Subject to receive any augmentation of Pension that he may be entitled to, by virtue of His Royal Highness the Prince Regent's Proclamation, dated 13th June 1815. 3rd June 1816 sig.'

I have covered the 1772 Manorial Court proceedings under John Barnes in the 1801/2 Land Ownership schedule. At that time John came into 3 acres of land in Highfield, two cottages, two other premises, and the three acres of Kitchen Croft. The last named was sold to William Radley in 1816. The 1816 transfer is recorded in the Edmonton Manor Minutes as follows, 'April 24th 1816. Received of Jane Barnes on the death of John Barnes 18s. Received of John Barnes 9s. Received of Wm. Radley on Surrender of Jane Barnes 15s.'

Robert Barclay (b. 1758) of Clapham died in 1816 and was buried on Church Hill (as was his son Robert in 1853). John Walker bought a partnership in the Limehouse brewing business of the local Taylor family, and the brewery thus became known by the long familiar name of Taylor Walker and Co..

1817

General

Princess Charlotte, the only child of the Prince Regent and his wife Caroline, died in childhood in 1817. The slump led to the Blanketeers' March, and other disturbances, such as riots in Derbyshire. Shots were fired at the Prince Regent after he opened Parliament, and a secret report to Parliament predicted that a rebellion was imminent, leading to the suspension of The Habeas Corpus Act. The first sovereigns were issued and, sadly, Jane Austen died.

Local

William Robinson tells us that, 'In the year 1817, the sum assessed upon the Hundred of Edmonton to the Land Tax was £4,845 12s 1d which is at the rate of 2s in the pound. The quota charged on this parish was £1401 19s 9d of which £957. 4s. 1¾ d has been redeemed: the sum now raised amounts to £444. 15s. 7¼ d only.'

At the Guildhall Library is the Dean and Chapter of St. Paul's Manorial Steward's Book for 1810 – 1817 (MS 20, 689). The handwriting isn't always very clear, but the following is my interpretation, 'On Febry. 6th 1817 I held a Court at Edmonton at Mr. Smith's Pauls House & admitted Mr. Knight of Norton Tolgate and I had some Converson with him about the Quit Rents where he said he had never received them he gave me the following list which he said he had received from Mr. Smith in his life time - late Steward.

Mr. Godman atty. Blackfriars Road Crescent – Wrangham - 2s 6d; John Davidson his land formerly Pinfolds; Pinfold Charles late Jarrett 2s. 6d; John Rowe – New River Compy. 6d; Clowes Joseph 1s. 0d; North Sarah now Knight 4d; Richd. Causton – Rented Finch lane 6d; Tashmaker (stet) £1. 2s. 8d Late Squire -; Late Galliard - ; Late Burton now Lucas 1s. 0d.; Sr. Jas Lake (now Frank) 10s 3d; Wm. Mellish 5s. 9d; Blackburn now Isaac Currie from 1812 5s. 0d; Clarke Cavendish 16s. 11d; Erwood – now Biggs & Leachman 4s. 4d.

In consequence of this new arrangement with Mr. Sperling – at the Court which I held Feby. 6. 1817 at the White Hart I admitted Mr. Knight at the Pauls House Edmonton & paid Mr. Leachman & Mr. Jos. Acott who attended as the Homage £1 cash. I after adjourned to the White Hart – there was no common there. I paid 10s 6d for the Room and I gave Corker whom I had appointed Bailiff £1.

In future I shall always procure 2 Copyhold Tenants for Edmonton & 2 for Tottm. hold the Edmonton Court at 11 & the Tottm. at 12 pay each £1 each which will cost £4- the Bailiff £1. The Room & perhaps some refreshment by way of lunch so that the £8 will I think cover all. I shall in future hold the Court in June when I have my Chair at Livery. I shall endeavour to hold all the Courts in June & July at furthest.'

At the LMA is the, 'Manor of Edmonton Middx. Court Book Commencing 12th June 1810' (document ACC 695/26). The minutes of a Special Court Baron of 14th May 1817 tell us that, 'At this Court the Homage find and present that Thomas Oliver late a Customary Tenant of this Manor is dead and that he died seized of (inter alia) all that close piece or parcel of meadow land now called or known by the Name of the Shoulder of Mutton Field situate and being at Winchmore Hill within this Manor and containing by admeasurement Six Acres two roods and sixteen perches abutting towards the North on Lands of Isaac Currie Esq. in his own occupation towards the West and Southwest partly on Lands in the occupation of the said Isaac Currie and partly on Green Dragon Lane ..... Left his lands, by a Will of 19th June 1802 to his wife Prudence.' There is also a map showing the land, from which I conclude that Shoulder of Mutton Field is a remnant of Plots 742 and 747 in the Enclosure Award. (Figure 16.)

Tom Mason's handwritten notes at the LHU tell us that "Mrs. Anna Hall, widow of the late Abraham Hall esq. of Aldermanbury" died, '1817 July 12 at Winchmore – hill, aged 70'.

1818

General

In this year the first iron ship was built on the Clyde. By now the British East India Co. effectively controlled India and Mary Shelley's 'Frankenstein' was published. Humphry Repton, who landscaped what are now the grounds of Grovelands Park, died in 1818.

Local

In 1819, in his *The History and Antiquities of Edmonton in the County of Middlesex*, William Robinson gives the following tables for the Parish of Edmonton -

Houses By Occupation (Date not given, but presumably 1818)

	By how many families The houses are occupied	Families chiefly employed in agriculture -	Families chiefly employed in trade & c.	All other Families not in these comprised
Church - street Ward	213	86	107	20
Fore - street Ward	519	151	241	127
Burv - street Ward	254	110	67	77
South - street Ward	369	169	93	107
Totals	1,355	516	508	331

It will be recalled that in the 1801 Census there were 950 families in Edmonton Parish, and that only 412 people - about one in twelve working people - were engaged in agriculture. The proportion working in the fields now seems to be much higher, including Bury Street Ward. Plates 62 & 63 do not date from this era, but perhaps reflect how many local people spent their days in 1818.

In 1818 James Lawford became the licensee of *The Orange Tree*. He took over from John Biggs, who had held the licence since 1795. Wyer Hall, which is covered in the section on properties in the Edmonton area, was demolished in 1818.

In his *History of Edmonton* Robinson says that in his Will of 12th April 1662, John Wild of Edmonton bequeathed some land to various people. On the 25th October 1731 the then trustees leased Sir Bybye Lake some of that land, which included five acres of arable land in Hag Field, for 999 years from Michaelmas 1732. In 1814 a Bill in Chancery was filed by the Edmonton vestry, 'to set the same aside; and by a decree, dated July, 1818, the said lease was ordered to be given up to the trustees to be cancelled, and the premises (as far as they could be ascertained) restored to their possession.....' (Hag Field is almost certainly a misprint for Highfield.)

"Soon as the morning trembles o'er the sky
Before the ripened field the reapers stand
In fair array." *(Autumn) Thomson.*

LOADING HAY.

Plates 62 (top) and 63. How the local fields might have looked in 1818

In the Census returns for 1801 only about 1 in 12 workers in the Parish were employed in agriculture, even though the utilisation of land denoted on the Enclosure Maps would suggest Winchmore Hill was agricultural. However, figures for 1818 from Robinson indicate that over 40% of households in Bury Street Ward, containing the village, were engaged in agriculture. So perhaps the scenes taken from old postcards might reflect how the local fields looked at the time.

William Radley had been gradually buying land in the angle formed by Hoppers Lane and 'Compton Road', paving the way for the Highfield House Estate. No one knows when Highfield House itself was built. It was clearly after 1801/2, when the E.E. Schedule was drawn up, and was in existence by 11th November 1818, when Radley made a will leaving "all my dwelling house commonly called Highfield House in the parish of Edmonton" to his wife, Margaret, for her lifetime.

At the LMA is the, 'Manor of Edmonton Middx. Court Book Commencing 12th June 1810' (document ACC 695/26). The minutes of the Court Baron of 12th May 1818 announce that Joseph Osborne had died. Under his reported Will of 1st June 1815 he left his land and property in Middlesex, Hertfordshire and Essex, including *The Dog and Duck*, to Thomas Boycott, James Maughan, John Thompson, and some in Trust for his nephew Osborne Delano.

1819

General

In August a peaceful rally of up to 80,000 people in Manchester campaigned for greater rights for industrial workers. David Starkey tells us that, 'the demonstrations had not threatened violence. The huge crowd was carefully marshalled, with brass bands accompanying each division playing patriotic tunes, like "God Save the King" and "Rule Britannia". And when it was the turn of the national anthem most members of the crowd respectfully took their hats off.' It ended with 11 people being killed by troopers' sabres, and about 400 wounded, in what came to be known as the Peterloo Massacre.

Further to this, Parliament passed the repressive Six Acts in an attempt to halt the spread of radicalism. These Acts included measures to ban meetings of more than 50 people, imposed a stamp duty on all newspapers, banned training in the use of weaponry, and empowered magistrates to search for, and seize, weapons. All this actually increased unrest. Parliament also passed the Factory Act, further regulating conditions in manufacturing.

Britain gained Singapore as a result of the British East India Co's. activities. James Watt, a key figure in starting the Industrial Revolution, died at the age of 83. Thomas Telford completed the Menai Straits Suspension Bridge. By 1819 there were an estimated 51,000 gas lights in London, and there was gas lighting in many towns. Victoria and Albert were born and Quaker Elizabeth Fry (1780 – 1845), who was no stranger to Winchmore Hill, compiled a report with her brother in 1819, urging prison reform.

The Parish Vestry dealt with all general parish matters, and met under the presidency of the Vicar, with the Churchwardens as his principal officers. At first the Vestry was "Open", when all ratepayers were entitled to take part in the deliberations, but under an Act of 1819 it became "Select", that is, composed of representatives duly elected by the ratepayers.

Local

In his *The History and Antiquities of Edmonton in the County of Middlesex*, of 1819, William Robinson says, 'Winchmore Hill is a large and pleasant village, situated on a considerable eminence. In the lane leading from Bush Hill, near a little thatched cottage, is a well, called 'Vicar's Well', so called from having been enclosed by a vicar of this parish. It is of antiquity, but what was the vicar's name, and in what year he enclosed it, is not at this day known (see section on Vicar's Well though). The water is very pure, always flowing, and was formerly in great estimation among the inhabitants of the adjacent villages. This village is long and straggling, and contains about forty or fifty houses, with a meeting house for the Quakers. Adjoining is a wood of about a mile over, which formerly belonged to Mr. Nicholl, who built Minchendon House, it is divided into twelve falls, one of which is cut down every year. There is a delightful walk through this wood which leads from this spot to Southgate.' He gives the following details relating to the Parish of Edmonton –

Marriages, Baptisms and Burials

Year	Marriages	Baptisms	Burials	Year	Marriages	Baptisms	Burials
1790		136	109	1804	30	132	110
1791		114	129	1805	21	111	112
1792		142	169	1806	25	128	122
1793	27	94	158	1807	28	128	129
1794	31	111	107	1808	46	146	149
1795	31	98	133	1809	39	136	115
1796	24	89	109	1810	36	117	151
1797	45	88	110	1811	36	155	145
1798	25	104	131	1812	36	129	137
1799	23	104	98	1813	30	137	141
1800	26	103	156	1814	27	128	139
1801	20	90	134	1815	44	151	130
1802	35	126	132	1816	44	152	125
1803	46	109	127	1817	37	156	132
				1818	51	181	134

Of the Rental and Rates of the Parish

The Rental of the parish is about £22,515 per annum, viz.

Church – street Ward valued at per Annum £4,656
Fore-street Ward do £6,019
Bury – street Ward do £5,745
South – street Ward do £6,095
£22, 515

Robinson says, 'The sum raised last year for the relief of the poor, amounted to £5,107 6s 9d which was raised by two half-yearly payments: - the one at 3s and the other at 3s 6d in the pound. The poor's rate varies, sometimes 3s at others 1s 9d and 1s 6d in the pound. The church rate, from Lady-day (25th March), 1818, to Lady-day, 1819, was at 6d in the pound.

The highway rate is sometimes 1s and at others 9d in the pound, as circumstances require; from the produce of which, the surveyors of the parish highways pay to the trustees of the Stamford Hill and Green Lanes turnpike roads, the sum of £110, per annum, under the provision in the act of parliament lately obtained by the trustees. The quote of the county rate paid by the parish in Sept. 1818, was £120 18s 6d the like quota to Feb. last, was £117 15s 1d.'

In his book Robinson also says, '......Sir James Winter Lake had a seat at Edmonton called 'The Firs' which has been some years pulled down. The estate has been sold, and is now the property of John Grant, Esq.' (Though see the relevant account in the map section).
Robinson informs us that in 1819 the Manors of Bowes, Dernford, Pauls House and Fordes were in the possession of the Dean and Chapter of St. Paul's. All held

a Court Baron and a View of Frankpledge. The lessee of the manor of Pauls House and Fordes at this time was Thomas Smith Esq., who had purchased the lease from James Vere Esq. and Mrs. Judith Teshmaker. (Remember the Dean and Chapter of St. Paul's Manorial Steward's records which read, 'On Febry. 6th 1817 I held a Court at Edmonton at Mr. Smith's Pauls House …')

The *Enfield Gazette and Observer* for 17th March 1939 contained an article by *Memorabilia*. He says, 'By courtesy of a friend I have been permitted to peruse a perfectly preserved map of the county of Middlesex, from an Actual Survey made in The Years 1818 and 1819 By C. Greenwood, London ……… Coming south to Winchmore Hill I find 'Butts Farm', last known as "Riverbank", Firs Lane, on the site of which stands one of the blocks of flats erected recently near the Laburnum Automatic Telephone Exchange ……… Whale Cottage marked near the *Chase Side Tavern* excites my curiosity because of its name, but from the Octogenarian Mr. John T. Downes, of 16, The Green, Winchmore Hill, I learn that it was in Cock Hill (now Eversley Park Road) a little distance below the tavern on the same side, the old cottage of Carter Page's nursery, but more interesting still is his statement that on the immediate opposite side of Cock Hill were the stocks…..'

In *The PGS Gazette* of 31st January 1936 'Memorabilia' tells us of three Manorial documents relating to land in Hoppers Lane. The earliest of the three deeds was dated 9th June 1772 and recorded that at the Courts of Edmonton Manor, the minor John Barnes was admitted tenant of three messuages and land on the death of his father Robert Barnes, who had died intestate. The second document recites that at a Manorial Court held on the 4th June 1816, John's widow Jane Barnes was admitted as tenant. The third document records that at a Court held on the 4th June, 1819, the three children of Jane Barnes, who had by then entered into possession on the death of their mother, sold three messuages or cottages to John Brown for £300, who was then admitted as tenant.

The Edwards Estates researchers for Devon House tell us of an inquest held at the *King's Head* in 1819: 'On View the Body of Robert Bishop, then and there lying dead. On the 15th July in the year aforesaid the said Robert Bishop being running nearby some pailings at the parish and County aforesaid and a cart drawn by three horses then coming near thereunto it so happened accidentally, casually and by misfortune that he the said Robert Bishop was jammed between the said cart and the said pailings by means whereof he the said Robert Bishop did then and there receive divers mortal bruises on the body of him the said Robert Bishop of which said mortal bruises he the said Robert Bishop then and there died. And so the jurors aforesaid do say that the said Robert Bishop in manner and by means aforesaid came to his death and not otherwise. Signed by the Coroner and 12 members of the jury including Richard Riley (who acted as foreman) and Daniel Harlow.'

Robert Bishop lived near *The King's Head* in what we now call Wade's Hill, and his widow continued to live there until her death in 1854. Her estate included 'all those six freehold messuages and premises with the gardens and appurtances thereto belonging situate and being in Winchmore Hill'. Richard Riley and Daniel Harlow are both mentioned in Horace Regnart's book *Memories of Winchmore Hill* as follows, 'Richard Riley was a plumber, painter and glazier but later became a grocer and had a post office ……… The shop now Stephens was kept earlier by Mr. Riley and later his daughter …. There was one postman, Daniel Harlow, who was an old man with a white beard in the 1870s….' Riley is listed in the 1826 Pigot's Directory.

The Friends Burial Ground in Church Hill contains the following headstones - 'Jonathan Hoare. Died 8th mo. 15 1819. Aged 66.', 'Mary Hoare. Died 1st

Mo. 21st 1819. Aged 58', which is situated next to, 'Samuel Hoare of Hampstead. Died 1825. Age 74 Years'. This, in turn, is next to a stone reading, 'Sarah Wife of Samuel Hoare. Hampstead. Died 1783. Aged 36 Yrs.' Both the Samuel Hoares, Senior and Junior, had given £50 towards the cost of rebuilding the Meeting House in 1790. In his books on the local Friends, Professor Olver tells us that the Quaker community was so small that in 1819 there were less than 15 families associated with the Meeting, although the building could accommodate 250 people – presumably because a gallery was then in existence.

Tom Mason's handwritten notes at the LHU record three deaths at 'Winchmore – hill' in 1819. On 8th June 'Thomas Holmes esq. many years of the excise office' died aged 88. On 26th August, 'Thos. Browne esq. formerly of Gould – square, & late of Stoke Newington' passed on, aged 78. On 28th October 'W. Cass esq.' passed away aged 76.

At the LMA are papers referenced ACC/588/10 concerning, 'Lease of a Messuage & c. at Winchmore Hill. Mr. Aaron Patrick and Miss Mary Peverell to Mr. John Parkinson. Dated 29th September 1819' John Parkinson was to pay a rent of £28-10s-0d. The document continued, 'The Schedule to which the above written Indenture refers – One Register Stove. One Bath Stove in the Parlour. Two Bedroom Stoves. One Common Kitchen Range. Bells all over the above mentioned Messuage or Dwelling house. A Pump and a Sink in the Kitchen. Locks and Keys to all the Doors......John Parkinson his executors and administrators or assigns shall and will from time to time and at times hereafter during the continuance of the said terms at his or their own proper costs and charges keep the said hereby demised messuage or tenement and the said Coachhouse Washhouse Stable and other the said premises in such real good and substantial repair.......21 years lease at £28 pa Tenement + ¼ Orchard, Coachhouse, Stable + Premises = £10-'

Aaron Patrick is shown as being of Enfield Highway, Mary Peverell of Hackney Road, Bethnal Green (Parish), John Parkinson of the Accountant Generals Office, Chancery Lane. Patrick and Miss Peverell appear to have come into the property by the Will of the late Samuel Patrick of Winchmore Hill. In the Edmonton Manor Court minutes for 8th May 1826, Samuel is revealed to be the father of Mary Peverell and brother of Aaron. He is listed in the E.E. Ownership Schedule.

The position of the house is given in the document, but it is impossible to locate its whereabouts from the old geography described. At the LMA are further papers ACC/588/14 dated 31st July 1821 from which it would appear that Parkinson sub-lets the land to John Radford of White Conduit Street, Pentonville for £125 for 21 years, with the consent of Patrick and Peverell. Presumably this is the John Radford who was prominent in the Winchmore Hill Independent movement.

Also at the LMA is the, 'Manor of Edmonton Middx. Court Book Commencing 12th June 1810' (document ACC 695/26). The minutes of the Court Baron of 1st June 1819 tell us that John Tugwell had died in possession of the 2r. 34p which had been Plot 1542 at the time of Enclosure. The minutes are a little confusing, however, because they also seem to suggest that the plot had been purchased from Copyholder Thomas Snelson, and that the transaction had been recorded in the Manor minutes of 4th June 1805. The 1819 minutes further say that under his Will of 20th February 1806, John left the Plot to his wife Martha Tugwell for her life, whence it would pass to his daughter Martha Richardson Yallowley.

1820

General

George 111 died on 29th January, aged 81, after 60 years on the throne, being succeeded by the former Prince Regent as George 1V. The Cato Street Conspiracy plotted to blow up the entire Cabinet. Local landowner William Mellish, who had sat as a Tory MP alongside George Byng since 1806, left the Commons in 1820. From 1820 the Little Ice Age slowly began to thaw.

Local

The 1819 diary contained the quote from Robinson that '... Sir James Winter Lake had a seat at Edmonton called 'The Firs' which has been some years pulled down. The estate has been sold, and is now the property of John Grant, Esq.' However, Tom Mason, in his 1948 *A Southgate Scrapbook* says that the mansion was demolished sometime between 1820 and 1830. The Mansion appears to still be marked on the 1822 O.S. Map (Figure 21).

Joseph Compton, a ship and insurance broker of Hackney, bought the house and associated land about half way down 'Compton Road', occupied by Miss Creswell's 'lawyer' Samuel Compton, in two stages. Ownership had been with Ann Dale at the time of Enclosure, and the first of Joseph's purchases was made in 1820.

In 1820 Thomas Clarke succeeded James Lawford as licensee of *The Orange Tree*. He retained the licence until succeeded by Ann Clarke in 1839. Tom Mason's handwritten notes at the LHU tell us that on '11th November 1820 Robert, 2nd son of John Vickris Taylor esq. died aged 21 at Southgate'. A paragraph from the Evangelical Magazine, dated 1820, reads that "The chapel at Winchmore Hill, having been closed for several months, was re-opened on Tuesday 26th September when two sermons were preached." We have no record of why this closure of the Independent Chapel (see Plate 23) took place.

The National Archives contain documents surrounding the Quaker John Decka of Roseville, the following being a substantial extract,

'I John Decka of Winchmore Hill in the County of Middlesex farmer do in the year of the Lord make and publish this to be my last Will and Testament that is To say to my Nephews John Coleman of Wimbledon in the County of Surry (stet) Ealiro printer and John Catchpool of Winchmorehill in the County of Middlesex Baker I give and devise all my Estate at Winchmorehill or elsewhere I may possess of

that is to say all my Copyhold estate consisting of a dwelling house and four acres of land in the occupation of John Pullen One half acre of land in the occupation of Joseph Osborn One cottage in the occupation of Daniel Isarlors (?) and our cottage in the occupation of Elizabeth Bell also a dwelling house Barn other buildings and land adjoining in my own occupation the whole including that on which the buildings stand/remaining about one acre. Also one acre of Copyhold land situated on Edmonton Common lately enclosed remaining about two acres in my present occupation as also all lands leases of land Goods Chattels plate wearing apparel ready money stock in trade business and effects of any kind whatsoever is thin to ever in trust for the following uses

that is to say first of all to discharge all debts demands on me or my Estate and then to dispose of the residue or remainder in manner following that is to say to my Sister Elizabeth Coleman I leave the sum of fifty pounds or if she be deceased to my heirs Mary Jeffery or to her children if she be deceased to the children of my late Sister Lydia Harvey the sum of fifty pounds to be equally divided among them share and share alike to my nephew William (stet) Catchpool I leave the sum of fifty pounds or to his surviving children if he be deceased to Edward Jiffins (?) of Winchmorehill I leave the sum of twenty pounds to be paid duly within six months after my decease and what may be left I leave as follows,

viz. One fourth part to my Nephew John Catchpool and the remaining three quarters my Nephew John Coleman. And thereby appoint my Nephews John Coleman and John Catchpool joint Executors to this my last Will and Testament in Witness whereof I have hereunto set my hand and Seal this twenty third day of the month called November, one thousand eight hundred and seven. John Decka signed sealed and delivered by the within named Testator as and for his last Will and Testament in the presence of Samuel Gibling, William Mahon James Pursell.

A: Whereas by my last Will and Testament I have appointed my Nephews John Coleman of Wimbledon in the County of Surry (stet) and John Catchpool of Winchmorehill in the County of Middlesex my Executors and whereas in the said Will are certain legacies directed for them to pay now I do hereby by this codicil revoke the legacy of fifty pounds to my heirs Mary Jeffrey legacy of fifty pounds to the surviving children of my deceased sister Lydia Harvey the legacy of fifty pounds to my nephew William Catchpool and the sum of twenty pounds to Edward Joffkins declaring the said legacies to be null and void. In witness whereof I have hereunto put my hand and seal this thirty first day of the month called July one thousand eight hundred and seventeen. John Decka.

B: It is my request and desire that after my decease there should be paid as a gift from me to my heir Mary Jeffrey the sum of fifty pounds to such of the surviving children of my deceased Sister Lydia Harvey fifty pounds Willm. Harvey who don't need any (?) in such sums to each of them when it is most wanted no one to have more than fifteen pounds to Sarah the wife of my nephew Willm. Catchpool fifty pounds by wordly allowance until the whole is dispensed or if she be deceased before the whole or any part is paid her the said Sum or remainder to be divided among her children that may be living in such proportion where it is most wanted also to Edward Joffins the sum of ten (?) pounds 7 My. 31 1817. John Decka.

C: In order that my nephew John Catchpool may remain in the business at Winchmorehill in which he is now engaged it is my desire that he may have the refusal of my estate at Winchmorehill consisting of my dwelling house and premises thereunto belonging two cottages a Barn with the land and gardens all in my possession for the sum of six hundred and ninety pounds dated this 20 of 10 M. in 1809 Since writing the above I have paid at (?) £50 to John Coleman £100 J. Catchpool should have the refusal for £600. 7 in 2 M. 1818 Jn. Decka NB the sum of £690 being due to my Sister Eliz. Coleman for which no interest has been paid for several years the provision in my will in behalf of my Nephew John Coleman may prove a (?) to him in that behalf.

1819 8 M.17. It is my desire that my Nephew John Catchpool should have the refusal of my Estate at Winchmorehill as specified on deceased this paper for five hundred pounds Jn. Decka. In the Goods of John Decka. 23rd Oct. 1820.'

'Appeared Personally Samuel Marsh of Broad Street (?) Cross in the County of Middlesex watchmaker and solemnly sincerely and truly declared and affirmed that he is one of the Dissenters from the Church of England commonly called Quakers and that he (?) and was well acquainted with John Decka late of Winchmore Hill in the County of Middlesex for some time before and up to the time of his death and also with his manner and character of handwriting and submission having several times seen him write and subscribe his name and having now carefully perused the paper writings hereto annexed marked A, B and C purporting to be and contain three codicils to the last will and testament ….. of the three codicils marked A, B and C and beginning ending and subscribed as aforesaid and also the subscriptions thereto and the whole of the handwrited memoranda written at the foot and base of the said codicil marked C is of the proper handwriting and subscription of the said John Decka. Saml. Marsh. On the day aforesaid this affirmation was made before me. J. Addams ….'

'Appeared Personally John Merrington of Union Court Old Broad Street in the City of London (?) and made Oath that he … and was acquainted with John Decka late of Winchmore Hill in the County of Middlesex …' a similar document of attestation to Marsh's, confirming codicil C as genuine.

'Proved at London with three Codicils 31 Oct. 1820 before the worshipful J. Addams Doctor of Laws and Surrogate by John Coleman and John Catchpool, the Executors to whom Administration was granted they having a solemn and sincere declaration or Affirmation according to Act of Parliament duly to Administer.'

1821

General

King's George 1V's Coronation took place on 19th July – the most lavish ever held until that date. Unfortunately his wife Caroline died that same year. A two year famine began in Ireland, whilst work started on the Stockton to Darlington railway. John Keats died in Rome, aged only 25. John Constable produced *The Hay Wain* and Michael Faraday published *The Principles of the Electric Motor*

Local

In his handwritten notes at the LHU Tom Mason records that on 28th June 1821 'the relict of Dr. Werner' died at Winchmore Hill. The second Minister of the Independent Church locally was the Rev. Thomas Humpage, who served from 6th December 1809 to 30th June 1821. He was succeeded by the Rev. Henry Pawling, who served from 1st October 1821 to 30th November 1842.

By 1821 the upper part of the Friends' Burial Ground (Figure 2), near the road, was full, and so they started to utilise the lower part, which had previously been used for grazing by a number of tenants, including Charles Bartholomew, who owned Enclosure Plot 71 a few yards down Church Hill.

An entry for the Edmonton Vestry Minutes for April 1821 read, 'It having been reported to this Vestry by the Overseers & Medical Gentlemen, that Mrs. S. Childs of Winchmore Hill inoculated many individuals to the annoyance of the neighbourhood, the which practice will, in all probability, bring a heavy burden on the Parish; Resolved – that she be written to, to discontinue such practice.' In Pigot's 1826 Directory Sarah Childs is listed as a furniture broker.

William Radley, who established the Highfield House Estate, died suddenly at that mansion, aged 72, on 28th January 1821. According to a brief notice in *The Times*, he had been "sincerely respected by all who knew him". He was buried in Edmonton churchyard on 6th February, and his death was reported to the Edmonton Manor Court Baron on 12th June 1821, when his widow, represented at the Court hearing by her son,

John Radley, was formally admitted as tenant.

The minutes of that Court Baron also tell us that, 'At this Court the Homage find and present that John Decka formerly of Winchmore Hill in the County of Middlesex Farmer late a Customary Tenant of this Manor is dead and that he died seized of all that Messuage or Tenement with the Appurtenances together with the Orchard Stable and Garden to the same belonging containing by estimation One Acre together with two Cottages or Tenements thereon lately erected and built by the said John Decka (being part and parcel of the Hereditaments and Premises to which he was at a general Court Baron holden in and for this Manor on the Twenty fourth day of May One Thousand and seven hundred and sixty eight admitted Tenant on a Surrender to him thereof made by Benjamin Young ....' Presumably we are here talking of Roseville and grounds.

The minutes also mention his 2a 20p Copyhold allotment on the Chase near the Quaker Poor. They say that at the Court of 13th Oct. 1803 he was admitted as a Copyhold tenant upon his purchase of 'Hereditaments' from John Barnes. Then the minutes quote Decka's Will, noted in detail in the diary for 1820.

At the LMA are papers referenced ACC/588/14 concerning the Lease of land by Aaron Patrick and Miss Mary Peverell to Mr. John Parkinson of 1819. In this further document dated 31st July 1821 it would appear that all three agree to the building and grounds being sub let to John Radford of White Conduit Street, Pentonville for £125 for 21 years.

1822

General

Robert Peel replaced Lord Sidmouth at the Home Office. By now there were seven gasworks in London, and frequently three or four gas companies supplied the same street, each with their own pipes under the pavement. John Nash's Royal Pavilion was completed in Brighton. William Wordsworth published 'A Description of the Scenery of the Lakes'.

Local

The 1822 O.S. Map is at Figure 21. The reader is invited to compare this map with the 1801/2 Enclosure Maps.

It is not my aim to do a detailed comparison, myself, here. However, I would point out the emergence of Brickley House at the corner of 'Hedge Lane' and Green Lanes. The farm in the crook of the join between Firs Lane and 'Hedge Lane' is marked as Huxleys, which survived for over a hundred years. A barrow, not shown on the 1801/2 Enclosure Map, is now indicated at the south west corner of what was Lake's field 367. Highfield House, curiously, is indicated as being on the southern edge of Barrow well Green, rather than where we know it to have been, just west of the modern day *Sainsbury's*. Fords Grove Mansion appears to be marked as Grove House, a name more usually associated with Grovelands mansion. By now *The Green Dragon Inn* had migrated to near its present position. The most westerly stretch of 'Houndsden Road' had now evolved.

At Plate 40 is a copy of the 1822 agreement by which James Wilson sold what had been Plot 101 in 1801 to John Udall for £750. The diary entry for 1825 reveals that Udall built a chapel on the land.

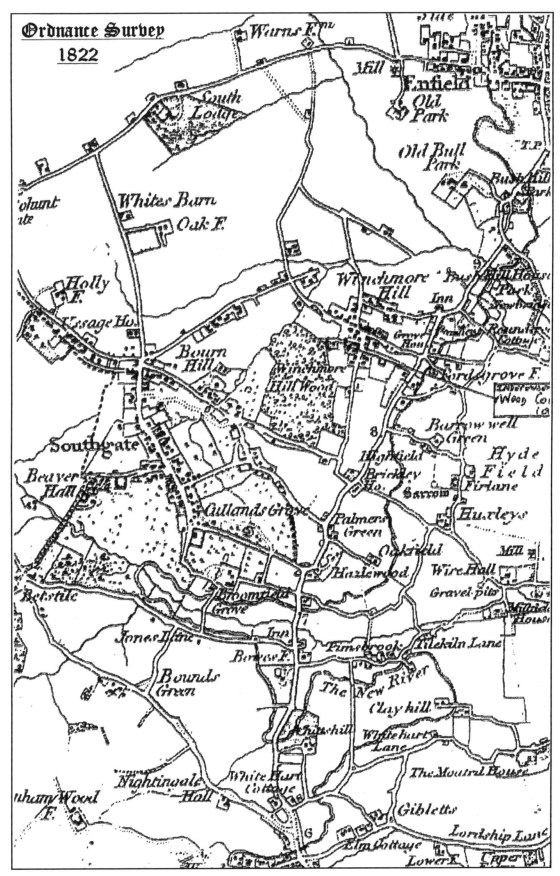

Figure 21. 1822 Ordnance Survey of Winchmore Hill

There seem to be many more buildings in the village than there were at the time of Enclosure.
(Not reproduced to scale.)

241

1823

General

Peel abolished the death penalty for 100 different crimes. In 1791 Roman Catholics had been granted freedom of worship, now Daniel O'Connell formed the Catholic Association. Charles Babbage invented a rudimentary calculator, whilst Charles Macintosh invented waterproof fabrics.

Local

'Pigot & Company's London & Provincial New Commercial Directory For 1823/4' contained, 'Coaches Winchmore Hill, Middlesex 7. See Palmer's Green. Palmer's Green, Middlesex 7 – Afternoon at half past 4, Four Swans, Bishopsgate St., through Southgate & Winchmore Hill.'

According to the late Tom Mason's notes in the LHU, on13[th] March the marriage took place between, 'Fred Cass esq. of Beaulieu – lodge, Winchmore – hill to Martha, daughter of John Dell Potter esq. of Ponder's - end.' That same month Sophia Taylor, daughter of John Vickris Taylor and his second wife Sophia Donnithorne, married Isaac Walker, the son of John Walker and Sarah Chorley. Mason further records that Jacob Yallowley (3rd) esq. died on 7th November 1823 at the age of 54. He was the husband of Martha Richardson Tugwell – 'Old Grandma Yallowley'.

In 1823 prison reformer Elizabeth Fry recorded in her Journal, 'Since I last wrote I have attended Winchmore Hill Meeting to my satisfaction together with my dear Sister Elizabeth, Wm. Allen and my Brother Samuel whose company I enjoyed.' In his book on the Quakers Professor Olver says that her family, the Gurneys, were inter – related with the Barclays, many of whom lived around Winchmore Hill, and of whom at least 46 rest in the Burial Ground.

At the LMA is document ACC/0824/6, labelled, 'Dated 1st May 1823. Sir William Curtis Bart. Counterpart Edward G.W. Tuck. Lease.' The document is an Indenture between Lord of the Manor Sir William Curtis, and Edward Gardner William Tuck of Edmonton, Master Gardener. Curtis lets out, for farming, four cottages and a small piece of land lying near Pinsbrook and Tanners End (Edmonton) and, 'those two Cottages or Tenements and the Shed or Blacksmiths shop thereto adjoining situate lying and being at Winchmore Hill in the said Parish of Edmonton' which Tuck had been occupying for some while. The lease was to run for 21 years from 25th December 1817, at the rate of £21 p.a., paid quarterly. There is then much 'legalese'. In the section on the map titled "From 'Station Road' to 'Vicars Moor Lane'" associated with the Edmonton Enclosure Act of 1800, I suggest that possibly the village blacksmith was based in one of the cottages on Elizabeth Taylor's Plot 110, on The Green.

1824

General

Following aggression from Burma, the Anglo-Burmese Wars began. Portland cement was patented by Joseph Aspdin of Wakefield. The Combination Acts forbidding Trade Unions, passed in 1799-1800, were repealed.

Local

In 1824 John Smith, landlord of *The King's Head*, was fined for being open, and selling beer, 'during the hours of divine service'. John Boards succeeded William Boards as licensee of *The Green Dragon*, to be succeeded, in turn, by Sarah Boards in 1828.

John Walker, grandfather of the seven cricketing bachelors of Southgate, died aged 58, on 9th May 1824. Sarah Thomasina Busk, wife of Edward, died at Fords Grove on 8th June 1824, at the age of 52. Local history writer Frederick Charles Cass (grandson of William) was born at *Beaulieu* in 1824.

The following is the start of an extract from a collection of Press cuttings at the LHU, labelled as being mostly from *The Gentleman's Magazine*, though not usually individually identified. Dated 1824 it runs, 'Freehold and Tithe-free Lands, Farm, and Houses, Winchmore-hill, and Chace-side, Southgate, offering most eligible investments, and now yielding low rents of about 300/- per annum, capable of considerable improvement at the expiration of the present leases. – By Mr. HOGGART, at the Auction Mart, on Friday, Nov 26, at 12, in 7 lots, by direction of the Executors -

Lot 1. A Valuable Freehold Estate, near to Winchmore-hill, and the Chace-side, Southgate, consisting of 2 excellent residences, one of them capacious, and both suitable for respectable families, delightfully situate in the midst of orchards, gardens, and surrounded by 33 acres of meadow and arable land, within a ring fence, and bounded by two good roads; on lease to Captain Bond for 31 years, of which 21 are now unexpired at £120 per annum. This rent may be called a ground rent.

Lot 2. A compact and very eligible Cottage Residence, or Pleasure Farm, adjoining lot 1, in a rural situation, being somewhat nearer to Winchmore-hill and the road leading to Southgate, with capacious barns, stables, and outbuildings, and several closes of fine meadow land, containing upwards of 16 acres; on lease to Mr. Russell, and held by him, with other lands, at the apportioned low rent of £651 – 12s – 4d per annum.

Lot 3. A desirable Freehold Estate, consisting of the capacious residence and premises, with a cottage in the occupation of Mr. F. Thompson, at Winchmore-hill, with a meadow, offices, and garden & let on lease for an unexpired term of 20 years, at a low apportioned rent of £77 per annum.

Lot 4. Two Fields, called Hoppet, and Nine Acres, at Winchmore-hill containing together upwards of 9 acres of meadow land; let to Mr. Alliston on lease, apportioned rent of £27 - 15s per annum.

Lot 5. A Freehold Field of fine Arable Land, containing 3a 2r 7p; let to Mr. Russell on lease, apportioned rent £4-7s-6d per annum.

Lot 6. Two Freehold Fields of Arable and Meadow, let to Mr. Pomfret, at £8 per annum.

Lot 7. An Arable Field, adjoining to lot 2, containing 2 acres and 25 perches, in the occupation of Mr. John Catchpool.

To be viewed by leave of the tenants; and particulars had of Messrs. Blunt and Roy, solicitors, Broad-street buildings; at the Mart, and of Mr. Hoggart, 62, Old Broad-street, Royal Exchange.'

It is difficult to say what or where Lot 1 is, but we know from the 1826 Diary section that Captain Bond also leased what had been Charles Bartholomew's Plot 1541 in the Edmonton Enclosure Schedule, and he might be the Edward Bond listed in that Schedule as the owner of Plot 1546. It also seems difficult to place the exact whereabouts of Lots 2 and 3, but Lot 4 seems less problematic. The 1801/2 Land Ownership Schedule indicates that William Tash of Broomfield sold Plots 69 ("The nine acres") and 70 (Hoppet) to Mr. Thompson. These Plots are in the vicinity of the modern day Paulin Drive and Broadfields Avenue. Lot 5 is said to contain 3a. 2r. 7p. I can't tie this in with any field in Winchmore Hill in the Ownership Schedule. Lot 6 talks of Mr. Pomfret. Page 23 of my *A Look at Old Winchmore Hill* reproduces a sketch by Dr. Cresswell from 1865 – 70 of the old *Retreat Inn* at the junction of what are now Green Moor Link and Green Dragon Lane, and then owned by a Mr. Pomfret. So perhaps these two Freehold fields were in that vicinity? Lot 7 talks of being in the occupation of John Catchpool. The 1834 sale Catalogue for The Grove Estate shows Catchpool occupying a plot of land about half way along the western side of Hoppers Lane. Possibly this is the site of Lot 7.

At the National Archives in Kew is the following Will, 'Martha Tugwell of Winchmore Hill in the County of Middlesex widow make this my last Will and Testament as follows & first I direct that my just debts and funeral expenses be paid and satisfied.

As to all my freehold property as well my present residence and grounds. Also a house and grounds nearly opposite (at same now in occupation of David (?) Gourloman (?) a Cottage and outhouses in Chase Lane at present in the occupation of Eustart and certain Allotments of land in the Chase as every other I give the same unto my daughter Martha Richardson Yallowley during her life and at her decease unto my granddaughter Martha Yallowley Abr Abiro and assigns for ever.

But if my said granddaughter Martha Yallowley should marry and should sit during the life of her husband without issue then I give my said freehold property to her husband his heirs and assigns for ever yet it is my will that if my son in law Jacob Yallowley should survive my said daughter Martha Richardson Yallowley his wife that he shall be allowed to occupy and have full possession of my present residence and grounds during his life provided he should prefer to reside there but not otherwise

and as to all the rest residue and remainder of my estate and effects whatsoever wheresoever I give (?) and bequeath the same unto my said grand daughter Martha Yallowley her heirs (?) administrators and assigns to and for her and their own use and benefit and I do nominate and appoint my said daughter Martha Richardson Yallowley and Robert Barnes floor cloth manufacturer No. 11 City Road Executist and Executor of this my will and revoking all former wills and other testimony dispositions by me at any time heretofor made. I do publish and declare this to be my last will and Testament …. said Martha Tugwell have hereunto set my hand this (/) day of October in the year of our Lord one thousand eight hundred and eighteen. Martha Tugwell. Signed in the presence of us who are her (/) and in the presence of oath have subscribed our names William Hammond, householder, John Udall, shopkeeper and Daniel Sashbridge, Gardener.

Proved at London 4th October 1824 before the worshipful Charles Coote Cator of Laws at Surrogate by the oaths of Martha Richardson Yallowley widow the daughter & Robert Barnes the Executors to whom an administration was granted being first sworn duly to administer.'

Son in law Jacob Yallowley (3rd) had died in 1823. His daughter Martha Yallowley married Robert Barnes. See the summary of family relationships at Figure 4.

1825

General

Parliament passed an Act to regulate cotton mills and factories whereby children under 16 were not allowed to work more than 12 hours a day. It also made those houses with less than eight windows exempt from the Window Tax. William Sturgeon invented the electro-magnet and the Menai suspension bridge was completed. The steam loco' 'Active' pulled the world's first goods/passenger train 27 miles on the Stockton to Darlington line, whilst the first horse drawn buses appeared in London.

Local

In 1811 the Clayton family had sold quite a large portion of the Old Park Estate to a Mr. Thomas Cotton. This portion extended from Windmill Hill to the Grangeway as far as the New River and included what is now Enfield Golf Course. The Estate came up for sale on Thursday 6th May 1825. Mrs. Elizabeth Lewis bought the 181 acres for £23,997. 8s. 0d in 1826.

At the LMA is the, 'Manor of Edmonton Middx. Court Book Commencing 12th June 1810' (document ACC 695/26). The minutes of the Court Baron held on 24th May 1825 announced the death of Henry Thompson. John Decka's nephews John Coleman and John Catchpool surrendered the 2a. 20p of Copyhold land near Winchmore Hill Gate that was shown as Decka's Plot 1581 in the Enclosure Award, William Good being admitted upon payment of a Fine of 13/4d and a Rent of 1d p.a..

The following is an extract from a collection of Press cuttings at the LHU, labelled as being mostly from *The Gentleman's Magazine,* though they are not usually individually identified. Dated 1825 the extract runs, 'Winchmore-hill, Middlesex - Delightful Freehold and part Copyhold Property, comprising two genteel Residences, Meadow Land and Building Ground - By W. LEIFCHILD, at Garraway's, on Thursday, May 26, at 12.

An elegant detached Residence, called Winchmore Villa, pleasantly situate in the preferable part of Winchmore-hill, Middlesex, approached by a circular carriage drive, and seated on the margin of a handsome lawn, with grounds tastefully disposed in pleasure walks, shrubberies, & c, ornamented by thriving plantations, capital greenhouse, excellent kitchen garden, well stocked with fruit trees, cucumber and melon ditto, and a small enclosure of fine meadow land. The house and premises are in complete repair, and perfectly adapted for the immediate reception of a respectable family.

Also a pleasant Country Residence, nearly adjoining the preceding, with lawns, pleasure grounds, kitchen garden & c. Also sundry handsome enclosures of superior meadow land and building ground, commanding extensive views of the surrounding country, and presenting particularly eligible sites for the erection of villas, being presumed to possess brick earth to a considerable depth. May be viewed on Mondays, Wednesdays, and Fridays between the hours of 11 and 2, with tickets only, which may be had at W. Leifchild's offices. Particulars will be ready for delivery 10 days previous to the sale, which may be had at Garraway's; on the premises; and at the offices of W. Leifchild, Enfield, Middlesex, where plans of the estate may be seen.'

Kelly's Directory for 1899-1900 lists a Winchmore Villa about six buildings up from *The Chase Side Tavern* at the foot of what is now Winchmore Hill Road (Chase

Side Road in 1825). It is impossible to say if this was the same building, but the location would give a commanding view over the surrounding countryside.

By chance I also came across another catalogue for the same Leifchild sale at the National Archives in Kew. It read, 'Particulars and conditions of sale of a delightful freehold cottage residence with early possession, called Vale Cottage, Winchmore Hill; which will be sold by auction by order of the proprietor, by W. LEIFCHILD on Thursday, the 26th May, 1825, at 12 o ' Clock, At Garraway's Coffee House, 'Change Alley, in one Lot.

A genteel and commodious residence, in the cottage style, pleasantly situated at Winchmore Hill, about Eight Miles from London; Approached by a Carriage Drive, and containing Four capital Bed Chambers, with Dressing Room; Drawing and Dining Room, Communicating by Folding Doors; Breakfast Room, Kitchen and Scullery, And other Domestic Offices; Chaise – house and Stable, with Lofts over; Small Yard, Cow-house, Piggeries, Coal – sheds, & c. EXCELLENT KITCHEN GARDEN; Capital Orchard, Stocked with thriving Fruit Trees, containing altogether about One Acre; Tythe free and exonerated from Land – tax. This desirable Residence is now in the Occupation of MANSFIELD BOWEN Esq. Tenant at Will, at the Rent of £40 per Annum. May be Viewed, and Particulars had at all the principal Inns in the Neighbourhood, and at W. LEIFCHILD'S Offices, Enfield, Middlesex.'

There are then a number of Conditions of Sale, number V. reading as follows, 'For such parts of the Property as consist of Allotment, under the Inclosure of Edmonton Common, the Vendor will produce no other Title than an extract of the Award shewing the Allotment and the Conveyance from the party to whom the Allotment was made, or the representation of such party. And for such parts of the Property as were formerly Copyhold, and are now enfranchised, the Vendors will not produce the Title of any of the Lords of the respective Manors.'

Kelly's Directory for 1899-1900 lists a row of three cottages on the west side of what is now Eversley Park Road as Vale Cottages, whilst today The Vale runs parallel to, and just north of, Winchmore Hill Road. One presumes, then, that Vale Cottage might well have been somewhere in this area, which had once been the Edmonton Allotment to the Chase.

Another National Archives document reads, 'I Jeremiah Bailey Junr. being very ill in body but sound in mind declare this as my last will and Testament that, is to say I give to my wife Mary Bailey all my real and personal property for her use and sole disposal surrounding my immortal soul to the favor and protection of my Creator I to this Testament have submitted my hand & seal this third day of September 1824 Jeremiah Bailey his x witness John Catchpool , Harrison Powell, George Watts.' The handwriting then becomes very poor, but it seems the Will was proven in 1825.

Also at the National Archives in Kew, amongst papers J90, is a sale catalogue for a, 'Cottage Residence and Small Dairy Farm Near Winchmore Hill and Chase Side, Southgate,' set, 'In a beautiful and picturesque situation, comprising Sixteen Acres with a roomy cottage residence and offices, productive orchard, garden, barn, stabling, and agricultural buildings, on lease to Mr. Charles Russell, which will be sold by auction by Mr. Hoggart, at the Auction Mart, on Thursday, the 22nd of December, 1825, at twelve o'clock, by direction of the Executors. To be viewed by leave of the tenant...... Subject to a Corn Rent of 5s 7d in lieu of Tithe....' Handwritten notes with the catalogue suggest the farm might well have been on Chase Side Road.

Edwards Estate's research reveals that by 1825 three small cottages bridged the gap between *The King's Head* and what we now call Devon House. The Poor Rate Book for 1825 shows shoe manufacturer J. Braggins as occupier of the latter premises, with G. Grace in the adjoining cottage. Ann Rook is in the middle cottage, and Daniel Baker in the one nearest *The King's Head,* where the landlord was J. Smith. Their research also tells us that members of the Beckett family were still known to be owners (though not necessarily occupants) of *The Kings Head* in 1825.

A headstone in the Friends Burial Ground, Church Hill, reads, 'Samuel Hoare of Hampstead. Died 1825. Age 74 Years'.

A History of Middlesex, of undisclosed authorship, includes the entry, 'Providence chapel was erected in 1825 in Vicar's Moor Lane by John Udall the elder, a member of a Winchmore Hill family which used its grocer's shop as a front for contraband goods. The chapel was registered by Independents (according to documents in the Guildhall), and the Udallite sect which worshipped there called itself Independent in 1851 .....The original chapel had 60 sittings.....(it) was rebuilt in 1888 in yellow brick with red brick dressings in the Gothic style.......' (1888 may be a misprint for 1883). The rebuilt Chapel is now a private residence with a listed façade. (See Plate 40.)

1826

Under an Act of 1789 the portion of Green Lanes in Edmonton Parish came under the turnpike trust looking after Fore Street, who made great improvements to it. In 1826 responsibility for the road passed to the Commissioners for Metropolitan Turnpike Roads.

Joseph Compton bought the house, and associated land, occupied by Miss Cresswell's 'lawyer' Samuel Compton, which had been owned by Ann Dale upon Enclosure, in two purchases. The first of these purchases was in 1820, the second in 1826.

The site of St. Paul's Church (pictured on the front cover) was donated by Walker Gray of Southgate Grove (now Grovelands) in 1826. The edifice was erected in 1826/7 at a cost of £4,249. 15s. 9d, of which £1,000 was raised by subscription, the remainder coming from the Church Building Commissioners, who were building in areas of expanding population. St. Paul's was one of a number of so-called 'Waterloo' churches dating from this period, and was built to a standard design known as 'Churchwarden's Gothic'. It was consecrated in 1828, the first baptism being in 1831.

Tom Mason's notes in the LHU say that on 11th February 1826 Joseph, the 2 year old youngest son of John Radford, died, followed two days later by Radford's wife Mary. In 1826 Robert Barnes and his wife Martha (nee Yallowley) had a baby girl named Anna, who went on to occupy the family home of Laurel Cottage at the top of Church Hill (Plot 54 on the Enclosure Map), where she died in 1901. This was the year, further to the 1825 entry, when Mrs. Elizabeth Lewis purchased 181 acres of Old Park Estate for £23,997 - 8s - 0d. In December 1827, she sold some of this.

At the LMA are the Edmonton Manor Books for 1826 – 44 (Ref. ACC/695/40). The record for 1826 contains many references to people listed in the 1801 Enclosure Schedule, and starts, 'Manor of Edelmeton otherwise Edelington otherwise Edmonton in the County of Middlesex to wit. The view of Frankpledge and general Court Baron of Sir William Curtis Baronet Lord of this Manor holden in and for this Manor on Tuesday in Whitsun week being the 16th day of May in the year of our Lord 1826 before Robert Spiller Wadeson Steward there. Jurors of our Lord the King William Acott, Edward Skekelthorpe, Thomas Leach, William Eaton, William English, George

Corker, Samuel Richards, George Oliver, George Galloway, William Cobbett, Richard Smith, William Gladwin, John Stanley, John Wright, Samuel Brown, John Brown, William Gates, Daniel Hayward, William Heath, John Jordan, George Gudgin, John Gibbons, William Williams and William Luck. Sworn.

First we present the common Fine. Also we present the undermentioned persons to serve the following offices for the year ensuing

	Constables	Headboroughs
Church St. Ward	John Beit	Edward Field
Bury St. Ward	Charles Alliston	John Gann
South St. Ward	William Gurney	William Mills
Fore St. Ward	William Rowley	John Crouch

	Ale Connors	Field Drivers
Church St. Ward	William Hinton	George Harwood
Bury St. Ward	Matthew Pain	Thomas Smith
South St. Ward	William Gates	James Bone
Fore St. Ward	George Galloway	John Booger

Constable for the Parish, Thomas Richards. Pound Keeper John Meadows....

...... This amercement is offered by us at the sum of Ten Shillings – William Acott Th. Leach Officers Sworn ..... The present Thomas Gabell for an encroachment by inclosing a part of the Waste before his House at Barnwells Green being 21 feet long by 20 feet broad being a public injury ...... We have viewed a certain piece of waste at the Bourne opposite Mr. Charles Harris Garden and are of opinion that the inclosure thereof would be a public injury ..... (Signed by the Jurors.)

And now the Court Baron Homage John Whitbread, Eleazer Booker Sworn ...... At this Court the homage find and present that Aaron Patrick and Mary Hudson formerly Peverell late two of the Copyhold or Customary Tenants of this Manor are Dead and that they died seized by all that piece or parcel of land ...... And the said Homage further find and present that the said Samuel Patrick made and published his last Will and Test. in writing the probate whereof under the Seal of the Perogative Court of the Archbishop of Canterbury bearing date the 8th day of January 1808 and presented at the Court holden in for (stet) this Manor on the 7 day of June 1808 whereby he devised as follows, "I give and devise unto my Dear Daughter Mary Peverell my brother Aaron Patrick and William Cobbett of Bury Street Edmonton aforesaid Gentleman and to their heirs and assigns all that freehold Cottage and Garden ground thereto belonging situate or standing and being at Enfield Highway in the said County of Middlesex and which is now or late was in the tenure or occupation of Wright and others.

Also all that half of an acre of freehold land situate lying and being at Winchmore Hill aforesaid and now in the tenure or occupation of my daughter Mary and all that copyhold Mess. or Tent. at Winchmore Hill aforesaid together with the garden ground & premises thereto belonging held by me of the Manor of Edmonton afsd. and now in my own occupation to hold to them the said Mary Peverell Aaron Patrick & William Cobbett. ...... The half acre of Freehold land situate at Winchmore Hill also to the use of my Grandson Henry Peverell and assigns for life. ..... my Grand daughter Frances Peverell...."

The Court then goes on to grant some or all of the land to Margaret Peverell, with an annual rent of 5/-. She paid Curtis a 16/- fine for this. The Court also announced the death of William Goslin, John Erwood and William Baker Naylor (brother of Thomas), and his Will.

E & G.N. Driver's catalogue for the sale of property at The Mart, Bartholomew Lane at noon on Friday 18th August 1826 includes the following for Winchmore Hill,

'Lot 1. A Valuable Copyhold Estate: Most delightfully situate at Winchmore Hill, in the Parish of Edmonton, in the County of Middlesex, and only about Eight Miles from London, comprising A Delightful Cottage Residence, Commanding most beautiful and rich Views over the surrounding Country, and fit for the occupation of a Family of Respectability, pleasantly placed at a gentle remove from the Road, from which it is screened by a Shrubbery, &c. with a Handsome Veranda extending along the Front and one end of the Cottage, with Lawns, Shrubberies, Pleasure Grounds, Garden and Paddock, containing in the whole about 2A. 2R 27P.

The Cottage contains on the Ground Floor, Entrance Hall, Dining Room, 21 Feet 10, by 14 Feet 9, with French Windows opening to Shrubbery, Drawing-room, 18 Feet by 14 Feet 6, with Bow Window opening to the Lawn, Water Closet, Cellar, Butler's Pantry, Store-room, Larder, Dairy, Kitchen, Scullery, and other domestic Offices. Above is a handsome Landing, lighted by Sky Light, with Four best Bed-rooms of good dimensions, Sitting-room, Nursery, and Two Smaller Chambers, neatly fitted up, and in good condition.

Detached are Summer House, Garden House, Wash or Brewhouse. In an enclosed Yard are Two Coach Houses, Four-stall Stable, with Loft over, Harness-room, Cart or Cattle Shed, Cow House, Poultry House, & C. The Garden is well stocked with thriving Fruit Trees, and the Pleasure Grounds are laid out with Gravel Walks and Luxuriant Shrubberies.

The above Premises are copyhold, of the Manor of the Rectory of Tottenham, in the County of Middlesex, And subject to a Trifling Quit Rent (which however has not been received for some Years) and to a customary Fine on Death or Alienation. They are in the occupation of Martin Esq., but let on Lease to Huntley Bacon, Esq., for a term of which 4 ¼ Years were unexpired at Midsummer, 1826, with a covenant to grant a further term of 2 Years, at the Lessee's expense, upon the same terms and conditions, at the very low clear annual Rent of £35, but of the estimated annual value of about £80. The Timber will be included in the Purchase.'

The 2a. 2r. 27p corresponds exactly with Charles Bartholomew's Plot 71 in the Edmonton Enclosure Schedule. Also on file is a Memorandum of 18th August 1826 which indicates that Lot 1 was sold for £800, though it isn't clear as to who the purchaser was.

'Lot 2: An allotment of land, containing 0 Acres, 1 Rood, 23 Perches, pleasantly situate a short distance from Winchmore Hill, abutting East upon the Road leading from thence to Southgate, and well adapted for Building, having a frontage of about 52 feet, in the occupation of Captain Bond, as Tenant from year to Year, at the annual Rent of £1. 0s. 0d. This Lot is held under the same Tenure, and subject to a trifling apportioned Quit Rent as Lot 1, and to the same Customary Fine. The Fence on the North side is to be made by the Proprietor of the adjoining Allotment.' The 0a. 1r. 23p corresponds exactly with Charles Bartholomew's Plot 1541 in the Edmonton Enclosure Schedule

'Lot 3. A Desirable Leasehold Estate: Also pleasantly situate at Winchmore Hill, and adjoining Lot 1, comprising A Residence, with Veranda in Front, Garden Pleasure Grounds and Paddock, containing on the whole about Two Acres. The house consists of a Dining-room, Drawing-room, Four Bed-chambers and a Dressing-room.

The Domestic Offices comprise Kitchen, Washhouse, pantry, Cellar, &c, with Coach-house and Stable.

The Premises are held for a Term of which 9½ Years were unexpired at Lady-day, 1826, at a Ground Rent of £6 6s per Annum. They are now in the occupation of the Rev. Mr. Pauling, but are let on Lease to Harvey Coombe, Esq. For the remainder of the said Term, at the low clear Annual Rent of £35 - 0s - 0d. Deduct Ground Rent £6 - 6s - 0d. Net improved Rent £28 - 14s - 0d.'

This is probably Hill House (Plot 72 adjoining Plot 71 on the Enclosure Map.) Rev. P. Henry Pawling was the Pastor for the Independents from 1st October 1821 to 30th November 1842, and is listed in the Pigot's Directory of 1826. At Enclosure the House was owned by John Tugwell, father of 'Old Grandma Yallowley', a bastion of the local Independents.

At the LMA are papers P/1826/09/050 concerning a case of assault - 'Middlesex to wit} The Information of Thomas Mantz taken on Oath, this Twenty sixth Day of August in the Year of our Lord One Thousand Eight Hundred and Twenty six - at the Police Office Worship Street, in the Parish of Saint Leonard Shoreditch, in the County of Middlesex, before me Henry Osborne Esq. One of His Majesty's Justices of the Peace in and for the said County of Middlesex, on the Examination and in the Presence and Hearing of William Reece brought before me and charged with an Assault.

The said Thomas Mantz on Oath says, I reside at Winchmore Hill, Stage Coachman Says, On Wednesday the 23rd of August instant the Prisoner was driving his Stage at Winchmore Hill a female on the outside was much frightened and I went up to endeavour to get her down, and while I was in the act of helping her down the Prisoner cut me with his whip, struck me with his fist and pushed me about the Road.

Sworn before me. A.J. Oborne. Tho. Mantz. Clerkenwell Sept. Sessions 1826. Information gst. William Reece for assault.' (I can't find a Mantz or Reece in the 1826 Pigot's Directory.)

Pigot & Co.'s London Directory - 1826

'Southgate & Winchmore Hill - (Middlesex)

Winchmore Hill is in the parish of Edmonton, eight miles north from London, and two miles east from Southgate; and as its name implies, is situated upon an eminence. The views from this spot are highly picturesque, and the air is very salubrious. Several highly respectable families reside at this place and in the immediate neighbourhood. The only place of worship here, is a chapel for dissenters, there are also some respectable schools, both boarding and day.

POST OFFICE, Winchmore Hill receiving house at Wm. Board's, the *Green Dragon*, from whence letters are dispatched at half past eight morning, and at half past three afternoon.

Nobility, Gentry and Clergy

Note - The names without address are in Southgate.

Alliston Chas. Esq.	Winchmore hill	Holmes Mrs. Jane	Winchmore hill
Arundell Jas. Chas. Esq.	Winchmore hill	Judkins Rev. Thomas Jas	
Austin Mrs.	Winchmore hill	Laing Jas. Esq.	
Bailiff Captain		Lewis Mrs. Winchester	Winchmore hill
Bond Captain	Winchmore hill	Lewis Mrs.	
Brown Geo. Hy. Esq.	Winchmore hill	Lugger Rev. Robert	
Buckingham and Chandos Duke of		Martin - Esq.	Winchmore hill
Busk Edw. Esq.	Winchmore Hill	Mellish Wm. Esq.	Bush hill
Butler J.L. Esq.		Padman Mrs.	Winchmore hill
Cass Fred. Esq.	Winchmore hill	Pawling Rev. Hy.	Winchmore hill
Catling Jas. Esq.		Pazeley Mrs. Jane	
Child Richard Esq.	Winchmore hill	Powys Henry P. Esq.	
Compton SI. Esq.	Winchmore hill	Radford John Esq.	Winchmore hill
Currie Isaac Esq.	Bush hill	Radley John Esq.	Winchmore hill
Curtis Sir Wm. Baronet		Schnider John P. Esq	
Curtis Thos. Esq.		Soulesby Wm. Esq.	Winchmore hill
Curtis Timothy Esq.		Taylor J.V. Esq.	
Desborough Henry Esq.		Teshmaker Mrs. Sh.	Winchmore hill
Egan Edw. Esq.		Tewart Edward Esq.	
Eykyn Jas. Esq.		Thompson Marmaduke Esq.	
Fawcett Mrs.	Winchmore hill	Walker Isaac, Esq.	Palmer's green
Gann John Esq.	Winchmore hill	Walker Mrs.	
Goad Geo. Esq.			
Gray Walker Esq.		Williams Mrs. Gregory	Palmer's green
Hewson Mrs.	Palmer's green	Warrick Edward Esq.	
Hoggart Charles Esq.		Yallowley Mrs.	Winchmore hill

Academies

Dickinson Cs. (gent's bdg)	Chase side	Rumsey Jas. Richd.	
Fleuret Benj. (boarding and day)		(gent's bdg.)	Eagle hall
Lloyd Rev. Wm. (gent's boarding)		Thomas Mrs.	
Pawling Mrs.		(ladies' bdg. & day)	Winchmore hill
(ladies' bdg. & day)	Winchmore hill	Thompson Francis	
		(gent's bdg.)	Winchmore hill

Inns and Taverns

Cherry Tree	Joseph Dale
Crown	Joseph Hoye
Green Dragon	William Boards, Winchmore hill
King's Head	John Smith, Winchmore hill

Surgeons

Hammond Wm. & Son

Wilkinson Charles

Tradesmen. Shopkeepers. &c

Acott, Wm. — Carpenter & builder
Allen, Edwd. — Carpenter & undertaker *Winchmore hill*
Allsop, Geo. — confectioner
Auty, Joseph — chair maker
Balaam, Geo. — Smith & bell hanger
Burton, John — Smith & farrier *Winchmore hill*
Bush, Geo. — butcher
Catchpool, John — Baker & corn dealer *Winchmore hill*
Childs, Sarah — furniture broker *Winchmore hill*
Cowles, Richd. — tinman, & c. *Winchmore hill*
Crane, Wm. — boot & shoe maker
Cuthbert, James — nurseryman
Denham, Js. — butcher *Winchmore hill*
Earl, John — butcher
Ellis, Abel — general dealer
Evennett, Wm. — Grocer & tea dealer, & agent to the Beacon Fire office
Flower, Elizabeth — butcher
Forster, John — boot & shoe maker *Winchmore hill*
Gates, Wm. — plasterer
Gladwin, Wm. — smith & bell hanger
Gudgin, George — wheelwright
Gurney, Wm. — brazier & tinman
Hanscombe, John — baker
Hedges John — baker
Horsell, James — general dealer
Horsey, Chas. — butcher *Winchmore hill*
Jifkins, Jas. — Corn & coal dealer *Winchmore hill*

Leach, Thos., — Carpenter & builder
Linwood, Wm. — Bricklayer
Long, Robt — general dealer in groceries, corn & coal
Love, Thomas — carpenter
Lowens, John — general dealer *Winchmore hill*
Lowing, Sophia — straw hat maker *Winchmore hill*
Manning, Thomas — carpenter & undertaker
Mays, Richard — wheelwright
Mills Wm. — corn & coal dealer
Petzold, Alice — boot & shoe maker
Pikesley, Joseph — baker
Phillips Lewis — tailor
Province, Thomas — tailor *Winchmore hill*
Richards, Samuel — auctioneer and agent to the Atlas Fire Office
Riley Richd. — painter, plumber & c. *Winchmore hill*
Sandilands, Robert — tailor
Sell John — carpenter & undertaker, *Winchmore hill*
Simmons, Abraham — fishmonger & poulterer
Skikelthorpe, Edwd. — plumber & c.
Tarrant, Wm. — saddle & harness mkr.
Taylor James — cooper
Udall, John — draper, haberdasher, grocer, & tea dlr. *Winchmore hill*
Wadkins, John — tailor
Whitman Wm. Henry. — corn & coal dealer
Wilkinson Jacob — linen draper

Coaches

To LONDON, from Southgate, THOMAS DANCER, from his own house, every morning at half-past eight; and twice on Sundays, to the *Four Swans,* Bishopsgate st. - from Winchmore hill, coaches leave the *King's Head* at half-past eight in the morning, to the *Four Swans,* Bishopsgate - street, daily.

Carriers

To LONDON, - From WINCHMORE HILL, WILLIAM HOLD, from his own house Mondays, Wednesdays and Saturdays, to the *Marlborough Head,* Bishopsgate street, and *White House,* Cripplegate.

Who were these people? – a.) The Great and the Good

Below I cover those families not listed in the E.E. Land Ownership Schedule.

Captain Bond

A Captain Bond is referred to as a tenant of Lot 1 of the sale documented at 1824 in the diary section, and also of Lot 2 in the sale catalogue documented in the 1826 diary section. There is an Edward Bond in the E.E. Ownership Schedule. Is the Captain that Edward, or a relative of his?

Frederick Cass Esq

See the section on Beaulieu in the Map Section - 'Highfield Road' to top of 'Firs Lane'.

The Child Family

In the churchyard at Church Street, Edmonton is a tombstone bearing the inscription, 'In memory of Ann wife of Richard Child of Winchmore Hill Gent. who departed this life on the 24th January 1837 in the 71st year of her age. She bore with Christian fortitude and resignation a protracted illness in a glorious hope of eternal happiness through a divine saviour. Also of the above named Richard Child who departed this life on the 24th May 1843 aged *76* years.'

Samuel Compton.

Today we remember Samuel in the name of Compton Road. Read more about him in the section on the Highfield House Estate.

Isaac Currie

In 1801 Bush Hill House (known before its demise as Halliwick) was in the hands of John Blackburn Jnr.. By 1826 the property was in the hands of City banker Isaac Currie.

Sir William Curtis (1752 – 1829)

Sir William is mentioned in the section on Edmonton Manor, which he became Lord of in 1800. Alan Dumayne, in his *Once Upon a Time in Palmers Green*, tells us quite a bit about Sir William, and I would refer the reader to that book for more details. The following is but a brief summary.

Alderman's Hill in Palmers Green is named after Alderman William Curtis, who lived in the fine Cullands Grove mansion, which Alan says was located slightly to the west of the junction of modern day Harlech Road (at its southern end) and Conway Road. It is thought to have been built in the first half of the 18th century. His grandfather had set up a business in Wapping, which his father inherited, specialising in the manufacture of ships' biscuits. William and his elder brother Timothy extended the business further, and they branched out successfully into banking. William was, apparently, a larger than life character who was a personal friend of the Prince Regent, later George 1V.

Curtis was appointed as an Alderman of the City of London in 1785 at the early age of 33, and was Sheriff in 1789. He became Lord Mayor in 1795, and was created a baronet in 1802. Curtis was a staunch Tory, and was elected as an MP for the City in 1790, holding the seat continuously for 28 years, until losing it in 1818. The following year he was elected MP for Bletchingley, but in 1820 he returned to represent the City. In 1826 he was elected to represent Hastings, though that December was forced to resign owing to ill health. Sir William retired from public life and went to live at his house in Ramsgate, where he died in 1829. The Cullands Grove Estate was purchased by J.D. Taylor, of Grovelands, and he demolished the mansion in 1840.

Mrs. Jane Holmes

This seems to be the lady who owned and ran a Mental Institution at Winchmore Hill, as outlined in the 1830 diary section.

The Rev. Henry Pawling

Pastor for the Independents from 1st October 1821 to 30th November 1842. In the property sale document in the 1826 diary section Pawling is shown as living at what appears to be Hill House. Presumably it was his wife who ran the Ladies boarding and day school in the village – perhaps at Hill House? It is said that he also ran a school, situated in Palmers Green.

Pawling was from Cornwall, and before he ministered at Winchmore Hill he did so at Thirsk in Yorkshire, and then East Budleigh in Devon. He apparently got tired of the 'constant changes in the village' of Winchmore Hill, and so he left to minister in Lenham, Kent, followed by Aston Tirrold, Berkshire. He retired to live at the home of his married daughter in Muswell Hill, until his death in 1869.

John Radford

John Radford was the Independent Church's Deacon from about 1800 to 31st October 1849. He is mentioned in the E.E. section on the map of The Green, as the original Church building was known to have been in that area. In the 1821 diary a legal document citing him as a lessee says he was of, 'White Conduit Street, Pentonville'. In 1828 Radford married Mary Padmore, widow of Isaac. In the section on *Roseville*, overlooking The Green, we learn that Radford acquired this small estate in 1830. His family retained it until 1921, though it did not necessarily live there. John left Winchmore Hill in 1849, the year after pulling down the original Meeting Place.

Mrs. Yallowley

The Yallowleys feature at Figure 4, and in the E.E. Ownership section on John Tugwell. This lady is Martha Richardson Yallowley, ('Old Grandma Yallowley'), mentioned in the Will of her mother Martha Tugwell, nee Richardson, in the 1824 diary. 'Old Grandma Yallowley' was a committed member of the local Independent community and in 1843, when the Chapel on The Green was under threat of closure, she wrote a 'begging letter' to Sir Culling Eardley Smith, bart. of Bedwell Park, Hertfordshire (near Hatfield), seeking support. Unfortunately she was unsuccessful, and the Chapel closed in 1843, being demolished by John Radford in 1848.

Who were these people? – b.) The Man in the street

The Catchpools

In 1838 the Friends published a paper by Irene L. Edwards entitled, *Two Hundred and Fifty Years of Winchmore Hill Meeting*. At P37 we read, 'From the

1827

General

Following his stroke, the Earl of Liverpool was succeeded as Prime Minister by George Canning, but he died only three months after taking up post. The third Tory PM for the year was Viscount Goderich (the Earl of Rippon). John Nash built Cumberland Terrace at Regents Park.

Local

The construction of St. Paul's Church, started in 1826, was completed in 1827. The Cass family left Beaulieu for Cat Hill in this year, selling the estate in 1832. John Donnithorne Taylor succeeded his father John Vickris in the Taylor Walker brewery in 1827. In December Mrs. Elizabeth Lewis sold a portion of Old Park Estate, now known as Grange Park, to Isaac Currie. She also sold 56 acres, between what is now Carrs Lane and the New River, to William Carr.

Albert Hill self published *Seventy - Two Years in Tottenham. Reminiscences* in 1899. Albert was a nephew of the famous Rowland Hill, owner of Bruce Castle and prime mover in the introduction of the uniform penny postage. (There is a statue in his honour in King Edward Street near St. Paul's Cathedral.) Albert was a master at his uncle's school for Boys at Bruce Castle, and lived in Tottenham for about ninety years until he died in 1917. It could be argued that the recollections of a Tottenham man have no place in a book on Winchmore Hill, but I have included some of Albert's observations as they shed light on the world of that time.

'If not the oldest resident in Tottenham now living, I must be very nearly so, being that I have now completed my seventy-second year of residence on the same spot, Bruce Castle and Priory Side being adjacent. Leaving Birmingham, my native place, at about 5 p.m., I reached Bruce Castle at noon the following day, April 23rd, 1827 (Shakespeare's birthday), after a tedious coach journey of nineteen-hours - a journey which would now be accomplished in five hours at the most. Tottenham was then a straggling village containing about five thousand inhabitants, thoroughly rural in all its surroundings. There was at that time no railway in the world, the maximum speed of travelling being that of the horse - at most ten or twelve miles an hour, ...

.... What a boon in my boyhood would have been the Lucifer matches and vestas which one is now pestered to buy by children in the streets and at railway stations! The only way to procure a light at the time I speak of was by use of the flint and steel - a process which occupied some minutes..... Our large sitting room at Bruce Castle (34 x 18 ft) was lighted, I remember, by two mould candles, which needed frequent use of the snuffers, an instrument long rendered obsolete by the composite candle, which snuffs itself ..... The only light carried from room to room was the tallow dip, now all but universally superseded by the paraffin lamp ...... For several years after coming to Bruce Castle, our only light was that of the murky oil lamp and the murky dip candle .....

..... Tottenham being on one of the main roads to the North, was traversed by five mail coaches running to Cambridge, Louth, Lincoln, York, and Edinburgh. It was a very pretty sight to see them spanking through the village, drawn by four spirited horses, heralded by the guard's horn. The coaches left St. Martin's-le-Grand *(near St. Paul's)* at 8 p.m., and used to pass the Lancasterian Girls' School (now the Marlborough Mission) at 8.35 to the minute ...... Before the Penny Postage (1840), letters were few, and were conveyed to and from London on horse-back, contained in a leathern satchel strapped behind the rider. That mode of conveyance proving insufficient, the post boys were replaced by mail carts, which were continued, I believe, until the opening of the extension of the Great Eastern Railway to Enfield in 1872 ....'

1828

General

Viscount Goderich was succeeded by the Duke of Wellington (Tory). Daniel O'Connell had formed the Catholic Association in 1823, and in 1828 was elected to Parliament. However, he refused to take his seat as the Oath he would need to swear was aimed against Catholics. A new Corn Law was introduced which allowed the import of foreign grain on a sliding system of duties according to the current price of British corn. James Nielson introduced the blast furnace. Regents Park was opened, and two London Colleges were founded – Kings College and University College, now both part of London University. University College (where I read Geology) welcomed all comers, regardless of their background.

Local

On 2nd June 1828 St. Paul's was consecrated as a Chapel-of-Ease to All Saints, Edmonton by the Rt. Rev. William Howley, D.D., Bishop of London, later to become Archbishop of Canterbury. The Curate from 1828 to 1834 was T. Bisland.

It was in 1828 that Sarah Boards succeeded John Boards as licensee of *The Green Dragon*. Joseph Horner followed her in 1833. According to Tom Mason's notes in the LHU John Vickris Taylor died aged 81 on 11th September.

At the National Archives, Kew is a box reference J90 which contains a series of slips (c. 3" x 7") testifying to the payments made by John Cross to Sir William Curtis, Lord of Edmonton Manor. Much of each slip was pre type printed. I here reproduce the content of one of these as an example. The regular type represents what had been pre printed on the slip, the words in itaelics having been completed in longhand,

'Manor of Edmonton, Com' Middx. The *25* Day of *March* 1828 RECEIVED then of *Mr. John Cross* the Sum of   Pounds *Three* Shillings and *four* Pence, for one Year's Quit Rent, due at Lady – day last; to Sir WILLIAM CURTIS Bart. Lord of the said Manor, by *John Meadow Bailiff.* N.B. The Bailiff will attend on WHIT – TUESDAY next, at the ANGEL, in Edmonton, to receive the Rents. JOHN MEADOWS, Bailiff.'

Along the right hand edge there are two columns showing what appear to be various sums received as rent. The right hand column totals 10s 8d, whilst the left hand column has only two sums totalling 3s 8d. Although the Bailiff's printed name is 'Meadows', the signature is clearly 'Meadow'!

Pigot & Company's Metropolitan New Alphabetical Directory for 1828

There is a map in the Directory portraying the local area, and I noted that Green Dragon Lane was marked as 'Chase Lane'. Postage rates were shown as: 15-20 miles = 5d; 20 - 30 miles = 6d; 30 - 50 miles 7d; 50 - 80 miles = 8d; 80-120 miles = 9d; 120 -170 miles =10d;170 - 230 miles = 11 d; 230 - 300 miles =12d; Each extra 100 miles = 1d more. One entry is, 'New Van, Waggon (stet). and Cart Conveyance List: Winchmore Hill, Middx. Southgate, Palmers Green, and Green Lane; Hold's, Wm. Luck's, Brook's, and Lowen's Carts daily.'

1829

General

With the Catholic Emancipation Act of 1829 Catholics were readmitted to Parliament on a non discriminatory basis. Home Secretary Robert Peel's Act for setting up the Metropolitan Police was passed in 1829, but its area initially extended no further north than Hackney and Newington. On July 4, 1829 George Shillibeer started Britain's first scheduled bus service in London, using horses.

Local

The poet Thomas Hood was born at Poultry, London in 1799, the son of a bookseller who had written two novels. In 1818 he became apprenticed to an engraver and so he was later able to illustrate his own poems with style. In 1821 Hood became sub-editor of *The London Magazine* and he devoted much time to his humorous work, whilst falling in with the literary set of Lamb, Coleridge, De Quincey and others. In 1828 his health began to fail and so, in 1829, a year or two after his marriage to Jane Reynolds (sister of John Hamilton Reynolds), he moved to Rose Cottage, in 'Vicars Moor Lane'. He stayed three years, near his close friend Lamb, but when the landlord didn't repair the cottage, Hood left, with later regrets. Part of the house was very old, and rumour had it that it was once occupied by Henry Cromwell, son of the Protector.

While living at Rose Cottage Hood published the first volume of *The Comic Annual*, illustrated mainly by his own humorous woodcuts. Some say that his poem 'Our Village' is about Winchmore Hill. After he left Winchmore Hill he lived in Wanstead and, when finances were a problem, two years in Coblenz, Germany, before moving to Ostend. He returned to England and one of his last works was Song of the Shirt published anonymously in Punch in 1844 - to general acclaim. In 1845 he died, 'the wittiest of poets and the most humane of wits - a devoted son and loving husband.'

The bulk of the Rose Cottage that Hood lived in was destroyed by the Germans in the Second World War, as recorded in Miss Bowman's account in my 1991 *Winchmore Hill Lives*. Today's premises at No. 59 Vicars Moor Lane bear a Blue Plaque reading, 'Thomas Hood 1799 – 1845. Poet and Humorist lived in Rose Cottage on this site.' (See plates 35 and 36.)

1830

General

Starkey tells us that, 'George 1V was unable to keep up the flurry of activity that marked the beginning of his reign. His health and mobility declined and his self indulgence grew, as he washed down vast amounts of food with even larger quantities of alcohol and dulled what little sense remained with even more frequent doses of laudanum. He died unlamented at Windsor on 26th June 1830 and, having been predeceased by his daughter and only child, was succeeded by his eldest surviving brother, William, Duke of Clarence.' Before his demise George 1V had started on the building of Buckingham Palace.

It was in 1830 that the Duke of Wellington's administration passed the Sale of Beer Act. This removed all taxes on beer and permitted anyone to open a beer shop upon payment of a two-guinea fee. This effectively ended gin smuggling, but encouraged 'ale house mania', and by the end of the year there were 24,000 beer shops in England and Wales. (In 1836 there were 46,000, plus 56,000 public houses.) Late in the year Lord Wellington resigned as Prime Minister, to be succeeded by the Whig Earl Grey.

Plate 64. The writer Charles Lamb

Charles's sister Mary is believed to have received treatment in the village during her fits of temporary insanity, probably at the Asylum situated, I suggest, at George Mordaunt's Plot 210 on Green Lanes. Charles and Mary were known to frequent Udall's first shop on The Green, and Charles, who died in 1834, is also mentioned in the 1830 Diary Section.

In 1830, Stephenson's 'Rocket', one of about 100 locomotives so far built in Britain to various designs, went to work on the newly opened Liverpool to Manchester Railway – the first in the world to carry passenger and freight. It established the 4' 8½ " gauge that has become standard in much of the world, revolutionised travel times, and started the demise of the canals. Meanwhile in London, Covent Garden was built.

In the period of 1829-31 fluctuations in wages and food prices resulted in riots and rick - burning, especially in the major agricultural areas of the south and east of England. The so called Swing Rioters turned their attentions to wrecking farming machines and attacking the landowners for introducing them.

Local

The January 2008 EHHS Newsletter featured an article by David Pam on Daniel Poyser's Farm, which was in the vicinity of Chase Farm in Enfield. Strictly speaking it is outside our area, but it is so close by that it perhaps offers us a clue as to what life was like for some in Winchmore Hill. Pam says that Poyser, 'treated his labourers somewhat worse than he treated his animals.' In about 1830 the labourers began to hit back, with threshing machines being destroyed and haystacks set ablaze. Charles Lamb (see Plate 64) was then living in Chase Side and wrote of events at Poyser's farm as follows, 'A great fire was burning last night … seven goodly stacks of hay, with corn barns proportionate lie smoking ashes and chaff ..... It was never good times in England since the poor began to speculate on their condition.'

In his *'Old' Southgate* of 1949 Herbert Newby tells us that, 'Before the building of the railways there was published in London a book for the benefit of the traveller on the highways. It was called "Paterson's Roads" I have one of the 18th edition published in 1830. It is a book of some 800 pages, crammed with information of the whole of England and Wales. Here is the itinerary for London to Enfield ..... Southgate Grove, Walker Grey Esq.; near which is Bone Grove, Harris Esq. .... This road, which is still called Green Lanes over a greater part of its distance, I have heard old coachmen describe as in a very poor condition in their young days. Some idea of roads in the early 19th century can be imagined by these warnings given by the author. "It is recommended to make previous enquiry as to the state of them as many of the cross turnpikes roads in winter time, and often in wet weather, rendered almost impassable."....'

City merchant Peter Pope Firth bought the Highfield House estate from Margaret Radley and her son, John, on 1 June 1830. On 2nd August 1830 he also bought the adjacent piece of freehold land previously belonging to Joseph Compton, and occupied by Miss Cresswell's 'lawyer Compton' (who Brenda Griffith-Williams tells us was associated with the Whitechapel firm of Compton and Sharp, plumbers and glaziers.) The freehold of all this land was granted to Peter Firth on 26th January 1831.

Frances Freeling, Thomas Hood's second daughter by his wife Jane Reynolds, was born in the village in 1830. Later in the century she and her brother Tom published several volumes of their father's work.

In 1796 David Barclay, Isaac Smith, Samuel Hoare, jun and Joseph Osgood gave £100 each to the local Friends. This was to be invested as a fund, the interest to be used as a supplement of one shilling a week for the resident doorkeeper, to help in his work of maintaining the building and its grounds. Any remainder was to be used for repairs as needed. This fund was further increased in 1830 by £100 from Robert Barclay, though I am not sure which one!

Robert Barclay of Bury Hill (1751 - 1830) was the nephew of David

Barclay of Cheapside, and is buried at Winchmore Hill. He did not go into the bank, but instead became the co-owner of the Anchor Brewery in Southwark, later to be known as Courage Brewery.

John Vickris Taylor moved to our area in about 1770, and married twice. He had a son, John Donnithorne, by his second wife Sophia Donnithorne, and on 13th January 1830 he married Elizabeth Henrietta Thompson at Edmonton Parish Church. Later in the decade they went on to become owners of The Grove.

On 6th April 1990 I noted that the plaque on the shed by the western wall to the grounds of Roseville read, 'J.C B.C. 1831'. The adjoining wall bore a plaque stating, 'J.R. 1830'. 1830 is the year that John Radford is deemed to have come into possession of *Roseville*. There is more on all this where I cover the story of *Roseville* in the section on the Enclosure map of The Highfield House Estate.

At the National Archives are two books (ref. HO 44/51) which relate to the running of Mental Institutions in the London area from 1829 onwards. Both the 1829 and 1830 books show the local one as being at, 'Winchmore – hill, near Green Lanes', the proprietor being shown as Jane Holmes, who is listed amongst 'the great and the good' in the 1826 Pigot Directory. No other staff are listed, presumably because there were only two inmates. Ann Page was admitted on 15th January 1826, whilst Dorothy Hulse was enrolled on 9th July 1826. The Metropolitan Commissioners visited the Asylum every few months, and wrote up their findings. The entry for their visit of 3rd March 1830 reads,

'Found the House in excellent order in every respect. Religious read every Sunday by Mrs. Holmes. The Commissioners direct Mrs. Holmes to point out to the Friends of her five Patients by whose authority they are placed under her care the absolute necessity of their compliance with the 30 Sec. of 9 Geo 4 Cap 41.. Signed Fred G. Calthorpe, J.R. Hume, Thomas Turner.'

This reference to five patients is at odds with the perpetual listing of only two patients, until the entry for 27th March 1831 reports, 'The Commissioners find this House as usual clean and comfortable. Mrs. Hulse died on Thursday last, only one Patient remains who is incapable of attending to Divine Service. G.J. Hampson. H.H. Southey. J. Bright.'

This Institution was presumably the one referred to in relation to George Mordaunt's Enclosure Plot 210, where today's Duncan Court stands, in the Map Section.

Main References used

Books and Booklets

Bath, Tony and Jennifer Bath; *Winchmore Hill Cricket Club - The First Hundred Years 1880 - 1980*

Boudier, Gary – *A – Z Enfield Pubs Pt. 2*, 2002. Self published.

Castleden, Rodney – *British History,* 1994. Parragon. ISBN 1 – 85813 – 418 – 8

Cresswell, Miss Henrietta – *Memories of a Lost Village,* 1912. Southgate Civic Trust.

Dumayne, Alan, *Fond Memories of Winchmore Hill,* 1990.

Evans, Professor Eric J.(Editor), *British History,* 2001. Starfire Books.
ISBN 1 – 844510 – 61 – 1.

Mason, Tom, *A Southgate Scrapbook*. 1948. Meyers, Brooks & Co. Ltd.

Olver, Professor A. David, *A History of Quakerism at Winchmore Hill.* 2002. Winchmore Hill Preparative Meeting.

Pam, David, *The New Enfield,* 1977. L.B. Enfield.

Pam, David, *Southgate and Winchmore Hill – A Short History,* 1982. L.B. Enfield.

Pam, David, *The Story of Enfield Chase,* 1984. Enfield Preservation Society.
ISBN 0 907318 03 7.

Ramsbotham, L.,Williams,I., Woolveridge,M., *The History of Winchmore Hill United Reformed Church 1742 – 1991.*

Regnart, Horace, *Memories of Winchmore Hill,* Meyers, Brooks & Co. Ltd. 1952.

Richardson, John, *The Local Historian's Encyclopaedia,*1986. Historical Publications.
ISBN 0 9503656 7 X.

Robbins, Michael, *Middlesex,* 1953. Phillimore & Co. Ltd. ISBN 1 86077 269 2.

Robinson, William, *The History and Antiquities of Edmonton in the County of Middlesex,* 1819.

Starkey, David, *Monarchy From the Middle Ages to Modernity,* 2006, Harper Press,
ISBN 0 – 00 – 724750 – 8.

Trevelyan, G.M., *History of England,* 1952 edition, Longmans, Green & Co.

Edmonton Hundred Historical Society (EHHS) Occasional Papers

No. 61. Griffith-Williams, B.M, *Highfield House, c1818-1952*, 2001. ISBN 0902922 61 0

No. 62. Pam, David, *Winchmore Hill A Woodland Hamlet,*2004 ISBN 0 902922 62 9

Southgate District Civic Trust

Oakleaves Bulletin No. 1, 1987; No. 2. 1996; No. 3. 2004.

Other Papers

Irene L. Edwards, *1688, Middlesex Village, to Suburb of London, 1938.   250 Years of Winchmore Hill Meeting.*

King, Archibald, *A Short History of Winchmore Hill Meeting House and Ground.*

Minutes of the Friends Meetings held at Friends House, Euston Road.

Winchmore Hill Bowling Club 1932 - 1982 - unlisted author(s).

Newspapers and Magazines

Gazette – The old *Palmers Green and Southgate (P.G. & S.) Gazette* and *Enfield Gazette*, particularly articles by Colonel Arthur Wills (often writing as 'Memorabilia') and Tom Mason. Also the more modern *Gazette*, particularly articles by David Pam.

E.H.H.S. Newsletters.

The Gentleman's Magazine.

Main Libraries used

Enfield Libraries: Local History Unit
Friends House, Euston Road
Guildhall Library
London Metropolitan Archives (LMA)
National Archives (N.A.) Kew

Main Private Papers used

Peter Brown
Alan Dumayne (courtesy widow Sheila)
David Hicks (courtesy custodian Stewart Christian)
Pauline Holstius

The above lists only the main sources.
I have tried to list other references as I have used them through the book.

The Art
of the
WWW

For Financial Advisers
a guide to
Marketing on the Internet

by

Richard Arundel

F.C.I.I., F.L.I.A. dip., M.C.I.M., M.C.I.J., A.L.A.M., (Hons).

1st Edition 1998

WITHERBY

PUBLISHERS

© Richard Arundel 1998
ISBN 1 85609 159 7
All Rights Reserved

Published and Printed by:
Witherby & Co. Ltd
32-36 Aylesbury Street, London EC1R 0ET
Tel No: 0171 251 5341   Fax No: 0171 251 1296

British Library Cataloguing in Publication Data
Arundel, Richard
The ABC of the World Wide Web – 1st Ed.
1.Title
ISBN 1 85609 159 7

DON'T PANIC

It's a funny thing this Internet. One minute no one had even heard of it and the next the whole world seems to be jumping on board and its about to leave us behind. And so the inevitable happens. Millions of people, in a blind panic, rush to get themselves onto the Internet just to say that they are there....

And then nothing....

Absolutely nothing happens at all. No one visits their web site. No one sends them e-mail messages. And when they do get onto the super highway it's a bit like the M25 at six in the evening, nothing moves.

Of course after all the initial hype the Internet has supplied the media with a never ending stream of great stories. The Internet is clogged up, congested, a waste of time and money. It's nothing but a lawless state full of perverts, terrorists and criminals. It's not safe for children, it's not safe for women, it's not safe to use your credit card... and so on.

Many of the people, who did jump in with a web site without thinking, don't know how to check to see if anyone is visiting their site, and if they did, they wouldn't know what to do about it. They forget to check their e-mail and then when they do, it's weeks out-of-date so no one sends messages anymore. In fact I suspect that, of the estimated 100 million people registered as Internet users world wide, a very large proportion have dormant accounts.

I don't want to put you off right at the beginning, but I do want you to know that this is a practical book. We are going to face up to the realities of the Internet. There is no point in me convincing you to get on-line and use the Internet if you go through the same experience I have outlined above.

The Internet is an enigma. On the one hand it is probably the most over-hyped phenomena of the twentieth century, while on the other it's probably the most underestimated phenomena of the twentieth century.

The Internet grew at a prodigeous pace simply because it was free. A modest monthly fee secures access and then no further charges, and in the USA, the birthplace of the Internet, there is no charge for the local telephone call to access the Internet.

There is still a great deal of free stuff on the Internet, but today the balance has tipped towards commercialism. This is the reason for this book. There is no point in investing time and money in technology unless there are commercial benefits for you.

My goal is to de-mystify the process. To remove the hype so that you can see what the Internet is, what it does and how you can use it as part of your business strategy.

What I'm not going to do is try and turn you into a "geek" or "anorak" full of incomprehensible computer jargon. If you need to understand the jargon you'll find an appendix at the back of the book. Unfortunately some jargon is necessary but I'll introduce it as the book progresses and you can look it up again later if you need to.

The Internet is not a fad. It's not something that's going to be here today and gone tomorrow. It's already been around for over thirty years, been a commercial service since 1991 and more money is being invested in developing the Internet than most of us can even comprehend.

Like it or not, you're going to be affected by the Internet and the related emerging technologies. But there's no rush. You do not need to spend a fortune getting involved. However, you do need to think about why you want to get involved and what the benefits will be.

The Internet is so easy to use that, and here's a bold claim, by the time you finish this short book you will know exactly what to do and how to make the Internet work for you. In fact I'll go further and say that by the time you finish this book you will be further ahead than half the people who are already on the Internet, even though right now you may not have even seen a web page.

Richard Arundel
April 1998

CONTENTS

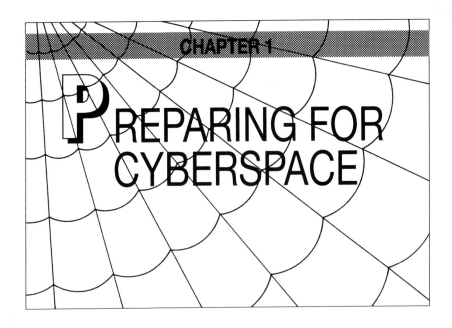

CHAPTER 1

PREPARING FOR CYBERSPACE

Forget the jargon, the Internet is simply a global communications system. It consists of twenty to thirty million computers all currently connected up to each other. (An educated guess, we don't really know the number). Anyone in the world can dial in to one of those computers or connect through a network and exchange information.

The information can be in any form that can be converted into a digital signal. It can be a picture, text, voice, video, animation, music, money or even a command to activate other electronic equipment.

Once you understand that the Internet is simply a global communications system open twenty-four hours a day, it helps to put everything else into perspective. It also helps you to understand why everyone involved in communicating information is excited about its potential. Sales and marketing is after all a communications process.

1

However, although the Internet has been around for thirty years, for the first twenty all the information that passed backwards and forwards was in the form of text. Although the Internet was born in the USA, it was an Englishman, Timothy Berners-Lee, who in 1989 was responsible for the development of the World Wide Web and the computer language, HTML, that enables us to view mixed media images and more importantly to link information dynamically across the globe.

That one development stimulated the creativity of the entire communications industry. Suddenly a new frontier had been created quickly attracting the name CyberSpace, a term first coined by science fiction writer William Gibson in his book "Burning Chrome." What we have created is a strange new parallel universe and probably the greatest jobs creation programme in the history of mankind.

Conquering the frontiers of CyberSpace

Unlike other frontiers such as science, the new worlds, the oceans and space, CyberSpace is man made. It represents the creative mind of man. The limitations of CyberSpace are quite literally the limitations of our imagination.

There are hurdles, there are some physical limitations. To enable billions of people to communicate electronically requires billions of miles of cable. There are physical limits to the speed that information can be sent electronically. There are political problems with a communication structure that ignores national boundaries. There are moral issues over the kind of information that can be freely transmitted around the world in seconds. CyberSpace is a reflection of the physical world so it's not surprising that the rogues and villains are as much in evidence here as elsewhere.

These obstacles and limitations are temporary. I became actively involved in working on the Internet in 1994, and many of the obstacles that existed then have gone, replaced by new ones. In a few years time they too will have disappeared, only to be replaced by others.

Years ago I heard an interesting quote in reference to conquering new frontiers. "The pioneers get the arrows, the settlers get the land". Right now the people making money are the early adopters, the pioneers, but they also take a lot of arrows. They are motivated as much by the desire to go where no man has gone before and to be a part of the creation of a new world, as they are by the lure of riches. They are here because their business is technology and communications.

What business are you in?

Before you embark on your venture into this new world, you need to be clear exactly what business you're in. I'm in the business of communications therefore I need to be a pioneer in this new communications frontier. I learn how to use the new technologies and apply my skills as a teacher in helping others take advantage of the new world.

Even then, I am not in the first wave of pioneers, those are the "geeks", which is not in any way to put them down. How could I when the head geek is now the world's richest man. I'm an applications specialist. It's my job to use the tools and turn them to business advantage.

I'm going to assume that your core business is as a financial advisor, which means you are in the people business. The Internet is only of value to you, if it enables you to communicate more effectively with people who are, or will become clients.

In this book I'm going to show you how to use the Internet and its associated technologies.

1.   To help you communicate with people.

2.   To secure useful and valuable information that you can communicate to your clients and prospects.

3.   As a new and exciting on-line trading environment.

Remember there's no rush. You don't need to panic. Most of your clients and prospects aren't using the Internet yet, but they will. You need to make sure that when they do go onto the Internet the only Financial Advisor they can communicate with is you. That the web site they go to, to seek information, is yours. That the information they need to keep them informed about financial aspects of their life, is the information you have directed them to. That when they decide to trade electronically, it will be with you.

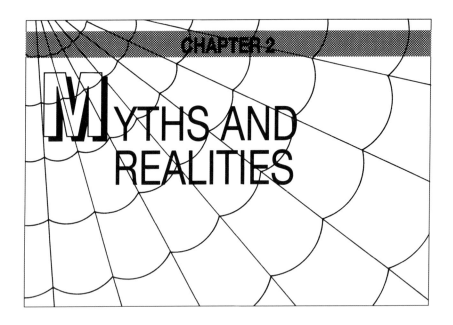

CHAPTER 2
MYTHS AND REALITIES

This chapter is a survival guide. I recently visited every financial advisor's web site I could find on the Internet. All of them were IFA sites and whilst at first there seemed to be quite a number, most of them might as well have not been there. At this moment, in early 1998, there are about 150 IFA web sites, which is less than 1% of the potential. Of those, less than 10% rank as good or better.

Why are there so many bad web sites? It's quite simple. Most people don't understand the Internet. They don't understand how it works or how to use it. They're being drawn in by the myths, creating sites, or more likely paying someone else to create a site, without any idea of what they're trying to achieve.

Let's explore some of the myths and realities so that even if you read nothing else you'll avoid wasting development money.

Myth 1: The Internet will give you access to millions of potential prospects.

This is the most common misconception about the Internet. It makes for a good sales argument but it exemplifies the lack of understanding of how the net works.

Firstly, no one knows how many people are on the Internet. Some people have access from work, which limits where they can go. Most people on the Internet live in the USA. Here in Britain about four to five million people have access, we think. But, research indicates that most people on the net don't use it very much, on average a couple of times a week for about an hour. Many use e-mail, but not the world wide web.

The second factor is that the number of people using the Internet has little to do with how many visit your site. The Internet is not like the physical world, people don't just accidentally go into your web site. They have to make a positive decision to go there. It's not like putting a poster up on a billboard and hoping people will see it. Visiting your web site requires active participation. Most of the pages on the Internet are probably never looked at by anyone other than the person who put them there.

Just because there are millions of people on the Internet doesn't mean that any of them will ever do business with you. Marketing on the Internet is a pro-active exercise and that's what you're going to learn in this book.

Myth 2: You can direct market to millions of people for free

Ooh! Careful. This ones true......... but!!!!

You can buy e-mail addresses by the bucket full. You will probably receive e-mail messages offering millions of e-mail addresses for a few hundred dollars to whom you can send bulk e-mail. Be warned! This is a complete no-no on the Internet.

Electronic junk mail is considered to be worse than physical junk mail. It even has its own special name - SPAM! Yes the very stuff of Monty Python fame. And spamming is considered one of the most heinous sins you can commit.

You can send bulk e-mail. But it has to be done carefully and in a well planned manner. If not, the chances are you will simply alienate your target market, cause your Internet Service Provider (the company who provides you with access to the Internet) a considerable amount of grief and end up losing your Internet account.

In Chapter 5 we will explore how to build your own e-mail directory and use e-mail to promote your business without offending and without breaking the unwritten code of Internet professionalism, called Netiquette.

Myth 3: The Internet is a great place for free advertising.

There are mountains of freebies on the Internet. You can get free software and free web space and you can put up free pages. Here are some examples of a typical Internet address for a free web site: Don't try to look them up, because they are not real, but you will come across real ones that are similar.

http://www.aol.com/members/myname

http://www.geocities.com/wallstreet/0956

http://www.freewebspace.com/personalfinance/cheap-IFA

The problem with these free sites is that they are really aimed at people who want a personal web site to promote their hobbies and family pictures, or voluntary organisations promoting their activities or people in minority groups. They are not intended as commercial sites and the address tells everyone, *"this is a free web site"*

But it's not free. You have to give something in exchange for the free site. You often have to allow the provider of your web site the right to advertise their services and their commercial advertising customers on your site. Instead of it looking like your company it looks like theirs. Remember *"there ain't no free lunch."*

And as to the site being free advertising, don't forget people seldom accidentally come to your web site, you have to bring them there. Just putting up a site doesn't advertise anything, it supports the rest of your advertising and marketing. You still have to work hard to get people to look at your pages.

If you use a free web site, the only people who get free advertising are the web providers who now have you actively promoting their services to all your clients, prospects and friends.

Myth 4: If you don't hurry you'll miss the boat.

Whatever anyone tells you, this is a myth. We're all on the nursery slopes of Internet developments and until most of your clients and the people you want to do business with use the Internet, you are going to have limited success in using this technology.

Things are moving fast, there is a learning curve and you need to be sure that you are keeping up with what's happening. The fact that you are reading this book means you're going to be ahead of most people. All business activities need time and careful planning or they will go wrong.

Myth 5: Internets full of "geeks and anoraks."

It is difficult to obtain research on exactly what is happening on the Internet. What there is seems to point to the same general picture. The people using the Internet are in social economic groups A and B. They are well off and intelligent. A high proportion are in the computer industry or in finance related markets.

Nearly 70% of Internet users are male but that is changing with significant growth in women going on the net. The average age of users is 35, but this is also changing with noticeable growth in the grey market, apparently because this is the best way to communicate with grandchildren! Most of the growth in new users is coming from the business community, not consumers.

If the Internet provides access to the younger social climbing A/B market and the affluent grey market (they need to be prepared to spend about a thousand pounds on a computer), and the business community, you can see why Financial Advisers cannot afford to ignore the Internet.

Myth 6: No one makes any money on the Internet.

The fact is that a lot of money is being made on the Internet. It is difficult to estimate total sales volumes now, but to put things into context, in December 1997 Dell Computers became the first company in the world to achieve sales of over $1,000,000 in a single day on the Internet.

What about Financial Advisers? I've not really had a chance to speak to many. I certainly do know one, Gaeia, the first IFA to have a web site, have been getting approximately one sale every week for the past three years. Garrison Discount Investments, also an early adopter, are now generating over 150 leads a week of which 20% are converted to business.

I have also spoken to others; who have spent thousands and got nothing. Having looked at a one hundred thousand-pound web site, I can understand why they have got nothing. You need to understand the medium and have a clear plan or your site will not work. That's where this book will help.

Myth 7: The Internet is not secure.

According to the credit card companies, using a credit card over the Internet is actually safer than using a credit card at a restaurant, although they won't say so publicly. It's easy for someone to see your credit card number when you use it in a store or over the 'phone. Most use of your credit card over the

Internet is automated. No one actually sees the transaction. To intercept credit card numbers on the Internet is not impossible but requires a considerable level of technical knowledge.

Unfortunately, the fact that it could be done, made for a good media story and the paranoia was born. Since then even greater levels of security and encryption has meant that credit card fraud on the Internet has been virtually eliminated. In fact there has not been a single case of major credit card fraud involving the Internet.

Over the past decade hackers, especially the fifteen and sixteen year old variety, have attracted more than their fair share of media attention. This is mostly because they've tended to try and hack some very sensitive places, but these are isolated incidents. If you plan to take money over the Internet, and that is beyond the scope of this book, you will need to spend time and money making your site secure to avoid the risk. But for all practical purposes you can assume that the Internet is safe.

Myth 8: I'm too old for this

This is the most common reason I hear for not using the Internet. It seems that most people over 40 believe that they are too old to get involved in the Internet because they missed out on computers at school. True, younger people have a natural feel for computers. However, if children from the age of five can master the technology then why can't an intelligent adult capable of running a business, also master it. There's a bit of a learning curve but with each new development it gets easier.

What you need to be prepared for is that things will take longer while you're learning. While you are unfamiliar with computers, unfamiliar with the jargon, unfamiliar with using a mouse, unfamiliar with navigating the superhighways, it's going to take a little more time to do everything.

Once they have mastered the basics and know their way around, most people wonder how they managed without the technology. So let's move on to the next step which is to get you on-line and start your journey into CyberSpace.

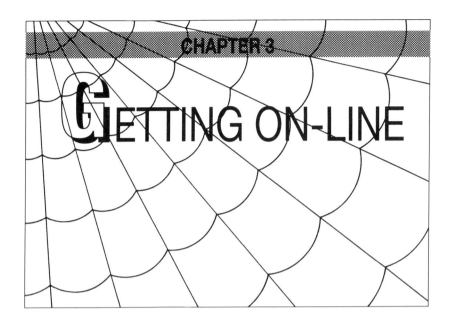

CHAPTER 3

GETTING ON-LINE

If you already have access to the Internet you may want to skip this chapter. However, if you have old versions of software you may still find that the disk that comes with this book very useful. It contains a library of up-to-date software as at April 1998. In fact the disk may be more recent than that.

If you are not on-line yet or if you are not a regular user of the Internet, I am sure you will find this chapter very useful.

The first step in mastering the Internet is simple, get on-line and use the Internet. This is important for a number of reasons

1. Experiencing the Internet as a user is the only way to understand how everything works in practice.

2. As you surf the net you will get a better feel for what makes a good web site and what makes a poor web site.

3. Although the Internet is easy to use there are tools you need to understand, and experience is the best way to learn how to use them.

4. There is some jargon. Some is essential, some is part of the culture, but the more you use the Internet the more familiar you will become with it.

5. Your competitors are on the Internet and using it is the only way to keep track of what they are doing.

6. An increasing number of your clients and prospects use the Internet and you need to establish an electronic relationship with them.

Getting on-line is straightforward, however to take advantage of the latest developments in communications and particularly the multimedia developments, you may need to upgrade your computer.

First you need a good PC

Most financial advisers have pretty good computers, with Pentium processors and Windows 95. If you are about to buy a new computer you will automatically get one that can cope with the Internet because that is all that's available now.

The problem comes if you have one that is a few years old. Computers have a life span of about three to four years and then they simply cannot cope with the new software. If you have one of those, you will need to think about upgrading. It's not essential to upgrade, but you will find some facilities not available to you unless you do, and everything will happen at a slower pace.

At the back of this book you will find a CD-ROM which contains all the software you need to get on-line. It supports most of the computers and operating systems you are likely to have. You will need a CD ROM drive and if your computer doesn't have one, you should think about upgrading. You can obtain a set of floppy disks if you contact **Primex on 01908 378999.**

The problem with recommending a specification for a computer is that it quickly goes out of date. These recommendations are based upon the position at the beginning of 1998. There is a companion section at my web site to support the book at http://www.arundel.co.uk/ABC where you will find an on-line guide to help you with updated information.

Recommended specification

If you are serious about using the Internet as a business tool, you do need a fairly high performance system. At least a Pentium 133 MHz but preferably a P233 MHz or better. You can use a slower machine, even a 486, but the performance will be frustratingly slow.

You need lots of memory, 32 MB of RAM or more. A machine with 16 MB of RAM will cope but it will be a little slow. Any less and you will struggle.

You need lots of disk space. I recommend 3 to 6 gigabytes. You do not need all this space to use the Internet, but you will find yourself loading more and more applications particularly if you decide to develop your own web site, which with new software like Microsoft FrontPage is becoming fairly easy to do.

To enable your computer to dial into the Internet you need a modem. The faster the better is the general rule and you should opt for 33.6 Kbs or 56 Kbs. As a minimum you will need at least a 14.4 Kbs modem.

Thinking about ISDN? Don't bother. The installation charges are too high, the quarterly rental is too high, the ISDN connectors are far more expensive than modems, Internet Service Providers often try to charge more for the connection, and it's not that much faster than a dial-up line.

By 1999 at least three new technologies will be available that are about 10 times faster than ISDN and probably cheaper. If you don't even know what ISDN is, you haven't missed anything.

Finally you should aim to have good multimedia capabilities.

A CD ROM, at least 8 speed, is an essential tool and without one you will not be able to use the installation disk that accompanies this book. Most software will not fit onto a floppy disk today, and in developing a web site you will almost certainly want access to libraries of graphics which are all on CD ROM.

Without a sound card you will be deprived of some of the most important new developments. The ability to communicate with voice over the Internet and to listen in to broadcasts, seminars, new bulletins, investment reports etc, that will become a regular feature of many web sites.

Finally I recommend that you get a good 15" SVGA or XVGA monitor, even 17" or more if you can run to that. Financial information sites particularly fill the screen with information and many others are demanding a good high resolution.

If this all seems rather a lot of power, don't panic. This specification is the standard multimedia machine of the day in 1998. How much will all this cost? You can get a good Internet ready machine for under £1000. However don't buy cheap, if that leaves you with no support. As a financial adviser you know the value of good service, so be prepared to pay to make sure you can get help when you need it. Computers do sometimes go wrong and when they do, help is essential.

Windows 95 Operating System

If you're not running Windows 95 you need to plan on upgrading soon, either to Windows 95 or Windows NT. or even Windows 98. Windows 3.1x is running out of time. An increasing number of products now support only Windows 95 or Windows NT.

On the first of January 2000 you will also discover another problem when the computer thinks that we have just returned to the year DOS - that's 1980, the year your computer thinks is the beginning of time. Alternatively you may have to change the date to stay in the 20th Century and then you really will have been left behind.

I have assumed that you are using a PC. Few Financial Advisers use a Macintosh. I use a PC and therefore most of the examples in this book will be PC related. However as most of what we are going to look at are marketing issues and have nothing much to do with the technology. The type of technology you use is largely irrelevant provided it gets you on-line and enables you to use the communication tools.

The disk supports the Macintosh operating system and includes all the communications software you will need to upgrade your system if you have an older version. It also supports Windows 3.1x. If you use Windows NT, you can get NT support later in 1998 by contacting **Primex on 01908 378999**

Internet service providers

Access to the Internet is achieved via an Internet Service Provider or ISP. You dial into the ISP system, and they route you onto the Internet to the destination you have requested.

Whilst it sometimes looks a little confusing, essentially there are two types of access providers.

On-line Service Providers

The first are the on-line service providers which you will almost certainly have come across, even is you don't have a computer, because they have been sending out "get on the Internet free disks" for a few years now. There are really only four on-line service providers in the UK. The biggest is America On-line, which recently acquired CompuServe, but still maintains a separate identity. This is probably because the services are incompatible and cannot be merged. The other two are Microsoft Network and newcomer Virgin Net.

All four provide access to the Internet, but in addition have a range of services exclusive to members. Both AOL and CompuServe provide their own proprietary software to access their on-line services. These services include travel, news, shopping, financial, business, entertainment, games, discussion groups, software libraries etc. In fact much the same as the services provided across the Internet, except that they are controlled and organised within the service.

MSN started with proprietary software but then switched to Internet technology when Microsoft failed to achieve the growth it expected and offers a similar range of services to AOL and CompuServe. Virgin offers a much more entertainment-based service.

Most on-line services offer 30 day free trials which you might like to try, but watch out for the charging structure if you decide to open an account. They have a variety of tariffs, some based on a low monthly change, but a high hourly charge after an initial free period. That charge can be over £2.00 an hour which is very expensive if, like me, you spend a lot of time on-line.

Local Internet Service Providers

Most people connect to the Internet via a local Internet service provider who generally provides access, web hosting and technical support services. There are hundreds of ISPs offering similar services. The key factors you need to consider are:

1. Do they provide local call access - either a local phone number or an 0845 number which is charged at local rates.

2. What is their modem to user ratio - they need a modem for each user accessing the system. If they have more than 30 users to every modem, you may have problems getting on-line at peak times.

3. What are their help desk opening times - If they are closed when you are usually on-line, you may occasionally find this a problem.

4. Do they have a 30 day trial and good easy to use installation software.

5. How much do they charge for access? You will find that services charge from £7.50 per month to £20 per month as a flat rate, depending upon what services they offer, so cost is usually not a major factor. Avoid ISPs who charge an hourly rate for being on-line.

The easy Internet CD with this book

The disk attached to this book is new. It is the most popular installation disk in the USA and Primex are the UK distributors as well as being a good medium sized access provider. The disk will automatically give you access to their service on a 30 day free trial, after which time you are free to sign up for, and pay for their service, or you can switch to a new provider of your choice.

The disk also provides all the software you are likely to need irrespective of the computer you use, which is why I selected it. It is there to help you get on-line if you are not already, and to make sure that you have access to all the latest browsing and e-mail software in case you want to upgrade.

Internet tools

Before you actually use the disk to go on-line we need to talk about some of the software you will be installing. Some of this is not essential yet, but it often comes as part of the package and is installed anyway.

- **E-mail** software enables you to send and receive e-mail messages and manage the e-mail addresses of your clients, prospects and friends.

- A **Browser** enables you to access web sites around the world and view information.

- **FTP** software enables you to transfer files to and from computers over the Internet.

- A **Web Editor** enables you to design your own web pages that you can put up on the Internet.

- A **Newsgroup Reader** enables you to participate in on-line discussions groups.

- **Chat** software enables you to participate in live on-line discussion by typing in your contribution.

- **Internet Phone** software enables you to speak to other users through your computer and exchange or share files and applications.

We are going to look at each of these types of software in Chapter 4. Now all you need to do is make a decision on which Browser you plan to use.

Which Browser?

'The Browser' is the software that enables you to view pages of text and graphics that comprise what is called the World Wide Web (WWW) or Web for short. Essentially there are only two, Microsoft Internet Explorer and Netscape Communicator. Both are currently at version 4, although Internet Explorer (IE4) is more than a browser. It is really an upgrade to Windows 95.

If you are using an older computer, and particularly if not using Windows 95, you will not be able to use the latest browsers. But don't worry the CD will sort that out for you. I recommend that you go for the latest versions of the software because they do include the entire suite of software listed above and they support most of the latest Internet developments.

So the choice is between Microsoft and Netscape. I use both although primarily IE4. The decision is one of personal preference. Both support largely the same function although there are some irritating differences that arise out of the commercial war between Netscape and Microsoft. Each company is developing its own new features, which they consider competitive issues.

For all practical purposes however they are the same. I prefer IE4 because it integrates with the Windows desktop and when a web site needs an ad-on software package, often called a Plug-in, Microsoft upgrades automatically, while Netscape often requires you to download, close the browser, install the plug in and then open the browser again.

Most of the examples I will be using in this book will be of IE4 and the other Microsoft tools, because they are the ones I am most familiar with.

Obtain your access code

Before you begin the installation you will need to 'phone Primex to obtain you personal access code. This provides you with a 30 day free trial access to the Internet. The number is **01908 378999.**

Tell them you have the disk with The ABC of the WWW by Richard Arundel.

You might want to write your access code here so that you don't lose it. You will also need to agree a Log-In Name and Password, which you will use to access your account in future. Make a note of them here.

ISP Configuration Code ....

Log in Name (Case Sensitive) ....

Password ....

Write in pencil so that you can erase later

You can obtain more information about Primex once you are on-line at their web site at - http://www.primex.co.uk

---

Easy Internet CD ROM set-up.

Whether you are using a PC or a Macintosh, simply follow these instructions to set up your computer for Internet access.

Step 1: Preparation

Close down any applications running on your system, open the CD ROM tray and place the Easy Internet CD ROM in the tray, text side up.

Step 2: Running Easy Internet CD-ROM

The CD should autostart, unless you have an older operating system , in which case you will need to run the program - *enet.exe.*

Windows 95 users: Click the start button, then choose *Run.* Type in the CD ROM drive letter followed by a colon and backslash and the filename "**enet.exe**" (e.g. *d:\enet.exe*)

Windows 3.1 users: From program manager, select *File,* then *Run,* then type in the CD ROM drive letter followed by a colon and backslash and the filename *"enet.exe"* (e.g. *d:\enet.exe*)

Macintosh users: Double click the *"enet.exe"* icon.

Step 3: Agree the Licence

Carefully read the licensing agreement and click the appropriate button if you agree or disagree. If you disagree, the program will close.

Step 4: Personal Configuration

Check that the Personal Configuration Wizard Window is open (click on the *Personal Config* button if necessary) and enter the following:

1.   In the box labelled **ISP Configuration Code** type in the code given to you by Primex. **Click next.**

2.   In the **Dial-Up Log-in Name** box enter your **Log-In Name.** This is case sensitive so type it in exactly as provided by Primex (You can agree a log-in name with Primex). Leave the "e-mail user name" box blank. **Click next.**

3.   **Your real name.**   This is the name that will appear on your outgoing e-mail - if you chose to you can enter a nickname. **Click finish.**

Step 5: Selecting and Installing Software (Optional)

Click on any of the programme titles in the *Available Titles* box and a description of the selected programme will appear in the information box along with pricing details if it is shareware. Shareware products are provided for you to try free, but if you like them you should pay for them. It's an honour system. Many shareware products are extremely good value.

This is where you need to decide if you want to use Microsoft or Netscape. I recommend that you undertake a full installation of the browser of your choice now, and look at some of the other software products on this disk later. I also recommend that you go for Internet Explorer 4 if you can, as this is the easiest to use and the one I will be using for most examples in the book.

For each programme that you wish to install, highlight the programme title in the *Available Titles* box and click the *Install* button. Some programmes require you to restart your computer after installation. Where that happens, follow the instructions to restart, and then run the programme *enet.exe* again as directed in Step 2 to continue installation and configuration.

Step 6 - Configuring your Computer after Installation

1. Click the button labelled 'Internet Config.' from the drop-down lists on the left-hand side of this window. Chose the National telephone location for local call access from anywhere in the UK and select the 0845 number appropriate to your modem. Leave this on the default number 0845 0798054 if you are unsure of the speed of your modem. Leave the box labelled "Use non-listed phone number" blank.

2. Check that the box labelled "Use server assigned IP address" is ticked

3. Click the icon labelled "Reconfig."

4. Check/uncheck the boxes in the programmes to be configured section as required (leave all the boxes ticked if you are unsure) and then click on the icon labelled "Configure."

5. When the configuration process is complete, close the Easy Internet programme by clicking the "Quit" or "Close" button on each window - you will be asked for confirmation before you finally close the programme.

This completes your easy Internet CD ROM set-up and installation.

Step 7 - Connecting to the Internet

Windows - Look for a *Primex Internet Solutions* connection icon on your desktop (Win 95) or in program manager in the program group *Dial-Up Connections* (Win 3.1x). Double-click on that connection icon, enter in your password, and choose the *Connect* button.

Macintosh - Choose *Apple Menu Item*, then *Control Panels*, then *PPP*. Enter your password then choose the *Connect* button.

After you connect, you can open and run any of the programs that you have installed.

And that's it! You are on-line surfing the Internet, you have started your voyage of discovery. But like any journey, if you begin without a map you are likely to get lost. So this is where this book suddenly becomes completely different from any you have ever read.

Part of the book is not here. It's on-line, and you cannot read it until you are on-line yourself. So in Chapter 4, I am going to guide you on your first journey, into the on-line world of Financial Services.

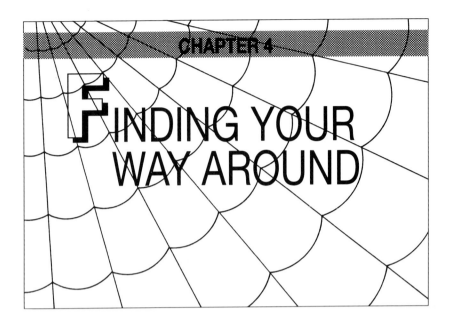

CHAPTER 4

FINDING YOUR WAY AROUND

The first time I went on-line it was a strange sensation. I had the feeling that everyone was watching me and would all be able to see when I made a mistake, especially when I decided to join an on-line conference. Then I realised that no one could see what I was doing except in the chat rooms, where everyone makes mistakes and no one cares.

The next problem was where to go and what to do. It took me a while to understand that the browser was just one tool, and that there were different tools for different jobs. In this chapter I want to briefly review the main tools that you will be using. There are others, but these are the most important.

Electronic Mail Software - e-mail

The first and most important tool is *E-mail* Software. This enables you to send and receive e-mail messages and manage the e-mail addresses of your clients, prospects and friends. There are dozens of e-mail packages around, many of which are very sophisticated and really designed for in-house e-mail systems in larger companies.

The main Internet mail packages today are Microsoft Internet Mail or Outlook Express, Netscape Messenger, Eudora Lite and Pegasus Mail. All five of these are on the CD, however when you installed your browser, it automatically installed and configured your e-mail software.

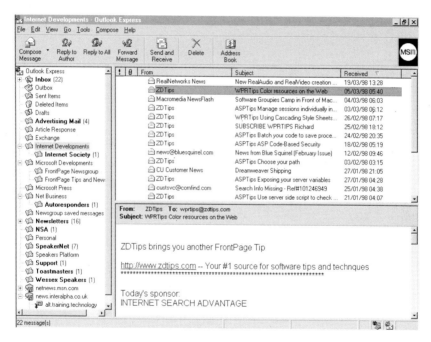

This is Outlook Express, which comes with Internet Explorer 4, and is the mail package I generally use. Others are similar. The left-hand column is the list of folders including the inbox, outbox, deleted messages, and folders of saved messages. It's a good idea to create new folders where you can to organise saved messages rather than allow them to build up in your inbox.

The top right hand window is the list of mail messages in the selected folder. This is particularly important, because I can see at a glance who the message is from and what the subject is. Sorting important mail from unimportant mail is therefore made very easy.

The bottom right hand window shows the text of the selected message without opening it. This enables me to simply tab down the list with the arrow keys, quickly checking mail and deleting junk mail in seconds.

One of the important features of e-mail is that you can reply to a message with considerable ease. Select the message, click on the "Reply To Author" button and type. The message is automatically addressed, and includes a copy of the incoming message so that all you need to do is answer and click "Send." You don't need to be on-line to use e-mail software. When you write your mail, it will be placed in your outbox until you go on-line.

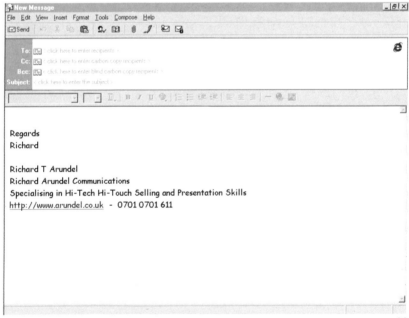

The diagram shows a typical blank message screen brought up by clicking "compose message". You can see that this already has a signature included, which I created as a standard. It allows a brief advertising message every time I send mail in the same way my headed paper does. The difference here is that I have included my Web address. It is underlined and coloured blue, which indicates a Hypertext Link. Point your mouse at this link, click and it will automatically fire up your browser and take you to my web site. We'll be looking at links in more detail later.

This message needs an address. Either type in an address or click the symbol beside the word "To", to access the address book.

A typical Internet e-mail address looks like this: richard@arundel.co.uk The first section is the user name, the @ sign indicates this is an Internet address. The next section is the domain name.

When you sign up with an Internet service provider, they will automatically provide you with an e-mail address. If you have used the disk, with this book, your e-mail address will be log-in-name@primex.co.uk. If you want your own domain name you can, and we will look at how in Chapter 7.

Send me an e-mail message now - ABC@arundel.co.uk

Want to try it out, send me an e-mail message now to this address. Keep it short and I will reply. And that's the basics of e-mail. In Chapter 5 we will look at how to use e-mail as a marketing tool.

Browsing the World Wide Web

The next important tool is the **Browser,** which enables you to access web pages and view information anywhere in the world. Again the technology is very easy to master.

There are dozens of browsers but the market is dominated by two. Until 1997, the dominant browser was Netscape. Today however that crown has passed to Microsoft.

Both browsers are good products and both handle 95% of the information on the Internet. The remaining 5% accounts for the differences. You have both on your disk, so it's really a matter of preference. I have both browsers installed on my computer.

The image below shows Microsoft Internet Explorer 4, browsing my home page. If you find my home page is different when you visit don't worry, one of the keys to success on the web is to keep things changing.

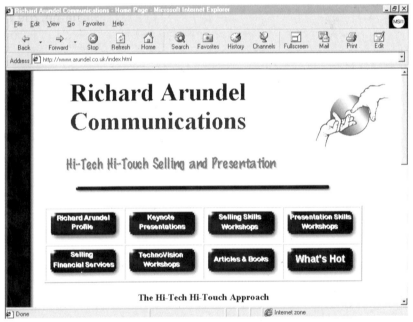

Browsers are simple to use. Type the address of a web site into the box labelled "address" or "location", hit return and you will instantly be transported to that site wherever it is in the world. The address is actually called a URL (Uniform Resource Locator) and looks like this - http://www.arundel.co.uk.

You do not need to type the http://. www.arundel.co.uk will get you there.

Surfing the net

There are four features of the browser you need to know at this stage to get around.

First are *Hypertext Links*. Every page on the Internet is linked to other pages. These links usually appear in a different colour and are underlined, or they may be images. You will spot them because when your cursor passes over them it changes, usually to a hand. If you click once on a link you will immediately be taken to the linked page. And that is how you surf the net.

The second is *Search.* Click on the search button and it brings up one of a number of links to large databases of Internet sites, where you can type in what you want to find and you will receive a list of possible matches. The more clearly you specify the request the better.

The third is the *Back Arrow* at the top left of the browser. Click on this and it takes you back to the previous page. Very useful if you find yourself lost.

And finally *Favourites or Bookmarks.* This is your personal directory of web addresses you want to revisit. Every time you find an Internet site that interests you, click on favourites or bookmarks, then "add" to record the address in your list. Your can organise this list into folders when it gets too long. You will find yourself frequently returning to interesting pages for more information or to check on new information.

With these tools you should be able to find your way around. In Chapter 6 we will look at using the browser to research the market-place and even find prospects. But for now, if you want to start looking around at financial services information I have created a section in my web site to support this book and provide a guided tour of the market-place at www.arundel.co.uk/ABC

Just type this address into the address box of your browser and join me on the web for a look around the financial services marketplace.

FTP - Transferring files across the net.

I'm not going to spend much time on this topic, because you may never use it. **File Transfer Protocol** or **FTP** is a method of moving files between two Internet sites. Many Internet sites have publicly accessible FTP areas holding material that can be downloaded.

The reason you are unlikely to use specialist FTP software is because your web browser can also download files from the web and from FTP sites. However the benefit of FTP comes when you need to upload and download a large number of files, for example when maintaining a web site.

There is a shareware package on the disk and if you decide to develop your own web site and do not use Microsoft FrontPage, you will use FTP to load your files on to the web host computer. Most software houses also have FTP sites where you can download upgrades and additional utilities.

Using a web editor to design a web site

When most people talk about using the Internet for business, what they mean is having their own web site to generate leads for new business and creating sales. I often receive e-mail messages asking where someone can learn to design a web site. Unfortunately there is a lot more to creating a web site than a quick course in design and we will be dealing with this in some detail in Chapters 7 and 8.

Web pages are created with a special language called HyperText Mark-up Language or HTML. It is a bit like a programming language, which creates a series of instructions to the web browser defining how to display and position text, which images to call and where to position them. Your word processor works with a similar language to enable you to format documents, but because it all happens in the background, you're not aware of it.

Web editors, are software packages, which to varying degrees let you design pages as you would with a word processor. In fact, If you have Microsoft Word 95 or Word 97 you already have a web editor built into the word processor, although I don't recommend it.

The value of most of the latest web editors is that they enable you to produce web pages without needing to learn HTML. FrontPage Express comes with Internet Explorer 4, Netscape Composer comes with Communicator 4 and Hot Dog 4 is also on the disk.

The illustration is FrontPage Express and the page you see in the window is as it looked when I designed it, and is probably as you will see it when you go to the web site. It will be redesigned from time to time so don't be concerned if it does look different.

FrontPage Express is very easy to use and you can quickly design a small site with it. However as the site gets bigger, and the number of pages grow, managing and maintaining the site becomes a problem.

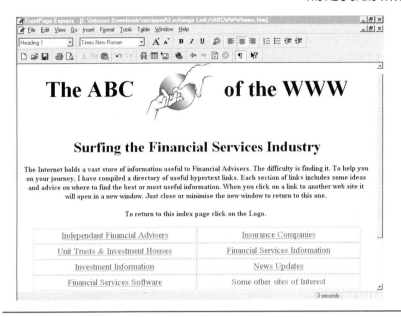

The Usenet and Newsgroups - On-line conferencing

The terms **Usenet** and **Newsgroups** are generally interchangeable, and describe, not a news service, but a system of on-line conferencing. Another term you may hear is **Bulletin Boards, BBS,** which are private versions of the same.

Essentially a newsgroup is a public e-mail exchange service. Instead of sending e-mail messages privately to a recipient, you POST the message on an electronic notice board for everyone else to see. Anyone can then comment on your e-mail and the reply will also be available for everyone to read.

To add structure to the whole thing, each newsgroup has a general theme, and everyone is requested to discuss those issues related to that theme or topic.

So for example here is a view of the newsgroup called **uk.finance**. You can see that a couple of Topic **Threads** have

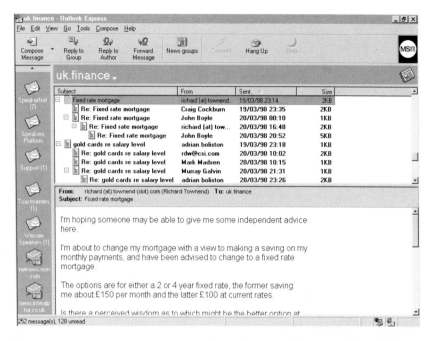

begun, one a request for independent advice on Fixed Rate Mortgages. The messages lower down, but inset, are responses to the question, and some of these responses have responses to them. Hence the term thread.

Its an on-line discussion but not live, in that you read the messages, and then post your comments often days after the original message was posted

Newsgroups can be a good source of information. You pick-up tips from people from all over the world, and many people have made lasting friendships as a result of meeting someone on a newsgroup. There have even been a few marriages resulting from these encounters.

From a practical point of view you have to be a little selective with the groups you join. There are literally thousands of newsgroups, some very useful, and some trite. Some have so many participants that you can become inundated with messages.

Most e-mail systems have a built in newsgroup reader, and there are specific newsgroup readers called **Free Agent** that can be found on the disk.

One thing you quickly learn about newsgroups is that the participants react badly to anyone who "cross posts". This means posting messages in a newsgroup that have no relevance to the topic, usually people trying to sell and advertise. The other "No No" is "spamming", which means sending advertising messages to a number of newsgroups simultaneously.

Netiquette, the unwritten Internet code, prohibits these practices and you are likely to find yourself on the receiving end of offensive messages and even have your Internet Service Provider close your account if you do it. I'll cover advertising and promoting yourself by e-mail and in newsgroups in more detail in Chapter 5.

Chat - CB Radio on the Internet

Chat is a little like newsgroups except that it happens in real time. As you type the message the other participants in the chat session can see what you write and can respond. Not a huge number of people participate in chat but those who do seem to be addicted. It's a bit like CB Radio on the Internet .

As with newsgroups the chat forums are set up by topic, although they tend to be more social than business focused. Many take place very late at night and quite a few are adult only.

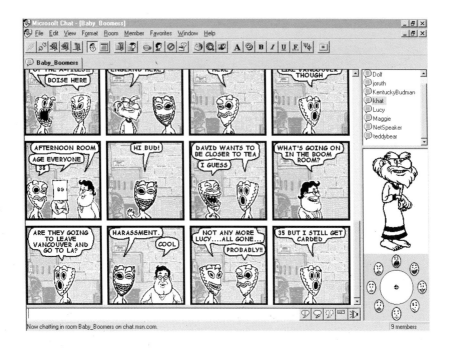

Microsoft attempted to make chat a little more fun with the launch of what they first called "comic chat" and then renamed Microsoft chat. You can choose to see the comments simply as a line of text or you can have the text automatically inserted into a speech bubble of a comic character, so that the chat session looks like an interactive cartoon strip. This software comes free with Internet Explorer 4, and there is also a shareware chat product on the disk called MIRC.

Chat can be fun, and it's a nice way to get to know people around the world. However it can also be very time consuming and if there are a lot of people in the chat room it can become very confusing.

Internet 'phone - The wave of the future

Finally, in this chapter I want to look briefly at using the PC and the Internet as an alternative to the 'phone. This might seem a bit of a fad, but it's much more than just an alternative to the 'phone. It is possible to transmit video signals and audio signals over the Internet and hold a conversation. The problem is the quality.

Full motion video requires 30 frames per second, while the Internet cannot support better than about 8 frames per second, and often much less. It's often more like a still picture that refreshes every couple of seconds. Voice on the other hand is much better, and although it can sound like an old radio system, it is acceptable.

What is more important is that you can share files and applications over the Internet. For example you could pass a spreadsheet down the line enabling a client to see the information and interactively work with you on changes to the spreadsheet. For example a portfolio analysis. Or you could share a word document, a will or partnership agreement and make changes on-line.

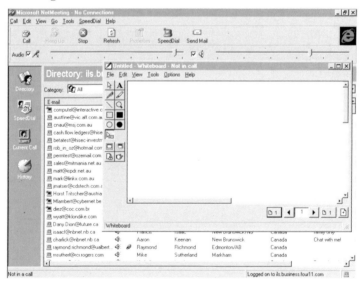

The problem is that in order to use the technology you both have to be on-line. The only way anyone can communicate with you if you are not on-line is to call you by 'phone and ask you to go on-line, or to pre-arrange an on-line meeting.

There are a large number of products now available and a communications standard has been agreed for voice communications, although there still seem to be incompatibilities. Microsoft Net Meeting comes with Internet Explorer, Cool Talk comes with Netscape and I-Phone is available on the Disk.

As the product and the speed of data transfer improves there is no doubt that this will be the communications medium of the future. The potential is stunning and I can see a day when you will conduct at least one client meeting every day using this technology, especially as it really doesn't matter where in the world the client is, you can still interact as if you are in the same room.

Keep your focus on business applications

So that is our brief tour of the basic tools of the Internet. As you can see most of them are easy to use. From a business perspective, e-mail, web browsing and creating your own web site are the clear winners, and in the remainder of the book we are going to focus almost entirely on those three topics.

So let's get under way and see if we can turn that simple e-mail package into a powerful business getting tool.

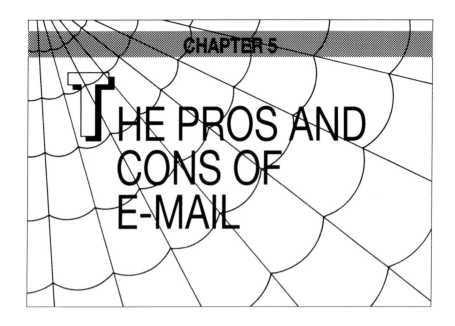

CHAPTER 5

THE PROS AND CONS OF E-MAIL

We've looked at the mechanics of e-mail and I hope by now that you have sent a few e-mail messages and received some replies!? If so, you will know how easy e-mail is to use, even if typing is not your strong suit.

Actually, the fact that most people who use e-mail are not good at typing is one of its advantages. Most messages can be read in a few seconds with no need to scroll the page. Why write a long letter when a simple "yes or no" gets the message across.

In this chapter, we are going to look at how e-mail can benefit your business, both as a communications and marketing tool. First however we need to look at two important issues, **Security** and **Compliance**.

Security and viruses

Let us put this into perspective. There are some security risks with e-mail but they are quite small and can easily be minimised.

e-mail Interception

It is possible for someone who knows what they are doing to intercept e-mail, although quite why they would want to is beyond me. They would need to know that you were involved in highly classified and sensitive information to warrant the effort.

If your e-mail is sensitive, then you can encrypt it. This means using a programme that scrambles the information so that it can only be read by someone who possesses a copy of the key needed to unscramble it. The two best known are VeriSign and Pretty Good Privacy (PGP), which you can obtain at the following addresses:

VeriSign   at   http://www.verisign.com   and   PGP http://www.pgpi.com

Virus Protection

Viruses are a real threat and one which insurance companies are particularly concerned about. In many offices, inserting an unchecked disk into a PC is sufficient to bring instant dismissal.

In reality though, there are more virus hoaxes around than viruses. If you receive an e-mail message telling you to immediately warn the world about a deadly new virus disguised as an e-mail message, with the subject "Good Times", "AOL4free", "Join the Crew", "Penpal Greetings", or some such title, ignore them. You can find more information at http://www.kumite.com/myths.

There is no way to trigger a virus simply by opening an e-mail message or any other text document. However, a file attachment can contain a virus that could damage your data and infect other computers. It seldom happens now but they exist. Protect yourself, by installing virus software like Dr Solomon's, Norton Anti-virus or McAfee. Most importantly, do not open file attachments, especially executable files, unless you know and trust the source and have virus checked the file.

Compliance issues

You need also to be aware of the compliance requirements when using e-mail as a basic communications mechanism. An important requirement is to include your status disclosure information etc, in each message.

Using Signatures

Signatures enable you to automate the process of adding footers to mail. All e-mail software has the facility to create a signature and some allow multiple signatures. The process for setting up a signature varies with each package, but you should find instructions in the help topics.

Set-up a signature immediately which satisfies your compliance advisor. That way you know that your e-mail will be signed-off with the correct information about who you represent, your status, how you are regulated and your contact information. You can also add a brief promotional message if you wish, but don't overdo this. You should definitely add your web address.

Some e-mail incorporates support for graphics, logo, background colours and even background music. Unfortunately, many of the people you write to will not be able to receive the information, or it may get completely scrambled. Even using fancy fonts can cause problems. The best approach is to keep it simple.

Compliance Records.

You need to keep records long-term to support your advice and dealings with clients. e-mail may be easy to use but it is also easy to delete. Hard disks do fail and files do become corrupted. I understand that many PIA inspectors are not comfortable with entirely electronic records.

Usually by default, your e-mail software automatically includes a copy of the original message with your reply and although it goes against the concept of electronic communications, you can print off the combined message and response and file the hard copy with your client file.

Building an e-mail database

When you installed your e-mail software, did you discover that you had no addresses to send e-mail to? When you don't use e-mail you tend not to think about asking for an e-mail address. Now that you have e-mail, you are going to need e-mail addresses from your clients, prospects, friends and anyone else you want to communicate with.

However they must be "Internet e-mail" addresses. One of the great benefits of the Internet is that it has forced a standard on the world for e-mail. It may not be the best protocol, but at least it's a standard and it's easy to understand. Unfortunately large numbers of people still have internal e-mail systems using IBM Mail, AT&T Mail, X400, CC Mail, Microsoft Exchange and so on. Some of these work well with the Internet and some don't. Whatever the case you need an Internet address.

That means it must be in the format <u>username@domain</u>. They won't be as simple as that. Some will have two or three sections before the @ and three or four sections after it, each with dots between them. Sometimes they include numbers, hyphens and underscores, but the key is the @ symbol. If there isn't an @ in the address, it's not an Internet mail address and you will not be able to send and receive to it.

Take Time to Organise e-mail Addresses

If you installed software from the disk, you probably installed one of the e-mail packages that comes with the browser, either Microsoft Outlook Express or Netscape Messenger. Neither of these has been designed to manage large numbers of e-mail addresses, although they are getting better. You therefore need to take a little time and patience to organise things as you go. Eudora Lite and Pegasus Mail, which are both on the disk, are slightly better at managing e-mail addresses, and you might want to look at them. You will also find more information at the ABC web site.

Recording e-mail Addresses

All e-mail software includes an address book and allows you to easily add addresses with a mouse click, or even automatically as you reply to incoming mail. Unfortunately the e-mail address does not easily identify the name of the person who sent the message. I have found that it is important always to go into the address book, and modify the properties to show the correct name and perhaps add the company name, 'phone number and some notes to keep your records clear.

45

Create Groups of e-mail Addresses

Organising your e-mail addresses into groups is essential for sending bulk e-mail. I always take the time to make sure that each time I add an e-mail address to my address book I automatically add the name to the appropriate groups. You might want to group people geographically, by age range, lifestyle, capital assets, social interests, membership of clubs etc. You might have a group for clients, prospects or for specific product promotions, investments, PEPS, pensions, mortgages etc.

You can add each person to as many groups as you want so that in future if you have a message you want to send to clients about a new pension opportunity, or a budget update, you can simply select the appropriate group.

Steps in Organising your e-mail Database.

1.   Become familiar with your e-mail software and learn how to record and manage names and addresses.

2.   Set up appropriate groups of contacts as an aid to future bulk e-mailing.

3.   Contact all your clients immediately to obtain their e-mail addresses.

4.   Prepare and send your first e-mail newsletter and write to those without e-mail addresses advising them of this new service, available once they are on-line.

5.   Update your fact-find form to ensure that you collect e-mail and web address from all your clients and contacts in the future.

Sending group e-mail and bulk e-mail

Sending unsolicited bulk e-mails over the Internet is a "no-no". It looks awfully tempting to send out hundreds of thousands of e-mail messages at very litle cost but it will rebound on you "big time".

Like it or not there is a negative attitude to unsolicited mail whether it's electronic or "snail" mail. Most of us can check a piece of mail, decide that it's of no interest and bin it in less than 5 seconds. With e-mail it's even quicker, but we can do more than just bin it.

One IFA software house told me that they occasionally receive one of their freepost envelopes back attached to a parcel containing three months back issues of Money Marketing and Financial Adviser. It's a protest from an IFA who objects to receiving unsolicited mail. Most people get occasional objections to junk mail. Reaction to junk e-mail is more active.

SPAM, Mail Bombs and Flames

The Internet use of the term SPAM originated as a term to describe indiscriminate posting of unrelated messages in newsgroups, but tends now to be universally applied to all forms of indiscriminate junk e-mail. People don't just quietly object to spamming.

First it's easy to return e-mail. You simply click reply and send. Unfortunately some people go beyond this. They attach a large file to the reply before they send it, or send thousands of replicas known as a "mail bomb." Others return what is called a "flame," an insulting and often offensive reply.

When I first got involved with using the Internet, I decided it would be a good idea to do a quick cheap mailing. I gathered together a hundred names and promptly sent out my mail shot.

I received:

1. One mail bomb, over a megabyte of junk.

2. One very angry flame.

3. One complaint from the organisation whose products I was promoting telling me not to send unsolicited mail with their name on it again.

4. One note from my Internet provider telling me if I did it again my account would be closed.

5. Not one single positive lead.

In the world of spamming, things have progressed. It is now possible to get software that will hide the sender, so that any flames or mail bombs are immediately returned to the sender.

However before you rush out to buy this software let me remind you who you will be joining if you choose to descend to the ranks of the people who insist on spamming the Internet. The top six spammer products are:

1. Access to pornographic sites or invitations to participate in intimate communications.

2. Multi-level marketing, business opportunities.

3. Invitations to participate in chain letters.

4. "Send me money and I'll tell you how to get rich on the Internet".

5. Ten million guaranteed e-mail addresses for "just $295".

6.   The very latest bulk e-mail management software that enables you to seek addresses on the Internet and mail them anonymously.

Spammers know they have to hide themselves away and make it difficult or impossible for anybody to track them down. Join them at your peril!

Mailing to clients and prospects

This does not mean that you cannot send bulk e-mail. It means you have to be very professional about it. I regularly receive bulk e-mails from a number of sources where I have agreed or asked them to keep sending the messages. I don't want my inbox filled with garbage but I'm quite happy to receive useful, helpful messages from people who are offering a valid service.

You already have a database of clients and prospects and I'm sure that you already send appropriate marketing letters to them from time to time. Approach bulk e-mailing in the same way. However, there are differences in the way you structure your communications. If you send long e-mail messages or large file attachments that take a long time to download you will alienate people.

There are four better options:

1.   Send short messages containing a hypertext link to a web page containing the information you wish to impart. Invite people to visit your page.

2.   Send a short message inviting people to request a larger e-mail or file containing more information.

3.   Send a short message asking people to phone your 0800 number and request the information by post.

4.   Send an auto-responder mail address.

Auto-responders

An auto-responder is the e-mail equivalent of a fax-back. You send a blank e-mail to an auto-responder address and the auto-responder instantly replies by sending the e-mail message to your mailbox. These are very popular in the United States but have not yet caught on here although they are growing in popularity. You can find out more about auto-responders at The ABC web site at www.arundel.co.uk/ABC

Electronic newsletters and memos

The problem with printed newsletters is the cost of printing, producing and mailing. Electronic mail eliminates those problems and provides you with a great opportunity to keep in touch with clients and prospects in a unobtrusive way. I subscribe to half a dozen electronic newsletters and memos that, through trial and error, I have found to be easy to scan and provide good quality tips and information.

Some newsletters are free and some make a charge for the information. Most paid for newsletters have an associated web site that enables you to see some previous editions before subscribing. Where they are free, they generally form part of a structured electronic marketing programme by the author.

Weekly Memos and Tips Bulletins

These are usually very short tips, the sort of thing I can read in less than a minute and pick up a simple tip that might help me immediately. They also remind me who sent them because at the end of the memo there's a little bit of advertising and a few suggestions of web-links I might like to visit.

Often they contain humour to brighten my Monday morning, but most importantly they contain useful information. Look through the information that flows through your office every day. Tips, news, comment, views, special offers, thoughts for the day. Pick out the best ideas, humorous anecdotes, off the wall news reports, interesting views, fascinating facts etc.

Seek sources of good useful tips on financial planning, ideas from abroad you could anglicise, business or investment management ideas, making the most of your retirement, staying healthy and fit longer. Insurance companies can sometimes be a good source of ideas.

Jot down your ideas through the week and at the weekend spend fifteen minutes writing out your weekly memo. Give it a simple title and then stick with it, so that people begin to recognise your memo. This is the basic process of establishing a brand awareness.

If you register at the ABC site I'll be happy to send you my weekly memo.

Surfs Up - Richard Arundel's Weekly tips on Web Marketing

This goes out on Friday and is designed to provide you with places to visit and ideas to consider over the weekend to make your Internet surfing more productive.

Newsletters

Newsletters are essentially the same as memos or tips but longer. e-mail is getting more creative but it's still not a good idea to send lots of graphics, pictures and sounds because so many people can't receive them. Most electronic newsletters tend therefore to be basic text. It's a good idea to keep each item relatively short, with links to web sites.

Even if you want to direct someone to web information on someone else's site, you might consider directing them first to your site where you can provide the link with information on what to do if they are interested. Get into the habit right from the beginning of directing people to your site as often as you can. Create an image of your web site as the first place your clients go for information on financial services issues.

One possibility is to use your e-mail newsletter as a promotion for a web version. Create an attractive newsletter on-line, with graphics, text, audio features, links to other sites, enquiry forms, calculators etc. Then create a text summary highlighting the main features with the URLs for the relevant pages. If many of your clients do not have web access, just expand the features on the newsletter, or provide an extended full text version at an auto-responder or to be sent on request.

Option to Remove

Make sure that you provide everyone with the option to honour that request. If you have your own e-mail domain, create an address e.g.remove@arundel.co.uk. At the bottom of your newsletter or memo, tell people that if they do not want to receive your mail to send a message to the remove address. If you do not have your own e-mail domain, then ask them to simply reply with a request for removal.

Keep your e-mail list confidential.

This is so obvious that I would not normally even mention it, except for the fact that I often receive e-mail messages that have been sent to a group of people with every e-mail address listed.

When I pointed this out, the sender was completely unaware this had been done.

Most people when sending e-mail to groups add all the addresses to the main "To": field at the top of the e-mail. Sometimes they use the carbon copy - "cc": field. (isn't it odd how a term sticks - no carbon paper required of course). Using this field has the same effect as "To", all the addresses are listed in each e-mail.

The best way to send bulk e-mail is to send the mail to yourself, and put the mailing list in the Blind Carbon Copy - bcc: field. Check that your e-mail software has such a field, and if not, I recommend that you change to one that does. Sending it bcc, means that other recipients are not made aware of the mailing list.

Securing a competitive edge

One of the challenges you face as a financial adviser, is that a number of direct insurers and brand marketers with significant capability in bulk mailing are competing for your business. Tesco, Virgin, M&S and others have the power to get to your client with very attractive offers. Any company operating a reward or loyalty card scheme doesn't just send a mailing, the bonus points they send are the equivalent of cash. They know the mail has a high chance of being opened.

Through their loyalty cards, they are also tracking lifestyles and spending. They know which people have children or pets, like gourmet food or drink a lot of wine etc. because they analyse spending profiles. That information together with the postcode enables them to target insurance and financial service markets on a systematic basis with "special offers." I suspect that your clients frequently respond to these offers although you could have provided them with a better deal. Unfortunately your clients may only hear from you once or twice a year.

Electronic mail gives you the ability to improve the relationship you have with your clients and remind them more frequently of the "Special Offers" you can provide. As most of your competitors are not collecting e-mail addresses yet, you have time to establish yourself electronically with your clients. Furthermore as it is the A/B market, not the large mass of consumers who are the early adopters of technology, this opens the way for you to target smaller groups of high net worth individuals very effectively and beat the competition.

Insurer communications

One thing that would really benefit all of us in the market-place is the ability to communicate more effectively with insurance companies. The main problems preventing this are the incompatibility of e-mail systems and the lack of an industry e-mail directory.

Most insurance companies use IBM mail, X400 or some other internally managed e-mail system that runs on their main frame computer. None, as far as I am aware, use Internet mail as the basis for the mail system, although many do now have gateways to the Internet. There are still quite a number of technical obstacles to be overcome with these gateways. In particular file attachments are often scrambled and e-mail sometimes just disappears.

The second problem is actually identifying who to send the e-mail message to. The whole concept of e-mail is that each person has an individual address. But if you have say a valuation request, who do you send the message to. Companies are still in the process of developing the internal procedures for routing mail to the right person and avoiding general queries building up in the mail box of someone who is on holiday, for example.

54

Different insurers also have different procedures. Some want mail routed to the local branch office, some to a general central office, others have different admin for different distribution systems, or even special departments for say a large network or tied agency.

If you're a tied agent or company representative, and you have e-mail, you may already have an e-mail directory within your company so that mail can be directed to the right person in the right department. For the independent intermediary community it's more difficult and this is where the Exchange will play a significant role. I'll be looking at the Exchange in Chapter 10.

It is worthwhile checking with your primary insurance contacts to see if they have an Internet e-mail directory available. Some now have a limited directory and they may be able to give you an address for their office and some specific departments you regularly deal with.

Managing in-coming mail and bulk mail

Most of what I've talked about in this chapter has been about out-going mail but of course you do have to watch incoming mail. After five years of regularly using e-mail I now have more electronic mail in the morning than "snail mail". And just as physical mail has to be sorted, sifted, filed and managed, so electronic mail needs the same disciplines.

Folders and Directories

There are no limits to the number of folders and directories you can create. You might want to create a folder for each insurance company. You might have an overall client folder within which you have sub-directories for each client. I find there are some people l receive an enormous amount of e-mail from and others its once in a blue moon, so I have a general client file and then some specific client files. Managing files effectively is important so take the time to think about it now and organise them.

Filters

One feature of Internet e-mail is the ability to automatically filter mail as it arrives. With Outlook Express and Internet Mail, for example, Inbox Assistant enables you to set a variety of instructions on how incoming mail is to be dealt with.

For example I receive two or three newsletters highlighting things happening on the Internet. These are not newsletters I want to read when they arrive, in the same way I don't read magazines the moment they hit my desk. I put them in a reading file. Outlook Express automatically directs all those newsletters into a newsletters file which I can view when I have time.

There are some people who persistently send me unsolicited mail. One told me if I sent them a message saying 'remove', they would take me off their list. I did, they doubled the amount of e-mail. So now Outlook immediately deletes all e-mail from that source.

Mailing lists

At some stage you will come across some of the legitimate mailing lists like LISTSERV and MAJORDOMO. You have to register to receive a particular regular mailing with these services. You can also buy lists, which are of people who have registered to receive information on a particular subject. Some result in occasional newsletters, some result in a veritable flood of e-mails, letters and newsletters.

Be just a little careful what you sign up for. It's easy to find yourself over-powered with incoming mail as has happened, on occasion, to me. Fortunately you can remove yourself from these lists quickly by following the instructions at the bottom of each newsletter.

Newsgroups

Newsgroups are not a primary tool in Internet marketing, but can be useful. The secret to success is in building relationships. The purpose of a Newsgroup is to enable people with similar interests to partake in a general discussion, making comments, asking questions and receiving advice.

I have already mentioned **uk.finance** that a number of advisers participate in. The people involved are not expecting anyone to sell to them. It's a discussion forum. If you like participating in newsgroups, enjoy the discussion and add valuable interesting content to the discussions, you will gain the respect of the group and may find yourself receiving a private e-mail message from participants asking for advice.

Blatant advertising will quickly upset everyone and destroy any likelihood of developing clients from this source. The way to advertise is with your signature. The same signature you use for your e-mail is fine, as this also protects you in the event that you make a comment that can be construed as professional advice.

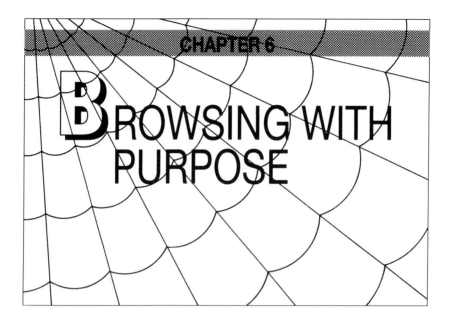

CHAPTER 6

BROWSING WITH PURPOSE

Don't drown in the surf

I hope by now that you have experienced "Surfing the Net" yourself. For many surfing has become more popular than watching television. And it can become quite addictive. It's easy to discover you have been on-line for four or five hours, that its now two o'clock in the morning and you are still surfing.

What I want to do in this chapter is put purpose into your browsing and help you discover how to make the web a valuable tool for business.

The concept of hypertext was developed as a business efficiency tool. When you think about how the brain works, we don't organise information in lists, we organise information dynamically. Everything we know links to other things we know, and some of those links are quite diverse. When we are researching and studying we don't read from cover to cover, we tend to go down one track and that prompts us to move off to another.

The world-wide web is organised to enable that process. You will find as you browse the Internet that when you encounter information you don't understand, often there are links to other pages providing explanations.

For example this entire book is available within the member section of the ABC Web Site. In the electronic version some jargon has a hypertext link to a page containing a definition, references to other web sites are all hypertext links. However a well-designed web site should not be cluttered with links otherwise it becomes difficult to stay focused on the main body content.

The Internet provides access to the entire global pool of information and finding the bit we want is not always easy. With a book or magazine we can flick through pages and use the incredible ability of our eyes to scan for information. Electronically we can't do that, so tools have been developed to help us.

General Surfing

Managing information electronically is a skill and the best way to learn it is to regularly surf the net. I don't mean hours every day, just some time every week to look around and become comfortable with the web.

I use the Internet almost every day. Searching for information, communicating with people, researching clients and prospects. As you become familiar with the Internet you realise you can learn a lot about an individual or a company by the way they organise their web site. More importantly you learn what works and what doesn't work as far as developing your own web site is concerned.

A number of web sites are clearly very expensive, the work of top design studios. Many make the "cool site" lists, even win awards, but they don't work. The pages take too long to download and the graphics detract from the message.

The same happens in paper publishing. How many times have you seen a company produce an expensive glossy art deco brochure which, when you read it, contains no valuable information. It's just a puff!

You will find that the successful sites, give something away to get people to come in. They don't give everything away, just enough for people to feel that they're getting good value, enough to encourage them to want to come back or to buy products and services. That is the essence of a good web site.

We are going to look at designing your own web site later, but use your time as you browse to note what works, what is likely to work for your clients and prospects and get some ideas for what you might like to do with your own site.

The Internet as a research tool

No one has any idea how many pages of information exist on the Internet and most of the information is of absolutely no value to you. It's probably of interest to someone or it wouldn't have been put there. What you need to be able to do is find the information you want and organise it in such a way that you can get back to it whenever you need it. To do this there are four basic tools:

1. The browser's navigation controls which speed up your ability to move around the Internet.

2.   Your favourites or bookmarks folder where you can record the web address of sites you've visited.

3.   Hypertext links which are the signposts people leave in their web sites to help visitors find the information they are looking for.

4.   Search engines that enable you to look up a key word or phrase across the Internet.

The basic browser navigation controls.

Essentially six controls help in navigation:

The Address/Location field

The exact location of the page you are viewing is displayed in this address/location field, usually at the top left of the browser although you can move it anywhere on the screen.

This is an active field. Type in the URL for a web page whether on the Internet, on your own PC or a local area network and the browser will instantly retrieve the page. For most web pages on the Internet all you need to do is type in **www** and the domain name.

This is the simplest and easiest way to find any web page, so you can see why it's so important that the URL for your own web site is easy to remember and easy to type.

The stop button

It's surprising how many times I use this button. Unfortunately some people design web pages under the misheld belief that we all like to watch paint dry. Any page or graphic which takes a long time to download is usually not worth the wait.

Sometimes a web site will warn you that a file will take a while to download, for example a PowerPoint presentation or a plug-in. When you know that, you can open up another browser and go off and do something else while you're waiting. It's when you find yourself waiting with no explanation that frustration grows.

When you visit a web site you'll notice some activity in the status bar in the bottom left hand corner of the browser. These are feed back messages to tell you what is happening, finding file, contacting web site, waiting for replies etc. When the page starts downloading the number of files still waiting to download is displayed.

Netscape and Microsoft provide different messages but they are generally quite self-explanatory. You can see when you are simply waiting for something to happen and if the wait gets too long just click the "stop" button, type in a new address or even re-try the same address. Sometimes a second attempt at the web site can get you in faster.

You'll also find this stop button usually kills irritating background music, animations, and other multimedia activity.

Home button

The home button is very useful and can be customised. The home setting is a page you can return to at any time and will be the page loaded when you first open your browser. If you've installed your software using the disk that came with this book, the default setting for your home button will be the Primex web site at www.primex.co.uk.

However, once you've developed your own web site you might use your own links page, where you keep addresses you frequently visit, as your home setting, or use the Financial Times or electronic Daily Telegraph.

I have created a special financial services links page at my web site designed as a starting point for financial advisers. From here you can go to any of the pages that I've just mentioned or anywhere else in the Financial Services market with a few clicks of the mouse. You might like to set the page as your home page.

In IE 3 or 4 in the address field type www.arundel.co.uk /abc/fslinks.htm. When you reach the page on the browser menu bar, click *View*, then *Internet Options* and that will give you a set-up screen. Under the general tab, click on *Use Current Page Settings* and, click *OK*. This will bring up the links page when you start the browser and anytime that you click 'home'.

If you are using Netscape Navigator, click *Edit* then *Preferences* for a similar set up screen.

Reload or Refresh Button

Once you have visited a site, the page is stored in a temporary file on you computer, called the **Cache**. When you visit that web site again, your computer will look in the cache and if it finds a valid page there, will load it from the PC saving time. However if the page has been updated since your last visit, you might be missing the most current information. Click "refresh" or "reload" and the computer will download the page again from its source.

I also try reload when a page is unusually slow at downloading or fails to download. Sometimes the second or third attempt gets through.

Backwards and Forwards Buttons

The backwards and forwards buttons on the left of the tool bar, take you back to the previous page viewed or forward to a page you've previously looked at. Sometimes the web site designer creates navigation controls on their page to enable you to move easily round their web site, but I find using the back button is much quicker.

With version 4 of Internet Explorer and Netscape Navigator, the backward and forward controllers are more sophisticated. If you click to the right of the arrow a small drop down menu appears listing the most recently visited pages so that you can click on them and jump back rather than having to tab back through each one.

There is also a feature called "History". Click on the "History" button in the tool bar for Explorer, or go to the communicator menu in Navigator and click history, and the list of all the sites you've visited over the past couple of weeks or more becomes available.

Right Click the Mouse - Open a New Window

If you 'right' click on the mouse in Windows 95, a small context sensitive navigation menu pops up. In a browser menu the feature I use most is *Open in New Window.*

Point your cursor to any hypertext link and 'right' click. From the menu that appears, select *Open in New Window* and the linked page will be opened in a new browser leaving the existing page where it is. This is particularly useful when using a search engine, or reviewing a number of links.

Favourites or bookmarks

Whenever you browse a web page on the Internet or on your PC or internal network, simply click the "favourites/bookmark" menu tag, then add to favourites or bookmark and this stores the details in your folder for future reference. To reuse the link, you simply select favourites or bookmarks and click on the link.

Internet Explorer gives you the option to decide in which folder to save the hypertext link. With Netscape you need to choose "file bookmark" first in order to select the folder.

Here are a couple more tips for keeping your links folder manageable.

The default name of the saved link will usually be the title of the web page as defined by the webmaster. That may not be a particularly useful name. If the webmaster has titled the page "home page," in a weeks time you will have no idea what that page was all about. With Internet Explorer, you can rename any page as you save it, so label the page with a meaningful name. If a web page needs a "password and user name" to get in, I usually add this to the name at the same time.

Unfortunately this is not so easy with Netscape, where you need to save the link then go into "edit bookmarks" to rename it.

My second suggestion is to organise your favourites/bookmarks into appropriate folders. I know this seems a rather obvious thing to say but very often I have found that even with a meaningful name, a link still wouldn't make sense but for the fact that I'd saved it in an appropriate file. I now have well over two hundred links in my favourites which would be unusable if not well organised.

The key to managing information is a good retrieval system. The quicker and easier it is to find information when you need it the more likely you are to use it and the more value your get from using the Internet.

Hypertext links and listings

One feature you'll find in most web sites is a links page. And I have found well managed links pages to be the most valuable resources available on the Internet. In fact the development of a good links page can be a major factor in getting people to regularly return to your site.

A superb example of this is Gaeia. Bridget Benson, who owns Gaeia, specialises in ethical investment and was the first IFA to have a site on the Internet. One of the features of her site is a huge list of links aimed directly at people interested in ethical and environmental issues. As this is one of my interests, I still use her site as a starting point when I want to research information on ethical or environmental issues.

Of course it doesn't just stop there. Much of Bridget's success in marketing her site is because many of the sites she lists reciprocate by listing her site. Bridget lists the Friends of the Earth site and Friends of the Earth lists her site, the same with Virtual Manchester. Because much of the Internet is based on people networking with each other, good reciprocal links can dramatically increase your hit rates, the number of visits to your site.

It's worth beginning to think about what sort of links would be of value to your clients and prospects, and look for ways which you can start creating reciprocal links with other web sites which might direct interested investors towards your site.

Listings sites

Some web sites specialise exclusively in providing listings. This is not quite the same as a search engine, which I'll come to later, it's a directory or magazine web site providing listings of other sites.

Within the financial services industry there are two such sites:

http://www.moneyworld.co.uk

http://www.find.co.uk

Both of these sites are aimed at consumers of financial services products in the UK and provide a very comprehensive listing of web sites in the UK financial services market-place and a few links to sites abroad. Listings on these sites are free, but if you want to stand out, you will need to pay for a banner advertising your presence, which is how they make their money.

Their success therefore depends on hit rates. The greater the number of visitors, the greater its value to an advertiser. Regular banner advertising is one of the key strategies that helps Garrison Discount Investments to secure 150 leads a week through the Internet.

One problem on both MoneyWorld and Find is that some of the links are broken. This may be because the web site no longer exists, or possibly because there is a technical fault. What I find strange is that some of those broken links have existed for over six months.

This suggests firstly that neither company checks the links on their pages. Secondly the IFAs in question have not bothered to check the links. Having a broken link is worse than having no link at all because it gives the impression that you have ceased trading.

What do we learn from all this? Marketing through the Internet is not a passive activity it is pro-active. You must constantly check what's happening and make sure that your electronic marketing is doing what you in the way you expected it to.

The ABC of the WWW Links Page

I mentioned earlier that I have also created a links page for the Financial Services Market. However my links page is not a consumer site, it's designed as an educational guide for financial advisers, as a support site for this book and the keynote presentations and training workshops I conduct.

One feature of my "Surfing the Financial Services Industry" page is the presence of guidelines to linked sites. These comprise a brief description, and highlights of what I consider are the best features for financial advisers. If you want to look at the guide notes, click on the "book" icon beside the link.

Making the most of search engines

Search engines are great in theory, but frustrating and sometimes difficult to use in practice. They are large databases of web pages, which you can search by typing in a key word or phrase that relates to what your looking for. I use search engines extensively but still find them challenging.

The search engine databases are compiled in one of two ways:

69

1.   Most people, when they put a site onto the web, register their site with the main search engines.

2.   Some search engines employ software called a **spider** which systematically searches out web sites around the Internet recording information about their contents.

Most databases are compiled electronically, although some are compiled by human researchers individually checking sites and registering them in appropriate directories.

The main search engines are:

Excite UK   http://www.excite.co.uk /

HotBot   http://www.hotbot.com

Yahoo UK   http://www.yahoo.co.uk

Lycros UK   http://www.lycos.co.uk

UK Index   http://www.ukindex.co.uk

Infoseek   http://www.infoseek.com

Alta Vista   http://www.altavista.digital.com

I find that different search engines produce different results. If I am doing research that requires me to use a search engine, I open two or three simultaneously and give each the same search criteria to see which one produces the best results for that particular topic. I therefore prefer to use my favourite list of search engines rather than use the search button on the toolbar.

Until 1997 most of the search engine results were American, most now have a UK specific site or the option to select which country you wish to search. Alta Vista does not, but it does allow you to translate most common languages on the Internet into English, including Japanese and Chinese sites, and vice versa. Sometimes the sense of what is being conveyed gets oddly transformed but it's clear enough to be understandable.

The main problem with search engines is the sheer volume of information. Type in a keyword and the search engine will tell you it has found 3,456,323 incidences of the word requested. Here are the first 10! Often the first ten responses are all different pages from the same company who mystifyingly seem extremely good at getting their site listed near the top.

You need a little patience and some creative thinking.

Define the search criteria as carefully as you can. Some search engines want a question as you would ask it in English, others want key words. In some you can put quotes around a phrase and the search engine will look only for that specific phrase, not the separate words. Others allow you a range of options while some always look for every word separately.

Yahoo is differently organised, using a tree structure. You start with the generic topic which gives a list of sub-headings, select a sub-heading and you move down to the next set of sub-headings and so on through the tree until you come to a list of sites.

You can see from this it's difficult to say that one particular search engine is better than another because they are all different and I tend to use most of them in equal measure.

Go on a tour

That completes our review of the browsing tools, so now it is time to take a tour and begin using the Internet as a research tool.

You might have heard about the congestion problems and be wondering when is the best time to use the Internet. Fortunately, the UK doesn't really get too congested at any time of the day. You may occasionally find difficulty dialling into your service provider between seven and ten in the evening. You may find congestion after three or four in the afternoon if you're visiting sites in the United States. The best guide is your own experience.

I recommend that you start at www.arundel.co.uk/ABC, and take the introduction to financial services tour you'll find there. Don't forget to set this page as your home page so that you can always return to the starting point at any time.

Prospecting on the Internet

Now that you have had a chance to get familiar with the tools, we can put them to some practical use in looking for prospects on the Internet. Where do we start?

Successful financial advisors on the Internet specialise. When you look at their web-site there is a clear focus, a mortgages service, discount investments, ethical investments etc. You need to adopt this focused approach even when you are using a browser as a means of finding new prospects.

Who makes an ideal client for you? Do you have a particular area of specialisation? Perhaps you're a financial planner or a specialist in corporate pensions or offshore investments, portfolio management, or mortgages. Perhaps you have a distinctly local service, working in a particular city or local community. Maybe you're a sportsman, golfer, sailor, or a marathon runner? Maybe you know a particular industry, the computer industry, advertising industry, medical market etc.

The moment you start searching the Internet with a specific focus you will start finding prospects.

Search your local community

As a good exercise in discovering the potential of the Internet in prospecting and to help you become familiar with the tools, start with some local research. Remember you can do this at any time of the day or night. As an example, let me relate a personal project, which I hope, will provide a model you can adopt.

I live in Winchester, Hampshire. I haven't lived there long so my contacts in the community are quite limited, particularly as most of my business is in the insurance industry rather than the local community.

My hobby is public speaking and I'm a very active member of Toastmasters International - www.toastmasters.org.uk . One of the first things I did when I came to Winchester was to set up a local community Toastmasters Club that is now running very successfully and we have a steady flow of new members attracted through Internet   activity.

As part of a recent recruitment drive I undertook some research on the Internet.

The first stage was simple, bring up three search engines, in this instance Excite UK, Hotbot set to search in Europe, and Yahoo UK.

My first search criteria was simply Winchester and up came a number of links to Winchester. I found links for the Winchester rifle and Winchester Cathedral which were not of any help. But I did find Winchester City Council and Hampshire County Council. I also discovered that IBM has a site promoting their local Hursley Training Centre. A lot of people visit the training centre so IBM has created a web site featuring local history, tourist information and a map listing most of the places to eat, drink and stay in Winchester. A very useful site.

The most important discovery was Hampshire County Council who have a huge web site listing all of the services currently available throughout Hampshire. Within it I found a list of every community association and club in Hampshire, with the contact names and address of the people who run them. Exactly what I was looking for. A list of people who may be called upon to speak in public in the course of their business or social life.

From this exercise I've begun producing a database of people in the local community. I've discovered that Hampshire Business Link is doing a large amount of work to help promote using the Internet within the local business community. This will open up channels for me to use electronic communications into local businesses but also identifies other people who need to speak in public in the course of their work.

I am able to start tracking developments in the growth of electronic communication within Winchester. I have created a web site for our public speaking club at www.arundel.co.uk/wessexspeakers One element of that web page is a links page and now I'm in the process of adding local interest links and building some local focus into the site.

I'm building an e-mail directory of prospects and centres of influence for toastmasters and we're now developing a newsletter to go out regularly to these people with tips on how to make meetings run better, improve presentations, use humour more effectively and tips on dealing with impromptu speaking. These are all things that people can learn if they join a toastmasters club but are of interest even if they don't. I need to be sure that I can send something to people that won't immediately be trashed.

Electronic Communications Supplement Existing Marketing

More often than not, my research has not produced an electronic communications route to people. So the information is being transferred into an ordinary contact management database; I use Act. We will send letters and even a printed newsletter where we cannot identify an electronic route.

We will be promoting our electronic services to identify an electronic address if one exists. The best route will be promoting the web site and offering our electronic newsletter on public speaking and meetings management.

I hope from this little case study that you now have some ideas for developing your own electronic marketing. What you have available is an additional set of tools to help build your business, not a replacement set. In every area of your marketing and client servicing you are going to find that the Internet can support and enhance what you are already doing.

On-line directories

Some of the most valuable resources on the Internet are the on-line directories. Unfortunately, the UK directories are not as advanced as those in the US. Here in the United Kingdom the main focus is on business information.

The Electronic Yellow Pages, EYP can be found at http://www.eyp.co.uk and Thompson's at http://www.inbusiness.co.uk. Both are organised on a regional basis and according to business category.

Companies House is now on-line at http://www.companies-house.gov.uk. Reed Information

Systems the publishers of Kompass and Kelly's have various on-line based services at http://www.reedinfo.co.uk. Dun and Bradstreet have a variety of UK services at http://www.dunandbrad.co.uk

A number of new directories are being developed which are entirely electronic, and provide extensive information for anyone prospecting for clients.

While some of the services are available directly via the Internet, some are only accessible via a separate dial up line or on CD ROM. Most of the business directories are not entirely free. Some allow simple searches free, but for the valuable information, names of current directors, business analysis, company reports, mailing lists of business categories, etc, there is often a fee.

The ABC Web Site

I said earlier that part of this book is on-line. This is the end of the paper edition of this chapter, the rest you need to go on-line for, but before you do, remember to have a look at your marketing. Decide who you are looking for and go on-line to the ABC Web site at www.arundel.co.uk/ABC and click on the "prospecting tour".

You will notice that part of the ABC site is free and provides general support to this book. There is also a member section, for which there is a fee. This is a monthly and entitles you to full access of the members section including training and seminars on-line, electronic books and a monthly news letter, High-Tech Touch Selling, and discussion groups.

CHAPTER 7

MARKETING YOUR WEB SITE

You are probably thinking, "That's odd. Have I missed out a chapter? How come we're talking about marketing a web site when we haven't even looked at how to build one?"

Well until you've sorted out your marketing strategy there isn't any point in starting to build a web site. Your web presence should be seen as a part of the overall marketing strategy of your business. Unfortunately having reviewed the UK IFA Internet presence, most advisers seem to be under the misapprehension that they can just put up a web site and wait for the business to come in. This will not happen.

Creating, maintaining and managing a web site needs to be done properly. Just putting up a web site because everyone else has, will do your business more harm than good. If you don't believe me go on-line now.

Type www.moneyworld.co.uk/ukpfd/out_ifa.htm in the address or location field. That URL will take you to the IFA directory at MoneyWorld.   Start anywhere and just begin looking at some of the web sites.

I had thought of illustrating a few sites here as a warning, but that would be unfair. I've no doubt that if anyone found themselves on my list of poor web sites, they'd very quickly change it. So here are some of the common problems I've encountered.

Typical problems with web sites

Error 404

You'll often come across this screen as you surf the web. It usually means that the site no longer exists at that server. The adviser may have closed the site but is still listed or may have moved to a new location but hasn't updated the list or notified the list manager.

If you do move or close your web site, make sure that you notify the webmaster at sites that have links to your address and get them to update the listing. If you move to a new ISP or change your URL by acquiring your own, make sure you create a simple redirection page at the old address, the same as you would if you changed your 'phone number.

File Listing or Missing Components

Sometimes instead of a web page you get a list of files. This usually indicates that the Webmaster doesn't understand the technology. There are certain rules that need to be followed, one of which is that the home page must be named in a specific way that suits the Host System. Often is must be called index.htm. Sometimes graphics are missing, usually because they are in the wrong directory on-line. Check your site by visiting it. If it doesn't display as you expected get it fixed before you promote it.

Business Card Sites

I feel quite angry when I see these. It is not that the advisers have put up a poor web site, often they have been sold a poor service. One particular company promotes a template service where IFAs can put in basic information about their business: name, address, e-mail address, contact name, list of products. In essence it's nothing more than you'd put on a business card. That's not a web site, that's a business card on the Internet.

You would be better off taking a box of your business cards, wandering down the high street, and handing them out. You'd get a much better response. If someone offers you a template web service, ask for the address of sample sites. Go on-line, look at them and ask yourself:

- "Would I tell my clients and friends to visit my site if it looked like this?"

- "Would a site like this add value to my business?"

- "What will be the likely outcome of a prospect coming to this web site?"

If you cannot give positive answers to these questions, forget it. The service is not going to benefit your business or enhance your marketing.

Cereal Box Sites

Just because there are some great tools to enable anyone to design and build a web site, doesn't mean that the design will be a good one. Unfortunately even employing design services doesn't mean the design will be good. So many sites try to incorporate every idea there is. The result is loud colours, backgrounds which obscure the writing, flashing signs, neon lights, irritating animated gifts and tacky background sounds.

Now there is nothing wrong with some of these features at the right time, and in moderation. When they come all at once on the same home page, do they really inspire confidence in your ability to manage clients money?

What is the image you want to present of your business? This is a shop front. When people come to your web site it is as important as 'phoning your business. What is the first impression they get? Don't let your site say "Amateur Financial Adviser" or "Cheapskate DIY man."

No One Visits My Site

One feature you'll find on a lot of web sites is **Counter**, an interactive meter that logs every visitor to the site,"*3475 people have visited this site since October 1997.*" I visited one site where the counter moved on like an odometer as I arrived, increasing the visitor count to 6. That's the sort of information I'd rather people didn't know.

I Sell Life Insurance - Wanna Buy Some?

90% of financial adviser sites I have visited don't actually say this, but that is the message they convey. The web site is just a list of products and services sold. There is nothing to draw people in; there is no advice, no attempt to establish rapport. In short there is no marketing, just an attempt to sell. This is a waste of money.

If you build it will they come?

You may remember Kevin Costner's "Field of Dreams," but on the Internet it doesn't work. If you just build it, they will not come, they won't even know you're there!

No one accidentally arrives at your web site. They come to your site because they have made a decision to do so. They have taken action, they have clicked on a "link" or they have typed in an address. They have visited your site because they wanted to.

And so the question you need to have an answer to by the end of this chapter is:

Why would anyone want to visit my web site?

I became involved in selling and marketing financial services in 1972, and almost the first thing I was told then was "no one ever buys life assurance".

Since then financial services education has changed things a little. People do buy financial services products. Direct Line, Virgin and M&S illustrate this. However, it does not happen without an enormous investment in marketing. The direct companies are successful because they aggressively market what they do through telesales, advertising, inserts and all manner of promotion to encourage people to take action. Some have added web sites to their armoury.

What do you want to achieve with a Web Site?

I mentioned earlier the importance of clearly defining your market. This is not a new idea developed as a result of the Internet, it's just that it is even more important when you try to market electronically. The fact that some people are making a lot of money marketing through the Internet gives great motivation for others to want to follow suit. The problem is that many jump in without defining what they are trying to achieve.

The key reasons for creating a web site are:

1.   To sell products and services.

2.   To generate leads.

3.   To provide client service and support.

4.   As part of a general advertising and PR campaign.

5.   "Everyone else has one so I suppose I should".

Selling on the Internet

If you plan to sell business directly over the Internet, then you need to do a great deal more than just put up a web site. There are security issues and expensive software requirements for handling money electronically. Also there are few role models to emulate, because few companies have been successful at selling financial services over the Internet. Attempting to sell directly on-line puts you right up there with the leading Internet pioneers.

There are some financial services products being sold on-line. I have bought travel insurance. Motor and other personal lines insurance are being traded, at least one PEP, http://www.netpep.co.uk and a number of unit trusts. The most successful financial service products trading on-line are stocks and shares. Try http://www.esi.co.uk, the Electronic Share Information Service, where you will also find links to other successful stockbrokers.

But if you are planning this route, you will also need high levels of customer and technical support. I would suggest that unless you have a budget of at least £100,000 to get started, and can afford to write it off if things don't work out, this is probably not the right route for you. Financial Services are not easy products to trade on-line, and certainly fall outside the scope of this book.

Generating Leads On-line

Using a web site as part of a lead generating process on the other hand is proving to be a very successful application, for a few IFAs. Most successful advisers use the Web site to deliver information and to encourage visitors to complete an on-line enquiry form.

People will visit the site for help and guidance and they want that help while they're on-line. The sort of help they are looking for is related to their interests. They are unlikely to visit the site because they want a sales pitch on why they should have more life insurance, or to read a puffy product brochure on personal pensions.

What is topical right now? It might be a feature on PEPs and ISAs. What can you do before PEPs are withdrawn, what will happen then? A briefing guide, with illustrations to help people understand the changes in regulations and perhaps some special offers on PEPs if they apply electronically. Or perhaps a special feature on the Capital Gains Tax changes and how you can take advantage of the new rules. Be topical and creative.

Having a specialist focus is a definite plus for a financial adviser. What is the typical profile of the clients you want to attract? And don't just say people with lots of money. Do you specialise in the corporate market, the grey market, family market, local community, a specific industry, offshore and expatriates, mortgages, ethical investments etc. Define your target market and organise your marketing, including your web site to appeal to those people.

It is worth noting that attempts to get visitors to complete a detailed fact find on-line have not been successful. Visitors seem unprepared to give extensive personal details without getting to know you. They are happy to provide general personal information, attitude to risk and details for an initial quotation. Make your enquiry form a request for information - a quotation, a report, a briefing. If it looks like an invitation for a call from someone trying to sell something, they will not respond.

If lead generation is your goal, then your objective must be to obtain basic prospect information and an understanding of their initial interest. One of the most important items of information you need is details of how the visitor wished to be communicated with, e-mail, post, 'phone through the office or at home.

Client Service and Support

80% of new business written by established advisers new business comes from making additional sales to existing clients, and most of the remainder is the result of referrals or recommendations from existing clients. It therefore makes sense to look at how your web site can help provide additional service and support to clients.

Do you send out a budget summary every year. That is easy to provide electronically, as are investment reports, newsletters, special reports on opportunities like windfall shares, or guides on self-assessment, buying property to let, offshore investing, making a will, business expansion, retirement planning etc. These can be creatively produced, including using an audio presentation with slides.

Talk to your clients and gain an understanding of what they want. What information would make visiting your site useful? Then promote the content with electronic newsletters or memos inviting clients to visit the web site.

The content doesn't have to be related to financial services. If you are keen on golf, you could provide golfing tips, reports on courses you have played, reports on local tournaments. You can take the same approach to any sporting, social or business interest you have in common with important clients and centres of influence. Content like this will give clients a reason to recommend the site to friends.

If you have a predominately local business and wish to maintain it as such, develop a local interest web site. What's on where, local history, places of interest, eating and drinking recommendations, other complimentary local businesses, photo' reports of local events, easy to do with a digital camera. Make the site a local focus point for clients and the people you would like as clients.

One key requirement for the future will be the provision of access to policy valuations. At present eight companies are able to provide some policy valuations to IFAs and a number of insurance companies provide such a service to their representatives. None offer this service directly to consumers.

One reason for this is the low take-up of Internet services by consumers. The other is a concern about Internet security. These services will become available in the near future. The Exchange already has an on-line Policy and Group Enquiry Service through its Common Trading Platform and this is expected to be available through their Extranet Service, soon.

PR and Advertising

Unless you are a large business with a high profile, this should not be the focus of your site. A web site is a support function for other promotional activity. If you want to advertise on the Web the best way is to pay for advertising banners on sites with high hit rates.

As for PR, when you develop your site you should think about your image. Make sure visitors receive a positive view of you and your business. Successful sites give something away to draw people in, and that is in essence the PR aspect of the site. Some very expensive corporate sites are entirely PR focused, designed to maintain name awareness and achieved by use of leading edge multimedia technology. Check out www.pepsi.com.

Everyone else has one so I suppose we should

This is probably the main reason for many sites today, although it is the worst possible reason. If you cannot see a clear business benefit from having a web site don't build one yet. Wait until you have a better understanding of the web and more of your clients and friends are on-line.

However don't write off electronic commerce just because you cannot see a benefit. Do your research; talk to clients and other advisers, especially those who are on-line. Everyone will eventually be using electronic communications, you need to identify how your business will benefit from doing so.

Give people a reason to visit

People are going to arrive at your site for one of 5 reasons:

1. They were invited to visit the site by you.

2. They were referred to the site by one of your clients or contacts.

3. They came across your site in a listing in another site.

4. They saw an advertisement with your URL or a hypertext link that attracted their attention.

5. They identified your site as a result of a search.

In looking at your objectives we have begun to consider the elements of the reason to visit. People are not necessarily going to come to your site because they want to buy insurance and yours was the first name they came across. They may come because you promote better than average investment returns, or discounted life insurance, or special deals for people over 65, or advice for first time buyers. The reason for visiting is likely to be something that sets you apart from the rest.

The Internet thrives on networking. Visitors will come to your web site because they've been given your URL. Throughout this book I've been listing Internet addresses, if you go to the ABC web site you'll find more web addresses. Every communication I send out to anyone has my web address on it, every time I write an article I publish my web address and my e-mail address. As often as possible when I speak I promote my web address.

People come to my web site because there is useful

87

information there that will benefit them. While they are at my web site I promote the services I offer and hope to stimulate business. But people come to my web site initially because there are some solutions to problems there.

Some of that information is free and some you have to pay for. Look at the successful IFA sites and you will see they follow the same process. When you arrive at the site there are newsletters, bulletins, useful bits of information to help people to understand investments, life assurance, pensions, tax planning and all the things to do with financial services. Helpful advice is provided free of charge in a generic way and then an offer to help in a specific way is made so that a visitor can chose to go further.

You have to draw people in to the site with a clear marketing message. Garrison offers discount investments, John Charcol offers mortgage advice, Gaeia offers ethical investments - they all sell financial services products but they have focused their marketing around a specific area. What is your specialisation, what makes you different, why should I come to your site, why should I do business with you?

Can your business support remote trading

One factor about using the Internet as a marketing tool often overlooked, is that people doing business via the Internet do not take account of its location. That means that you could receive enquiries from anywhere in the world and the clients expect you to be able to trade remotely. Garrison finds that about ten percent of their leads come from offshore, the rest come from all around the United Kingdom.

So before you leap into web based marketing, you need to look at your business processes and decide whether you have the ability or the desire to cope with business remotely. This means that you and your staff, and you will need staff, need to know how to convert leads over the 'phone, by post and electronic mail. This may need a different business process, even if the enquiries are local.

You can still use electronic marketing to support your current process, but you must make a decision about how you will handle an enquiry from someone three or four hundred miles away? If you are not organised to convert leads remotely you run the risk of wasting a lot of time and losing business.

Look at the success of Direct Line, Virgin, John Charcol. All promotion is supported by an 0800 number usually manned beyond normal business hours. If you 'phone John Charcol's mortgage enquiry line, you will be routed to someone who can handle your enquiry either at a central office or, with the assistance of some clever software, to the nearest branch or franchise office. All these businesses have web sites they are building into their remote marketing strategy.

When people see your promotion on the Internet, they want to act now. That means an easy to complete enquiry form or a free-phone enquiry line and a support system to ensure that the enquiry is handled immediately.

Organise Yourself For Remote Trading

Most large companies in the financial services industry have a remote trading strategy. I am aware of a number of IFA firms who are working on this, as are some larger tied businesses. I am not aware of many smaller firms, tied or independent, who see this as a major part of their business strategy. That is a mistake. Whether you plan to use a web site to market your business or not, remote trading will play an ever increasing role in your business.

Most experience suggests that you are going to convert about 20-25% of leads, however as you are not selecting prospects, many will be enquiries for low premium levels.

Considering the average hourly rate required of a financial adviser at around £100 to £150 per hour, guess who should not be handling incoming enquiries?

Enquiries need to be handled by a much less expensive resource. You'll notice at the Garrison site a button marked "execution only" and most advisers, who are remote trading, have some level of execution only business. But it's not just remote leads that need rethinking. How do you make a profit on top-up business, if a senior adviser does all the work?

I am not going to address this topic in detail in this book however. I plan to provide case studies and additional support in the members section of the ABC web site based on feedback from advisers successfully using the web and undertaking other remote trading activities. I will look at one aspect of remote trading, providing a rapid response to enquiries.

Rapid Response

People using the Internet expect actual or near instant response. If I want a software package, I expect to pay for it and download it immediately. If I want a quote I expect to be able to input the information and get it back immediately. This is not always possible, but you need to keep control of the process. Most advisers offering quotes do so on the basis that the quotation will be dispatched by return. Which means it has to be dealt with on the day it is received, a 24 to 48 hour response.

Anything longer than that is too slow. You need to have a system for handling incoming enquiries, a step by step process that enables all your staff to respond to an enquiry with the appropriate marketing pack, telephone call or e-mail response.

Web based marketing is a significant business decision, an alternative or additional strategy to aid your current marketing. It stimulates remote trading and dealing even with existing clients and you need to be organised to handle that if you want to use the Internet to help generate new business.

Why should you get your own domain name?

One essential thing you need in marketing a web site is your own domain name. I touched on this in Chapter 2, and now I want to look at it in a little more detail.

When a web hosting company allocates you space on their server they will allocate to you a sub-domain within their domain. The following examples are not real addresses but show what a sub-domain might look like with a fictitious host

www.adviser.host.com

www.host.com/adviser

www.host.com/ifanet/adviser

Now these examples might look easy to remember, but often they are quite complex.

http://www.host-net.co.uk/commercial/~adviser-jones

How much better to have - http://www.jones.co.uk

The problem is of course that **jones.co.uk** has already gone. Which is where we need to get creative.

Apart from the ease of remembering the name and clearly

indicating that this is your own domain, it frees you from being tied to any particular web hosting company.

If you are allocated a sub-domain by a host and you want to move to another host, you cannot take the name with you. That means you will have to:

- Change all your business stationery, business cards, advertising, brochures and anything else on which you have printed or publicised your domain name.

- Inform all your existing clients and contacts of the change in domain name.

- Re-register your web site with all the search engines and other listings you have found.

- Maintain a web account at the original site for about a year to redirect anyone you cannot inform, or where listings fail to update addresses.

If you have your own domain name, you simply move to a new host, they will point your domain name to their computer, and no one will even know you have made the change. The domain name is yours for life, subject to you paying the annual fee.

So let us look at what domain names are and how you can get your own, even before you have a web site.

Understanding URLs

Uniform Resource Locator or URL is the technical name for an Internet address. In fact it's a little more than that because every single page of information on the Internet has a unique URL. Part of that URL is the domain name. So let's break down the URL for my site into its constituent parts so that you understand what it all means.

<u>http://www.arundel.co.uk</u>

First how do you tell someone your URL? You do not need to tell people the first part, the http://. As you'll see later, they don't need this to find a web page. So when someone asks me for my web address, it's "**www dot arundel dot co dot uk.**"

Protocol

This first part of the URL, **http://**, indicates that this is "hypertext transfer protocol". You don't need to type this into your browser because this is the default for web addresses.

You will see other protocols that you will need to type in. ftp:// indicates 'file transfer protocol". gopher:// is a protocol that dominated the Internet prior to the introduction of the World Wide Web although you're unlikely to come across it very often now.

Host Computer

The next section of the URL denotes the host computer, or server as it is known, usually **www** by convention. This is not always the case and you will come across addresses that begin with say, **home**. This indicates a separate host computer or a sub-domain of the host computer. When you rent space on a server, your address will almost certainly begin **www**.

Domain Name

The next section of the URL is the important part. This is the domain and comprises two parts, the 'Name' and the 'Generic Top Level Domain' or gTLD. Let me deal with the Top Level Domain first.

The domain name is actually read from right to left, so this is the first part. The gTLD in my case is **.uk**. However the UK naming body has allocated a range of second level domains to provide an increased availability of names. **.co** is the second level domain indicating a commercial organisation in the United Kingdom. The current UK Domains are:

.co.uk - for general commercial organisations.

.ltd.uk - for limited companies.

.plc.uk - for public limited companies.

.ac.uk - for educational establishments.

.org.uk - for non-profit making organisations.

.net.uk - for network organisations and Internet service providers.

.uk.com - a sub-domain of the .com international top level domain for the UK.

In addition there are some domains strictly reserved for government and military bodies.

The true top level domains are those issued in the US, of which there are only four commercially available at present, although this is about to be increased once the political and administration issues are resolved. These are extremely popular not just because of the demand in the US, but because they are seen to denote an international business. These are the four main gTLDs:

.com - commercial domains for companies and the most common top level domain.

.org - non-commercial organisations and others that don't fit elsewhere.

.net - network related companies and Internet service providers.

.edu - this was originally for all educational establishments, but now more restricted.

There are other Top Level Domains but these are restricted, for example:

.gov - US federal government organisations

.mil - US military organisations.

Due to the enormous demand for **.com** addresses especially, most of the good names have already been used. Remember a URL has to be unique, so that once one person has bought a **.com** name, no one else can have it, unless they want to embark on a complex international legal process. Even then, unless you can clearly demonstrate that you own the name with world-wide trademarks etc, it is very difficult to take a name from someone who has registered it. You can always try to negotiate or buy it from them.

To overcome the serious name shortage new top-level domains are now about to be released. The proposed seven new gTLDs which were, at the time of writing, due to be available any time, are:

.firm - for businesses or firms.

.store - for businesses offering goods to purchase.

.web - for organisations involved in World Wide Web related activities.

.**arts** - for organisations involved in cultural and entertainment activities.

.**rec** - for recreational and entertainment focused organisations.

.**info** - for suppliers of information services.

.**nom** - for personal domains.

The reason for going into this in so much detail is that you may need this information in order to secure a useful and memorable domain name that relates to your business. The question is which top-level domain do you chose for your business.

In the main you will probably want a **.co.uk** or a **.ltd.uk** address unless you intend to market yourself as an international organisation, in which case you might want to consider **.com** or one of the new top level domains.

The part of the domain name that you can create is the name, in my case **arundel**. This name can consist of up to 22 letters, numbers or dashes, (under score or a hyphen, but cannot begin or end with a dash). If you see domain names split with dots these are sub-domains allocated by the host provider.

Before we look at how you actually go about getting your own domain name, let me deal quickly with one last piece of jargon you will encounter, and which confused me no end until I understood what it was all about.

Internet Protocol Numbers

The Internet doesn't actually understand a URL. Like most computers the Internet likes to work with numbers, therefore every address has a number, called an Internet

Protocol Number or IP Number. They look like this 123.456.789.2.

When you type in a URL, the first thing that happens is that your browser accesses what is called a Domain Name Server or DNS. This is a large database of URLs and their matching IP numbers. Your Internet Service Provider will have one, or will direct your request to one automatically.

Occasionally you will see IP numbers in the status bar when you are browsing and if you have to reconfigure your dial-up connection you will need to enter two. More importantly, when you buy a UK domain name you must provide two IP numbers to allocate your name to, which your host will usually organise for you.

Obtaining your own domain name

It is very possible that the domain name you would like has already been taken. So the best place to start is on-line where you can check the names you would like for availability. If they are not taken you can move to the next stage of getting one registered, if not then you will need to be a little creative.

First let's consider what sort of name you want for your electronic business. The most important rule is that it is memorable. Short names are usually easier to remember and easier to type. If you type in an address incorrectly it will not be recognised. One of the longest names I have seen that works was www.webpagesthatsuck.com. 16 characters which you might have to read twice to understand, but it is very descriptive and memorable.

You can use acronyms for your name but avoid them if no one knows what they mean. If you are planning to market your name by advertising, it may be worth thinking about a new name that's easy to market.

You first choice might be your current company name, especially if you are primarily marketing to existing clients. Often this will be your name or two or three names together. How do we cope with more than one name? Although, you cannot have spaces between names, you can have a dash (not the underscore) or you can join the words up. The underscore can be used in file names.

For example **cyberspace** or **cyber-space**.   These are different names. I like to avoid dashes if possible. Internet names are not case sensitive, they always default to lowercase. However you can market the name any way you like. So it's easy to market **CyberSpac**e which enables us to use two names joined up, but still look separate when promoted.

Now we can attach the name to the Top Level Domain, giving more options.

Both of the options above could be **.com** or **.co.uk** giving us six options, of which I can tell you three have already been taken and one is still available at time of writing. If none of these options are available for your name, you can go on to try **.org, .org.uk, .uk.com**. If you are a Limited Company or Public Company, you can use **.ltd.uk** or **.plc.uk**. However you must use your registered name for these.

The most popular names are .com and .co.uk, and to check these out you can go to www.webscape.co.uk. Roger Phillips the owner of WebScape was an IFA and is now a UK host and ISP with some experience in putting financial advisers on the Internet. Garrison, IFA Direct and the IFA Association use them to design and host their web sites. As these are all good sites, they can be recommended.

You will find an item WHOIS, at their site which enables you to check your own domain name. Simply type in the name you want to use and a search will be made of the appropriate databases. If the name you want is available, e-mail WebScape will arrange to secure the name and hold it until you have decided where you want to host your web site.

There is a fee of £80 for a **.uk** name for two years and then £40 per year from year three onwards. In addition WebScape make a £40 fee for administration. You do not have to use their service to host your site, but with their experience, I would certainly talk to them. **.com** addresses have just reduced in price to $70 initial and $35 per annum.

If you are unsuccessful in finding the name you want here, you can always look further and consider other top level domains. www.alldomains.com specialise in providing Internet names. Their site enables you to check every domain available and provides access to all the national naming bodies so that you can do the registration yourself and avoid the administration fee. You will need to provide two valid IP Protocol numbers if you do your own UK registration.

Well I hope this has not confused you too much. It's not as complex as it might at first appear, but believe me, getting your own domain name, and doing it **NOW**, is important. Domain names are currently being registered at the rate of over 17,000 a day.

Promote your site

Clearly you do need a web site before you can start to promote it, and we're going to look at building the site in the next chapter, but remember the web site is part of your overall marketing strategy not a replacement for it.

You need to make sure you promote your URL everywhere you can. On a recent trip to the States I even saw a URL emblazoned above the shop front of an adviser. Make sure you include it in newsletters, electronic or paper, on mail shots, at seminars and in any printed advertising you do. Have it on your business card, your headed paper, on every e-mail you send.

Print it on flyers, on all your brochures and literature, on your business stamp, on the back of application forms, on special marketing bulletins you send out to clients. Put it everywhere. The more you promote your web address the more people will go to your site and the more likely you are to do business.

You can also advertise and of course with a web site the best place to advertise is on the Internet. There are three ways to advertise: two are often free and the other can be more expensive than prime time television advertising.

I'll deal with the cheap versions first;

Search Engine Registration

You need to list your web site with every search engine that is likely to be used by your clients. There are about a dozen important ones. Your web host will also usually provide a registration service and that is definitely worth considering.

Alternatively you can get software which will do the job, one that I've used is called ExploIT. This is often available with free CDs on magazines and you can get this from: http://www.exploit.com.

However you handle the search engine registration do regularly check the main search engines manually to see that you at least appear with a search on your business name. It can take up to a month for you to appear in the system.

Most registration requires that you provide:

A brief description of your business, this means brief. Sometimes the first 250 characters, sometimes 50 or a 100 words. Get the description of what you do down to the first short sentence and then expand, that way you get the key information into every search.

Keywords, usually at least 20 keywords and phrases that people searching for your business might use. Make the first 20 the important ones, some search engines allow more. Try some searches yourself and see what turns up to get some ideas

Directory Listings

There are a number of private directories like www.moneyworld.co.uk and www.find.co.uk which are electronic consumer finance magazines. You should clearly make sure you are registered with these.

There are a number of other directories worth considering. For example you may find there is a directory for your local community. Virtual Manchester is a good example. Many of these sites actively promote local businesses.

Like all marketing, it's a matter of searching and identifying the best places to be. Have a look at where other financial advisers and financial services organisations are listed? It will take some time to build an effective strategy for networking your site but it's worth the effort. Make sure that you have a section of your site which promotes other local businesses, so that you can facilitate reciprocal listings.

You can find more information and ideas on promoting your web site at my web site - www.arundel.co.uk/abc

Advertising

Some web sites receive an enormous number of hits every day. Good examples are Netscape and Microsoft which are the default home settings in millions of browsers. As both web sites are accessed well over a million times a day, the cost of advertising is high. But web advertising does work. Del computers advertises extensively on web sites.

On a smaller scale Garrison Discount Investments advertises regularly at both MoneyWorld and Find and get 150 enquiries a week. However there is little hard research and no long-term track record with Internet advertising, so there is a degree of trial and error.

There are a number of electronic newspapers like The Telegraph, The Times, The Financial Times now running on the Internet which carry advertising. The local community sites also carry advertising as do Electronic Yellow Pages and Thompsons.

However, it is important before you start advertising your web site, to remember no one does business on the Internet by accident, it is done by design. People who go to your web site go there because they've decided to. It is important that your site is attractive and interactive, and that you can cope effectively with the enquiries. Let's see now how you can achieve that.

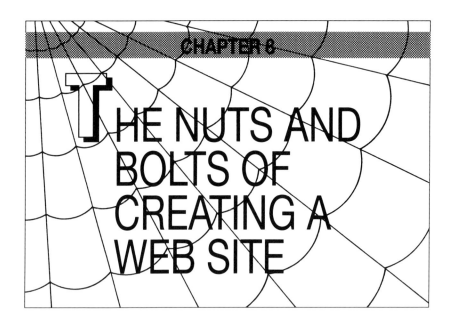

CHAPTER 6

THE NUTS AND BOLTS OF CREATING A WEB SITE

At the beginning of this book I said don't panic. There's no need to rush to build a web site. Although the progress of the Internet has been dramatic we are still at the beginning.

If you plan to be a financial adviser for the next ten years one thing is inevitable, you will be marketing electronically. It may not be called the Internet then and as to what tools and techniques we will use to represent ourselves electronically, I can only guess.

Web sites won't look much like they do today. They will be more like television programmes with sound, music, video and on-line interaction. Your clients won't phone, they'll use a Personal Communications Workstation or whatever we call it. And the tools on your computer will enable you to do things which today require advanced programming techniques and multi-media studios.

Does this sound fantastic? In 1969 I was issued with a calculator, a cylindrical machine requiring no batteries or mains power. I pushed a few levers and turned a small handle at the side. A £200 pound state of the art pocket calculator. For the equivalent price today I can buy a Pentium II 333 MHz with 128 Mb of RAM, a 14 Gb hard drive, a 21" monitor, a 32 bit sound system, full screen MPEG video, 56 Kbs modem and loaded with all the software needed to run a business. Just to put that into perspective that desktop computer, which I can buy for just over £2000, has more disk space than the entire insurance industry in 1969.

Don't underestimate how much things can change, and it's because things will change so much that you need to start building a web site today. You need to begin learning how to use the electronic tools I've talked about in this book.

You won't need to become a programmer. I'm not and don't need to be. You will need to understand how to put a web site together. You will need to be aware of the tools and techniques available. You will need to understand how to communicate electronically with your clients, prospects, staff and other professionals in the industry. You will need to keep yourself at the forefront of business developments.

If you do, you will discover ways to do business that previously you were unaware of. Opportunities will present themselves that unless you are involved you simply would not understand. My objective with this chapter is not to teach you how to design a web page, but to help you to understand how to develop a web marketing strategy that supports your business objectives.

Selecting a web host

The first thing you will need, is a web host. This is where you will site your web page so that people can access it 24 hours a day. Unless you are a company of significant size with IT resources, I suggest that you don't even think about using your own server. You will need an expensive leased line, a fast network computer and fairly expensive server software.

I also recommend that you avoid "Free Web Sites". I discussed these in Chapter 2 and I don't think they create the kind of image that you will want to present.

A good web host service will cost about £150 to £300 a year for about 5 to 10 Mb of disk space, depending upon what other services are provided. You are unlikely to need more space than that. There are a number of other things to check out with a web host. Some are essential, some are good to have if you can get them.

Virtual Web Space and Domain Registration

You will want to use your own domain name, which means that you want "virtual web" space. This is essential. Although it is easy to register you own domain, it can make things easier if your host provides the service, but make sure that you own the domain name.

Location of the Web Host

You can have a web host anywhere in the world, but if most visitors to your site are likely to be local, it can make sense to use a local host. To reach your web site visitors have to pass through a number of routers and these are the bottlenecks. The further the host is away from your visitors, the greater the number of "hops" to reach your server and the slower the connection. You might also check how many "hops" to the backbone, the fast information superhighway. More than 3 or 4 and your visitors might experience a slow connection.

Technical Support

You will need technical support at some time and you will want to be able to speak to someone and not have to send an e-mail message. Check on hours of availability of support and what charges if any are made. General technical support should be free.

Size of the Company

Make sure you are dealing with a full-time web hosting company. It doesn't take many staff to run a web hosting company, but you don't really want one that's a part-time business. If they are also an Internet Service Provider, that is a good sign.

Access Logs and Reports

Make sure the web host can provide you with good information on who is coming to your site and what pages they are viewing. This will not give you e-mail addresses, but will tell you your hit rates and identify what is popular.

Promotion and Design Services

At the very least it is helpful if the host company can help you register your site with the main search engines. Even if you are planning to produce your web site yourself, having a web host who can provide design services will be useful. There will be some things that need more skill than you have time to learn, and you need someone to turn to.

Client References

Most web hosts promote their list of clients, so there should be no problem in identifying a number of their clients you can speak to about the service. Check out some of the sites and see if there are any delays. Look at some sites they have designed, preferably in the financial services industry, and talk to the clients about the service they receive.

Microsoft FrontPage Extensions

If you plan to use Microsoft FrontPage, and I recommend that you do, you need a "web host" who has a FrontPage server extensions on their server. We will look at FrontPage later. The web space may cost more, but it is worth it if you want ease of maintenance of your site.

Secure Server

You may be requesting sensitive information from clients, and you may even decide to sell some contracts on-line and therefore want to take money electronically. A secure server encrypts information and therefore provides peace of mind.

CGI Scripts

CGI means Common Gateway Interface. It is a way of providing interactivity on a site. If you are using FrontPage, you will have less need for CGI scripts, but there are some things you might want to do that needs them. Some hosts do not allow them. The best option is a host who has a library of scripts and also provides support it writing and incorporating them into your web site.

Database Access

If you want to provide visitors with access to information in a database, you will probably need technical help. If your web host has database search facilities and can provide technical support this might be very useful for you.

Auto-Responders/Mail Responders

Not all web hosts provide mail responders/auto-responders, especially in the UK. If you plan to them as part of you marketing strategy it would be helpful if your web host provides them, although not essential. You can obtain this service from a specialist autoresponder host.

Everything you need to know about HTML

All web pages are created using HTML which stands for HyperText Mark-up Language. It's a simple page formatting language created by Tim Berners-Lee when he worked in Switzerland at CERN. It comprises a series of instructions to a web browser on how to present a page of text, and where to position graphics and other multimedia applications.

When I put together my first web page I did learn some basic HTML. It took a few days of quite hard work trying to remember all the different commands and then success. But three months later I could hardly remember any of it.

I soon quickly discovered that tools have been developed for people like me who don't want to learn and remember HTML. If you do have a "geek streak" in you there are hundreds of books on the topic. But with so many software packages available to enable you to produce a web page without knowing a single line of HTML code, I recommend you wait to see if your really do want to learn it.

Web editors

A web editor is a software package designed to help people to create web pages. There are two types.

The first is designed for those people who do understand HTML, but don't want the bother of typing in all the commands. These web editors automatically create the correct code and you just fill in the text. The problem is that you cannot see what the page will look like until you view it in a browser.

The second type of web editor is a WYSIWYG editor, which stands for What You See Is What You Get. These web editors operate like a word processor or a desk top publisher. You create the web page the way you want it to look and the editor produces the HTML code in the background for you to up load onto your web host.

There are three web editors available on the disk which came with this book, and another I recommend that is not on the disk.

Microsoft FrontPage Express

FrontPage express comes as part of Microsoft Internet Explorer 4. You can open it from the start menu or from within Internet Explorer 4 by clicking on the 'edit button' on the tool bar. At any time while browsing a web page, click 'edit' and FrontPage Express will open the page you are viewing in the editor. You can then edit the page and save it to disk, which enables you to plagiarise other web pages.

Let me add a note of caution here about copyright. Copying HTML code and modifying it has been accepted practice on the Internet since its days as a free system.

109

Now that it's much more commercial, you should be cautious. Everything on the Internet is copyright by its author and you do need permission to use it, which is often freely given in exchange for your agreement to promote the source. You should be safe if all you are doing is copying a general page design and not the text and graphics, but if in doubt, ask.

Netscape Composer

If the Netscape Browser is your preference, there is a similar WYSIWYG editor with Netscape Communicator 4.0, called Composer. You can find it via the start menu and can design quite complex web pages without needing to know any HTML code.

Hotdog

On the disk you'll find another very popular web editor Hotdog Pro. I will admit to not having used Hotdog other than a brief look some time ago, my personal preference being for the full version of FrontPage. The reviews for Hotdog are extremely good.

Microsoft FrontPage 98

FrontPage 98 is not on the disk, but is the web editor I recommend if you are planning to build and maintain your own web site. No other web editor comes even close. It is part of Microsoft Office although supplied separately.

Apart from being a good WYSIWYG editor, its other main value is FrontPage Explorer, a web site design and management package. This enables you visually organise the structure of your web site, to check all the links to make sure they're working and to edit your pages directly on the server, as well as on your PC. This makes it relatively easy to modify your site content on a day to day basis.

FrontPage will take time to master in the same way that you needed to master Word or PowerPoint. But once you understand the product, it is easy to use both as an editor and as a manager and certainly a product you or a competent member of staff would have no real problem using.

Why not just have a go?

I suggest you have a go at designing a few pages. They're easy to produce once you have browsed a few pages to get the idea. Microsoft and Netscape have some on-line support and tutorials and you will find links to other tutorial at the Primex Web Site. Why not grab a page from the Internet that you like and edit it or try to design one from scratch.

At my web site at http://www.arundelco.uk/abc you'll find a few tips and hints about using FrontPage Express and a simple web site you are quite welcome to copy, edit and use for your own.

Poor Richards web site

Quite by accident, I came across a book entitled Poor Richards Web Site by an English author called Peter Kent, who now lives in Colorado. You can understand how the name attracted me. It is one of the best books I have ever bought, and is undoubtedly the best there is right now on helping anyone build a business orientated web site, without needing to become a "geek" in the process.

This practical, down to earth book covers everything you

need to know and along with FrontPage 98 is a must if you are planning to build and maintain your own web site.

You can find details at http://www.poorrichard.com and the impressive thing about Peter Kent's business is that if you order the book on-line, even though it has to come from Colorado, it will arrive within about 48 hours and the postage is very reasonable. Peter Kent writes about the importance of delivering fast service off the Internet and he walks his talk.

The book is also now available in the UK, and as it is now on the best-seller lists in the US, I suspect that it may be available in most bookshops. You should still check out the web site, because there is a wealth of additional useful information there.

DIY versus web design services

The alternative to building your own site is to employ the services of a design agency. There are hundreds to chose from, some good and some not so good. At my web site I will be building a directory of recommended web designers who have experience in building good sites for Financial Advisers, based upon feedback I get from advisers, so pop in and have a look, or even let me know about your experiences.

The advantage of using a web design firm is that you don't need to get involved in the technicalities of building a web site. You brief the designers and they'll produce the site. However a word of caution. Having looked at many of the web sites it's quite clear there are design companies with a goal to just get you on the net with a site, whether it works or not.

The only reason for creating a web site is because it is part of your overall marketing strategy and is designed to achieve specific business objectives. Putting a business card on the web does more harm than good.

At the time of writing this book one company that stands out is WebScape at http://www.webscape.co.uk who, as I mentioned in the previous chapter, have already designed and hosted a number of IFA sites including Garrison Discount Investments and the IFA Association. Not all of their clients web sites get my vote as great web sites, but they are definitely taking things in the right direction.

The Exchange will be providing a bespoke design service for larger IFAs later in 1998 and a template service to smaller firms at the same time. I will be looking at the Exchange in more detail in Chapter 10. One advantage with the Exchange will be its access to client support services, including the possibility of on-line policy valuations.

If you plan to take the DIY route you will need to buy a book such as Poor Richards Web Site, you need to become familiar with web editing and management tools such as FrontPage 98 and then use some of the design recommendations that we're now going to cover.

If you're going to chose the agency route, the rest of this chapter will give you a better idea on how to brief a design agency and make sure that they deliver what you want. If you can negotiate a fixed fee for the design of a web site that would be the best position. The greatest danger of anything to do with software development is that it always seems to take twice as long and costs twice as much as was originally planned.

And this is not always the fault of the programmers. First, the brief is often fuzzy and is then interpreted technically, missing the business objectives. Second, clients often change their mind as things develop and all changes take time and cost money.

The clearer you can make your brief the better. Get some examples of the sort of features you are looking for. A good web designer could cost £400 to £500 a day, and programmers

£250 a day upwards depending upon skill.   Whatever their price, check their work, get some references and talk to their clients.

There are package deals available including design of the site, half a dozen pages including a form to capture visitor information and feed it back, registration of a domain name and registration of the site at most of the leading search engines. WebScape for example charge about £1000 for that package.

The cost of design will focus your mind on the value and benefits of having a web site. But before you think it's cheaper to do it yourself, remember they can probably produce web pages three to four times faster than you can. As a financial advisor, your time costs at least £100 per hour, so it may work out a lot cheaper to get someone who knows what they're doing to create your site.

At the end of the day it's down to personal preferences. If you have a bit of a "Geek Streak," and I admit to that, you might be tempted to have a go yourself, but just watch the time and the knowledge requirements.   There may come a point when you need to make the decision to bring in someone who knows the technology and get on with the business of marketing financial services electronically.

Organising information

Lets start with an overview of how you're going to organise your web site. And as the web is a communications tool, it makes sense to look at some basic principles of communication used by journalists.

Get Attention!

First, You've got to get attention and quickly. It's the same with all marketing. Good headlines or graphics are the key. You probably have about five seconds to get attention from the point at which visitors arrive at your web site. That means the web site has to come up quickly, grab interest, pull people in and make them want to find out more about what's within. But that doesn't mean lots and lots of whizzy graphics. People come to your web site because they're looking for content, looking for answers, looking for solutions. They need to feel very quickly that this could be the right place.

Convert Attention to Interest

Having grabbed their attention, you've got about 30 seconds to convert that into interest. But with a web site you have something extra that's not available with paper - interaction. What you need to do within about 30 seconds of a visitor arriving at your site, is stimulate them to take some action, to do something that takes them deeper into your web.

This is why Chapter 7 on marketing your web site is placed ahead of this chapter on designing it. You must understand your market, have appropriate messages to suit them and provide the kind of content that you know will draw people in and encourage them to want to find out more about what's inside.

Structure of a web site

When I'm designing a web site I tend to work with diagrams, which is one of the reasons I like FrontPage. It enables me to start designing the structure of the site with a simple organisation tree.

Every site is going to be different, so what I will do now is present a few ideas of the basics that I have seen work, and some general considerations you need to bear in mind when creating the structure.

The home page

The first and the most important page of your web site is the home page. This is where it all starts. This is the page at which people arrive when they type your URL into the address/location field of their browser. It is your shop front and the first impression clients and prospects will get of your business.

This is where getting their attention and converting it to interest happens. Don't make the home page too big, visitors should hardly need to scroll the page. You may have noticed that some web pages are very long. Most experience shows that people don't like to scroll. They would much rather click and go to another page, which also encourages interaction. Provide small bites of information and then encourage action.

Because it's important to get people quickly involved, it is important that you do not load your home page with enormous graphics that take forever to download. If you have to wait, it's usually not worth it, so keep your home page simple.

Some of the most successful sites make their home page a newsletter. Not with long articles, but with headlines and short, very short paragraphs, quick and easy to read. An up date on what's happening in the market-place, news and views. Visitors can scan to pick up some ideas. If an item grabs their attention, they can click on the 'headline' to look deeper.

At the same time you need a site map. Create a menu with a series of buttons that enable people to move deeper into your site. Not so many that it becomes confusing, but enough to make it clear where to go and what to do.

The image of your home page is really a matter of personal taste. I don't like cereal box designs and I don't like overbearing backgrounds, but you have to design for what you like. The more you use the Internet, the more you'll come across sites you like and designs you can emulate.

Site navigation controls

Make it easy for people to find their way around your site. A lot of visitors who come to your site will be new, and not have a good understanding of the basic navigation controls we covered in Chapter 4. Whilst most people will come to your site as a result of typing in your URL, or being directed to your home page, some will come from a link at another site which may direct them to the middle of your site. Coming via a search engine means an even greater possibility of that happening.

So make sure you provide good navigation on every page. One of the worst sites I have ever seen provided just one navigation control; a button enabling me to move forward to the next page. It was like a bad slide presentation, pages of text and forward controls. I never did make it to the end.

All of your second level pages should have an overall site navigation panel if possible. This can be a series of buttons down the side or along the top of the page. Of course, if the page scrolls down, the navigation controls will disappear and you have two options for overcoming this. You can either put the navigation controls at the bottom of the page as well as the top, or you can use "Frames."

Using "Frames" means that instead of just having a single page, you effectively put two, three or four pages of different sizes altogether within one view. So you could have a banner across the top, you could have an index or menu down the left and the actual body of your page to the right in the largest of the panels. Make sure you don't use too many frames as it can look very complex and confusing.

The downside to frames is that not all browsers support them. However as Internet Explorer 3 and 4 and Netscape Navigator 3 and 4, do support frames and about 80% of people seem now to be using one of these browsers, my guess is you'd be pretty safe.

The best way to check your navigation controls is to get someone to look at the site to give you feedback on how easy it is to move around and what they would have found more useful and helpful.

Graphics

I mentioned graphics earlier and there is no doubt that you should use graphics because they add a great deal of interest to the page. Graphics can be used as links, and animated graphics add action to the page. But it is easy to over do it and make the whole site a dog's dinner. The creation of graphics is a specialist field and it is in this area that I tend to turn for help from someone experienced.

Most advisers who attempted to do their own desktop publishing a few years ago, when it was all the rage, found the same problem. Whilst the tools are there to enable us to deliver good graphical content, it needs someone who has basic design skills and an artistic flair to do a good job with the tools.

Fortunately products like FrontPage 98 and Hotdog come with graphic support, FrontPage 98 in particular has a feature called "themes". This comprises a library of professionally designed web templates from which you can select. These are on the same principle as the templates provided with Word and PowerPoint. The FrontPage design themes includes headings, graphics, buttons and layouts, and can be modified quite easily.

Most web graphics use one of two graphic standards, GIFs or JPEGs. GIFs are normally used for bright coloured images using up to sixteen colours, e.g. small icons and animations. JPEGs are used for the photographic images. Both are compressed image files which means that they take up much less space than the image would normally use. However they can still be quite large and often take 30 seconds to a minute download, which can be a real problem when there are a number of graphics on a page.

There are a few things you can do to avoid long waits for graphics. When a graphic image has been downloaded to your computer it is stored in a temporary file called the "cache". If the same graphic is used on another page the computer will reuse the image from its cache, which loads immediately. So when you design pages, try to reuse graphics as much as possible

When images are inserted into a web page you can provide an alternative text title. You will have often noticed when a graphic starts to load, a frame appears first and then the graphic is revealed in a slow wipe down. If there are a number of graphics, giving a brief description of what the picture is, helps the user to see what's coming.

By seeing the descriptions visitors can make a decision about whether they want to wait or go onto the next page. The buttons which are hypertext links to other pages are graphic and it's often these that we're waiting to see. If the name of the button appears quickly, the visitor can see the link and click without having to wait for the graphic. Make it easy for visitors to use your site and they'll come back.

The whizzy bits

Some of the graphics are not straight forward, and some components on web sites are quite complex. It might be a programme that operates a graphic or scrolls text. You will hear about CGI Scripts, Java and Java Scripts, Active X Controls,

Shockwave Animations, Shockwave Movies, Dynamic HTML etc.

Most of the expensive, sophisticated sites use an abundance of these utilities. Some simpler elements are available in FrontPage 98. Some are only supported by the latest browsers. A number of the advanced techniques that work with Internet explorer won't work with Netscape and vice versa.

To be honest they are not essential. You need an interesting informative site that draws your clients in, gets them to stay and hopefully interact with you. If you want to make it highly entraining as well, you can, but it will cost you. Either you will need to employ someone with programming skills, or you will need to invest time to learn them.

Unless you have the time or the money, I recommend you stick to a good basic web site that can be supported by the majority of browsers. Remember *"the pioneers get the arrows the settlers get the land!"*. It's probably a good idea to let the pioneers play with the new technologies while they're expensive and wait for the tools that will enable the rest of us to be able to use them at the click of a 'mouse' in a years time.

Capturing information

To add business value to your web activities, the most important thing you can do is to capture visitor names and e-mail addresses, which you can then use in one-to-one electronic marketing, as we discussed in Chapter 5. You can't force people to give you information, but if you ask, most will provide it.

You can do this in one of two ways. The simplest approach is to use a request for information form. On clicking an appropriate button visitors will be presented with an easy to complete enquiry form requesting their name, address, e-mail, telephone number etc. In addition you then provide either a free format text box in which they enter brief details of what they want, or a list of options from which to select.

The easier you make the form to complete the better. Use pop-up menus where possible so that visitors do not have to type things in, but can select from a list and send the message to you. That form will populate a database or an e-mail, which will then be forwarded to you so that you can respond.

This type of interaction is very easy to create with FrontPage 98. If you are not using FrontPage then it becomes a little more complex and you need to use a CGI script, which are small programs on the host computer. Your web host may have an appropriate script, but I recommend that you use a web design company to help you. Your Web Host may be able to provide this service. They are not complex but it does take time to learn how to write them and correct your early mistakes

The second approach to capturing e-mail addresses is to make a part of your site private. Perhaps for clients only or just to require registration in order to use it. This is a technique used by a number of insurance companies and on-line newspapers.

Again this is a simple thing to set up using FrontPage but requires CGI scripts otherwise. If you are briefing a web designer tell them that as soon as possible after people enter your site you want to try and capture their e-mail address in the most unobtrusive way possible. They might register for your monthly newsletter, they would need to register and submit information if they were requesting a quote or a personalised report.

Think about what you could provide your prospects and clients that might be of interest or value in exchange for providing you with their e-mail address. It's a fair exchange most people are prepared to make.

If you decide to create a private section at your site you will need to introduce a validation process and agree or issue a user name and password. In future, to gain access to this part of your site, clients will need to provide their user name and password which will be checked against a database before allowing them admission.

If you go to The Norwich Union web site, and http://www.norwich-union.co.uk and click on 'IFA First', you will discover that you need to register and obtain a user name and password. The same applies at the Scottish Provident site and Standard Life, both of whom have IFA only sections.

One of the advantages of a client or members only section is that it creates an air of exclusivity and increases the perceived value of the information within, especially if you have to "qualify" for membership, i.e. being a client.

It is important to promote the value of becoming a member in the public section of the site, and create a sense that "you are definitely missing something important, if you are not a member". Encourage visitors to want to become your clients in order to gain access to the exclusive and valuable information available within.

Make it personal

One of the things I don't see enough of on IFA web sites is an attempt to make the site personal.

You're communicating with people, developing an on-line one-to-one relationship. Brigid Benson at Gaeia does just this. A small picture of herself, click on the picture and it takes you to a brief biography of her work with women in business and in the ethical and environment fields with such organisations as Friends of the Earth.

But why not go beyond this. Photographs of your office, the people in the office, meetings or corporate hospitality events with clients, involvement in local community or charity events. Create a clear sense that when dealing with your firm, clients are dealing with real people, not technology.

You need to create a high-tech high-touch environment. When visitors come to your site don't just provide bland information about financial services, introduce them to, or remind them of, the people who will be looking after their financial future.

The Internet has great scope for this. You can create a audio welcome greeting, even a narrated PowerPoint presentation is easy to produce. You simply create the PowerPoint presentation in Office 97, narrate using a microphone plugged into your PC and then using a software product called Real Presenter convert it into a file that will play over the Internet. You can see an example and get more details at my web site.

Consider how you can make your site more fun and a bit more personal. Let visitors see who they are doing business with, while remaining professional an informative.

News views and tips

In Chapter 5 we looked in some depth at the value of newsletters, and I suggested then that one way to handle this is to create a newsletter on your web site and then e-mail a short summary with links to clients and prospects to attract them to the site.

Another useful feature might be to create special bulletins or help guides on significant events. Keep an archive on previous newsletters. Develop a library of business, investment or retirement tips. Keep your eye on the national and financial press to see what the topics of the day are.   Instead of complaining about poor advice in the press, create your own news comment.   Pick up on key stories and write your own personal finance column.

Looking at your business specialisation and the profile of your average clients should give you lots of clues as to how to organise the news view and tips within your site to attract regular visitors.   This is your chance to become a regular columnist.

Product and service guides

Most current IFA web sites have a list of products.   Life Assurance, Pensions, Unit Trusts, Mortgages etc.   Click on any of these links and you are taken to a page which tells you what they are and why you should buy some.   The successful sites don't provide electronic product brochures, they provide electronic product guides.   Your guide to PEPS or ISAs, your guide to retirement planning etc.   Make them informative, helpful, non-technical guides and follow the format of a needs interview rather than a product sales presentation.

Look at the information direct companies are providing to their clients, or the sales aids your own company or other life offices provide as sales support.   This is the sort of information which could well be converted into attractive interactive web pages to provide helpful and useful consumer advice, and encourage visitors to want more information.

Have a look at http://www.mortgages-on-line.co.uk. When you arrive at their home page rather than the usual list of technical mortgage options and interest rates, they offer some very simple options.   First Time Buyer, Home Movers, Buying to Let.

The options relate to the prospective clients current need.

They click on the button that will lead to a solution, not one that adds to the dilemma by providing more complex information and decisions. Follow the links and you find helpful articles, calculators and of course a simple enquiry form.

I am not suggesting that this or any of the web sites I have singled out for praise could not be improved, they certainly can. Mortgages-on-line has a couple of monster pages of text that I think are far too long. The point is that they draw people in and they focus on needs. They are trying to help people, not sell to them.

This may seem obvious, but when you design your web site, please, please, don't forget your selling skills 101 training, it's just as important on-line as face-to-face. Organise your site to appeal to the interest and needs of your target market.

Calculators

Calculators are a very useful addition to any Financial Advisers web site. These are actually small programs, usually written in a language called JAVA that are run from the web page. Quite simply they allow the visitor to calculate important financial events, the cost of moving home, the cost of a mortgage, income required for retirement etc. The sort of simple needs analysis calculations you might conduct on a laptop computer at the point-of-sale.

These are simple, interactive and give the client useful personalised information. You can see examples of calculators at both Gaeia and Mortgages on-line. It you are interested in adding a couple of calculators to your site you might like to have a look at Ian Dicksons site http://www.moneyweb.co.uk where he has two JAVA script calculators available. You might need some technical help in incorporating them into your site.

I have come across a huge number of them in the US, but

125

they are not appropriate for the UK and they are extremely expensive, but as I become aware of calculators you can obtain and use in the UK, I will provide more information at my web site.

Links page

There is a bit of disagreement over the value of providing links to other sites at your web site. Some people believe that all you do when you provide links to other web sites is to encourage visitors to leave your site and go somewhere else.

I don't entirely agree with this view. One of the things I want to achieve with my web site and one of the things you need to achieve with yours, is to get people to regularly come through the site on their way to wherever they are going.

The problem with the electronic world compared to a shop front, is that no one actually passes by. On the Internet people have to make a decision to come to you. Now if I can get people to pass through my web site frequently, then I can put up notices and promotional offers, so that they might think, "ooh, what's that? I think I'll stop and have a look". This happens all the time to me when I go to the MSN http://www.msn.co.uk site which is a great example of how to capture passing trade.

The links page is one way of achieving this. I've created a fairly extensive links page specifically designed for Financial Advisers to help you find your way around and reach sites that might be of interest. Unlike MoneyWorld and Find, I am not setting out to reach consumers with the site, so the links are mostly business to business information and marketing related sites.

I sell Hi-Tech, Hi-Touch Selling, Marketing and Presentation Skills Services so I need people visiting my site who are involved in sales and marketing. I will unashamedly tell you that at my links page you will come across advertising and promotion items and you will be encouraged to join the members section of my site for which you will be asked to pay a modest fee.

Think about the kind of links that will be valuable to your clients and prospects. They might be interested in information they can get from the Inland Revenue or HMSO. They might be interested in city and financial news, they might be interested in business information services. Perhaps you socialise with your clients, so they might be interested in golf, football or other sporting information.

If, like many Financial Advisers, your business is focused in the local community, then make your site is a centre for local community and business information. Make sure there are links from your site to important sites carrying local information, like the Chamber of Commerce and speak to the webmasters of these sites and see if you can get a reciprocal listing helping to promote your site. Become an active member of the local virtual community. Promote other peoples businesses and in turn encourage them to promote yours.

The most important group of people to promote on your site are of course, your clients. Don't just provide links, provide recommendations and summaries of what they do. It is a powerful testimonial to your business, if you have a strong client list of local businesses. Do check that you can mention them as clients, but make it clear you are promoting their businesses.

Get the networking bug and you will see hit rates on your site dramatically increase.

Discussion forums

Discussion forums, which are like private newsgroups, make a useful addition to any web site, because they encourage interaction. Everyone is encouraged to post comments or ask questions on your electronic bulletin board and anyone can respond to those messages. You should moderate the discussion, providing topics for discussion and answering questions, but encourage others to contribute as much as possible.

You can have a lively debate on the pros and cons of the latest budget or the impact of new legislation, or your thoughts on local issues, in fact anything you as a group feel inclined to discuss. You should also remove posts you feel are inappropriate. Start with a single general discussion group and then as themes develop, create a specialist topic discussion group.

Discussion groups can grow quite large, and as the information might enable visitors to gain significantly without being a client, I recommend that this is always a private area for clients and registered visitors.

On-line seminars

With my background as a trainer and professional speaker, I have become very interested in the delivery of training and seminar material over the Internet. You will see within my web site on-line training features in the form of narrated PowerPoint presentations, on-line books and interactive training sessions.

Over the next few years, we are going to see significant developments in this area and in particular the concept of delivering on-line business seminars either live or recorded.

Many intermediaries use seminars as a means of promoting business and creating referrals, and now this can be done on-line.

The technology that has made this possible is streamed audio and video. To play an audio or video file directly off the Internet you need some additional software and the most popular is Real Player which you can obtain free from http://www.real.com.

You can present a live on-line seminar at a specific time and although relatively easy to do, this does require your web host to have a Real Server, a software system to support live broadcasting. It can also be a little impractical getting people to log on at a specific time.

Much easier is to stream a narrated PowerPoint presentation, so that anyone can click on it and listen to the seminar when they want to. You could do the same with a video presentation, but you will experience problems with video quality.

To stream a PowerPoint presentation, simply create the presentation in PowerPoint 97, and record a narration directly onto your PC. You can either record the entire presentation as say a half-hour seminar, or you can break it into three or four shorter separate presentations, which I think is a better approach.

You will need some software to convert the presentation into a streamed presentation called Real Presenter, which costs $29 from http://www.real.com. Once this software is installed, converting the PowerPoint presentation to a streamed file is achieved by simply clicking on a 'menu item' in PowerPoint.

Once the file is linked to a web page, a visitor simply clicks on 'the link', the PowerPoint presentation opens and the narration begins to play. They will need Real Player so you should also insert a link on your page to the Real Player software. This way your visitor can quickly download the player, which is a once only requirement and takes about 10 minutes.

I believe this will add significantly to your site. It is easy to deploy, it is interactive, provides useful information and is personal - it is you speaking. Some messages are easier to put across using slides and voice than by trying to get someone to read the topic and look at diagrams. If you are interested in doing this, have a look at the presentation on my web site.

If you are unfamiliar with PowerPoint, it is a slide making software package, which comes with Microsoft Office and you need the latest version Office 97. Another feature of PowerPoint, is the ability to create a slide presentation on-line without narration, so that people can browse through them. You will find that I have used this in a number of instances on my site where you will find more detailed suggestions for using PowerPoint.

Planning and research first

Of necessity this chapter has been an overview of what you can do with your web pages. I've been working on the Internet now for four years and I'm learning something new every day. The best way to learn what you can do with your site is to regularly use the Internet and see what other people are doing.

Start by drawing up a plan for how your web site might appear. I found it was a good idea to draw a diagram, a sort of organisation chart starting at the home page and opening out down through the other threads in the site.

With this chart I then began searching the Internet looking at what competitors and other businesses were doing. As I looked I noted and bookmarked pages to create a resource that I was then able to use for ideas and even templates for my pages.

I said at the beginning of the book that there is no rush, it is a learning process. My objective with this book has been to help you get on-line, understand the tools for managing information on-line, and start to use them in building your on-line strategy.

In the next chapter, I am going draw together the threads of the book and summarise them in 10 simple tips, which will help you to build an effective profitable strategy for marketing on the Internet.

CHAPTER 9

10 TIPS FOR EFFECTIVE INTERNET MARKETING

If you are new to the Internet and have read the book this far, I wouldn't be surprised if your head were swimming. It's a huge amount to take in. It took me about six months before I felt comfortable using the Internet. It took even longer to learn how to use the technologies as business tools and I'm still learning.

The most important lesson I have learnt is that the basics of marketing still apply even when everything is in a state of constant change. I see a lot of mistakes and in every case the reason is a departure from basic marketing principles.

So where do you go from here? You are on-line, you have surfed the net, you have started sending e-mail and you have started planning your web site. But it still seems a bit complex. To help simplify everything I have summarised the book into 10 simple tips to keep your journey into marketing in cyberspace on track.

Beyond these basic tips there are no limits. It is a new frontier. An opportunity for everyone to expand their creativity. Be prepared to dare to be different, to step outside of what you know and are familiar with and enter the 21st Century

Tip 1 - Think People not Technology

This is the most important tip of all. No matter how sophisticated the technology, the Internet is a global communications system. Its overriding purpose is to enable people to communicate with each other more effectively.

Use the technology to enhance relationships. Look for ways to use the power of Internet networking. Look at your current sales and marketing and consider how you can use technology to improve the relationships with your prospects and clients.

Tip 2 - Use the Internet Regularly

Handling information electronically is different to handling information physically. You can flip through pages of text, scanning with your eyes, but searching through screens of web pages is much slower and more cumbersome.

Using the Internet regularly puts you at the receiving end of communications, seeing things as your clients will. What do you like on the net, what do you dislike? What gets your attention, what turns you off, what entertains you? In this new frontier success comes by being creative and innovative, and remembering that we are experiencing a communications revolution, not a technology revolution.

Tip 3 - Buy a Good Domain Name

URLs are unique. Once the name you want has gone, that's it, you've lost it. Check out www.webscape.co.uk or www.alldomains.com for the current availability of the name you want, and buy it now. They will hold the name for you until you are ready to use it. Alternatively you can ask your local ISP or your Web Host to sort the name for you, but make sure that you will own the name. Chose a UK top level domain name unless you want to promote your services internationally.

Tip 4 - Clearly Define Your Market

There are probably about 100 million people using the Internet and none of them will even visit your web site unless you convince them to. And if you are successful in bringing large numbers of prospective clients to your site, could you cope? People using the Internet expect fast response,. If they request information they expect it immediately or at worst within 48 hours.

Do you want to build a remote trading business dealing with hundreds of enquiries throughout the UK or even across the world every day? Or are you looking to develop a local market? Do you want your web site to generate leads or service existing clients? Who are you trying to reach with the Internet and why?

Decide what sort of products you want to sell. Create a profile of your ideal client. Talk to your clients and find out what they expect from a web site and then go about producing it. If the site is popular with clients, it helps to secure your relationship and will become a source of referral business.

Try to find a unique slant to your marketing. Perhaps you specialise in some particular area of business, ethical

135

investments, portfolio management, mortgages, retirement planning, financial planning, discount investments. Perhaps you specialise in a particular market, offshore investments, corporate and business clients, medical market, a geographical location or specific industry. Perhaps there is a common hobby or interest amongst your clients, golf, football, sailing, health and fitness,

Make your site different and appeal to the people you want to attract. Provide useful services at your web site not just a catalogue of products, for example an advice service to small businesses.

Tip 5 - Build an Electronic Communications Database

Get into the habit of collecting e-mail and web addresses. You need your clients web addresses so that you can keep up-to-date with what they are doing in their businesses. You'll be surprised at how many business opportunities you can identify as you start to look through web sites.

More important is the clients e-mail address. Everyone who uses the Internet has an e-mail address, it comes automatically with every account. Make sure your web page requests e-mail addresses before giving out valuable information, or create a members area which requires registration.

Knowing their e-mail address you can mount an electronic marketing campaign, provided you observe the simple rules of netiquette. Keep e-mail short, send a link to more information on a web site or let them request the longer e-mail report. Make sure you have permission to send e-mail promotions.

The secret to success in electronic marketing is using the technology to build the relationships not to push products. Make sure you organise your e-mail addresses into appropriate groups as you would with any direct marketing list, don't send information to people that is irrelevant

Tip 6 - Send Electronic Newsletters Regularly

The idea of building an e-mail database is to give you a list of people who are unlikely to be offended when you write. Create an electronic newsletter, but make it different from ordinary newsletters. Monday morning investment tips, business improvement tips, active retirement ideas, better business communications, tax saving tips, even improving your golf game.

Study your target market, what will interest them, what will get their attention, what will get them reading the newsletter? Add some humour, a fantastic fact or an odd news report. Make sure you include a link to appropriate pages at your web site. What sort of information coming regularly to your e-mail box, would you look forward to reading?

Make sure you include your web address in your newsletter, and point to new and recently updated pages. For example you might do a short tip on a current investment opportunity, with a link to your on-line investment newsletter or investment report so that they just click 'the link' to take them straight to your web page.

Tip 7 - Get Attention Quickly

Our ability as consumers to process information is quite stunning. Look how quickly you process mail, in the morning and with electronic communications it's even quicker. When e-mail arrives we can see immediately who it's from and the subject matter. One hit of the delete key and it's gone. When writing electronic mail and designing your web site think, "how can I get attention quickly?"

137

1 - Write good subject headings

Think more about the heading than the content. You want your headline to jump out of the list and prompt them to think - "ooh what's that?". The same applies to headlines on your web page. Write things that make people want to know more so that they are encouraged to interact, open the e-mail, click on 'a link', respond to a message.

2 - Solve problems don't create them

Everything you do in sales and marketing should offer a solution to someone's problem. The more you understand the person, the more you'll understand their needs, the better able you are to create headlines that look interesting.

No-one is really interested in your products, they are interested in what the products will do for them. Make sure that your web content and your e-mail content focuses on helping people, provide information to help solve their problems or satisfy their needs.

3 - Tell the story in the first paragraph

Use journalistic techniques when you write material. Put the whole story in the first one or two paragraphs. Draw people into the information telling them what it's all about quickly, then expand. The idea of hypertext is to draw people deeper and deeper into information.

What you must not do is to leave the good bit to the end. Most people don't reach the end. If you work on the principle of grabbing attention, expanding your story with illustrations, examples and anecdotes then summarise your story, you'll get attention, hold peoples interest and they'll want to do business with you.

You have 5 seconds to gain attention, 30 seconds to stimulate interest.

Tip 8 - Make it Interactive.

Communicating electronically is different to communicating with paper. We're not passive with electronic information, we're interactive. As we read electronic information we have a mouse and keyboard available. If it bores us, we leave, but we also like to do something. We like short bites and then interaction.

When writing content for newsletters, and web pages think. "How can I get them to do something?". But don't overdo it and fill the page with too many hypertext links or they'll lose the thread. Consider organising your home page as a newsletter that you regularly up date with new leading stories.

Create a simple menu structure to enable people to see where they're going at your site. Give lots of guidelines through the site, links back to your home page, links to other related features, navigation controls that make it easy for them to find what they want.

Ask people to register and give them a reason for doing so. You can do this very simply on your home page. You might have a hypertext heading HOT FIVE INVESTMENT TIPS with a brief paragraph. But when they click 'the link' up pops a registration box or an intermediate page that says, "why not register to receive our investment tip of the week?"

Provide a simple on-line enquiry form and make it easy to complete with pop-up menus for completing fields. You can use this to enable visitors to request personalised investments reports, mortgage quotations or information pack.

Not everything has to be electronic. Provide an 0800 number for people who prefer to talk to someone, and make sure your addresses are prominently displayed throughout the site and in your e-mail signature. You might consider a freepost address makes dealing with you easier. Use the electronic tools to promote seminars and open evenings. Consider the merits of creating a discussion group or on-line seminars and make sure everyone has to register for these.

Always be on the look-out for ways to get visitors to your site, to become involved, to do things, to interact and find creative ways to encourage them to register their name and e-mail address.

Tip 9 - Be up to date not Leading Edge

The latest multi-media web tools are fun, but being leading edge is expensive and limits your market. A lot of people don't have browsers that can cope. You are a financial services business not a demonstration site for the latest shockwave animation techniques. Leave the leading edge stuff to the "geeks" and "pioneers". The tools to enable you to do inexpensive multimedia will be along soon enough.

Don't try to work to the lowest level of technology. Some people don't keep up-to-date, but your site will suffer if you make them your target audience. Everyone can accept e-mail. So create a modern and professional look and make sure your home page loads quickly. Draw people into the site then you can offer things that may take a little longer to load. And remember that once a graphic is loaded it can be reloaded quickly on another page, so reuse elements as often as you can.

Tip 10 - Keep the Audience Coming Back.

Finally watch your Hit Rate. Make your site interesting, up-to-date and well maintained enough to encourage visitors to come back. You should be up-dating information at least once a month, preferably once-a-week. If you have a lot of clients on-line, consider up-dating on a daily basis.

That means someone needs to maintain the site. Its easy to think "oh! I'II do something at the weekend", but it gets overlooked. Web maintenance needs to be an active part of your business.

Its worth considering employing an assistant, who writes reports, deals with day-to-day enquiries, executes only sales, increases and updates, someone who frees the adviser to handle client meetings. Web maintenance and newsletter writing is an ideal part of such a persons job. When your electronic marketing is successful, you may not be able to cope without an assistant.

One final reminder.

We live in a world of instant gratification, "I want it now!". If someone comes to your site, asks for information and a week later, is still waiting, don't expect to see them again. The fastest way to make sure that people come back and keep on coming back is to deliver exceptional service and demonstrate that your technology is just a tool.

What matters most to you, are people.

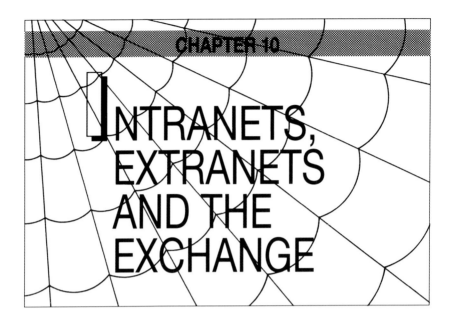

CHAPTER 10

INTRANETS, EXTRANETS AND THE EXCHANGE

The Internet is a constantly changing environment. Even as I wrote this book, which took little more than a month, I had to make changes to reflect new developments during that time. One of the reasons for creating a supporting web site is to keep the book up-to-date on-line.

In this final chapter I want to explore some the developments that are happening alongside the Internet and in response to some of the practical difficulties in managing the Internet , but which may have an even greater long term effect on your business.

Commercial problems of the Internet

Essentially whilst the public Internet gives electronic access to a vast and growing number of people, there are commercial problems which severely impede its efficiency and potential as a business communication medium. The key problem areas for businesses fall into three categories:

Security, congestion and management control.

Security

I said earlier in the book that the Internet can generally be considered safe. In order to hack into a server you would probably need a lot of luck or some inside information and you would need to be fairly expert in computer and communications technology.

Unfortunately there are people who have luck, access to inside information, exceptional technical skills coupled with criminal or malicious intent. Not long ago I searched around the on-line hacking community and within fifteen minutes found full details on how to hack an FTP site, how to obtain confidential information and how to break into mobile phone networks.

For people with the skill and the intent, the Internet does provide scope to access computer systems illegally. The early Internet technology in particular was very insecure, although it has now being significantly improved. Despite this there have been a number of high profile security breaches. The Labour Party web site and the Pentagon in the US immediately spring to mind.

The simplest way to improve security is not to allow anyone to dial into the system, which can make a lot of sense. In a company the requirement is often to allow communication within the company and access out to the Internet, rather than allowing access into the system.

The other security issue, which particularly concerns insurance companies is the risk of virus contamination to their main frame systems, which could be considerably damaging, particularly from a PR point of view. The easiest way to get a virus into a company is to attach it to an e-mail.

Congestion

In one particular area the Internet is a victim of its own phenomenal success. The rate at which people have been opening Internet accounts, and the pace at which new networks have been connected has been outstanding. Unfortunately, the growth has outpaced the ability of the technology to support the people who want to use it.

You may have already experienced the congestion, especially if you have attempted to browse information in the US late in the afternoon or early in the evening, when usage is at its absolute maximum. I have experienced occasions when I have been totally unable to access Microsoft's site.

The problems will be eased as more bandwidth is provided by the telecommunication companies but they are in a constant race against the continuing growth in usage. The estimated number of people on the Internet at the moment is probably around a hundred million but there are predictions suggesting that by the early twenty-first century that number will reach two billion.

Add to this the thirst for more bandwidth to support the demand for fast access to multimedia applications, and I suspect that we will face congestion problems on the Internet for a long time to come.

Management Control

The final area of concern from a commercial perspective is management control of staff using the Internet. You will already know if you've been on the Internet how easy it is to become completely oblivious of time and find that you have spent hours on-line. Many companies have discovered that providing unlimited access to the Internet has caused a fall in productivity of up to 20%.

What we need to be able to do is exercise some control over staff usage of the Internet. We want to allow access to web sites that are appropriate and beneficial in improving efficiency, but restrict their access to those sites that are of commercial value, but this is difficult to implement.

Intranets

The solution to these problems is to be found in developing an Intranet, and accounts for the fact that Intranet growth for the past two years has actually outstripped Internet growth.

An Intranet is quite simply the use of Internet technology within a private network, for example within a company's local area network. One of the primary benefits of the Internet is the ease of which information can be shared amongst people who need it. Within a company, sharing and accessing information can be a real challenge, particularly as so much related information is often held in different places around the organisation.

However it was exactly this problem which led Timothy Berners-Lee to develop HTML and the web in the first place. The Internet allows information to be dynamically linked, so that by installing an Intranet, information can be shared with everyone else and related information in different departments can be linked, speeding up communications considerably.

The creation of simple web editing tools like FrontPage '98 means that information sharing can be achieved very easily. Word processor documents, slide presentations, spreadsheets and database applications can all be easily converted to web pages with a click of a button.

But in addition to the productivity and file sharing benefits, an Intranet overcomes many of the security, congestion and management control issues.

The network administrator can allow communication between the Intranet and the Internet, but they can do so in a much more controlled way.

1. An audit trail is created for all use of the Internet. The fact that the company has a record of which Internet sites have been visited and by whom, is often a sufficient deterrent to personal use of the Internet.

2. The company can provide set links to approved Internet sites and restrict access, so that only those sites or parts of those sites can be visited.

3. The technology used to secure the site is called a "Firewall," a combination of software and hardware which enables users inside the company to go out into the Internet but prevents people from outside of the company coming in via the same connection.

4. The Intranet can allow incoming e-mail to its internal mail server, but anti-virus software can be installed both at the server to scan all incoming mail attachments, and on each workstation to scan attachments when they are opened.

147

Commercial networking

Throughout this book I have stressed the value of networking. The Internet is not about technology it is all about people, communicating with each other, trading with each other and sharing information. And it is no different when we move into the world of Intranets.

The first stage in networking comes in looking at the contacts a company has with its suppliers and customers. There are a variety of ongoing services which any business needs, travel and accommodation, fleet management, insurance, office supplies, computer services and supplies, banking services etc. If these suppliers have developed on-line trading services, then it makes sense to provide electronic access by providing a link from one Intranet to another.

Because of the ease with which any company with a Local Area Network (LAN) can set up an Intranet, and the benefits of connecting to suppliers and customers to deliver electronic commerce facilities, they have become increasingly popular. Most large companies either have an Intranet or are in the process of creating one.

This provides a great opportunity for Financial Advisers who specialise in the corporate market. Many organisations welcome the opportunity to have access to the current details of their staff pension scheme, so that members of staff can check their own benefits and values when they want to.

But the opportunity extends beyond business to business information. Most companies of any size also provide their staff with access to a range of consumer services on special terms and many Financial Advisers have negotiated such affinity schemes.

With electronic links to its main suppliers, businesses can

offer staff access to travel services, computer supplies, on-line banking, car leasing and even on-line shopping at the supermarket. Insurance and financial services are obvious services to offer staff through this electronic network.

Because these services are provided electronically, eliminating large amounts of administration, it becomes easy for suppliers to provide discounted terms. In fact they are demanded, because once the supplier is available via the company Intranet, competition is effectively locked out.

I hope warning bells are ringing. The future for financial services in the corporate market means providing access into on-line transaction services that eliminate paper work and deliver exclusive competitive products. If you are unable to deliver an electronic service to your corporate clients someone else will.

Extranets

The next step from an Intranet is an Extranet. Essentially an Extranet is a commercial business to business private Internet service, and you can probably see how they evolved as a natural extension of networking trading partners.

However the concept of the Extranet goes beyond just linking services on an *ad hoc* basis, to creating an entire business to business trading environment. They are still rather new and few major Extranets exist. One that, at the time of writing, is about to be launched is the new Exchange Extranet for the IFA sector of the financial services marketplace which we will look at later in this chapter.

The concept of the Extranet is broadly similar to the Intranet. It has the same benefits in that users dial into the Extranet over a private network rather than through the public Internet, therefore access from within the Extranet into the

Internet can be controlled. The difference is that it is a private wide area network, rather than sited on a company's local area network.

Rather than just linking the trading partners of one company the Extranet brings together a business sector so that electronic commerce capabilities are delivered to the entire sector. This means that smaller companies, without the resources to develop their own infrastructure, can benefit equally with the larger competitors.

Extranets can allow access into the Internet, and in some instances also provide a consumer site to allow members to promote their services on the Internet, but still retain the security elements of the Extranet which it accesses separately. This means that although consumers can reach the public areas of the Extranet, there is no access through into the private areas.

An Extranet provides the same level of management control over access to the Internet, although they can usually allow individual members to set their own parameters. Some might want to allow full Internet access but only to certain staff, while others have restricted access and some have no access to the Internet.

The Exchange

I have mentioned the Exchange a number of times and if you are an IFA you will probably already use the CTP and Videotex services. If you are a tied agent or company representative you will probably have heard of the Exchange, but may not know what it is or what it does.

Because it's role in the financial services marketplace is so significant I felt that it was important to include a section on the Exchange. If you are tied, you at least will understand what technology is about to become available in the IFA marketplace, and if you are an IFA, you will have a better understanding of how this development will impact your businesses.

I have been retained as an independent consultant by the Exchange since shortly after its launch in 1991, and have been instrumental in helping IFAs to understand the technology and how to use it since that time, which has provided me with a considerable insight into the difficulties of automating a marketplace.

My objective here is simply to provide a little history of the development and an outline of what will be happening with the launch of the new Extranet service. As more information becomes available I will be providing updates on my web site for those of you who are interested.

Lets start with a brief look at what the Exchange is, and why it was formed.

The Impact of Regulations

As a result of the Financial Services Act in 1988, any support services provided by an insurer to an IFA, and not directly related to the promotion of products, were required to be considered as part of commission and disclosed. This effectively barred insurance companies from individually providing commercial support to IFAs.

Concerned that this would place IFAs at a disadvantage, a group of 20 of the leading insurers formed two initiatives to collectively provide assistance to the independent marketplace.

The two organisations formed through this alliance were:

IFA Promotions - The objective of IFAP was to promote the value of independent advice and assist IFAs with help in marketing.

Origo Services - The objective of Origo (not an acronym) was to assist IFAs and insurers in improving business efficiency with particular emphasis on automating the business process.

The challenge facing Origo Services then was significant. Approximately 25,000 IFAs with vastly differing states of technology from nothing to very sophisticated in-house networks were using a variety of different operating systems.

The only common technology in the market was Videotex with two services providing on-line quotations and some embryonic electronic trading. Although incompatible systems both provided essentially the same services and were paid for by insurers based on the number of quotations requested by IFAs. Most of the services were free to IFAs.

Formation of The Exchange

Origo approached AT&T and BT, owners of the competing services with a proposal to merge and create a joint initiative to develop an electronic trading environment. BT chose not to participate and a Joint venture was agreed between Origo (67%) and AT&T (33%) to form, in early 1991, a separate commercial organisation, the Insurance Trading Exchange, trading as The Exchange. The BT Service was withdrawn in 1992

The Exchange continued to support and develop the videotex service, but directed most of its attention to developing the Common Trading Platform (CTP); a windows based software package designed as the core of a new electronic trading environment.

The first stage was the development of new quotation services and the enhancement of the existing services.

This has largely been achieved, although the videotex service is still being supported, probably until the end of 1998.

The second stage was the development of electronic forms and the infrastructure to enable new business to be traded electronically. This project met a number of obstacles, cultural, political and technical and to date no significant levels of new business are traded electronically. The software is now in place, but overcoming the cultural resistance is difficult, particularly as IFAs do not see electronic processing of new business as a priority.

IFAs are reluctant to use the service complaining that not enough products and insurers are represented. Insurers are reluctant to invest in developing more electronic products until more IFAs use the service - Catch 22.

The Retail Regulatory Review

1995 saw a major shift in the role of The Exchange with the Retail Regulation Review requirement that all products offered to clients were to be supported with full disclosure of values, commissions and the effect of expenses. This meant that each quotation and Key Features Document (KFD) had to be approved by the company as compliant and provided at the point of sale before a sale could be completed.

In response, The Exchange developed a network linking its quotations bureau to 50 insurance company systems to provide electronic access to these quotations.

The Quotations Service

To obtain a quotation, IFAs complete the client details in the CTP (This information can be pulled in from an integrated IFA back office system). IFAs can request single company quotations, or a comparative list of all, or a group of companies offering the product.

CTP submits the requests to The Exchange bureau, which forwards them to the appropriate insurer machines. A typical quote request is completed in less than 2 minutes. Once the required quotation is selected a compliant key features document can be printed. The result has been a dramatic increase in the level of electronic quotations.

Currently The Exchange has 10,000 active user accounts across a broad band of IFA firms. 550 products from 60 product providers are supported, including 10 Unit Trust companies. IFAs now request over 4 million quotations a month from The Exchange and the service is accessed over 12,000 times every per day. Current estimates indicate that 40% of IFA business written is quoted through The Exchange.

Electronic Processing of Business

The quotation information together with any information in a integrated back office system, can be automatically passed to an electronic application form. This form can then be printed, partly or fully completed. It is the next step of electronically forwarding the information to the company that has met a variety of obstacles, some technical, some political and some simply resistance to change.

Electronic Products

In 1996, GA Life withdrew all manual support for term assurance. Since that time all its term business quotations have had to be obtained through The Exchange, but on terms better than were previously available. The result has been an 11-fold increase in business. Five other companies have since enhanced their term assurance contracts with similar improvements in business. Following the GA initiative, the pace of change and demand for enhanced products has been forced by a group of twenty large intermediary firms.

Policy Servicing

In addition to providing quotations and electronic processing of new business, The Exchange also provides access to policy information for a small but growing range of products. Nine companies offer instant values, mostly for investment bonds. Four provide a much wider range of services including most maturity, surrender and paid up values for all life and pension products.

The service should eventually enable IFAs to request up to date values on a client's entire portfolio in a single on-line session. Unfortunately the usual problem of IFAs wanting more insurers on the service before they use it and insurers wanting more usage from IFAs before they invest in developing the service, is slowing progress.

On the Group Pension side, three insurers took the initiative of developing a service that has now been joined by another three companies. This group enquiry service is becoming a very important part of The Exchange service for IFAs in the group market.

The Limitations of the Service

There are some limitations to the existing CTP service. In order to create a quotation request off-line, the PC workstation at the IFA office needs to hold a significant amount of data and be regularly updated. The library of forms and product details has to be distributed to IFAs every month and requires six weeks to three months lead-time in testing software and CD ROM production and distribution. This slows the insurers ability to deliver new products and services to the market.

The growth of the Internet has created significant possibilities for improving speed to the market and allowing a much greater mix of multimedia capabilities in the creation of sales and marketing materials. In addition, since the first development of the CTP, the IFA marketplace has matured greatly, with over 80% of IFAs now using up-to-date technology capable of supporting the new browsing software.

The Exchange Extranet

For the past year, The Exchange has been actively designing, building and testing the next stage of its development, the creation of an industry wide Extranet service for the IFAs and Insurers. This Extranet is probably the largest commercial Extranet project in the world.

Based on the existing infrastructure, and running in parallel with the Videotex and CTP services, the Extranet enables IFAs to access information using a web browser. The existing quotation services will be progressively migrated to the new service but the range of each service will be expanded to include much more electronic point-of-sale support.

In 1998, The Exchange was the subject of a successful management buy-out and the market has opened up, allowing other competitors to emerge. However with the strength of its existing relationships, and the extensive network with insurers it is unlikely that any significant competitor will emerge in the short-term.

At the time of writing the first preview version of the

Extranet service has been released to selected large intermediaries for testing and comment. The second pilot scheme will soon follow with commercial release due in the second half of 1998.

What Does all this Mean to IFAs?

I dwelled a little on the historical development, simply to outline the extent of the technology network that has already been developed by The Exchange. It is because it is able to simply apply Internet technologies to this existing infrastructure that it is able to deliver significant benefits to the market in a relatively short time.

Benefits of the Extranet

The most important benefit of the Extranet is that it instantaneously provides a common communications network for the marketplace, because it uses standard technologies. Browsers, Internet e-mail, chat and all the technologies we have already considered in detail.

There is no additional learning curve. If you have already used a browser, you will be able to use the Extranet service. If you have used e-mail, you will be able to communicate with the entire industry.

Lets consider the specific service benefits briefly.

Industry e-mail

Insurance companies are already switching to Internet mail and the Exchange will deliver to everyone a complete directory of insurer e-mail contacts. As this is controlled by the insurance companies, you do not need to know which companies want mail centrally and which want it at branch level. You look up the insurance company and select the appropriate e-mail address based on the content and send.

Every registered user of The Exchange automatically receives their own e-mail address, resulting in an immediate industry wide mail directory for all IFAs. Have you tried to find someone's e-mail address on the Internet?

However because this is all within a secure Extranet, it also means that the addresses cannot be searched and used by the Internet Spammers, keeping you relatively free from junk mail. If you give anyone your e-mail address there is always a chance that it may be reused by a junk mailer, but if you keep it secret that would be like making your business telephone line ex-directory.

Another advantage of an e-mail service controlled through an Extranet, is that The Exchange can install virus checking software on the system to ensure that all e-mail passing through the system is clean, an issue of concern to insurers. It is still a good idea to make sure that you take personal responsibility for virus security and install virus software on your own systems though.

Aggregation of Content

The business process consists of a number of documents and sales aids. Using Internet technologies and its capabilities for rich multimedia function, The Exchange can deliver a wide range of information and tools to support the electronic business process. So that quotations can be supported with marketing materials, calculators, bulletins, fund and investment information, company analysis and even audio and video content.

Additional content is added by insurers relevant to the

quotations requested and because information can be made instantly available to the marketplace, it will always be the most up to date available.

Third Party Services

Until now, third party services could only be delivered through The Exchange if specifically developed to support the exchange technology. Now, using Internet technology, the tools to develop content are freely available and in a standard that everyone can receive.

The Exchange is negotiating with a number of third part content providers to secure exclusive products for users of the Extranet. Already Financial Adviser will be providing a new electronic news service for IFAs and the research department is developing a product database, based upon its Aequos service. Others are being considered.

Development of Insurer Services

Insurers have generally been limited to using the Videotex service to deliver there own bespoke services. Some have now developed Internet sites with IFA sections within them. The Extranet provides a standard environment that enables them to develop significant new content, on their own sites and link it through the Extranet. Other insurers are much happier about delivering services through a secure environment than using the Internet, and we will undoubtedly see an increase in IFA content from insurers currently without an Internet presence

Faster Distribution of Products

Speed to market is becoming a major issue for most insurers. As new opportunities arise, insurers need to be able to react in a timely fashion. Internet technologies mean that they control their timetables and can maintain much greater secrecy over their product launch, than is possible when electronic support needs a three month lead time, which is the current position.

The better bandwidth available through an Extranet also means that they can use multimedia tools more reliably, and I suspect that over the next couple of years you will see quite a shift in creativity as insurers begin to master the new technology.

Internet Access

Part of the plans include providing IFAs and insurers with access to the Internet via the Extranet. This will be of considerable value because of the issues we looked at earlier in terms of security, congestion and management control. With staff accessing the Internet via The Exchange Extranet, users have the ability to set levels of control over the type of access allowed. Thus some staff can be restricted to accessing insurer sites only, others can have access to other support sites, some can have full access if needed.

IFA Web Content

Finally The Exchange has quite well advanced plans to assist IFAs in the development of consumer sites.

One part of their service will be the provision to larger IFAs of a full design and consultancy service to develop and host custom channels, or bespoke web sites. The value to larger IFAs here is the now extensive experience that The Exchange is accumulating in Internet and Intranet developments and the ability to incorporate some of The Exchange functionality into their sites.

Another service will be the development of a range of templates for smaller IFAs so that sites can be developed relatively inexpensively. The advantage of the Exchange service will be the ability to include access to on-line policy valuations and other tools once those services are incorporated into the Extranet.

The Exchange have a number of plans for developing support for IFAs wishing to develop consumer sites and it will be worth while keeping a regular check on what services are available.

Remember, I said, "don't panic." This is one of the reasons. No one else can deliver these services to IFAs in the time frame, but when they are available they will make your site, as far as client servicing is concerned, at the leading edge of the marketplace, without you needing to become a "geek" in the process.

The Exchange Consumer Site

However, "Don't Panic", does not mean "Don't Act". The most significant new development from The Exchange will be a new consumer personal finance site specifically designed to promote the value of independent advice and link consumers with IFAs. This development is quite well advanced now and involves a number of major partners which will virtually guarantee the success of the site.

One feature of this site will be links to IFA sites. It will be a competitive consumer market-place providing helpful information and one in which IFAs will need to compete for their share of the business. Make sure that you have an attractive well designed website and that you use the principles I have outlined in this book and this will increase your competitive position when this site is launched later in 1998.

Where do you go from here?

I hope by now, you are beginning to feel more comfortable with the Internet, and that some of its mysteries have been revealed. If you have read all the book and used the disk, you should have some clear ideas of where you want to go.

What you need to do is continue to regularly use the Internet, looking for ideas to develop your site content. You need to encourage your clients to use the Internet and begin communicating with them electronically, especially with a regular newsletter. You need to get into the habit of using the Internet for research and prospecting. You need to keep an eye on developments so that as new services are available, you will have a clear idea of how you want of use them and can quickly gain competitive advantage.

Finally, do look in regularly at my web site. This book was already out of date as it was published, despite the fact that it was produced in a little over a month. I mentioned at the beginning, that part of this book is on-line. It's more than that.

The on-line service extends the book, keeps it regularly up-to-date and provides you with a finger on the pulse of the electronic marketplace from the perspective of a Financial Adviser. See you on-line.

http://www.arundel.co.uk/abc

THE JARGON BUSTER
GLOSSARY OF INTERNET TERMS

There is an extended on-line version of this glossary updated regularly at www.arundel.co.uk/abc .

ActiveX

A programming language developed by Microsoft for producing interactive content in web pages, Not very well supported in Netscape.

Acronyms

Abbreviations for long terms using the first letter of each word, often used for frequently typed phrases such as BTW for By The Way

America On-line (AOL)

The largest commercial on-line service, having recently taken over CompuServe.

applet

Small programmes written using Java programming language, designed to run within a browser, rather than stand alone.

ARPANet

Advanced Research Projects Administration Network. The forerunner to the Internet, developed in the late 1960's and early 1970's by the US Department of Defence as an experiment in wide-area networking that would survive a nuclear war.

ASCII

American Standard Code for Information Interchange. This is the accepted world-wide standard for the code numbers used by computers to represent all the upper and lower-case Latin letters, numbers, punctuation, etc. There are 128 standard ASCII codes.

backbone

The high speed line or series of connections between an information provider and the Internet Network. The size of these backbones relative to the number of users dictates the quality of service.

Banners

Small rectangular advertisements usually found on sites with high levels of regular traffic.

Bandwidth

Defines the maximum amount of data, in the form of text, images, video, sound etc, that can be sent through a connection before it becomes full: usually measured in bits-per-second.

baud

One of the terms used to define the speed of a modem and is equal to one signal per second.

BBS

Bulletin Board System. A BBS is a meeting and announcement, or conferencing system that enables discussions and the exchange of files

binary

Files comprised of data that is not text such as image files and software applications.

bit

Binary Digit. The smallest single component of computer data, represented as a 1 or a 0.

bps

Bits Per Second. The standard measure of transmission speed through a modem. A 28.8K modem transmits at 28,800 bps

Bookmarks

A method of recording interesting Internet sites when visited with the Netscape browser to make revisiting them easier.

Browser

A software package that enables users to browse text, graphics, audio and video on the Internet. The first browser developed was Mosaic. Today there are two leading browsers, Netscape Navigator and Microsoft Internet Explorer.

Byte

A set of bits that represent a single character, generally there are eight or 10 bits to a byte.

CERN

Conseil EuropÇenne pour la Recherche NuclÇaire, the European Laboratory for Particle Physics in Geneva, Switzerland, where Timothy Berners-Lee developed the World Wide Web technology.

CGI

Common Gateway Interface, software routines to enable web access to external programs like databases, used for example to process interactive forms or search databases.

Channels

Web sites which enable users to subscribe and automatically receive content when the site is updated and store it for future viewing.

Chat

An Internet tool that facilitates real time interactive communication between users.

cookie

Encoded data that a web site sends to a browser and is stored on the hard disk tracking a users visiting habits and increasingly used by advertisers to accumulate user data and build user profiles.

connect time

The amount of time a computer is connected to an on-line service.

client

When your computer requests information from another computer on the Internet, it is known as the client, and the computer providing the information is known as the server.

compression

One of a number of techniques for reducing the size of a file to enable it to take up less space on a disc and to be transmitted more quickly over a network.

Common Trading Platform (CTP)

A windows based financial services system developed by The Exchange, to enable IFAs to obtain and publish comparative quotations, key features documents, application forms and other sales support documents, via a private network within the financial services marketplace.

CompuServe (CIS)

One of the largest and the oldest commercial on-line services, although now merging with AOL.

CompuServe Information Manager

The unique CompuServe, a graphical interface for Mac and Windows. Usually abbreviated CIM.

Cyberspace

Originated by science fiction author William Gibson in his novel "Burning Chrome", the word Cyberspace is now used to describe the virtual world of on-line services in particular the Internet.

dial-up account

A ISP account enabling users to access the Internet dialling over a normal phone line using a Modem.

domain name

The unique Internet address which enables users to access web sites. It is important for everyone who plans to develop a web site to own their own domain name.

domain name server (dns)

A computer which holds a database of domain names and their associated IP number and enables sites to be identified when a user types the Internet address into their browser.

e-mail

Electronic mail messages, which are usually in a text form, but increasingly include graphics, and sound.

header: The area in an e-mail message that contains information about who that message came from, when it was sent, etc.

subject: A single line which outlines the content of the e-mail. Making the subject clear is important,

body: The area where a message goes in an e-mail.

signature: A space that automatically includes several lines of text on an e-mail or newsgroup post. These are easily created by the user and can include e-mail address, snail mail address, phone numbers and regulatory information.

bounce: When e-mail fails to be delivered and is returned

Encryption

A method of encoding data to prevent unauthorised access, most commonly used on the Internet to protect e-mail

Exchange Extranet

New financial services Extranet developed by the Exchange to support IFAs. The Exchange service provides complete aggregated content to support the sale and servicing of financial services products through independent intermediaries.

Extranet

A private network using Internet technologies. An Extranet is protected from unauthorised access by "firewalls". It usually provides business-to-business services to associations or specific markets of customers and suppliers.

FAQ

Frequently Asked Questions. Documents that list answers to the most common questions on a particular subject.

Favourites

A method of recording interesting Internet sites when visited with the Microsoft browser to make revisiting them easier.

finger

An Internet software program used to locate people on other Internet sites. The most common use is to determine if a person has an account at a particular Internet site.

firewall

A combination of hardware and software that protects a network from Internet hackers and other potential security breaches.

flame

An offensive over reaction to an activity that breaches netiquette, most frequently a response to an unsolicited e-mail or posting of junk messages in a newsgroup.

freeware

Copyrighted software but available at no charge from the software's author and often available over the Internet.

FTP

File Transfer Protocol is a common method of moving files between two Internet sites.

gateway

A host computer that connects networks that communicate in different languages. For example, a gateway connects a company's local area network to the Internet.

gif

Graphical Interchange Format is a graphical file format for images which originated with CompuServe and now one of the most popular formats due to the small size of the graphic file. Particularly used in the creation of animations. (Animated gif files)

gopher

The primary search tool before the development of the World Wide Web.

hacker

Usually applied to someone who illegally accesses computers, often quite young, but very bright computer experts with an unquenchable thirst for the secrets of other machines.

Home Page

The first page or shop front of a web site which provides an introduction to the site and directions to finding information at the site.

host

Any computer on a network that is a storehouse for services available to other computers on that network.

HTML

HyperText Mark-up Language is the basic language used to build pages on the World Wide Web.

http

HyperText Transport Protocol. The protocol (rules) computers use to transfer hypertext documents.

hypertext

Text or graphics in a document that contains a hidden link to other text, pages or web sites anywhere in the world.

Interactive Broadcasting

The provision of broadcast type content via Internet technologies, comprising text, audio, animation and video, which enables the user to interact with the content and define what they receive.

Internet

The global collection of approximately 100,000 inter-connected networks that use the TCP/IP protocols and that evolved from the ARPANet of the late 1960's and early 1970's.

interstitials

Full-page ads that run for about 10 to 12 seconds when you click a link and are considered more intrusive than the normal "banner" ad.

Intranet

A private network using Internet technologies usually within a company to provide information service to employees and other authorised corporate users.

IP

Internet Protocol. The rules that provide basic Internet functions.

IP number

Internet Protocol Numbers are a unique set of numbers consisting of four parts separated by dots allocated to each computer and web site on the Internet. Example: 182.981.525.9

IRC

Internet Relay Chat is a system that enables users to communicate in real time through common interest groups, a bit like CB radio with computers.

ISDN

Integrated Services Digital Network. A set of communications standards that enable moderately fast communications over a single phone line but at a high cost.

Java

A programming language developed by Sun Microsystems to create applets, or programs that can be distributed as attachments to Web documents.

JPEG

Joint Photographic Experts Group. The name of the committee that designed the photographic image-compression standard used extensively for photographic images on the Internet.

kbps

kilobits per second is speed rating for computer modems that measures (in units of 1,024 bits) the maximum number of bits the device can transfer in one second.

LAN

Local Area Network. A computer network limited to the same area, normally the same building.

Leased-line

A phone line that is rented for exclusive 24-hour, seven-days-a-week use from one location to another.

link

Short for hypertext link and is usually highlighted with a different colour than the surrounding text in the web page.

listserv

An Internet application that automatically "serves" mailing lists by sending electronic newsletters to a stored database of Internet user addresses.

login

Noun: The account name used to access a computer system.

Verb: The act of connecting to a computer system.

mirror site

A site that exactly matches the contents of another Internet site. Used to lessen the load on a popular site.

modem

A communications device, its name derived from "Modulator, Demodulator," which allows computers to talk to other computers through the 'phone system.

moderator

The person who vets contributions to a moderated newsgroup before they are posted.

Mosaic

The first WWW browser available for the Macintosh, Windows and UNIX with the same interface. Mosaic opened the Internet to non-technical users.

multimedia

Any web content that uses a combination of text, sound, graphics, video or animation.

NCSA

The National Center for Supercomputing Applications at the University of Illinois in Urbana-Champaign, where the first browser capable of displaying graphics, named Mosaic, was developed.

Net

An abbreviation for the Internet

netiquette

The unwritten code of rules for interaction on the Internet, particularly within newsgroups, chat and by e-mail.

newbie

An inexperienced user or someone new to the Internet.

newsgroups

On-line discussion groups, of which there are upwards of 20,000, in which people participate in discussing a wide range of topics of common interest.

newsreader

Software program used to read newsgroups and to follow and delete threads.

One-to-One Marketing

Commercial communications to individually identified Internet users based upon analysis of profiles that detail the interests and habits of the user.

off-line

The state of being disconnected from the Internet.

on-line

The state of being connected to the Internet via telecommunication lines.

packet switching

The technique of breaking data into identifiable small chunks so that it can be transmitted over the Internet, sharing lines with other data and passing down different routes to be reassembled at the destination.

page

One section of a WWW site containing text, sounds, videos, animations, etc.

PGP

Pretty Good Privacy. A way of encrypting information sent through the Internet to secure privacy.

POP

Post Office Protocol. A protocol for storing and receiving e-mail.

PoP

Point of Presence. A site equipped with tele-communications equipment, modems, leased lines and Internet routers which provides access to the Internet for a providers customers. .

protocols

Computer rules that provide uniform specifications so that hardware and operating systems can communicate. Regardless of the underlying language, the basic protocols remain the same.

post

To send a message to an on-line publication or community, generally a newsgroup or discussion forum.

plug-in

An additional program application designed to extend the browser to display or play content produced in other specific applications - e.g. Shockwave or Real Player.

protocol

A system of rules or standards for communicating over a network, particularly the Internet.

public domain

Software that is free to be used, distributed or modified.

Push Technologies

A reversal of the traditional Internet concept, where the content provider sends personalised information automatically to the user based on identified user interests rather than the users request.

RealAudio and RealPlayer

A commercial software program that plays audio or video on demand, without waiting for long file, transfers being a technique called streaming. For example RealPlayer enables radio programmes to be received anywhere in the world, and training seminars on video or with narrated PowerPoint presentations to be broadcast.

router

A network device that enables the network to re-route messages it receives that are intended for other networks. The network with the router receives the message and sends it on its way exactly as received.

search engine

A software program that allows a user to search the Internet by entering in keywords. You should register your web site with as many search engines as possible to improve potential business.

self-extracting archive

A compressed file that needs no special software to uncompress it. You can uncompress it just by clicking on it.

server

When you request information from an Internet location, that computer serves the information to your computer known as the client. The term server can describe either the specific software that delivers particular information or it can refer to the machine on which the software is running.

shareware

Software provided free of charge for evaluation which should be paid for if retained and used. It is an honour system of distribution and payment is usually made directly to the author.

site

> The location of any Internet resource. Like WWW site, ftp site, etc.

SLIP/PPP

> Serial Line Internet Protocol/Point-to-Point Protocol. The basic rules that enable PCs to connect, usually by dial-up modem, directly to other computers that provide Internet services.

smileys

> A feature of Chat and Newsgroups using symbols constructed from punctuation and text to describing tone, body language or feelings
>
> > :-) (happy)
> > :-((sad)
> > ;-) (Wink)

snail mail

> Traditional mail via the post office or couriers.

spam

> Originally used to describe the action of posting a commercial message to a number of newsgroups simultaneously where the message has nothing to do with the newsgroup topic, but now describes any form of unsolicited e-mail.

Streamed audio/video

> Sound and or video files that can be played directly over the Internet without the need to download and play.

Subscriptions

> The facility to instruct your browser, currently Internet Explorer 4, to automatically check a web site for changes and download defined pages for later viewing off-line.

surf

> Slang term for "browsing the Internet", although often used to refer to browsing without a specific purpose.

T-1

> A leased-line connection carrying data at up to 1,544,000 bits-per-second. At maximum capacity, a T-1 line could move a megabyte in less than 10 seconds. T-1 is the speed commonly used to connect networks to the Internet .

T-3

A fast and expensive leased-line connection that can carry data at 45,000,000 bits-per-second.

TCP/IP

Transmission Control Protocol/Internet Protocol. The group of protocols that defines The Internet . Originally for the UNIX operating system, TCP/IP software is now usable for every major kind of computer operating system.

Terminal Adapter

An electronic device that interfaces a PC with an Internet host computer via an ISDN phone line.

thread

A group of messages on a newsgroup that relate to each other.

timeout

In a SLIP connection, after a certain amount of idle time, depending on the software being used, the connection will disconnect.

UNIX

The computer operating system that was used to write most of the programs and protocols that built the Internet.

URL

Uniform Resource Locator. A term which means your Internet address. It is essential that you promote your URL on every paper or electronic document you publish.

Usenet

Another name for Internet Newsgroups.

VRML

Virtual Reality Modeling Language, a set of codes used for writing the files for three-dimensional virtual reality programs.

virus

A malicious, human-created program that searches out other programs and "infects" them by embedding a copy of itself and can replicate itself on other computers. Some viruses result in harmless messages others can destroy files on the computer's hard disk.

WAIS

> Wide Area Information Servers. A distributed information retrieval system that is sponsored by Apple Computer, Thinking Machines and Dow Jones, Inc.

Web

> Short for the World Wide Web.

wizard

> Computer-based help provides step-by-step guides though a task, often to support installation or configuration of software.

WWW

> WWW) (W3) (the Web) An Internet client-server distributed information and retrieval system based upon the hypertext transfer protocol (http) that transfers hypertext documents across a varied array of computer systems.

WYSIWYG

> What You See Is What You Get. A term to describe a software application that enables you to work with information in the form that it will eventually be published.

The ABC of the WWW for Financial Advisers

The Easy Internet CD ROM

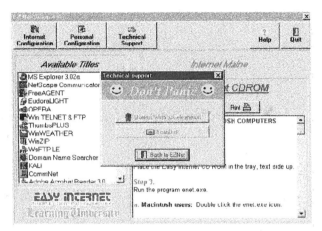

Getting online, whether you have a PC or a Macintosh couldn't be easier.

The Easy Internet CD inside the back cover of this book, is the worlds No 1 product to get you on the internet. Distributed in the UK by Internet Service Provider Primex Ltd, this CD contains all the software described in this book, and a comprehensive library of top shareware and freeware products.

This CD is designed for people with no experience.

Call Primex for your access code, username and password - **01908 378999**

Close all applications, place the disk in the CDROM tray, text side up and follow the instructions. The CD will automatically configure your PC for you.

If the disk doesn't start automatically refer to Chapter 3.

Primex provides 30 days free access to the Internet.

Call their *support desk* if you have any problems. - **01908 643597**

Check their *web site* for tips and help online **http://www.primex.co.uk**

The **Companion Web Site** for this book is at.

http://www.arundel.co.uk/ABC

The ABC of the WWW for Financial Advisers

A Guide to Marketing on the Internet